"I think there was something strange about your father's letter."

Lord Eversley's voice indicated he was deep in thought.

Deborah was stung by his comment. "He committed suicide, Robert!" she cried. "Of course the letter was strange—he was distraught!"

"That's not what I mean," Eversley went on stubbornly. "I mean suggestive. Mysterious."

In her mind's eye, Deborah saw the letter, and quite suddenly certain phrases stood out: "I comforted myself with the thought...He has no proof...We were so young and so deeply in love!...At the last, as at the beginning, I will rob him of his victory...."

Deborah frowned. "Yes!" she said. "I don't know why I didn't see it at once."

Eversley reached out for Deborah's hands and held them tightly as he looked deeply into her eyes.

"Deborah, my sweeting," he said. "You must think very carefully. Have you any family scandals? Any skeletons in the closet?"

She did not answer at once and when she did, her words sent shivers down both their spines.

"I don't know, Robert. But I think we're about to find out."

TOLLIN'S DAUGHTER

ELIZABETH MICHAELS

Harlequin Books

TORONTO • NEW YORK • LONDON
AMSTERDAM • PARIS • SYDNEY • HAMBURG
STOCKHOLM • ATHENS • TOKYO • MILAN

PROLOGUE

THE LIBRARY DOOR SLAMMED. Footsteps sounded and light blossomed as a candle on the corner of the desk was lit. The man who had entered the room shrugged out of his dripping greatcoat and threw the garment carelessly over the chair which stood before the empty hearth.

The man moved to the long windows behind the desk and twitched back damask draperies to stare out at the night. The rain had finally stopped, he saw; the clouds were beginning to roll away and the first tentative light of dawn showed in the east. His hand tightened convulsively on the heavy material for a moment, then he closed the draperies and turned abruptly away.

The gentleman next turned his attention to the fireplace. He soon had a respectable blaze going in the grate, its cheerful crackle strangely at odds with the man's sombre expression. He rubbed his hands together and stared down into the fire, oblivious to the water which dripped from his greying hair and the steam which had begun to rise from his soaked clothing. A deep sigh shook his shoulders; he pulled from his pocket a yellow, dog-eared document, and held it out as though he would cast it into the flames.

Many long moments passed as the man's hand remained poised over the hearth. When at last he turned away, the paper was still clutched in his fingers. "No, by Jove!" he said aloud, his expression determined. A decision made, he crossed the room and with an ironic smile slid the paper into the binding of an old Bible which occupied a position of honour in the library. Then he turned back to the desk and sank into the chair behind it.

He took up a pen, pulled a pile of foolscap toward him, then sat for all of a quarter hour, the ink drying on the nib. When at last he began to write, the lines beside his mouth deepened and, for just a moment, a grimace of pain twisted his features. "My dearest Deborah," he began.

As I sit down to write this letter—the most difficult I have ever written!—it seems impossible to explain to you how all this happened, how things came to this point. I often look back and wonder, if I had been kinder, if I had tried to understand—but no matter. Never think to hide from the past, my Deborah. It will find you, wherever you go, whatever you do. I laugh to think of all the times, over the years, that I comforted myself with the thought, *He has no proof.* I was wrong, my sweet girl, so horribly, criminally wrong! Your mother was wiser than I—she always knew. How can I properly explain, how can I make you see the way things were, and that any action at the time seemed justifiable? We were so young, and so deeply in love!

The man stopped; he buried his face in his hands, and a dry sob shook his shoulders. Then he lifted his head, dashed the tears from his eyes, and continued his letter:

I know the pain which you will feel when you learn of what I have done. I know the shame which I bring down upon your innocent head, and for that I beg your forgiveness, my child. I do what I must. The secret will die with me, but by then it will not matter. Violence has ever been difficult for me, and when I contemplate the aftermath—I must be strong. At the last, as at the beginning, I will rob him of his victory.

Oh, Deborah! We shall not meet again in this life, for to look at your face would only weaken my resolve. Goodbye, my Deborah, goodbye!

The man folded and sealed the letter, and inscribed a name on the outside. Then he opened a small drawer in the desk and slid back an indistinguishable wooden panel in the back of the drawer. He placed the letter safely within this compartment, and shut it up tight. Only then did he open the box which lay on the desk top before him, to reveal a pair of elegant, silver-chased pistols. "For Deborah!" he whispered to himself, and rising to his feet, took the pistols firmly in his hands.

CHAPTER ONE

"AUNT SARAH! What are you doing?"

The small, silver-haired woman jumped, and shrank even farther back into the cluster of potted palms which sheltered her. The hall was deserted. Most of the guests invited for the evening had already arrived and were in the ballroom dancing, or in the study, where card tables had been set up for the gentlemen. "Deborah!" she said. "You startled me, child."

"Oh, Aunt Sarah, look at you," Miss Deborah Tollin said scoldingly, her satin skirts whispering as she hurried to her aunt. "Why are you hiding?"

"I am not hiding, Deborah," Sarah Beldon said with a great deal of dignity. "I am just, er, resting."

"Oh, Sarah," Deborah said, concern in her blue eyes. "There's no need to hide. Oh, excuse me, rest." She coaxed a reluctant smile from her aunt.

"I'm so uncomfortable in such a large crowd," her aunt confessed. "I'm just not accustomed to it."

"But, Aunt!" Deborah said in surprise. "You've chaperoned me at dozens of affairs since my coming-out—balls, routs, drums, alfresco parties...."

"That's quite different, my dear," Sarah said with a shaky laugh. "At someone else's entertainment, I am merely another spinster aunt. I can sit comfortably along one wall, watching while the young people flirt and dance, and no one pays the least bit of attention to me." She shuddered delicately. "But this is your ball, Deb, your night! With your father gone, I have to take a much more active role than I should like." She met her niece's gaze squarely. "People will talk, Deb. I don't want you to be hurt by my mistakes."

"Nonsense," said Deborah briskly. "The past is in the past—let's leave it there, shall we?" She tucked her aunt's arm into her own and began leading the older woman toward the brightly lit ballroom. "And if anyone should say something unkind to you, I want you to promise to tell me. Will you, Aunt Sarah?"

"Deborah, this is no time to make a scene..." Sarah began worriedly.

Deborah opened her eyes wide. "Me? Make a scene? How can you think such a thing of me, Aunt?" She bent her head closer to Sarah's. "What I should do, though, is point out to any woman unkind enough to tease you—for it would be a woman, don't you agree? No gentleman would be so ill-mannered. I would simply point out to the lady, oh so gently, how aged she must be even to recall such old news."

Sarah gave a gurgle of laughter. "You are too, too bad, Deborah."

"Agreed!" said Deborah instantly. "But no more roundaboutation, Aunt Sarah. We have guests to see to." Deborah paused in the doorway of the ballroom and anxiously scanned the crowd. "I do hope that Timothy will come," she said lightly. "I have been longing to see him."

"But he's not the one whom you're waiting for, is he, my dear?" Aunt Sarah asked gently. "Oh, never look so surprised, love. I am not quite so blind that I don't see—"

"Aunt Sarah, don't!" Deborah said, blushing hotly. "And I don't know what you're talking about."

"Really?" Sarah teased. "Perhaps I am merely imagining things, but I could have sworn that you had become more than fond of—"

"Deb?"

Deborah Tollin turned around. "Timothy!" she cried, grateful for the interruption. "I'd begun to think you weren't coming!"

"What? And miss your ball?" The young man sauntered lazily up to the two women. Brown eyes twinkling, he tweaked Deborah's cheek. "Hello, brat!" He swept Sarah up in a hug. "'Lo, Aunt Sarah! Where's Uncle Geoffrey?"

"In the country still," Deborah said, tucking her arm into his. "Papa had pressing business to attend to. He said to tell you that he expects you to stand in his stead, and to—what was it he wrote, Aunt?"

Sarah took Timothy Stewart's other arm. "He said that he expected you to protect Deborah from her more impetuous admirers," she said. "And you may need to. I notice young Rankin is here tonight. He's head over heels, poor boy."

Timothy halted. "Rankin?" he said incredulously. "You can't be encouraging him, Deb. Lord, the man's a looby. If his father weren't as rich as Croesus, he'd be in Bedlam!"

"Shh!" Deborah said. "Timothy, you're awful! I'm not encouraging Lord Rankin." She laughed up at the young man. "But even if I were, 'twould be none of your affair."

"Yes, it would. I'm the closest thing to a brother you'll ever have, Deb, so it's up to me to—"

"Give overbearing lectures, tease me unmercifully, and be as odiously rude to me as you please? Yes, yes, I know, Timothy. I often rue the day that our fathers acquired neighbouring estates," Deborah said.

"Admit it, Deb—you adore me," Timothy said. "Admit it, or I'll go and tell young Rankin you're mad for him."

"I admit it, I admit it!" Deborah said, throwing up her hands. "I do love you, but I often wonder how I've kept from murdering you all these years."

"Aunt Sarah will protect me," Timothy said. "She was ever my champion, weren't you, Aunt Sarah?"

"Indeed, yes," Sarah said. "I remember the time you tried to drown him in the horse trough, Deborah—"

"I never did!" Deborah gasped.

"Yes, you did," Timothy said. "Dashed near did the trick, too. If it weren't for Aunt Sarah, I'd be dead now, and you'd be in gaol, my girl."

"Miss Tollin?"

Deborah stopped, and bright colour flooded her cheeks. Then she whirled about so fast that Timothy blinked.

"My...my lord," she said breathlessly. "I had not thought to see you here this evening."

Timothy raised an enquiring brow in Sarah's direction; Sarah ignored him.

"Am I so late, then?" Lord Robert Eversley bowed over Deborah's hand, a smile lurking in his green eyes. "Forgive me! I had not made allowances for the traffic. I should have known that your ball was bound to be a sad crush." He turned to Aunt Sarah. "Miss Beldon. In looks, as always, I see."

It would be wrong to say that Sarah blithered, though she did seem somewhat flustered. As the peer bent his auburn head over her hand, she said, "My lord! Such a surprise...that is to say, not a surprise, for we certainly invited you, but...a pleasure! Yes, a pleasure, to be sure."

Timothy Stewart's eyes twinkled. "Very prettily put, Aunt Sarah," he drawled.

"Lord Eversley, may I present Timothy Stewart?" said Deborah. "Timothy is my oldest and dearest friend—we grew up together. Timothy, Lord Robert Eversley."

The two men surveyed each other. Timothy saw a gentleman much above the average in height, with the lean figure and browned complexion of a sportsman. His clothing did not reflect his obvious interest in the outdoors, however; no tailor but Weston could have made his perfectly cut black frock coat, and though his neckcloth did not reach the heights prescribed by the most modish of men, it was impeccably starched and skilfully arranged.

For his part, Eversley saw what he could only characterize in his own mind as a fashionable fribble. Though Timothy's innate good taste would never allow him to go over the line, he affected every excess of costume which was currently the rage. From the watch fobs dangling from his waistcoat, to the neckcloth which only just allowed him to turn his head, Timothy was every inch the young buck on the town.

"Stewart." Eversley nodded politely.

"Charmed, my lord," said Timothy, vastly amused by the faint disapproval he detected in Eversley's eyes. "Deborah, my love, don't forget to save me a waltz," he said to the somewhat puzzled young lady. "I won't be gainsaid, my girl, so don't think to escape me." He offered his arm to Sarah. "Aunt Sarah, shall we? I can't resist the opportunity to parade around the room with the second most beautiful woman here. Your servant, Eversley." With a nod and a wave, they were gone.

Deborah felt suddenly shy. "I've known Timothy forever," she said. "He's a sad scamp, I fear."

"Indeed," said Eversley dryly. Deborah looked up at him suspiciously, but he only smiled down at her with such warmth that she coloured. "Did you really think I wouldn't come this evening?" he asked softly. "Tell the truth now."

"I hoped... I mean, I wondered... Oh, I don't know what I mean!" Deborah said in confusion. She did not meet his eyes.

"Well, never mind," said Eversley, hard put to hide his exultation. "But later this evening, Deborah—may I call you Deborah?—later this evening, Deborah, we will discuss the matter at greater length."

TIMOTHY JERKED BACK his head in the direction from which they had come. "Our little Deborah aims high," he remarked.

"She does not," Sarah said hotly. "She's every bit as wellborn as Eversley. One of Geoffrey's ancestors fought at Crécy, I'll have you know. Her birth and breeding entitle her to look as high as she might wish for a bridegroom."

"Hold, Aunt, hold!" Timothy said, laughing. "I meant nothing by it, I promise you. Simply that Eversley has been long on the market and, so far at least, most successful at eluding capture."

"Capture!" Sarah sniffed. "My Deborah would never lower herself to 'capture' anyone. For your information, Timothy Stewart, if I know one thing about my Deborah, it's this: she will never marry for anything but love."

Timothy's expression softened. "Good luck to her, then," he said. "There's no one more deserving to love and be loved than our girl, eh, Aunt Sarah?"

Sarah watched the young man, a troubled look on her face. "What of you, Timothy?" she said. "When are you going to find love?"

"Dear Aunt, I find love every day," the young man said lightly. "Problem is, it never lasts long."

"Pooh!" said Aunt Sarah. "Shop girls and opera dancers. Any young gentleman of fashion must have his flings."

"Aunt Sarah!" said Timothy, shocked but amused. "A lady doesn't speak of such things."

Sarah smiled sadly. "There are those," she said quietly, "who would not put me in the category of lady."

Timothy looked troubled. "Never say so, Aunt Sarah—not after so many years."

She shrugged. "Some people have long memories," she said simply.

They strolled in silence for a moment. "I have often regretted," he said finally, "as I know my father did, his part in your..."

"Ruin?" Sarah supplied. "You shouldn't nor should he have," she said. "We were young, and in love, and very, very foolish."

Timothy turned to face her. "Tell me the truth, Aunt," he said intently. "Is my father the reason you never married?"

Sarah smiled shakily. "Partly," she admitted. "But he was blameless, Timothy. Remember, it was my father who chased us to the border and brought me home. If it had been up to your papa, we would have wed."

"I never understood what your father had against the marriage," Timothy said, brow furrowed. "After all, my father was—or would have been—a suitable mate for you, by birth and fortune."

"Ah, but Stewart was another like yourself," Sarah said. "A little wild, and terribly hot to hand. I could have tamed him, I think, but my father disagreed." She blinked away the tears which had risen to her eyes. "That is why I have always felt so close to you, Timothy. In another world, a better world, I might have been your mama."

Timothy took both her hands in his. "Well, Aunt Sarah, as my own mother died so long ago I can scarce remember her, let us just say that you have the job. If you want it, that is?"

"Oh, Timothy." Sarah was forced to take out her handkerchief and dab at her eyes. "You sweet, sweet boy."

"Come now, no tears tonight," Timothy said heartily. "This is the night of Deborah's triumph, and I, for one, refuse to spend it wailing and moaning over the past. Are we agreed?"

"We are," said Aunt Sarah. "But, Timothy—" she stretched up and kissed his cheek "—thank you."

Timothy and Sarah continued their progress through the crowd. Sarah stopped from time to time to speak to this lady or that gentleman in performance of her duties as hostess, however uncomfortable she might have been with the role.

Timothy smiled and bowed as was necessary, and did his best to stand in Deborah's father's stead.

"Good evening, Miss Beldon, Mr. Stewart," said a calm voice.

Timothy Stewart's smile froze. He turned to the young lady who had spoken with every appearance of reluctance. Sarah looked back and forth between them, perplexed.

Lady Margaret Rawlings occupied a unique position in London society. A fiery-haired, green-eyed beauty of excellent birth, she had first come to Town at the tender age of sixteen to play hostess for her widowed father. She had been surprisingly successful. The ton had become quite accustomed to seeing her at the head of her father's table, and more than holding her own at his brilliant political dinners. So accustomed, in fact, that when Lord Rawlings died, and his daughter set up housekeeping with no more than an aged cousin to lend her countenance, no one had so much as raised an eyebrow. To be sure, it was as much the young lady's apparent indifference to men as her renowned tact which allowed her to take liberties no other unmarried woman of her age would dare. So it was that Lady Margaret found herself in the enviable position of being one of the foremost hostesses in a city which lived for amusement, without the unpleasant necessity of taking a husband for propriety's sake.

Timothy bent stiffly over her hand. "My lady," he said shortly. He bowed to her escort. "My lord."

The elegant Marquess of Pembroke raised an arched brow in Timothy's direction. "Stewart," he nodded. "Miss Beldon. It appears that you have a triumph on your hands."

Sarah smiled shyly. "Coming from such a social force as yourself, my lord, that is high praise indeed."

"Oh, I am past the age to make a mark on society," said Pembroke, uttering a patent falsehood. "It's young bucks like Stewart and my son who set the mode today. How is my son, by the way, Stewart?"

"Burle is very well, sir. We just returned from a short jaunt out of town. I'm sure he'll be calling on you."

Something suspiciously like a twinkle appeared in Pembroke's eye. "To be sure, to be sure. A spot of rustication, my boy?"

Timothy raised his head. "The young woman," he said forcefully, "accosted us only because of a misunderstanding. I deeply regret that your niece was subjected to such a scene, my lord."

Pembroke blinked. "What?"

Lady Margaret said smoothly, "Just a misunderstanding, Uncle. A...lady, spoke to Mr. Stewart and me when we were driving in the Park, several weeks ago." She met Timothy's gaze squarely. "I thought nothing of it."

Timothy flushed. "You are too good, my lady. Your uncle will, I am sure, agree with me that the incident was unpardonable. Now, if you'll excuse me? Your servant, my lord." He bowed jerkily, and he and Aunt Sarah moved away, she more mystified than ever.

"Niece?" said Pembroke to his companion.

Lady Margaret shrugged, apparently unconcerned. "A friend of Mr. Stewart's—his mistress, to be blunt—merely spoke to us, 'tis all. He makes a great deal too much of the matter." She did not look at her uncle.

Pembroke checked a startled exclamation. "I think not," he said finally. "The boy should not allow his—" he paused "—his friends such license."

"I doubt that he knew her intentions," Lady Margaret said lightly. "At any rate, 'tis monumentally unimportant to me what Mr. Stewart's friends do, or who they are, for that matter."

"Good," said Pembroke firmly. "I'm quite fond of the boy, Maggie, you know that, but I tell you straight out and to your face, he's not for you."

Lady Margaret laughed; if the smile did not quite reach her eyes, her uncle did not notice. "We are agreed on that, then," she said. "Mr. Stewart is far too stubborn and full of himself to be any woman's husband. Now, Uncle mine, shall we dance?"

"We shall indeed," said the marquess, and the pair twirled off into the laughing, glittering crowd.

"MY LORD! You startled me."

"I do seem to have that effect on you. I wonder why?" Lord Eversley said. He closed the French doors behind him and stepped out to join Deborah on the terrace. "A lovely night, is it not?"

"Yes," Deborah said. "Such a refreshing change from the ballroom—it's so fearfully hot!"

"I'm ashamed to admit that I've hoped the heat would overwhelm you," Eversley said. "I've been trying to get you alone all evening."

"Oh?" was all that Deborah could think of to say.

"Lord Rankin seems to have taken it upon himself to foil my plans, however," Eversley said dryly. "I'm expecting him to join us here at any moment."

"He has been rather a nuisance, hasn't he?" Deborah said honestly. "He never even speaks to me, you know. Just follows me around and makes calf eyes at me."

"I can understand that," Eversley said. "You are quite, quite beautiful." The darkness hid Deborah's blush. "No, don't move away!" he said urgently, and stepped closer to the girl. "You know why I'm here, don't you?"

"I—I—" Deborah stammered.

Eversley took her hand. "I've been very patient, sweet Deborah."

"Have you?" she said faintly.

"Yes," he answered. "The first moment I saw you, two months ago, I knew." He stepped out of the shadows, so that the moonlight lit his smile, and his eyes, staring down into Deborah's own.

"My lord! I can't . . . I don't . . ." She pulled her hand out of Eversley's and half turned away.

"What is it, Deborah?" Eversley asked. "Are my words unwelcome? Did you not know that I've been longing to speak?"

Deborah spread her hands. "I don't know how to explain!" she said. "Perhaps I can begin by telling you about my parents."

"Your parents? I don't understand."

"My father and mother eloped," Deborah began.

"You can't think that would matter to me!" Eversley protested. "I know I have the reputation of being, well, proud and high in the instep, but I assure you, Deborah—"

"That's not what I meant," Deborah hastened to assure him. "It's just . . . Oh, my lord, I envy them that!"

"Elopement?" Eversley sounded surprised.

"No, of course not!" Deborah said. "To be so in love that one doesn't stop to count the cost," she said. "To be so deeply attached to another that nothing else matters. Can you understand?"

"I can," Eversley said after a moment's hesitation. "And I gather you don't feel that way about me?"

Deborah ignored his question. "People say," she said carefully, "that you have decided to set up your nursery, that you realize your responsibility to your name and your family, and have determined to find a bride this season."

"People," said Eversley acerbically, "show a great deal of impertinence!"

"Be that as it may, my lord, I shouldn't wish . . . That is to say, you should wait . . . I know that marital love is not fashionable, my lord, but you should do yourself a great disservice if you married for anything less!" Deborah finally blurted.

"Can it be that you don't know?" Eversley said, astonishment in his voice. "Can it be that you are unaware of my feelings? From the moment we met, Deborah Tollin, I was lost. I felt as though my heart had stopped that first night and then started again, beating so hard and so fast that I thought it would burst. I've waited so long for you!'' He stepped out of the moonlight and closer to Deborah. ''I don't want you because you are wellborn or plump in the pocket,'' he said, ''though you are. And I don't want you because I think you would be a good mother to my children, though I do. I want you because I am deeply, deliriously in love with you, and because I think that no other woman could possibly make me happy.''

''You . . . you do?''

''I do. And I thought . . . I had dreamed—'' he stepped closer and recaptured Deborah's hand ''—I believed,'' he murmured, turning her hand over and pressing a kiss onto her palm, ''that you felt the same for me.'' He took her chin between strong fingers. ''Was I wrong, my sweet?''

''No,'' Deborah whispered. ''No, my lord, you were not.''

Eversley chuckled softly. ''Do you think you could bring yourself to call me Robert, Deborah? As I am just about to kiss you, it seems only fair.''

''Yes, Robert,'' Deborah said meekly and eagerly lifted her face.

A long silence ensued. When at last Eversley lifted his face from Deborah's and tenderly tucked back into place the black curls which had gone awry, Deborah said ruefully, ''Have I given you a disgust for me, my love? I should have demurred; a lady always demurs, and says, 'Oh, sir, this is so sudden,' or, 'I must consult my father,' or something equally foolish.''

'''My love,''' Eversley repeated. ''I like the sound of that, sweeting. As for demurring, pray do not repine over the matter. Should anyone question me, I will swear that you kept me dangling for weeks.''

''Thank you, sir.'' Deborah lightly ran her finger along the line of Eversley's jaw, which compelled him to kiss her again.

"About your father, though..." Eversley said when at last he lifted his lips from Deborah's. "Will he forgive me, do you think? I know I should have asked him for your hand first, but I just couldn't wait."

Deborah smiled. "I'll tell you a little secret, Robert, but you must promise not to mention it to Papa."

"So sworn," Eversley said gravely.

"He told me weeks ago that you would offer for me. He said that you looked at me just the way he had looked at Amanda, my mother."

"An astute gentleman," Eversley remarked. "And did you believe him?"

"I didn't dare," Deborah said. "The disappointment would have crushed me, you see, if you hadn't."

This time it was Deborah who boldly reached up to Eversley and the two figures, dark against the moonlight, melted into one.

"Oh, Robert!" Deborah sighed. "We shall be so very, very, happy."

"Deborah! Deborah! Where are you?" Aunt Sarah rushed out onto the terrace; the light spilling out through the open French doors showed the tears streaming from her eyes. "Oh, my poor girl! There's been an accident, and Geoffrey is—Geoffrey is—" Her shoulders shook. "Oh, Deborah!"

CHAPTER TWO

DEBORAH TOLLIN STARED UP at the portrait which hung over the mantelpiece. "There are two of these portraits, you know," she said, as though speaking to herself. "Papa..." Her voice faltered for a moment. "Papa liked the original so much that he had the artist do a precise copy, to hang at Shaftsworth. He always said that the painter had exactly captured my mother." She tipped her head to one side. "I have been told that I am very like her, but I must confess, I think it untrue. Oh, I do have her black curls, but her eyes were much bluer than mine, and she was more lovely than I shall ever be."

"I don't think so," Lord Eversley said lightly.

She ignored him. "How deceiving portraits are," she reflected. "One would think that they would reveal their subjects, but they don't, do they?"

"Oh, I don't know," Eversley said, happy to see Deborah's mind, at least for the moment, on something other than the tragedy. "A man may hide much, but his eyes give the truth away."

"Do they, Robert?" she asked bleakly. "Then why didn't I know? I should have known."

Eversley groaned. "What an oaf I am, sweeting," he said. "I didn't mean...I was speaking of generalities...can you forgive me?"

Deborah blinked rapidly and shook her head. "There is nothing to forgive, Robert," she said, with a forlorn attempt at normality which touched Robert's heart. "After all, I must become...accustomed to things, mustn't I? You'll think me very foolish, I know, but sometimes it all doesn't seem quite real to me."

"I don't think you foolish at all," Eversley said gruffly. "Far from it, love."

For perhaps the thousandth time, Eversley wondered how Geoffrey Tollin could have done such a thing to the daughter he had professed to love. Deborah had been devastated by the news of her father's suicide. Eversley could only be glad that Geoffrey had done the deed at his country estate, Shaftsworth, and not here in Town, where Deborah would have been the one to discover the body. As it was, Eversley had been deeply concerned by the effect the news had had on Geoffrey's daughter. For three days, she had refused to leave her bedchamber, or to see any but her maid; it was not until the funeral, that morning, that she had left the solitude of her room. Eversley was shocked by the changes a few short days had made in his beloved. Always slender, she had become positively frail. Her eyes, once so lively and full of spirit, were listless and sad, surrounded by the dark shadows of grief. Watching her valiant struggle to hide her sorrow, Eversley cursed the memory of the man he had once admired.

"Can I get you anything, sweeting?" Eversley asked Deborah. "Something to eat, perhaps? You must keep your strength up, you know."

"No, thank you, Robert," Deborah said absently. "But if you desire something, do ring for Danson—he'll be only too happy to bring you anything you like." She stared into the fire, lost in thought.

"Deborah?"

"Hmm?"

"Deborah, listen to me."

Deborah looked up. "What is it, Robert?"

Eversley took a deep breath. "Deborah, I think that we should be married, very quietly of course, but as soon as possible." He watched Deborah's face closely for her reaction.

"But, Robert," she said blankly, "we can't."

"Oh, I know that it's customary to wait a year after a death in one's immediate family," Eversley acknowledged impatiently, "but, in this case at least, I think custom should go hang." He put his arms tenderly around the girl. "I want to take care of you, Deborah," he murmured, his face pressed against her sweet-smelling curls. "It breaks my heart to see you so unhappy."

For just a moment, Deborah crushed her face against Eversley's broad chest. "Oh, my dear, I don't deserve such devotion," she whispered tearfully.

"Nonsense," Eversley said. "Of course you do. You're the sweetest, dearest—"

Deborah twisted in her seat, away from Eversley. "Don't, Robert!" she cried. "I can't bear it." She began to weep softly.

"My dear," said Eversley, "what is it? No, my love, no, don't cry. What's wrong?"

"Papa killed himself, Robert," Deborah said. "Can you imagine how desperately unhappy he must have been? How alone he must have felt? And I—" her voice was filled with self-loathing "—I, so involved with my balls and my dresses, and what entertainment I should attend, that I never even noticed. Oh, Robert, I shall never, ever forgive myself!"

"Deborah Tollin!" Eversley snapped. Deborah's head flew up; she was not accustomed to being spoken to in that tone of voice.

"Do not, pray, speak such gudgeon to me," he said sternly.

"I beg your pardon?" Deborah said faintly.

"You heard me. Do not, if you please, attempt to take responsibility for something which was out of your hands," Eversley said, maintaining his scolding tone with some difficulty. "You are not God, Deborah. You could have done nothing to prevent your father's death."

"But, Robert," Deborah said doubtfully, "I should have realized . . . I should have known . . ."

"How?" Eversley asked. "Your father was a determined man, Deborah, and a determined man can always keep a secret."

"From a stranger, perhaps," Deborah said bitterly. "But not from his only child. You said yourself, the eyes always tell the truth."

Eversley silently cursed his own glib tongue, but only said gently, "Don't blame yourself, my love. It wasn't your fault."

"If only I knew why he did it! What could have driven him to such an extreme, Robert?" Deborah asked desolately.

"It doesn't matter," Eversley said. "You will probably never know what influenced your father to act as he did, and I think that the sooner you accept that, the better off you will be. I know something else, too, Deb—your father would not have wished you to blame yourself."

Deborah sat silent for so long that Eversley began to wonder if he had taken too harsh a tone with the girl. Then she heaved a deep sigh and said, smiling faintly at Eversley, "You're right, of course, Robert. You always are, it seems."

"Never say that, my dear!" Eversley said hastily, a smile lighting his green eyes. "If there is anything more unpleasant than someone who is always right, I don't know what it is."

"Not to me," Deborah declared. "To me you are a knight *sans peur et sans reproche*. How lucky I am to have you!"

"You still have not answered my question, you know," he said. "Will you marry me, Deborah? Right away?"

Deborah pulled away from his embrace and rose to take an agitated turn about the room. "I'm sorry, Robert," she said finally. "Much as I would like to, I may not. 'Twould be too disrespectful, to marry so soon after my father's death.''

Geoffrey Tollin ill deserved such loyalty, Eversley thought, particularly from the innocent daughter who would have to live with her father's dishonour. But he said only, ''May I not persuade you, my love? 'Tis most important to me!''

Deborah took his hands. ''Please don't press me, Robert,'' she said. ''It's very hard to refuse you, but I feel that I must. Can you understand?''

''I can. Your scruples do you credit,'' he said, and smiled the smile which had first drawn Deborah to him. ''But be warned, Deb, I don't give up quite so easily as this!''

TIMOTHY STEWART pulled up his horse and took a deep breath of the sweet morning air. The Park was deserted; no person of fashion would think of venturing out for any reason so early in the day, much less only to go riding. This was the precise reason that Timothy was to be found here every morning; he found the solitude a welcome change from the crowds and confusion of the social scene.

Another lone rider broke out of the trees and began to canter up the path toward Timothy. What he saw made him stare, then frown, then spur his horse to meet the rider.

''What are you doing here?'' he said without preamble. ''Where's your groom?''

''I sent him home,'' Lady Margaret Rawlings said calmly.

''Dash it, Mar—my lady, you shouldn't be out riding alone,'' he said. ''Who knows whom you might encounter here at this time of day, and with no one to protect you!''

''I need no protection,'' the woman said, and smiled at Timothy. ''I'm safe with you, Timothy.''

''No, dash it all, you're not!'' Timothy blurted. ''With my reputation, you'd need only to be seen here alone with me to be ruined.''

Lady Margaret shrugged gracefully. "I care not," she said.

"You...care...not?" Timothy repeated incredulously. "Margaret, have you run mad?"

Lady Margaret smiled wistfully. "In a way," she said obscurely.

Timothy grabbed her bridle and forced her mount to turn around. "I shall take you home," he said grimly, "and pray God no one sees us on the way." He glared at her. "Will you come peacefully, or must I drag you?"

"Yes, Timothy," Lady Margaret said meekly.

"What?"

"Yes, I'll come peacefully," she said.

"Good," Timothy growled.

They cantered along in silence for several moments, then Lady Margaret ventured a glance at her companion through lowered lashes. "Won't you even talk about it?" she asked.

"Talk about what?" They left the Park and cantered through the traffic which was still relatively light.

"Timothy," she protested, "it wasn't so awful. Just a little...." She giggled. "In truth," she confessed, "I thought it rather comical."

"Comical? Comical?" Timothy spluttered. "If I needed any more proof that I'm a bad influence on you, this is it!"

"I did have a sense of humour before I met you, actually," Lady Margaret said apologetically. "Don't think too badly of me for it, will you?" Timothy did not answer her. He stared straight ahead, his mouth set in a grim line.

"Alas!" she said. "I can see that I have sunk myself beneath reproach in your eyes. Papa always said that my unfortunate tendency toward levity would be my undoing." A twist of Timothy's lips, quickly suppressed, was her reward. Emboldened, she pulled up her horse. "Timothy," she said earnestly, "really, 'twas not so bad! The lady—"

"Person," Timothy corrected her coldly. He did not stop, so Lady Margaret was obliged to spur her horse to catch up with him.

"The 'person' just thought that I was trying to steal you away from her," Margaret said. "I can understand her anger." She looked at Timothy; his face was set in a stony mask. "Surely you don't think that you are the first young gentleman to keep a mistress? All gentlemen do it. I will grant you, it is not quite the thing for the lady to have approached you while you were with me, but if I can forget it, why can't you?"

"Does the marquess know you are here?" Timothy asked, ignoring her question.

"Of course not."

"I thought as much," he said.

"Need I remind you, Timothy, that the Marquess of Pembroke, my uncle, is neither my guardian nor my trustee," Margaret said angrily. "My life and my fortune are my own!"

"I wish you joy of them, my lady," Timothy said. They had reached the Rawlings' town house. "Good morning, Lady Margaret," he said, and rode away.

"Men!" said the lady, uttering an ageless lament. "Men!"

THE BUTLER OPENED THE DOOR and cleared his throat portentously. "Mr. Roger Henderson, milord," he announced.

Lord Alexander Burle leapt out of the chair into which he had folded his long, lanky frame, pale eyes bulging in alarm. "H-H-Henderson?" he stammered. "Here?" He looked round the room rather wildly, as though he expected the aforementioned gentleman to jump out from underneath a table.

"In the small sitting room, actually, milord," said the butler, much accustomed to his young master's fits and starts. "Shall I show him up?"

"Er, that is to say, could you not have told him that I was out?" Burle asked plaintively. "Henderson, of all people!" he wailed.

"I'm afraid, my lord, that you neglected to inform me that you were not at home," the butler said with every appearance of regret.

"Oh, very well," said Burle, with a long-suffering sigh. "Show him in, then, Jennings. And bring more brandy!" he called, as the servant quietly closed the door.

Burle turned to his guests. "Forgive the interruption, my friends. Roger Henderson—a friend of my father's, known him since I was a lad. A diverting old gentleman, to be sure," he explained, his breezy words at odds with his crestfallen expression.

Timothy Stewart chuckled richly, one brow raised eloquently. "Indeed, Burle," he said, "it's evident how very amusing you think the gentleman. Why, by your trepidation, one might think—"

Whatever observation Stewart had been about to make was cut short by the opening of the door. Mr. Henderson entered the library to find Burle gesticulating wildly at his friend, while Stewart looked angelically off into space. "Harrumph!" said Mr. Henderson, and stared at a blushing Burle from under beetling brows.

"Oh!" Burle squeaked. "That is to say, how good it is to see you again, sir. My father will be most sorry to have missed you, I'm sure. May I offer you a brandy?"

"'Tis a pity that I've missed Pembroke, but, er, yes, a brandy would be excellent," he said gruffly, his attention on Burle's two friends. A pointed glance at Burle was all that was necessary for the young lord to hasten to perform introductions.

"Sir Cyril, may I present to you Mr. Roger Henderson? Mr. Henderson, Sir Cyril Dennison," Burle said. Sir Cyril, a gentleman in his forties with a bland, round face, nodded politely. "And Mr. Timothy Stewart."

Henderson frowned. "Timothy Stewart, eh?" he said, not quite able to keep the disapproval out of his voice.

Stewart smiled charmingly at Henderson. "Why, yes, sir. Have we met?" he asked, winking at Burle.

Henderson ignored the question and turned to Burle. "Where have you been keeping yourself, lad? Haven't seen much of you of late."

"Timothy and I have been in the country," Burle said. "We came back to Town three or four days ago for Miss Tollin's ball, then went right back to Lord Duncan's."

"Duncan's, eh?" Henderson said. "I pity you, lad."

"No need, sir," Timothy put in gaily. "Lady Duncan was not present."

Henderson turned to stare at Timothy. "A gentleman," he said heavily, "does not speak so of a lady."

"Of course, sir, you're quite right," Timothy said, eyes gleaming. "Forgive me. I should not have assumed that you referred to Lady Duncan when you offered your condolences." Henderson's mood was helped neither by the knowledge that he had indeed been referring to Lady Duncan, a veritable dragon of a woman, nor by Sir Cyril's appreciative chuckle. He glared at Timothy.

"Ah, er..." Burle, fairly babbling with distress, looked miserably from one man to the other. "That is to say...come and speak to Sir Cyril!" he said, placing a hand clumsily on Henderson's sleeve and moving him away from Stewart. For a moment, it seemed as though Henderson would resist the young peer's attempt to play peacemaker, but his long-standing affection for Burle finally overcame his stubbornness, and he allowed himself to be led across the room and guided into conversation with Sir Cyril.

By the time Burle returned to Stewart's side, Stewart had apparently forgotten Henderson's hostility and was lazily flipping through a book of poetry which stood on a side table. "Do you know, Burle," he remarked to his friend, "I think I should become a poet."

"What?"

"A poet," repeated Stewart patiently. "My name would look quite well, I think, embossed in gold on the cover of a tome such as this," he said, waving the book. "And the ladies, of course, find poets, whatever their method or manner, to be the most romantic creatures." Stewart sighed dreamily. "I think it might suit me, to be tenderly cossetted by some fair handmaiden of Erato, while waiting for inspiration to strike!" He grinned at Burle. "Well, my friend? What think you?"

"I, um, perhaps..." Stewart burst into delighted laughter. "Are you just joking, then, Timothy?" Burle asked, relieved. "I am never quite sure what to make of the things you say."

"You're a good friend, Burle, and a complete hand, but your sense of humour leaves much to be desired," Stewart said, shaking his head. "You're quite as bad as old Henderson, and I can say no worse than that."

Burle's face fell. "About Henderson, Timothy," he said awkwardly, "he doesn't mean to be uncivil, I'm sure but, well, he's just a very strict-minded old gentleman. You mustn't think anything of it—his whole family is like that. He's rather a good sort, actually." Stewart fixed his friend with a sceptical eye and Burle hastened to add, "You might think I wasn't terribly fond of him, by my demeanour when he first arrived, but you'd be wrong, Timothy, truly. 'Tis just that I've known him practically since I was born, and—" Burle smiled sheepishly "—well, he makes me feel an absolute cawker."

Stewart laughed aloud and clapped Burle on the back. "Think no more of it, I pray you, Burle. I daresay my reputation has preceded me, for you know what tattlemongers Londoners are." He rolled his eyes. "Let a man but break his fast, and the gossips will have it that he's eaten a banquet!" Timothy shrugged. "Perhaps as Henderson comes to know me better, he will perceive my many sterling qualities," Stewart said dryly. "If not, well..." He spread his hand eloquently.

Across the room, as Henderson watched Stewart speak to the lanky young Burle, he observed the latter's clear admiration for his less wellborn friend. Henderson's brow furrowed, and he did not hear Sir Cyril address him until the other man had repeated himself twice. "Eh? What was that?" he said finally, catching the end of Sir Cyril's remark.

"I said, you seem troubled by Stewart's presence," said Sir Cyril calmly. "Did you not know that he and Burle had struck up an acquaintance?"

"No, I did not, and I cannot like it," Henderson said bluntly. "I am very much surprised that Pembroke allows it." He referred to the Marquess of Pembroke, Burle's father and his own very good friend.

"Frankly, Mr. Henderson, I agree with you," Sir Cyril said. "Though he is still received everywhere..."

"He is," Henderson acknowledged, "but that, Sir Cyril, I take to be only a sign of the dissolute times in which we live. This Stewart is no more than a wastrel, a shameless here-and-therian who lives for gaming and the pursuit of women. Why, 'tis common knowledge." Henderson angrily dashed back the rest of his brandy. "A disgrace, I call it, that such a one should be allowed to lead Burle down the primrose path. Burle is too good a lad, too good by far, to be so corrupted."

Sir Cyril nodded. "Quite right, Henderson," he said, then, "By the way, I understand you are to be felicitated. Your nephew is to wed?"

Henderson's attention had been on Timothy and Burle, but at these words his eyes snapped back to Sir Cyril, his face turning a deep shade of purple. "What?" he blustered. "What was that?"

Burle, overhearing, hurried across the room to the two men. "What is it?" he asked worriedly. "May I—"

"What did you say?" Henderson asked Sir Cyril again savagely.

Sir Cyril raised a haughty brow. "I merely offered you my congratulations upon the betrothal of your nephew, Lord Eversley," he said coolly. "I fail to see what you could find offensive in that."

"Is Eversley engaged?" Burle asked, surprised. "To whom, I wonder?"

"Miss Deborah Tollin," Sir Cyril explained. "The engagement was made on the night of her ball."

"Deb, engaged to Eversley?" Stewart said to himself. "Well, I'll be damned!"

The colour in Henderson's face faded from deep purple to dull red. "Allow me to beg your pardon again, Sir Cyril," he said formally, and bowed jerkily from the waist. "I had thought Miss Tollin's recent bereavement would preempt any engagement—'twas my mistake." He bowed again, and set his glass down on a nearby table.

"What bereavement?" Timothy Stewart asked. When Henderson turned to leave without answering, the young man placed himself squarely in Henderson's path and repeated firmly, "What bereavement?"

Mr. Henderson answered coldly, "Geoffrey Tollin was buried this morning. If you will kindly step aside?"

Stewart didn't move. "I don't believe it," he scoffed. "Uncle Geoffrey is as healthy as I am."

"*Uncle* Geoffrey?" Henderson echoed, caught by surprise. "Are you related to Miss Tollin, then?"

"No, no, but we've known each other since we were children," Stewart explained impatiently. "What happened to Deborah's father? Was there an accident?"

"You might say so," spat out Henderson bitterly.

"Timothy..." Burle began.

"If I have raised a difficult subject, sir..." Sir Cyril said.

Stewart ignored Burle and Sir Cyril. "What happened?" he asked, his gaze fixed unswervingly on Henderson.

"Tollin shot himself." Henderson's simple words seemed to reverberate in the suddenly silent room.

"My God!" Burle gasped.

Stewart took an involuntary step back. "How can that be?" he whispered. "Are you sure?"

"I attended his funeral myself," Henderson said, then asked witheringly, "Are you quite satisfied, Mr. Stewart?" With a sketchy bow in Burle's direction, he headed for the door.

"Do you mind, Mr. Henderson, if I accompany you?" Sir Cyril asked, taking up his hat and cane. "Perhaps we might stop at White's for a brandy."

Mr. Henderson grunted, and taking that as consent, Sir Cyril bid the two young men a polite good day, and he and Mr. Henderson departed.

"I can't believe it," Stewart said. "Uncle Geoffrey, dead by his own hand. I can't believe it."

"I'm sorry, Timothy," Burle said sincerely. "Lord, what a thing to have happen. How dreadful for his daughter!"

"Deborah," said Stewart, much struck. "Poor lass." He turned to Burle. "You must allow me to excuse myself, Burle. I know that we had an engagement, but under the circumstances..."

"Pray don't trouble yourself about it, Timothy," Burle said quickly. He laid a hand on his shaken friend's sleeve. "If there's anything that I can do...?"

"Thank you, Burle," Timothy said, "but there's nothing anyone can do now, I'm afraid. Poor Deborah!"

CHAPTER THREE

DEBORAH TOLLIN, followed at a discreet distance by a bored footman, walked slowly down a path which skirted the edges of Green Park. A few cows grazed quietly on the well-kept grass; the milkmaids in their pretty gowns, engaged to dispense the cows' milk to any thirsty passersby, loitered and gossiped in the nearly empty park.

The peace of the enclosure was broken by a horseman who rode in and pulled his mount to a halt. The milkmaids giggled in delight at the sight of the handsome young rider, clearly a gentleman of the quality. He was unaware of their regard, standing in his stirrups to scan the park until his eyes alighted on a black-clad figure moving slowly away from him. He spurred his mount and crossed the park at a canter, sliding gracefully from the saddle when he reached the pedestrians. He clapped a hand on the footman's shoulder and motioned the man to be silent, then stepped quietly ahead of the servant and called, "Deborah!"

The girl whirled around, and a smile of pure joy transformed her sad face. "Timothy!" she cried, and flew into the open arms which awaited her.

Timothy Stewart smoothed back the few curls which had slipped out from under the black velvet bonnet and whispered, "My poor Deb. What a terrible time you have had of it!"

"Oh, Timothy!" Deborah smiled, but tears glistened in her eyes. "How glad I am to see you, my friend."

"Forgive me for being so long about it," Timothy said soberly. "I had no idea!" He hugged Deborah tightly before releasing her. "I'm so sorry, Deb, so devilish sorry," he said awkwardly.

"Yes," said Deborah heavily. "As am I."

"Of all men, Uncle Geoffrey is the last I should have thought . . . that is to say, it is so hard to believe . . ." Seeing Deborah's face twist in misery, Stewart hastily changed the subject. "Lord, Deb, whatever possessed you to choose Green Park for your walk?" he asked, in as normal a tone as he could manage. "I've searched all over London for you, I'll have you know. Aunt Sarah told me that you had gone out for some air, but I naturally assumed that she meant in Hyde Park. I went up and down Rotten Row a dozen times, trying to catch sight of you, before I realized that you might be here, and so came to investigate." The expression on his face clearly demonstrated the sophisticated Londoner's distaste for the unfashionable, into which category Green Park definitely fell.

"Let us just say," Deborah said coldly, "that I prefer the company here."

Timothy's mouth fell open. "Prefer the company of a bunch of dashed cows?" he said, stupified. "Come now, Deb! Doing it rather too brown, don't you think?" He stopped. "Oh," he said.

"Oh, indeed," Deborah said ironically.

After a moment Timothy asked gently, "Has it been very bad, my dear?"

Deborah shrugged. "Not at all," she said. "I am merely invisible, you see. Apart from Lord Eversley, no one, not one of my friends or acquaintances, not one of Papa's, has called since his death. We have not received a single message. No cards have been left, no enquiries made. Do you blame me for avoiding Hyde Park? Lord knows what kind of reception I'd meet with, and frankly—" she essayed a shaky smile "—I don't feel up to the effort of exuding defiance, right at the moment."

"Infamous!" Timothy fumed. "The inequity, the sanctimonious posturing..." He pulled himself to a halt and took a deep breath. "Enough," he said, to himself as much as Deborah. "If they can do without us, then we can certainly do without them." Deborah squeezed his arm gratefully.

Timothy smiled down at Deborah, and they walked along in silence for several minutes, enjoying the warm sun and the gentle breeze that wafted through the open park. "Deborah?" he said finally, his gaze fixed firmly on his shoes.

"Yes?"

"Have you any idea why Uncle Geoffrey did it?"

Deborah said pensively, "I've asked myself that question a thousand times. I've racked my brains, trying to remember anything that he might have said or done, but to no purpose. I have no idea what made him take such a desperate measure, or what caused him to believe that there was no alternative."

"Might it have been money, do you think?" Stewart asked, surprising Deborah. "He would not be the first gentleman to have been driven to the wall by gaming debts. Are you in need, Deb? Because if you are, I daresay that I could come through with the ready." He grinned. "I have had the most marvellous run of luck at cards recently—you might as well benefit from it." Timothy looked sternly at Deborah. "And you needn't think that your pride must cause you to refuse. If you will not accept a loan from such an old friend as I, well, things have come to a sorry pass, indeed."

Deborah blinked rapidly. "Timothy Stewart," she said, in a husky voice, "you are the kindest, dearest, most thoughtful—"

Timothy held up a hand. "Please, brat!" he said laughingly. "I assure you, Deb, I never would have offered if I had known that you were going to turn maudlin on me. And I notice," he added shrewdly, "that you have not answered my question. Are you pockets-to-let?"

Deborah smiled at the young man. "No, Timothy, I am not," she told him. "Papa's solicitor assures me that everything is in order." She smiled dazzlingly at Timothy through her tears. "Thank you," she said simply.

"Don't be a goose, Deb," Timothy said lightly. "Someone has to keep an eye on you. Speaking of which," he went on with a crooked grin, "pray allow me to offer you my congratulations, Miss Tollin. A brilliant match—I am quite overwhelmed, I promise you." He bowed from the waist. As he raised his head, he was surprised to see Deborah frown and bite her lip. "Why, what's wrong, my sweet?" he asked.

"Oh, Timothy, everything is in such a muddle," Deborah said. "I scarce know which way to turn."

"What, then? Has Eversley cried off?"

"No, he has not," Deborah said, rather more sharply than she had intended. "But he should have, don't you see, Timothy? His family...his good name...the gossip..." She shrugged hopelessly.

"Don't be such a looby," Timothy said. "Lord, Deb, you should know that a scandal never lasts. By this time next week, you'll be supplanted by some heiress running off with a fortune hunter, or the birth of a duke's by-blow."

"I wish it were true," said Deborah bitterly, "but we both know better than that, Timothy."

"Well, perhaps not by next week," Timothy conceded, "but certainly—" He broke off, and turned to stare at a copse of trees on the far side of the park.

"What is it?" asked Deborah curiously. "Is something wrong?"

"No," said Timothy slowly. "At least, I don't think so. I had the strangest feeling, just now, that someone was watching us. I must have imagined it."

They walked in silence for several more moments, the footman trailing behind with Stewart's mount, before Deborah tried again. "Can't you see how wrong it would be for me to marry Eversley as things stand? To bring disgrace as my dowry—I couldn't bear it."

"Now, Deb, you mustn't let pride dictate—"

"Why not?" Deborah interrupted. "You have."

"That is a different situation entirely," Timothy said stiffly.

"Is it?" Deborah asked.

"Eversley won't care about the gossip," Timothy said, holding to his point. "He doesn't seem the type to back down in the face of a little opposition."

"That's all the more reason for me to break our engagement," Deborah said earnestly. "I know that Robert would never cry craven. 'Twas his nobility of character that first drew me to him."

"Nobility of character?" Timothy repeated. "Good Lord, you must love the man to spout such intolerable pap!" His eyes took on an irrepressible twinkle. "Truly, Deb, you might have told me that you desired a fusty old parson-type to wed. I should have made myself over years ago, had I known."

Deborah gasped in outrage. "Eversley is no parson," she said hotly. "He is handsome, and witty, and brave..." She trailed to a shamefaced halt as Stewart broke into laughter.

"Then perhaps it was not his nobility of character which was quite the first thing that drew you to him?" he teased.

Deborah could not help but smile. "Perhaps not," she owned, then her smile died. "Still, Timothy!"

He held a finger to her lips. "No more," he said. He took her hands in his own and looked down at her seriously. "Let me give you some good advice, my sweet," he said. "Wait a bit. This is not the moment to be making a decision which will affect your happiness for the rest of your life. You need time to think."

Deborah sighed. "Oh, Timothy, 'tis all so complicated."

"Isn't it just, though?" Timothy said, and tucked Deborah's arm back into his own. "Now," he said firmly, "you may tell the footman to take my horse and be off, for I intend to see you home myself. You need cheering up, my girl, and I'm just the man for the job."

A short time later, Deborah entered the drawing room, glancing back over her shoulder at Timothy, who followed. "Timothy Stewart, you are too, too bad," she scolded. "To say such a thing to me—you should be quite ashamed of yourself!"

"Should I, my fair one?" came his lazy drawl. "But only a female could truly appreciate that story, and what other female ears would I dare sully with such an outrageous tale?"

Deborah gave a gurgle of laughter. "I must confess, I would have given a monkey to see her face when she learned—"

"Good day, Deborah," Lord Eversley said evenly.

Deborah's head snapped around, and she stopped dead in her tracks. The guilty knowledge that she had just now been discussing her fiancé with Timothy made her stammer, "Robert! Wh—what a surprise."

"So it seems, Deborah, though I can't think why," he said.

Timothy bowed. "Hello, Eversley," he said. "Congratulations. You're a lucky knave, to be sure." The dislike in Eversley's eyes made him grin broadly.

Eversley forced himself to be courteous. "So I am," he said. He turned to Deborah. "I wonder, love, what scandalous tale Mr. Stewart was telling you to make you laugh so? Such hilarity should be shared."

Deborah blushed. "Oh, no, Robert, it was nothing, nothing at all."

"A mere bagatelle," Timothy agreed blandly.

"Timothy!"

"Don't fret, Deb. I'm quite sure that nothing I might say would affect Lord Eversley's opinion of me by one whit." Timothy laughed. "Would it, my lord?"

Eversley felt his composure deserting him, but he managed to say, "I am glad to see that you've been outdoors, Deb. The fresh air can only do you good."

"Exactly what I have been telling her," Timothy said, with an unholy twinkle in his eye. "Now, you must agree to go driving with me tomorrow, Deb. Even his lordship thinks that it would do you good."

Deborah, flustered, said, "Oh, no, Timothy, really, I don't think I care to..."

Stewart shook his head. "I'm afraid I'll not be refused, Deborah, my love. You must."

Eversley could feel the colour rising in his face. "If Deborah does not wish to accompany you—" he began coldly.

"Oh, no!" Deborah squeaked, then, "I should love to go, truly, Robert. Thank you, Timothy. 'Tis most kind of you to offer."

"My pleasure," said Timothy, highly amused by Eversley's angry flush, and the hand he could see opening and closing behind the peer's back. He judged it time, however, to beat a strategic retreat. "I shall leave you now, Deb, to enjoy a comfortable cose with his lordship," he said, bestowing a brilliant smile on that irritated gentleman. "Until tomorrow, my dear." He pressed a kiss onto Deborah's hand, much to her mystification and Eversley's chagrin. *"Au revoir!"*

Eversley ground his teeth as Timothy Stewart sailed happily out of the room. "How can you tolerate such a coxcomb, Deborah?" he burst out as the door closed behind Stewart.

Deborah looked hurt. "Why, Robert," she said, "Timothy is my friend. I most certainly do not think him a coxcomb." A warm look came into her eyes. "He is a dear," she said softly. "No matter how low I feel, he always manages to lift my spirits."

"I wish that I might be such a comfort to you."

Deborah stared at Eversley. "Did I not know you better, Robert, I would say that you were jealous. Of Timothy, of all people!" she added, with an involuntary trill of laughter.

"I am not jealous!" Eversley snapped. "Forgive me if I beg leave to tell you, my dear Deborah, that you are blind, as so many ladies have proven to be, to Mr. Stewart's many faults."

Belatedly noticing the tension in Eversley's shoulders and the set, angry look on his face, Deborah said soothingly, "I realize that Timothy has acquired the reputation of being somewhat, er, frivolous..."

"Frivolous? Hah!" Eversley snorted.

"Frivolous," Deborah repeated firmly. "If you knew him a little better, Robert, you would realize that he is merely high-spirited, as I'm sure he has every right to be."

"No, Deborah," said Eversley cuttingly. "To be perfectly blunt, your friend Timothy is a ne'er-do-well, no more and no less. He wastes his time, and his substance, on the pursuit of women and the laying of wagers; to be fashionable is his only ambition. He embodies everything that is worst about English manhood. I am surprised, quite frankly, that your father allowed you to pursue an acquaintance with one so eminently unsuitable."

Deborah leapt to her feet in outrage. "How dare you?" she gasped. "How dare you say such things about one whom I love as a brother? I won't have it, Eversley, I won't!"

"Then we must agree to differ, Deborah, for that is how I see your dear friend Timothy," Eversley said implacably. "I shall not forbid you to see him, though."

"What?" Deborah cried. "You shall not forbid me to see him? I agree, Lord Eversley, that you shall not forbid me, for you have not that right!'' She stood with arms akimbo, blue eyes flashing. ''Do not think to come the tyrant with me, my lord. I'll not tolerate it!''

''Need I remind you, Deborah, that as your betrothed, I have certain rights?'' Eversley said frigidly, every bit as infuriated as his bride-to-be.

''Ahem.'' Unnoticed by the pair in their anger, the drawing-room door had opened, and a red-faced Danson stood on the threshold, his gaze fixed somewhere off in the distance.

Deborah could have wept with frustration. ''Yes, Danson?'' she asked. ''What is it?''

''A caller for you, Miss Deborah,'' the butler replied.

''Miss Deborah will be along in a moment, thank you,'' Eversley said coolly, not unaware of the servant's disapproval. ''That will be all, Danson,'' he said firmly, when the butler seemed inclined to linger. After the door closed behind the man, Eversley shook his head. ''You allow your servants too much freedom, Deborah. They have become woefully impertinent.''

''Is that quite all, my lord?'' Deborah hissed. ''Or perhaps there is another subject upon which you might care to lecture me?''

'''Tis a pity that your father never broke you to the bridle, my girl,'' Eversley said disdainfully. ''He's left me the job, and I don't thank him for it.''

''Now we come down to it,'' Deborah said, face ashen. ''My father. It's not only Timothy you disapprove of, is it? It's my father, and the disgrace which he's brought down on your precious name. Isn't it, Eversley?''

''You are being ridiculous, Deborah,'' Eversley said, and took up his hat and cane. ''I can only presume that the strain of the last few days has been too much for you. I think it better that we drop the subject.''

''Oh, do you? Well, let me tell you, the—''

"I called today to inform you that I am obliged to go into the country for a few days, possibly a week," he continued inexorably. "I shall be obliged to pass by Shaftsworth on my way. Is there any commission which I may execute for you there? No? Very well, then." He moved toward the door, and paused with his hand on the knob. "Will you not wish me Godspeed, my dear?" he asked mockingly.

"Godspeed, my lord!" Deborah said from between clenched teeth. "And do not," she called after his disappearing back, "pray do not hurry home on my account!"

"THERE YOU ARE, Deborah, my love!" Sarah Beldon rose to her feet and hurried toward her niece. "We have wondered what was keeping you. Only look who has come to call—Mr. Henderson!"

Deborah extended her hand politely to Robert Eversley's uncle. "How do you do, sir?"

"Tolerably well," Roger Henderson replied gruffly, looking at Deborah from beneath drawn brows. "I wish to speak to Miss Tollin alone," he said bluntly.

Deborah was mystified, but amenable. "Certainly, sir," she said calmly. "That is, if my aunt has no objection?"

"But, Deborah," Sarah protested hesitantly, "'tis not quite the thing. For propriety's sake..."

"Spending a moment or two in conversation with Mr. Henderson will not adversely affect my reputation, I'm quite sure," Deborah said ironically. "Please, Aunt Sarah...?"

"Very well." Sarah rose stiffly to her feet and left the library without another word.

Even after Sarah had left the room, Henderson did not speak. He looked down at the floor uncomfortably, clenching and unclenching his fists.

"Let me pour you a glass of brandy, Mr. Henderson," said Deborah. "My father brought it home from France himself. He says...said—" her smile wavered for a moment "—that it was the best he'd ever tasted."

She carried a glass of the amber liquid carefully across the room, and watched Henderson so hopefully as he tasted it that he felt obliged to respond. "Good," he said. "Quite drinkable."

Deborah sank into her chair with a happy sigh. "I'm so glad you like it," she said. Henderson grunted, and drained the brandy in one swallow. Deborah was faintly surprised. Though she did not, of course, drink brandy herself, she knew that it was meant to be savoured, not gulped. Still, when Henderson put down his empty glass, she jumped to her feet to refill it.

Henderson coughed and picked it up again. "Very good," he said grudgingly. "Superior, in fact."

"Well," said Deborah, "what is it that you wished to discuss, Mr. Henderson?"

Eversley's uncle winced, and he drank down his second glass, only a little more slowly than the first. "I wish to discuss...that is to say...might I trouble you for another drop of this?"

"Of course," said Deborah, and complied. Her eyes widened as Henderson once again drained his glass. By the time he had finished swallowing the brandy, Mr. Henderson's colour had risen dramatically, and his eyes had taken on a somewhat glassy sheen. Deborah, observing the change, asked anxiously, "Are you all right, Mr. Henderson? You look—-unwell."

"I," said Henderson with a great deal of dignity, "am perfectly well, I promish...promise you." He corrected his pronunciation with rather more effort, Deborah thought, than should have been required.

"Are you quite sure?"

"Quite," he said, straightening his clothing and blinking owlishly. "In fact," he declared, "I cannot recall when last I felt so well!"

"I see," said Deborah doubtfully. Her experience with inebriated gentlemen was severely limited, but she was be-

ginning to suspect that she should not have been quite so
beforehand with the decanter. "I know," she said, bright-
ening. "Shall I send for the tea tray?" She seemed to recall
that food was thought to have a salutory effect upon those
who had had too much to drink.

Mr. Henderson could barely repress a shudder. "No!" he
said too quickly, then, "But perhaps...a bit more brandy?"
He held out his glass.

Deborah hesitated, then, with an inward shrug, filled the
proffered receptacle. It was not for her to tell Eversley's beloved uncle that he was castaway. She watched with something approaching awe as Mr. Henderson drank the brandy
and set the glass down with a crash.

"There now!" he said, looking round the room as though
he were not quite sure how he had got there. "What was I
shay...saying?" Deborah thought it wisest not to answer;
she folded her hands in her lap and fixed her gaze expec-
tantly on her guest.

Mr. Henderson rose to his feet and began to pace unsteadily back and forth. "Miss Tollin, I have come here today for a reason," he began sententiously.

"So I had supposed," Deborah murmured, then ducked
her head when Henderson frowned at her, and said hastily,
"Do go on, sir!"

"As I was saying," Henderson articulated carefully, "I
have come here today for a reason. 'Tis not a pleasant one,
no, nor a comfortable one. But never let it be said, Miss
Tollin, that any Henderson put pleasure before duty."

Deborah followed Mr. Henderson's less-than-smooth
navigation of the library with a fascinated eye. He barely
missed a small table as he circled the room, and the width of
his turn all but sent him stumbling into the fireplace. A
muttered curse at an impertinent end chair proved to be
Deborah's undoing; never before had she heard a gentleman tell a piece of furniture that he would "meet you in

hell, sir!'' Her stifled giggle caused Mr. Henderson to throw his shoulders back and direct an outraged glare at her.

"Yes, I don't doubt that a shense...sense of duty is a laughing matter to you, my girl!'' he said.

"Mr. Henderson, I didn't—''

"But it is not a joke to all of us, I beg leave to tell you. Do you think I enjoy poking my nose into Eversley's affairs, when I know well that he'd send me to the devil for it? But a man must do his duty, aye, and a lady, too!''

"Have you come to show me my duty, sir?'' asked Deborah, all amusement wiped from her face. "I suppose I should thank you.''

"Don't thank me. Give up my nephew,'' Henderson said brutally. "It's no good, holding him to a betrothal made before your father's suicide. Surely you agree. Oh, he'll marry you, make no mistake about that—his word is his bond. But he deserves better than to have his name besmirched, and that it will be if he weds you, Miss Tollin.''

Deborah had become very pale. "Does he know that you're here?'' she whispered.

"Of course not!'' Henderson said scornfully. "Game as a pebble, the lad is, and would call me out if he knew I'd spoken to you. But I couldn't let him ruin his life without making a push to stop it, that I could not.''

Deborah bowed her head. "But I love him,'' she said quietly.

"If you love him,'' Henderson said, "you'll spare him the pain of enduring your shame with you!''

"I am so tired,'' Deborah said quite irrelevantly. "So very, very tired.''

"Well, Miss Tollin? What say you? Will you call off the engagement?'' Mr. Henderson, sensing Deborah's weakness, leaned over her chair for emphasis. The move proved to have been ill-considered. Quite abruptly his skin took on a distinctly greenish cast; he blinked his eyes once or twice, gulped, and with a frantic, "Pray-excuse-me-Madam-I-fear-

that-I-am-unwell,''was gone, the sound of his running
footsteps echoing down the hall.

When Sarah returned to the library, all agog to learn what
had transpired between her niece and Mr. Henderson, she
found Deborah, alone in the darkened chamber, crying as
though her heart would break.

CHAPTER FOUR

TIMOTHY STEWART SAUNTERED into the Tollins' drawing room the next morning, whistling a merry tune which was all the rage in Town. From head to toe, Mr. Stewart was the picture of the fashionable young man about Town. His starched collar points rose to the perfect modish height, but not one inch farther; his canary yellow pantaloons were *le dernier cri*, and the figured waistcoat he wore could be called neither too timid nor too bold.

"'Lo, Deb," Timothy said to his seated friend. "Ready to go?"

"What?" Deborah seemed lost in thought; she brought herself out of her reverie with difficulty. "Oh, no, Timothy, I'm afraid I really don't feel up to—"

"I told you that I wouldn't take no for an answer," he interrupted. "We shall go driving together today, you and I, no matter what excuses you devise." His eyes took on a wicked twinkle and he said mischievously, "Why, even Lord Eversley approves. Did he not tell us so, just yesterday?"

The change in Deborah at the mention of Eversley's name could not be missed; the colour leeched out of her cheeks, and her face took on a pinched, unhappy look. Timothy took an involuntary step forward. "What is it, my pet?" he asked. "Have you—"

They were interrupted by a visibly disturbed Danson, who all but ran into the room. "What is it, Danson?" Deborah asked listlessly.

"I was seeking your aunt, miss," the butler said. "I had thought her to be here." He turned to go, but stopped on the threshold, clearly the victim of indecision; he eyed Timothy speculatively.

"Is there something that I might help you with, Danson?" asked Timothy.

"With Miss Deborah's permission," Danson said. "As you are such a good friend to the family..." He looked to the girl for approval; Deborah shrugged indifferently. Danson crossed the room to speak in Timothy's ear.

"I'll be damn...dashed!"

"What is it, Timothy?" Deborah asked, interested despite herself. "Has something happened?"

"I'll say!" Timothy said. "Lead on, MacDuff!" he told Danson. "Or do I mean lay on?" he asked himself. "No matter. Let us go!"

Danson led Timothy out of the drawing room. Deborah trailed along behind them, puzzled but wryly amused by Danson's instinctive desire for male leadership. The servant led them along the hall, down a broad staircase and up to the heavy door of the library. Here, all words seemed to fail Danson; he merely grimaced and threw open the door. Deborah gasped, Timothy exclaimed wordlessly, and the two of them stepped inside.

The library was a shambles; it looked as though someone had tried, quite literally, to tear the room apart. The heavy draperies had been slashed, the rugs were in tatters, and in several places, the very panelling had been pried away from the wall. The books had been pulled from the shelves and hurled to the floor. The contents of the desk had been removed and thrown about the room. Deborah turned round and round, staring at the destruction, unable to speak. Timothy regarded the ruins judiciously, poking at the mess on the floor with an elegantly shod foot and whistling tunelessly under his breath.

"When—how—" Deborah stammered finally, help-lessly.

Timothy turned to Danson, still hovering anxiously in the hall outside. "Well, Danson?" he asked evenly. "What can you tell us about all this?" He waved a hand.

"I assure you, sir, I know nothing about it, nothing at all!" Danson said hastily.

"Be of good cheer, Danson," Timothy said. "I was not accusing you. I merely wondered when the, er, disorder was discovered."

"This morning, sir," Danson said, his equanimity restored. "Just before I came upstairs to the drawing room, miss," he said, belatedly remembering to whom he owed his explanation.

"And when was the last time the library was used?" Timothy asked.

"Late yesterday afternoon," Deborah said unexpect-edly. Timothy raised an amused brow in Deborah's direc-tion, but she did not elaborate.

"Exactly so, miss," Danson said. "And of course I came in last night before retiring, to see that the windows were properly locked, which they were."

"No signs of trouble at that time, Danson?" Timothy asked, wandering across the room.

"I should say not, sir!" replied the servant in scandal-ized tones.

"It seems the window was forced open," Timothy com-mented, examining the aforementioned aperture through his quizzing glass.

"But why?" asked Deborah, greatly agitated. "I can un-derstand theft, I suppose, if one were hungry or desperate enough. But why such useless destruction? What possible end could it serve?"

Timothy caught Deborah's eye and lifted one shoulder in Danson's direction. For a moment, Deborah did not com-prehend her friend's meaning. Then she said, "That will be all, Danson. Mr. Stewart and I will break the news to Miss Beldon. I'm sure she'll inform you when she wishes you to begin to set the room to rights. Thank you, Danson.'' The butler hesitated for a moment, then left the library. Deborah turned back to Timothy. "What on earth..." she began.

"I thought it best that Danson should leave, thinking all this no more than a particularly messy case of burglary," Timothy said. "No sense in causing unnecessary speculation in the servants' quarters, is there?"

Deborah shook her head in confusion. "I don't understand, Timothy," she complained. "What else could it be?"

"I don't know, Deb, but I do know this—no proper burglar would be mad enough to hang about the scene of a crime, cutting rugs and curtains to ribbons," Timothy said. "No, my dear, whatever this was, it was no ordinary robbery." He looked about the room again. "Obviously," he said slowly, "whoever did it was looking for something, something which they thought hidden."

"That's absurd, Timothy," Deborah scoffed. "What could anyone possibly think hidden in our rugs, of all places?"

"That, I don't know," Timothy said, shaking off his introspection. "But what I do know," he said briskly, offering Deborah his arm, "is that even this occurrence, unexpected as it was, will not, I repeat, not, keep me from taking you out to the Park today. Shall we, my dear?"

Deborah had to smile at his perseverance. "Oh, but Timothy," she protested, "how can I? Aunt Sarah will be upset, when she finds out."

"Which she will not, until we tell her," Timothy responded. "We've already instructed Danson not to mention the matter to her, and what are the chances that she'll come in here on her own while we're gone?"

"Almost nonexistent," Deborah admitted. "She's never cared for the library—too many books."

"Well, then, there you have it," Timothy said cheerfully. "We're off."

The inevitable reaction was setting in. Deborah, regarding the destruction around her, looked closer and closer to tears. "Oh, Timothy," she said, "who would do such a thing?"

Timothy took her arm in a strong grip, and turned her around. "Come along, my girl," he said. "We'll discuss it later."

"But—"

He pressed a finger to her lips and smiled down at her. "No buts, no delays, no excuses," he said. "Whether you like it or no, my dear Deb, I am determined—quite determined—to keep you from sinking into despair." *And a fine task,* he thought as they left the library, *you've chosen for yourself, you poor sod!*

BENEATH A TALL STAND of trees, in a country lane not many minutes from the city, a dark coach had pulled off the road. No crest marred the smooth shine of the coach's door and its windows were tightly shuttered, giving no clue as to the identity of the occupant.

A coachman sat quietly on top of the coach, smoking a pipe, his hat pulled low over his eyes to block out the sun. He exhibited no signs of impatience; indeed, had it not been for the regular puffs of smoke which drifted away from him, one would have thought him asleep.

Then the drowsy stillness of the lane was disturbed. The sound of footsteps could be heard, and a disgruntled mumbling, too low to be distinguished. The coachman lifted his hat from his eyes to briefly but thoroughly inspect the figure that appeared around a bend in the road. Satisfied by what he saw, he dropped the hat back into place without a word.

As the newcomer opened the door of the coach, an intruding beam of sunlight shone on a gold-headed cane, and made a jewel nestled in the folds of the occupant's neck-cloth twinkle. Then the door closed, and an impenetrable darkness fell inside the coach.

"Well, my friend?" the occupant asked in cultured tones. "What news have you for me?"

"None at all, I'm afeared, milord," was the hoarse response. "I done just wot yer told me, but there weren't nothin' t'find."

"Come now, Jack," said the gentleman. "I find it difficult to believe that you didn't find anything." His voice held a delicate hint of menace.

"I swear t'yer, milord, I didn't find nothin'!" the ruffian whined. "I wouldn't lie t'yer lordship, that I wouldn't."

"Wouldn't you, Jack? I wonder," was the gentleman's reflective comment. Then came the sound of a dull thud, and a strangled cry.

"My leg! Yer've broken my leg!"

"I doubt that, my dear Jack. 'Tis merely a bruise, I'm sure. But were it broken, my lad, you would have no one to blame but yourself," the refined voice said gently. "It appears that you've forgotten how terribly unwise it is to cross me. Now, I will ask you once again—what have you for me?"

"Nothin' like wot yer sent me fer!" the injured man warned him, but there was, nonetheless, the rustle and clank of pockets being emptied and objects laid out for inspection.

One of the shutters on the coach windows was opened a crack; the light fell on a dirty, stringy-haired man of indeterminate years, who blinked blindly in the sudden illumination, and on a motley collection of items spread out on the seat beside him. A hand emerged from the still-darkened corner of the coach; eagerly it flipped through the tangled collection of small silver items, one or two ancient-looking books, and a multitude of handwritten papers. Each paper was carefully perused, then thrown to one side until all had been examined. "Is this the lot?" the gentleman asked harshly. "Think well before you lie to me again, Jack!"

"That's all, milord, I swear it!" the man said, with the indefinable ring of truth in his voice. "I took the silver and such fer meself, thinkin' that yer'd not object, milord, but all the papers wot I found is right 'ere." A dirty finger tapped the pile. "And a terrible 'ard time I 'ad of it, milord, 'avin' to be so quiet, wot with it bein' the dead o' night and all," he confided, then added hastily, "But I done it jest the way yer said; 'tweren't nothin' 'idden in that room, milord!" His voice held a note of pride at a job well done.

The gentleman said nothing for a long moment. Then he sighed and closed the shutter. "Very good, Jack," he said. "You did well. Stealing the silver will convince the household that it was no more than an ordinary robbery. Though I warn you, Jack," he added silkily, "if ever we do business again, I will expect you to do exactly as I tell you, no more and no less. Do you understand?"

The dirty man hastened to assure the speaker that he did, indeed, understand. There was the clink of coins, and the man thanked his employer profusely.

"I should not be surprised," said the gentleman calmly, "if I were to have further work for you at some later time, friend Jack. If, or should I say, when I do, I will contact you in the usual way. Good day, Jack." Thus dismissed, Jack bade farewell and departed. The gentleman sat in the dark for quite some time, tapping a manicured nail thoughtfully against his teeth, before raising his cane to rap sharply on the roof of the coach, signalling his man to drive on.

LORD ROBERT EVERSLEY whipped up the horses, and neatly took the sharp corner through the gates of The Green Dragon. The high-stepping black stallions upheld his lordship's reputation as a rare judge of horseflesh; they also exactly suited the glossy black enamelled phaeton he drove, though his cronies would have been much surprised to see him driving such a vehicle outside Town.

Apparently he felt the same way. "Whatever possessed me," he asked his groom, "to take the phaeton on this trip?"

The servant, with the freedom born of having placed his lordship on his first pony, chuckled and said, "Sheer wrongheadedness, I should wager, milord."

"You will have your little jests, won't you, Tom?" growled Eversley.

"I'll need a joke or two, with you in the temper you're in, milord," responded Tom boldly. "Don't recall when last I seen you in such a takin'!"

"Unless you desire to see me in even more of a taking, as you put it, you'll oblige me by keeping your opinions to yourself!" barked Eversley.

The groom drew himself up stiffly. "Indeed yes, milord!" he said. "I beg your pardon, milord!"

Eversley heaved an exasperated sigh. "Oh, for God's sake, Tom, don't you poker up on me. I've had quite enough of that for one day."

"I shouldn't dream of it, milord," replied the aged servant, too correctly. "Pray forgive me, milord."

"I shall have to apologize to you, shan't I?" asked Eversley with a rueful grin. "Very well, then. Forgive me, my friend. That bad temper you remarked on has made me prickly as an old bear, and I'm truly sorry for it."

"Aw, go along with you," said the groom. "I've known you since you were breeched, ain't I? Who knows your fits and starts better than I do?" He slanted a glance at the back of his master's head. "I would like to know what put you in such a stew—I got my suspicions, needless to say."

Eversley laughed. "I'm sure you do!" he said.

Tom nodded wisely. "You're just like your father, Lord rest his soul," he said. "There was ne'er a truer or finer gentleman born, but oh, that temper! Once he got himself worked up, there weren't no tellin' how long it would take him to cool down again. Sometimes,'' he added reflectively, ''it took weeks.''

''I remember,'' said Eversley softly. ''He wasn't the most comfortable of gentleman, was he?''

''But a right 'un, through and through,'' Tom averred loyally.

''That he was,'' agreed Eversley, and they rode along in silence for a time.

''Tell me this, Tom,'' Eversley said finally. ''You knew my parents all their married life. Did you ever know my mother to look at another man?''

''Never,'' Tom said instantly. ''As far as her ladyship was concerned, the sun rose and set on your papa.''

Eversley scowled.

''Which is not to say, mind, that her ladyship never had no gentleman companions, so to speak,'' Tom continued. ''Why, a lady so sweet and kind couldn't help but make friends. 'Twas as natural to her as breathin'.''

''I'll daresay my father didn't take very kindly to that.''

''Oh, posh,'' Tom scoffed. ''What were her ladyship's friends to him? He knew she loved him. Your father weren't no fool,'' Tom added after a moment.

Eversley looked long and hard at the groom. ''Meaning what?''

''Meanin','' answered Tom calmly, ''that there is times when I don't see much of a resemblance between you and his late lordship.''

''That's going too far, Tom,'' Eversley burst out. ''Why, you're as much as calling me a fool—I won't stand for it!'' He whipped the horses roughly, and cursed as the leader stumbled, then recovered.

''There's no call to take it out on the horses, milord,'' said Tom sharply. ''Maybe I spoke as shouldn't, but it's mortal hard to see you makin' such a gudgeon of yourself, and out of nothin' more than jealousy.''

"Jealousy?" sputtered Eversley. "Why, you old rascal, I'm no more jealous of Stew—of anyone, than I am of you!"

"Is that so, milord? Then tell me why you were shoutin' at poor Miss Deborah so loud that the whole household could hear? Shamin' the poor lady in front of her servants. It ain't right, milord, that it ain't." Tom shook his head solemnly.

"Damn you, Tom! Do you think that you may sit here and tell *me* how to behave?" White with fury, he twisted round to meet the old man's gaze. "I don't care how long you've—"

Tom's eyes widened as he looked over Eversley's shoulders. "Watch out!" he gasped. "Milord, watch out . . . !"

CHAPTER FIVE

LORD BURLE SAT UP straight in his seat. "I'll be dashed!" he exclaimed.

Lady Margaret Rawlings did not look up from the embroidery with which she was engaged. "I sincerely hope not," she said calmly, her fingers busy with the brightly coloured silks.

Lord Burle reread the paragraph which had so surprised him, his finger moving along slowly beneath the print. "There it is, though," he acknowledged, then let the journal drop. "Poor girl!"

"Who is a poor girl, dear?" asked Lady Margaret patiently.

"Miss Tollin," Burle explained. "And right on top of her father's death. Does seem rather hard!"

"I only wish I knew what you were talking about, Alex," the redheaded girl said.

Lord Burle picked up the paper again, and showed it to Lady Margaret. The prominent London journal had been folded open to a page containing social announcements and carefully phrased titbits of gossip.

"Yes?" she prompted.

One of Burle's long fingers poked at a particular paragraph. "Look, here it is, Maggie," he said. The young woman quickly read the indicated text.

"How distressing," murmured Lady Margaret.

"I must admit, I never would have thought it of Eversley," remarked Burle candidly. "That he should end the betrothal isn't so surprising, I suppose, but he might have waited a little longer—the girl's father is barely cold in the ground. It shows a sad want of feeling, in my opinion.''

"I should say so," Lady Margaret agreed. "The poor child—how she must feel." She read the paragraph again, her pretty brow puckered.

"You, calling her a child?" Burle teased. "Why, she can't be more than three or four years younger than you are, Greybeard!"

"Five years," Lady Margaret corrected him, "and our cases are completely different."

"Timothy will be livid over this," Burle predicted, tapping the newspaper. "I wish there was something I could do for the girl, for his sake if no one else's."

Lady Margaret lowered her gaze back to her embroidery. "Timothy?" she said. "Would that be Timothy Stewart?"

Burle nodded. "He's quite close to the girl—they're practically like brother and sister. Timothy took Mr. Tollin's death very hard," Burle said.

Lady Margaret pursed her lips thoughtfully. "Perhaps we should try to do something to help, Alex."

"Yes, we should!'" Burle answered enthusiastically. "We should...we should... What should we do?"

"At the very least, we should show the ton that the child is not completely friendless," Lady Margaret said decisively. "You know—call on her, perhaps take her for a drive in the Park. It's a pity that her mourning prevents her from attending Almack's. The surest way to silence the gossips would be to parade her before their very faces."

"What an excellent notion, Maggie," Burle said happily. "It can only do the girl good, and Timothy will be pleased. You're quite a good sort, Lady Margaret, do you know that?" He smiled. "Of all my cousins, and Lord knows I've enough of them, you are my absolute favourite."

Margaret bowed her head. "I thank you, my lord," she said dryly, "but you are making a great deal out of nothing, you know. 'Tis a simple act of charity, no more, no less." She regarded her embroidery dispassionately. "The question is, how shall I explain my sudden interest in Miss Tollin? She'll think it strange if I suddenly call on her when we're scarce acquainted."

"I could have Timothy introduce you," Burle suggested helpfully.

The faintest of blushes coloured Lady Margaret's fair skin. "No, no, that won't be necessary!" She busied herself for a moment, untangling the skeins of silk which littered the seat beside her, then said, "I know—I'll tell her that I was acquainted with her papa, which is true, though only slightly, and that I have only just now learned of his death. Will that do, do you think, Alex?"

"I'd believe it," he said stoutly.

Lady Margaret hid a smile. Her dearly loved cousin was not the most perspicacious of gentlemen. "Good," she said, "then we are agreed. And mind, Alex, this is just between the two of us."

"Done," said Burle. "We'll stand by the girl, and let the proud Lord Eversley go straight to the devil!"

LORD EVERSLEY SMILED apologetically at the grizzled old man. "You must forgive me for imposing on your hospitality in this rag-mannered way, Perkins," he said. "I assure you, had there been any alternative—"

Perkins said gruffly, "Beggin' yer pardon, milord, but seein' as 'ow yer t'wed Miss Deborah, I can't see as 'ow yer shoulda gone anywhere but here in yer troubles."

"And how," Eversley asked with a smile lurking in his eyes, "did you know about the betrothal?"

"Ah," said Perkins wisely, "us who serve 'ave our little ways, milord!" With a grunt, he cut the boot off Eversley's foot, causing the peer to grimace and clutch at the sides of the sofa on which he lay. "Ah, that's a right sore 'un, I'll wager," the old man said, regarding Eversley's swollen purple foot and ankle with something approaching satisfaction. "Lucky yer are, t've been so close to Shaftsworth when it 'appened," the stableman told Eversley. "How did you say it 'appened, agin?" he asked curiously.

Eversley flushed. "Er, a driving accident," he said, nonplussed.

"Driving, eh? I didn't see no livestock tied to that there cart wot brought you, milord. Wot did yer do with yer 'orses?"

"Luckily my groom was uninjured in the, er, accident," Eversley replied. "I had the devil of a time convincing him to stay with my equipage, but I finally managed the thing by assuring him that I'd be as well taken care of by you, Perkins, as I would be in my own home."

"And so you'll be, milord, and so you'll be!" Perkins said, clearly pleased by Eversley's confidence. "Me missus is fixin' a pullet fer yer dinner right now, and I'll make a bed up fer yer lordship. It may not be quite wot yer used ter, seein' as 'ow there's only the missus and meself t'see t'yer," Perkins warned him, "but we'll make do."

"I'm sure that everything will be fine," said Eversley, and dug into his pocket for a coin. "By the way, will you see to it that the lad who brought me gets this? It was good of him to take me so far out of his way."

Perkins bobbed his head in acknowledgement and left the library, to hurry along Eversley's dinner and open up one of the better bedchambers for his lordship.

Eversley sighed and poured himself a glass of the brandy which Perkins had thoughtfully left close at hand. He leaned his head back against the leather of the sofa, and gave himself up to a rueful recollection of the day just past.

His groom's shouted warning had, alas, been too late; by the time Eversley had turned his attention back to the road, the lumbering coach approaching had been almost upon them. By way of some extremely skilful driving, Eversley had kept both his horses and his groom from serious harm. He himself had not been quite so fortunate. Perkins had ventured the opinion that no bones had been broken, but he had pronounced his lordship's ankle to have been severely sprained, and predicted that Eversley would be abed for at least a fortnight, if not longer.

Eversley sighed again and opened his eyes. It might have been worse, he supposed; he might have had his accident farther from Shaftsworth, or in another part of the country altogether, and been forced to subject himself to the uncertain hospitality of some hastily chosen inn. At least here he could be sure of decent accommodations, and at least a modicum of devotion on the part of the servants, for Deborah's sake if not his own.

The library door opened, and Perkins bustled back into the room. "I've the drawin' room open now, yer lordship," he said. "Just lean on me, and we'll have yer moved in a trice, with no trouble."

Eversley looked surprised. "Must I?" he asked the old man. "I'm quite comfortable here, I promise you, and to be frank, I'd just as soon not joggle this ankle any more than I must."

Perkins shrugged. "Yer must suit yerself, t'be sure, milord," he said unconcernedly. "Me missus just thought, wot with the tragedy and all, yer might be better somewheres else. Fer meself," the grizzled stableman confided, "I ain't squeamish 'bout sech things."

"Oh," said Eversley weakly.

"If that's all, yer lordship," said Perkins hopefully, "I'll see t'yer bedchamber?" Eversley waved a distracted hand, and the servant once again left the room.

Eversley picked up his brandy glass and hastily swallowed the contents. He looked around the room again. Where had Geoffrey Tollin done it, he wondered. In the wing chair which stood before the hearth? Had he been sitting behind the great desk when he ended his life, or had he stood, in the centre of the room perhaps, staring out the windows at his beloved estate as he squeezed the trigger? There was no outward sign of exactly where in the room the death had occurred; whatever mess there had been had been dealt with efficiently by Perkins and his thus-far invisible wife.

For the first time, Eversley noticed how very quiet the great house was. Though he knew that Perkins must be somewhere about, and that Mrs. Perkins was only as far away as the kitchens, the silence was so thick that he might just as well have been alone in the building. Had Geoffrey sat here this way, Eversley wondered, with the sound of his own heartbeat echoing in his ears, feeling as though he were the last man on earth? Eversley felt the first stirrings of pity for Deborah's late father. How tragic, he thought, to die so very lonely a death.

Suddenly the hair on the back of Eversley's neck stood straight up, and a strangled exclamation escaped him. He had never been a superstitious man; indeed, his friends and family knew Lord Eversley as the most pragmatic of beings. But now, with no warning, he was filled with the eerie certainty that he was no longer alone in the library.

He tried to fight the feeling. He hastily sat up and swung his feet off the leather sofa, though not without considerable pain. "This is ridiculous," he told himself sternly. "Of course there's no one else here." Grimacing, he rose to his feet, and looked round the room warily. His conviction had not lessened; he felt another presence in the room more strongly by the moment. "It must be the brandy," he muttered. "That's it—the brandy must be tainted." An inspiration struck him. "I'll write a letter to Deborah, which will distract me. What a capital notion—a letter of apology!" He hopped painfully across the room to the desk.

The injured peer took up pen and paper and commenced to write. "My dearest Deborah," he began. "I write to you today to apologize for my churlish behaviour when last we met. I behaved like a fool, my darling girl, and I can only pray your indulgence for..."

His lordship heard a sound and jerked his head up, but too late. A faint acrid odour, a blinding flash of pain, and Eversley knew no more.

"YOU WHAT?" Timothy Stewart all but drove his curricle off the road in his surprise, and was obliged to spend the next several minutes attempting to bring his excellent, if sadly high-spirited horses back under control. Through all Timothy's efforts, Deborah stared stoically ahead, her face a mask.

When finally Timothy had his pair in hand and the curricle again rolled sedately along, he turned his attention back to his passenger. "Tell me this again, Deb," he said. "I'm not sure that I quite grasp your words."

Deborah shrugged. "What is so difficult to grasp, Timothy?" she asked. "I have broken my engagement to Eversley. What more needs to be said?"

"A great deal more, my dear Deborah," Timothy said indignantly. "What made you decide so suddenly? I thought you promised me that you would think it over."

"I did think it over," Deborah said flatly.

"Not for very long," Timothy protested. When Deborah did not respond, he tried again. "Does Eversley know?" Deborah shook her head. "Well, then," said Timothy, with something very like relief in his voice. "The betrothal is not broken, really, not until you inform Eversley. And I think it a good thing, I don't mind telling you, Deb. You've made much too hasty a decision, in my opinion."

Deborah did not say anything; she merely opened her reticule, and handed Timothy a scrap of paper containing the paragraph which had been published that morning. With a puzzled frown, Timothy took the cutting and as best he could while controling restive horses, ran his eyes over the lines of print. What he saw made him exclaim angrily, "You sent a notice to the papers, Deb? Without even telling Eversley? A fine way to behave, my girl!"

Deborah flinched at Timothy's harsh words. "I don't need you to judge my actions, Timothy Stewart," she responded hotly. "And I'll thank you to remember that I am quite capable of making my own decisions."

"Are you, now," drawled Timothy. "One would never know it by this." He waved the paper. "Of all the addle-headed, ill-conceived..." He shook his head in disgust.

"I knew you wouldn't understand," Deborah said.

"Does Aunt Sarah know about this?" Timothy demanded. Deborah shook her head. "Oh? And when were you thinking of telling her?" he asked witheringly. "Or did you plan to let her read it herself, with her morning tea, perhaps?"

Deborah looked stricken. "I never thought of that," she admitted.

Timothy regarded her with a frown, then pulled the curricle to the side of the road. "Now," he said ominously, "you are going to tell me exactly what precipitated this decision of yours—and no excuses, my girl."

Deborah shook her head. "What does it matter...?" she began.

"It matters a great deal to me!" snapped Timothy. He favoured Deborah with another long look, then said shrewdly, "It has something to do with Eversley's uncle calling on you, I'll wager. Aunt Sarah told me Henderson had been to see you." Deborah stared straight ahead, stubbornly refusing to answer. "I'll tell you this once, Deborah Tollin," he warned her. "I do not care, no, not in the least, if we must sit right here all day—you will answer me, I promise you." When Deborah still said nothing, he shrugged. "So be it."

Timothy leaned comfortably back in his seat and began to whistle under his breath. He seemed perfectly at ease in the open carriage; the stares of curious passersby did not appear to trouble him in the least. The sun shone down steadily out of a cloudless sky and though it was beginning to become rather too warm, in Deborah's opinion, her companion showed no signs of discomfort. Indeed, Timothy appeared to enjoy the heat; he smiled complacently at Deborah and turned his face, eyes shut, toward the light—like a great, purring cat, Deborah thought in disgust. She herself was beginning to feel the effect of the sun; a black velvet cloak and heavy black bonnet were not, she discovered, the ideal ensemble in which to enjoy an unseasonably warm day. Surreptitiously, she wiped a rivulet of perspiration from the back of her neck and sternly told herself to think cool thoughts. Timothy continued to drowse happily in the sun's rays.

"This has gone on long enough," Deborah announced when at last she could stand it no longer. "Take me home immediately, Timothy," she shrilled. "Right now, I say!"

Timothy opened one eye. "I shall take you home," he said politely, "when you have told me exactly what transpired between Mr. Henderson and yourself, and not a moment before. Until then..." He grinned at his unwilling passenger.

"This is infamous!" Deborah cried. "You shall not coerce me, Timothy Stewart, no, not though I die for it," she finished dramatically.

"You shall not die," Timothy said, in a perfectly friendly manner, "only, perhaps, freckle a bit." He laughed heartily as Deborah's hand flew to her nose.

"Ooh!" Deborah ground out, teeth clenched tightly together. "I hate you! I hate you!" She pummelled Timothy with closed fists.

He caught her fists in his hands. "Nonetheless, Deb, you shall tell me in the end, you know," he said with perfect equanimity. "You always do." He smiled at her again, more sympathetically, and gently tucked a stray wisp of hair back under the brim of her bonnet. "Come, Deb," he invited. "I'm only trying to help, you know."

Timothy's tenderness succeeded where threats had failed. All the fight went out of Deborah suddenly, and her shoulders slumped despairingly.

"Buck up, old girl," Timothy said bracingly. He whipped a handkerchief out of his pocket and pushed it into Deborah's hand. "Just tell me. I promise, I shan't eat you!"

Hesitantly, her voice faltering at times, Deborah told Timothy about Mr. Henderson's call, and what he'd had to say on the subject of his nephew's betrothal. Timothy's mouth hardened as he listened. He bit back a curse when Deborah relayed the more hurtful of the gentleman's comments, but he gave a reluctant shout of laughter at the end, when Deborah described the man's hasty departure. "It's not funny, Timothy," Deborah protested weakly, when Timothy's merriment had subsided a bit.

"Ah, but it is, Deb," he said, still chuckling. "The old devil got exactly what he deserved, for interfering in a matter which was none of his concern. If it's any consolation to you, I daresay Eversley will be furious with Henderson when he finds out."

"But he won't find out," Deborah said, once again in control of her emotions. "I don't want Eversley to know that his uncle ever called on me," she insisted, much to Timothy's surprise.

"Why not?" Timothy asked. "After the things Henderson said to you . . ."

"However much he might have hurt me, he did it only out of love for Eversley," Deborah said. "And he was right, right in every instance."

"But, Deb—"

"It's done, Timothy," she said wearily. She did not meet his eyes. "The notice has already been printed. The betrothal is broken." Deborah ventured a smile. "It may have been," she added, with an unsuccessful attempt at levity, "the shortest engagement in history. What was it, four days? Five?"

Deborah's white, pinched face belied the lightness of her tone; Timothy had not the heart to press her any further. "True," he agreed easily. "You may have set some sort of record, my dear." He took up the reins again and set the horses in motion. "I think," he said, with another glance at Deborah, slumped in her seat, "that I shall take you home now, Deb. Redoubtable as you are, my sweet, I fear that between one thing and another, you have had rather more excitement of late than is good for you."

"Thank you, Timothy," Deborah whispered.

"And Deb, don't worry about telling Aunt Sarah. I'll break the news to her myself," he added. "She's always had a soft spot for me. I daresay she'll be a little upset, but I'll put it right, never you fear."

Deborah dabbed her eyes with Timothy's handkerchief. "You're so good to me, Timothy," she said thickly. "I don't deserve it."

"And I don't deserve to have you turn into a dashed watering pot," Timothy said hastily. "Give over, Deb, do. It's embarrassing to ride in an open carriage with a female who's crying. Makes people wonder what set her off, don't you know." Deborah obligingly wiped her eyes, and tried to smile. "That's better," said Timothy approvingly. "And as for being grateful to me, you should wait to see what price you pay for my kindness before you thank me, my pretty." He accompanied these words with such a broad and theatrical leer that Deborah could not help but give a gurgle of laughter.

With peace, if not peace of mind, restored, Timothy did his best to distract Deborah's thoughts during the ride home. He played the fool wonderfully, never giving a sign of the worry which chased round and round in his head: what would the proud Eversley think of being jilted, and in so public and humiliating a way?

CHAPTER SIX

"LORD EVERSLEY! Oh, milord, open your eyes!"

Eversley slowly came back to himself at the sound of the woman's entreating voice, but lay with his eyes closed for a long moment, trying to identify the source of the blinding pain in his head, and the lesser throbbing in his ankle.

"Oh, please, milord!" the woman said, then, "I hold you responsible for this, Mr. Perkins. You should not have left him in that room alone."

"Now, Martha," came the rumbling tones of the stableman, "yer makin' a great deal out 'a nothin'. His lordship more n' likely jest took a little faintin' spell. Coulda 'appened anywheres!"

"That room is cursed," the woman said clearly, "and you never should have left him there."

Eversley finally felt enough recovered to open his eyes. He found himself stretched out on a freshly made bed, in what was clearly one of Shaftsworth's better bedchambers. A plump, pleasant-faced woman hovered anxiously over him, Perkins at her elbow. She gave a sigh of relief at the sight of her patient's opened eyes.

"Do not, I beg you, Mistress Perkins, scold your good husband on my account," Eversley said with the ghost of a smile. "He is quite right. I am feeling very much more the thing now."

Mrs. Perkins was not deceived. "Begging your pardon, milord," she said crisply, "but you do not look 'quite the thing.' Is your head paining you?"

"A trifle, perhaps," Eversley admitted, lifting a hand to touch the back of his head, "but 'tis nothing to signify, I promise you."

"Mr. Perkins," said his wife decisively, "pray go to my kitchen, and fetch me the bottle which stands on the table by the hearth—the brown bottle, if you please. My elixir will do wonders for his lordship." Her husband bobbed his head in agreement, though not without rolling his eyes in Eversley's direction.

After Perkins had left the room, Mrs. Perkins busied herself with straightening Eversley's bedcothes and tenderly wiping his forehead with a damp rag. "There, now, milord," she said soothingly, "you just lie back and rest until Mr. Perkins returns. Though he is the most reliable of men, my Perkins is not the fastest, by any means."

Eversley had a curious sense of unreality. "So you are Mrs. Perkins," he said. "I have heard a great deal about you from Deborah, you know, and all of it good."

"Oh, milord, I don't know how I'll ever face Miss Deborah again," Mrs. Perkins said, and all but wrung her hands in distress. "Poor Mr. Geoffrey," she said. "We should have taken better care of him, Mr. Perkins and I, while he was here. Then maybe he wouldn't have . . ."

"I'm quite sure that Deborah would not wish you to hold yourself responsible," Eversley said kindly. "It wasn't your fault. You must not blame yourself."

"If there's blame to affix," Mrs. Perkins said darkly, "I say it's that cursed room what's responsible!"

"Come, now, Mrs. Perkins . . ." Eversley said reasonably.

"I know, I know, you think me mad," the woman said, "but I tell you, milord, there's strange things have been happening in that library of late. Even before Mr. Geoffrey's . . . even before his death, things were not right there. I'd go in to dust or to lay a fire, and it would be as though someone were watching me, all the time. Or Mr. Perkins would lay something down for just a moment, and when he went back, it'd be gone. And what happened to you there today, I should like to know?" she demanded, adding a belated, "milord."

Eversley frowned. "I can't exactly remember," he admitted, his hand stealing unconsciously to the back of his head. "I was lying on the sofa..."

"Mr. Perkins found you slumped over the desk," Mrs. Perkins told him.

"That's right," Eversley said. "I sat down to write a letter to Deborah... but that's all I remember," he finished.

"Well, it's very strange," Mrs. Perkins said ominously, as the door opened and her husband reentered the room.

"Here y'are, Martha," he said, handing his wife the brown bottle. "Is that the one yer wanted?"

"Indeed it is," she said with a smile. "Thank you, my dear. Now, milord," Mrs. Perkins said briskly, pouring a small amount of brownish liquid into a glass, "you drink this, get a good night's sleep, and I guarantee that the pain in your head will be gone by morning. No argument, now, milord," she said, when Eversley seemed inclined to protest. "This will set you to rights before you know it."

Seeing that he had very little choice in the matter, Eversley acquiesced as gracefully as he could. He drank the foul-tasting liquid, and allowed Mrs. Perkins to help him to settle himself before she left the room. As her husband was about to follow her out the door, he stopped, and digging into a pocket, turned back to the bed.

"Oh, milord," the stableman said, holding out his hand, "'ere be that letter what yer was writin' in the libery. I thought yer might be wonderin' what become of it."

"Thank you, friend Perkins," Eversley said drowsily, the potion already beginning to affect him. Perkins nodded and tiptoed out of the bedchamber. On the edge of sleep, barely conscious of what he was doing, Eversley glanced at the letter.

"My dearest Deborah," it read. "As I sit down to write this letter—the most difficult that I have ever written!—it seems impossible to explain to you how all this happened..."

MR. ROGER HENDERSON sat in his bedchamber, the *Morning Chronicle* spread across his knees. He had picked up the paper in the midst of dressing. He sat now in his shirtsleeves and smallclothes, unaware of his valet's pained expression, his attention focussed on the short paragraph which informed all London of the end of the engagement between his nephew, Lord Robert Eversley, and Miss Deborah Tollin.

"Damn," Henderson said aloud, "but the chit moves apace!" No uninformed observer, seeing his gloomy expression, would have guessed that the item had been sent to the journal as a result of his prompting. "Damn!" he said again.

"Did you wish something, sir?" his valet asked anxiously.

"Nothing, nothing," Henderson replied testily. "Take yourself off, Thompson, and don't come back until I call you." After his man had left the room, Henderson crumpled the paper into a ball and hurled it into the corner. "The devil take all women!"

Mr. Henderson irritably took up a neckcloth, and set himself to finish dressing. "I ask you, what was the hurry?" he enquired of his reflection in the mirror. "That's the trouble with women. They never take the time to think things through. Always rushing around in a pother, without an idea in their heads of what they're doing..." With a fervent curse, he ripped the crumpled neckcloth off and sent it to join the offending newspaper in the corner. His fury spent, he slumped dejectedly on the corner of the bed.

The truth of the matter was that Mr. Henderson had begun to think that his visit to Miss Tollin had been extremely ill-advised, on a number of scores. As soon as the throbbing headache and vile nausea to which he had awakened the next morning had subsided, he had realized the error of his ways; the more he thought on the matter, the more convinced he became that he had interfered intolerably with Eversley's affairs, and that his nephew would not thank him for it. To be sure, he still considered that marriage to the scandalous Miss Tollin would bring Eversley only pain, but he was forced to acknowledge that it was Eversley's life, and that the boy had the right to live it as he chose.

Thompson reentered the room and waited patiently for his master to notice him. "Eh?" Mr. Henderson said, when finally he caught sight of his valet. "I thought I told you not to disturb me."

"You have a caller, sir," Thompson said. "The Marquess of Pembroke, sir."

"Very well, show him in," Mr. Henderson said absently, his mind on other matters.

"Here, sir?" Thompson stammered in amazement. "Are you quite sure, sir?"

"Pray do as you are told, Thompson!" Mr. Henderson barked.

The valet bowed and left the room. His master resumed his brown study, and did not look up when the door opened again.

"Roger!" came a hearty voice. "What? Still not dressed? You are a lazy dog!"

Mr. Henderson came to himself with a jerk. "Pembroke," he said blankly. "What are you doing here?" He looked down at himself, realized that he was still not properly attired, and leapt to his feet.

The marquess threw back his head and roared with laughter. His resemblance to his son, or rather, the son's resemblance to his father, was striking; they had the same long, lanky frame, the same slightly bulging brown eyes. But, where Burle was physically unprepossessing, to say the least, his father was the picture of civilized elegance. This favourable impression was created not only by his clothing, though his dress was everything it should be, but also by his calm belief in his own position, and the sure knowledge that he was a social force to be reckoned with, which lent the marquess a confidence which was most attractive.

Pembroke clapped his friend on the back. "Did I startle you, Roger?" he asked, still chuckling. "Your man did show me up, you'll recall."

"And I'll know why," Henderson muttered furiously, shrugging into his frock coat. "To bring a visitor into my bedchamber...has he lost his senses? He will lose his position, that I promise you!"

The marquess looked surprised. "Softly, my friend, softly," he advised. "Surely there's no harm done? I assure you, I am not offended in the least. On the contrary, I think it a good jest."

"Nonetheless, Pembroke..." Henderson said, his expression adamant.

The marquess regarded his friend thoughtfully for a moment or two. "What's wrong, Roger?" he asked bluntly.

Henderson did not meet his eyes. "That fool Thompson..." he began.

"Do not, pray, have me believe you are so upset over the minor mistake of a servant," Pembroke said shrewdly. "I know you a little too well to credit such nonsense. What's troubling you?"

Henderson turned away from the marquess uneasily. "Why should anything be troubling me?" he said, more sharply than he had intended.

Pembroke's eyebrows flew up. "No reason," he responded coolly.

His back to the marquess, Henderson winced; he had not intended to offend his friend, only to avoid discussing family business with an outsider.

"Do forgive me, Roger," Pembroke added dryly. "I did not mean to pry, of that you may be sure."

Henderson turned to him. "Don't be a gudgeon," he said gruffly. "Of course you weren't prying. I'm just a stubborn old fool." Inspiration struck. "What's really troubling me," he confided falsely, "is Burle."

Once again Pembroke's brows were raised in surprise. "Burle?" he said. "What has my son to say to anything?"

"Or rather," said Henderson, "it's Burle's friends who are the trouble. Specifically, one friend—that Stewart fellow."

"Stewart?" the marquess said, then frowned. "I don't know what you've heard, Roger, but—"

"No more than have you, Pembroke, and that's enough to know that the man's a reprobate," Henderson blustered. "And yet you allow your son, your heir, to associate with him."

Pembroke looked faintly relieved. "There's no real harm in the boy, Roger," he said. "He's a bit wild, I'll grant you, and if I had a daughter, I wouldn't let him within twenty feet of her. But Burle is not my daughter, he's my son, and I respect him too much to try to choose his friends for him."

"Burle's just a boy. He doesn't see what Stewart is, and it is your responsibility to show him the right way to go on," Henderson said heavily. "If a close relative of mine were about to make a mistake, I would do anything in my power to prevent it."

Stung by Henderson's reproach, the marquess snapped, "Would you really, Roger? Then I strongly suggest that you look to your nephew. He is far closer to being beyond the bounds than Burle, or Stewart, for that matter, will ever be!"

Henderson glared at the peer. "What do you mean?" he demanded.

Pembroke sighed, and rubbed a hand over his face. "I'm sorry," he said. "I spoke without thinking."

Henderson stepped closer to the marquess, his expression fierce. "Tell me!" he said.

It was Pembroke's turn to move away from Henderson. He began to fiddle uncomfortably with his cane. "There has been some talk in the clubs," he began.

"Yes?" prompted Henderson.

"'Tis being said that it was unkind of Eversley to break his engagement to the Tollin girl so soon after her father's death," Pembroke said carefully.

"What?" cried Henderson.

"No one faults him for not wishing to go through with the wedding, given the scandal, but it is felt that he might have handled the matter a trifle more discreetly," Pembroke said.

"Eversley did not end the betrothal!" Henderson spluttered.

"Now, is it likely that Miss Tollin would have been the one to end it, when to do so would destroy any last chance of acceptance for her?" Pembroke asked reasonably. "The girl couldn't be that foolish."

"Whether you credit it or no, Pembroke," Henderson said with clenched teeth, "I tell you, it was she who broke the engagement, and sent the announcement to the paper."

Pembroke shrugged. "She may have been the one to send the actual announcement to the *Chronicle*," he said, "but it seems naive to suppose that she would have done so had considerable pressure not been brought to bear on her."

Henderson looked as though he were about to explode. "Lies, damnable lies!" he shouted. "And you believe them," he added accusingly.

"Roger!" said the marquess.

Henderson stared pugnaciously at his taller friend. "I take it ill, Pembroke, very ill indeed, that you are so quick to think the worst of Eversley."

Pembroke met Henderson's gaze squarely. "Roger, you and I have been friends for a very long time," he said, with great affection in his voice. "If you tell me that the Tollin girl was not, er, persuaded to sever the connection between herself and your nephew, then I believe you, and shall challenge anyone whom I hear say otherwise.'' He paused, then asked gently, ''But can you, in all honesty, tell me that she came to this decision quite on her own, my friend?''

Henderson was obliged to look away from the marquess's probing brown eyes, afraid that his guilt would show on his face. ''Damn you, Pembroke,'' he muttered, with the sick feeling in his stomach that he had, without intending it, done his nephew a great deal of harm.

DANSON OPENED the drawing-room door. ''You see, Deborah?'' said Sarah Beldon bracingly. ''First Lady Margaret, and now, unless I am very much mistaken, yet another caller. It's just as I told you—the ton will forget all about…what happened. It's already starting.'' Sarah turned to Danson. ''Well, Danson?'' she asked. ''Who is it?''

''Miss, I…I…'' Danson stammered, face pale.

''I believe,'' came a voice from the threshold, ''that Danson is having a little trouble deciding how to announce me.''

Deborah and Sarah both gasped aloud. Timothy Stewart stood there, a charming smile on his face, both blackened eyes all but swollen shut. His hands, placed casually on his hips, were cut and bruised, his clothing was torn and dirtied. He winced as he moved toward the two women.

''Timothy!'' Deborah cried. ''Oh, you poor dear!'' She flew across the room to her friend's side and helped him into a comfortable chair. ''What happened?''

''Dam—dashed if I know,'' he said with a rueful smile. ''Or rather, I do have a suspicion or two. But before we get into that, I would give anything for a cup of tea.'' Sarah gave the order to the anxiously hovering Danson, and as the man left the room, Timothy went on reflectively, ''Isn't it strange that in times of trouble, one turns instinctively to the remedies of one's youth? I once had a nurse who thought that any ill, no matter how grave, could be healed by a hot cup of tea.'' He grimaced as he shifted position, and added lightly, ''I must say, I do hope that she was right.''

Deborah and Sarah waited, none too patiently, until Danson had left the tea and departed. As soon as the door had closed behind the servant, Deborah demanded, ''Well? Tell me!''

Timothy took a long, restoring swallow of the hot liquid, and set the cup down. ''This morning,'' he began, ''I went to White's, to meet Burle.''

''Lord Burle did this?'' Deborah squeaked.

''Of course not, you gudgeon,'' Stewart said. ''Will you let me tell the story, please?'' He grinned at Deborah, and continued, ''We stayed at the club for several hours, gossiping and drinking chocolate, and playing the odd hand or two of piquet.''

''Gambling so early in the day?'' said Sarah. ''You are incorrigible, Timothy.''

''So I am,'' he agreed affably. ''At any rate, after I left the club—several hundred pounds the richer, I might add—I decided to stop at my rooms for a moment to leave a note for a friend whom I was expecting to call on me there.''

''And?'' Deborah prompted, all but wriggling with impatience.

Timothy shrugged. ''And,'' he said calmly, ''there was someone waiting for me. He must have been there for hours—my rooms were in a shambles.''

''But who?'' asked Sarah. ''And why?''

''That, Aunt Sarah, is a very good question,'' Timothy answered. ''Who it was, I don't know. I was taken completely by surprise, more's the pity. I was too busy attempting to defend myself to get a good look at the blighter. As to why...'' He paused and eyed Deborah and Aunt Sarah thoughtfully.

"Does it have something to do with us, Timothy?" Deborah asked, her voice steady, though her hands were clasped anxiously in her lap. "Please be honest!"

"As he was leaving, the man stopped to finish the search which I had interrupted. He thought that I was unconscious, and I very nearly was," Timothy admitted. "But I could hear him mumbling to himself."

"What did he say?"

"He said a great deal. He seemed to be one of those people who keep up a constant stream of conversation with themselves," Timothy said. "Only one bit of it caught my attention, though. He was grumbling about 'impossible jobs' and 'coves what dream things,' and I distinctly heard him say, 'It ain't at the girl's and it ain't at Shaftsworth and it ain't 'ere. Where the—where is it?'"

"But whatever can this ruffian be looking for?" Sarah asked. "None of this makes any sense!" She rubbed her forehead fretfully.

"This explains the destruction in the library," Deborah said. "You were right, Timothy, about it being more than just a random burglary."

"You are taking all of this very calmly, the two of you," Sarah said pettishly. "I should like to know what you propose we do about this persecution."

"I suggest," said Timothy, watching Deborah's face closely, "that we repair to Shaftsworth."

"Shaftsworth?" began Sarah in an outraged tone. "Good Lord, Timothy, why—"

"Oh!" Deborah gasped, the colour draining from her face. She crossed the room to kneel before Timothy's chair. He took her hand and squeezed it, a tender, knowing expression on his face. "You think that this has something to do with Papa, don't you, Timothy?"

"Yes, I do, love," he said gently. "I have no proof of it, but I am as certain as I can be that there is a connection between Uncle Geoffrey's death and these apparently random burglaries." He smiled cheerfully and tweaked Deborah's cheek. "And I'll make you a solemn promise, my girl—I'll find that connection at Shaftsworth, or die trying."

CHAPTER SEVEN

THE GENTLEMAN TAPPED a riding crop against his buckskin-clad leg. "So," he said. "It wasn't there." He swung out of the saddle and slapped himself free of the dust which a five-mile ride from London had raised. "How very unfortunate."

"Aye, well may yer say that, milord," Jack complained, gingerly rubbing his sore jaw. "That cove was right 'andy with 'is fives, that 'e were!"

The horseman seemed unimpressed by Jack's complaint. "My concern is the item for which we search," he murmured. "Frankly I did not really expect . . . but no matter." He looked at Jack. "You are quite sure, then, that it was not there?" he asked.

"I looked everywheres, milord," Jack hastened to assure him. "Everywheres!"

"Well," said the gentleman briskly, "there is no point in repining. We, or rather I, must simply rethink our strategy." He ran an idle hand over the glossy neck of the magnificent roan stallion that waited by his side.

"Er . . . milord . . ." Jack said hesitantly.

The rider focussed an alert gaze on his confederate. "Yes?" he said sharply.

"Ain't it possible the gentleman burnt it?" Jack asked. "If 'e knew wot it was yer was after . . ."

The gentleman's lips curled. "I think not," he said contemptuously. "Geoffrey was always an indecisive weakling, even as a boy. He would never have had the determination to do any more than make a feeble attempt to hide the truth. No, the document still exists, I'm certain of it.''

Jack's attention had wandered. "Look, milord!" he said excitedly. "Look!" He pointed through the stand of trees in which he and his employer had chosen to meet, to the pretty village green that lay stretched out below them. "It's them," he said. "Them wot we been watchin'!"

Jack's employer stepped forward. He watched the tiny, far-off figures of Deborah and her aunt emerge from a travelling coach, and then Stewart, who had been riding alongside the coach, climb stiffly from the saddle to escort the ladies into the inn which was the village's only commercial enterprise. "Just as I thought," said the gentleman, with great satisfaction in his voice.

"Where be they goin', milord?" Jack asked. "Do yer think they found it? They must 'ave—"

"Shut up, Jack." The gentleman watched until all three figures had disappeared into the inn. He stood staring down at the green for another long moment, before laughing softly to himself. "This is excellent," he said. "Excellent!"

"I don't know wot yer thinks is so excellent," Jack said sullenly. "Looks to me like they be runnin' off on yer."

"But then, you are a fool, Jack," the man said affably. At the sight of Jack's suddenly murderous expression, he raised one aristocratic brow. "Have I wounded your tender sensibilities, my friend?" he jeered. "I do apologize."

Jack clapped a weathered hat onto his stringy hair and spat out, "To 'ell with yer, me fine lord, and may yer rot there!" He began to turn away from the other man, only to howl with pain as a riding crop slashed down across his cheek. Clapping a hand to his bleeding face with an inarticulate snarl, Jack reached for his pocket. He stopped short as he caught sight of a gleaming silver pistol, levelled at his chest.

"I'm not yet finished with you, my dear Jack," his companion said calmly, the gun fixed steadily on Jack's heart. "I have not spent quite all of my time waltzing at Almack's, you know. My years on the Continent taught me a thing or two about defending myself, and about how to bring a recalcitrant dog to heel."

Jack spread his hands appeasingly. "D-don't shoot... milord," he stammered hastily. "I didn't mean no 'arm."

The gentleman caused the gun to disappear as quickly as it had appeared. "Of course you didn't," he said mockingly. "You should strive to be less precipitate, friend Jack. That hasty temper will be the death of you yet." He sighed. "I do grow weary of teaching you these little lessons, but perhaps it is as well. You won't so underestimate me the next time, will you?" Jack assured his master that he would not. "As to why I am so happy to see our dear friends travelling," the man continued, "the reason is simplicity itself: they are, as I'm certain you've deduced by now, on their way to Shaftsworth, which is precisely where I wish them to be."

"Why?" Jack asked sullenly. "Yer told me there weren't nothin' t'be found at Shaftsworth."

"I told you that I could find nothing there," the horseman corrected Jack. "They may succeed where I have failed." He chuckled richly. "Particularly," he added, "as I have left them a little something which will set them frantically a-searching."

"Wot?" Jack asked, interested despite himself.

"Why, the letter, of course," the gentleman said. "Admit it, Jack, you thought me mad to leave the letter at Shaftsworth, didn't you?" Jack shuffled his feet uncomfortably; the gentleman looked deeply satisfied. "But I was right. If we cannot find what we seek, then we must elicit the aid of Geoffrey's near and dear ones in the search." He climbed gracefully back into the saddle. "I always thought it most likely that we'd find it at Shaftsworth—that, after all, is where Geoffrey died. And who better to find what Geoffrey has hidden than his own daughter?" The man stared down at Jack unseeingly. "Dear Geoffrey," he said, his tone curiously gentle. "He thought to have bested me, but he was very, very wrong."

LADY MARGARET RAWLINGS adjusted the angle of her parasol, and nodded her head graciously to the occupant of a carriage just leaving the Park. Without letting her smile falter, she murmured to Burle, "Poor woman, she must be blind. Look at that quiz of a bonnet."

Lord Burle squinted at the fast-disappearing carriage, and shrugged. "Didn't look so bad to me," he remarked. "But then, I've always been rather fond of that shade of puce."

His cousin shuddered delicately. "Alex," she said flatly, "you should thank God that you have Uncle to help dress you. One cringes at the thought of what you would inflict on an undeserving public otherwise."

"I do, Maggie, I do," Burle said, guiding his phaeton skilfully around a pair of soldiers who had pulled over to converse with a blushing young debutante, despite her fiercely frowning companion. "Though it's deuced uncomfortable sometimes, being the son of a man who cuts such a fine figure as Father. So very hard to live up to, don't you know."

"So it is, Alex," Margaret agreed sympathetically, and squeezed his arm. "But you do a fine job, coz. Really."

"No, I don't," Burle said. "I know that I don't. I shall never be so well dressed, or well respected, or so...well, just so civilized as Father." He moved his thin shoulders uncomfortably for a moment, then grinned at Lady Margaret. "I try not to let it bother me. No, no, don't look at me that way, Maggie," he protested. "My father is absolutely first-rate, I could never ask for better. I just wish..."

"That you could be more of a first-rate son to him?" Lady Margaret supplied. Burle nodded his head sheepishly.

His cousin startled him by remarking blightingly, "What a cawker you are, Alex."

"Aye, that I am," Burle agreed gloomily.

Margaret's fair skin turned pink with embarrassment. "That's not what I meant, and you know it. Uncle couldn't be more pleased with you if...if...if nothing! He positively dotes on you."

"All right, all right." It was Burle's turn to flush. "Dash it all, Maggie, no need to make such a fuss. I promise you, I don't waste time repining over my inadequacies."

"It just maddens me when you undervalue yourself so," Lady Rawlings replied, her attention caught by something else. "Pull over, Alex, do. There's Lady Duncan. A horrible creature, but she always knows all the most delicious gossip. Good day, Lady Duncan," she called.

"Good day, Lady Margaret. And Lord Burle." Lady Duncan, notorious for her social aspirations, simpered at Burle. "How lovely to see you, and such a divine day for a drive, don't you agree, my lord?"

"Er, uh, yes," Burle stammered. "Indeed it is." He looked to his cousin for rescue.

"Tell us the latest *on dit*, my lady," Lady Rawlings begged prettily. "You are always in the know."

Lady Duncan preened, and smoothed the skirt of her gown, a hideous concoction of lace and purple satin totally unsuited for a simple drive in the Park. "Well," she began in a hushed, confiding tone, "of course you must have heard about poor Lord Driver? Lost his entire fortune, playing piquet with a certain—person, shall we say? Poor Lady Driver is devastated, of course—as much by the notion that a demimondaine won the money, I think, as the fact that it was lost." Lady Duncan tittered unpleasantly. "But then, men will be men, won't they, Lord Burle?" She stared pointedly at Margaret's cousin.

"I beg your pardon?" Lady Margaret said frigidly.

"Eh?" Burle was confused.

"You misunderstand me, my lady," Lady Duncan said hastily. "I was referring to this unfortunate matter of Lord Burle's friend, Mr. Timothy Stewart."

"What about Timothy?" Burle asked. Lady Margaret said nothing, her face carefully blank.

"Why, this business of him and Miss Tollin," Lady Duncan exclaimed archly. "Surely you knew?"

"What business?" Burle demanded.

"Well!" sniffed Lady Duncan. "I'm sure there's no need to be rude."

"Pray forgive my cousin, Lady Duncan," Lady Margaret said quietly. "Concern for his friend is uppermost in his mind. He had no intention of being impolite."

"Of course," Lady Duncan said, unbending. "I do so hate to be the bearer of bad tidings." Her avid look gave this the lie. "But," she said, leaning forward eagerly, "if you didn't hear it from me, you would from someone else, and perhaps someone without my sensitivity."

"Indeed," said Lady Margaret, hard put to keep her dislike hidden.

Lady Duncan's eyes glittered. She motioned to her coachman to draw her vehicle a little closer to Lord Burle's phaeton. "The fact of the matter is, my dear Lady Margaret," she said confidently, "that Mr. Stewart and that Tollin chit have run off together!" Lord Burle stifled an exclamation, Lady Rawlings gasped, and Lady Duncan said triumphantly, "Yes, yes, 'tis shocking, is it not? Of course, one could not expect any better from such a creature as Miss Tollin, for blood will always tell. But that Mr. Stewart would do such a thing . . . well, I suppose it just shows that his reputation is not undeserved."

"I don't believe a word of it," Burle said bluntly, glaring at Lady Duncan. "Timothy would never do such a thing, nor would Miss Tollin."

Lady Duncan tittered again, her expression unpleasant. "I'm sure your loyalty does you credit, my lord, but I assure you, 'tis quite true. They were seen leaving Town by, oh, any number of people. The brazen hussy didn't even trouble to try to hide their destination—they went to Shaftsworth, Miss Tollin's estate.'' Lady Duncan shook her head, and assumed a pious expression. ''One might almost pity the child. She knew she'd never receive another respectable offer after Eversley cried off, so she took Stewart up on one which was, quite obviously, far from respectable.''

''Alone?'' Lady Margaret asked tersely. ''Did they go alone?''

''Well, no,'' Lady Duncan admitted reluctantly. ''That aunt of hers was with Miss Tollin, but that is of no consequence.'' She waved a hand. ''Everyone knows what Miss Beldon is. Why, she ran off with Stewart's own father, not so many years ago.''

''Well over twenty years ago, as I recall,'' Lady Margaret said dryly.

''Twenty years or one, the woman is no better than she should be.'' Lady Duncan looked smug. ''Miss Tollin may well have persuaded her aunt to go along to lend them countenance, but she will find that society is not so easily fooled.''

''Why, you—you—'' Burle sputtered.

Margaret laid a restraining hand on her cousin's arm, and turned to the lady in the other carriage. ''In other words,'' she said clearly, ''you are maligning the character of a young lady who has gone on a perfectly innocent trip, suitably chaperoned, with a young man she has known from the cradle.'' Her green eyes swept coldly up and down the woman before her. ''You, madam, are despicable.''

Lady Duncan paled, then flushed. ''You may be content to believe such nonsense, my dear Lady Margaret,'' she hissed, ''but I promise you, 'tis my opinion which will prevail among the ton, not yours!'' She rapped her driver rather harder than was necessary with her parasol, and her carriage pulled quickly away.

"But how could they?" Burle asked, deeply distressed. "How could they think...? How could they say...?"

"Very easily, Alex," Margaret said wearily. "Here in London, for every Pembroke, fair-minded and tolerant, there are a hundred Lady Duncans, ready, nay, anxious! to believe the worst." She shook her head. "Sometimes this place sickens me," she said quietly.

"But we must do something, Maggie!"

"What?" Margaret asked gloomily. "What can we do?"

"One thing I can do, Maggie," said Burle decisively, "is to speak to my father. He'll know what's best done, I'm sure of it."

"That is an excellent notion, Alex," his cousin said approvingly. "If anyone can think of a way out of this coil, it will be Uncle."

They drove along in silence for a time, Burle's brow furrowed in thought, Lady Margaret's gaze fixed on the far distance. More than one occupant of the Park attempted to greet the popular pair, only to be passed by, unseen and unheard. They were actually on their way out of the Park when Burle startled his cousin by giving a whoop of delight.

"I have it, Maggie, my love!" he cried. "I have it."

Lady Margaret eyed Burle warily. "Have what, my dear?" she asked.

"The solution to Timothy's problem, of course," Burle said. "What else? I don't know why I didn't think of it right off." He chuckled.

"Alex," Lady Margaret began, "I really don't think—"

"That I'm capable of solving a problem? For shame, coz!"

"That is not what I was going to say," Margaret stated with great dignity.

"Well, whatever you were going to say, just wait a moment, won't you?" Burle begged. "This plan is absolutely foolproof. After all, it would have to be, wouldn't it, if I'm involved?''

"Alex!" Lady Margaret protested, half laughing.

"Just listen, Maggie," Burle commanded. "This is what I was thinking..."

SARAH BELDON WEARILY sank down onto one of the trunks piled in the centre of Shaftsworth's lofty entrance hall. "Thank God we're here," she groaned. "I've never been so glad of anything in my life as I was to hear us rattling over that old bridge at the end of the drive. One more moment on the road would have killed me!"

Timothy Stewart pulled off his gloves. "Come now, Aunt Sarah, it wasn't that bad," he said, and grinned. The purple-and-yellow bruises on his face, while healing, still lent his smile a gruesome aspect.

"All very well for you," Sarah responded darkly. "You were astride, not cooped up for hours in that stuffy, swaying carriage."

"True," Timothy acknowledged, "but I assure you, dear Aunt, 'twas not the most comfortable of journeys for me, either. My unknown assailant saw to that. I vow I feel worse right now than I did the day he beat me."

"Poor boy!" said Sarah, relenting. "I have been thinking only of myself. How odiously selfish."

Timothy feigned alarm. "Oh, no, Aunt Sarah, you mustn't coddle me," he said. "''Twould quite spoil my character. Deborah, come and give me a much-needed dose of unkindness—Aunt Sarah is threatening to unman me.'' He looked behind curiously when the girl did not answer. "Deb?"

Deborah stood silently in the centre of the hall, her arms wrapped tightly about herself, blue eyes shadowed. As Timothy watched, she looked toward the library and shuddered, a haunted expression on her pale young face. Timothy silently damned himself for an insensitive fool; he should have remembered that this was the first time the girl had been home since her father's suicide. He took a step toward her, but before he could speak, the Shaftsworth stableman bustled into sight.

"Miss Deborah!" Perkins cried, his grizzled face split by a grin. "I thought it were yer coach I seen comin' up the drive. Welcome."

Deborah stepped forward, both hands held out to the old family retainer. "Perkins," she said warmly. "How well you look."

Perkins blushed ferociously. "Yer lookin' right fit yourself, miss, and a sight fer sore eyes." He hesitated for a moment, then began clumsily, "Me and the missus, Miss Deborah, we—"

Whatever he had been about to say was cut short by the arrival of his good wife, who hurried into the foyer drying her hands on her spotless white apron. "Perkins!" she called. "Where are you?" She stopped short at the sight of the two women and Timothy Stewart, and the colour drained from her normally ruddy cheeks. "Miss Deborah," she said faintly. "I...I..." Her voice failed her, and she burst into tears.

Deborah looked amazed; a glance at her aunt told her that Sarah had no more idea of the reason for Mrs. Perkins's tears than she. Deborah hurried over to the housekeeper. "Mrs. Perkins, what is it?" she asked gently. "Please, Mrs. Perkins, don't cry."

"How can you ever forgive us, Miss Deborah?" Mrs. Perkins sobbed. "Your poor father..."

"Here, now, Martha, yer be upsettin' Miss Deborah," her husband said. "Give over, do!"

"You mustn't blame yourself, truly, Mrs. Perkins," Deborah said. "There wasn't anything you could have done."

"We should have seen...we should have known..." Mrs. Perkins said brokenly.

"Now, that ain't true, Martha," Perkins said bracingly. "Mr. Geoffrey was always one t'keep 'imself t'imself. Ain't that right, Miss Sarah?" The look he turned on Sarah could only be described as entreating.

"Exactly, Perkins," Sarah said briskly, rising from her trunk and crossing to Mrs. Perkins's side. "Martha," she asked the woman, "how long have we known each other?"

Martha was puzzled by the abrupt change of subject, but answered promptly. "Since you first came to live at Shaftsworth, Miss Sarah, nigh on a quarter century ago."

"And in all that time, have I ever lied to you?" Sarah continued patiently.

Mrs. Perkins looked shocked. "Why, of course not!" she exclaimed.

Sarah smiled sadly at Perkins's wife. "Then believe me now when I tell you that there was nothing that you could have done," she said. "Geoffrey was far too fond of both you and your husband to ever think of distressing you with his problems." Aunt Sarah met Mrs. Perkins's gaze squarely. "I am only grateful, " she told the woman, "that you were here to make his last days comfortable, as I'm certain that you did."

"But . . ." Mrs. Perkins protested faintly.

"That's enough, Martha," Aunt Sarah said kindly. "No more repining, if you please."

"Yes, Miss Sarah," Mrs. Perkins said dutifully, and wiped the last tears from her plump cheeks. She looked around at the bags and trunks strewn around the hall and turned to her husband. "Perkins," she said, with a return to her normal tone, "see Miss Sarah and Miss Deborah up to the drawing room, then help Rose and Mary take these trunks and such abovestairs."

"Mary and Rose are not with us this trip," Aunt Sarah told the housekeeper uneasily. "They, er, asked if they might be allowed to visit their parents while we were at Shaftsworth."

Mrs. Perkins tut-tutted. "This is what comes of allowing sisters to be employed together," she said with satisfaction; she and the two lady's maids had never dealt well together. "But to be so inconsiderate as to go off together, leaving you poor ladies to fend for yourselves, well, you should never have allowed it, Miss Sarah."

Deborah and Aunt Sarah exchanged uncomfortable glances; they could not tell Mrs. Perkins that they had felt it unfair to bring the maids into a potentially dangerous situation, and so had offered the sisters an unasked-for vacation.

"Well, never you mind," Mrs. Perkins said contentedly. "Lazy as the two of them are, we shall get along quite well without them."

Aunt Sarah sank back down onto her trunk. "I'm sure you're right, Martha," she said, and vainly attempted to stifle a yawn. "For myself, all that I require is a hot meal and clean linens on my bed," she told the housekeeper. "I feel as if I could sleep the clock round."

"And so you shall, Miss Sarah," the housekeeper said briskly. "Perkins, see to Miss Sarah and Miss Deborah's baggage, if you please. I shall go and start dinner, and then just run and make up the beds. You ladies take yourselves to the drawing room, and everything will be ready in a trice, I promise you."

"Is there anything which I might do, Perkins?" Timothy asked helpfully. "I know that we caught you unprepared— I'd be more than happy to lend a hand. Perhaps I could go and open up the drawing room for Aunt Sarah and Deborah?"

"No need o' that, Mr. Stewart," Perkins said gruffly, "though I thank yer kindly for the offer. The drawin' room is already open, on account o' his lordship."

"His lordship?" Aunt Sarah repeated blankly. "What lordship?"

Perkins looked sheepish. "I forgot ter tell yer, Miss Sarah, in all the excitement," he admitted.

"Deborah!" The joyous cry echoed in the spacious hall. "What a wonderful surprise!"

Three backs stiffened into shocked rigidity, then slowly turned toward the curving staircase at the opposite end of the long hall. Sarah gasped aloud, her face ashen, and clasped her hands anxiously together. Timothy whistled soundlessly and thrust his fists deep into his pockets. Deborah, after a fleeting moment during which her eyes had lit with pleasure and her lips curved into the beginning of a smile, looked as though she had been struck.

Lord Eversley struggled down the stairs, leaning heavily on a carved Malacca cane, his ankle carefully bandaged. "By Jove, Deb, I am glad to see you!" he called happily.

Without a word, with only the whispery rustle of her black bombazine skirts to break the sudden silence, Deborah Tollin closed her eyes and sank to the floor in a faint.

CHAPTER EIGHT

"I DON'T KNOW about this, Alex," Lady Margaret Rawlings said doubtfully as her cousin helped her out of the travelling coach. "It seemed a good notion when we were back in London, but..."

"Did it?" Burle asked. "Then why did you fight it so hard? It took me all of two hours to convince you." He leapt out of the coach. "Don't worry—it will all go off smooth as silk, you wait and see." He turned back and addressed the driver. "The right front wheel, now, John, and don't overdo it—just enough to be believable, if you please." The coachman nodded and touched his hat.

Burle returned his attention to Lady Margaret and gallantly offered her his arm. "Well, coz?" he said. "Shall we?"

She sighed. "Very much against my better judgment," she said, "we shall."

Lady Margaret Rawlings and Lord Burle set off walking. It was not the best of days for strolling along a dry country road; the sky overhead was a menacing shade of grey, and the air was still and oppressive. Lady Margaret's chic green travelling gown and matching velvet pelisse were not the ideal ensemble for such dusty work, and indeed, the pair had not even lost sight of the coach before Margaret stopped. "How much farther is it, Alex?" she demanded.

"Not a very great distance, Maggie," Burle said, careful not to meet her eyes.

She was not so easily fooled. "What exactly do you mean by 'a very great distance'?" she asked. He made no response. "Alex!"

"We have to make it look real, don't we?" Burle asked plaintively. "In the interests of verisimilitude—"

Lady Margaret threw up a hand. "Don't tell me any more," she said. "I must have been mad!" she muttered to herself, and grimly set off again.

Burle squeezed her hand. "You're a right 'un, Maggie, no doubt about it," he said, and grinned down at her. She could not help but smile back, and harmony was restored, at least for the moment. Then Burle said, "Do you mind if I ask you a rather personal question?"

"Of course I don't," she said. "Ask away."

"How is it that you have never married?" he asked. "That is to say," he added hastily, "it seems inexplicable. You are beautiful and intelligent, an accomplished hostess, everyone loves you, and your fortune is more than respectable. You must have had dozens of offers. How is it that you never accepted one?"

Margaret shrugged. "No one for whom I really cared ever asked," she answered simply.

"Do you mean that you have, in fact, met a gentleman for whom you've developed a *tendre*?" Burle supplied helpfully. Lady Rawlings blushed as red as her hair. "Aha!" he cried. "I knew it! There is such a gentleman, isn't there?"

"Whatever are you jabbering about, Alex?"

"Don't try to scare me off the scent, Maggie," Burle said, supremely unaffected by her irritation. "It won't work, you know—I've known you for far too long. In fact, that's what first made me suspect."

"Suspect what?"

"Why, that you were in love," Burle told her innocently.

"In love! Alex, how can you say such a thing? How . . . how positively vulgar," his cousin sputtered.

"Is it vulgar to fall in love, Maggie?" Burle asked with interest. "Then pray tell me why you thought it so marvellous when Eversley and Miss Tollin were betrothed? You said 'twas just like a fairy story."

"That was different," Lady Margaret snapped. "Their affection was mutual."

"Oh," said Burle. "Is that the way of it, then. I'm sorry, coz."

Margaret closed her eyes, then stamped her foot on the packed dirt of the road. "You...you...cad!" she cried, and, snatching up her skirts, forged angrily ahead of Burle.

"Maggie, don't be angry. I didn't mean to pry!"

The first fat drops of rain plopped onto the dry ground as Burle hurried after his cousin, calling her name and adjuring her to wait. "Maggie, please!"

John the coachman hunched his shoulders against the steadily increasing downpour and cursed the foul weather. But as he watched the two disappear down the road, honesty forced him to reflect that he'd rather be where he was than running along in the rain, trying to soothe an angry female.

THERE WAS A SHARP RAP on the bedchamber door. "Come in!" called Eversley eagerly, hastily smoothing back his auburn hair. He ran a hand over his shaven chin, silently blessing Perkins's skills as a valet, and straightened the pile of cushions on which his ankle and foot rested.

The door opened and Timothy Stewart sauntered into the room, impeccably groomed, his hands thrust deep into his pockets.

"Oh, it's you," said Eversley, unable to keep the disappointment out of his voice.

"Well," said Timothy philosophically, "I hardly expect you to be thrilled to see me."

"Forgive me, Stewart," Eversley said, surprising Timothy. "I had thought it might be Deborah, you see."

"I can quite understand your disappointment, then," Timothy acknowledged cheerfully, and perched on a corner of Eversley's bed. "I'm a sorry substitute indeed." He regarded Eversley's swathed limb with more curiosity than compassion. "How is it?" he asked.

Eversley grimaced. "It would have been fine by now, had I not taken that ridiculous tumble down the stairs last evening," he admitted ruefully. "When I saw Deborah faint, though, I quite forgot about my ankle. I wanted only to help her as quickly as I could. What an absolute dolt she must think me." Eversley cocked an eyebrow at Timothy. "Would it be too rude of me to ask what happened?"

Timothy touched the bruises on his face. "These?" he said. "Just a small disagreement with an intrepid housebreaker—tedious, but far from fatal." He looked away from Eversley. "You'll never know how surprised we were to look up last night and see you standing at the top of the stairs. How is it that you happen to be at Shaftsworth?" Timothy watched Eversley intently out of the corner of his eye.

Eversley frowned, not unaware of Timothy's close, if surreptitious, regard. "It's coincidence, really," he answered warily. "I had a driving accident not far from here and was reduced to begging transportation from a farmer's boy. I thought it sensible to have him bring me here, rather than to some unknown, and most probably uninhabitable, inn. It seemed perfectly unexceptionable—Deborah and I are betrothed, after all."

"To be sure," said Timothy noncommittally, and stared thoughtfully down at Eversley. The faint sounds of horses pounding up the drive and a moment later the bang of the knocker against the front door did not appear to disturb his reverie.

Eversley bore the scrutiny well, lifting his chin and meeting Timothy's gaze squarely. After several moments, he asked, a little defiantly, "Well, Mr. Stewart? Shall I do?"

Timothy had the grace to blush. "Ah ... I was thinking of something else," he said.

"Such as what kind of a husband I shall make Deborah?" Eversley guessed. "A good one, I promise you."

"It's certainly none of my affair ..." Timothy began.

Eversley shook his head and smiled, and for the first time, Timothy began to perceive what Deborah saw in his lordship. "That's what I thought," he said ruefully. "I was quickly brought to see the error of my ways. Deborah was furious! She thinks of you as a brother, you know."

Timothy looked extremely uncomfortable. "It is in that guise that I've come to speak to you today," he began stiffly.

With a twinkle in his eye, Eversley said, "And you're not enjoying it overmuch, are you? Very well, then let me help you with the thing." He dropped the bantering tone and looked gravely at Stewart. "I love Deborah with all my heart. I plan to spend the rest of my life trying to make her happy."

"No, no, you misunderstand me!" Timothy said. "I must tell you—"

The bedchamber door crashed open, and Roger Henderson stormed into the room, his face red, the veins in his neck bulging angrily.

"Uncle Roger!" cried Eversley. "What ... ?"

Roger Henderson ignored his nephew. "You!" he shouted, pointing at Timothy.

"Uncle Roger, what's wrong?" Eversley, seriously alarmed, struggled to sit up straighter. Timothy reached out to help the peer by propping a pillow up behind him.

"Stay away from him, you devil!" Henderson roared, and leapt to his nephew's side.

"Roger, get hold of yourself," said Lord Pembroke, who had entered the room behind Henderson, along with Sir Cyril Dennison. All three men were dressed for riding, and covered with the dirt which hard travel raises.

"Damned scoundrel!" said Henderson, nose to nose with Timothy. "Horsewhipping's too good for you!"

"Uncle Roger, please," said Eversley. "What has Stewart done? He is not—"

"He is Deborah's lover!" Henderson bellowed.

In the sudden silence, the first drops of rain could be heard hitting the open windows which looked out over the park. Sir Cyril Dennison muttered something incomprehensible, and moved to shut the windows with a slam; the noise seemed to break the spell that had fallen upon the inhabitants of the bedchamber.

"You lie, sir," said Timothy from between clenched teeth. "Were it not for your advanced age, I would teach you truthfulness at the end of my sword."

"Advanced age!" repeated Henderson, on the verge of an apoplexy. "I'll show you who is aged, you insolent young puppy!"

"That's enough, Uncle Roger," said Eversley, pale but firm. "Pray forgive my uncle, Mr. Stewart; I can't imagine what—"

"Now that is outside of enough!" burst out Henderson. "Should you apologize to the cad who has stolen your fiancée and made a whore of her?"

Eversley tried to rise, and only Pembroke's restraining hand kept him from leaping out of the bed at Henderson. "Shut your mouth, damn you!" he shouted at his enraged uncle. "You'll not speak of her that way. I shan't allow it."

"You shall hear me, Eversley, if I have to sit on you to make you listen," Roger Henderson said grimly. "When the chit first broke her engagement to you, I have to admit, I felt badly about it. She had done it for love of you, I thought, and though it was necessary, I regretted it." He laughed bitterly. "What a fool I was. She was just anxious to be rid of you, so that she could run off with her paramour, this—this—" Words failed him as he pointed a shaking finger at Timothy.

Eversley shook his head dazedly. "I don't understand. She has broken our engagement? When? How?"

"The notice was in the papers," said Pembroke gently. "Just after you left London."

"No sooner was the deed done than she was off with him," Henderson said, scowling at Timothy. "You're well rid of her, my boy. She's no better than a damned—"

"That is quite enough," said Timothy, the twitching of a muscle in his cheek testifying to the difficulty he was experiencing in keeping a rein on his temper. "You are wrong about Miss Tollin, Henderson, as wrong as you can be. 'Twould be laughable, were it not so unspeakably foul." He turned to leave the room. Eversley reached up and grasped his wrist in a strong clasp.

"Is it true?" he asked quietly, his face white. "Has she broken our engagement? Are you her lover?"

Timothy hesitated. "Yes... No... Let me explain," he said.

Eversley's face closed. "I see," he said coldly. He looked Timothy up and down insultingly. "And I had thought to have misjudged you!"

Timothy looked as though he would say more, then shrugged and left the bedchamber. Pembroke stepped forward and laid a hand on Eversley's shoulder.

"I'm sorry, lad," he said. "The news cannot have been welcome to you, particularly at such a time." Eversley turned his face away from the marquess.

"Well, you'll not spend another night in this house, that I do promise you," Henderson blustered. "We'll be on our way as soon as our horses are ready."

"I think not, Roger," said Sir Cyril, still standing by the windows. "Look!"

The other three men turned their attention to the outdoors. They had been too intent on their conversation to notice that the wind had risen dramatically, and that the rain had turned into a downpour. Even as they watched, the first bolt of lightning split the sky, followed not many seconds later by a deafening roar of thunder. So heavy was the rain that the park directly outside the windows could barely be distinguished, and the stables, situated a short distance from the house, were completely invisible.

"Traveling in this weather is out of the question," said Sir Cyril in his precise way. "Particularly if your nephew is to accompany us, Henderson. We shall have to spend at least the night here."

"What? Beg hospitality from that whore and her lover? I will not!" Mr. Henderson vowed.

Pembroke frowned and poked Henderson in the ribs. When the latter turned to glare at him, the marquess nodded toward the bed. Eversley was lying with his eyes closed, his head back against the pillow. So white was his face, and so strained his expression, that Henderson took an involuntary step toward him. Pembroke shook his head and said lightly, "Roger, my friend, we have no choice in the matter. Unless you are able to grow gills and swim, I fear that we shall be forced to pass the night at Shaftsworth."

"So we shall," Henderson mumbled unhappily. "But at first light, come what may, we shall be on our way, and to hell with Miss Deborah Tollin!"

"AUNT SARAH, please, calm down and tell me what happened," Deborah begged her aunt. "You're not making sense, my dear."

"They just burst in," Aunt Sarah said wildly. "Henderson, and Lord Pembroke, and some other gentleman..."

"Sir Cyril Dennison," supplied Timothy, coming down the stairs into the entrance hall.

"They burst right in, and when I asked where they were going," Sarah went on, "Henderson spun around and positively grimaced at me, and said that he had come to rescue his nephew from this 'den of iniquity'!"

"Den of iniquity?" Deborah repeated incredulously. "Why would he say that? Didn't he explain himself?"

"I told you, he just stormed right by me!" Sarah said.

"Well," said Deborah firmly, "I do not know what is going on, but I intend to find out." She picked up her skirts and turned toward the stairs, only to have Timothy stand before her, blocking her path.

"No, Deb," he said flatly. "Stay away from them. I don't imagine they'll be here much longer."

"I'll do no such thing," Deborah said indignantly. "This is my home. I should like to know what is going on in it, if you don't mind."

Timothy sighed. "Very well, then, come into the dining room, and I'll try to explain it to you as best I can."

"Excuse me." Lord Pembroke, tall and slender, came down the stairs. He crossed the hall, ignoring both Timothy and Sarah, and stopped in front of Deborah. "Miss Tollin," he said without preamble, "I am forced to beg accommodation from you for myself and my two companions, due to the inclement weather."

Deborah flushed to the roots of her hair at Lord Pembroke's brusque tone.

"Come now, my lord," protested Timothy.

Lord Pembroke raised his quizzing glass in Timothy's direction. From his expression, one would never have supposed that he and Timothy were well acquainted, that they had, in fact, been quite fond of each other. "Have you something to say to me, young man?"

Timothy placed a hand on Lord Pembroke's sleeve. "Lord Pembroke," he said. "You know me. Can you believe what Henderson has said? Can you?"

Pembroke's only response was to stare pointedly at the hand on his sleeve until it dropped, then to turn away. "Well, Miss Tollin?" he asked. "May we, however reluctantly, rely upon your hospitality?"

Timothy's expression hardened. "Do not use that tone of voice with Miss Tollin, my lord," he said coldly. "I warn you..."

Deborah stepped forward and shook her head at her friend. "Hush, Timothy," she said, then with great dignity, "You are, of course, welcome to stay as long as you wish, my lord, as are Mr. Henderson and Sir Cyril. I fear that you may not be as comfortable as could be hoped, though. At the present time, we have only a skeleton staff here at Shaftsworth."

The marquess forbore to comment, but one haughtily raised brow spoke volumes.

Deborah went white where she had been red, but said only, "I shall send my housekeeper up to prepare rooms for you and your companions. If there is anything you need, pray do not hesitate to ask."

Lord Pembroke frowned. He looked long and hard at Deborah, who returned his gaze fearlessly. He opened his mouth to speak, but before he could utter a word, a loud knock was heard on the front door. Sarah hurried over to the entrance and swung the door open.

"Good day, Miss Beldon," came a faint voice. "May we come in?"

Sarah appeared to have lost her powers of speech. She waved a hand and stepped out of the way.

Lady Margaret Rawlings picked up her sodden skirts and stepped into the house with as much dignity as she could muster. Her shoes made a squishing sound as she stepped onto the tiled floor of the entrance hall; the feather which adorned her bonnet and had once curled so charmingly about her face, now hung limp and broken, dripping water down her back. Lord Burle was in no better condition. Soaking wet, his new green frock coat and bright yellow small-clothes so saturated that their colours had begun to run, he had the look of something out of a nightmare. As he stepped through the door, he sneezed violently.

Timothy burst out laughing at the sight of the woebegone pair on the threshhold. Lady Margaret's head flew up at the sound, and her fair skin turned a bright shade of red. "Mr. Stewart!" she snapped. "How very gracious of you to greet us so kindly."

"Yes, really, Timothy," Deborah scolded as she hurried to welcome the cousins. "How can you be so unfeeling? 'Tis unforgivable!" She turned her attention to Lady Margaret. "My poor Lady Margaret, what on earth has befallen you? No, no, don't tell me—there will be time enough for that later, after we have you out of these wet clothes. Come along, my lady, up to my bedchamber. We'll have you all dry and comfortable in no time." She tucked Margaret's arm under her own. "Aunt Sarah, pray tell Martha to prepare two, no, five, more rooms. Timothy, will you please see to... Lord Burle, isn't it?" She smiled warmly at Burle, reducing him to a state of stuttering idiocy, then swiftly disappeared up the stairs, Lady Margaret in tow.

"By God," breathed Burle reverently, staring up the stairs after Deborah, "but she is a beauty!"

"That she is, Burle, that she is," Timothy agreed. He draped an arm around his friend's shoulder. "If you'll step into the library with me, my friend, I'll pour you a brandy, and you can explain to me what odd concatenation of events brought you to Shaftsworth."

The marquess of Pembroke stepped out of the shadow of the staircase. "Not," he said, "before you explain it to me, my son!"

CHAPTER NINE

THE KITCHEN DOOR OPENED, and Martha's husband blew in on a gust of wind and rain. "Perkins!" cried Martha, hurrying to his side. "Oh, Perkins, you're soaking wet," she scolded, helping him out of his saturated outer clothing.

"Of course I am, woman," he grumbled good-naturedly. "There be a gale abroad!"

"Well, come sit by the fire, and I'll get you some tea," Martha fussed. "You need to get warm."

"Only a minute, mind," Perkins warned her, "fer there's more t'do out there. This is goin' t'be a powerful bad storm."

Deborah had come into the kitchen to tell Mrs. Perkins of their extra guests. "Oh, Perkins, surely there's no need for you to go back out tonight?" she said, dismayed. "It's so cold and wet. Can't your chores wait until morning?"

"No, miss," Perkins said gravely. "Things is right bad out there. The bridge is already washed out, and if it don't let up, the stables might be in danger o' flooding."

"What?" cried Deborah. "How can that be? It's only been raining for a couple of hours."

"Yes, that's true, Miss Deborah, but it's been a powerful wet spring," Perkins explained. "I been watchin' that bridge and worryin' fer weeks."

"Is there any danger to us?" Deborah asked. "Is there anything we should be doing?"

Perkins shook his head. "The house itself is up 'igh enough to be out of danger. Like I said, though, I'll be keepin' a close eye on those stables." He stood up and gulped down the last of his tea, then shrugged back into his wet coat. "If yer needs me, Martha, I'll be with the 'orses," he said. "Don't fret yerself, 'bout this, Miss Deborah. We just needs t'sit tight and wait it out." With the slam of a door, he was gone.

Martha wrung her hands. "I do hate the thought of Perkins out all alone in this weather," she said. "Anything could happen!"

"Don't worry, Martha," said Deborah. "I'm going to ask Timothy to go out and help him." She sighed. "This does mean, though, that our guests won't be leaving tomorrow. If that bridge is out, they'll be here until it's fixed."

"We'll manage, Miss Deborah, never you fear," said Martha decisively, then more hesitantly, "But if you could ask Mr. Stewart to help Perkins...? He'd never admit it, but my husband isn't the man he used to be, I'm afraid. He doesn't see as well as he once did, and his hearing's a little off, too." She lifted her chin proudly. "Don't misunderstand me, Miss Deborah. In normal times, there's not a better or more loyal worker to be found anywhere." She looked out the window at the driving rain and shivered. "But these are not normal times, are they?"

"Of course not," said Deborah. She squeezed Martha's hand reassuringly. "And of course Perkins is the best of stablemen. Do you think I don't know that? But in this weather, he'll need all the help he can get, and then some. Don't worry; I'll send Timothy out to help him right away."

"Thank you, Miss Deborah, that does set my mind at rest," Martha said gratefully. "Now you run along and put your feet up before dinner. You're looking a mite peaky, if you don't mind my saying so."

"Are you quite sure you won't need me, Martha? I could lend you a hand..." Deborah said, looking around the kitchen doubtfully.

The housekeeper laughed. "Begging your pardon, miss, but I think you'd be more of a hindrance than a help. Get along with you, now. Scat!" Martha watched her mistress leave the kitchen and closed the door behind her, then turned back to her kitchen. "Nine people!" she sighed. "Lord, give me strength, for it just might kill me!"

"SO YOU SEE, FATHER, we were really lucky to be so close to Shaftsworth when it happened," Burle said earnestly. "Else we might have been wandering around for who knows how long, and in this awful weather, too."

Pembroke eyed his only son consideringly for what seemed to Burle an eternity, then took a long sip of his brandy. "I see," he said finally. Burle breathed a sigh of relief, but too soon, for his father said musingly, "There's only one thing I'm mildly curious about, Alex—where were you going?"

"What?" asked Burle stupidly.

"After all, you must have been on your way to somewhere when your accident occurred," said Pembroke reasonably. "Where?"

"Er, that is to say," mumbled Burle. "Simpson!" he squeaked.

Pembroke raised one arched brow. "Simpson?" he repeated.

"We were on our way to visit Maggie's old nanny," Burle said. "That's it, Maggie's nanny, Mrs. Simpson." He appeared to be highly pleased with himself.

"Oh?" said Pembroke gently. "And exactly where does this Simpson person reside?"

Burle was overset. "Ah...ah..."

Pembroke chuckled gently. "Just as I suspected," he said.

"I can't think what you mean, Father." Burle recovered himself quickly. "What did you suspect?"

"No matter," the marquess said, and fixed his son with a judicious eye. "Tell me, Alex..." he began.

"Yes, sir?"

"Are you quite happy living in London?"

"Oh, yes," Burle said. "It's something like! Full of fun and interesting people, and always a new diversion to, er, divert one."

"Indeed," said Pembroke. "And your rooms are satisfactory, are they?"

"That they are!" His son nodded emphatically. "I do believe your man of business found the best bachelor digs to be had in Town. Not too far away from anything, but not so close that one is overrun by a bunch of cits. Cosy, but not too small, not fussy, but comfortable. They're perfect."

"I am gratified," Pembroke murmured. "And your allowance—adequate, I pray?"

Burle blushed. "Yes, sir. I'm the envy of all my cronies—you're dashed generous, don't you know." He stopped. The marquess was watching him closely, a smile playing about his lips. Burle blushed again. "Oh!" he said. "I see. You think I should tell you, since you're so...in return for..."

"Good evening, Uncle," said Lady Margaret, closing the door silently behind her. "What a lovely surprise, to find you here."

"Is it, my dear?" Pembroke asked, rising from his chair to press a kiss onto Lady Margaret's forehead. "I beg leave to doubt it." He smiled down at his niece and tweaked her cheek lightly.

"Oh, Uncle," Lady Margaret said reproachfully, sending Burle what Pembroke could only have described as a speaking glance. "How you do tease!"

Pembroke ignored this, saying as he settled back into his seat, "You have come in the nick of time, Margaret, as ever. As I recall, you have always been partial to rescuing your cousin."

"Oh?" Lady Margaret replied brightly. "Are you in a scrap, then, coz? But how entertaining!"

Burle looked miserably unhappy. His father took pity on him, and said to Lady Margaret, "Alex here was just about to tell me where this nanny of yours lives."

"Nanny?" echoed Lady Margaret blankly.

Lord Pembroke's smile widened. "Mrs. Simpson," he supplied helpfully.

"You know, Maggie...Mrs. Simpson," babbled her cousin, with suitable grimacings and pointed glances at his father. "Whom we were on our way to visit. When the wheel broke?"

Lady Margaret's brow cleared. "Oh!" she said. "Alex, you great silly, she wasn't my nanny, she was the housekeeper!" Her wide green eyes were innocent as she turned them on her uncle. "Honestly, I do despair of your son at times."

"I am not," her uncle replied calmly, "completely unfamiliar with that emotion myself." As Burle sat up to protest, his father held up a hand. "Do be at ease, Alex. You've borne the standard manfully, and now you've earned your just reward. I believe that Margaret and I shall converse for a time. You will excuse us, my son?"

Burle looked at his cousin helplessly. "Maggie?"

"Do go, Alex," said Lady Margaret instantly, a martial light in her eyes. "It will be my great pleasure to speak with my uncle."

"I've always wondered," the marquess said thoughtfully after Burle had left, "if perhaps your father did not allow you a tad too much freedom. Regretfully, my dear, I have lately become convinced of it."

Margaret smiled broadly at her relative. "Have you, Uncle?" she drawled. "And upon what grounds, may I ask?"

"I experienced my first twinge of unease," he said, "during your unfortunate romance with Mr. Stewart."

All traces of amusement were wiped from Lady Margaret's face, and her back stiffened alarmingly. "I beg your pardon?" she said frigidly.

"Do not, pray, attempt to come the lady with me," her uncle advised her pleasantly. "I know that your father did not appoint me your guardian, but surely I may be allowed to be concerned for you?" Margaret did not seem inclined to concede the point. "I will grant you, no one who was not intimately acquainted with you would ever have been aware of your interest in Stewart," Pembroke continued. "But to one who has known you, and may I add, loved you, since you were a babe, 'twas painfully obvious."

"I don't know what you're speaking of," she said.

"Then just let me talk, and you listen," said the marquess. "At any rate, I was greatly disturbed by what I saw between yourself and Stewart, greatly disturbed indeed, but I thought that your common sense—"

"You are imagining things," Margaret said.

"But I thought that your common sense had overcome your infatuation, and that you had had the wisdom to sever that connection," he went on firmly. "But now, here you are, out of nowhere, and dragging my unfortunate son along behind you. Have you taken leave of your senses, Maggie?"

She shrugged. "This is your tale, Uncle," she said bitterly. "You tell it."

"Very well, then," said Pembroke. He leaned forward. "Are you so lost to pride, my dear, that you actually followed that rake Stewart to Shaftsworth?"

Lady Margaret leapt to her feet. "I believe *you've* run mad!" she cried. "First of all, there never was any romance between Mr. Stewart and myself. Never. Secondly, even if there had been, as you yourself have pointed out, 'twould be none of your concern! And thirdly—" she turned back, skirts in hand, chin trembling despite her defiant glare "—Timothy Stewart is not a rake!" She stamped her foot, then swept out the door.

The marquess looked deeply distressed. "Oh, my dear girl," he said, shaking his head. "Oh, my poor, dear girl."

THE MAN SHIVERED uncontrollably, and attempted to huddle farther under the tree which lent him such inadequate shelter. The frequent bolts of lightning which lit the sky made the Londoner flinch, and the booming cannonade of thunder caused him to shudder even more violently.

"'E's mad!" Jack muttered, hugging himself and bowing his head against the rain. "Stay close, 'e says, and wait for me signal. 'As the soddin' lunatic looked out a window o' late? I couldn't see 'is signal if 'e burned the cursed 'ouse down!" He scowled ferociously, then pulled a flask from his pocket and took a long, satisfying swallow. He sighed, replaced the flask, and returned to watching the dim outline of the house, which was all that could be distinguished through the driving rain. "Yer 'as ter admit, though, 'e's as good 'as 'is word," Jack said, resuming his soliloquy. "'E got 'imself invited ter the place, jest like 'e said. If 'e could do that, may'ap it will go off the way 'e planned."

A bolt of lightning which garishly illuminated the landscape shook Jack's newfound faith. He hastily took another swallow of gin, and, instead of replacing the flask in his pocket, held it in his hand, ready for his next libation. "'E's mad!" Jack said again. "'Ow long does 'e expect me ter wait, I wonder? I'd 'ave ter be a bleedin' fish ter stay out 'ere all night!" He took another long drink and, back against the tree, slid slowly down to sit in the mud.

"I should leave, that's wot I should do," Jack mumbled to himself, oblivious now to the rain and the howling wind. "I ain't no fool, ter wait 'ere forever at 'is 'ighness's beck an' call! Yeah, I should..." He stopped; one hand crept up to finger the healing wound on his right cheek.

An earsplitting crack of thunder sounded. In the relative silence which followed, Jack heard the high-pitched scream of a frightened horse, and, a moment later, the faint sound of galloping hoofs. By the time he had stowed his flask away and struggled unsteadily to his feet, his mount was long gone. "Damn that soddin' jade of an 'orse!" Jack said weakly, and staggered heavily. "Damn 'er to 'ell!" Lightning again lit the sky, illuminating Shaftsworth and the stables which stood nearby; Jack blinked owlishly, and suddenly grinned. "That's it!" he said. "'E did say ter stay close—couldn't be no closer 'n that!" Laughing at his own wit, one hand placed protectively over the pocket which held his flask, Jack began to slowly weave his way toward the stables, and shelter.

CHAPTER TEN

DEBORAH TOOK A DEEP BREATH, then rapped gently on the door. She did not wait for a response, but straightening her shoulders, lifted her chin and swung the door firmly open.

Eversley, his head turned away on the pillow, said tiredly, "What is it, Perkins? I don't need anything right at the moment, thank you."

"It's not Perkins," Deborah said.

Eversley's eyes flew open, and he winced as if he had been struck. Then his lips curled in a sneer, and he said, "My esteemed hostess. To what do I owe this dubious honour?"

The colour rose to Deborah's cheeks. "How are you, my lord?" she asked. "Did you pass a comfortable night?"

"This sudden concern for my feelings is most touching," Eversley said sarcastically. "I am quite overwhelmed, I promise you."

"I did not think that you would be glad to see me," Deborah said, "but I did rely upon your courtesy."

"You have me there, Miss Tollin," Eversley said. "Whatever I may feel, it is incumbent upon me to be polite, isn't it?"

Deborah was silent for a moment, then she began hesitantly, "I know that you are very angry with me..."

Eversley snorted. "Angry does not begin to describe the way I feel toward you."

"But you don't understand!" Deborah said, clasping her hands and beginning to pace in agitation.

"Ah, but I do see, quite clearly," Eversley said unpleasantly. "I was not available to warm your bed, so you turned to the first man who was. I was a fool. It sickens me to recall how innocent and pure I once thought you. My only consolation is that you had the poor judgment to choose Stewart, who will surely use you and abandon you, as you so richly deserve."

Deborah stopped and stared blankly at Eversley. "Robert," she said faintly. "You cannot believe that!"

Eversley bit his lip. "What else am I to believe?" he asked bitterly. The pain in Deborah's eyes made him look at her more closely. He said haltingly, "Deb, if you have an explanation for the way you behaved... if there is some reason... ?"

Deborah closed her eyes for a split second, then shrugged. "No," she said harshly. "I have no explanation. You're absolutely right, about everything. And if Timothy does desert me, well, there are many more men in the world, are there not?" She turned away from Eversley's scrutiny. Walking toward the windows, she said lightly, "At first I thought that I should be quite happy to marry you, for to be a lady of rank and wealth could not help but be pleasant, and you are rather handsome, you know, Eversley. But then it occurred to me that if I could have you, then surely I could find a gentleman of even higher birth. As for good looks, if one cannot find them in marriage, then one must simply look elsewhere!" She whirled round and looked at Eversley, her eyes glittering. "Don't you agree?" she asked sweetly. Without waiting for an answer, she went on, "And then, of course, there was that quarrel we had, the day that Timothy and I met in Green Park. I saw that you would be a jealous sort of husband, and that would never do, no, not for me. I wish for a man who will be willing to—" she tittered inanely "—look the other way, shall we say? So I decided to break the engagement. And there was Timothy, so devilish handsome, so eager to please. I'm sure that you quite understand, don't you, my lord?''

Eversley opened and closed his mouth several times before his voice finally emerged. "Get out!" he shouted hoarsely. "Get out of here, do you hear me? Or, so help me God, I'll—I'll—"

Deborah sniffed indignantly. "There's no need to become violent. I'll leave you now, Robert, for you are obviously not well. Good day, my lord."

"Wait!" Eversley scrabbled frantically through the drawer in the table next to his bed. He laughed as he found what he was looking for, and hurled the folded paper at Deborah. "I had not thought to give you this, thinking that it would wound you too deeply," he said triumphantly, "but I was wrong. It could not affect you in the least, my dear, for you have no heart. Read it, lovely Deborah, read it and laugh at another poor fool who loved you!"

Clutching the paper tightly in her hand, Deborah did not say another word, but turned and swept out of the room.

"To hell with you!" Eversley bellowed after her, his body trembling with rage. "To bloody hell with you!"

With the sound of his voice echoing in her ears, Deborah stopped outside the closed doors and buried her face in her hands, her shoulders shaking.

"You! What are you doing here?" came a hostile voice.

Deborah lifted her head to find Mr. Henderson standing before her, his chest thrust out angrily. "If you will recall, Mr. Henderson," she bit off angrily, "this is my home!"

"Don't think I can forget that unhappy fact for a moment," Henderson retorted. "Were Eversley not so banged up, I would leave this house today—if I had to swim to do it!"

Deborah felt suddenly drained. "I am very well aware of that," she said wearily. "I'm sorry that you're compelled to remain here, but even you will admit that there is nothing I can do about it. Now, if you will excuse me."

"I want to know what you were doing in Eversley's room!" Henderson demanded.

"Then I suggest," snapped Deborah, "that you ask your nephew." Then she turned her back on him and was gone.

Mr. Henderson opened the bedchamber door and immediately exclaimed, "Here, now, Eversley, stop that!"

Lord Eversley ignored his uncle. He swung his legs over the edge of the bed and tried gingerly to stand.

Henderson hurried to Eversley's side. "Damned fool," he scolded his nephew. "What are you doing, trying to get up? You must give it time to heal, gudgeon!" Gently, Henderson lifted the swathed ankle back onto the pile of pillows. "'Twill never mend if you don't let it rest."

"I must get up," Eversley declared. "I'll not spend another minute in this house."

Henderson frowned. "I know just how you feel, lad, but there's no help for it," he said. "Even if you could get up, which you cannot, there's no place to go. Until this rain lets up enough for the bridge to be repaired, here we are and here we stay."

"It is intolerable," said Eversley distinctly, "that I be obliged to stay here."

"Aye," agreed Henderson, "but tolerate it we must. Believe me, Robert, were there any other way..." Mr. Henderson worriedly watched his nephew's face. "I'm sorry," he said helplessly.

After a moment, Eversley reached up to grip his uncle's shoulder reassuringly. "It's not your fault," he said with a wan smile. "I do wish that we could leave Shaftsworth, but the Fates have apparently aligned themselves against us. So be it." His grip tightened. "You will tell me, though, the instant we can leave? The very instant?"

"You have my word on it, lad," promised Henderson, covering Eversley's hand with his own. "Now rest, and let that blasted ankle heal. I'll be in to see you later."

Eversley nodded and closed his eyes. Mr. Henderson tip-toed silently out of the bedchamber.

LADY MARGARET RAWLINGS leaned her head on her hand and stared dreamily off into space. She was nestled in a deep armchair in the drawing room, her feet tucked underneath her, a book forgotten on her lap. She did not stir when Timothy Stewart entered the room, nor when he crossed to stand beside her chair. She seemed quite unaware of his presence.

"Good afternoon, Lady Margaret," he said, smiling down at her. "Whatever are you thinking of, with such a smile on your face?"

Lady Margaret flushed hotly, and jumped to her feet so quickly that one of her slippers was left in the chair. "Ti—Mr. Stewart!" she cried. "Fie on you, sir, for skulking about so."

"*Au contraire*, my lady," he said easily, reaching down to capture the empty slipper. "I was not skulking. You were merely engrossed. Come, tell me, what were you thinking of?"

"That," she said sharply, "is none of your affair. May I trouble you for my slipper, please?" She held out an imperious hand.

Timothy frowned consideringly, and shook his head. "No, I think not," he said. "Not until you tell me what brought that soft smile to your lips. Would that it were I," he added lightly.

Lady Margaret's green eyes flashed fire. "Oh, really?" she said bitingly. "That was not at all my impression. Give me my slipper!"

It was Timothy's turn to flush. "Of course, my lady," he said, and handed her the item with a bow. "You are quite right. Pray forgive me."

Lady Margaret bit her lip. "No," she said stiffly, "forgive me. I was too harsh." Her face was hidden as she bent gracefully to replace her shoe.

"You are most gracious," Timothy responded, his face carefully expressionless.

Lady Margaret resumed her seat, and an uncomfortable silence fell on the pair. The sound of the rain thrumming against the window filled the drawing room, and she shivered involuntarily.

"Are you cold?" Stewart asked instantly, and squatted down beside the young woman's chair. He took up a poker to stir the fire, but before he could do so, Lady Margaret reached out and touched his arm shyly.

"I am sorry," she said softly. "I'm afraid that my temper sometimes gets the better of me." Her face took on a wistful expression. "My father often scolded me for it."

"As well he should have," Timothy said with a forgiving grin. "There is nothing worse then a tempery woman. Although," he added, reaching out to twirl a lock of her hair gently around his finger, "with that red hair, I suppose you have no choice but to be a harridan!" He leaned toward her, his eyes gleaming. "A beautiful, tempting harridan, to be sure," he murmured, "but still a woman to lead a man a merry dance."

"Am I?" asked Lady Margaret, curiously breathless. "Am I beautiful and tempting?" Her hand tightened on Stewart's sleeve.

"My lady... Margaret..." he breathed.

"Yes, Timothy?" Her lips were a scant inch from Stewart's own.

"I...I..." Timothy threw himself to his feet and away from Lady Margaret. His back to her, he said, "Once again I have forgotten myself. Your pardon, my lady."

"But, Timothy!" Lady Margaret blinked back the tears. "Please!"

"We have been over this before," Timothy said bleakly "Do not forget that you are a lady of birth and breeding and I, no more than today's scandal."

"You cannot think that I believe all this nonsense about you and Miss Tollin?" Lady Margaret said. "I know you too well!"

"For me, this is merely the latest scandal among many," Timothy said wearily. "You know it, my lady. No one who cared for you would let you become involved with a man of my reputation—ask your uncle. He will tell you what I am. Your father, were he alive, would call me out for allowing myself such familiarity with you, and he would, alas, be right."

The lady's eyes sparkled. "My father," she said acerbically, "was not such a fool as to believe everything he heard. Nor am I, Mr. Stewart." She rose to her feet and took a hesitant step toward the young man. "Please, Timothy," she said yearningly. "I have been so unhappy."

"Don't!" he broke in sharply, and strode toward the window, his back stiff. "Don't embarrass either one of us by saying any more."

Lady Margaret's shoulders sagged, and she sank back into her seat. "As you wish," she agreed unhappily. She took up her book and stared blindly at the pages.

"Now what is this?" Timothy said, in a completely different tone. He cupped his hands around his eyes and peered out the window into the rain and deepening darkness.

"What is what?" Lady Margaret asked listlessly.

"Come and see," he commanded, and the young woman rose obediently to her feet and crossed the room to the window.

"I see nothing," she said, acutely aware of the strong young body so close to her own.

"Look," he said. "There's a light in the stables."

"Where?"

"Over there," he said impatiently. "You can just make it out. Do you see?"

"Yes," said Lady Margaret. "You're quite right. I didn't notice it at first."

"Now, who could that be?" Timothy wondered.

"Perkins, I should think," she said. "Who else would be out there?"

"That's just it," Stewart said with interest. "I was just out in the stables with Perkins, lending him a hand with the horses."

"That was kind of you, Timothy," she said softly. "Particularly as you are not feeling quite the thing." She touched his bruised cheek gently.

Timothy jumped as if her fingers had scalded him. "I'm fine," he said, "just a little sore, that's all. The point is, when we came in, Perkins told me that he was in for the night. He was most grateful, he said, that he wouldn't have to see to 'them cursed 'orses,' as he put it, until morning."

"He must have forgotten something," Lady Margaret suggested.

Timothy turned away from the window with a determined expression. "Well," he said, "if Perkins is out there working still, then I am going out to help him."

"Oh, but Timothy!" she protested. "You shouldn't be out in such weather."

"And Perkins, a man of sixty, should be?" Timothy retorted. "I would not have thought you so heartless, Mar—my lady."

"But he is a servant," Lady Margaret said in confusion. "He must be accustomed to such conditions, mustn't he?"

"True," Timothy acknowledged, "and in the ordinary run of things, I shouldn't dream of being anything more than an ordinary, selfish houseguest. But Perkins and his good wife are single-handedly seeing to the needs of—how many? Nine of us?"

"You're right, of course." Lady Margaret smiled sheepishly at Timothy. "How unselfish you are."

"Don't think too highly of me," Timothy said with a grin, "Deborah had to ask for my help before I realized how overworked they were." He started to leave the room, then stopped, and turned back. "Lady...Margaret," he said awkwardly, "I wish, that is to say...we may be friends, may we not?"

"Yes, Timothy," she said. "We may be friends." He waved a hand and was gone. It was not until the door had closed firmly behind him that Lady Margaret bent her head and began quietly to weep.

THE MARQUESS OF PEMBROKE looked up and down the deserted hallway, then slipped into the library and closed the door gently behind him. He sighed happily when he saw that the room was deserted, and congratulated himself upon finally finding a place apart from the cloud of dislike and anger which hung over the rest of the household. To a man of Pembroke's urbane outlook, such an atmosphere was distasteful under the best of circumstances; when it involved his oldest friend, and a young man of whom he had once been very fond, it was an extreme trial. So great a trial, in fact, that Pembroke could not have waited with more anticipation for the moment when he, Henderson, Dennison and, of course, Eversley, could bid a final farewell to Shaftsworth and its occupants.

With that happy day in mind, he crossed the room to the windows which stood behind the desk, only to have his hopes dashed. The rain still poured steadily, as it had all morning, with no sign of a break in the clouds, or even a lessening of their density. Pembroke grimaced, then his features relaxed. No good had ever come of regret, he reflected, and turned his attention to an examination of the Shaftsworth library.

The chamber was a pleasant one. Despite its size, it had a cosy air that Pembroke found a refreshing change from the rest of the draughty house. He wandered over to an ornately carved lectern which stood near the fireplace and idly flipped open the Bible that rested upon it. The volume was an aged one, long in the family, he guessed from the spidery, old-fashioned handwriting on the inside cover which proclaimed the book to belong to one Oliver Tollin and his good wife, Jane. The Tollins were, or at least had been, a family of much pride. Just inside the front cover was a meticulously drawn and quite detailed family tree, which began with the aforementioned Oliver and Jane. Pembroke amused himself for some moments by tracing out the more obscure branches of the family, which, he saw, included Burlinghams, Lathams and even the odd Witherspoon or two. Following one of the branches with his fingertip, he exclaimed aloud; at the very spot where Deborah Tollin's name, and that of her mother, should have been inscribed, there was a hole cut in the page. The vandalism could not have been accidental for the edges of the cut were too precise, the two names, and no more, too carefully removed. Pembroke shook his head in distaste. Who would disfigure such an obviously treasured family heirloom, he wondered, and for what reason? For a moment, he debated whether or not to call it to the attention of someone in the household. No, he decided, for it was none of his affair, and could only add to the general air of dislike and mistrust which prevailed at Shaftsworth. Closing the Bible firmly and turning away from the lectern, he focused his attention on the leather-bound volumes which filled the shelves of the library. Having chosen a suitable work, he settled into a comfortable armchair and was soon engrossed in his reading.

Some time later, Lord Pembroke had the feeling that he was being observed. Without looking up, he said absently, "Yes? Who is it?" There was no answer. He lifted his head impatiently and repeated, "Who is it, I say?" Pembroke looked around the room. Save for himself, the library was empty. He shrugged and returned to his novel.

The marquess had not read very many more pages before he again felt as if he were being watched. He tossed the book down with an irritated growl and snapped, "All right! You've had your little joke, now come out!" No one answered him, so he rose and searched the spacious chamber, even going so far as to look under the desk and behind the draperies, but there was no one to be found.

Pembroke frowned, slowly resumed his seat, and picked up the book which he had been reading. But he was unable to attend to the story. The perception that he was not alone grew stronger and stronger, until he found himself actually straining to hear a sound, any sound, in the silence. His vigilance was rewarded. He heard a sliding noise, then a faint click which seemed to come from the direction of the massive stone fireplace. In a flash he was on his feet and across the room.

A fire burned cheerfully in the grate, the hearth was neatly swept, the mantelpiece dusted, and the andirons gleamed with polish. The marquess ran a hand over the contents of the shelves and shook the screen which was neatly folded to one side of the fire, but could not reproduce the sounds he had heard. Though he no longer sensed that he was being watched, Pembroke felt a sudden chill and, despite the heat of the fire, shivered convulsively.

"Father?"

Pembroke whirled around. "Burle!" he snapped, more sharply than he had intended in his relief. "Damn you, sir! Do you think yourself amusing?"

Burle blinked. "I beg your pardon, my lord?"

"This little game you've been playing—the flat of my sword might teach you better manners!" Pembroke glared at his only child.

Burle looked bewildered. "But, Father, I haven't been playing any game," he said plaintively. "I don't know what you're talking about."

"Do you deny that you've been lurking about, trying to startle me?" his father demanded. "Do you?"

"But I just this moment arrived," Burle said. "Honestly, Father!"

Pembroke hesitated for a moment, then clapped his son on the shoulder. "I'm sorry, Alex," he said more reasonably. "Forgive me my temper."

Burle's brow cleared. "Of course," he assured his father. "But what happened?"

Pembroke turned back to frown at the fireplace. "I could swear..." he began, then shrugged. "Never mind. Were you looking for me, my boy, or just exploring?"

Burle did not answer; he was staring up at the portrait of the late Mr. Tollin and his deceased wife, Amanda, which hung over the mantel. It had apparently been painted when the young pair were first wed; they had the happy, starry-eyed look of two people deeply in love. "You can see where Miss Deborah gets her beauty," Burle noted. "She bears a remarkable resemblance to her mama."

"Miss Deborah?" Pembroke repeated, raising one eloquent brow. "I had not thought that you and the young lady were that well acquainted."

Burle blushed. "It happens that Miss Deborah," he said defiantly, "has been all that is gracious to me. I'm sure that you wound her deeply, Father, by believing—"

"I very much doubt," interrupted Pembroke coldly, "that my beliefs are of any consequence at all to the young lady—or should I say, person?"

"Now, really, Father, you go too far," Burle scolded. "This is precisely why I have come to speak to you today—you are committing a grave error!"

Pembroke inclined his head regally. "You are entitled to your opinion," he said, and turned his attention rather pointedly back to his book.

Burle was not to be dissuaded. "May we not discuss this, Father?" he coaxed. "One gentleman to another?"

Pembroke hesitated, then nodded. "I suppose so," he grumbled reluctantly, "though I warn you now, Alex, there's no point to it."

"I'll take that chance," Burle retorted, with a smile which transformed his homely face and warmed his father's heart. "I know that if you will only stop and think about all this, you'll see how absurd it is." He leaned forward intently. "You know Timothy Stewart, father. You used to like him, I think, didn't you?"

"I'll admit that I found Stewart pleasant company," Pembroke said cautiously. "But the truth will out, Alex, and he's shown us all what he's made of, more's the pity. He is a bounder and a cad, and I deeply regret the kindness that we—I—have shown him in the past."

Burle's face was pale. "Father, you can't mean that!"

"Why not, Alex? Could you have thought that I would condone his actions? Granted, I was fond of him once, and the girl does seem to have cooperated wholeheartedly. But he has seduced a lady of birth, and that is still, even in these jaded times, unacceptable behaviour." Pembroke eyed his son shrewdly. "You'll forgive me, lad, if I point out to you that you are not the most experienced of men? Of course you think Stewart a trump. You've not yet known enough bounders to recognize the breed."

Burle's cheeks burned, but he held his temper. "I realize that you have seen far more of the world than I have, sir, but I do know Timothy, and I know that he would never do anything to hurt Miss Deborah, not for any consideration."

Pembroke sighed. "But he has done just that, Alex. Were this little jaunt of theirs the most innocent of excursions, which I am not by any means prepared to accept, it has still utterly destroyed Miss Tollin's reputation with the ton.''

''But they have been constantly chaperoned!'' Burle exclaimed. ''Does that count for nothing?''

Pembroke shrugged. ''If Sarah Beldon thinks her consequence sufficient to excuse such a questionable venture,'' he remarked, ''then she is most sadly mistaken.''

Burle gripped the arms of his chair in frustration. ''Can you not see how small-minded you are being?'' he demanded. ''How terribly unfair?''

''How, Alex?'' asked Pembroke evenly. ''Is it unfair to expect gentlemen, and yes, ladies, too, to obey the rules of polite society? Without such rules there would be no civilization, only chaos.''

''We are not speaking of rules, Father, or of civilization,'' Burle said in great disgust. ''We are speaking of truth and justice. The fact of the matter is that Timothy and Miss Deborah have done nothing worse than what Maggie and I did in coming to Shaftsworth, or has that thought not yet occurred to you?''

''I don't think... That is to say... The cases are not the same.'' It was Pembroke's turn to flush.

''They are, and you know it,'' Burle said. ''Will I be an outcast, Father? Will Maggie be a ruined woman?''

''Of course not,'' Pembroke responded irritably. ''Don't be absurd.''

Burle spread his arms wide. ''The rules of polite society are flexible, it seems,'' he said ironically.

''Perhaps when you're older, Alex, you'll, er, understand,'' Pembroke blustered.

Burle's lips tightened, and he rose stiffly to his feet. ''I am not a child, Father,'' he said, with a dignity which showed, more clearly than words, how deeply Pembroke had hurt him. ''You have no right to treat me as one. Excuse me, please.'' He turned to leave the library.

"Alex!" said the marquess surprised. "I didn't mean…"

"I have always known that you thought me a fool," Burle said quietly. "How I wish that there was something I could do to change that opinion." He closed the door behind him.

CHAPTER ELEVEN

"BY GOD, DENNISON, but this is the very devil of a place," Roger Henderson said tensely, turning away from the window and letting the curtain fall back into place. Sir Cyril Dennison's lips twitched, but he did not interrupt his friend. "We've already spent one night here, and it's been raining all day. At this rate, we'll be trapped here a fortnight."

Sir Cyril shrugged and held his glass up, letting the light of the fire warm the brandy's amber depths. "It could be worse, you know, Henderson," he remarked. "Despite the lack of servants, they've managed to make us very comfortable."

Henderson scowled. "I'd sooner be drowning, out there in the rain," he retorted, flinging an arm toward the window, "than forced to remain under the roof of...of..." He closed his eyes, his expression pained.

"You may wish yourself out in the weather, but I do not," Sir Cyril said promptly. "I much prefer to be here, by a warm fire, digesting the efforts of a talented cook and enjoying an excellent brandy." He raised his glass in Henderson's direction.

Henderson looked curiously at his friend. "I must confess, Dennison, I was surprised when you agreed to accompany me on this unpleasant journey," he admitted. "With your love of creature comforts, I had thought that you would not stir from your cosy London hearth." He flushed at Sir Cyril's amused look and added awkwardly, "I do appreciate it, I promise you."

It was Dennison's turn to look nonplussed. "Don't be an ass, Roger," he advised Henderson. "I was flattered that you asked me, considering the brief span of our acquaintance and the delicacy of the situation." He wriggled uncomfortably in his seat. "Besides, I thought that you might need me," he confessed. "I know this Stewart to be a rum 'un, from personal experience."

Henderson's eyebrows soared. "You do?"

Sir Cyril settled back in his seat. "Do you recall," he began, "the day that Burle introduced us?" Henderson nodded. "Well, the three of us, Burle, Stewart and I, had just returned from a few days in the country. Lord Duncan's place—perhaps you know it? At any rate, it was there that I first met Stewart, introduced to him by Burle, whom I had met shortly after my return from the continent, some six months ago. I found the young man, Stewart that is, to be amusing company, and was inclined to think him a good sort."

"This is his method," Henderson said darkly. "He has certainly deceived Burle with his charming ways."

"He has," Sir Cyril agreed soberly. "To continue, the party was of the most ordinary, with all the usual amusements. Save for a stretch of perfectly beastly weather, there was nothing the least bit noteworthy about the gathering. There were no ladies present—just the four of us, Burle, Stewart, Lord Duncan and myself. We had fallen into the habit of having a hand or two of cards every evening after dinner. There was not a great deal of money involved, just enough to keep the game interesting. Not, that is, until the last night of our stay." Dennison rolled the brandy glass reflectively between his fingers. "We had rather a special dinner that evening, as we were to leave the next morning, including Lord Duncan, who was to meet his lady in London. I regret to say that we were all, myself and Duncan included, rather the worse for drink by the time we sat down to play." Henderson made a strangled sound, but did not speak. After a moment, Sir Cyril went on, "The game started off normally enough, with the customary small stakes. But something seemed to have come over young Mr. Stewart that night. He bet more and more recklessly with each successive hand, damning us for cowards until we matched his extravagance." Sir Cyril pulled a long face. "It may be that we were partly to blame for what followed. I believe that is why Lord Duncan insisted that we forget the entire matter, later on."

"What matter?" Henderson demanded. "Do get to the point, Dennison!"

"Well," said Sir Cyril, "the hours seemed to fly by. All of us became totally engrossed in the game, none more so than Stewart. He was losing badly, of course—with the way in which he was betting, he would have had to have the devil's own luck to hope to do so much as break even. He seemed not to care, though. When a hand went against him, he would simply laugh and call for the play to continue."

Henderson leaned forward, enthralled. "And?" he prompted.

Dennison looked supremely uncomfortable. "I really should not be telling you this," he said uneasily. "Lord Duncan swore us to secrecy."

"Lord Duncan be damned!" Henderson expostulated. "It's too late to change your mind now, Dennison."

"You're right," admitted Sir Cyril. He lowered his voice confidentially. "The final hand was for an enormous sum of money—close to a thousand pounds, I should guess."

"Good Lord!" exclaimed Henderson weakly.

"Exactly, my dear Henderson," said Sir Cyril dryly. "By that point, we were all too flown with wine and excitement to realize how absurd the stakes had become." He sighed. "When the play ended, Stewart had won. Lord Duncan cursed him for a lucky dog, but none of us thought anything of his win, save to rue our own bad luck."

"Are you saying . . . ?" Henderson breathed.

"When Stewart reached out to gather in his winnings," Sir Cyril said heavily, "a card slipped out of his sleeve. A low card, and his hand full of royalty."

Roger Henderson looked stunned. "A rogue and a scoundrel I knew him, but a common cheat? I would never have credited it," he said, shaking his head. "And you say that Lord Duncan swore you to secrecy? Why, in God's name?"

"As I said, I believe that Lord Duncan felt partly responsible, for allowing the boy to drink so deep at his table," Sir Cyril answered. "I would also wager that Duncan did not want his wife to learn of the considerable sum of money which he had lost that evening. She surely would, were the matter to become general knowledge. Lady Duncan's sources of information are, er, impeccable."

The ghost of a smile crossed Henderson's face. "That they are."

"A most formidable woman, to be sure," said Sir Cyril smoothly.

"I can understand Lord Duncan's motive in keeping silent, but what was yours?" asked Henderson bluntly. "You should have told. Damn it all, Stewart should not have been allowed to return to the society of gentlemen!"

"Need I remind you, Henderson, that I was honouring the wishes of my host?" asked Dennison frostily. "It seems no more than his privilege to decide what was to be done." He met Henderson's gaze with a challenging stare.

"You're right, I suppose," agreed Henderson, rubbing his chin, "but it doesn't seem right, somehow. Someone should have said something."

"Burle was only too happy to agree to the plan, not unsurprisingly," Sir Cyril commented calmly.

"Burle—I had quite forgotten about him." Henderson swung round to frown mightily at Sir Cyril. "Never tell me that Burle countenanced this lie? I'll not believe it!"

"Oh, Burle," said Sir Cyril dismissingly. "He is loyal to his friend. He insisted that it was an accident, that Stewart had unknowingly scooped up the card when he reached out for his winnings. In fact, Lord Duncan pretended to agree with Burle, then spoke to me privately later on about remaining silent." Dennison drank the rest of the brandy. "No one else has learned the truth, excepting only Pembroke, of course."

Henderson's head jerked. "Pembroke knew?" he said blankly.

"Duncan did agree, finally, that Burle's father must be told." Sir Cyril spoke modestly. "The marquess has a right to know just what Stewart is."

"But how can that be?" Henderson asked himself aloud. "When Pembroke took such convincing that Stewart had seduced the Tollin female? When he defended the scum so eloquently!"

"It may be that Lord Duncan has not written. 'Tis quite understandable that he should wish to postpone an unpleasant task," Sir Cyril speculated. "It has not been so very long."

"But Pembroke did receive a letter from Duncan." Henderson was clearly agitated. "Don't you remember? He mentioned it to us, a week or so ago, at the club."

"Ah, well, I'm sure that there is some reasonable explanation for all this," Sir Cyril said comfortably. He rose to his feet. "After all, a man of the marquess's position has other matters which demand his attention." He gestured helplessly. "Perhaps he simply forgot."

Henderson shook his head. "To forget such a thing? Not Pembroke!"

Sir Cyril Dennison clapped his friend on the shoulder. "I shouldn't trouble myself about it, if I were you," he counselled. "As long as Pembroke knows now what a rapscallion this Stewart is, there's no harm done, is there?"

"I BEG YOUR PARDON?"

"I said," repeated Lady Margaret Rawlings patiently, "I wonder if you have seen Mr. Stewart today." She coloured a little under Sarah Beldon's quizzical scrutiny, but her gaze did not falter.

"Well, no, Lady Margaret, as it happens I have not," Sarah answered politely. "But then, that is not surprising. I have been busy in the kitchens, helping Mrs. Perkins, for most of the morning."

"But don't you think it rather strange, that no one should have seen him today?" Lady Margaret pressed her. "I do!"

Sarah regarded the young redhead with mild surprise. "Why would you think that strange, my lady?" she asked. "I'm sure that it is the most common thing in nature for a young man to lie long abed, particularly a young gentleman from London."

"That is not Timothy's way," Lady Margaret declared vigorously. "He's no lazy young fop, wasting his time sleeping the day away. And since he isn't," she finished confusingly, "then where is he?"

Sarah shook her head. "I don't have the faintest idea what you're talking about," she said. "And furthermore, my lady, I don't think it wise in you to show such familiarity with . . . Deborah!" she cried in relief and hurried across the hall to her niece's side. "Perhaps you may be of some assistance to Lady Margaret," she said. "I should like to help, truly, but Mrs. Perkins is waiting for me, I'm afraid." With a significant look in Deborah's direction, she hurried away.

"Yes, my lady?" Deborah asked perfunctorily. "How may I be of help?"

Lady Margaret took a step closer to Deborah, her brow wrinkled. "Forgive me, Miss Tollin, but are you quite well?"

Deborah pushed the limp curls back from her forehead and smiled unconvincingly. "I'm fine, aside from a slight headache," she said. "And please, call me Deborah, won't you?"

"Only if I may be Margaret to you," Lady Margaret said. "Are you sure that you're not ill?" she asked sceptically.

"Quite sure," Deborah said a little curtly, then smiled to take away the sting of her words. "But what is troubling you, my—Margaret?"

The concern on the lady's face deepened. "It's Mr. Stewart," she said.

Deborah was surprised. "Timothy?" she repeated. "What's wrong with Timothy?"

"I'm not sure. That is to say, perhaps nothing." In a few short words, Margaret told Deborah of Timothy's trip to the stables the night before, and of her own concern when he had not appeared for breakfast. "Your aunt thought me mad, I know," she said, biting her lip, "but I have this feeling..."

"You're quite right, it is strange for Timothy to miss breakfast," Deborah said thoughtfully. "Perhaps I should just go and tap on his door to make sure he's all right."

Lady Margaret blushed again. "I already did, and there was no answer," she said, ignoring Deborah's quickly suppressed look of surprise. "Furthermore, though it was shameless of me, I opened the door and looked in his room," she continued defiantly. "The bed had not been slept in, Deborah!"

"Perkins might already have made it up, I suppose," Deborah said doubtfully.

"He didn't," she said flatly. "I asked."

"And no one else has seen him this morning?" Deborah enquired. Lady Margaret shook her head. "That is strange," acknowledged Deborah. "What's to be done?"

"I suggest we go out to the stables and have a look round," Lady Margaret said. "Don't you agree?"

"Wouldn't it be better to ask one of the gentlemen to do it?" Deborah frowned. "After all, if there were some kind of trouble..."

"I don't think there's a man in this house who would lift a finger to help Timothy, aside from Burle," Lady Margaret said, "and he is shut away with his father at the moment. No, I think that we should investigate the matter ourselves."

"Very well," said Deborah. "Let me run upstairs and get my wrap."

"I'll wait for you here," said Lady Margaret with a nod.

Deborah ran lightly up the stairs, the distress of the previous evening banished, at least momentarily, by the mystery of Timothy's whereabouts. She entered her bedchamber and snatched up a warm cloak. As she turned to leave the room, Deborah stooped to retrieve a piece of paper which lay on the floor next to the bed where she had thrown herself after her meeting with Eversley to fall instantly into an exhausted sleep. She unfolded the paper, reflecting wryly that nothing Eversley had written could be worse than the things he had said to her. With unbelieving eyes, her hands shaking uncontrollably, she read, "My dearest Deborah..."

Lady Margaret paced the deserted hall, the serviceable cloak which she had thrown over her shoulders billowing out behind her as she strode forcefully back and forth. As the tones of a clock striking the hour echoed in the empty space, she turned toward the stairs, determined to go and fetch her dilatory hostess. Before she could do so, however, she heard the library door opening, and she slipped silently into the shadow of the stairs.

Margaret heard Burle's wounded tone. "I am not a child, Father. You have no right to treat me as one. Excuse me, please."

Pembroke spoke. "Alex! I didn't mean..."

"I have always known that you thought me a fool," Margaret's cousin said quietly. "How I wish that there were something I could do to change that opinion!" Burle closed the door behind him and ran up the stairs, so close that Margaret could have touched him.

"Damn!" swore Pembroke explosively, so loudly that he could be heard through the closed door. "Damn it all!"

"Oh, Alex," said Lady Rawlings to herself, with both sadness and amusement. She took a tentative step in the direction which Burle had taken, then stopped. One crisis at a time, she told herself firmly, and looked again for Deborah. The girl was nowhere in sight, so, squaring her shoulders resolutely, Margaret opened the heavy front door and slipped silently out into the storm.

"PERKINS!" scolded the housekeeper, hurrying to her husband's side. "Have you gone daft, standing there dripping all over my clean floor? Here, you great nobby, take your things off and come sit by the fire." All the while she was helping Perkins to remove his outer clothing, settling him in a capacious rocking chair which stood before the massive kitchen hearth, and thrusting a cup of steaming tea into his gnarled hands.

"Aye, lass, that's enough," Perkins said absently. "Quit yer fussin', now, do."

"I don't know why I shouldn't fuss," Mrs. Perkins said good-naturedly. "In and out of those stables at all hours, and in this weather, too. You're too old for this nonsense, Perkins, too old by far."

"That's as may be, Martha," responded Perkins with a twinkle in his eye, "but I'm only two years older'n yer, don't ferget!"

Mrs. Perkins sighed gustily. "I wish that I could," she told him, "but these old bones won't let me."

Perkins grinned crookedly. "Yer bones look just fine ter me, lass," he said, and leered ridiculously.

A snort of laughter escaped Mrs. Perkins. "Get along with you, now," she said with mock severity, her colour high. "I've too much to do to listen to your taradiddles." She leaned over the large pot of soup stock that stood simmering on the stove, humming under her breath as she stirred the fragrant liquid.

Mr. Perkins stared into the roaring fire, drinking his tea, his brow furrowed in thought. "It's right strange, Martha," he said finally.

"What's that, dear?" asked Mrs. Perkins, her mind on her soup.

"The stables," Perkins said impatiently. "Somethin' out there ain't right."

"What?"

"I don't know," Perkins confessed, and another long silence fell on the kitchen. "It's like someone's been rummagin' about," he said slowly. "Things ain't where they should be."

"Well, wasn't Mr. Stewart out helping you yesterday?" Mrs. Perkins suggested practically. "He might not have put things back exactly as he found them."

Perkins shook his head emphatically. "No, it weren't 'im," he said definitely. "'E's a good, careful worker, is Mr. Stewart. 'E put everythin' back as 'e found it. Shoulda been a stableboy," he finished inconsequentially.

"Perkins, you are too ridiculous," Mrs. Perkins said with a laugh. "Imagine, calling a gentleman a stableboy. He'd not thank you for the compliment, I think!"

"Be that as it may, it weren't 'im what left things awry," Perkins said stubbornly. "Not that things were awry, exactly, 'tis just—" he shrugged helplessly "—things 'ave been 'andled," he said.

"I shouldn't worry about it, if I were you, Perkins," Mrs. Perkins said comfortably, stopping for a moment to rub her husband's shoulders. "You've been working very hard since all these guests arrived, and perhaps you just didn't put things away exactly as you thought."

•

"'Tis possible, I suppose," Perkins said doubtfully. "I would 'a sworn, though..." He rose heavily to his feet. "I think I'll just go and have another look," he said. "Better safe 'n sorry, they say."

Mrs. Perkins planted her hands on her ample hips and shook her head. "Oh, no, you don't, Perkins," she said firmly, and pushed her husband back into his seat. "I'll not have you out in this weather any more than you absolutely have to be." The boom of thunder punctuated her words. "You see?" she added triumphantly. "It isn't fit for man nor beast out there. No, no, don't fuss at me! Just sit still, and I'll fetch you a bowl of my good soup."

Perkins knew better than to argue with his wife when she set her jaw in that determined way, so he settled himself back into his seat. "Whate'er yer say, lass," he said, his tone a mixture of resignation and amusement. "Right lucky that I love a bossy woman, though, ain't it?"

"Bossy? I am not!" protested Martha hotly. "I'm just thinking of..." She stopped, and waved her finger in her husband's face. "Thomas Perkins!" she scolded. "You should be ashamed of yourself, teasing me so."

Before Perkins could answer, however, the kitchen door flew open and an ashen-faced Sarah Beldon flew into the room. "Martha!" she gasped. "Come quickly!"

Mrs. Perkins stepped toward her, thoroughly alarmed. "Miss Sarah! What is it?"

"It's Deborah—there's been some kind of accident! I found her lying on her bedchamber floor, and I can't revive her, Martha! Hurry!"

CHAPTER TWELVE

LADY MARGARET BLEW into the stables on a howling gust of wind. Blinded by the driving rain, thunder booming in her ears, she barely managed, using all her strength, to slam the heavy door shut behind her. She leaned against the closed door, dazed by the force of the weather. Had she had any idea how fierce the storm was, she thought, she would never have had the courage to leave the shelter of the house. After a moment or two she felt somewhat restored, and, straightening her cloak, she looked curiously about.

Illuminated only by the dim light admitted through two small, dirty windows, the stables were dark and gloomy. Margaret blessed the forethought that had made her thrust a candle and the means to kindle it into her pocket before leaving the house, and hastened to light it.

The horses whinnied softly as she crossed to the stalls, and one friendly creature nuzzled her shoulder gently as she passed. Aside from the sounds made by the horses and the steady roar of the gale without, the building was quiet, and seemed peaceful; Margaret began to think that she had come on a fool's errand. It was only a reluctance to undertake the harrowing return to the house which prompted her to venture farther into the depths of the building.

During a momentary lull in the storm, however, there was a sound at the door. In a split second Margaret had extinguished her candle and dropped to her knees behind the last horse stall. She only had time to reflect that she would feel a perfect gudgeon if it were only Perkins, before she heard the unmistakable sounds of someone entering and slamming the door shut as she herself had done only moments ago. There was a scratching sound, and a light appeared, casting grotesquely large shadows on the wall behind her.

The young woman held her breath as she heard a male voice call softly, "Jack! Jack! Damn it, Jack, where are you?" Footsteps approached her hiding place; she wiggled as far back into the corner as she could, and almost cried out in relief as another, coarser voice responded, and the footsteps retreated.

"'O's there?" it asked roughly. "Wot do yer want?"

"Who do you think it is, you half-wit?" the first man snarled. "Get down here."

Peeping over the top of the stall, Lady Margaret could not see the first man, by his tone a gentleman, but she did see someone climbing unsteadily down from the loft above. She dared not look too long, but she got the impression that the second man was shabbily dressed and extremely dirty and, it appeared, drunk, for he staggered heavily as he reached the ground.

"I got out here as quickly as I could," came the more cultured tones. "Have you run mad, Jack? That was a damned reckless way to get a message to me. What was so urgent that it couldn't wait until this evening?"

"That Stewart cove," the man called Jack slurred. "'E were sniffin' round out 'ere last night, so I coshed him one. 'E's up above."

"What? You fool!" Margaret heard the thud of a heavy blow, and the dirty man whimpered.

"I didn't 'ave no choice!" Jack whined. "'E walked right in on me. I couldn't let 'im run off, could I?"

"If you hadn't been drunk, he never would have seen you," snarled the first man. "I warn you, Jack, I won't tolerate any more mistakes." His voice dropped to a purr. "Have you forgotten your little lesson so soon, my friend?"

"No, milord, I ain't fergot," was his obsequious answer. "I'll do whate'er yer say, milord, that I will!"

"What's done is done," the gentleman said. "The question is, how are we to deal with young Stewart now?"

Margaret felt that she almost recognized the speaker, but the sounds of the storm outside made it impossible to identify the voice positively.

"Wot question?" Jack asked, and laughed. "We should kill 'im, that's wot we should do."

Margaret gasped aloud, then froze with fear. Apparently the two men had not heard her, though, for after a moment's pause, the gentleman continued speaking.

"No," the other said, "or at least, not yet. It's too early in the game to resort to such desperate measures." His voice took on a reflective tone. "'Tis a pretty problem you've set for me, Jack, my lad. You are quite fortunate that I am such a tolerant fellow."

"I told yer, milord, I didn't . . ." Jack began defensively.

"Enough," the first man said coldly. "Shut up, and let me think."

Margaret strained to hear what was happening at the other end of the stables. Slowly, cautiously, she edged out to the end of the stall wall, and risked a quick look at the two men. This time, the gentleman was in her line of sight, but he had his back to her, and in the murky light she could not be certain who he was. His long cloak and tall beaver hat even disguised his height and build.

"Is Stewart conscious?" the man asked curtly.

Jack made a seesawing motion with his hand. "'E starts to come around every few 'ours, but I just cosh 'im and 'e's back out agin." He giggled. "It's the only fun I've 'ad since I got 'ere!"

The gentleman ignored Jack's last comment. "Did Stewart actually see you?"

Jack nodded. "That 'e did, milord," he said, his cheerfulness fully restored. "Walked right in on me, like I said."

"Then we can't just let him go, but we can't, er, dispose of him, either," the first man mused. He started to turn, so Margaret ducked quickly back to her corner. "My affairs are at a very delicate stage, right at the moment. I can't afford to have anything go wrong." Margaret heard footsteps striding back and forth impatiently.

"A very pretty problem, indeed, Jack," the man continued. "But perhaps—" a hand reached over the stall wall and jerked Margaret roughly to her feet "—Lady Margaret will be good enough to help us solve it?"

DEBORAH OPENED HER EYES and frowned at the ceiling. What was she doing in bed? The last thing she remembered was... She frowned again.

"Deborah, thank God!" Aunt Sarah leaned over her niece's bed. "What a fright you've given us, love!" Martha and Perkins hovered anxiously behind Sarah, peering over her shoulder at their supine mistress.

"Aunt Sarah," said Deborah faintly. "What happened?"

"I don't know, sweeting," her aunt answered. "I came up to ask you something, I don't recall what at the moment, and found you stretched out on the floor, unconscious."

Deborah struggled to sit up. "I'm sorry to have frightened you, Aunt Sarah," she said. "But I feel quite well now, I promise you."

"You may not feel ill at the moment, Deborah," said her aunt, pushing her firmly back into the pillows, "but a well person does not swoon for no reason."

"I was reading something, I think," Deborah said slowly, "something import—" The colour drained from her face, and she raised a shaking hand to cover her mouth. "I remember!" she burst out. "Father... where is it? Where is it?" She looked frantically around the room.

"Might this be what you were looking for, Miss Deborah?" Mrs. Perkins asked, holding out a crumpled paper which she had picked up from the floor.

Deborah all but snatched it out of her housekeeper's hand, tears streaming unheeded down her face. She clutched it tightly, her knuckles showing white against the creamy foolscap. Her eyes widened in horror as she reread the fateful letter.

"Deborah, what is it?" exclaimed Sarah. Deborah did not appear to hear her aunt; she only stared down at the paper, her hand shaking uncontrollably. "Deborah!"

"In spite of everything, I thought that it was just a mistake," Deborah whispered. "I thought that perhaps . . . an accident . . . that somehow, something had happened which he'd never intended . . ." She raised her face to Sarah. "How could he do it?" she cried. "How could he do this to me?" She rolled over and buried her head in her arms, sobbing.

Aunt Sarah and Martha exchanged alarmed looks over Deborah's head, and Sarah gently took the paper from her niece. She became as pale as Deborah as she read it and sank slowly down onto the side of the bed. "My God!" breathed Sarah, aghast. "It's from Geoffrey—written the night he died!" She swayed unsteadily until the housekeeper put a strong arm around her.

Martha deemed it time to take control. "Perkins," she said briskly, "go down to the kitchen and make a pot of tea, as hot and strong as you can. Miss Sarah, you come along with me."

"No," protested Sarah weakly, her face the colour of putty. "Deborah needs me."

"You'll be of no use to Miss Deborah or anyone else if you don't put your feet up and rest for a moment," Martha told her. "You've had a terrible shock; I won't allow you to make yourself ill."

"But Deborah . . ."

"I shall see to Miss Deborah, never you fear," Martha responded soothingly. "Haven't I looked after her since she was a babe?"

"Yes, but..." Sarah said.

"No buts, if you please," said Martha, helping Sarah to her feet. "Miss Deborah, I'll be right back, as soon as I see your aunt settled in her own room." She took Sarah by the arm and the two left the room.

Deborah sat up and lifted herself unsteadily to her feet. It was impossible for her to just lie there, with her thoughts all in a whirl. She slowly left her bedchamber and made her way downstairs to the library.

She looked around the room. "Oh, Papa," she whispered. "How could you leave me? I don't understand!" She slumped against the stand and rested her forehead on the cool leather of the family Bible. "Wasn't there some other way?" she asked the empty room.

"Deborah?"

The girl jumped and turned. "Eversley!" she gasped. "How you startled me. What are you doing out of bed?"

"The letter—you mustn't read it!" Eversley hobbled across the room.

Deborah pushed him down into a chair unceremoniously. "It's too late for that," she said, all the while lifting his leg tenderly up onto an ottoman. "You should be very happy, my lord," she added bitingly. "You have wounded me every bit as much as you intended. My felicitations."

"Deborah, I'm sorry," Eversley said. "Dash it all... I was so very angry."

Deborah tugged on the bellpull. "It matters not, Eversley," she said, suddenly exhausted. "At the very least, we may be grateful that we are through hurting each other." She turned back toward the fireplace.

"Deborah, must it be this way?" he asked yearningly. "We both spoke in haste. Might we not—"

"No!" Deborah all but shouted. "How much more must we both suffer before you will be satisfied, Robert? It is finished."

"Very well." Eversley's expression was unreadable. "I must apologize again for giving you your father's letter in such a way. It was unforgivable, I know."

Mrs. Perkins hurried back into the room. "Here I am, Miss Deborah, and what may I ask are you doing down here? I told you..." Martha caught sight of Eversley. "And my lord! You too should be abed."

"I needed to speak to your mistress, Mrs. Perkins," said the peer. "Now, if you will be good enough to fetch Mr. Perkins, perhaps he might help me back to my room? I fear I overdid it just a trifle, coming downstairs."

"Indeed I will," said Martha. "And you should come with me to find him, Miss Deborah, for it isn't meet that you should be alone with his lordship, now that, well, you know..." she finished lamely, for it was not her place, she knew, to point out improprieties to her mistress.

Eversley looked hard at Deborah and shook his head ever so slightly; she was puzzled, but readily said, "Pray do not trouble yourself about it, Martha. I will stay here, to bear Lord Eversley company while he waits."

Martha looked doubtful for a moment, then shrugged and left the room.

"I am sorry, you know, Deborah," Eversley said quietly.

"I know," she said, without meeting his eyes.

"An apology is not the only thing which brought me here, though," Eversley told her. "There was something else—" He stopped.

"What is it?" Deborah asked wearily.

"Does it strike you," he continued carefully, "that some of the things your father wrote were rather strange?"

Stung, Deborah cried out, "He committed suicide, Robert! Of course the letter was strange—he was distraught."

"That's not what I mean," Eversley went on stubbornly. "I mean suggestive. Mysterious."

In her mind's eye Deborah saw the letter, and quite suddenly certain phrases stood out as though written in fire:

I comforted myself with the thought... *He has no proof*... We were so young, and so deeply in love!... At the last, as at the beginning, I will rob him of his victory.

Deborah frowned. "Yes!" she said. "I don't know why I didn't see it at once."

He nodded. "I noticed it when I first read the letter," he said. "That business about proof, and all those references to the past. It doesn't ring true somehow."

"He said," Deborah murmured, "that the secret would die with him. What secret?"

"I don't know," Eversley replied, "but I'd wager that it had something to do with your mother."

"You're right," Deborah nodded. "He mentioned her several times."

"Was there ever any scandal associated with her?" Eversley asked warily.

Deborah did not take offence. "Not really," she answered. "Oh, she and Father did elope, but that was so long ago, and they were so happily married, I shouldn't think that anyone would remember."

"No family scandals?" Eversley pressed. "No skeletons in the closet?"

Deborah's brows wrinkled in thought. "Well," she said slowly, "originally, Amanda—that was my mother's name, Amanda. I've always called her that, since she died when I was so young. At any rate, Amanda was originally courted by my father's brother, James. But when Amanda met my father, it was love at first sight, so they were betrothed, and later they eloped."

"I didn't know that your father had a brother," Eversley said in surprise.

"Oh, he left the country, shortly after my parents were wed," Deborah said. "He was something of a black sheep, or so I gathered. Father never liked to speak of him. He died in America some years ago." Deborah paused for a moment, then remarked thoughtfully, "I wonder, could this have had something to do with the break-in?"

"What break-in?" Eversley asked sharply. Deborah quickly told him of the assault on her London house, and of the destruction of the library.

"And Timothy was accosted, too," she finished eagerly. "The ruffian quite mauled him. I'm convinced that there is a connection."

Eversley's face went rigid at the mention of Stewart's name; Deborah could have kicked herself. "I'm far more inclined to believe that Stewart was attacked by some irate father or husband," he said stiffly. "Lord knows, he has offended enough of them."

Deborah judged it wiser not to defend Stewart at the moment, nor to tell Eversley that the break-in was why she and Timothy had come to Shaftsworth in the first place. Why anger him more, she thought, when he was bound not to believe her anyway?

"The burglary in London, though," Eversley ruminated. "That does sound suspicious. Was anything taken?"

Deborah shrugged. "A few trifles, nothing of any value, and a great deal of worthless paper—old letters, estate papers, even some blank sheets of foolscap, as I recall."

"Hmm," Eversley said. "Clearly they were looking for some sort of document."

"And just as clearly they did not find it," Deborah stated decisively. Eversley looked at her quizzically. "You would have known if you had seen the room," she said. "Though some of the destruction was obviously a by-product of the search, some of it was quite sickeningly pointless. Even at the time, it struck me as pique of some sort on the robber's part." Deborah began to pace excitedly. "It all begins to make sense, Robert. Don't you see? They must have—" Whatever point Deborah had been about to make was interrupted by the reappearance of Martha and Perkins.

Before Perkins and Eversley left the room, Deborah said, "Thank you, Robert," and shyly touched his hand. "Thank you for everything. I know that it cannot have been easy for you to come to me, in light of . . . everything which has happened."

"I would have done the same for anyone, anyone at all," Eversley retorted, more gruffly than he had intended.

Deborah's face fell, and she silently watched Perkins help his lordship out of the room.

BURLE SLAMMED the bedroom door behind him and grimaced in satisfaction at the loud bang which echoed down the empty hall. To hell with Pembroke! He'd waste no more time trying to convince his stubborn sire of Timothy Stewart's basic soundness; only let this cursed rain stop, the young man resolved, and he'd put Shaftsworth behind him without a backward glance. Aye, and his father, too.

Restlessly Burle circled the room. Perhaps he should look for Maggie; she was a good listener, and he was certainly in need of a sympathetic ear, after his father's amiable ridicule. His mistake had been in returning to the library after his hasty exit, to attempt a reconciliation with his father. Burle's face burned as he recalled the marquess's condescending words.

"Alex," Pembroke had said wearily, "we have run over this ground once too often. You cannot change my mind."

"But there must be a way to make you see how iniquitous this is," Burle had said. "To condemn a man with no evidence . . ."

The ghost of a smile had crossed the marquess's face. "And what would you consider to be evidence, my son?"

he asked. "To catch Stewart and Miss Tollin in the act? Even considering Stewart's, ah, proclivities, that's a bit much to hope for, I think."

Burle had blushed hotly. "Please, Father," he had burst out. "You do them both an injustice!"

Pembroke had lifted his shoulders in a shrug. "And here we are again," he had observed. "The subject were best closed between us, lad, for we only end up chasing our own tails every time we discuss it."

A thought had occurred to Burle. "All along, Father, your main grievance against Timothy has been that he and Miss Deborah have treated Lord Eversley abominably, has it not?"

"In the main, yes," Pembroke had answered calmly.

"Very well, then. Let us, for the moment, stipulate that Timothy and Miss Deborah have come to Shaftsworth for illicit purposes," Burle had said carefully.

One eyebrow soaring, Pembroke had only remarked, "How delicately worded, my boy. Go on."

"Gladly," Burle had said. "Your whole argument collapses on this one simple point, Father—how can they have been said to have wounded Eversley, when he had already broken the engagement between himself and Miss Deborah before she and Timothy ever left town?" He had leaned back triumphantly. "Just answer me that."

Pembroke had hesitated. "Your point is well taken, but—"

"But what?" Burle had cried, and bounced to his feet. "But what?"

"Roger won't see it that way, I'm afraid," Pembroke had said. "He'll never forgive the two of them for making Eversley look the fool. Besides, he staunchly maintains that it was Miss Tollin who severed the relationship."

"We are not speaking of Mr. Henderson, Father, or his opinions," Burle had responded tensely.

"I must stand with Roger, Alex," Pembroke had said. "Surely you can understand that. We have been friends practically all our lives."

"I see," Burle had said coldly. "Then 'tis simply a matter of whose opinion is more important to you, Henderson's or your own son's. And you have made your choice, haven't you, Father?"

"Alex, Alex, calm down," his father had said soothingly. "Don't let this drive a wedge between us, my boy. Long after you've forgotten who this Stewart is, we shall still be father and son, you know."

"Thank you so much," Burle had responded stiffly. "It is perfectly conceivable that you should be friends with the odious Mr. Henderson for twenty years, but I could never be capable of the same level of devotion, could I? No, I'm sure that you think I'll forget all about Timothy as soon as something comes along to distract me. Perhaps you'd care to offer me a sweet, Father, to hasten the process?"

"Alex!" his father had protested, seeming genuinely hurt. "There's no need to take such a tone. You don't understand—"

"Of course I don't!" Burle had interrupted rudely. "Truth to tell, my lord, I often wonder how you could have sired a child so lacking in your own intelligence. Did I not know my mother better..."

The memory of the hurt and outrage on his father's face at that unkind comment, and the unsatisfactory parting which had quickly followed, made Burle shake his head now, and aim a vicious kick at the andiron in the empty hearth.

The andiron fell straight down. With a muttered curse, the young man bent to straighten it, then watched, open-mouthed, as the brickwork at the back of the fireplace slid slowly back, revealing a narrow staircase.

Burle's eyes lit up. He thrust his head eagerly into the opening and looked up and down. It was too dark to see more than a few steps in either direction. Silently blessing Perkíns for neglecting to light a fire in his room that morning, Burle snatched a lit candle and happily entered the opening, all thought of his unhappy conversation with his sire gone from his mind.

CHAPTER THIRTEEN

"WHAT'S THIS?" Mr. Henderson grumbled as he entered the dining room. "Where is everyone?" The long table was more than half-empty; Henderson, Sir Cyril Dennison and Lord Pembroke were the only guests present. Sarah Beldon sat at the head of the table, looking tired and unwell.

"As I was just telling Sir Cyril, Mr. Henderson," Sarah said with as much equanimity as she could muster, "Deborah begs your pardon, but she is far too ill to come to table."

Henderson snorted. Lord Pembroke could not help but smile down into his wineglass as his friend muttered, "Damnably rude, but what can one expect? The chit probably daren't face us."

Sarah flushed, but she lifted her chin high and fixed a challenging stare on Pembroke. "And what of your family, my lord?"

Pembroke looked unconcerned. "What of them, Miss Beldon?" he asked.

Sarah waited until Perkins had served the first course and left the room before continuing. "You'll pardon me for saying so, my lord, but such behaviour was not tolerated when I was a girl."

Pembroke raised one slightly scornful brow. "How true, ma'am," he murmured.

Sarah's colour deepened, but she did not demur. Waving a hand to indicate the empty chairs, she said, "To treat another's home as though it were a hostelry is not at all the

thing," she said boldly. "Surely Lord Burle and your niece
might at least have had the courtesy to notify us that they
would not be down for dinner. When one considers how
very short-staffed we are at the moment..."

"An excellent soup," Pembroke remarked. Sarah bit her
lip in vexation. "As to my son and Lady Margaret," he
continued, "I believe that we may allow them their little
foibles, as they are not here of their own choosing."

"That is true, my lord," Sarah shot back. "After all,
their wheel might have broken farther down the road, and
then they would have been forced to beg hospitality from
someone else, wouldn't they?"

It was Pembroke's turn to look embarrassed. He bowed
his head and, smiling faintly, acknowledged, "A flush hit,
Miss Beldon. You are quite right, of course. 'Twas most inconsiderate of them not to have told you their plans, and
more rude of me to try to defend them. I do beg your pardon."

Sarah looked inordinately pleased. "Think no more of it,
my lord," she said. "We must simply endeavour to enjoy
our dinner without them."

Henderson somewhat spoiled the mood of the moment
with a loud and disgusted snort, and Sir Cyril hastened into
the breach. "Wherever Burle and Lady Margaret have taken
themselves off to, they shall miss a fine meal," he said dip-
lomatically. "Your housekeeper is to be commended, Miss
Beldon. She has done you proud, and all but single-
handedly, as I understand."

"Aye," remarked Henderson with a sneer. "But then,
brothels are often known for the quality of their victuals."

Sarah gasped. Sir Cyril shook his head, and Pembroke
protested, "Now, really, Roger, that is too much. There is
no call for—"

"There is no call for you to forget what has brought us
here!" Henderson exclaimed. "This woman is no better
than a procuress." He stopped, then added accusingly,

"You may find it consistent with your honour, Pembroke, to sit here and pretend that we are merely dinner guests making polite conversation, but I do not."

"Roger, that is hardly fair," Pembroke said mildly.

"Excuse me, my lord," Sarah said, rising unsteadily to her feet. "If Mr. Henderson finds it so very unpleasant to share a meal with me, then I will spare him that necessity." She turned to leave the table, then stopped, and said over her shoulder, "It is amazing to me, Mr. Henderson, that you and Eversley could be even remotely related to each other. Whatever his failings, your nephew has never wanted for courtesy!"

"She was absolutely right, you know, Roger," Pembroke said quietly after Sarah had left the room. "I have never known you to be so discourteous, or so cruel."

"I have never known you to be so disloyal," Henderson retorted.

"Henderson, give over," Sir Cyril said softly. "This is hardly the time or the place." Both Henderson and Pembroke ignored him.

"How have I been disloyal?" Pembroke asked, his eyes never leaving Henderson's. "Tell me, Roger."

"What of Lord Duncan's letter, eh?" Henderson demanded. "What of that?"

The marquess looked blank. "Lord Duncan's... What has Lord Duncan to say in all this?"

"Do you deny that Lord Duncan warned you, weeks ago, that Stewart was a liar and a cheat? Do you?" Henderson demanded. "You might have prevented Eversley's heartbreak, if only you had spoken."

Pembroke shook his head in confusion. "I don't know what you're talking about," he said. "I haven't seen Duncan since, Lord, I don't remember when."

"You had a letter from him, not two weeks ago," Henderson said. "I daresay you thought that I had forgotten it."

Pembroke raised his eyebrows at Henderson's vehemence. "Truth to tell, I had forgotten. But what of it, Roger? I did receive a letter from Lord Duncan, but why on earth should you think that it concerned Stewart? You're not making sense, man."

"I'll tell you what makes no sense," Henderson shouted, red-faced and trembling with anger. "That you should choose to protect a boy you barely know, at the expense of a lifelong friend! Well, to hell with you, my lord!"

"I think, Roger," said Pembroke coldly, his eyes like steel, "that you had best stop and think before you say any more." Henderson pointedly turned his shoulder toward Pembroke, at which action the marquess flushed darkly. "Do you know," he continued, pushing himself away from the table, "I had begun to think that the conclusions we had come to about Stewart might be wrong. Now I am convinced of it. Your prejudice, Roger, has blinded you to the truth. Burle was quite right. I, for one, plan to go to him right now and tell him so. Pray excuse me, gentlemen." He stood up and made for the door.

Henderson stared down at his plate, deathly pale where before he had been red. He half rose to his feet and reached out a hand as though to detain his old friend, but the door slammed, and Henderson sank back into his seat.

He did not see his companion raise his glass delicately to his lips, or the smug smile which crossed Sir Cyril's face as he silently toasted the departed marquess.

LORD PEMBROKE PAUSED in the foyer, and looked across to where the front door of Shaftsworth had just blown open with a bang. "Margaret!" he called. "Just a moment!"

Lady Margaret started at the sound of Pembroke's voice, and jumped guiltily away from the doorway. "Uncle!" she said. "You startled me."

"Do you have any idea where Burle is?" Pembroke asked, intent on his own thoughts.

"What?" said Margaret blankly. "Any idea... No, no, I do not," she replied in a relieved tone, and made as if to climb the stairs.

"I don't understand it," Pembroke mused. "I've looked all over the house for him, and he's nowhere to be found. And he wasn't at dinner, either. You must admit, Margaret, 'tis most unlike Alex to miss a meal." He brightened. "Perhaps he's with Stewart—that's it, of course! Do you know where Stewart is, then, Margaret?"

"No!" she cried. Pembroke looked surprised at her vehemence, and she added in a more moderate tone, "That is to say, how would I know?"

"True," Pembroke agreed mildly. "But where could they have taken themselves off to? I've searched the whole—" He stopped, and smote himself lightly on the forehead. "The stables," he chided himself. "Of a certainty, the stables—they must have gone to check on the horses. I'll find them there, I'm sure."

"You won't, Uncle, not in the stables," Lady Margaret said, clutching at Pembroke's arm. "I just came from the stables—there's no one there, I promise you."

Pembroke looked amazed. "What on earth were you doing in the stables, Margaret?" he asked. He suddenly noticed her rain-drenched cloak, wind-blown hair, and the mud which covered her from the waist down. "For that matter," he said with a frown, "what were you doing out of doors at all?"

Lady Margaret turned away from her uncle. "Nothing," she said stubbornly.

"Margaret..." Pembroke said warningly.

Her chin lifted, and she turned round to meet Pembroke's gaze coolly. "I felt the need of some fresh air."

"What? In this weather? Have you run mad, child?" he demanded.

She waved a hand carelessly. "I was bored," she said. "I thought it might be diverting to venture out into the storm." A shaky laugh escaped her. "It was."

"Bored?" Pembroke echoed. "Bored? I don't believe it," he said bluntly. "You are not quite so foolish as that, Margaret. What really sent you outside?"

"You may believe it or not, Uncle, as you choose," she said. "But at any rate, you'll not find Burle, or Stewart, in the stables."

Pembroke stared at his niece for a long moment. "Were I not so concerned about Alex, I would get to the bottom of this mystery, my dear, of that you may be sure," he said dryly. "As it is, though—" he shrugged "—you may count yourself fortunate that I have other matters to attend to."

"Indeed," said Margaret tiredly, and, shoulders drooping, picked up her skirts.

"I'll help you upstairs," the marquess said, and lent her his arm. "Go to bed, child. You look exhausted." The peer watched Lady Margaret walk slowly down the upstairs hall. Then he turned to enter the drawing room, his forehead wrinkled.

"Damn it all!" Pembroke demanded of the empty room, slamming the door shut with an angry kick. "Where is he?"

Lady Margaret Rawlings, meanwhile, silently eased the bedchamber door shut behind her and leaned against it for a moment, weak with relief. Then she shrugged the heavy, wet cloak off her shoulders and set to work. She found a battered portmanteau in the wardrobe, threw it on the bed and began to hurriedly stuff it full of the contents of the drawers.

"I must keep my head," she told herself. "There's no one but me to save him, but how? How? Stay calm, my girl, stay calm! You'll need all your wits about you." She finished with the dresser and turned to the wardrobe, folding the clothes haphazardly as she thrust them into the bulging portmanteau. Only once did she stop, to run her hands lovingly over the fabric of a shirt thrown carelessly across the foot of the bed. She buried her face in it for an instant, then folded it hastily and put it away. "None of that, now, Margaret," she said. "There is no time for hysteria!"

"Stewwwwart!"

Margaret gasped aloud as the ghostly voice filled the room, and whirled away from the bed, looking wildly around her.

"Stewwwwaaart!"

"Who is it?" she cried bravely. "Who's there?"

There was a creaking sound, and a section of wall next to the fireplace slid out of sight. A grinning Burle emerged, covered with dirt, a crown of cobwebs adorning his hair. He stopped short at the sight of his cousin. "Maggie! What are you doing here?" Margaret could only gape idiotically. Burle's brows snapped together in a frown. "What are you doing in Timothy's room?" he demanded fiercely. "Answer me, I say!"

Suddenly it all seemed too much for Margaret. She sank onto the bed and burst into tears.

"Maggie!" Burle flew across the room to her side. "What is it, my dear?" He knelt beside her. "Don't be afraid, coz, just tell me."

"It's all too horrible," Margaret sobbed. "They said they'll kill him if I don't do as they tell me. But, oh, Alex, I'm so afraid that they'll kill him anyway!"

"Kill who? I mean, who will kill who? Whom," he corrected himself. "Dash it all, Maggie, what are you talking about?" He looked around the room. "And why are you packing Timothy's things? What's going on?" he demanded.

"They said if I told anyone they'd cut Timothy's throat," Margaret whispered hoarsely. "I don't know what to do!"

"I know what you should do," Burle said firmly. He pulled out his handkerchief, only slightly the worse for wear, and handed it to the girl. "Wipe your eyes, take a deep breath, and start at the beginning," he told her. "And don't leave anything out."

Lady Margaret wiped her eyes. She looked hard at Burle, seeming to take his measure, then began. "I was concerned about Timothy..." She quickly outlined her trip to the stables, and the horrifying discovery she had made there.

"Good Lord!" breathed Burle. "Tell me quickly, Maggie, who is it? Who is the scoundrel in our midst?"

"That," she said stoically, "I cannot tell you, Alex."

"What?" cried her cousin, outraged. "What do you mean, you cannot tell me? You must!"

"I cannot." She took his hands in her own. "Don't you see, Alex? You could never look at...him and pretend not to know. Your honesty, should I tell you, could cost Timothy his life!"

Burle's forehead wrinkled, then relaxed, and he smiled ruefully at his cousin. "You're right, of course, Maggie," he owned. "The first time I saw the cad, I should probably leap for his throat. No matter, then. How can I help?" he asked simply.

"Oh, Alex, I don't know!" she wailed. "What can we do?"

A despondent silence filled the room, but only for a moment. Then Burle gave a shout of laughter. "I have it," he chortled. "I have it!"

Lady Margaret was torn between hope and despair. "Another of your ideas, Alex?" she said. "This is too serious a matter—"

"Never fear, Maggie, this plan will work," Burle promised his cousin confidently. "We'll need to enlist an assistant, but that won't be a problem. Listen now, and see if you don't agree that I am a genius...."

JACK PULLED THE STOPPER out of the crystal decanter of brandy and poured himself another glass, spilling the dark liquid all over the hand which held the glass. He blinked owlishly at Timothy Stewart, who lay stretched out on the loft floor, securely bound, his eyes alert over the filthy gag which silenced him.

"Yer thought yer was smart, didn't yer?" Jack gloated drunkenly. "Sneakin' around, pokin' yer nose where yer 'ad no business. The joke's on yer, though, ain't it? Tis a shame yer'll not live to enjoy it!" He giggled inanely, and took another long pull from his glass.

Timothy's eyes fixed thoughtfully on the decanter which lay close by the villain's side. He was sure that it had not been in the loft when last he had been conscious, and there was no sign that Jack, dry as a bone, had left the shelter of the stables to procure it. Jack saw the direction of his gaze, and giggled again. "Yer wondering 'ow the likes o' me got 'old o' such a thing, ain't yer?" His dirty hand caressed the bottle lovingly. "Ain't yer?" he repeated. Timothy's eyes spoke volumes.

Jack stared at his captive, closing one eye to improve his vision, then staggered to his feet. "I feels like a little company, so ter speak," he announced, and advanced on Timothy. "No 'arm in takin' this off, no 'un 'ear yer if yer screamed yer 'ead off." The crash of thunder punctuated his words. "And if 'is 'igh-and-mighty lordship don't like it, too damned bad!" He whipped the rag away from Stewart's face.

Timothy took a long, deep breath. "Thank you, my good man," he said, smiling calmly at Jack. "That rag has been used, too recently I fear, to clean the horse stalls. The smell was, er, unpleasant." He looked carefully around him.

"Don't be gettin' no ideas, now," Jack warned. "'E'd kill me if I let yer get away. I'd rather take care o' yer now than face 'im."

Timothy let this pass without comment and said only, "Now that I can ask, where did you get that decanter?"

'No 'arm in tellin' yer, I reckon—yer'll never live ter tell no 'un else," Jack decided. "I got it down 'ere." He pointed at the ladder which led down into the stable proper.

Timothy raised one eyebrow incredulously. "If they keep such things in the stables here, one can only wonder what they use in the house," he remarked.

Jack guffawed. "That's a good 'un, it is! One can only wonder... That's a good 'un! No, I don't mean in the stables, I got it out o' the 'ouse, o' course," he said.

"Oh? Were you an invited guest, my friend, or did you just drop by?" Timothy asked.

"I comes and goes as I pleases in that 'ouse," Jack bragged, puffing out his chest and jerking a thumb toward the manor. "Many's the night, aye, and the day, too, that I've made meself at 'ome 'ere, and no 'un the wiser!"

"Come now, Jack," Timothy said. "One night, yes, or even two, but you couldn't possibly manage to break into Shaftsworth night after night without being discovered. It just isn't possible."

"'Oo said anythin' 'bout breakin' in? I just walks in, without so much as a by yer leave," Jack boasted.

"Unless you are able to walk through walls..." Timothy shrugged his shoulders delicately. "Frankly, I fail to see how you managed the thing."

"Are yer callin' me a liar?" Jack snarled. He whipped a blade out from somewhere in his clothing and waved it at Timothy menacingly.

"You misunderstand me, gentle Jack," Timothy hastened to assure him. "I merely confess myself mystified. Enlighten me, my friend, do!" He bestowed his most charming smile on his captor.

The dirty man's chest swelled with pride. "Don't mind if I do—yer sure as 'ell won't be tellin' no 'un about it," he cackled, then leaned forward confidingly. "It's a secret passage," he whispered hoarsely. "Runs all through the 'ouse, it do, and right on out 'ere to the stable. Now wot do yer think of that?''

Timothy's eyes widened in surprise. "And you discovered this passage yourself, Jack? Bravo!" He watched the man's face closely.

"Now 'ow would the likes 'o me ever find out such a thing?" Jack asked with a yawn. "No, it were—" He caught himself and waved a finger waggishly at Timothy. "Yer almost made me tell, and that 'ud never do," he admonished the younger man. "'Cause if I 'ad told yer, I'd 'a 'ad ter kill yer now, 'stead 'o waitin' till later. Yer lady friend wouldn't like that, now, would she?" He slid farther down on his spine, and leaned his head back against the wall. "Not that it matters," he mumbled sleepily, his eyes closing heavily. "Now or later, yer as good as dead, me fine cove, as good as dead!" The brandy glass slipped from his limp fingers, and a loud snore competed with the thunder outside.

No sooner had Jack's eyes closed than Timothy began to struggle furiously to free himself from the stout ropes which held him. "We shall see about that," he murmured grimly. "We shall just see."

CHAPTER FOURTEEN

"Now are you sure that you know what to do?" Burle asked his cousin anxiously. "We can't afford any mistakes!"

Lady Margaret nodded. "I'm sure," she said, her voice steady.

"And you're to wait half an hour, don't forget," Burle reminded her. "Exactly thirty minutes—that will give me plenty of time to go and enlist Father's aid." He looked worried. "I only hope that he'll help."

"Of course he will," Margaret said heartily. "Whatever differences the two of you may have had, the marquess will not fail us, never fear."

Burle nodded. "I hope you are right." He turned at the door and said once more, "Don't forget, Maggie—thirty minutes."

"I won't forget," Margaret said impatiently. "Just hurry!"

Burle took his cousin at her word; he was tapping at his father's bedchamber door before too many more seconds had passed. There was no answer. "Now, where else would he be?" Burle asked himself. "The drawing room, perhaps?"

He hurried down the hall only to be stopped, hand on the drawing-room door, by a voice calling his name.

"Burle! Oh, Burle!" Sir Cyril Dennison hurried up, his normally expressionless face wrinkled in a frown. "Excuse me for troubling you, Lord Burle, but have you seen Mr. Henderson, or your father?"

"No, I'm afraid not, Sir Cyril," Burle replied politely.

"Oh, dear, this is most upsetting, most upsetting indeed," Sir Cyril said. "I do hope there hasn't been any trouble."

"Trouble? Why, what's wrong?" Burle asked. "Has something happened?"

"I hope not, but frankly, my lord, I am worried," Sir Cyril said, with the air of one speaking despite himself. "Mr. Henderson and the marquess quarrelled violently over dinner."

"Mr. Henderson and my father?" Burle said in surprise. "No, that cannot be—they are the closest of friends! I've never known them to disagree, certainly not seriously."

"Well, they have this time," Dennison said promptly. "I scarce was able to keep them from blows at the table, and Roger left the dining room vowing to 'beat some sense into that damned scoundrel, Pembroke.'"

"Now, really, Sir Cyril, that is coming it much too brown," Burle protested. "Mr. Henderson would never use such intemperate language..." He faltered, recalling the many verbal tirades which he had witnessed in Henderson's company. "Well, at any rate, not about my father," he finished feebly.

Sir Cyril shrugged. "If you had heard them shouting at each other, my boy, you would not be quite so sanguine," he said.

The chiming of the clock in the foyer reminded Burle of his mission. "I haven't time to pursue this matter further with you, Sir Cyril, but I am absolutely sure that your fears are groundless," he told the obviously sceptical older man. "Perhaps later, when I am not quite so pressed for time..." He swung open the door as he spoke, and stopped short on the threshold.

The marquess lay on the floor before the hearth, the back of his head cut and bloodied. Leaning over him, his hand just reaching out to touch the unconscious man's head, was Roger Henderson.

"You murderous knave!" gasped Burle, and flew across the room to his father's side. "Get away from him!" He thrust Henderson away from the marquess's inert form.

"What..." sputtered Henderson. "What are you saying, lad? I just came in—"

"And viciously attacked my father!" Burle cried, cradling Pembroke tenderly in his arms. "Dennison, get Aunt Sarah and Mrs. Perkins. Quickly!" Sir Cyril obediently hurried off.

"Have you lost your mind, Burle?" stormed Henderson, his face a deep shade of crimson. "Are you honestly accusing me of this crime? Me, his oldest friend?"

Burle, meanwhile, had loosened his father's stock and made him as comfortable as he could. "Don't bother denying it," he said, white with fury. "Unless you are also going to deny quarrelling over dinner and telling Sir Cyril that you would beat some sense into that—what was the phrase, Henderson?—damned scoundrel, Pembroke!"

Henderson flushed an even deeper red. "Well," he admitted slowly, "I own that I was angry, damned angry!" Aggressively, he stepped toward Burle. "But if you think that I would creep up on a man and bash him over the head like some kind of base-born coward—"

"I never would have thought it," Burle spat, "but since this business with Timothy began, you seem to have become a different person. I no longer know what you might do!"

Henderson glowered at the mention of Stewart, but doggedly continued, "Why would I do it, Alex? True, we argued, and I was furious, I don't deny it. But why should I suddenly decide, at this late date, to try to kill your father? 'Tis absurd!"

"I don't know. Perhaps you were so blind with anger—" Burle was interrupted by the entrance of Sarah and Mrs. Perkins, suitably appalled by the sight which met their eyes. They pushed Pembroke's son to one side and began to bathe the wound on the unconscious man's head.

Henderson followed the younger man stubbornly. "Look!" he said, pointing to Pembroke's position on the floor. "He's facing the doorway. I couldn't have entered the room without his seeing me. Is it likely, Burle, that he would have watched me walk up to him with the aim of striking him and done nothing to defend himself? Is it?"

For the first time Burle looked uncertain. "You might have hidden your intentions from him, until you were within striking distance," he said feebly.

Henderson raised his eyebrows. "In such a passion as you have me, is it likely that I could have practised such dissimulation? Come now, Burle," he said ironically. "You know me too well to believe that. For good or for ill, I wear my feelings on my face." Solemnly he looked Burle in the eye. "I'm innocent," he said. "I swear it."

Burle's shoulders sagged. "Of course you are," he said unhappily. "What can I have been thinking? Oh, sir, I do apologize. To have accused you of such a thing."

Henderson dropped his hand heavily on Burle's shoulder. "No need, my boy, no need," he said, a little too heartily. "'Twas only the shock." He turned toward the women. "How is he?" he asked.

"He's beginning to come round," Sarah said. "We must move him abovestairs, though, and settle him into his bed." She shook her head doubtfully. "Another invalid. I don't know how we'll manage, I'm sure I don't!"

"Ah, well, Miss Sarah, these things are sent to try us," Mrs. Perkins said calmly. "Mr. Henderson, if you'd be so good as to take his head? But gently, sir, gently! And, milord, you may support your good father's feet. I'll just take him about the middle, here, to lighten the load. There, now, are we ready? All right, then, when I say—''

The clock outside sounded the half hour. Burle gasped and pulled away from his father's feet, which he had been about to lift. "My God, I must go!" He looked around the drawing room wildly. "Dennison, you must come with me,'' he cried. "No time to explain—just do as I say!'' He grabbed Sir Cyril's sleeve and began to pull the man out of the room.

"Burle, where are you going?'' asked Henderson, outraged. "What could be more important than your father? Burle!'' he shouted, but the young man was gone, taking Sir Cyril Dennison with him.

LORD EVERSLEY SHRUGGED into his dressing gown and cautiously lowered his foot to the floor. A delighted smile lit his face; although the pain was far from gone, it had lessened greatly since his excursion to the library, and the ankle had the indefinable sensation of being finally on the mend.

Eversley looked consideringly around the room and, hobbling over to the fireplace, took up a poker and used it as a cane. "Now,'' he said to himself as he opened his bedchamber door, "to find Deborah and delve more deeply into this mystery.''

The peer could not help but groan as he contemplated the stairs, but care and caution brought him safely down. His biggest fear, that he might encounter his Uncle Roger, had proven unfounded. The old gentleman had been irate to learn of Eversley's earlier conversation with Deborah; when he had informed Henderson that he had gone to the girl to apologize, Eversley had very much feared that his uncle would suffer apoplexy. Fortunately that disaster had been averted; Henderson had told Eversley sternly that his injury must have gone to his brain, and ordered his nephew to stay in bed, or else. Or else what, Eversley could only imagine; he grinned as he contemplated what his uncle would do, were he to see Eversley disobeying him so soon.

Eversley opened the library door and frowned when he found the chamber empty. He was about to leave the room when he heard Henderson's voice in the upstairs hall. As quickly as he could, he stepped into the library and eased the door shut silently.

He listened at the door. He could hear feet clattering down the stairs, and they appeared to be coming in his direction. "Damn!" he muttered. "Uncle Roger will probably tie me down if he finds me out of bed again." Eversley looked around for a place to hide and noticed a shadowed niche between the fireplace and the stand which held the family Bible. He squeezed himself into the spot, while thinking to himself that he would feel a perfect fool if anyone actually caught him there. All his alarm was for naught, however; he heard the front door open and close, and all was silent again.

Eversley breathed a sigh of relief, but too soon, for, moving out of his hiding place, he caught his sleeve on the corner of the Bible and sent it crashing to the floor. "Damn!" he said again, and bent to retrieve the fallen volume.

For several long moments, Eversley remained bent over, staring at a piece of parchment which had slipped out of the binding of the Bible when it was knocked over. When he straightened, his face was paper white. "Oh, my God!" he whispered to himself. "That's it! Deborah!" He turned and stumped out of the library, apparently no longer concerned with Roger Henderson's anger or location. He took the stairs at a speed which would have seemed impossible to anyone who had seen him move so cautiously just a few minutes before.

At the top of the stairs he turned and made his way unerringly to Stewart's door. "Stewart!" he cried, banging on the door. "Stewart, open up! I have to speak to you!" He heard a loud metallic clunk from inside the bedchamber, and a strange, sliding sound. "Stewart!" He knocked harder, but in vain.

Without hesitation, Eversley swung open the door. "Stewart, I need your help," he said without preamble. "Deborah's in trouble, serious trouble, and I know..." Whatever else he had been about to say was left unspoken. The room was empty. With a frown of puzzlement he clumped farther into the chamber. "Now where the devil did he go?" Then he pulled up short.

The back wall of the fireplace had disappeared; the flickering light of a candle which could still barely be seen in the passage beyond, and a scrap of lace caught on the edge of the opening indicated that someone, if not Stewart, had left the bedchamber in this novel way.

For only a moment did the man stand indecisive; then, with a muttered, "This place is a madhouse!" Eversley crossed to the dark opening and, clumsily pushing himself through, disappeared within.

"ROBERT, I KNOW you're angry, but please answer me," Deborah whispered urgently. "It's important!" There was no response. She pressed her ear against Eversley's bedchamber door and knocked again; there was nothing to be heard from within. "Robert, if you don't answer me, I am going to enter," she warned. "I need to talk to you about my father's letter." Still her former fiancé made no sound. Squaring her shoulders, she said, "Very well, then, I did warn you!" and she opened the door.

A moment later she shut the door behind her, her expression puzzled. Where could Eversley have taken himself off to? Her brow furrowed. That uncle of his was behind this, she'd warrant. Henderson was probably so anxious to leave Shaftsworth that he'd forced Eversley out of bed before the injured man was ready. She strode angrily to the end of the hall and twitched back the curtain. The rain was still falling, though less heavily than before.

"Does he think that Eversley can travel in this weather?" she asked the empty air. "And what of the bridge? Shall poor Robert be forced to swim back to London?" She walked determinedly toward the drawing room, the colour high in her cheeks. "It is past time, Mr. Henderson, that you and I had a little chat."

Roger Henderson, meanwhile, turned away from the window and let the heavy curtain fall back into place. Still raining; still no chance to leave. He was beginning to think, quite seriously, that the place was bewitched. Just look at all that had happened! If anyone had ever told him that he could come to the point of blows with his oldest and dearest friend, he would never have believed it, no, not for any reason. Then to find Pembroke stretched out, insensible, on the floor—such things simply did not happen in a well-ordered household. And what could possibly have come over Burle? Deserting his father at such a moment, with no explanation, without so much as a by your leave, when Pembroke could have been at death's door. It surpassed belief.

"Mr. Henderson!" Deborah's tone was icy.

Henderson lifted his gaze entreatingly to heaven. Good Lord, not her, not now. "Pray excuse me, ma'am," he said tightly. "I have business elsewhere." He made as if to leave the room.

"No," she said deliberately, "I do not excuse you. In fact, you might just as well make yourself comfortable, for I have one or two things I should like to discuss with you." She closed the door and planted her body solidly against it.

Henderson hesitated for a moment, then, with an ill-humoured shrug, sat down; short of bodily moving the chit, he had no choice but to obey.

"Very good," Deborah said. "I think—" she glared at Roger "—that it is past time you and I came to an understanding."

"There is no possibility of that, miss," Henderson said coldly. "I could never understand you, not if I lived to be a thousand."

"The feeling is mutual, I assure you," Deborah said. "Nevertheless, for Robert's sake, we must lay our enmity to rest, or at least—" she smiled fleetingly "—give it a day or two of holiday."

"In a day or two," Henderson replied, returning glare for glare, "I fervently hope to be many, many miles from Shaftsworth, Miss Tollin, and from you."

"Exactly," retorted Deborah furiously. "You hope to be miles away, and what if Eversley is still unable to travel? Why, you will drag him from his sickbed regardless, won't you? Won't you?"

"If I were prepared to do that," Henderson snapped, "we should have been back in London days ago. And very much the better for it, I might add." He heaved himself to his feet. "You are very anxious to be rid of us, Miss Tollin, I know, but no more anxious than we are to leave you behind, of that you may be sure. As soon as Eversley is on his feet again..."

Deborah looked uncertain. "I don't understand this," she said.

"What the devil are you talking about?" Henderson demanded.

"Where is Eversley, Mr. Henderson?" she asked.

"Why, in his bed, of course," Henderson responded. "Where else should he be?"

"I don't know, but he's not in his bedchamber," Deborah said firmly. "I know that for a fact—I just came from there."

"Perhaps he simply did not want to speak to you," Henderson said. "I should quite understand his feeling."

Deborah blushed. "That's what I thought, so I looked into his room," she said. "He wasn't there."

"Then where in blazes is he?" Henderson blustered.

"I don't know. That's why I came looking for you." Deborah shivered. "There's something strange going on," she said. She looked at the older man. "I'm frightened," she whispered.

Henderson started for the door. "Don't be," he said gruffly. "I'm sure that Eversley just decided to...to...stretch his legs," he finished lamely. "I'll find him."

"May I come with you?" Deborah could not meet Henderson's eyes.

"Oh, for— Come along, come along," he agreed reluctantly. "You're making a great deal out of nothing, though." He held the door open for the girl. Her back to him, Deborah did not see Henderson frown, or the apprehensive look which he cast back into the drawing room as he closed the door quietly behind them.

CHAPTER FIFTEEN

"...So you see, stealth is of the essence," Burle finished earnestly. "Timothy's life may depend upon it."

"I see," said Sir Cyril in his precise way. The rain had lessened enough to allow the two men to confer quietly in a stand of trees near the stables, thereby allowing Burle to explain the situation, or as much of it as he could, to his companion. "Have you any idea who this snake in the grass is?" Sir Cyril asked Burle.

The youth shook his head. "No, Maggie wouldn't tell me," he admitted.

"Where is Lady Margaret?" Sir Cyril enquired. "As intrepid as she has proven herself to be, I'm surprised that she did not insist on accompanying you on your search."

Burle's only response was to grab Sir Cyril suddenly by the arm, and pull him deeper into the copse in which they stood. "I thought I saw someone looking out," he said nervously. "It's important that you remain hidden. Your entrance must come as a complete surprise to those within." He gestured toward the stable.

"Indeed," said Sir Cyril. "Then I suppose we had best get on with it, eh, my boy?"

Burle nodded eagerly. "Now remember, I will go first. Wait until you see Timothy's gaoler come down from above, then burst in. Agreed?" He turned to go, then turned back to Sir Cyril with a sheepish grin. "I almost forgot," he said, digging in a pocket. "You'd best take this—you might need it." He handed Sir Cyril a small pistol. "Guard it well. 'Tis the only weapon I have. Belongs to my father," he explained. "He always carries it when he travels."

"How very far-sighted of him," Sir Cyril remarked. "Go now, Burle, and don't worry. I'll be here to back your play." He watched the young lord open the stable door and creep inside. Then, whistling softly to himself, Sir Cyril turned away from the stables and made his way back to the house.

"'Tis no use," Deborah said dispiritedly. "They're nowhere to be found." She and Henderson were in the library, having completed a search of the house.

"But this is ridiculous," Henderson said. "Where could they all have gone? Robert, Lady Margaret, Burle, Sir Cyril, even that cad Stewart has disappeared!"

"Thank God that Aunt Sarah and Mrs. Perkins are with the marquess, else he would likely have vanished, too," Deborah said. A bubble of hysterical laughter escaped her. "No doubt you and I shall be the next to go!"

Henderson frowned at his hostess. "Buck up, now, my girl," he said sternly. "'Tis no time to be losing control of yourself. A cool head, that's what's called for here."

His commanding tone of voice seemed to reach Deborah. She straightened her shoulders and said, "Of course. You're quite right."

Henderson surprised Deborah, and himself, by patting her on the shoulder. "That's better," he said. "Now, I believe our next step should be to search—"

"Search? Why? What's amiss?" asked Sir Cyril, sauntering into the library. "Have I missed more excitement?"

Deborah gasped aloud. "Where have you been?" she cried. "Where are the rest of them?"

Sir Cyril raised his eyebrows haughtily. "My dear Miss Tollin," he said, "pray calm yourself."

Roger Henderson took a step toward him. "Where have you been?" he asked. "And where is Burle?"

"I must say, had I known that I would be subjected to this inquisition, I never would have gone with Lord Burle in the first place," Sir Cyril protested mildly. "As to where the young man is at the present, I have no idea."

"But he bore you off with such urgency," pressed Henderson. "It must have been important."

Sir Cyril shrugged. "So it would have seemed, yet as soon as we left the house, Burle mumbled something about 'compelling business' and ran off. I tried to follow him, but age will tell. He soon lost me. I waited around for a time, hoping that he would return, but the rain soon drove me back inside," he finished.

"Did you see anyone else while you were out of doors?" Deborah asked. "Anyone at all?"

"Of course not," Sir Cyril said. "Who would venture out in this weather, were they not compelled to?"

"Where can they have gone?" Deborah exclaimed.

"I do wish," said Sir Cyril plaintively, "that someone would tell me what is going on."

"It appears," Henderson told him, "that quite a few of our fellow guests have . . . wandered off."

"Disappeared," Deborah corrected him bluntly.

"How very interesting," Sir Cyril murmured. "Which ones, I wonder?"

"Lord Burle, Stewart, my nephew Eversley and Lady Margaret," Henderson said. "We've searched the whole house—they're nowhere to be found."

"Indeed," said Sir Cyril thoughtfully. "Might they not simply have gone outside?"

"As you yourself said, who would go out in this weather?" Henderson reminded him. "No, I think that these absences, occurring as they have right after the attack on Pembroke, must be viewed with suspicion."

"And who *did* attack the marquess?" Deborah demanded. "It must have been one of us."

"Surely not," Henderson demurred. "Perhaps the servants . . . ?"

"Mr. and Mrs. Perkins," said Deborah coldly, "have served my family since well before I was born. It is vile of you to even suggest that they might be responsible for assaulting the marquess. Besides," she added reasonably, "what possible motive could they have for such an attack?"

"This would not be the first time that seemingly devoted servants have suddenly turned bad," Sir Cyril suggested. "Who can truly say that they understand the lower classes?"

"No," said Deborah flatly. "I would sooner believe that it was you—" she pointed a finger at Sir Cyril "—or you." She indicated Henderson.

"At any rate," said Henderson briskly, "Pembroke is not our immediate concern. Miss Sarah and the housekeeper have promised to stay in his room with him until I come back."

"I just thought of something—where is Mr. Perkins?" Deborah asked, dread in her tone. "He didn't turn up during our search, either. You don't suppose . . ."

"He could be in the stables, looking after the horses," Henderson said doubtfully. "We mustn't jump to conclusions."

"He's perfectly safe," said Sir Cyril. "When I was searching for Burle, I saw him going in the kitchen door."

"All right, then, to the kitchen we go," said Deborah. "Perhaps Perkins can shed some light on this mystery."

Sir Cyril moved toward the door. "If you'll excuse me," he said, "I think I shall go upstairs and get into some dry clothing. I'm quite drenched."

"Oh, no," responded Henderson quickly. "Until we discover what is going on around here, I think that we should all three stay together."

"I agree," said Deborah. She essayed a shaky laugh. "We don't want you to go missing, too!"

"I hardly think it necessary—"

"Please," Deborah said. "Please, Sir Cyril?"

"Well—" he said with a sniff, "if you insist!"

"I do." Henderson was firm. He clapped Sir Cyril on the back. "Consider it a favour to me," he said, in as jovial a tone as he could manage. "For I swear to you, if one more person disappears from this house, I shall go stark, staring mad!"

LORD EVERSLEY STOPPED; some instinct made him press himself against one wall of the damp, foul-smelling passageway. He heard a loud scraping noise ahead of him, then two voices; some trick of acoustics made it sound as if the speakers were right next to him.

"'Ey!" growled a crude, suspicious voice. "'Ow did yer find out about this way in ter the stables? Yer been snoopin' around on us, missy?"

"Of course not." Eversley recognized Lady Margaret's disdainful tone. "Your master showed it to me."

The man seemed to accept this; "'Bout time yer come back," he complained. "I were thinkin' that yer might 'a squealed on us—that 'ud be right bad luck fer yer friend."

"I did just as I was told," Burle's cousin said. "See? Here is Timothy's portmanteau, all packed and ready."

"'Is lordship'll be glad ter see that," came the man's voice. "Yer done good, missy."

"Let me talk to Timothy," Lady Margaret said imperiously. "I want to make sure that he's all right."

"Oh, no, yer don't," the man said. "'Is lordship says yer ain't ter come back in. Just go back ter the 'ouse, 'e says, and keep yer trap shut. Else your friend 'ere'll end up a corpse." He cackled happily.

Eversley crept quietly in the direction of the two speakers as Margaret said, "I must see him." She sounded desperate. "Just for a moment. I won't even speak to him, if you don't want me to. Please!" Eversley could see light coming round what was apparently a final bend in the secret passage, but he dared venture no farther without knowing if he would be seen.

There was a momentary silence, then the man chuckled menacingly. "'Ow bad do yer want it, missy?" he asked. "Bad enough ter be friendly ter a poor cove wot's feelin' right lonely? Eh, missy?"

Lady Margaret's voice rang out in the quiet space. "Take your hands off me, you swine. Take them off me, I say!" Eversley started round the corner, but stopped when Margaret added contemptuously, "Your master will kill you if you hurt me!"

"Yer ain't gonna tell 'im, is yer, missy?" The man's voice took on a disgusting whine. "I was just 'aving a little fun. No 'arm done, is there, missy?"

"If you don't let me see Timothy, I'll tell," Lady Margaret said clearly. "I'll tell, and he'll kill you for interfering with his plans."

The man snarled, "'E'll kill me for lettin' yer talk to the pretty boy, too!"

"Dead is dead, is it not, Jack? That is your name, isn't it?" Margaret said sweetly. Eversley grinned in admiration. "And he will never find out that you let me see Timothy—I certainly won't tell."

The man hesitated, then said, "All right, come on. But just for a minute, do yer 'ear? 'E might ... wot's that? Get back in there, someun's comin'! Tryin' ter get me killed, was yer?" This last in a virulent whisper. "I'll pay yer back fer that, yer poxy jade!" Eversley heard the sound of a loud slap, and then a scraping noise which indicated, he surmised, that the hidden door to the stable had been closed.

Eversley peered cautiously around the corner and saw Margaret hammering on the rough panel which had been closed in her face. "Let me in!" she cried. "Let me in!" There was no response from the stable. She sank to her knees in the mud, and frantically began to dig at the bottom of the door, trying in vain to slide it open.

"Lady Margaret?" called Eversley softly, peering cautiously around the corner. "Lady Margaret!" He gestured to the startled young woman, motioning her deeper into the passageway.

"Thank God you're here!" she said, tugging on his hand. "There's not a moment to lose—Burle will be here any minute, and he is counting on us—on me—to spirit Timothy away while he distracts the guard." Her eyes lit up as she caught sight of Eversley's makeshift cane. "We can use that to pry the door open." She pulled him toward the end of the passageway.

Eversley went with her, but shook his head when she tried to take the poker out of his hand. "First," he suggested, "I think it would be wise to reconnoitre a bit." He pointed to a crack in the boards of the stable wall.

"We must hurry!" Margaret breathed. Eversley ignored her as he pressed his eye to the crack.

"Unfortunately," he whispered after a moment, "the time for haste has passed." Margaret pulled him away from the wall and looked herself.

Inside the stable, Jack was bending over Burle's inert body, expertly searching the young man's pockets. "Yer fool," Jack muttered as he worked. "Wot'd yer want ter come out 'ere fer? This place be as busy as 'yde Park!" Satisfied that Burle carried no weapon, Jack looked down at his uninvited guest and shook his head. "'Is lordship won't like this a bit."

The scene made Lady Margaret gasp and press a hand to her mouth. Eversley led her gently away from the door, far enough down the corridor that they need not worry about being overheard.

"What will we do now?" Margaret's face was ashen, and she trembled with the cold.

"You must tell me what is going on," her companion told her. "I can't help you, or Burle, until you do." Margaret told the peer her story, starting with her decision to search for Stewart in the stables, and ending up with Burle leaving her in Timothy's room, to go and enlist his father's aid. "I see," said Eversley slowly, his brow puckered. "Who was it, my lady?" he asked bluntly.

"You must call me Margaret," she hedged, not meeting his gaze.

Eversley lifted her chin with one finger, and stared unflinchingly into her eyes. "Who was it?" he asked again.

"Sir Cyril," she whispered unhappily. She buried her face in her hands. "He said he'd kill Timothy if I told!"

"Sir Cyril?" Eversley sounded puzzled. "But why? Why?"

"He did make one strange comment," Margaret volunteered. "He said," she closed her eyes, and repeated in a singsong voice, "'I won't let Geoffrey beat me, not this time, not when the old man is finally on my side!' Then he laughed, a horrible, vengeful sort of laugh." She shivered.

"Of course," Eversley said. "What a fool I am, not to have realized it."

"Realized what?" Margaret asked. "What should you have realized?"

"No time for explanations," he said briskly. "Come, my lady, we've work to do!" He turned back in the direction of the house, and held out an arm to Lady Margaret.

"But where are you going? We must rescue them!" Margaret was frantic.

"Somehow I think that we shall need more brawn than a woman and a man half-crippled can provide," he said dryly. "Never fear, though. I've a deep yearning to become better acquainted with this Jack fellow." Eversley lightly touched the finger-marks still visible on Lady Margaret's face. "And to beat Sir Cyril Dennison at his own game."

"BURLE! I SAY, BURLE, wake up!"

Lord Burle slowly opened his eyes. He found himself lying on his side, apparently in the loft of the stables, his hands bound tightly behind his back; far to his left, against the wall, he could just see two feet, also bound, whose owner seemed to be attempting to wriggle toward him. When Burle tried to roll over to see his fellow prisoner, a stabbing pain in his head made him wince and hastily cease all movement. "Timothy, is that you?" he whispered. "Lord, my head is killing me! What happened?"

"That's what I should like to know," Timothy Stewart retorted sharply. "What in hell are you doing here?"

Burle could not help but smile. "Trying to rescue you," he confessed. "Not very successfully, I'm afraid."

"All by yourself? And how did you find out I was here?" Stewart asked. "Damn it all, Burle, you shouldn't have..." He stopped, and breathed a gusty sigh of exasperation. "Start at the beginning," he said more patiently, "and don't leave anything out."

"Very well," Burle said stiffly, offended. "Maggie told me that you were being held—"

"Maggie!" Timothy exploded. "Don't tell me you've involved her in all this? Burle, what were you thinking of?"

"If you'd only listen for a moment," Burle told him, "you'd see that she involved me, not the other way around! Let me explain; Maggie came out here, to the stables, to look for you—"

"What?" Stewart roared. "Are you run mad, Burle? How could you let her—"

"Timothy, shut up!" Burle shouted.

"'Ey!" Jack yelled from below. "If yer don't shut yer mouths, I'll be up and cosh yer both!"

"How could you let her come out here alone?" Timothy berated Burle, albeit more quietly. "Of all the harebrained, positively juvenile stunts—"

"Stop!" Burle spoke between clenched teeth. "Not one more word," he said tightly. "If you want to know what happened, I'll tell you. But if you so much as open your mouth to speak, I swear I'll let you die of frustration before I say another word." He waited a moment. Stewart was silent, so he went on, "My cousin did not consult me before coming out to investigate. If she had, I would, of course, have stopped her. As it was, I only found out about it by accident, when I surprised Maggie in your bedchamber, packing up your clothes." He quickly told Stewart the rest of the story, including the assault on his father, and finished up by saying, "I can't imagine what happened to Sir Cyril. He was supposed to follow me in, by way of reinforcement. I hope he's all right."

"I'm sure he's fine," Stewart said grimly. "He's the devil behind all this—didn't Maggie tell you?"

"What? But I thought... What an ass I am!" he groaned.

"Sir Cyril is our man, all right," Timothy said. "The only question is, what is he after?"

"Whatever he does want, there'll be no one to say him nay, at this rate," Burle pointed out gloomily. "My father is laid up, you and I are well out of the way, and Eversley's still abed with that blasted ankle. Who'll protect the ladies from this scum?" he asked Timothy. "Eh? Tell me— Oh, no!" he gasped. "Maggie!"

"What about Maggie?" Timothy was thoroughly alarmed. "What about her? Answer me, damn you!"

"She was to have come through the secret passage," Burle whispered, aghast. "And to have helped you escape, while Sir Cyril and I created a diversion. Oh, Lord, she'll walk right into their arms!"

"Did Sir Cyril know that she was coming?" Timothy demanded fiercely.

"No. He asked me, but somehow I never really answered him," Burle said.

Timothy blew out a sigh of relief. "She's safe, then," h
said. "You were unconscious for some time, Burle. Had sh
come into the building, I should have heard her." He gav
a crack of relieved laughter. "I heard you, from the mo
ment you opened the door!" he said. "Don't ever devot
yourself to a life of crime, my friend—you haven't the skill
for it."

"Well, thank you very much," Burle responded. "I tr
to rescue you, and am I thanked for my efforts? No, not
bit of it."

"Wait a minute. What secret passage?" Timothy asked

Burle had finally wriggled himself far enough to be abl
to see his friend's face. "'Tis the greatest thing in nature
Timothy," he said enthusiastically. "The whole place i
riddled with hidden doors, peepholes and passageways. It'
beyond belief!"

"That explains it," Timothy remarked thoughtfully
Burle looked at him quizzically, but Timothy only shook hi:
head. "And you say that one of these passageways runs ou
here?" he asked. Burle nodded. "Well, then," Timothy saic
cheerfully, "we've only to wait, and try to prepare our
selves to be as much help to our rescuers as we may."

"What rescuers?" Burle said. "I just finished telling you
there's no one left to—"

"Never fear, Burle," Timothy said confidently. "Mag
gie'll find a way to help us. She's a right 'un, she is!"

"But how can..." Burle stopped, and eyed his frienc
speculatively. "Maggie, is it? And she's a right 'un, eh?
hadn't realized you two were so friendly."

Timothy amazed Burle by blushing hotly. "I have al
ways, er, admired her."

"So that's the way the wind blows," Burle said softly
"Congratulations!" He grinned.

Timothy looked unaccustomedly eager. "What do yo
mean?" he demanded. "Has she said anything? Did sh
tell... Never mind!" he added, before Burle could answer

"We must apply ourselves to the problem at hand," he said, as much to himself as to Burle. He began to wriggle more energetically, trying to get his back, and his bonds, closer to his fellow prisoner. "And trust," he said under his breath, "that Maggie can get to us before Sir Cyril!"

CHAPTER SIXTEEN

EVERSLEY REACHED OUT and tugged on Lady Margaret's skirts. "Wait a moment," he hissed. "I hear voices." He carefully examined the side wall of the passageway. With a grunt of satisfaction, he swung a small wooden lozenge out of the way, and pressed his eye against the opening.

"What is it, Eversley?" Margaret whispered urgently. "What do you see?"

"Shh!"

On the other side of the wall, Eversley's uncle was speaking sternly to Perkins. "Under no circumstances are you to leave the women and the marquess alone," Henderson was saying. "Not until I come and tell you that it is safe. Do you understand?"

"'Ere now!" Perkins protested hotly. "What about me duties? What about them 'orses, out there in the stable? I ain't seen to 'em all day."

Eversley could not help but grin as his relative snapped back, "Never you mind about the horses, my man—just do as you're told." A bristling Perkins stared back at Henderson for a long moment, breathing heavily, then left the kitchen, grumbling softly to himself. Eversley's smile faded, however, and his brows slammed together as Sir Cyril Dennison stepped into view.

"I quite fail to see what has made you so upset, Henderson," the man said in a faintly complaining tone. "After all, if Stewart and Lady Margaret have chosen to go off together, well, I don't think that it's really any of our affair, do you?''

"Lady Rawlings and Timothy have not snuck off to an assignation," Deborah said angrily. "Something has happened to them, I tell you!"

"You may prefer to believe that an accident has kept Mr. Stewart from your side, my dear," Sir Cyril said smoothly, "but I scarcely think that your jealousy should be reason to throw the whole household into an uproar."

"My jealousy? My jealousy?" Deborah said incredulously.

"That's absurd, Dennison," Henderson said unexpectedly. "Even if we ignore the absence of Stewart and Lady Margaret, what of Burle? And Eversley? What about the attack on Pembroke? You can't explain all that away!"

Sir Cyril shrugged. "I saw Burle myself, safe and sound, not thirty minutes ago," he said carelessly. "Where Eversley is, I have no idea, but surely no one in his condition could travel very far." Eversley smiled grimly. "As to the marquess," Sir Cyril continued, then stopped.

"Yes?" Henderson prompted him impatiently.

"Forgive me, Henderson, but are you not the prime suspect in his attack?"

It was Henderson's turn to bridle. "What's that? Just what are you trying to say, Dennison?"

Inside the passageway, Lady Margaret pulled on Eversley's sleeve. "Eversley," said she, sotto voce, "if you don't tell me what's going on, I shall scream."

"Press your ear to the wall and listen," Eversley responded, and returned his attention to the kitchen.

"...so quick to anger," Sir Cyril was saying. "I merely point out that you both have good reason to be overly concerned about our companions." He shivered dramatically. "For myself," he went on, "I want nothing more than to go to my chamber and get out of these wet clothes."

Deborah, who had thus far remained silent, startled Eversley by saying suddenly, "They must be in the stables."

"Damn it, Deb, not now!" Eversley muttered under his breath.

"It's the only place left," she said reasonably. "We've searched everywhere else. What alternative is there?"

"You're right, of course," Henderson agreed. Eversley was hard put to stifle a groan. "We should go and have a look, I suppose."

"I think not," interrupted Sir Cyril pleasantly.

"But really, Sir Cyril," said Deborah turning, "I don't see..." She froze as she saw the small but deadly-looking pistol which was fixed unwaveringly on herself and Henderson.

"How unfortunate it is that you should insist on visiting the stables so soon," Sir Cyril remarked. "I knew that it was only a matter of time, of course, but I had hoped to have the chance to change my clothes and perhaps have a bite to eat, before you thought of it. Ah, well!" he observed. "Such is life."

"But—what—why—" Deborah stammered, unable to take her eyes from the weapon in Sir Cyril's hand.

"Not just yet," he said. "First, I think that perhaps we should all pay a visit to the stables, since you are so very anxious to do so." He smiled winningly. "And, lest you think somehow to disarm me, Henderson..." He grabbed Deborah and pressed the barrel of the gun against her throat.

Margaret laid a restraining hand on Eversley's shoulder as his fists clenched and unclenched with rage.

"Never think that I should hesitate to use it," Sir Cyril warned Henderson. "I should not, I promise you. On the contrary, it would solve all my problems. But that can wait. Shall we go, my friends?" He nodded toward the door.

Eversley could only watch in impotent fury as Henderson, Deborah and Sir Cyril left the kitchen and disappeared into the fast abating storm.

SARAH SHIVERED CONVULSIVELY. "It's still raining," she told Perkins and his wife, "though not, perhaps, quite as hard."

Perkins, sitting before the fire, nodded his head. "We seen the worst of it, I'll wager," he prophesied. "Though I don't doubt there'll be a rare sight o' clean-up, afore all is said and done."

His good wife leaned over the bed on which Pembroke was stretched out. "The poor gentleman seems a little better," she announced. "His colour has improved, and he seems now to be more asleep than unconscious." She wiped his forehead one last time, then dropped the wet rag into a basin of bloody water which stood on a table beside her.

"That is good news!" Sarah exclaimed. "Though I must admit, how the marquess came to hit his head in the first place, I can't imagine."

Perkins gave a crack of laughter. "Lor' bless you, ma'am, he didn't 'it his 'ead—he were coshed."

"Perkins," Martha scolded him. "Quiet, now, man!"

"Aw, Martha, yer know it be true," Perkins complained. "It couldn't 'a been no accident."

"Surely you're mistaken, Perkins," Sarah demurred. "Who would do such a thing? No, I cannot countenance it."

Mrs. Perkins bit her lip, then spoke. "Well, Miss Sarah," she said reluctantly, "it does appear...that is to say, it is most peculiar—" She stopped.

Sarah's eyes widened, and her cheeks paled. "Do you really think so, Martha?" she asked breathlessly. The housekeeper nodded. "But who? How? Why?"

"Aye, now, that be the question!" Perkins reflected gloomily, staring into the fire.

"Of course, I did wonder why Mr. Henderson should insist so strenuously that we remain with the marquess," Sarah mused, "but I never dreamed...I merely thought the gentleman a tyrant," she finished, in so woebegone a tone that Martha Perkins was obliged to turn away, lest her mistress see her smile.

Perkins cleared his throat. "I been thinkin' and thinkin'," he said, "and I can't rightly see 'ow it could 'a been any but that Sir Cyril what done the job on 'is lordship. Though for the life 'o me," he added, "I can't think 'o why!"

Sarah gasped and turned angrily toward the stableman. "Really, Perkins, that is outside of enough. Shame on you, to lay such a crime at Sir Cyril's door, and with no evidence."

"Well," he answered, "I don't know nothin' 'bout no evidence, but I did see 'im sneakin' into the drawin' room, directly after 'is lordship went in." Perkins nodded toward the bed. "Looked right suspicious, 'e did, too. 'Course, I didn't pay no mind to it at the time, but, thinkin' back on it ..." He shrugged. "Looked right suspicious, 'e did," the man repeated stubbornly.

"Still, Perkins," Sarah said reproachfully. "To say something so slanderous, and about a guest in our home! I am most disappointed in you, most disappointed, indeed."

Mrs. Perkins was quick to defend her mate. "If you'll excuse my saying so, Miss Sarah," she said, "I think that you should pay heed to what Perkins has to say. We both know that he's not the imaginative type. If he thinks that Sir Cyril behaved suspiciously, well, we should listen."

"I am forced to agree with your housekeeper, Miss Beldon."

The two women spun around. Perkins leapt to his feet, and all three of them converged on the bed. "Your lordship!" cried Sarah. "How are you?"

The marquess grimaced expressively. "I have been better, thank you, Miss Beldon," he answered. "However, I daresay I shall live to bore my friends and disappoint my heirs yet a while. Speaking of heirs," he added, "where has mine taken himself off to?"

Sarah shrugged. "I'm sure I have no idea," she said disapprovingly. "The manners of these young men! Rushing off on some errand with his sire at death's door, and dragging Sir Cyril away with him, with no more than a—"

"What? You say he went off with Sir Cyril? Damn!" Pembroke exclaimed, and sat bolt upright.

"My lord, you mustn't..." Sarah tried to force Pembroke back against the pillows; he ignored her, and fixed a keen, if somewhat bloodshot, gaze on Perkins.

"You were quite right about Dennison," he told the gratified servant, swinging his legs off the bed. "He was the one who attacked me." He winced as he bent to tug on his boots; Perkins knelt and lent him a hand. "Where's Henderson?" Pembroke asked.

"Now, that be a right good question," Perkins answered thoughtfully. "'Im and Miss Deborah, and that Sir Cyril, come bustin' into the kitchen and told me ter get up here quick, and not ter leave 'til they told me it were safe. There be somethin' right strange goin' on, milord, that I'll swear ter."

"I'm very much afraid you're right, my friend," Pembroke agreed. He swayed dizzily for a moment as he rose to his feet; then, steadying, he crossed to the wardrobe and began to rummage about inside it.

"My lord, you should not be out of bed," Sarah protested weakly. "Your injury...the bleeding!"

"Madam, I should very much prefer a bloody head to a dead son," Pembroke answered shortly, and slammed shut the wardrobe door. "Blast!" he said. "My pistol's gone."

Unexpectedly Martha Perkins spoke up. "Do not trouble yourself, my lord," she said calmly, and turned her back on the gentleman. The rustle of material, a flash of petticoat, and she spun round, a small pistol in her hand. Pembroke laughed. "When we found you unconscious, I was a little worried," Mrs. Perkins explained. "So, when I went for bandages, I stopped and picked this up." She met Pembroke's gaze unflinchingly. "What are you going to do?"

"Try to find them and tell Henderson what Sir Cyril has done," Pembroke told her. "First, though, I think we must look for reinforcements, eh, Perkins? Perkins?"

"'Ellfire . . . and . . . damnation!" exclaimed Perkins, staring intently into the fire. "I'll be a . . ." Whatever Perkins was to say was forgotten as he began to beat ferociously at the fire which blazed in the hearth. "Get water!" he ordered his wife, who brought him the basin without question. Perkins threw the liquid on the flames, and stepped back.

The other occupants of the bedchamber could only stare, agape, as first Lady Margaret, then Eversley, emerged hastily through the steam and smoke which filled the fireplace.

"WELL, WELL, WELL," said Sir Cyril happily. He straightened up from binding Henderson and Deborah, then looked down at the pair, propped against the wall of the stable. "Here we are at last, all comfortable and cosy."

"But why?" asked Deborah, meeting Sir Cyril's gaze squarely, her voice steady.

Sir Cyril raised one eyebrow. "You are a cool one," he said, a grudging admiration in his tone.

"Wot I want ter know is," said Jack petulantly, "wot're we gonna do with these two?" He jerked his head toward Henderson and Deborah. "I can't be watchin' all o' them!"

"Patience, friend Jack, patience," Sir Cyril admonished gently. "All in good time. At the moment, though, I am conversing with Miss Deborah." He turned back. "You were saying?" he prompted.

Deborah shrugged. "I confess myself outwitted," she said. "I cannot imagine why you have brought us here."

"I think him mad!" barked Henderson, glaring at Sir Cyril. "He must be, to think he'll get away with this."

"You are a fool, Henderson," Sir Cyril said contemptuously. "No, worse than a fool—a slave to convention. Everything you hear, you believe. Everything you believe, you act upon. Have you any notion how easy it was to use you?" he sneered. "I wished to separate Miss Tollin—" he bowed in Deborah's direction "—from Eversley, so I played on your fears of what the ton would think. It was pathetically easy to send you running to the chit, demanding that the engagement be broken." Henderson had the good grace to blush. "I wished to complete Miss Tollin's isolation from society," Sir Cyril continued, "so I encouraged you, and a few others, to indulge in scurrilous gossip about what was basically an innocent excursion, properly supervised, with a childhood friend. I wished to discredit Stewart, so I told you a pack of lies about the lad cheating at cards. You must be the most gullible creature ever born, to believe such hogwash!"

"But why?" cried Deborah. "Why?"

"Don't be rude, now, Miss Deborah," Henderson said, exercising iron control over his temper. "Let Sir Cyril tell us the story in his own way."

Sir Cyril seemed pleased. "Very well," he said. "Where to start?" He leaned against a post and crossed his legs at the ankles.

"First of all," he began, "you should know that my name is not Sir Cyril Dennison. It is Tollin, James Tollin." Deborah gasped. "Yes, that's right, my dear, your long-lost uncle. You thought me dead, didn't you? Or should I say, Geoffrey let you think that I was dead." He smiled mirthlessly. "My dear brother Geoffrey. We were always enemies, you see. From the moment I was born, I resented him. I resented his wit, his charm, his inheritance, but most of all, I resented the love which our father bore him." James Tollin pushed himself erect, and strode back and forth before the captives. "The old man didn't care a whit for me—Geoffrey was all he wanted. I often wonder why he bothered to have another son—perhaps he had hoped for a daughter. At any rate, he all but ignored me, so busy was he doting on Geoffrey."

Deborah opened her mouth to speak. Henderson shook his head at her, and she subsided.

"It all came to a head when we met Amanda," Deborah's uncle continued softly. "God, she was beautiful!" He surveyed his niece dispassionately. "You are very like her," he said flatly, and turned away. "I met her before Geoffrey, actually, at an alfresco party on the first day of summer." His eyes were unfocussed; he seemed to be looking back in time. "She liked me very well, to that I would swear. I, of course, loved her at first sight. Then she met Geoffrey." He was now totally lost in his narrative; he snarled at the empty air before him. "That was the end of Amanda's regard for me. No sooner did she lay eyes on my brother than I was forgotten. On the day they became betrothed, she begged me to wish her happy. I can still see her, so pretty in her blue velvet dress, standing there telling me how much she loved Geoffrey."

"Uncle . . ." whispered Deborah.

"Something snapped in me at that moment," James Tollin went on. "I was determined to have my revenge on my brother, aye, and on she who had spurned me, too. So I took her.'' He stopped.

''What do you mean?'' demanded Henderson, enthralled by the tale despite himself. ''What do you mean, you took her?''

''I mean,'' the man said deliberately, ''I picked her up, threw her over my saddle and rode off with her. At the first town we came to, I hired a coach and set off for Scotland.'' He sighed. ''Her terror was wonderful to see—she pleaded with me to return her, promised that she'd wed me anyway, if I'd just take her home. The lying jade! Did she think me fool enough to believe that? No, I said, we're for Gretna Green, where they are not overscrupulous about having the bride's consent to a marriage.''

Deborah, her sympathy for her uncle forgotten, said, ''But your wicked scheme came to naught, didn't it? My father saw to that, I'll wager.''

James Tollin smiled. ''On the contrary, my dear, everything went exactly according to plan. We arrived safely in Scotland, and Amanda and I were wed. There! I've surprised you, haven't I? No more than the odious Geoffrey, though—you should have seen his expression when finally he caught up to us and I waved our marriage lines in his face. It was exquisite, to see the pain in his eyes and Amanda's.''

''But—but—'' Deborah stammered. ''I don't understand . . . Was there a divorce?''

''Now we come to the crux of the matter,'' her uncle exclaimed in satisfaction. ''No, my sweet, there was no divorce,'' he said. ''Geoffrey simply took my wife—my wife!—and threatened to kill me if I didn't leave the country. He had got hold of certain, er, incriminating letters of mine, the publication of which would have landed me in Newgate. So I was forced to do as he wished. I left England, and he took Amanda home and let it be known that they had eloped. Since they were already affianced, it was a nine days' wonder, or scandal I should say, then all was forgotten." He looked at Deborah. "Nine months later, you were born."

What little colour was left in Deborah's face drained away. "No! No!"

James Tollin's lips curled. "No, I am not your father," he said. "Unfortunately, Geoffrey caught up with us before the marriage could be consummated. That makes you happy, does it?" he asked Deborah. "I find that surprising, I must say—one would not think you anxious to be a bastard." Deborah looked thunderstruck. "Ah, you hadn't thought of that, had you? How does it feel, dear Deborah, to be born on the wrong side of the blanket? You simply must tell us."

Deborah lifted her chin proudly. "Better to be Geoffrey Tollin's bastard," she spat, "than your legitimate child."

"Bravo, girl!" Henderson cried. "Bravo!"

"Shut up, damn you!" Tollin aimed a vicious kick at the helpless gentleman. "Shut up!" He turned back to Deborah, his composure regained. "How admirable," he said. "But have you thought the matter through, dear child? Or perhaps you simply have never seen a copy of your grandfather's will."

"What has that to say to anything?" Deborah asked disdainfully.

"Quite a lot, my dear. My esteemed father made his will long before you were born, indeed before Geoffrey and Amanda had ever met. But not, alas, before he had become disillusioned with his younger son." James Tollin shrugged. "He was quite anxious that none of his worldly possessions should come to me, so he left me out of the document completely, naming as his heirs his son Geoffrey and the legitimate—" he stressed the word "—issue of

Geoffrey's body. Now do you understand?" He leaned over his niece, his eyes glittering. "You are nothing, my beautiful Deborah, and nobody!"

CHAPTER SEVENTEEN

"TIMOTHY, DID YOU HEAR THAT?" Burle was appalled by what he had heard. Sir Cyril's voice, as well as those of Deborah, Henderson, and the odious Jack, were clearly audible in the loft. "The poor thing, who would ever have believed it?" Burle looked over at his friend, who had applied himself even more savagely to his bonds since hearing Sir Cyril enter the stable with his prisoners.

"There," Stewart grunted, slipping the last coil of rope from his bruised and abraded wrists. "I've got it." He crawled silently to Burle's side and began to undo that young man's hands, but held a finger to his lips when Burle opened his mouth. "Shh! I want to hear this," Timothy mouthed.

Down below, Deborah was speaking. "Well," she retorted defiantly, "if I am a nobody, so too are you! I may not have Shaftsworth, but you won't have it, either."

"Wrong again," James said easily.

"That's correct, I'm afraid," Henderson said unexpectedly. "If your uncle was not specifically excluded by name, then he would be next in line to inherit. One can only assume that your grandfather failed to take legal advice before making his will."

"Quite true." Deborah's uncle nodded. "The old man hated solicitors and had as little to do with them as possible. For that," he murmured, "I can only be profoundly grateful."

"How glad I am," Deborah said sadly, "that Papa is not here to see...to see..." She could not finish.

"I do feel a tad cheated by Geoffrey's untimely demise," James agreed, "although I daresay I should not!" He laughed aloud.

Timothy's eyes narrowed; he sucked in his breath between his teeth.

"Someun's comin'," Jack said loudly from his post by the door. "It be that Lady Margaret."

"Maggie? No! We must—" Stewart stopped Burle's exclamation by the simple expedient of placing his hand over the young man's mouth until he had subsided.

"Do you want them to come up here and find us loose?" Timothy whispered fiercely. "We'll do her more good free, I promise you." Burle nodded. Timothy released him, and crawled to the window to watch Lady Margaret's approach.

"BE YE READY NOW, MILADY?" Perkins asked, scowling at Lady Margaret. "I don't like this, no, and I ain't afraid to tell yer. 'Tain't right, sendin' a lady into such a place!" He jerked his head toward the stables.

"Now, Perkins, don't carry on," the lady in question said staunchly, though her skin was ashen. "You know we all agreed that I should have the best chance of making it into the building without being searched." She reached down to check, through her skirt, the pistol strapped securely to her calf with a wide band of sheeting. "Were you or any of the gentlemen to turn up, they'd be bound to find the gun first thing. As it is, I may have a chance of smuggling it in undiscovered. I hope," she added wryly.

"I know, I know, but I still don't like it," Perkins grumbled. "And what's more, neither do his lordship, the marquess."

"I'm very much aware of that fact," Lady Margaret said. "But it is much the best plan that we came up with, and so you must admit, Perkins, as my uncle finally did."

"Aye, miss," Perkins acknowledged gloomily.

"I am still concerned, though, that Sir Cyril may bind me," the young lady said worriedly. "It would be too, too distressing to get all the way in and still be unable to do any good."

"Well, as to that, milady, just remember what milord Eversley showed yer," Perkins reminded her. "All ye has to do—" he turned around and demonstrated "—is strain yer muscles, like, while they be tying yer. Then, when ye relax, them ropes should be loose enough to slip yer 'ands out."

"Yes, yes, I remember," Lady Margaret said, and took a deep breath. "I am a little nervous," she confessed.

Perkins surprised both the lady and himself by patting her clumsily on the shoulder. "Well, I think yer doin' just fine," he said gruffly. "Ain't many ladies what 'ud 'ave the brass t' do what yer doin'."

"Thank you, Perkins." She smiled gratefully.

Perkins blushed and ducked his head to check his time-piece. "Well, milady," he said reluctantly, "it be time, I'm afeared."

Lady Margaret took another deep breath and lifted her chin proudly. "Wish me luck," she said, and without a backward glance, began to stride purposefully toward the stables.

"May God be with ye, milady!" called Perkins softly, and stepped back into the trees.

"JUST AS I THOUGHT," Timothy said, and motioned to his friend to join him. Burle made it to the window just in time to see Perkins disappear from view in a nearby copse of trees as Lady Margaret opened the door of the stable.

"They must have a plan," Burle said. "Jolly good."

"It won't be so good," Stewart promised grimly, "for whoever allowed Maggie to become involved in this. They'll answer to me for it, curse 'em!"

"Oh?" Burle looked amused. "Shall they now?"

Stewart blushed. "Just shut up, will you, Burle?" he said rudely. "I'm trying to listen."

"Now, I wonder what brings you back out here?" James Tollin was asking Margaret. "I smell a rat, my lady!"

"Don't be absurd." Timothy could not help but smile at the defiance in Lady Margaret's tone. "What threat can I be to you? You hold my friends to hostage."

"I do," he admitted. "Still—"

"But you have not finished your tale," Deborah said hastily. "Do go on."

"Bless you, Deb," Timothy murmured to himself.

"We still have no notion of what brought you back to England, or of why you have brought us here," Deborah said coaxingly to her uncle.

"As to that, the Americas had become...uncomfortable for me," the man said carelessly. "So I came to the Continent. I was in Paris, wondering what to do with myself, when I began to hear talk among the English tourists, of *la belle Tollin*. Imagine my surprise. Up until that time, I had had no notion that you existed, my dear. But when they told me of you, of your beauty and grace, well! I knew that I had the weapon of my brother's destruction in my hand. I lost no time in returning to England."

"To blackmail Geoffrey, I have no doubt," Henderson said contemptuously.

"Suffice to say," the former Sir Cyril said, "that Geoffrey was aware of the damage it would do his beloved daughter to be named a bastard, and chose to compensate me for my silence." He sighed. "It was financially rewarding, but alas, emotionally unsatisfying."

Burle glanced over at his companion, but Timothy Stewart did not appear to be listening; he rubbed his chin, deep in thought, and stared blankly off into space.

Down below, Deborah's uncle continued. "It was not enough for me to beggar Geoffrey," he said. "No, I wanted to destroy him, totally and forever."

"You killed him, didn't you?" Deborah's voice was chilling. "I never believed that he shot himself. You did it, didn't you?"

"Why, my dear Deborah—" James's tone was light "—how clever you are, my sweet! Yes, I shot him, but only because he did something very, very foolish. He stole something of mine, something which I needed rather badly."

"The marriage lines," Henderson burst out. "That has to be what Geoffrey took. It's the only thing which makes sense!"

James nodded. "That's right—the marriage lines that prove my niece a bastard. I must have them. I will have them!"

"I still sez 'e burnt the rubbishin' paper," Jack grumbled thickly. "E'd 'ave 'ad ter be all about in 'is 'ead ter 'a saved it."

"No," said Deborah and James together.

"He would never have done that." Deborah was adamant. "Hide the paper, yes, but destroy it? No. He wouldn't, I know it."

"I agree completely," said Deborah's uncle. "I always told Geoffrey that his benighted sense of honour would be the ruin of him. Appears that I was right! Now, 'tis simply a matter of determining where he put the thing. I believe that you can help me there, Deborah."

Unnoticed by the speakers, Lady Margaret had edged closer to Mr. Henderson. Keeping a wary eye on James Tollin and his henchman, she pressed her thigh against his.

Henderson jumped. "Here, now, my lady," he whispered, "I know you're frightened, but—"

"Shh!" She fixed him with a compelling stare, and wriggled a little closer.

"What the dev— Oh!" He felt the hard pistol jabbing against his leg through her skirts, and at the same moment, her cool fingers touching his wrists. She began to tug at the rope which bound him.

They both froze in horror as Jack stumbled over. "'Ere now, wot're yer doin'?" he asked. "A little rub an' grab?" The man laughed coarsely. "Yer turn me down, then go fer this old bag o' bones?" He raked his eyes offensively over Lady Margaret, then stepped closer. "I'm the lad fer yer, sweetheart, not 'im. I've got more in me pocket than this old..."

"Jack! Get back by the door," James Tollin said coldly, barely glancing at Lady Margaret and Henderson. "And stay there, do you hear me?"

Henderson could barely contain a sigh of relief as Jack returned to his post by the entrance, and her uncle spoke again to Deborah.

"So, my dear," he said pleasantly, "where is it?"

Deborah tossed her head. "How should I know?" she asked. "And even if I did, can you really believe that I would tell you?"

"Oh, yes," James Tollin stared down at his niece implacably. "You will tell me, my dear, I assure you."

"I think not!"

"Not even if I drag Eversley down from the house and, er, decorate him?" James purred. A wickedly sharp knife appeared in his fingers and he began to toy with it lovingly. "I am a man of much patience, Deborah, but I grow weary of this game. I will have what I want." Without a moment of hesitation, Deborah's uncle spun round and threw the knife.

Roger Henderson cried out and dropped the pistol which he had just raised in Tollin's direction; he cursed the streaming wound in his arm, and glared impotently at his attacker.

"A most commendable try, Roger, but you needn't have bothered," James said coolly, stooping to pluck the knife from Henderson's wound and scoop up the pistol. He looked down at Henderson and Lady Margaret, and his eyes narrowed. "Jack," he said, without removing his gaze from the pair, "go and stand by the secret door. I believe that we shall be having a visitor."

"Damn!" whispered Stewart. "I was afraid of this. We must stop—"

But it was apparently too late; Stewart and Burle heard the creaking sound of the panel below swinging open, then a moment or two of loud scuffling and the cries of Deborah and Lady Margaret.

Burle started as he heard his father's voice. "Damn you, Dennison!" the marquess said weakly.

"I must see what's happening, Timothy," Burle mouthed frantically. "I must!" He started toward the ladder which led below and cautiously peeped over the edge.

The sight which met the young peer's eyes did nothing to reassure him; he saw his father, hands already bound, being pushed down next to Lady Margaret.

"Call the groom, Deborah," Tollin said calmly. Deborah only stared at the man. "Call him, or I'll blow the marquess's head off." He pressed the barrel of Henderson's pistol firmly against Pembroke's temple. Deborah said nothing. "Do you doubt my resolve, niece?" the armed man asked, and cocked the pistol.

"Perkins! Come in!" she shouted. "Please, Perkins, now!"

The elderly groom cautiously opened the door. He was quickly overcome and bound, to join the group leaning against the wall of the stable.

"So here we all are," said James Tollin. "Excepting only Eversley, of course, and he may remain safely in his bed, for the moment at least."

"I'm going down, Timothy," Burle said decisively. "No, no, don't argue with me—it's now or never. I'm going to try to leap down on Jack. If I manage the thing, it will be up to you to deal with Tollin." He grinned crookedly. "I've left you the harder task, you see. He's the one with the pistol!"

Timothy hesitated for only a moment, then nodded. "We'll have to jump, if we're to go down together," he said. "Simultaneous attack is our only chance. You're going to have to land right on Jack. That way, Tollin won't be able to shoot for fear of hitting him. I'll try to hit the floor and roll into Tollin. I can't reach him in one leap."

Burle nodded and reached out to clasp Timothy's hand. "Good luck, Timothy!" he said.

"Aye," said Timothy, and grimaced wryly. "For England, and Saint George!"

The two men positioned themselves at the head of the ladder and leapt from the loft through the opening.

EVERSLEY STOOD OUTSIDE the stable, his hair plastered against his face by the rain. Cautiously he raised his head to peer through the dirty glass of the window; he bit back a curse as he realized that their plan, hatched so confidently, had gone badly awry. He could see Pembroke, hands bound, seated on the floor along with the other captives. His uncle Roger had one hand clapped over his arm, but the bright blood seeped slowly out through the old man's fingers.

He limped around to the door of the stable and carefully, slowly, looked in through the small wooden hatch set in the door. Jack had his back to the portal; Sir Cyril, or Tollin, as Eversley now knew him to be, was standing farther down the stable, in front of the captives. Eversley tried the door gently. It was latched.

Suddenly Eversley saw Burle and Stewart plummet down through the opening from the loft. Stewart immediately disappeared from Eversley's view; Burle landed directly on top of Jack. The two men fell to the floor and rolled from side to side, struggling for a knife which had appeared in Jack's hand. Eversley turned the handle of the stable door and swung it open a few inches. About to rush in, he heard a shot ring out, and then another. Jack and Burle both jerked, then lay still.

"Hold!" cried Tollin. "Do you wish to die, as your friend has just done?" He appeared to be speaking to Stewart. Eversley saw the young man rise to his feet, his face working. "Much better," Tollin said approvingly. "Gratuitous violence has ever been a dislike of mine." Deborah's uncle walked over to kick contemptuously, first Jack's body, then Burle's.

Eversley could wait no longer. He pushed the door ajar and plunged through the opening, his foot forgotten, unaware that he was shouting hoarsely. He plowed directly into Tollin, knocking the man off his feet with the violence of his assault. Tollin reached frantically for the pistol which Eversley's charge had knocked from his hand. Timothy Stewart leapt to Eversley's aid and kicked the gun out of reach.

"Don't interfere," Eversley grunted, aiming a blow at Tollin's head. "He's mine!" Timothy bowed and stepped back. In only a moment it was over, and James Tollin lay motionless on the dirt floor. Eversley took the precaution of pocketing Tollin's pistol, then turned away.

"Robert!" Deborah sobbed helplessly. "Oh, Robert!"

Pembroke ceased the furious struggle to escape his bonds. "Burle," he whispered, his face ashen. "Oh, my son, my son!"

Stewart had knelt over his friend. "He's alive, sir," he said. He checked Burle's inert body. "The bullet seems to have been deflected by Jack's body. Burle's bleeding a bit, but it doesn't look too bad." As he spoke, he whipped off his neckcloth and efficiently bound the wound. "I think he'll be all right."

Pembroke bowed his head; he seemed not to care that tears were streaming down his face. "Thank you," he said, to no one in particular.

Stewart checked Tollin's henchman. "Jack's dead," he said.

No one paid any attention to him. Eversley had crossed to Deborah, and held the still-sobbing girl gently in his arms. "There now, pet," he murmured. "There, now. It's all over. Nothing to be afraid of."

"Oh, Robert, I was so frightened!" Deborah lifted her face. "I thought he would kill us all!"

"Timothy!" Margaret screamed.

Yet another shot rang out. With a surprised expression, Timothy, his back to Tollin, crumpled slowly to the floor.

"Fools," James Tollin said dispassionately. "Did you think you could be rid of me that easily?" He got slowly to his feet, but the barrel of the tiny gun he held didn't waver from Eversley. "I had this made on the Continent. Cunning, isn't it? It only holds two shots, but two would be enough, don't you agree?"

Eversley seemed inclined to chance it, but Tollin moved the gun so that it pointed at Deborah. "Don't try it, my buck. Your little love would never survive the attempt. Sit down, won't you?"

Eversley reluctantly sank onto the floor beside Deborah. Tollin moved about the stable, making a pile of hay and the rags used to clean bridles and saddles.

"What are you doing?" Henderson asked, still belligerent despite his situation. "Eh, you blackguard?"

"He plans to set the building on fire and leave us all here to die," Eversley said bluntly. "I'll wager he intends Jack to stand in for his own unsightly corpse—so passes Sir Cyril Dennison, and the heiress to Shaftsworth, victims of a tragic fire. Then, when a suitable amount of time has passed, James Tollin reappears and inherits everything. Is that the rough outline of your plan, Tollin?"

"More or less," the man affirmed. He struck a spark and lit the pile. "You drove me to it yourself, Deborah," he said, "by refusing to give me the marriage lines. It's on your head, niece."

"But I don't know where they are!"

"It's unimportant," Tollin shrugged, and winced as the wound in his head began to bleed a little more freely. "With you dead, I'll inherit, anyway."

The fire caught and began to spread rapidly; despite all the rain, the building was old and tinder-dry. Tollin looked around the stable appraisingly. "Have I done everything, now?" he asked himself. "Ah, yes, just one more detail to take care of." He bent over to pick up Eversley's forgotten fire iron. "Regretfully, I must put you to sleep now, my lord," he said. Eversley stared up at Tollin. "Never think that you could overcome me before I shot Deborah; you couldn't," Tollin said. Eversley raised his hands; Tollin brought the heavy iron crashing down onto his head.

It was beginning to be difficult to breathe in the stables; the flames had raced up the walls, and were devouring the dry beams overhead. "Well, *mes amis,* it is time for me to bid you farewell," James Tollin said cheerfully. "My advice to you all is to breathe deeply, and let the smoke do the job before the flames." With a jaunty wave of the hand, Sir Cyril Dennison, né James Tollin, jerked open the stable door. At the threshold he turned back. *"Au revoir,* my friends," he said. "I hope..." Whatever it was that James Tollin had hoped would never be known; the draught from the open door had made the fire explode, and his figure was outlined in light for a moment before the fiery beam above the doorway gave a groan, and fell with a crash on his head.

Deborah shrieked in horror. "Oh, my God! We must save him!" She struggled frantically against her bonds.

"It's no use, Miss Tollin," said Henderson gently. "The man is beyond our help, I'm afraid."

Lady Margaret had apparently given up all hope. She wriggled and twisted, and propelled her body across the floor until she sat next to Timothy. Leaning forward, she kissed him softly on the lips. "I love you, Timothy," she said quietly.

Perkins grunted. "We ain't done yet, yer ladyship," he said grimly. "That we—Look!"

The secret door slid open; looking for all the world as though she were entering a London ballroom, Sarah Beldon, one hand fastidiously holding her skirts aloft, stepped into the stable.

CHAPTER EIGHTEEN

"BUT HOW DID YOU ever have the courage, Mrs. Perkins?" They were all in the drawing room, Stewart and Burle stretched out on facing divans, the rest of the group scattered about the room. "I would have been frightened witless!" Lady Margaret was frankly admiring.

"How could I be afraid, when the mistress was so brave?" Mrs. Perkins said, bustling about the room with tea and toast for all. "It was all Miss Sarah's idea. She said she wouldn't sit around, waiting for someone else to kill her or save her."

"Your idea, Aunt Sarah?" said Deborah, agog. "I can scarce believe it."

"I must surmise," responded Sarah sharply, "that you have harboured quite as poor an opinion of me as your uncle apparently did. To think he forgot all about Mrs. Perkins and me, only on account of our age and our sex! 'Tis a lowering thought."

"A mistake which none of us will ever make again," Timothy said. "I've always known you to be a heroine in disguise, Aunt Sarah."

"Flatterer!"

"Well, whoever's notion it was, 'twas a good one," Eversley said, the bandage which was wrapped about his head white against his hair. "We shouldn't have lasted much longer out there. Once Tollin opened the door..." A gloomy silence fell on the group.

"What I should like to know," said Sarah, in an obvious effort to change the subject, "is how our Timothy survived his shooting. Do tell, my boy!"

Timothy laughed, then groaned. "A dashed flask of brandy did the trick," he said. "It deflected the bullet."

"Now why would you carry the flask stuck into the back waist of your pants?" Pembroke asked, taking his eyes off his son for the first time since entering the room. "Seems a trifle inconvenient. Wouldn't a pocket have been more comfortable?"

"I moved it when I was working on the horses," Timothy explained. "I had my coat off, and felt the need of a little, er, refreshment. So I took a swallow, and stuck it into the back of my pants, where I promptly forgot all about it."

"I, for one, am profoundly grateful that you did," Margaret said softly. Timothy blushed.

"Do you know," Pembroke said, "I'm still not sure that I understand everything that happend. For instance, what of the letter that Mr. Geoffrey Tollin wrote? Was it a forgery?"

"No," said Deborah, shaking her head. "It was Father's handwriting, I'm certain of it."

"I have a theory about that," said Eversley, then he hesitated, lifting one eyebrow questioningly at Deborah.

Though her colour deepened, she said instantly, "After all that we have been through together, you need not scruple to speak in front of my friends, Robert."

"I think," he said slowly, "that Geoffrey was going to kill, or attempt to kill, his brother."

"No!" Deborah gasped.

"Remember the letter, Deb," Eversley said. "Geoffrey spoke of his hatred of violence, and of the aftermath of his actions. But there is no aftermath to suicide, only death."

"Perhaps he was thinking of the consequences for Miss Deborah," Pembroke suggested.

"I think not," Eversley responded. "He also said 'the secret will die with me, but by then it won't matter.' He expected to die, not by his own hands, but on the field of honour—duelling, you see."

"It does make sense," Timothy agreed.

"Aye," said Perkins unexpectedly. "Yer in the right of it, milord, I'll wager. Not two days before the accident, I come upon Mr. Geoffrey, a-cleanin' 'is pistols, with such a look on 'is face! Not sad, or mopin', like, but grim, grim as death."

"It was all so unnecessary," Deborah said sadly. "My father died to save my good name, and to keep me from losing Shaftsworth. It was all for naught. My good name was lost the instant I learned of my illegitimacy. I have no right to Shaftsworth."

"Balderdash," Eversley said flatly. "You're talking a lot of nonsense, my pet, and you know it. Scum like Tollin could never take anything from you—you are too good, too fine. You belong at Shaftsworth—you, and your children, and your children's children after you, carrying on the Tollin tradition."

"But I am illegitimate, Eversley," Deborah said despondently.

"You are your father's daughter," said Pembroke. "Have you thought this through, my dear?" he asked. "With your uncle dead, if you disqualify yourself from inheriting, Shaftsworth will go to the Crown by default. Are you prepared to let the home of your ancestors go that easily?"

"I agree with Father," Burle said weakly. When every head in the room swivelled in his direction, the young peer's ashen cheeks coloured. "Don't look so surprised—I'm not dead yet!" He swung his gaze to Deborah. "What I mean to say is, well, you're a Tollin, Miss Deborah, and you deserve to have Shaftsworth. Besides, I for one don't believe a word that lying scoundrel said."

Eversley smiled gently at Deborah. "Think of it as one final service you may render your father, Deb—to accept the gift which he gave his life to defend. This has all been horrible for you, and you have borne the burden with grace and breeding. Don't throw it away now, and for no purpose."

"Very well," she said dully, and turned away.

"Well," said Mrs. Perkins practically, "Perkins and I will take ourselves off to see about heating hot water and putting on some dinner."

"I'll come with you, Martha," Sarah said, seeming none the worse for wear. "You'll need an extra pair of hands, I'll wager."

"Aye, and after, I'll see about gettin' ter the village ter have the bridge fixed, now that the rain is stopped," Perkins added.

"Has it? I had not noticed," Deborah said. "I think we are all in need of a rest. Shall we go to our rooms, La—Margaret?"

"Not just yet, if you please, Miss Deborah," Henderson stood. pulled on the lapels of his filthy frock coat and harrumphed once or twice. "Well," he said, then paused. "Well...I have some apologizing to do," he said, his face beet-red. "First of all, to you, Mr. Stewart."

Timothy jerked his head up. "You do?"

"Yes, I do. I misjudged you, lad, and for that I'm sorry," Henderson said, meeting Timothy's gaze squarely. "I'm an old fool, and that's the right of it, my boy."

Eversley hid a smile at Stewart's discomfiture. "I...that is to say..." Timothy said, "think nothing of it, sir. I do present the appearance of a shameless here-and-therian."

"Still, that's no excuse," Henderson said, and gravely extended his hand to the supine Timothy. The two men shook hands and grinned at each other sheepishly.

"And as for you, Miss Deborah," Henderson said, swinging round so abruptly that Deborah started, "high-

born or bast...not, sick or well, a better wife for my nephew
don't exist, and I hope to welcome you into the family very
soon." He crossed the room and bowed deeply before the
flabbergasted girl.

"Ah, yes," said Eversley smoothly, "that was very nicely
done, Uncle, very nicely indeed. Now, if you will excuse
Deborah and I, we have a matter or two to discuss." He held
out his hand to Deborah. Seemingly against her will, she
took it and helped him to his feet. The pair left the drawing
room.

Henderson laughed. "Go to it, lad!" he called out after
them. "Always was one to throw his heart over, that boy,"
he said. Still chuckling, he took himself off to his bedchamber.

The drawing room was quiet for a long moment after
Henderson left. Burle seemed to be dozing, while his father
sat comfortably in an arm chair, eyeing Stewart and Lady
Margaret Rawlings thoughtfully.

"Well, Margaret," he said finally, "it seems that you were
right about this young man—" he nodded toward Timothy
"—and I was wrong. My apologies, my dear."

"Thank you, Uncle," Margaret said. "It is good of you
to own it."

"By your actions in the stable, I gather that felicitations
are in order?"

"Yes," said Lady Margaret boldly.

"By no means, sir," Timothy said, just as quickly. "Lady
Margaret has conceived a certain fondness for my company, but I assure you, it has gone no further than that."

"And why not?" Pembroke asked.

"I beg your pardon?"

"I said, why not?" Pembroke repeated patiently.

"But sir...you cannot have considered...I am not a fit
candidate for my lady's hand!" Timothy protested.

"In the normal run of things, I would agree with you," Pembroke said. "But, after the quite disgusting display my niece made of herself not long since, marriage is the only solution, I fear."

"You've no choice, Timothy," Burle said, opening his eyes. "She's bagged you, fair and square."

Timothy tried once more. "Truly, my lord . . . In her own best interests . . ."

"But, Timothy! Don't you want me?" Margaret dissolved in tears.

The ensuing scene of love and reassurance caused Pembroke to tell Stewart sharply to have the courtesy at least to make love to the girl in private. The couple agreed and, with Margaret tenderly supporting her love, went off in search of that privacy.

Burle and Pembroke were left alone. "How are you feeling?" asked Pembroke.

Burle grimaced. "It hurts a bit," he admitted, "but I daresay the pain will strengthen my character." He grinned feebly.

"Your character," said his father, "is fine just as it is. You showed great bravery today, lad."

Burle's eyes bulged. "I?" he said. "I did nothing . . ."

"It was your idea to leap from the loft, Stewart told us," Pembroke said. "It was you who went out, quite intrepidly, to beard the lion in his den, so to speak." He met his son's gaze squarely. "It has always pained me," he said quietly, "that you thought I had no regard for you."

"Father, I—" Burle began.

"I have not demonstrated it as I ought, of late," Pembroke owned. "I should have believed you about Stewart, and for that, I am profoundly sorry." He gripped his son's hand tightly. "But never doubt my love for you, or my respect—they are both boundless. You frightened me to death today, Alex. I couldn't bear to lose you!"

What the son saw in his sire's eyes made him return tha[ ]tight grip, and promise incoherently never to trouble hi[ ]parent in such a manner again. As the two men smiled a[ ]each other, misty-eyed, Lord Burle reflected dizzily that i[ ]had, after all, been a very good day.

"DEBORAH."

"Yes, Robert?" Deborah stood before Eversley, hand[ ]behind her back, eyes on her shoes.

"Why did you break our engagement? Oh—" he held u[ ]a hand to stop Deborah from speaking "—I know all abou[ ]Uncle Roger trying to pressure you into it. But I know you[ ]too, Deb, and I know that if your mind had been made up[ ]he wouldn't have been able to sway you. And no rounda[ ]boutation, if you please. Just tell me the truth."

"It seemed—" she spoke in a troubled voice "—it seeme[ ]my duty."

"Your duty to break my heart?" he said lightly. "Com[ ]now, Deb. Surely not."

She lowered her head even more. "You deserve a lad[ ]above reproach, not the ruined daughter of a suicide," sh[ ]said.

"Your father didn't commit suicide," Eversley pointe[ ]out.

"That's true. Not the daughter of a suicide, but a bas[ ]tard," she said bitterly. "That is an improvement, isn't it[ ]And penniless to boot."

"I thought we had settled the matter of the estate, and o[ ]your birth?"

"You compelled me to keep Shaftsworth, and my fa[ ]ther's fortune. You can't force me to do more than spen[ ]what I must to keep up the house and grounds," she re[ ]torted. "No matter what you say, the estate isn't mine, an[ ]I won't treat it as though it were."

"Very well, then. You may save it for one of our sons,"
Eversley said cheerfully. "I daresay by the third or fourth
one, even my fortune will be a trifle the worse for wear!"

"We'll have no sons," Deborah whispered. "Your children should not have to suffer the shame of a mother born
on the wrong side of the blanket." One great tear fell onto
the polished floor in front of his feet.

"Say that you don't love me, Deb," Eversley commanded, and lifted her chin. "Look into my eyes and tell me
that you don't love me every bit as much as I love you!" She
turned away from him. "I thought as much," he said. "It
will never be over between us, Deborah Tollin, not as long
as we have minds and hearts and spirits." He took her in his
arms. "You have proved your worth a thousand times over,
my love," he said. "If our sons have a tenth of your bravery and fortitude, I shall be a proud father indeed!" A
muffled sob was her only answer. "Even if everything which
your uncle said was true, can you understand that I don't
care?" he pressed her. "You are the only woman for me."

"I can't, Robert. I can't!"

"You can, Deb. You must. If you will not wed me for
your own sake, do it for mine. My life would be—" his voice
faltered for a moment "—desolate, without you." Deborah protested weakly, but Lord Eversley was deaf to her
pleas. He bent his head to hers until their lips met, and for
several moments the library was quiet. Then he raised his
head and added with a chuckle. "Besides, my sweet, we
have no choice. If I do not marry you, Uncle Roger will
never forgive me!" He kissed her again. "Have I convinced you, Deb?"

"You have." Deborah hesitated, then asked, "Do you
think, Robert…is it possible that Uncle James was lying?"

"I should not be surprised." Eversley said, telling the lie
without a moment's hesitation. "I should not be surprised

at all." He wiped the tears and the soot gently from Deborah's cheeks.

Deborah laughed shakily. "I must look a sight! May I go and wash and change before we tell everyone? You don't mind, do you, Robert?"

"Not at all, my love," he said. "There's something I need to take care of anyway. Go ahead. Run along."

Lord Robert Eversley waited until Deborah had left the room, then crossed to the portraits of Geoffrey and Amanda Tollin which hung on one wall of the library. "What would you have me do, Geoffrey?" he asked aloud. "What shall I do?"

As though in answer, a phrase from Geoffrey Tollin's final letter appeared in Eversley's mind. "At the last, as at the beginning," Geoffrey had written, "I will rob him of his victory."

"Very well, then!" Eversley said. He took from his pocket the document which had caused so much pain and trouble, the missing marriage lines, and threw it into the fire.

"She's safe now, Geoffrey," he said aloud. "Deborah is safe at last."

Harlequin Regency Romance™

COMING NEXT MONTH

#19 LUCINDA by Blanche Chenier
Lucinda Edrington is down at the heels and must sell
her family home to pay her brother's debts. Her new
neighbour, Lord Sarne, would like to help, but is
constantly attended by a woman with designs on him.
In an effort to keep Lucinda and Lord Sarne apart, a
rumour is circulated that Lucinda was born on the
wrong side of the blanket. Lord Sarne, however, sees
through the deception and rescues Lucinda from her
various misadventures just in time to propose a
marriage she never dreamed possible.

#20 THE VICAR'S DAUGHTER by Eva Rutland
With her father so ill, Christina Frame appeals to the
Earl of Wakefield to finance his recovery in Spain.
The earl agrees to do so if Christina will marry his
profligate son, Domenic Winston, Viscount Stanhope.
Christina and Domenic agree for reasons of their
own. While Domenic intends to pursue the freedom
that marriage allows, he soon finds himself too busy
to do so. So busy is he that he does not realize that he
has fallen in love with the wife he had tried so hard to
avoid until it is almost too late.

A compelling novel of deadly revenge and passion
from Harlequin's bestselling international
romance author Penny Jordan

POWER PLAY

Eleven years had passed but the
terror of that night was something
Pepper Minesse would never
forget. Fueled by revenge against
the four men who had brutally
shattered her past, she set in
motion a deadly plan to destroy
their futures.

Available in February!

 Harlequin Books ®

HPP-1A

H A R L E Q U I N
American Romance®

**Beginning next month
Share in the**

Rocky Mountain Magic

Join American Romance in celebrating the magical charm of the Colorado Rockies at a very special place— The Stanley Hotel. Meet three women friends whose lives are touched with magic and who will never be the same, who find love in a very special way, the way of enchantment.

Read and love
#329 BEST WISHES by Julie Kistler, February 1990
#333 SIGHT UNSEEN by Kathy Clark, March 1990 and
#337 RETURN TO SUMMER by Emma Merritt, April 1990

ROCKY MOUNTAIN MAGIC—All it takes is an open heart.
Only from Harlequin American Romance

All the Rocky Mountain Magic Romances take place at
the beautiful Stanley Hotel.

RMM-1

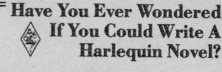

Harlequin Superromance®

LET THE GOOD TIMES ROLL...

Add some Cajun spice to liven up your New Year's celebrations and join Superromance for a romantic tour of the rich Acadian marshlands and the legendary Louisiana bayous.

Starting in January 1990, we're launching CAJUN MELODIES, a three-book tribute to the fun-loving people who've enriched America by introducing us to crawfish étouffé and gumbo, zydeco music and the Saturday night party, the *fais-dodo*. And learn about loving, Cajun-style, as you meet the tall, dark, handsome men who win their ladies' hearts with a beautiful, haunting melody....

Book One: *Julianne's Song*, January 1990
Book Two: *Catherine's Song*, February 1990
Book Three: *Jessica's Song*, March 1990

February brings you...

PENNY JORDAN

valentine's night

Sorrel didn't particularly want to meet her long-lost cousin Val from Australia. However, since the girl had come all this way just to make contact, it seemed a little churlish not to welcome her.

As there was no room at home, it was agreed that Sorrel and Val would share the Welsh farmhouse that was being renovated for Sorrel's brother and his wife. Conditions were a bit primitive, but that didn't matter.

At least, not until Sorrel found herself snowed in with the long-lost cousin, who turned out to be a handsome, six-foot male!

Also, look for the next Harlequin Presents Award of Excellence title in April:

Elusive as the Unicorn
by Carole Mortimer

HP1243-1

Introduction to Optical Electronics

Holt, Rinehart and Winston Series in Electrical Engineering, Electronics, and Systems

Other Books in the Series:

Introduction to Optical Electronics

AMNON YARIV

Professor of Electrical Engineering
California Institute of Technology

HOLT, RINEHART AND WINSTON, INC.

New York   Chicago   San Francisco   Atlanta
Dallas   Montreal   Toronto   London   Sydney

PHYSICS

Preface

The fast growing field of quantum electronics can be divided roughly into two broad categories. The first is concerned chiefly with the atomic aspects of the problem. These include the study of energy levels, lifetimes, and transition rates in laser media; also the mechanisms and the physical origins of phenomena such as Raman and Rayleigh scattering and second-harmonic generation. This branch of the field leans heavily on the formalism of quantum mechanics and has consequently become the domain of the physicist and, to a lesser extent, the physical chemist.

The second category deals with the *coherent interactions of optical radiation fields with various atomic media*. Here we tend to accept the existence of certain physical phenomena and concern ourselves with their implications and applications. The physical properties may now be represented by parameters characteristic of the material. Two typical examples are: (1) the analysis of power output and frequency pulling in laser oscillators in which the physical phenomena of spontaneous emission and atomic dispersion are important, and (2) the problem of optical second-harmonic generation and phase matching in which the complicated quantum mechanical considerations involved in understanding the optical nonlinearity are lumped into the nonlinear constant.

This second aspect of quantum electronics is more closely linked to applications and has consequently attracted the attention of the applied physicist and the electrical engineer. In this area, a good deal of the emphasis is on optics rather than on quantum physics and many of the concepts encountered here have their counterparts in radio and microwave electronics. For this reason I have decided to refer to the subject matter as optical electronics and to choose the same name for the book's title.

The book is aimed at students in the senior year or in the first year of their graduate studies. This is done in the belief that the ever-increasing role of coherent optics in science and technology will require an early exposure to this area on the part of most electrical engineering and applied physics students. With this in mind, I have undertaken to present the material without the use of quantum mechanics. Instead of inventing quasi-classical substitutes for quantum mechanical concepts, I decided to ask the student to accept on faith certain statements whose justification can only be provided by quantum mechanics. Somewhat to my own surprise, I found that this was necessary only when introducing the concepts of stimulated and spontaneous transitions. The rest of the material can then be treated using classical formalism. The level of mathematical sophistication required in this book is kept, hopefully, to what one may expect of a fourth year student of electrical engineering or applied physics. An introductory knowledge of atomic physics and of electromagnetic theory would be helpful, although the basic results are derived in the text.

I am grateful to Drs. U. Ganiel, R. MacAnally, and S. Kurtin for critical comments and suggestions on the manuscript, and Mrs. R. Stratton for her competent and patient typing.

AMNON YARIV

Pasadena, California
January 1971

Contents

1

Electromagnetic Theory

1.0 Introduction

In this chapter we derive some of the basic results concerning the propagation of plane, single-frequency, electromagnetic waves in homogeneous isotropic media, as well as in anisotropic crystal media. Starting with Maxwell's equations we obtain expressions for the dissipation, storage, and transport of energy resulting from the propagation of waves in material media. We consider in some detail the phenomenon of birefringence, in which the phase velocity of a plane wave in a crystal depends on its direction of polarization. The two allowed modes of propagation in uniaxial crystals—the "ordinary" and "extraordinary" rays—are discussed using the formalism of the index ellipsoid.

1.1 The Complex-Function Formalism

In problems that involve sinusoidally varying time functions we can save a great deal of manipulation and space by using the complex function formalism. As an example consider the function

$$a(t) = |A| \cos (\omega t + \phi_a) \qquad \text{(1.1-1)}$$

where ω is the circular (radian) frequency[1] and ϕ_a is the phase. Defining the complex amplitude of $a(t)$ by

$$A = |A|e^{i\phi_a} \tag{1.1-2}$$

we can rewrite (1.1-1) as

$$a(t) = \mathrm{Re}\,[Ae^{i\omega t}] \tag{1.1-3}$$

We will often represent $a(t)$ by

$$a(t) = Ae^{i\omega t} \tag{1.1-4}$$

instead of by (1.1-1) or (1.1-3). This of course is not strictly correct so that when this happens *it is always understood* that what is meant by (1.1-4) is the *real part* of $A \exp(i\omega t)$. In most situations the replacement of (1.1-3) by the complex form (1.1-4) poses no problems. The exceptions are cases that involve the product (or powers) of sinusoidal functions. In these cases we must use the real form of the function (1.1-3). To illustrate the case where the distinction between the real and complex form is not necessary, consider the problem of taking the derivative of $a(t)$. Using (1.1-1) we obtain

$$\frac{da(t)}{dt} = \frac{d}{dt}\left[|A|\cos(\omega t + \phi_a)\right] = -\omega|A|\sin(\omega t + \phi_a) \tag{1.1-5}$$

If we use instead the complex form (1.1-4), we get

$$\frac{da(t)}{dt} = \frac{d}{dt}(Ae^{i\omega t}) = i\omega Ae^{i\omega t}$$

Taking, as agreed, the real part of the last expression and using (1.1-2), we obtain (1.1-5).

As an example of a case in which we have to use the real form of the function, consider the product of two sinusoidal functions $a(t)$ and $b(t)$, where

$$a(t) = |A|\cos(\omega t + \phi_a)$$
$$= \frac{|A|}{2}[e^{i(\omega t + \phi_a)} + e^{-i(\omega t + \phi_a)}]$$
$$= \mathrm{Re}\,[Ae^{i\omega t}] \tag{1.1-6}$$

and

$$b(t) = |B|\cos(\omega t + \phi_b)$$
$$= \frac{|B|}{2}[e^{i(\omega t + \phi_b)} + e^{-i(\omega t + \phi_b)}]$$
$$= \mathrm{Re}\,[Be^{i\omega t}] \tag{1.1-7}$$

---

[1] The radian frequency ω is to be distinguished from the real frequency $\nu = \omega/2\pi$.

with $A = |A| \exp (i\phi_a)$ and $B = |B| \exp (i\phi_b)$. Using the real functions, we get

$$a(t)b(t) = \frac{|A|\,|B|}{2} \left[\cos (2\omega t + \phi_a + \phi_b) + \cos (\phi_a - \phi_b) \right] \quad \textbf{(1.1-8)}$$

Were we to evaluate the product $a(t)b(t)$ using the complex form of the functions, we would get

$$a(t)b(t) = ABe^{i2\omega t} = |A|\,|B|e^{i(2\omega t+\phi_a+\phi_b)} \qquad \textbf{(1.1-9)}$$

Comparing the last result to (1.1-8) shows that the time-independent (dc) term $\frac{1}{2}|A|\,|B| \cos (\phi_a - \phi_b)$ is missing, and thus the use of the complex form led to an error.

Time-averaging of sinusoidal products.[2] Another problem often encountered is that of finding the time average of the product of two sinusoidal functions of the same frequency

$$\overline{a(t)b(t)} = \frac{1}{T} \int_0^T |A| \cos (\omega t + \phi_a)|B| \cos (\omega t + \phi_b) \, dt \quad \textbf{(1.1-10)}$$

where $a(t)$ and $b(t)$ are given by (1.1-6) and (1.1-7) and the horizontal bar denotes time-averaging. $T = 2\pi/\omega$ is the period of the oscillation. Since the integrand in (1.1-10) is periodic in T, the averaging can be performed over a time T. Using (1.1-8) we obtain directly

$$\overline{a(t)b(t)} = \frac{|A|\,|B|}{2} \cos (\phi_a - \phi_b) \qquad \textbf{(1.1-11)}$$

This last result can be written in terms of the complex amplitudes A and B, defined immediately following (1.1-7), as

$$\overline{a(t)b(t)} = \tfrac{1}{2} \operatorname{Re} (AB^*) \qquad \textbf{(1.1-12)}$$

This important result will find frequent use throughout the book.

1.2 Considerations of Energy and Power in Electromagnetic Fields

In this section we derive the formal expressions for the power transport, power dissipation, and energy storage that accompany the propagation of electromagnetic radiation in material media. The starting point is

---

[2] The problem of the time average of two nearly sinusoidal functions is considered in Problems 1.1 and 1.2.

Maxwell's equations (in MKS units)

$$\nabla \times \mathbf{h} = \mathbf{i} + \frac{\partial \mathbf{d}}{\partial t} \tag{1.2-1}$$

$$\nabla \times \mathbf{e} = - \frac{\partial \mathbf{b}}{\partial t} \tag{1.2-2}$$

and the constitutive equations relating the polarization of the medium to the displacement vectors

$$\mathbf{d} = \epsilon_0 \mathbf{e} + \mathbf{p} \tag{1.2-3}$$

$$\mathbf{b} = \mu_0 (\mathbf{h} + \mathbf{m}) \tag{1.2-4}$$

where $\mathbf{i}$ is the current density (amperes per square meter); $\mathbf{e}(\mathbf{r}, t)$ and $\mathbf{h}(\mathbf{r}, t)$ are the electric and magnetic field vectors, respectively; $\mathbf{d}(\mathbf{r}, t)$ and $\mathbf{b}(\mathbf{r}, t)$ are the electric and magnetic displacement vectors; $\mathbf{p}(\mathbf{r}, t)$ and $\mathbf{m}(\mathbf{r}, t)$ are the electric and magnetic polarizations (dipole moment per unit volume) of the medium; and ϵ_0 and μ_0 are the electric and magnetic permeabilities of vacuum, respectively. We adopt the convention of using lowercase letters to denote the time-varying functions, reserving capital letters for the amplitudes of the sinusoidal time functions. For a detailed discussion of Maxwell's equations, the reader is referred to any standard text on electromagnetic theory such as, for example, Reference [1].

Using (1.2-3) and (1.2-4) in (1.2-1) and (1.2-2) leads to

$$\nabla \times \mathbf{h} = \mathbf{i} + \frac{\partial}{\partial t} (\epsilon_0 \mathbf{e} + \mathbf{p}) \tag{1.2-5}$$

$$\nabla \times \mathbf{e} = - \frac{\partial}{\partial t} \mu_0 (\mathbf{h} + \mathbf{m}) \tag{1.2-6}$$

Taking the scalar (dot) product of (1.2-5) and $\mathbf{e}$ gives

$$\mathbf{e} \cdot \nabla \times \mathbf{h} = \mathbf{e} \cdot \mathbf{i} + \frac{\epsilon_0}{2} \frac{\partial}{\partial t} (\mathbf{e} \cdot \mathbf{e}) + \mathbf{e} \cdot \frac{\partial \mathbf{p}}{\partial t} \tag{1.2-7}$$

where we used the relation

$$\frac{1}{2} \frac{\partial}{\partial t} (\mathbf{e} \cdot \mathbf{e}) = \mathbf{e} \cdot \frac{\partial \mathbf{e}}{\partial t}$$

Next we take the scalar product of (1.2-6) and $\mathbf{h}$:

$$\mathbf{h} \cdot \nabla \times \mathbf{e} = - \frac{\mu_0}{2} \frac{\partial}{\partial t} (\mathbf{h} \cdot \mathbf{h}) - \mu_0 \mathbf{h} \cdot \frac{\partial \mathbf{m}}{\partial t} \tag{1.2-8}$$

Subtracting (1.2-8) from (1.2-7) and using the vector identity

$$\nabla \cdot (\mathbf{A} \times \mathbf{B}) = \mathbf{B} \cdot \nabla \times \mathbf{A} - \mathbf{A} \cdot \nabla \times \mathbf{B} \tag{1.2-9}$$

results in

$$-\nabla \cdot (\mathbf{e} \times \mathbf{h}) = \mathbf{e} \cdot \mathbf{i} + \frac{\partial}{\partial t}\left(\frac{\epsilon_0}{2}\mathbf{e} \cdot \mathbf{e} + \frac{\mu_0}{2}\mathbf{h} \cdot \mathbf{h}\right)$$
$$+ \mathbf{e} \cdot \frac{\partial \mathbf{p}}{\partial t} + \mu_0 \mathbf{h} \cdot \frac{\partial \mathbf{m}}{\partial t} \qquad \text{(1.2-10)}$$

We integrate the last equation over an arbitrary volume V and use the Gauss theorem [1]

$$\int_V (\nabla \cdot \mathbf{A})\, dv = \int_S \mathbf{A} \cdot \mathbf{n}\, da$$

where $\mathbf{A}$ is any vector function, $\mathbf{n}$ is the unit vector normal to the surface S enclosing V, and dv and da are the differential volume and surface elements, respectively. The result is

$$-\int_V \nabla \cdot (\mathbf{e} \times \mathbf{h})\, dv = -\int_S (\mathbf{e} \times \mathbf{h}) \cdot \mathbf{n}\, da$$
$$= \int_V \left[\mathbf{e} \cdot \mathbf{i} + \frac{\partial}{\partial t}\left(\frac{\epsilon_0}{2}\mathbf{e} \cdot \mathbf{e}\right) + \frac{\partial}{\partial t}\left(\frac{\mu_0}{2}\mathbf{h} \cdot \mathbf{h}\right) + \mathbf{e} \cdot \frac{\partial \mathbf{p}}{\partial t} + \mu_0 \mathbf{h} \cdot \frac{\partial \mathbf{m}}{\partial t}\right] dv$$
$$\text{(1.2-11)}$$

According to the conventional interpretation of electromagnetic theory, the left side of (1.2-11), that is,

$$-\int_S (\mathbf{e} \times \mathbf{h}) \cdot \mathbf{n}\, da$$

gives the total power flowing *into* the volume bounded by S. The first term on the right side is the power expended by the field on the moving charges, the sum of the second and third terms corresponds to the rate of increase of the vacuum electromagnetic stored energy $\mathcal{E}_{\text{vac}}$ where

$$\mathcal{E}_{\text{vac}} = \int_V \left[\frac{\epsilon_0}{2}\mathbf{e} \cdot \mathbf{e} + \frac{\mu_0}{2}\mathbf{h} \cdot \mathbf{h}\right] dv \qquad \text{(1.2-12)}$$

Of special interest in this book is the next-to-last term

$$\mathbf{e} \cdot \frac{\partial \mathbf{p}}{\partial t}$$

which represents the power per unit volume expended by the field *on* the electric dipoles. This power goes into an increase in the potential energy stored by the dipoles as well as to supply the dissipation that may accompany the change in $\mathbf{p}$. We will return to it again in Chapter 5, where we treat the interaction of radiation and atomic systems.

Dipolar dissipation in harmonic fields. According to the discussion in the preceding paragraph, the average power per unit volume expended by the field on the medium electric polarization is

$$\overline{\frac{\text{Power}}{\text{Volume}}} = \overline{\mathbf{e} \cdot \frac{\partial \mathbf{p}}{\partial t}} \qquad \text{(1.2-13)}$$

where the horizontal bar denotes time-averaging. Let us assume for the sake of simplicity that $\mathbf{e}(t)$ and $\mathbf{p}(t)$ are parallel to each other and take their sinusoidally varying magnitudes as

$$e(t) = \text{Re}\,[Ee^{i\omega t}] \qquad \text{(1.2-14)}$$

$$p(t) = \text{Re}\,[Pe^{i\omega t}] \qquad \text{(1.2-15)}$$

where E and P are the complex amplitudes. The electric susceptibility χ_e is defined by

$$P = \epsilon_0 \chi_e E \qquad \text{(1.2-16)}$$

and is thus a complex number. Substituting Equations (1.2-14) and (1.2-15) in (1.2-13) and using (1.2-16) gives

$$\begin{aligned}
\overline{\frac{\text{Power}}{\text{Volume}}} &= \overline{\text{Re}\,[Ee^{i\omega t}]\,\text{Re}\,[i\omega Pe^{i\omega t}]} \\
&= \tfrac{1}{2}\,\text{Re}\,[i\omega\epsilon_0\chi_e EE^*] \qquad \text{(1.2-17)} \\
&= \frac{\omega}{2}\,\epsilon_0|E|^2\,\text{Re}\,(i\chi_e)
\end{aligned}$$

where in going from the first to the second equality we used (1.1-12). Since χ_e is complex we can write it in terms of its real and imaginary parts as

$$\chi_e = \chi_e' - i\chi_e'' \qquad \text{(1.2-18)}$$

which, when used in (1.2-17), gives

$$\overline{\frac{\text{Power}}{\text{Volume}}} = \frac{\omega\epsilon_0\chi_e''}{2}\,|E|^2 \qquad \text{(1.2-19)}$$

which is the desired result.

We leave it as an exercise (Problem 1-3) to show that in anisotropic media in which the complex field components are related by

$$P_i = \epsilon_0 \sum_j \chi_{ij} E_j \qquad \text{(1.2-20)}$$

the application of (1.2-13) yields

$$\overline{\frac{\text{Power}}{\text{Volume}}} = \frac{\omega}{2}\,\epsilon_0 \sum_{i,j} \text{Re}\,(i\chi_{ij}E_i^*E_j) \qquad \text{(1.2-21)}$$

1.3 Wave Propagation in Isotropic Media

Here we consider the propagation of electromagnetic plane waves in homogeneous and isotropic media so that ϵ and μ are scalar constants. Vacuum is, of course, the best example of such a "medium". Liquids and glasses are material media that, to a first approximation, can be treated as homogeneous and isotropic.[3] We choose the direction of propagation as z and, taking the plane wave to be uniform in the x-y plane, put $\partial/\partial x = \partial/\partial y = 0$ in (1.2-1) and (1.2-2). Assuming a lossless ($\sigma = 0$) medium, Equations (1.2-1) and (1.2-2) become

$$\nabla \times \mathbf{e} = -\mu \frac{\partial \mathbf{h}}{\partial t} \qquad (1.3\text{-}1)$$

$$\nabla \times \mathbf{h} = \epsilon \frac{\partial \mathbf{e}}{\partial t} \qquad (1.3\text{-}2)$$

$$\frac{\partial e_y}{\partial z} = \mu \frac{\partial h_x}{\partial t} \qquad (1.3\text{-}3)$$

$$\frac{\partial h_y}{\partial z} = -\epsilon \frac{\partial e_x}{\partial t} \qquad (1.3\text{-}4)$$

$$\frac{\partial e_x}{\partial z} = -\mu \frac{\partial h_y}{\partial t} \qquad (1.3\text{-}5)$$

$$\frac{\partial h_x}{\partial z} = \epsilon \frac{\partial e_y}{\partial t} \qquad (1.3\text{-}6)$$

$$0 = \mu \frac{\partial h_z}{\partial t} \qquad (1.3\text{-}7)$$

$$0 = \epsilon \frac{\partial e_z}{\partial t} \qquad (1.3\text{-}8)$$

From (1.3-7) and (1.3-8) it follows that h_z and e_z are both zero; therefore, a uniform plane wave in a homogeneous isotropic medium can have no longitudinal field components. We can obtain a self-consistent set of equations from (1.3-3) through (1.3-8) by taking e_y and h_x (or e_x and h_y) to be zero.[4] In this case the last set of equations reduces to Equations (1.3-4) and (1.3-5). Taking the derivative of (1.3-5) with respect to z and

---

[3] The individual molecules making up the liquid or glass are, of course, anisotropic. This anisotropy, however, is averaged out because of the very large number of molecules with random orientations present inside a volume $\sim\lambda^3$.

[4] More fundamentally it can be easily shown from (1.3-1) and (1.3-2) (see Problem 1.4) that, for uniform plane harmonic waves, $\mathbf{e}$ and $\mathbf{h}$ are normal to each other as well as to the direction of propagation. Thus, $\mathbf{x}$ and $\mathbf{y}$ can simply be chosen to coincide with the directions of $\mathbf{e}$ and $\mathbf{h}$.

using (1.3-4), we obtain

$$\frac{\partial^2 e_x}{\partial z^2} = \mu\epsilon \frac{\partial^2 e_x}{\partial t^2} \tag{1.3-9}$$

A reversal of the procedure will yield a similar equation for h_y. Since our main interest is in harmonic (sinusoidal) time variation we postulate a solution in the form of

$$e_x^{\pm} = E_x^{\pm} e^{i(\omega t \mp kz)} \tag{1.3-10}$$

where $E_x^{\pm} \exp(\mp ikz)$ are the complex field amplitudes at z. Before substituting (1.3-10) into the wave equation (1.3-9) we may consider the nature of the two functions $e_x^{\pm}$. Taking first e_x^{+}: if an observer were to travel in such a way as to always exercise the same field value, he would have to satisfy the condition

$$\omega t - kz = \text{constant}$$

where the constant is arbitrary and determines the field value "seen" by the observer. By differentiation of the last result, it follows that the observer must travel in the $+z$ direction with a velocity

$$c = \frac{dz}{dt} = \frac{\omega}{k} \tag{1.3-11}$$

This is the *phase velocity* of the wave. If the wave were frozen in time, the separation between two neighboring field peaks—that is, the wavelength—is

$$\lambda = \frac{2\pi}{k} = 2\pi \frac{c}{\omega} \tag{1.3-12}$$

The e_x^{-} solution differs only in the sign of k, and thus, according to (1.3-11), it corresponds to a wave traveling with a phase velocity c in the $-z$ direction.

The value of c can be obtained by substituting the assumed solution (1.3-10) into (1.3-9), which results in

$$c = \frac{\omega}{k} = \frac{1}{\sqrt{\mu\epsilon}} \tag{1.3-13}$$

or

$$k = \omega\sqrt{\mu\epsilon}$$

The phase velocity in vacuum is

$$c_0 = \frac{1}{\sqrt{\mu_0\epsilon_0}} = 3 \times 10^8 \text{ m/s}$$

whereas in material media it has the value

$$c = \frac{c_0}{n}$$

where $n \equiv \sqrt{\epsilon/\epsilon_0}$ is the *index of refraction*.

Turning our attention next to the magnetic field h_y, we can express it, in a manner similar to (1.3-10), in the form of

$$h_y^\pm = H_y^\pm e^{i(\omega t \mp kz)} \tag{1.3-14}$$

Substitution of this equation into (1.3-4) and using (1.3-10) gives

$$-ikH_y^+ e^{i(\omega t - kz)} = -i\omega\epsilon E_x^+ e^{i(\omega t - kz)}$$

Therefore, from (1.3-13),

$$H_y^+ = \frac{E_x^+}{\eta} \qquad \eta = \sqrt{\frac{\mu}{\epsilon}} \tag{1.3-15}$$

In vacuum $\eta_0 = \sqrt{\mu_0/\epsilon_0} \simeq 377$ ohms. Repeating the same steps with H_y^- and E_x^- gives

$$H_y^- = -\frac{E_x^-}{\eta} \tag{1.3-16}$$

so that in the case of negative $(-z)$ traveling waves the relative phase of the electric and magnetic fields is reversed with respect to the wave traveling in the $+z$ direction. Since the wave equation (1.3-9) is a linear differential equation, we can take the solution for the harmonic case as a linear superposition of e_x^+ and e_x^-

$$e_x(z, t) = E_x^+ e^{i(\omega t - kz)} + E_x^- e^{i(\omega t + kz)} \tag{1.3-17}$$

and, similarly,

$$h_y(z, t) = \frac{1}{\eta}[E_x^+ e^{i(\omega t - kz)} - E_x^- e^{i(\omega t + kz)}]$$

where E_x^+ and E_x^- are arbitrary complex constants.

Power flow in harmonic fields. The average power per unit area— that is, the intensity (W/m^2)—carried in the direction of propagation by a uniform plane wave is given by (1.2-12) as

$$I = \overline{\mathbf{e} \times \mathbf{h}} \tag{1.3-18}$$

where the horizontal bar denotes time averaging. Since $\mathbf{e} \parallel x$ and $\mathbf{h} \parallel y$, we can write (1.3-18) as

$$I = \overline{e_x h_y}$$

Taking advantage of the harmonic nature of e_x and h_y, we use (1.3-17) and (1.1-12) to obtain

$$I = \tfrac{1}{2}\,\mathrm{Re}\,[E_x H_y^*] = \frac{1}{2\eta}\,\mathrm{Re}\,[(E_x^+ e^{-ikz} + E_x^- e^{ikz})]$$
$$\times [(E_x^+)^* e^{ikz} - (E_x^-)^* e^{-ikz}]$$
$$= \frac{|E_x^+|^2}{2\eta} - \frac{|E_x^-|^2}{2\eta} \tag{1.3-19}$$

The first term on the right side of (1.3-19) gives the intensity associated with the positive $(+z)$ traveling wave, whereas the second term represents the negative traveling wave, with the minus sign accounting for the opposite direction of power flow.

An important relation that will be used in a number of later chapters relates the intensity of the plane wave to the stored electromagnetic energy density. We start by considering the second and fourth terms on the right of (1.2-11)

$$\frac{\partial}{\partial t}\left(\frac{\epsilon_0}{2}\mathbf{e}\cdot\mathbf{e}\right) + \mathbf{e}\cdot\frac{\partial \mathbf{p}}{\partial t}$$

Using the relations

$$\mathbf{p} = \epsilon_0\chi_e\mathbf{e}$$
$$\epsilon = \epsilon_0(1 + \chi_e) \tag{1.3-20}$$

we obtain

$$\frac{\partial}{\partial t}\left(\frac{\epsilon_0}{2}\mathbf{e}\cdot\mathbf{e}\right) + \mathbf{e}\cdot\frac{\partial \mathbf{p}}{\partial t} = \frac{\partial}{\partial t}\left(\frac{\epsilon}{2}\mathbf{e}\cdot\mathbf{e}\right) \tag{1.3-21}$$

Since we assumed the medium to be lossless, the last term must represent the rate of change of electric energy density stored in the vacuum as well as in the electric dipoles; that is,

$$\frac{\mathcal{E}_{\text{electric}}}{\text{Volume}} = \frac{\epsilon}{2}\mathbf{e}\cdot\mathbf{e} \tag{1.3-22}$$

The magnetic energy density is derived in a similar fashion using the relations

$$\mathbf{m} = \chi_m\mathbf{h}$$
$$\mu = \mu_0(1 + \chi_m)$$

resulting in

$$\frac{\mathcal{E}_{\text{magnetic}}}{\text{Volume}} = \frac{\mu}{2}\mathbf{h}\cdot\mathbf{h} \tag{1.3-23}$$

Considering only the positive traveling wave in (1.3-17) we obtain from (1.3-22) and (1.3-23)

$$\frac{\overline{\mathcal{E}_{\text{magnetic}}} + \overline{\mathcal{E}_{\text{electric}}}}{\text{Volume}} = \left(\frac{\epsilon}{2}\right)\overline{(e_x^+)^2} + \left(\frac{\mu}{2}\right)\overline{(h_y^+)^2}$$

$$= \frac{\epsilon}{4}|E_x^+|^2 + \frac{\mu}{4}|H_y^+|^2$$

$$= \frac{\epsilon}{4}|E_x^+|^2 + \frac{\mu}{4}\frac{|E_x^+|^2}{\eta^2}$$

$$= \tfrac{1}{2}\epsilon|E_x^+|^2 \tag{1.3-24}$$

where the second equality is based on (1.1-12), and the third and fourth use (1.3-15). Comparing (1.3-24) to (1.3-19), we get

$$\frac{I}{\overline{\mathcal{E}}/\text{Volume}} = \frac{1}{\sqrt{\mu\epsilon}} = c \qquad (1.3\text{-}25)$$

where $\overline{\mathcal{E}} = \overline{\mathcal{E}_{\text{magnetic}}} + \overline{\mathcal{E}_{\text{electric}}}$ is the total field energy density. In terms of the electric field we get

$$I = \frac{c\epsilon|E|^2}{2} \qquad (1.3\text{-}26)$$

1.4 Wave Propagation in Crystals—The Index Ellipsoid

In the discussion of electromagnetic wave propagation up to this point, we have assumed that the medium was isotropic. This causes the induced polarization to be parallel to the electric field and to be related to it by a (scalar) factor that is independent of the direction along which the field is applied. This situation does not apply in the case of dielectric crystals. Since the crystal is made up of a regular periodic array of atoms (or ions) we may expect that the induced polarization will depend, both in its magnitude and direction, on the direction of the applied field. Instead of the simple relation (1.3-20) linking $\mathbf{p}$ and $\mathbf{e}$, we have

$$P_x = \epsilon_0(\chi_{11}E_x + \chi_{12}E_y + \chi_{13}E_z)$$
$$P_y = \epsilon_0(\chi_{21}E_x + \chi_{22}E_y + \chi_{23}E_z) \qquad (1.4\text{-}1)$$
$$P_z = \epsilon_0(\chi_{31}E_x + \chi_{32}E_y + \chi_{33}E_z)$$

where the capital letters denote the complex amplitudes of the corresponding time-harmonic quantities. The 3×3 array of the χ_{ij} coefficients is called the electric susceptibility tensor. The magnitude of the χ_{ij} coefficients depends, of course, on the choice of the x, y, and z axes relative to that of the crystal structure. It is always possible to choose x, y, and z in such a way that the off-diagonal elements vanish, leaving

$$P_x = \epsilon_0\chi_{11}E_x$$
$$P_y = \epsilon_0\chi_{22}E_y \qquad (1.4\text{-}2)$$
$$P_z = \epsilon_0\chi_{33}E_z$$

These directions are called the *principal dielectric axes of the crystal.* In this book we will use only the principal coordinate system. We can, instead of using (1.4-2), describe the dielectric response of the crystal by means of the electric permeability tensor ϵ_{ij}, defined by

$$D_x = \epsilon_{11}E_x$$
$$D_y = \epsilon_{22}E_y \qquad (1.4\text{-}3)$$
$$D_z = \epsilon_{33}E_z$$

From (1.4-2) and the relation

$$\mathbf{D} = \epsilon_0 \mathbf{E} + \mathbf{P}$$

we have

$$\epsilon_{11} = \epsilon_0(1 + \chi_{11})$$
$$\epsilon_{22} = \epsilon_0(1 + \chi_{22}) \qquad \text{(1.4-4)}$$
$$\epsilon_{33} = \epsilon_0(1 + \chi_{33})$$

Birefringence. One of the most important consequences of the dielectric anisotropy of crystals is the phenomenon of birefringence in which the phase velocity of an optical beam propagating in the crystal depends on the direction of polarization of its **e** vector. Before treating this problem mathematically we may pause and ponder its physical origin. In an isotropic medium the induced polarization is independent of the field direction so that $\chi_{11} = \chi_{22} = \chi_{33}$ and, using (1.4-4), $\epsilon_{11} = \epsilon_{22} = \epsilon_{33} = \epsilon$. Since $c = (\mu\epsilon)^{-1/2}$, the phase velocity is independent of the direction of polarization. In an anisotropic medium the situation is different. Consider, for example, a wave propagating along z. If its electric field is parallel to x, it will induce, according to (1.4-2), only P_x and will consequently "see" an electric permeability ϵ_{11}. Its phase velocity will thus be $c_x = (\mu\epsilon_{11})^{-1/2}$. If, on the other hand, the wave is polarized parallel to y it will propagate with a phase velocity $c_y = (\mu\epsilon_{22})^{-1/2}$.

Birefringence has some interesting consequences. Consider, as an example, a wave propagating along the crystal z direction and having at some plane, say $z = 0$, a linearly polarized field with equal components along x and y. Since $k_x \neq k_y$, as the wave propagates into the crystal the x and y components get out of phase and the wave becomes elliptically polarized. This phenomenon is discussed in detail in Section 9.2 and forms the basis of the electrooptic modulation of light.

Returning to the example of a wave propagating along the crystal z direction, let us assume, as in Section 1.3, that the only nonvanishing field components are e_x and h_y. Maxwell's curl equations (1.3-4) and (1.3-6) reduce, in a self-consistent manner, to

$$\frac{\partial e_x}{\partial z} = -\mu \frac{\partial h_y}{\partial t}$$

$$\frac{\partial h_y}{\partial z} = -\epsilon_{11} \frac{\partial e_x}{\partial t} \qquad \text{(1.4-5)}$$

Taking the derivative of the first of Equations (1.4-5) with respect to z and then substituting the second equation for $\partial h_y/\partial z$ gives

$$\frac{\partial^2 e_x}{\partial z^2} = \mu\epsilon_{11} \frac{\partial^2 e_x}{\partial t^2} \qquad \text{(1.4-6)}$$

If we postulate, as in (1.3-10), a solution in the form

$$e_x = E_x e^{i(\omega t - k_z z)} \qquad\qquad \text{(1.4-7)}$$

then Equation (1.4-6) becomes

$$k_x{}^2 E_x = \omega^2 \mu \epsilon_{11} E_x$$

Therefore, the propagation constant of a wave polarized along x and traveling along z is

$$k_x = \omega \sqrt{\mu \epsilon_{11}} \qquad\qquad \text{(1.4-8)}$$

Repeating the derivation but with a wave polarized along the y axis, instead of the x axis, yields $k_y = \omega \sqrt{\mu \epsilon_{22}}$.

The index ellipsoid.   As shown above, in a crystal the phase velocity of a wave propagating along a given direction depends on the direction of its polarization. For propagation along z, as an example, we found that Maxwell's equations admitted two solutions: one with its linear polarizations along x and the second along y. If we consider the propagation along some arbitrary direction in the crystal the problem becomes more difficult. We have to determine the directions of polarization of the two allowed waves, as well as their phase velocities. This is done most conveniently using the so-called index ellipsoid

$$\frac{x^2}{(\epsilon_{11}/\epsilon_0)} + \frac{y^2}{(\epsilon_{22}/\epsilon_0)} + \frac{z^2}{(\epsilon_{33}/\epsilon_0)} = 1 \qquad\qquad \text{(1.4-9)}$$

This is the equation of a generalized ellipsoid with major axes parallel to x, y, and z whose respective lengths are $2\sqrt{\epsilon_{11}/\epsilon_0}$, $2\sqrt{\epsilon_{22}/\epsilon_0}$, and $2\sqrt{\epsilon_{33}/\epsilon_0}$. The procedure for finding the polarization directions and the corresponding phase velocities for a *given* direction of propagation is as follows: Determine the ellipse formed by the intersection of a plane through the origin and normal to the direction of propagation and the index ellipsoid (1.4-9). The directions of the major and minor axes of this ellipse are those of the two allowed polarizations[5] and the lengths of these axes are $2n_1$ and $2n_2$, where n_1 and n_2 are the indices of the refraction of the two allowed solutions. The two waves propagate, thus, with phase velocities c_0/n_1 and c_0/n_2, respectively, where $c_0 = (\mu_0 \epsilon_0)^{-1/2}$ is the phase velocity in vacuum. A formal proof of this procedure is given in References [2] and [3].

To illustrate the use of the index ellipsoid, consider the case of a uniaxial crystal (that is, a crystal which possesses a single axis of threefold, fourfold, or sixfold symmetry). Taking the direction of this axis as z,

---

[5] These are actually the directions of the **D**, not of the **E**, vectors. In a crystal these two are separated, in general, by a small angle; see References [2] and [3].

symmetry considerations[6] dictate that $\epsilon_{11} = \epsilon_{22}$. Defining the principal indices of refraction n_o and n_e by

$$n_o{}^2 \equiv \frac{\epsilon_{11}}{\epsilon_0} = \frac{\epsilon_{22}}{\epsilon_0} \qquad n_e{}^2 \equiv \frac{\epsilon_{33}}{\epsilon_0} \qquad \textbf{(1.4-10)}$$

the equation of the index ellipsoid (1.4-9) becomes

$$\frac{x^2}{n_o{}^2} + \frac{y^2}{n_o{}^2} + \frac{z^2}{n_e{}^2} \qquad \textbf{(1.4-11)}$$

This is an ellipsoid of revolution with the circular symmetry axis parallel to z. The z major axis of the ellipsoid is of length $2n_e$, whereas that of the x and y axes is $2n_o$. The procedure of using the index ellipsoid is illustrated by Figure 1-1.

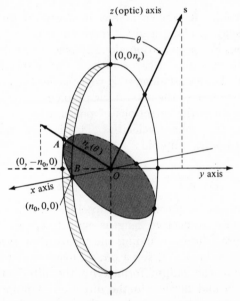

Figure 1-1   Construction for finding indices of refraction and allowed polarization for a given direction of propagation **s**. The figure shown is for a uniaxial crystal with $n_x = n_y = n_o$.

The direction of propagation is along **s** and is at an angle θ to the (optic) z axis. Because of the circular symmetry of (1.4-11) about z we can choose, without any loss of generality, the y axis to coincide with the projection of **s** on the x-y plane. The intersection ellipse of the plane normal to **s** with the ellipsoid is crosshatched in the figure. The two allowed polarization directions are parallel to the axes of the ellipse and thus

[6] See, for example, J. F. Nye, *Physical Properties of Crystals* (Oxford University Press, New York, 1957).

correspond to the line segments OA and OB. They are consequently perpendicular to **s** as well as to each other. The two waves polarized along these directions have, respectively, indices of refraction given by $n_e(\theta) = |OA|$ and $n_o = |OB|$. The first of these two waves, which is polarized along OA, is called the *extraordinary wave*. Its direction of polarization varies with θ following the intersection point A. Its index of refraction is given by the length of OA. It can be determined using Figure 1-2, which shows the intersection of the index ellipsoid with the y-z plane.

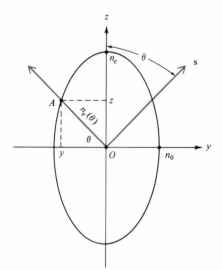

Figure 1-2   Intersection of the index ellipsoid with the z-y plane. $|OA| = n_e(\theta)$ is the index of refraction of the extraordinary wave propagating in the direction **s**.

Using the relations

$$n_e{}^2(\theta) = z^2 + y^2$$

$$\frac{z}{n_e(\theta)} = \sin\theta$$

and the equation of the ellipse

$$\frac{y^2}{n_o{}^2} + \frac{z^2}{n_e{}^2} = 1$$

we obtain

$$\frac{1}{n_e{}^2(\theta)} = \frac{\cos^2\theta}{n_o{}^2} + \frac{\sin^2\theta}{n_e{}^2} \qquad \textbf{(1.4-12)}$$

Thus, for $\theta = 0°$, $n_e(0°) = n_o$ and for $\theta = 90°$, $n_e(90°) = n_e$.

The ordinary wave remains, according to Figure 1-1, polarized along the same direction OB independent of θ. It has an index of refraction n_o. The amount of birefringence $n_e(\theta) - n_o$ thus varies from zero for $\theta = 0°$ (that is, propagation along the optic axis) to $n_e - n_o$ for $\theta = 90°$.

The normal (index) surfaces.   Consider the surface in which the distance of a given point from the origin is equal to the index of refraction of a wave propagating along this direction. The surface is called the normal (index) surface. The normal surface of the ordinary wave is a sphere, since the index of refraction is n_o and is independent of the direction of propagation. The normal surface of the extraordinary wave is an ellipsoid. In a uniaxial crystal it becomes an ellipsoid of revolution about the optic (z) axis in which the distance $n_e(\theta)$ to the origin is given by (1.4-12). The intersection of the normal surfaces of a positive ($n_e > n_o$) uniaxial crystal with the **s-z** plane is shown in Figure 1-3.

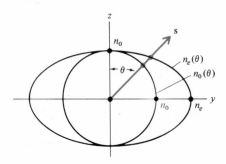

Figure 1-3   Intersection of s-z plane with normal surfaces of a positive uniaxial crystal ($n_e > n_o$).

■ **PROBLEMS**

1-1   Consider the problem of finding the time average

$$\overline{a^2(t)} = \frac{1}{T} \int_0^T a^2(t)\, dt$$

of

$$a(t) = |A_1| \cos(\omega_1 t + \phi_1) + |A_2| \cos(\omega_2 t + \phi_2)$$
$$= \mathrm{Re}\,[V_a(t)]$$

where

$$V_a(t) = A_1 e^{i\omega_1 t} + A_2 e^{i\omega_2 t}$$

and $A_{1,2} = |A_{1,2}|e^{i\phi_{1,2}}$. $Va(t)$ is called the *analytic signal* of $a(t)$. Assume that $(\omega_1 - \omega_2) \ll \omega_1$ and integrate over a time T, which is long compared to the period $2\pi/\omega_{1,2}$ but short compared to the beat period $2\pi/(\omega_1 - \omega_2)$.[7] Show that

$$\overline{a^2(t)} = \tfrac{1}{2}[V_a(t)V_a^*(t)]$$

---

[7] When this condition is fulfilled, $a(t)$ consists of a sinusoidal function with a "slowly" varying amplitude and is often called a quasi-sinusoid.

1-2 Show how we can use the analytic functions as defined by Problem 1-1 to find the time average

$$\overline{a(t)b(t)} = \frac{1}{T}\int_0^T a(t)b(t)\,dt$$

where $a(t)$ is the same as in Problem 1-1, and the analytic function of $b(t)$ is

$$V_b(t) = [A_3 e^{i\omega_3 t} + A_4 e^{i\omega_4 t}]$$

so that $b(t) = \mathrm{Re}\,[V_b(t)]$. Assume that the difference between any two of the frequencies ω_1, ω_2, ω_3, and ω_4 is small compared to the frequencies themselves. *Answer:* $\overline{a(t)b(t)} = \frac{1}{2}\,\mathrm{Re}\,[V_a(t)V_b^*(t)]$.

1-3 Derive Equation (1.2-21).

1-4 Starting with Maxwell's curl equations [(1.2-1), (1.2-2)] and taking $\mathbf{i} = 0$, show that in the case of a harmonic (sinusoidal) uniform plane wave the field vectors $\mathbf{e}$ and $\mathbf{h}$ are normal to each other as well as to the direction of propagation. *Hint:* Assume the wave to have the form $e^{i(\omega t - \mathbf{k}\cdot\mathbf{r})}$ and show by actual differentiation that we can formally replace the operator ∇ in Maxwell's equations by $-i\mathbf{k}$.

1-5 Derive Equation (1.3-19).

1-6 A linearly polarized electromagnetic wave is incident normally at $z = 0$ on the x-y face of a crystal so that it propagates along its z axis. The crystal electric permeability tensor referred to x, y, and z is diagonal with elements ϵ_{11}, ϵ_{22}, and ϵ_{33}. If the wave is polarized initially so that it has equal components along x and y, what is the state of its polarization at the plane z, where

$$(k_x - k_y)z = \frac{\pi}{2}$$

Plot the position of the electric field vector in this plane at times $t = 0$, $\pi/6\omega$, $\pi/3\omega$, $\pi/2\omega$, $2\pi/3\omega$, $5\pi/6\omega$.

■ **REFERENCES**

[1] Ramo, S., J. R. Whinnery, and T. Van Duzer, *Fields and Waves in Communication Electronics*. New York: Wiley, 1965.

[2] Born, M., and E. Wolf, *Principles of Optics*. New York: Macmillan, 1964.

[3] Yariv, A., *Quantum Electronics*. New York: Wiley, 1967, p. 295.

2

The Propagation of Rays and Spherical Waves

2.0 Introduction

In this chapter we take up the subject of optical ray propagation through a variety of optical media. These include homogeneous and isotropic materials, thin lenses, dielectric interfaces, and curved mirrors. Since a ray is, by definition, normal to the optical wavefront, an understanding of the ray behavior makes it possible to trace the evolution of optical waves when they are passing through various optical elements. We find that the passage of a ray (or its reflection) through these elements can be described by simple 2×2 matrices. Furthermore, these matrices will be found to describe the propagation of spherical waves and, in the next chapter, of Gaussian beams such as those which are characteristic of the output of lasers.

2.1 The Lens Waveguide

Consider a paraxial ray[1] passing through a thin lens of focal length f as shown in Figure 2-1. Taking the cylindrical axis of symmetry as z, denoting the ray distance from the axis by r and its slope dr/dz as r', we can relate the

---

[1] By paraxial ray we mean a ray whose angular deviation from the cylindrical (z) axis is small enough that the sine and tangent of the angle can be approximated by the angle itself.

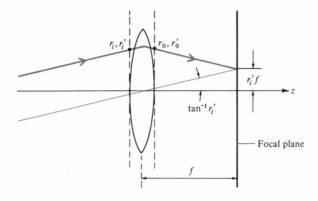

Figure 2-1   Deflection of a ray by a thin lens.

output ray (r_{out}, r'_{out}) to the input ray (r_{in}, r'_{in}) by means of

$$r_{out} = r_{in}$$
$$r'_{out} = r'_{in} - \frac{r_{out}}{f} \qquad \text{(2.1-1)}$$

where the first of Equations (2.1-1) follows from the definition of a thin lens and the second can be derived from a consideration of the behavior of the undeflected central ray with a slope equal to r'_{in}, as shown in Figure 2-1.

Representing a ray at any position z as a column matrix

$$\mathbf{r}(z) = \begin{vmatrix} r(z) \\ r'(z) \end{vmatrix}$$

we can rewrite (2.1-1) using the rules for matrix multiplication (see References [1]–[3]) as

$$\begin{vmatrix} r_{out} \\ r'_{out} \end{vmatrix} = \begin{vmatrix} 1 & 0 \\ -1/f & 1 \end{vmatrix} \begin{vmatrix} r_{in} \\ r'_{in} \end{vmatrix} \qquad \text{(2.1-2)}$$

where $f > 0$ for a converging lens and is negative for a diverging one.

The ray matrices for a number of other optical elements are shown in Table 2-1.

Consider as an example the propagation of a ray through a straight section of a homogeneous medium of length d followed by a thin lens of focal length f. This corresponds to propagation between planes n and $n + 1$ in Figure 2-2. Since the effect of the straight section is merely that of increasing r by dr', using (2.1-1) we can relate the output (at $n + 1$) and input (at n) rays by:

$$\begin{vmatrix} r_{out} \\ r'_{out} \end{vmatrix} = \begin{vmatrix} 1 & d \\ -1/f & (1 - d/f) \end{vmatrix} \begin{vmatrix} r_{in} \\ r'_{in} \end{vmatrix} \qquad \text{(2.1-3)}$$

Notice also that the matrix corresponds to the product of the thin lens matrix times the straight section matrix as given in Table 2-1.

Table 2-1 RAY MATRICES FOR SOME COMMON OPTICAL
ELEMENTS AND MEDIA

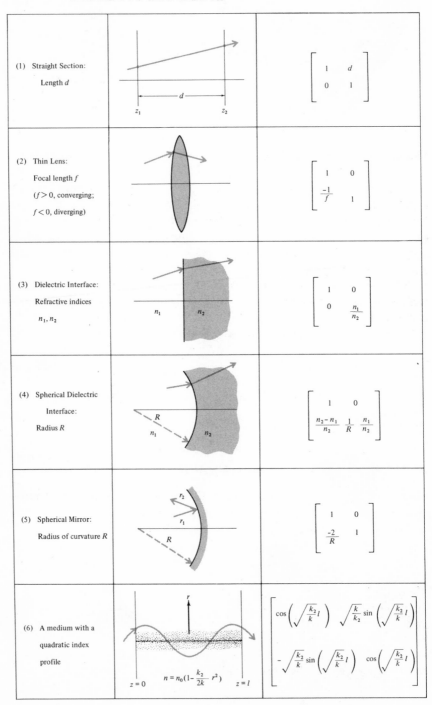

(1) Straight Section: Length d		$\begin{bmatrix} 1 & d \\ 0 & 1 \end{bmatrix}$
(2) Thin Lens: Focal length f ($f > 0$, converging; $f < 0$, diverging)		$\begin{bmatrix} 1 & 0 \\ \frac{-1}{f} & 1 \end{bmatrix}$
(3) Dielectric Interface: Refractive indices n_1, n_2		$\begin{bmatrix} 1 & 0 \\ 0 & \frac{n_1}{n_2} \end{bmatrix}$
(4) Spherical Dielectric Interface: Radius R		$\begin{bmatrix} 1 & 0 \\ \frac{n_2-n_1}{n_2}\frac{1}{R} & \frac{n_1}{n_2} \end{bmatrix}$
(5) Spherical Mirror: Radius of curvature R		$\begin{bmatrix} 1 & 0 \\ \frac{-2}{R} & 1 \end{bmatrix}$
(6) A medium with a quadratic index profile	$n = n_0(1 - \frac{k_2}{2k}r^2)$	$\begin{bmatrix} \cos\left(\sqrt{\frac{k_2}{k}}\,l\right) & \sqrt{\frac{k}{k_2}}\sin\left(\sqrt{\frac{k_2}{k}}\,l\right) \\ -\sqrt{\frac{k_2}{k}}\sin\left(\sqrt{\frac{k_2}{k}}\,l\right) & \cos\left(\sqrt{\frac{k_2}{k}}\,l\right) \end{bmatrix}$

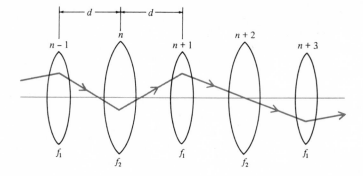

Figure 2-2 Propagation of an optical ray through a biperiodic lens sequence.

We are now in a position to consider the propagation of a ray through a biperiodic lens system made up of lenses of focal lengths f_1 and f_2 separated by d as shown in Figure 2.2. This will be shown in the next chapter to be formally equivalent to the problem of Gaussian-beam propagation inside an optical resonator with mirrors of radii $R_1 = 2f_1$ and $R_2 = 2f_2$ which are separated by d.

The section between the planes n and $n + 2$ can be considered as the basic unit cell of the periodic lens sequence. If we limit ourselves, at the moment, to planes n, $n + 2$, $n + 4$, ..., and denote them as planes s, $s + 1$, $s + 2$, ... (so that $\Delta s = 2\Delta n$), from (2.1-3) we have

$$\begin{vmatrix} r_{s+1} \\ r'_{s+1} \end{vmatrix} = \begin{vmatrix} 1 & d \\ -\dfrac{1}{f_1} & \left(1 - \dfrac{d}{f_1}\right) \end{vmatrix} \begin{vmatrix} 1 & d \\ -\dfrac{1}{f_2} & \left(1 - \dfrac{d}{f_2}\right) \end{vmatrix} \begin{vmatrix} r_s \\ r'_s \end{vmatrix} \qquad \textbf{(2.1-4)}$$

or, in equation form,

$$r_{s+1} = A r_s + B r'_s$$
$$r'_{s+1} = C r_s + D r'_s \qquad \textbf{(2.1-5)}$$

where A, B, C, and D are the elements of the matrix resulting from multiplying the two square matrices in (2.1-4) and are given by

$$A = 1 - \frac{d}{f_2}$$

$$B = d\left(2 - \frac{d}{f_2}\right)$$

$$C = -\left[\frac{1}{f_1} + \frac{1}{f_2}\left(1 - \frac{d}{f_1}\right)\right] \qquad \textbf{(2.1-6)}$$

$$D = -\left[\frac{d}{f_1} - \left(1 - \frac{d}{f_1}\right)\left(1 - \frac{d}{f_2}\right)\right]$$

From the first of (2.1-5) we get

$$r'_s = \frac{1}{B}(r_{s+1} - Ar_s)$$ (2.1-7)

and thus

$$r'_{s+1} = \frac{1}{B}(r_{s+2} - Ar_{s+1})$$ (2.1-8)

Using the second of (2.1-5) in (2.1-8) and substituting for r'_s from (2.1-7) gives

$$r_{s+2} - (A + D)r_{s+1} + (AD - BC)r_s = 0$$ (2.1-9)

for the difference equation governing the evolution through the lens waveguide. Using (2.1-6) we can show that $AD - BC = 1$. We can consequently rewrite (2.1-9) as

$$r_{s+2} - 2br_{s+1} + r_s = 0$$ (2.1-10)

where

$$b = \tfrac{1}{2}(A + D) = \left(1 - \frac{d}{f_2} - \frac{d}{f_1} + \frac{d^2}{2f_1f_2}\right)$$ (2.1-11)

Equation (2.1-10) is the equivalent, in terms of difference equations, of the differential equation $r'' + Ar = 0$, whose solution is $r(z) = r(0)\exp[\pm i\sqrt{A}z]$. We are thus led to try a solution in the form of

$$r_s = r_0 e^{isq}$$

which, when substituted in (2.1-10), leads to

$$e^{2iq} - 2be^{iq} + 1 = 0$$ (2.1-12)

and therefore

$$e^{iq} = b \pm i\sqrt{1 - b^2} = e^{\pm i\theta}$$ (2.1-13)

where $\cos\theta = b$.

The general solution can be taken as a linear superposition of $\exp(is\theta)$ and $\exp(-is\theta)$ solutions or equivalently as

$$r_s = r_{\max}\sin(s\theta + \alpha)$$ (2.1-14)

where $r_{\max} = r_0/\sin\alpha$ and α can be expressed using (2.1-8) in terms of r_0 and r'_0.

The condition for a stable—that is, confined—ray is that θ be a real number, since in this case the ray radius r_s oscillates as a function of the cell number s between $r_{\max}$ and $-r_{\max}$. According to (2.1-13), the necessary and sufficient condition for θ to be real is that [5]

$$|b| \leqslant 1$$ (2.1-15)

In terms of the system parameters we can use (2.1-11) to reexpress (2.1-15) as

$$-1 \leqslant 1 - \frac{d}{f_2} - \frac{d}{f_1} + \frac{d^2}{2f_1 f_2} \leqslant 1$$

or   **(2.1-16)**

$$0 \leqslant \left(1 - \frac{d}{2f_1}\right)\left(1 - \frac{d}{2f_2}\right) \leqslant 1$$

If, on the other hand, the stability condition $|b| \leqslant 1$ is violated, we obtain, according to (2.1-10), a solution in the form of

$$r_s = Ae^{(\alpha_+)s} + Be^{(\alpha_-)s} \qquad\qquad \textbf{(2.1-17)}$$

where $e^{\alpha\pm} = b \pm \sqrt{b^2 - 1}$ and since the magnitude of either $\exp(\alpha_+)$ or $\exp(\alpha_-)$ exceeds unity, the beam radius will increase as a function of (distance) s.

The identical-lens waveguide.   The simplest case of a lens waveguide is one in which $f_1 = f_2 = f$; that is, all the lenses are identical.

The analysis of this situation is considerably simpler than that used for a biperiodic lens sequence. The reason is that the periodic unit cell (the smallest part of the sequence that can, upon translation, recreate the whole sequence) contains a single lens only. The (A, B, C, D) matrix for the unit cell is given by the square matrix in (2.1-3). Following exactly the steps leading to (2.1-11) through (2.1-14), the stability condition becomes

$$0 \leqslant d \leqslant 4f \qquad\qquad \textbf{(2.1-18)}$$

and the beam radius at the nth lens is given by

$$r_n = r_{\max} \sin(n\theta + \alpha)$$

$$\cos\theta = \left(1 - \frac{d}{2f}\right) \qquad\qquad \textbf{(2.1-19)}$$

Because of the algebraic simplicity of this problem we can easily express $r_{\max}$ and α in (2.1-19) in terms of the initial conditions r_0 and r_0', obtaining

$$(r_{\max})^2 = \frac{4f}{4f - d}\left(r_0{}^2 + dr_0 r_0' + df r_0'{}^2\right) \qquad\qquad \textbf{(2.1-20)}$$

$$\tan\alpha = \sqrt{\frac{4f}{d} - 1} \bigg/ \left(1 + 2f\frac{r_0'}{r_0}\right) \qquad\qquad \textbf{(2.1-21)}$$

where n corresponds to the plane immediately to the right of the nth lens. The derivation of the last two equations is left as an exercise.

The stability criteria can be demonstrated experimentally by tracing the behavior of a laser beam as it propagates down a sequence of lenses spaced uniformly. One can easily notice the rapid "escape" of the beam once condition (2.1-18) is violated.

2.2   The Propagation of Rays between Mirrors [6]

Another important application of the formalism just developed concerns the bouncing of a ray between two curved mirrors. Since the reflection at a mirror with a radius of curvature R is equivalent, except for the folding of the path, to passage through a lens with a focal length $f = R/2$, we can use the formalism of the preceding section to describe the propagation of a ray between two curved reflectors with radii of curvature R_1 and R_2, which are separated by d. Let us consider the simple case of a ray which is injected into a symmetric two-mirror system as shown in Figure 2-3(a). Since the x and y coordinates of the ray are independent variables, we can take them according to (2.1-19) in the form of

$$x_n = x_{\max} \sin{(n\theta + \alpha_x)}$$
$$y_n = y_{\max} \sin{(n\theta + \alpha_y)} \tag{2.2-1}$$

where n refers to the ray parameter immediately following the nth reflection. According to (2.2-1), the locus of the points x_n, y_n on a given mirror lies on an ellipse.

Reentrant rays.   If θ in (2.2-1) satisfies the condition

$$2\nu\theta = 2l\pi \tag{2.2-2}$$

where ν and l are any two integers, a ray will return to its starting point following ν round trips and will thus continuously retrace the same pattern on the mirrors. If we consider as an example the simple case of $l = 1$, $\nu = 2$, so that $\theta = \pi/2$, from (2.1-19) we obtain $d = 2f = R$; that is, if the mirrors are separated by a distance equal to their radius of curvature R, the trapped ray will retrace its pattern after two round trips ($\nu = 2$). This situation ($R = d$) is referred to as symmetric confocal, since the two mirrors have a common focal point $f = R/2$. It will be discussed in detail in the next chapter. The ray pattern corresponding to $\nu = 2$ is illustrated in Figure 2-3(b).

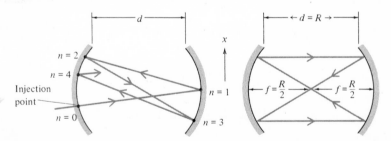

Figure 2-3   (a) Path of a ray injected in plane of figure into the space between two mirrors. (b) Reentrant ray in confocal ($d = R$) mirror configuration repeating its pattern after two round trips.

2.3 Rays in Lenslike Media [7]

The basic physical property of lenses that is responsible for their focusing action is the fact that the optical path across them $\int n(r, z)\, dz$ (where n is the index of refraction of the medium) is a quadratic function of the distance r from the z axis. Using ray optics, we account for this fact by a change in the ray's slope as in (2.1-1). This same property can be represented by relating the complex field amplitude of the incident optical field $E_R(x, y)$ immediately to the right of an ideal thin lens to that immediately to the left $E_L(x, y)$ by

$$E_R(x, y) = E_L(x, y) \exp\left[+ik\,\frac{x^2 + y^2}{2f}\right] \qquad \text{(2.3-1)}$$

where f is the focal length and $k = 2\pi n/\lambda_0$.

The effect of the lens, therefore, is to cause a phase shift $k(x^2 + y^2)/2f$, which increases quadratically with the distance from the axis. We consider next the closely related case of a medium whose index of refraction n varies according to[2]

$$n(x, y) = n_o\left[1 - \frac{k_2}{2k}\,(x^2 + y^2)\right] \qquad \text{(2.3-2)}$$

where k_2 is a constant. Since the phase delay of a wave propagating through a section dz of a medium with an index of refraction n is $(2\pi\,dz/\lambda_0)n$ it follows directly that a thin slab of the medium described by (2.3-2) will act as a thin lens, introducing [as in (2.3-1)] a phase shift proportional to $(x^2 + y^2)$. The behavior of a ray in this case is described by the differential equation that applies to ray propagation in an optically inhomogeneous medium [8],

$$\frac{d}{ds}\left(n\,\frac{d\mathbf{r}}{ds}\right) = \nabla n \qquad \text{(2.3-3)}$$

where s is the distance along the ray measured from some fixed position on it and $\mathbf{r}$ is the position vector of the point at s. For paraxial rays we may replace d/ds by d/dz and, using (2.3-2), obtain

$$\frac{d^2r}{dz^2} + \left(\frac{k_2}{k}\right)r = 0 \qquad \text{(2.3-4)}$$

If at the input plane $z = 0$ the ray has a radius r_0 and slope r_0', we can write the solution of (2.3-4) directly as

$$r(z) = \cos\left(\sqrt{\frac{k_2}{k}}\,z\right)r_0 + \sqrt{\frac{k}{k_2}}\,\sin\left(\sqrt{\frac{k_2}{k}}\,z\right)r_0'$$

$$r'(z) = -\sqrt{\frac{k_2}{k}}\,\sin\left(\sqrt{\frac{k_2}{k}}\,z\right)r_0 + \cos\left(\sqrt{\frac{k_2}{k}}\,z\right)r_0' \qquad \text{(2.3-5)}$$

---

[2] Equation (2.3-2) can be viewed as consisting of the first two terms in the Taylor-series expansion of $n(x, y)$ for the radial symmetric case.

That is, the ray oscillates back and forth across the axis, as shown in Figure 2-4. A section of the quadratic index medium acts as a lens. This can be proved by showing, using (2.3-5), that a family of parallel rays entering at $z = 0$ at different radii will converge upon emerging at $z = l$ to a common focus at a distance

$$h = \frac{1}{n_0} \sqrt{\frac{k}{k_2}} \cot\left(\sqrt{\frac{k_2}{k}}\, l\right)$$ (2.3-6)

from the exit plane. The factor n_0 accounts for the refraction at the boundary, assuming the medium at $z > l$ to possess an index $n = 1$ and a small angle of incidence. The derivation of (2.3-6) is left as an exercise.

Equations (2.3-5) apply to a focusing medium with $k_2 > 0$. In a medium where $k_2 < 0$—that is, where the index increases with the distance from the axis—the solutions for $r(z)$ and $r'(z)$ become

$$r(z) = \cosh\left(\sqrt{\frac{k_2}{k}}\, z\right) r_0 + \sqrt{\frac{k}{k_2}} \sinh\left(\sqrt{\frac{k_2}{k}}\, z\right) r'_0$$

$$r'(z) = \sqrt{\frac{k_2}{k}} \sinh\left(\sqrt{\frac{k_2}{k}}\, z\right) r_0 + \cosh\left(\sqrt{\frac{k_2}{k}}\, z\right) r'_0$$ (2.3-7)

so that $r(z)$ increases with distance and eventually escapes. A section of such a medium acts as a negative lens.

Physical situations giving rise to quadratic index variation include:

1.   Propagation of laser beams with Gaussian-like intensity profile in a slightly absorbing medium. The absorption heating gives rise, because of the dependence of n on the temperature T, to an index profile [9]. If $dn/dT < 0$, as is the case for most materials, the index is smallest on the axis where the absorption heating is highest. This corresponds to a $k_2 < 0$ in (2.3-2) and the beam spreads with the distance z. If $dn/dT > 0$, as in certain lead glasses [10], the beams are focused.

2.   The absorption of pump light in solid laser rods, such as ruby, gives rise to an $n(r)$ that decreases with r (for $dn/dT < 0$) and hence causes pumped laser rods to act as lenses.

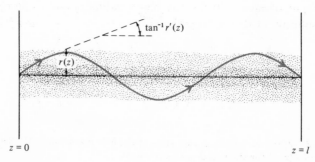

Figure 2-4   Path of a ray in a medium with a quadratic index variation.

3.   Dielectric waveguides made by sandwiching a layer of index n_1 between two layers with index $n_2 > n_1$. This situation will be discussed further in connection with injection lasers in Chapter 7.

4.   Optical fibers produced by cladding a thin optical fiber (whose radius is comparable to λ) of an index n_1 with a sheath of index $n_2 < n_1$. Such fibers are used as light pipes.

5.   Optical waveguides consisting of glasslike rods or filaments, with radii large compared to λ, whose index decreases with increasing r. Such waveguides can be used for the simultaneous transmission of a number of laser beams, which are injected into the waveguide at different angles. It follows from (2.3-5) that the beams will emerge, each along a unique direction, and consequently can be easily separated. Furthermore, in view of its previously discussed lens properties, the waveguide can be used to transmit optical image information in much the same way as images are transmitted by a multielement lens system to the image plane of a camera.

2.4 Propagation of Spherical Waves [7]

In this section we derive the simple laws governing the propagation of spherical wavefronts in the geometrical optics approximation. These relations will be compared in the next chapter with those that apply to the propagation of Gaussian beams.

Consider the spherical wave shown in Figure 2-5. If propagation is from z_1 to z_2, the radius of curvature increases from R_1 to R_2 or by $z_2 - z_1$. The evolution of R is thus given by

$$R(z_2) = R(z_1) + (z_2 - z_1) \tag{2.4-1}$$

The convention regarding the sign of R is that $R(z) > 0$ when the center of curvature of the phase front at z occurs at $z' < z$, as is the case in Figure 2-5.

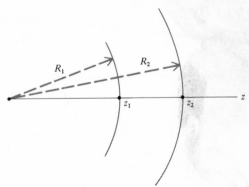

Figure 2-5   Spherical wavefronts emerging from a point source.

Considering next the passage of a spherical beam through a lens or lenslike medium, we take advantage of the relationship

$$R(z) = \frac{r(z)}{r'(z)} \tag{2.4-2}$$

between the ray (defined as the normal to the phase front) parameters and the radius of curvature of a spherical wave and use the ray transformation law (2.1-2)

$$\begin{vmatrix} r_2 \\ r_2' \end{vmatrix} = \begin{vmatrix} A & B \\ C & D \end{vmatrix} \begin{vmatrix} r_1 \\ r_1' \end{vmatrix}$$

to obtain

$$R_2 = \frac{A R_1 + B}{C R_1 + D} \tag{2.4-3}$$

Equation (2.4-3) is of major importance. It tells us that if the elements A, B, C, and D that relate the rays at two different planes are known, they can be used as in (2.4-3) to find the change in the radius of curvature of a spherical wave between these two planes. Relation (2.4-3) will be found, in the next chapter, to hold in the case of Gaussian beams as well. As an example, if we use the matrix

$$\begin{vmatrix} A & B \\ C & D \end{vmatrix} = \begin{vmatrix} 1 & z_2 - z_1 \\ 0 & 1 \end{vmatrix}$$

governing the propagation of rays through a homogeneous section occupying $z_1 \leqslant z \leqslant z_2$, we obtain (2.4-1). If, on the other hand, we use (2.1-2) for the propagation of a ray through a thin lens, we obtain

$$\frac{1}{R_2} = \frac{1}{R_1} - \frac{1}{f} \tag{2.4-4}$$

where R_1 is the radius of curvature of the incoming wave, while R_2 is that of the outgoing one.

■ PROBLEMS

2-1   Derive Equations (2.1-19) through (2.1-21).

2-2   Show that the eigenvalues λ of the equation

$$\begin{vmatrix} A & B \\ C & D \end{vmatrix} \begin{vmatrix} r_s \\ r_s' \end{vmatrix} = \lambda \begin{vmatrix} r_s \\ r_s' \end{vmatrix}$$

are $\lambda = e^{\pm i\theta}$ with $\exp(\pm i\theta)$ given by (2.1-12). Note that, according to (2.1-5), the foregoing matrix equation can also be written as

$$\begin{vmatrix} r_{s+1} \\ r_{s+1}' \end{vmatrix} = \lambda \begin{vmatrix} r_s \\ r_s' \end{vmatrix}$$

2-3 Derive Equation (2.3-6).

2-4 Make a plausibility argument to justify (2.3-1) by showing that it holds for a plane wave incident on a lens.

2-5 Show that a lenslike medium occupying the region $0 \leqslant z \leqslant l$ will image a point on the axis at $z < 0$ onto a single point. (If the image point occurs at $z < l$, the image is virtual.)

2-6 Derive the ray matrices of Table 2-1.

■ REFERENCES

[1] Pierce, J. R., *Theory and Design of Electron Beams*, 2d Ed. Princeton, N.J.: Van Nostrand, 1954, Chap. 11.

[2] Ramo, S., J. R. Whinnery, and T. Van Duzer, *Fields and Waves in Communication Electronics*. New York: Wiley, 1965, p. 576.

[3] Yariv, A., *Quantum Electronics*. New York: Wiley, 1957, p. 230.

[4] Siegman, A. E., *An Introduction to Lasers and Masers*. New York: McGraw-Hill, 1968.

[5] Kogelnik, H., and T. Li, "Laser beams and resonators," *Proc. IEEE*, vol. 54, p. 1312, 1966.

[6] Herriot, D., H. Kogelnik, and R. Kompfner, "Off-axis paths in spherical mirror interferometers," *Appl. Opt.*, vol. 3, p. 523, 1964.

[7] Kogelnik, H., "On the propagation of Gaussian beams of light through lenslike media including those with a loss and gain variation," *Appl. Opt.*, vol. 4, p. 1562, 1965.

[8] Born, M., and E. Wolf, *Principles of Optics*, 3d Ed. New York: Pergamon, 1965, p. 121.

[9] Gordon, J. P., R. C. C. Leite, R. S. Moore, S. P. S. Porto, and J. R. Whinnery, "Long-transient effects in lasers with inserted liquid samples," *J. Appl. Phys.*, vol. 36, p. 3, 1965.

[10] Dabby, F. W., and J. R. Whinnery, "Thermal self-focusing of laser beams in lead glasses," *Appl. Phys. Letters*, vol. 13, p. 284, 1968.

3

Propagation of Gaussian Beams

3.0 Introduction

The propagation of rays and spherical beams through lenses and lenslike media was discussed in the preceding chapter. A closely related topic of fundamental importance in quantum electronics is the propagation of optical beams. These beams usually take the form of planelike waves whose energy density is localized, for reasonable propagation distances, near the propagation axis. The output of laser oscillators will be found to consist of one or more of such beams. This is also the form of the fields set up by feeding electromagnetic energy into a resonator formed by two curved reflectors. The understanding of the characteristics of these modes is thus a prerequisite to the study of many laser-related phenomena.

3.1 The Wave Equation

The most widely encountered optical beam is one where the intensity distribution at planes normal to the propagation direction is Gaussian. To derive its characteristics we start with the Maxwell equations in a

30

homogeneous charge-free medium so that $\nabla \cdot \mathbf{E} = 0$.

$$\nabla \times \mathbf{H} = \epsilon \frac{\partial \mathbf{E}}{\partial t}$$

$$\nabla \times \mathbf{E} = -\mu \frac{\partial \mathbf{H}}{\partial t}$$

(3.1-1)

Taking the curl of the second of (3.1-1) and substituting the first results in

$$\nabla^2 \mathbf{E} - \mu\epsilon \frac{\partial^2 \mathbf{E}}{\partial t^2} = 0 \qquad (3.1\text{-}2)$$

where we used $\nabla \times \nabla \times \mathbf{E} \equiv \nabla(\nabla \cdot \mathbf{E}) - \nabla^2 \mathbf{E}$ and $\nabla \cdot \mathbf{E} = 0$. If we assume the field quantities to vary as $\mathbf{E}(x, y, z, t) = \text{Re}\,[\mathbf{E}(x, y, z)e^{i\omega t}]$—that is, a pure monochromatic radiation—the wave equation (3.1-2) becomes

$$\nabla^2 \mathbf{E} + k^2(\mathbf{r})\mathbf{E} = 0 \qquad (3.1\text{-}3)$$

where

$$k^2 = \omega^2 \mu\epsilon \left(1 - i\frac{\sigma}{\omega\epsilon}\right) \qquad (3.1\text{-}4)$$

where we allowed for the possible dependence of k on position $\mathbf{r}$. We have also taken k as a complex number to allow for the possibility of losses ($\sigma > 0$) or gain ($\sigma < 0$) in the medium.[1]

We limit our derivation to the case in which $k^2(\mathbf{r})$ is given by

$$k^2(\mathbf{r}) = k^2 - kk_2 r^2 \qquad (3.1\text{-}5)$$

where k_2 is some constant and $k = 2\pi/\lambda$, where λ is the wavelength of a TEM (transverse electromagnetic) plane wave propagating in the medium. Furthermore, we assume a solution whose transverse dependence is on $r = \sqrt{x^2 + y^2}$ only so that in (3.1-3) we can replace ∇^2 by

$$\nabla^2 = \nabla_t^2 + \frac{\partial^2}{\partial z^2} = \frac{\partial^2}{\partial r^2} + \frac{1}{r}\frac{\partial}{\partial r} + \frac{\partial^2}{\partial z^2} \qquad (3.1\text{-}6)$$

The kind of propagation we are considering is that of a nearly plane wave in which the flow of energy is predominantly along a single (say, z) direction so that we may limit our derivation to a single transverse field component E. Taking E as

$$E = \psi(x, y, z)e^{-ikz} \qquad (3.1\text{-}7)$$

we obtain from (3.1-3) and (3.1-5), in a few simple steps,

$$\nabla_t^2 \psi - 2ik\psi' - kk_2 r^2 \psi = 0 \qquad (3.1\text{-}8)$$

---

[1] If k is complex (say, $k_r + ik_i$), then a traveling electromagnetic wave has the form of $\exp[i(\omega t - kz)] = \exp[-k_i z + i(\omega t - k_r z)]$.

where $\psi' = \partial\psi/\partial z$ and where we assume that the transverse variation is slow enough that $k\psi' \gg \psi'' \ll k^2\psi$.

Next we take ψ in the form of

$$\psi = \exp\{-i[P(z) + \tfrac{1}{2}Q(z)r^2]\} \tag{3.1-9}$$

which, when substituted into (3.1-8) and after using (3.1-6), gives

$$-Q^2r^2 - 2iQ - kr^2Q' - 2kP' - kk_2r^2 = 0 \tag{3.1-10}$$

If (3.1-10) is to hold for all r, the coefficients of the different powers of r must be each equal to zero. This leads to [1]

$$Q^2 + kQ' + kk_2 = 0$$

$$P' = -\frac{iQ}{k} \tag{3.1-11}$$

The wave equation (3.1-2) is thus reduced to Equations (3.1-11).

3.2   The Gaussian Beam in a Homogeneous Medium

If the medium is homogeneous, we can, according to (3.1-5), put $k_2 = 0$, and (3.1-10) becomes

$$Q^2 + kQ' = 0 \tag{3.2-1}$$

Introducing the function $s(z)$ by the relation

$$Q = k\frac{s'}{s} \tag{3.2-2}$$

we obtain directly from (3.2-1)

$$s'' = 0$$

so that

$$s' = a \qquad s = az + b$$

or, using (3.2-2),

$$Q(z) = k\frac{a}{az + b} \tag{3.2-3}$$

where a and b are arbitrary constants, we will find it more convenient to deal with a parameter q, where

$$q(z) = \frac{k}{Q(z)} = \frac{2\pi}{\lambda Q(z)} \tag{3.2-4}$$

so that we may rewrite (3.2-3) in the form

$$q = z + q_0 \tag{3.2-5}$$

From (3.1-11) and (3.2-4), we have

$$P' = -\frac{i}{q} = -\frac{i}{z + q_0}$$

so that

$$P(z) = -i \ln \left(1 + \frac{z}{q_0} \right) \qquad \text{(3.2-6)}$$

where the arbitrary constant of integration is chosen as zero.[2]
Combining (3.2-5) and (3.2-6) in (3.1-9), we obtain

$$\psi = \exp \left\{ -i \left[-i \ln \left(1 + \frac{z}{q_0} \right) + \frac{k}{2(q_0 + z)} r^2 \right] \right\} \qquad \text{(3.2-7)}$$

We take the arbitrary constant of integration q_0 to be purely imaginary and reexpress it in terms of a new constant ω_0 as

$$q_0 = i \frac{\pi \omega_0^2}{\lambda} \qquad \lambda = \frac{2\pi}{k} \qquad \text{(3.2-8)}$$

The choice of an imaginary q_0 will be found to lead to waves whose energy density is confined near the z axis. With this last substitution let us consider, one at a time, the two factors in (3.2-7). The first one becomes

$$\exp \left[-\ln \left(1 - i \frac{\lambda z}{\pi \omega_0^2} \right) \right] = \frac{1}{\sqrt{1 + \frac{\lambda^2 z^2}{\pi^2 \omega_0^4}}} \exp \left[i \tan^{-1} \left(\frac{\lambda z}{\pi \omega_0^2} \right) \right] \qquad \text{(3.2-9)}$$

where we used $\ln (a + ib) = \ln \sqrt{a^2 + b^2} + i \tan^{-1} (b/a)$. Substituting (3.2-8) in the second term of (3.2-7) and separating the exponent into its real and imaginary parts, we obtain

$$\exp \left[\frac{-ikr^2}{2(q_0 + z)} \right] = \exp \left\{ \frac{-r^2}{\omega_0^2 \left[1 + \left(\frac{\lambda z}{\pi \omega_0^2} \right)^2 \right]} - \frac{ikr^2}{2z \left[1 + \left(\frac{\pi \omega_0^2}{\lambda z} \right)^2 \right]} \right\} \qquad \text{(3.2-10)}$$

If we define the following parameters

$$\omega^2(z) = \omega_0^2 \left[1 + \left(\frac{\lambda z}{\pi \omega_0^2} \right)^2 \right] \qquad \text{(3.2-11)}$$

$$R = z \left[1 + \left(\frac{\pi \omega_0^2}{\lambda z} \right)^2 \right] \qquad \text{(3.2-12)}$$

$$\phi = \tan^{-1} \left(\frac{\lambda z}{\pi \omega_0^2} \right) \qquad \text{(3.2-13)}$$

---

[2] This amounts to fixing the oscillation phase ϕ of the final solution of

$$E(x, y, 0) [\cos (\omega t - kz) + \phi]$$

as zero.

We can combine (3.2-10) and (3.2-9) in (3.2-7) and, recalling that $E(x, y, z) = \psi(x, y, z) \exp(-ikz)$, obtain

$$E(x, y, z) = \frac{\omega_0}{\omega(z)} \exp\left[-i(kz - \phi) - r^2\left(\frac{1}{\omega^2(z)} + \frac{ik}{2R}\right)\right] \quad \textbf{(3.2-14)}$$

This is our basic result. We refer to it as the *fundamental Gaussian-beam solution*, since we have excluded the more complicated solutions of (3.1-3) by limiting ourselves to transverse dependence involving $r = (x^2 + y^2)^{1/2}$ only. These higher-order modes will be discussed separately in Section 3.6.

From (3.2-14), the parameter $\omega(z)$, which evolves according to (3.2-11), is the distance r at which the field amplitude is down by a factor $1/e$ compared to its value on the axis. We shall consequently refer to it as the beam "spot size." The parameter ω_0 is the minimum spot size. It is the beam spot size at the plane $z = 0$. The parameter R in (3.2-14) is the radius of curvature of the very nearly spherical wavefronts[3] at z. We can verify this statement by deriving the radius of curvature of the constant phase surfaces (wavefronts) or, more simply, by considering the form of a spherical wave emitted by a point radiator placed at $z = 0$. It is given by

$$E \propto \frac{1}{R} e^{-ikR} = \frac{1}{R} \exp\left(-ik\sqrt{x^2 + y^2 + z^2}\right)$$

$$\simeq \frac{1}{R} \exp\left(-ikz - ik\frac{x^2 + y^2}{2R}\right), \quad x^2 + y^2 \ll z^2 \quad \textbf{(3.2-15)}$$

since z is equal to R, the radius of curvature of the spherical wave. Comparing (3.2-14) with (3.2-15), we identify R as the radius of curvature of the Gaussian beam. The convention regarding the sign of R is the same as that adopted in Chapter 2; that is, $R(z)$ is negative if the center of curvature occurs at $z' > z$ and vice versa.

The form of the fundamental Gaussian beam is, according to (3.2-14), uniquely determined once its minimum spot size ω_0 and its location—that is, the plane $z = 0$—are specified. Its spot size ω and radius of curvature R at any plane z are then found from (3.2-11) and (3.2-12). Some of these characteristics are displayed in Figure 3-1. The hyperbolas shown in this figure correspond to the ray direction and are intersections of planes that include the z axis and the hyperboloids

$$x^2 + y^2 = \text{const. } \omega^2(z) \quad \textbf{(3.2-16)}$$

They correspond to the direction of energy propagation. The spherical surfaces shown have radii of curvature given by (3.2-12). For large z the

---

[3] Actually, it follows from (3.2-14) that, with the exception of the immediate vicinity of the plane $z = 0$, the wavefronts are parabolic, since they are defined by $k[z + (r^2/2R)] = \text{const.}$ For $r^2 \ll z^2$, the distinction between parabolic and spherical surfaces is not important.

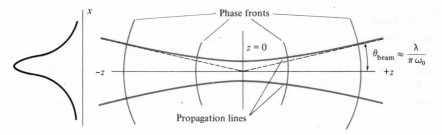

Figure 3-1 Propagating Gaussian beam.

hyperboloids $x^2 + y^2 = \omega^2$ are asymptotic to the cone

$$r = \sqrt{x^2 + y^2} = \frac{\lambda}{\pi\omega_0} z \qquad (3.2\text{-}17)$$

whose half-apex angle, which we take as a measure of the angular beam spread, is

$$\theta_{\text{beam}} = \tan^{-1}\left(\frac{\lambda}{\pi\omega_0}\right) \simeq \frac{\lambda}{\pi\omega_0} \qquad (3.2\text{-}18)$$

to an area of dimension $\simeq \pi\omega_0$. This last result is a rigorous manifestation of wave diffraction according to which a wave which is confined in the transverse direction to an aperture of radius ω_0 will spread (diffract) in the far field ($z \gg \omega_0^2/\lambda$) according to (3.2-18).

3.3   The Transformation of the Gaussian Beam

The *ABCD* law.   We have already established that the propagation of a Gaussian beam through a homogeneous medium is described by Equations (3.2-11) and (3.2-12). We can combine these two relations into a single equation by using (3.2-11) and (3.2-12) to identify the two terms in the exponent of (3.2-10). The result is

$$\frac{1}{q(z)} = \frac{1}{q_0 + z} = \frac{1}{R(z)} - i\frac{\lambda}{\pi\omega^2(z)} \qquad (3.3\text{-}1)$$

where, we recall,

$$k = \frac{2\pi}{\lambda} \quad \text{and} \quad q_0 = i\frac{\pi\omega_0^2}{\lambda}$$

According to (3.3-1), once the value of $q(z)$ at some plane (say z_1) is known, we can find its value at any other plane z_2 by

$$q(z_2) = q(z_1) + (z_2 - z_1) \qquad (3.3\text{-}2)$$

and then use (3.3-1) to obtain the beam spot size $\omega(z_2)$ and its radius of curvature $R(z_2)$. The parameter q is usually referred to as the complex radius of the Gaussian beam.

Equation (3.3-2) is identical in form to (2.4-1), so in passing through a homogeneous medium, q transforms exactly as the radius of curvature R of a spherical wave. Furthermore, in passing through an ideal thin lens, the Gaussian-beam spot size $\omega(z)$ remains unchanged, while $[R(z)]^{-1}$, following (2.4-4), changes by $-f^{-1}$, as shown in Figure 3-2. Using (3.3-1) we find then that in passing through a thin lens, $q(z)$ transforms according to

$$\frac{1}{q_2} = \frac{1}{q_1} - \frac{1}{f} \tag{3.3-3}$$

where q_1 is the complex beam parameter of the incoming Gaussian beam and q_2 that of the outgoing wave.

The formal similarity between (3.3-2) and (3.3-3) on the one hand and (2.4-1) and (2.4-4) on the other shows that q transforms in the same way as the radius of curvature R of a spherical wave. It follows that the values of q at any two planes are related to each other, as in (2.4-3), by [1]

$$q_2 = \frac{Aq_1 + B}{Cq_1 + D} \tag{3.3-4}$$

where $A, B, C,$ and D are the elements of the matrix relating a paraxial ray at plane 2 to plane 1 as follows:

$$r_2 = Ar_1 + Br_1'$$
$$r_2' = Cr_1 + Dr_1'$$

A Gaussian beam in a lens waveguide.   To illustrate the power of the $ABCD$ law, as Equation (3.3-4) has come to be known, we consider the propagation of a Gaussian beam through a sequence of thin lenses, as shown in Figure 2-2. The matrix, relating a ray in plane $s + 1$ to the plane $s = 1$ is

$$\begin{vmatrix} A_T & B_T \\ C_T & D_T \end{vmatrix} = \begin{vmatrix} A & B \\ C & D \end{vmatrix}^s \tag{3.3-5}$$

where (A, B, C, D) is the matrix for propagation through a single unit cell $(\Delta s = 1)$ and is given by (2.1-6). We can use a well-known formula for the

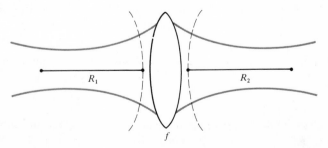

Figure 3-2   Transformation of a Gaussian beam in passing a thin lens.

sth power of a matrix with a unity determinant [2] (unimodular) to obtain

$$A_T = \frac{A \sin{(s\theta)} - \sin{[(s-1)\theta]}}{\sin\theta}$$

$$B_T = \frac{B \sin{(s\theta)}}{\sin\theta}$$

$$C_T = \frac{C \sin{(s\theta)}}{\sin\theta}$$

$$D_T = \frac{D \sin{(s\theta)} - \sin{[(s-1)\theta]}}{\sin\theta}$$

(3.3-6)

where

$$\cos\theta = \frac{1}{2}(A+D) = \left(1 - \frac{d}{f_2} - \frac{d}{f_1} + \frac{d^2}{2f_1 f_2}\right)$$

(3.3-7)

and then use (3.3-6) in (3.3-4) with the result

$$q_{s+1} = \frac{\{A \sin{(s\theta)} - \sin{[(s-1)\theta]}\}q_1 + B \sin{(s\theta)}}{C \sin{(s\theta)}q_1 + D \sin{(s\theta)} - \sin{[(s-1)\theta]}}$$

(3.3-8)

The condition for the confinement of the Gaussian beam by the lens sequence is, from (3.3-8), that θ be real; otherwise, the sine functions will yield growing exponentials. From (3.3-7), this condition becomes $|\cos\theta| \leqslant 1$, or

$$0 \leqslant \left(1 - \frac{d}{2f_1}\right)\left(1 - \frac{d}{2f_2}\right) \leqslant 1$$

(3.3-9)

that is, the same as condition (2.1-16) for stable-ray propagation.

3.4 Propagation of a Gaussian Beam in a Medium with a Quadratic Index Profile

Consider a medium whose index of refraction varies as

$$n(r) = n - \tfrac{1}{2}n_2 r^2$$

(3.4-1)

where r is the radial distance from the cylindrical axis of symmetry; see References [1], [3], and [4]. We can relate n_2 to k_2 as defined in (3.1-5) by[4] $k_2 = k_0 n_2$ so that the propagation equation (3.1-10) becomes

$$Q^2(z) + kQ'(z) + k^2 n_2 = 0$$

(3.4-2)

The steady-state $Q'(z) = 0$ solution is

$$Q = -i\sqrt{kk_2}$$

(3.4-3)

---

[4] This follows from replacing (3.1-5)—that is, $k^2(r) = k^2 - kk_2 r^2$—by its approximate form for small r, $k(r) \simeq k - \tfrac{1}{2}k_2 r^2$, and then using the equivalent definition $k = (\omega/c_0)(n - \tfrac{1}{2}n_2 r^2) = k_0(n - \tfrac{1}{2}n_2 r^2)$.

where the sign was chosen so as to yield a real spot size ω in the relation

$$\frac{1}{q} = \frac{Q}{k} = \frac{1}{R} - i \frac{\lambda}{\pi \omega^2} \tag{3.4-4}$$

It follows from (3.4-4) that the steady-state solution (3.4-3) corresponds to a Gaussian beam with planar wavefronts ($R = \infty$) but with a constant Gaussian spot size

$$\omega = \left(\frac{\lambda}{\pi}\right)^{1/2} \left(\frac{k}{k_2}\right)^{1/4} = \left(\frac{\lambda}{\pi}\right)^{1/2} \left(\frac{n}{n_2}\right)^{1/4} \tag{3.4-5}$$

so that the natural tendency of a finite-diameter beam to spread (diffract) is counterbalanced by the index variation.

It is interesting to derive the last result using the $ABCD$ law. According to this law, the complex beam radius $q(z)$ is related to its value at $z = 0$ by

$$q(z) = \frac{Aq(0) + B}{Cq(0) + D} \tag{3.4-6}$$

where A, B, C, and D are the elements of the ray matrix appropriate to a lenslike medium of length z and are given by (2.3-5) as

$$A = \cos\left(\sqrt{\frac{k_2}{k}}\, z\right)$$

$$B = \sqrt{\frac{k}{k_2}} \sin\left(\sqrt{\frac{k_2}{k}}\, z\right)$$

$$C = -\sqrt{\frac{k_2}{k}} \sin\left(\sqrt{\frac{k_2}{k}}\, z\right) \tag{3.4-7}$$

$$D = A$$

The condition for a steady-state propagation is $q(z) = q(0) = q$, which, using (3.4-6) and (3.4-7), yields

$$q^2 = -\frac{k}{k_2} \tag{3.4-8}$$

which, since $q = kQ^{-1}$, reduces to (3.4-3).

3.5 Propagation in Media with a Gain Profile

We can account for the existence of optical gain or loss in a medium by adding an imaginary part to the propagation constant so that the propagation factor becomes

$$e^{-ikz} = e^{-i(k_r \pm i\alpha)z} = e^{ik_r z} e^{\pm \alpha z}$$

If the gain (or loss) varies quadratically with the radial position r, we can take $k(r)$ as

$$k(r) = k_r \pm i(\alpha_0 - \tfrac{1}{2}\alpha_2 r^2) \tag{3.5-1}$$

so that if we assume $k_2 r^2 \ll k$ in (3.1-5), we have $k_2 = i\alpha_2$. Equation (3.5-1) corresponds to a propagation factor

$$\exp\left[-ik_r z \pm \left(\alpha_0 - \frac{\alpha_2}{2}r^2\right)z\right]$$

The steady-state solution for the complex beam radius is, according to (3.4-3),

$$\frac{1}{q} = -i\sqrt{\frac{k_2}{k}}$$

which, using $k_2 = i\alpha_2$ and Equation (3.3-1), yields the value of the steady-state spot size and radius of curvature

$$\omega^2 = 2\sqrt{\frac{\lambda}{\pi\alpha_2}}$$

$$R = 2\sqrt{\frac{\pi}{\lambda\alpha_2}}$$

(3.5-2)

Therefore, unlike the case of the index profile, the radius of curvature is finite and we have the slightly unusual case of a nonspreading beam with spherical wavefronts.

A gain profile such as that described by (3.5-1) occurs naturally in some gas lasers due to a radial distribution in the electron density [2]. Experimental data in support of the first of Equations (3.5-2) showing a linear dependence of ω^2 on $\alpha_2^{-1/2}$ is shown in Figure 3-3.

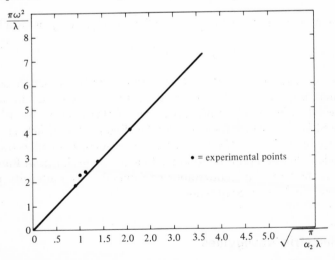

Figure 3-3 Theoretical curve showing dependence of beam radius on quadratic gain constant α_2. Experimental points were obtained in a xenon 3.39-μm laser in which α_2 was varied by controlling the unsaturated laser gain. (After Reference [5].)

3.6 High-Order Beam Modes

The Gaussian mode treated up to this point has a field variation that depends only on the axial distance z and the distance r from the axis. If we do not impose the condition $\partial/\partial\phi = 0$ (where ϕ is the azimuthal angle in a cylindrical coordinate system (r, ϕ, z)) and take $k_2 = 0$, it can be shown straightforwardly that the wave equation (3.1-3) has solutions in the form of

$$
\begin{aligned}
E_{m,n}^{(x)}(x, y, z) = {} & E_0 \frac{\omega_0}{\omega(z)} H_m\left(\sqrt{2}\,\frac{x}{\omega}\right) H_n\left(\sqrt{2}\,\frac{y}{\omega}\right) \\
& \times \exp\left[-ik\frac{x^2 + y^2}{2q(z)} - ikz + i(m+n+1)\phi\right] \\
= {} & E_0 \frac{\omega_0}{\omega} H_m\left(\sqrt{2}\,\frac{x}{\omega}\right) H_n\left(\sqrt{2}\,\frac{y}{\omega}\right) \\
& \times \exp\left[-\frac{x^2 + y^2}{\omega^2(z)} - \frac{ik(x^2 + y^2)}{2R(z)} - ikz \right. \\
& \left. \hphantom{\times \exp\left[\right.} + i(m+n+1)\phi\right]
\end{aligned}
\tag{3.6-1}
$$

where H_m is the Hermite polynomial of order m, and $\omega(z)$, $R(z)$, $q(z)$, and ϕ are defined as in (3.2-11) through (3.2-13).

We note for future reference that the phase shift on the axis is

$$
\theta = kz - (m+n+1)\tan^{-1}\frac{z}{z_0}
\tag{3.6-2}
$$

$$z_0 = \pi \frac{w_0^2}{\lambda}$$

The transverse variation of the electric field along x (or y) is seen to be of the form

$$
E \propto H_n(\zeta)e^{-\zeta^2/2}
\tag{3.6-3}
$$

with $\zeta = \sqrt{2}\,x/\omega$. This form is identical to that of the harmonic-oscillator wave functions, a problem solved in any introductory course in quantum mechanics [6]. The author took advantage of this analogy by using harmonic-oscillator wave-function curves for Figure 3-4, which shows the field (E) and intensity ($|E|^2$) distribution of some low-order transverse laser modes. Photographs of actual field patterns are shown in Figure 3-5. Note that the first four photographs correspond to the intensity plots of (a), (b), (c), and (d) in Figure 3-4.

3.7 Dielectric Waveguides

In Section 3.5 we showed that a medium with a quadratic variation of the index of refraction can support a confined optical beam. It was also shown that such a medium is the continuum analog of a sequence of thin lenses,

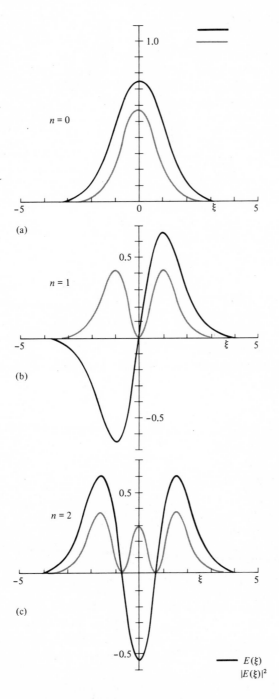

Figure 3-4 Plot of field distributions (solid lines) and intensity distributions (dashed lines) of some low-order transverse modes.

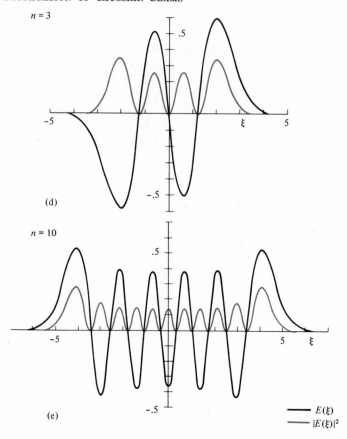

Figure 3-4 (*Continued*)

so the confinement may be understood in terms of periodic focusing of the otherwise diffracting beam.

A closely related form of confined optical propagation exists in the so-called dielectric waveguide. It consists in practice of a rectangular dielectric cylinder embedded in one or more media of lower indices of refraction. An example of such a guide is shown in Figure 3-6.

Dielectric waveguides have been studied extensively in the microwave regime [7]. The interest in their optical properties is more recent and is prompted by the role that such waveguides play in p-n junctions and junction lasers (see References [8]–[10]) as well as by their potential application in compact optical "circuits," in which the guiding and processing of coherent light will be accomplished in small-volume solid structures [11].

In this chapter we analyze the simple case of a two-dimensional dielectric waveguide, which consists of a sheet of dielectric constant ϵ_i sandwiched between two infinite layers with a dielectric constant ϵ ($< \epsilon_i$).

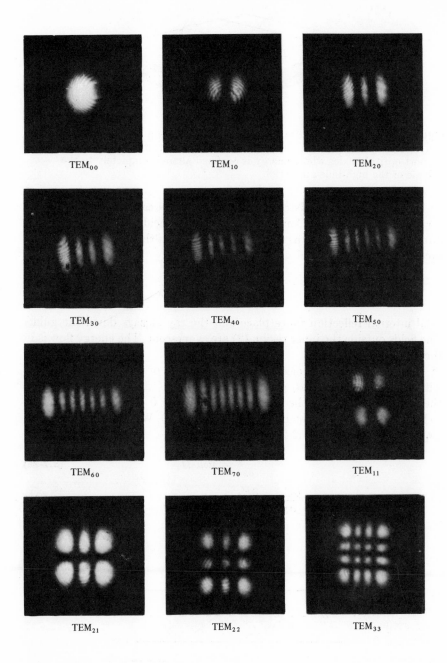

Figure 3-5 Some low-order optical-beam modes. (After H. Kogelnik and W. Rigrod, *Proc. IRE*, vol. 50, p. 220, 1962.)

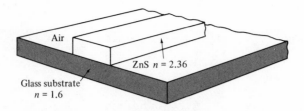

Figure 3-6 Optical dielectric waveguide consisting of a ZnS ($n = 2.36$) rectangular cylinder resting on a glass ($n = 1.6$) substrate. This structure can support optical modes whose energy is confined almost completely to the volume of the high-index material.

The reason for the existence of confined modes can be appreciated by a ray-optics argument. Consider a ray that is incident on the dielectric interface from the inside, as shown in Figure 3-7. If the angle of incidence θ exceeds the critical value

$$\theta_c = \sin^{-1}\frac{n_1}{n_2} = \sin^{-1}\frac{1}{\sqrt{\kappa}} \qquad (3.7\text{-}1)$$

total internal reflection takes place and the ray zigzags down the guide. The fields outside the inner region (2) are evanescent. The energy flow is in the z direction.

In the more rigorous electromagnetic analysis of this problem we start with Maxwell's equations, given by (1.2-1) and (1.2-2). We assume that the fields do not vary in the y direction, so $\partial/\partial y = 0$. We limit the problem to harmonic time variation in the form of exp ($i\omega t$). With these restrictions, Equations (1.2-1) and (1.2-2) can be written as

$$\frac{\partial E_y}{\partial z} = i\omega\mu_0 H_x \qquad (3.7\text{-}2a)$$

$$\frac{\partial E_x}{\partial z} - \frac{\partial E_z}{\partial x} = -i\omega\mu_0 H_y \qquad (3.7\text{-}2b)$$

$$\frac{\partial E_y}{\partial x} = -i\omega\mu_0 H_z \qquad (3.7\text{-}2c)$$

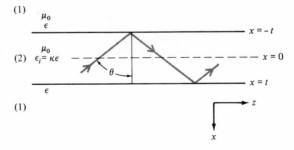

Figure 3-7 Dielectric waveguide.

$$\frac{\partial H_y}{\partial z} = -i\omega\epsilon E_x \qquad \textbf{(3.7-2d)}$$

$$\frac{\partial H_x}{\partial z} - \frac{\partial H_z}{\partial x} = i\omega\epsilon E_y \qquad \textbf{(3.7-2e)}$$

$$\frac{\partial H_y}{\partial x} = i\omega\epsilon E_z \qquad \textbf{(3.7-2f)}$$

Next we assume that the variation in the z direction is represented by the factor $\exp(-i\beta z)$; thus in (3.7-2) we may replace $\partial/\partial z$ by $-i\beta$. An inspection of (3.7-2) reveals that we may obtain two self-consistent types of solutions. The first will involve only E_y, H_x, and H_z, and is referred to as transverse electric (TE) solutions, since the electric field (E_y) is restricted to the transverse ($z = $ const.) plane. Maxwell's equations (3.7-2) for this case reduce to

$$E_y = -\frac{\omega\mu_0}{\beta} H_x \qquad \textbf{(3.7-3)}$$

$$\frac{\partial E_y}{\partial x} = -i\omega\mu_0 H_z \qquad \textbf{(3.7-4)}$$

The second type of solution is transverse magnetic (TM) and involves only H_y, E_x, and E_z. Maxwell's equations in this case are

$$H_y = \frac{\omega\epsilon}{\beta} E_x \qquad \textbf{(3.7-5)}$$

$$E_z = -\frac{i}{\omega\epsilon} \frac{\partial H_y}{\partial x} \qquad \textbf{(3.7-6)}$$

Analysis of TE modes. We assume a solution for E_y in the form of

$$E_y = A \exp[-p(|x| - t) - i\beta z] \qquad |x| \geqslant t \qquad \textbf{(3.7-7)}$$

and

$$E_y = B \cos(hx) \exp(-i\beta z) \qquad |x| \leqslant t \qquad \textbf{(3.7-8)}$$

where p and h are constants to be determined. From (3.7-4) we obtain

$$H_z = -\frac{ipA}{\omega\mu_0} \exp[-p(|x| - t) - i\beta z] \qquad |x| \geqslant t$$

and

$$H_z = -\frac{iBh}{\omega\mu_0} \sin(hx) \exp(-i\beta z) \qquad |x| \leqslant t$$

Requiring that E_y be continuous at $x = \pm t$ gives

$$A = B \cos(ht) \qquad \textbf{(3.7-9)}$$

whereas the continuity of H_z at $x = \pm t$ imposes the condition

$$pA = hB \sin(ht)$$

which, using (3.7-9), gives

$$pt = ht \tan(ht) \qquad \textbf{(3.7-10)}$$

The field components obey a wave equation that can be derived from (3.7-2). If we take the derivatives of (3.7-2a) and (3.7-2c) with respect to z and x, respectively, the resulting equations and (3.7-2e) give

$$\frac{\partial^2 E_y}{\partial z^2} + \frac{\partial^2 E_y}{\partial x^2} + \omega^2 \mu_0 \epsilon E_y = 0 \qquad \text{(3.7-11)}$$

In the region $|x| \leqslant t$ we have $\omega^2 \mu \epsilon_i = \kappa k^2$, and thus from (3.7-8) and (3.7-11) we get

$$\beta^2 = \kappa k^2 - h^2$$

For $|x| \geqslant t$, (3.7-7) and (3.7-11) give

$$\beta^2 = k^2 + p^2$$

Combining the last two relations leads to

$$(pt)^2 + (ht)^2 = (\kappa - 1)k^2 t^2 \qquad \text{(3.7-12)}$$

The transcendental pair of equations, (3.7-10) and (3.7-12), can be solved for p and h. This can be done graphically by drawing (3.7-12) on a pt vs. ht plot. The result is a circle with a radius of $\sqrt{\kappa - 1}\, kt$. The allowed modes of propagation correspond to the intersection (or intersections) of the curve $pt = ht \tan(ht)$ with the circle. The transverse-mode variation is, according to (3.7-7), described by the factor $\exp[-p(|x| - t)]$, so the modes are confined *only* when $p > 0$. The graphical solution described above is illustrated in Figure 3-8.

The parameter $\sqrt{\kappa - 1}\, kt$, which corresponds to the radius of the circles in Figure 3-7, can be written also as

$$2\pi \sqrt{\frac{\epsilon_i - \epsilon}{\epsilon}} \left(\frac{t}{\lambda}\right)$$

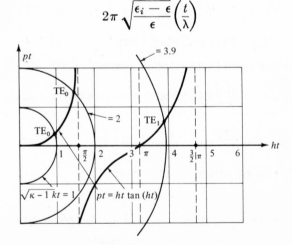

Figure 3-8   Graphical solution for determining parameters p and h of even TE modes in a symmetric dielectric waveguide. These parameters are determined by the intersections of $pt = ht \tan(ht)$ and $(pt)^2 + (ht)^2 = (\kappa - 1)k^2 t^2$.

where $\lambda = 2\pi/k$ is the free propagation wavelength in the external medium (1). In a given structure this parameter is determined once the frequency is chosen. At low frequencies such that

$$0 < \sqrt{\kappa - 1}\, kt < \pi \qquad \qquad \textbf{(3.7-13)}$$

only one confined ($p > 0$) mode exists. The transverse parameter h of this mode is contained in the interval

$$0 < ht < \frac{\pi}{2} \qquad \qquad \textbf{(3.7-14)}$$

The mode is designated as TE$_0$, as shown in Figure 3-8.

When the parameter $\sqrt{(\kappa - 1)}\, kt$ falls within the range

$$\pi < \sqrt{\kappa - 1}\, kt < 2\pi \qquad \qquad \textbf{(3.7-15)}$$

we get two intersections. One corresponds to a value of $ht < \pi/2$ and is thus a lowest-order TE$_0$ mode. In the second mode,

$$\pi < ht < \frac{3\pi}{2} \qquad \qquad \textbf{(3.7-16)}$$

and consequently, has one zero crossing in the region $|x| < t$. This is the so-called first-order, even TE$_1$ mode. Both of these modes correspond to the same frequency and can therefore be excited simultaneously. Further increases in $\sqrt{\kappa - 1}\, kt$ bring additional modes into the propagation regime.

From (3.7-14) and (3.7-16) we conclude that no modes exist with $\pi/2 < ht < \pi$. The reason is that we limited ourselves at the outset to solutions of the form of (3.7-8) that are even in x. Another family of modes—the odd modes—results when we take the fields in the form of

$$\begin{aligned} E_y &\propto \sin{(hx)} \exp{(-i\beta z)} & |x| &\leqslant t \\ E_y &\propto \exp{[-p(|x| - t) - i\beta z]} & |x| &\geqslant t \end{aligned} \qquad \textbf{(3.7-17)}$$

These solutions have values of ht corresponding to the regions $\pi/2 < ht < \pi$ and $3\pi/2 < ht < 2\pi$, which are "avoided" by the even TE modes. As $\sqrt{\kappa - 1}\, kt$ is increased gradually additional modes, which alternate between even and odd, are thus brought in. Further discussion of these modes, as well as of TM modes, is relegated to the problems.

■ PROBLEMS

3-1   a. Show, using the $ABCD$ law, that a stable biperiodic lens sequence—that is, one satisfying the condition (3.3-9)—can propagate a Gaussian beam that repeats itself after every two lenses.
b. Show that this beam must have, next to any lens, a radius of curvature R equal to twice the focal length of the lens. Show also that R changes sign in passing through the lens.

c. Assume that the lens waveguide of (a) is replaced by two mirrors having radii of curvature $R_1 = 2f_1$ and $R_2 = 2f_2$ and separated by d.
d. What is the significance of this mode?

3-2 Derive Equation (3.4-8).

3-3 Derive the propagation characteristics, as in Section 3.7, for
a. Odd TE modes.
b. Odd TM modes.
c. Even TM modes.

Show that the lowest-order odd TE and TM modes cannot be confined (that is, have $p > 0$) below some critical "cutoff" frequency.

3-4 **a.** In Figure 3-7 assume that a perfect conductor occupies the plane $x = 0$. What kind of TE and TM modes can this structure support? (*Hint:* Show that only even TM and odd TE modes can exist. These have properties identical to the corresponding modes in the symmetric waveguide, as shown in Figure 3-7.)
b. Can we have TE propagation at arbitrarily low frequencies? Justify your answer.

3-5 Show that as $\sqrt{\kappa - 1}\, kt \to \infty$, $\beta \to \omega\sqrt{\mu_0 \epsilon_i}$ for TM and TE modes.

■ REFERENCES

[1] Kogelnik, H., "On the propagation of Gaussian beams of light through lenslike media including those with a loss or gain variation," *Appl. Opt.*, vol. 4, p. 1562, 1965. This article contains many other relevant references.

[2] See, for example, M. Born and E. Wolf, *Principles of Optics*, 3d Ed. New York: Pergamon, 1965, p. 67.

[3] Pierce, J. R., "Modes in sequences of lenses," *Proc. Nat. Acad. Sci. U.S.*, vol. 47, p. 1808, 1961.

[4] Tien, P. K., J. P. Gordon, and J. R. Whinnery, "Focusing of a light beam of Gaussian field distribution in continuous and periodic lenslike media," *Proc. IEEE*, vol. 53, p. 129, 1965.

[5] Casperson, L., and A. Yariv, "The Gaussian mode in optical resonators with a radial gain profile," *Appl. Phys. Letters*, vol. 12, p. 355, 1968; W. R. Bennett, "Inversion mechanisms in gas lasers," *Appl. Opt. Suppl. 2, Chemical Lasers*, vol. 3, 1965.

[6] See, for example, R. B. Leighton, *Principles of Modern Physics*. New York: McGraw-Hill, 1959, p. 133.

[7] See, for example, R. E. Collin, *Field Theory of Guided Waves*. New York: McGraw-Hill, 1960, p. 470.

[8] Yariv, A., and Leite, R. C., "Dielectric waveguide mode of light propagation in *p-n* junctions," *Appl. Phys. Letters*, vol. 2, 55, 1963.

[9] Anderson, W. W., "Mode confinement in junction lasers," *IEEE J. Quantum Electron.*, vol. QE-1, p. 228, 1965.

[10] Stern, F., in *Radiative Recombination in Semiconductors*. Paris: Dunod, 1964, p. 165.

[11] Tien, P. K., R. Ulrich, and R. J. Martin, "Modes of propagating light waves in semiconductor films," *Appl. Phys. Letters*, vol. 14, p. 291, 1969.

4

Optical Resonators

4.0 Introduction

Optical resonators, like their low-frequency, radio-frequency, and micro-wave counterparts, are used primarily in order to build up large field intensities with moderate power inputs. A universal measure of this property is the quality factor Q of the resonator. Q is defined by the relation

$$Q = \omega \times \frac{\text{field energy stored by resonator}}{\text{power dissipated by resonator}} \tag{4.0-1}$$

As an example, consider the case of a simple resonator formed by bouncing a plane TEM wave between two perfectly conducting planes of separation l so that the field inside is

$$e(z, t) = E \sin \omega t \sin kz \tag{4.0-2}$$

According to (1.3-22), the average electric energy stored in the resonator is

$$\mathcal{E}_{\text{electric}} = \frac{A\epsilon}{2T} \int_0^l \int_0^T e^2(z, t) \, dz \, dt \tag{4.0-3}$$

where A is the cross-sectional area, ϵ is the dielectric constant, and $T = 2\pi/\omega$ is the period. Using (4.0-2) we obtain

$$\mathcal{E}_{\text{electric}} = \tfrac{1}{8}\epsilon E^2 V \tag{4.0-4}$$

where $V = lA$ is the resonator volume. Since the average magnetic energy stored in a resonator is equal to the electric energy [1], the total stored energy is

$$\mathcal{E} = \tfrac{1}{4}\epsilon E^2 V \tag{4.0-5}$$

Thus, designating the power input to the resonator by P, we obtain from (4.0-1)

$$Q = \frac{\omega\epsilon E^2 V}{4P}$$

The peak field is given by

$$E = \sqrt{\frac{4QP}{\omega\epsilon V}} \tag{4.0-6}$$

The main difference between an optical resonator and a microwave resonator—for example, one operating at $\lambda = 1$ cm ($\nu = 3 \times 10^{10}$ Hz)—is that in the latter case one can easily fabricate the resonator with typical dimensions comparable to λ. This leads to the presence of one, or just a few, resonances in the region of interest. In the optical regime, however, $\lambda \simeq 10^{-4}$ cm, so the resonator is likely to have typical dimensions that are very large in comparison to the wavelength. Under these conditions the number of resonator modes in a frequency interval $d\nu$ is given (see Problem 4-8 or, for example, Reference [2]) by

$$N \simeq \frac{8\pi\nu^2 V}{c^3}\,d\nu \tag{4.0-7}$$

where V is the volume of the resonator. For the case of $V = 1$ cm^3, $\nu = 3 \times 10^{14}$ Hz and $d\nu = 3 \times 10^{10}$, as an example, Equation (4.0-7) yields $N \sim 2 \times 10^9$ modes. If the resonator were closed, all these modes would have similar values of Q. This situation is to be avoided in the case of lasers, since it will cause the atoms to emit power (thus causing oscillation) into a large number of modes, which may differ in their frequencies as well as in their spatial characteristics.

This objection is overcome to a large extent by the use of open resonators, which consist essentially of a pair of opposing flat or curved reflectors. In such resonators the energy of the vast majority of the modes does not travel at right angles to the mirrors and will thus be lost in essentially a single traversal. These modes will consequently possess a very low Q. If the mirrors are curved, the few surviving modes will, as shown below, have their energy localized near the axis; thus the diffraction losses caused by the open sides can be made small compared with other loss mechanisms such as mirror transmission.

4.1   The Fabry–Perot Etalon

The Fabry–Perot etalon, or interferometer, named after its inventors [3] can be considered as the archetype of the optical resonator. It consists of an infinite plane-parallel plate of thickness l and index n which is immersed in a medium of index n'.[1] Let a plane wave be incident on the medium at an angle θ' to the normal, as shown in Figure 4-1. We can treat the problem of the transmission (and reflection) of the plane wave through the etalon by considering the infinite number of partial waves produced by reflections in the two end surfaces. The phase delay between two partial waves— which is attributable to one additional double trip—is given, according to Figure 4-2, by

$$\delta = \frac{4\pi n l \cos\theta}{\lambda_0} \tag{4.1-1}$$

where λ_0 is the vacuum wavelength of the incident wave and θ is the internal angle of incidence. If the complex amplitude of the incident wave is taken as A_i, then the partial reflections B_1, B_2, and so forth, are given by

$$B_1 = rA_i \qquad B_2 = tt'r'A_ie^{i\delta} \qquad B_3 = tt'r'^3A_ie^{2i\delta} \qquad \cdots$$

where r is the reflection coefficient (ratio of reflected to incident amplitude), t is the transmission coefficient for waves incident from n' toward n, and r' and t' are the corresponding quantities for waves traveling from n toward n'. The complex amplitude of the (total) reflected wave is $A_r =$

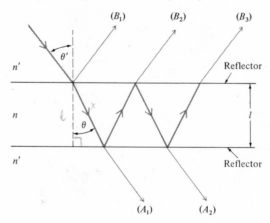

Figure 4-1

---

[1] In practice, one often uses etalons made by spacing two partially reflecting mirrors a distance l apart so that $n = n' = 1$. Another common form of etalon is produced by grinding two plane-parallel (or curved) faces on a transparent solid and then evaporating a metallic or dielectric layer (or layers) on the surfaces.

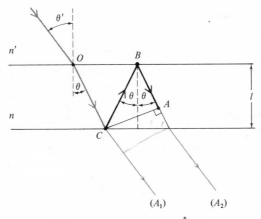

Figure 4-2   Two successive reflections, A_1 and A_2. Their path difference is given by

$$\delta L = AB + BC = l\frac{\cos 2\theta}{\cos \theta} + \frac{l}{\cos \theta} = 2l\cos\theta$$

$$\longrightarrow \delta = \frac{2\pi(\delta L)n}{\lambda_0} = \frac{4\pi nl\cos\theta}{\lambda_0}$$

$B_1 + B_2 + B_3 + \cdots$, or

$$A_r = \{r + tt'r'e^{i\delta}(1 + r'^2e^{i\delta} + r'^4e^{2i\delta} + \cdots)\}A_i \qquad \textbf{(4.1-2)}$$

For the transmitted wave,

$$A_1 = tt'A_i \qquad A_2 = tt'r'^2e^{i\delta}A_i \quad A_3 = tt'r'^4e^{2i\delta}A_i$$

where a phase factor, $\exp(i\delta)$, which corresponds to a single traversal of the plate and is common to all the terms, has been left out. Adding up the A terms, we obtain

$$A_t = tt'(1 + r'^2e^{i\delta} + r'^4e^{2i\delta} + \cdots) \qquad \textbf{(4.1-3)}$$

for the complex amplitude of the total transmitted wave. We notice that the terms within the parentheses in (4.1-2) and (4.1-3) form an infinite geometric progression; adding them, we get

$$A_r = \frac{(1 - e^{i\delta})\sqrt{R}}{1 - Re^{i\delta}}A_i \qquad \textbf{(4.1-4)}$$

and

$$A_t = \frac{T}{1 - Re^{i\delta}}A_i \qquad \textbf{(4.1-5)}$$

where we used the fact that $r' = -r$, the conservation-of-energy relation that applies to lossless mirrors

$$r^2 + tt' = 1$$

as well as the definitions

$$R \equiv r^2 = r'^2 \qquad T \equiv tt'.$$

R and T are, respectively, the fraction of the intensity reflected and transmitted at each interface and will be referred to in the following as the mirrors' reflectance and transmittance.

If the incident intensity (watts per square meter) is taken as $A_i A_i^*$, we obtain from (4.1-4) the following expression for the fraction of the incident intensity that is reflected:

$$\frac{I_r}{I_i} = \frac{A_r A_r^*}{A_i A_i^*} = \frac{4R \sin^2(\delta/2)}{(1-R)^2 + 4R \sin^2(\delta/2)} \qquad \textbf{(4.1-6)}$$

Moreover, from (4.1-5),

$$\frac{I_t}{I_i} = \frac{A_t A_t^*}{A_i A_i^*} = \frac{(1-R)^2}{(1-R)^2 + 4R \sin^2(\delta/2)} \qquad \textbf{(4.1-7)}$$

for the transmitted fraction. Our basic model contains no loss mechanisms, so conservation of energy requires that $I_t + I_r$ be equal to I_i, as is indeed the case.

Let us consider the transmission characteristics of a Fabry–Perot etalon. According to (4.1-7) the transmission is unity whenever

$$\delta = \frac{4\pi nl \cos\theta}{\lambda_0} = 2m\pi \qquad m = \text{any integer} \qquad \textbf{(4.1-8)}$$

Using (4.1-1), the condition (4.1-8) for maximum transmission can be written as

$$\nu_m = m \frac{c_0}{2nl \cos\theta} \qquad m = \text{any integer} \qquad \textbf{(4.1-9)}$$

where $c_0 = \nu\lambda_0$ is the velocity of light in vacuum and ν is the optical frequency. For a fixed l and θ, Equation (4.1-9) defines the unity transmission (resonance) frequencies of the etalon. These are separated by the so-called free spectral range

$$\Delta\nu \equiv \nu_{m+1} - \nu_m = \frac{c_0}{2nl \cos\theta} \qquad \textbf{(4.1-10)}$$

Theoretical transmission plots of a Fabry–Perot etalon are shown in Figure 4-3. The maximum transmission is unity, as stated previously. The minimum transmission, on the other hand, approaches zero as R approaches unity.

If we allow for the existence of losses in the etalon medium, we find that the peak transmission is less than unity. Taking the fractional intensity loss per pass as $(1 - A)$, we find that the maximum transmission drops from unity to

$$\left(\frac{I_t}{I_i}\right)_{\text{max}} = \frac{(1-R)^2 A}{(1-RA)^2} \qquad \textbf{(4.1-11)}$$

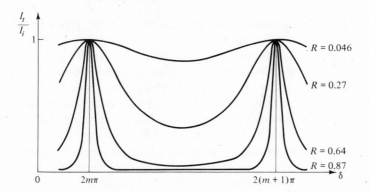

Figure 4-3 Transmission characteristics (theoretical) of a Fabry–Perot etalon. (After Reference[4].)

The proof of (4.1-11) is left as an exercise (Problem 4-2).

An experimental transmission plot of a Fabry–Perot etalon is shown in Figure 4-4.

4.2 Fabry–Perot Etalons as Optical Spectrum Analyzers

According to (4.1-8), the maximum transmission of a Fabry–Perot etalon occurs when

$$\frac{2nl \cos \theta}{\lambda_0} = m \tag{4.2-1}$$

Taking, for simplicity, the case of normal incidence ($\theta = 0°$), we obtain the following expression for the change $d\nu$ in the resonance frequency of a given transmission peak due to a length variation dl

$$\frac{d\nu}{\Delta\nu} = -\frac{dl}{(\lambda_0/2n)} \tag{4.2-2}$$

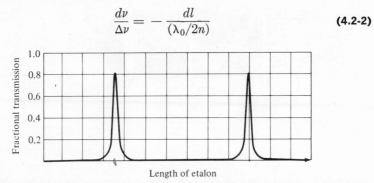

Figure 4-4 Transmission characteristics of a Fabry–Perot etalon at 6328 Å as a function of the etalon optical length with $R = 0.9$ and $A = 0.98$. The two peaks shown correspond to a change in the optical length $(nl) = \lambda/2$. (After Reference [5].)

where $\Delta\nu$ is the intermode frequency separation as given by (4.1-10). According to (4.2-2), we can tune the peak transmission frequency of the etalon by $\Delta\nu$ by changing its length by half a wavelength. This property is utilized in operating the etalon as a scanning interferometer. The optical signal to be analyzed passes through the etalon as its length is being swept. If the width of the transmission peaks is small compared to that of the spectral detail in the incident optical beam signal, the output of the etalon will constitute a replica of the spectral profile of the signal. In this application it is important that the spectral width of the signal beam be smaller than the intermode spacing of the etalon ($c_0/2nl$) so that the ambiguity due to simultaneous transmission through more than one transmission peak can be avoided. For the same reason the total length scan is limited to $dl < \lambda_0/2n$. The operation of a scanning Fabry–Perot etalon is demonstrated in Figure 4-5, and Figure 4-6 shows intensity vs. frequency data obtained by analyzing the output of a multimode He–Ne laser oscillating near 6328 Å. The peaks shown correspond to longitudinal laser modes, which will be discussed in Section 4.5.

It is clear from the foregoing that when operating as a spectrum analyzer the etalon resolution—that is, its ability to distinguish details in the spectrum—is limited by the finite width of its transmission peaks. If we take, somewhat arbitrarily,[2] the limiting resolution of the etalon as the separation $\Delta\nu_{1/2}$ between the two frequencies at which the transmission is down to half its peak value, from (4.1-7) we obtain

$$\sin^2\left(\frac{\delta_{1/2} - 2m\pi}{2}\right) = \frac{(1-R)^2}{4R} \qquad \textbf{(4.2-3)}$$

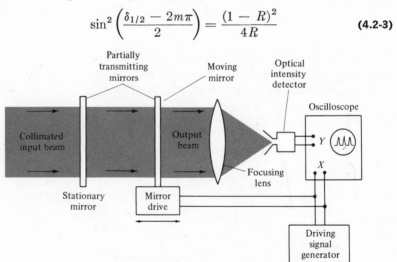

Figure 4-5   Typical scanning Fabry–Perot interferometer experimental arrangement.

---

[2] For a more complete discussion concerning the definition of resolution, see Reference [4].

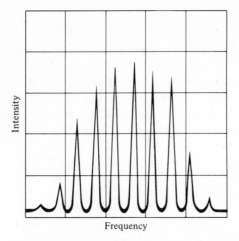

Figure 4-6 Intensity versus frequency analysis of the output of an He-Ne 6328 Å laser obtained with a scanning Fabry–Perot etalon. The horizontal scale is 250 MHz per division.

where $\delta_{1/2}$ is the value of δ corresponding to the two half-power points—that is, the value of δ at which the denominator of (4.1-7) is equal to $2(1 - R)^2$. If we assume $(\delta_{1/2} - 2m\pi) \ll \pi$, so that the width of the high-transmission regions in Figure 4-3 is small compared to the separation between the peaks, we obtain

$$\Delta \nu_{1/2} = \frac{c_0}{2\pi nl \cos \theta} (\delta_{1/2} - 2m\pi) \simeq \frac{c_0}{2\pi nl \cos \theta} \frac{1 - R}{\sqrt{R}} \qquad \textbf{(4.2-4)}$$

Or using (4.1-10) and defining the etalon finesse as

$$F \equiv \frac{\pi \sqrt{R}}{1 - R} \qquad \textbf{(4.2-5)}$$

we obtain

$$\Delta \nu_{1/2} = \frac{\Delta \nu}{F} = \frac{c_0}{2nl \cos \theta \, F} \qquad \textbf{(4.2-6)}$$

for the limiting resolution. The finesse F (which is used as a measure of the resolution of Fabry–Perot etalon) is, according to (4.2-6), the ratio of the separation between peaks to the width of a transmission bandpass. This ratio can be read directly from the transmission characteristics such as those of Figure 4-4, for which we obtain $F \simeq 26$.

Numerical example—design of a Fabry–Perot etalon. Consider the problem of designing a scanning Fabry–Perot etalon to be used in studying the mode structure of a He–Ne laser with the following characteristics: $l_{\text{laser}} = 100$ cm and the region of oscillation $= \Delta \nu_{\text{gain}} \simeq 1.5 \times 10^9$ Hz.

The free spectral range of the etalon (that is, its intermode spacing) must exceed the spectral region of interest, so from (4.1-10) we obtain

$$\frac{c_0}{2nl_{\text{etal}}} \geqslant 1.5 \times 10^9 \qquad \text{or} \qquad 2nl_{\text{etal}} \leqslant 20 \text{ cm} \qquad \textbf{(4.2-7)}$$

The separation between longitudinal modes of the laser oscillator is $c_0/2nl_{\text{laser}} = 1.5 \times 10^8$ Hz (here we assume $n = 1$). We choose the resolution of the etalon to be a tenth of this value, so spectral details as narrow as 1.5×10^7 Hz can be resolved. According to (4.2-6), this resolution can be achieved if

$$\Delta\nu_{1/2} = \frac{c_0}{2nl_{\text{etal}}F} \leqslant 1.5 \times 10^7 \qquad \text{or} \qquad 2nl_{\text{etal}}F \geqslant 2 \times 10^3 \qquad \textbf{(4.2-8)}$$

To satisfy condition (4.2-7), we choose $2nl_{\text{etal}} = 20$ cm; thus (4.2-8) is satisfied when

$$F \geqslant 100 \qquad\qquad\qquad \textbf{(4.2-9)}$$

A finesse of 100 requires, according to (4.2-5), a mirror reflectivity of approximately 97 percent.

As a practical note we may add that the finesse, as defined by the first equality in (4.2-6), depends not only on R but also on the mirror flatness and the beam angular spread. These points are taken up in Problems 4-2 and 4-4.

Another important mode of optical spectrum analysis performed with Fabry–Perot etalons involves the fact that a noncollimated monochromatic beam incident on the etalon will emerge simultaneously, according to (4.1-8), along many directions θ,[3] which correspond to the various orders m. If the output is then focused by a lens, each such direction θ will give rise to a circle in the focal plane of the lens, and therefore each frequency component present in the beam leads to a family of circles. This mode of spectrum analysis is especially useful under transient conditions where scanning etalons cannot be employed. Further discussion of this topic is included in Problem 4-6.

4.3   Optical Resonators with Spherical Mirrors

In this section we study the properties of optical resonators formed by two opposing spherical mirrors; see References [6] and [7]. We will show that the field solutions inside the resonators are those of the propagating Gaussian beams, which were considered in Chapter 3. It is, consequently, useful to start by reviewing the properties of these beams.

The field distribution corresponding to the (m, n) transverse mode is

---

[3] Each direction θ corresponds in three dimensions to the surface of a cone with a half-apex angle θ.

given, according to (3.6-1), by

$$E_{m,n}^{(x)}(\mathbf{r}) = E_0 \frac{\omega_0}{\omega(z)} H_m\left(\sqrt{2}\,\frac{x}{\omega(z)}\right) H_n\left(\sqrt{2}\,\frac{y}{\omega(z)}\right)$$

$$\times \exp\left[-\frac{x^2+y^2}{\omega^2(z)} - ik\frac{x^2+y^2}{2R(z)} - ikz + i(n+m+1)\phi\right]$$

(4.3-1)

where the spot size $\omega(z)$ is

$$\omega(z) = \omega_0\left[1 + \left(\frac{z}{z_0}\right)^2\right]^{1/2} \qquad z_0 = \frac{\pi\omega_0^2}{\lambda} \qquad \text{(4.3-2)}$$

and where ω_0, the minimum spot size, is a parameter characterizing the beam. The radius of curvature of the wavefronts is

$$R(z) = z\left[1 + \left(\frac{\pi\omega_0^2}{\lambda z}\right)^2\right] = \frac{1}{z}[z^2 + z_0^2] \qquad \text{(4.3-3)}$$

and the phase factor ϕ is as follows:

$$\phi = \tan^{-1}\left(\frac{\lambda z}{\pi\omega_0^2}\right) \qquad \text{(4.3-4)}$$

The sign of $R(z)$ is taken as positive when the center of curvature is to the left of the wavefront, and vice versa. According to (4.3-1) and (4.3-2) the loci of the points at which the beam intensity (watts per square meter) is a given fraction of its intensity on the axis are the hyperboloids

$$x^2 + y^2 = \text{const.} \times \omega^2(z) \qquad \text{(4.3-5)}$$

The hyperbolas generated by the intersection of these surfaces with planes that include the z axis are shown in Figure 4-7. These hyperbolas are normal to the phase fronts and thus correspond to the local direction of energy flow. The hyperboloid $x^2 + y^2 = \omega^2(z)$ is, according to (4.3-1), the locus of the points where the exponential factor in the field amplitude

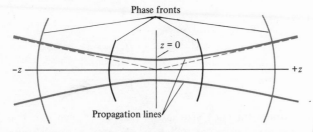

Phase fronts

$z = 0$

$-z$ $+z$

Propagation lines

Figure 4-7 Hyperbolic curves corresponding to the local directions of propagation. The nearly spherical phase fronts represent possible posi reflectors. Any two reflectors form a resonator with a transverse field distribution given by (4.3-1)

is down to e^{-1} from its value on the axis. The quantity $\omega(z)$ is thus defined as the *mode spot size* at the plane z.

Given a beam of the type described by (4.3-1) we can form an optical resonator merely by inserting at points z_1 and z_2 two reflectors with radii of curvature that match those of the propagating beam spherical phase fronts at these points. Since the surfaces are normal to the direction of energy propagation as shown in Figure 4-7, the reflected beam retraces itself; thus, if the phase shift between the mirrors is some multiple of 2π radians, a *self-reproducing stable field* configuration results.

Alternatively, given two mirrors with spherical radii of curvature R_1 and R_2 and some distance of separation l, we can, under certain conditions to be derived later, adjust the position $z = 0$ and the parameter ω_0 so that the mirrors coincide with two spherical wavefronts of the propagating beam defined by the position of the waist ($z = 0$) and ω_0. If, in addition, the mirrors can be made large enough to intercept the majority (99 percent, say) of the incident beam energy in the fundamental ($m = n = 0$) transverse mode, we may expect this mode to have a larger Q than higher-order transverse modes, which, according to Figure 3-3, have fields extending farther from the axis and consequently lose a larger fraction of their energy by "spilling" over the mirror edges (diffraction losses).

Optical resonator algebra.   As mentioned in the preceding paragraphs, we can form an optical resonator by using two reflectors, one at z_1 and the other at z_2, chosen so that their radii of curvature are the same as those of the beam wavefronts at the two locations. The propagating beam mode (4.3-11) is then reflected back and forth between the reflectors without a change in its transverse profile. The requisite radii of curvature, determined by (4.3-3), are

$$R_1 = +z_1 + \frac{z_0{}^2}{z_1}$$

$$R_2 = +z_2 + \frac{z_0{}^2}{z_2}$$

from which we get

$$z_1 = +\frac{R_1}{2} \pm \frac{1}{2}\sqrt{R_1{}^2 - 4z_0{}^2}$$

$$z_2 = +\frac{R_2}{2} \pm \frac{1}{2}\sqrt{R_2{}^2 - 4z_0{}^2}$$

(4.3-6)

For a given minimum spot size $\omega_0 = (\lambda z_0/\pi)^{1/2}$, we can use (4.3-6) to find the positions z_1 and z_2 at which to place mirrors with curvatures R_1 and R_2, respectively. In practice, we often start with given mirror curvatures R_1 and R_2 and a mirror separation l. The problem is then to find the minimum spot size ω_0, its location with respect to the reflectors, and the mirror spot sizes ω_1 and ω_2. Taking the mirror spacing as $l = z_2 - z_1$, we can solve (4.3-6) for z_0^2, obtaining

$$z_0^2 = \frac{l(-R_1 - l)(R_2 - l)(R_2 - R_1 - l)}{(R_2 - R_1 - 2l)^2} \tag{4.3-7}$$

where z_2 is to the right of z_1 (so that $l = z_2 - z_1 > 0$) and the mirror curvature is taken as positive when the center of curvature is to the left of the mirror.

The minimum spot size is $\omega_0 = (\lambda z_0/\pi)^{1/2}$ and its position is next determined from (4.3-6). The mirror spot sizes are then calculated by the use of (4.3-2).

The symmetrical mirror resonator.   The special case of a resonator with symmetrically (about $z = 0$) placed mirrors merits a few comments. The planar phase front at which the minimum spot size occurs is, by symmetry, at $z = 0$. Putting $R_2 = -R_1 = R$ in (4.3-7) gives

$$z_0^2 = \frac{(2R - l)l}{4} \tag{4.3-8}$$

and

$$\omega_0 = \left(\frac{\lambda z_0}{\pi}\right)^{1/2} = \left(\frac{\lambda}{\pi}\right)^{1/2}\left(\frac{l}{2}\right)^{1/4}\left(R - \frac{l}{2}\right)^{1/4} \tag{4.3-9}$$

which, when substituted in (4.3-2) with $z = l/2$, yields the following expression for the spot size at the mirrors:

$$\omega_{1,2} = \left(\frac{\lambda l}{2\pi}\right)^{1/2}\left[\frac{2R^2}{l(R - l/2)}\right]^{1/4} \tag{4.3-10}$$

A comparison with (4.3-9) shows that, for $R \gg l$, $\omega \simeq \omega_0$ and the beam spread inside the resonator is small.

The value of R (for a given l) for which the mirror spot size is a minimum, is readily found from (4.3-10) to be $R = l$. When this condition is fulfilled we have what is called a symmetrical *confocal resonator*, since the two foci, occurring at a distance of $R/2$ from the mirrors, coincide. From (4.3-7) and the relation $\omega_0 = (\lambda z_0/\pi)^{1/2}$ we obtain

$$(\omega_0)_{\text{conf}} = \left(\frac{\lambda l}{2\pi}\right)^{1/2} \tag{4.3-11}$$

whereas from (4.3-10) we get

$$(\omega_{1,2})_{\text{conf}} = (\omega_0)_{\text{conf}} \sqrt{2} \tag{4.3-12}$$

so the beam spot size increases by $\sqrt{2}$ between the center and the mirrors.

Numerical example—design of a symmetrical resonator.   Consider the problem of designing a symmetrical resonator for $\lambda = 10^{-4}$ cm with a mirror separation $l = 2m$. If we were to choose the confocal geometry with $R = l = 2m$, the minimum spot size (at the resonator center) would be, from (4.3-11),

$$(\omega_0)_{\text{conf}} = \left(\frac{\lambda l}{2\pi}\right)^{1/2} = 0.06 \text{ cm}$$

whereas, using (4.3-12), the spot size at the mirrors would have the value

$$(\omega_{1\ 2})_{\text{conf}} = \omega_0\sqrt{2} \simeq 0.084 \text{ cm}$$

Assume next that a mirror spot size $\omega_{1,2} = 0.3$ cm is desired. Using this value in (4.3-10) and assuming $R \gg l$, we get

$$\frac{\omega_{1,2}}{(\lambda l/2\pi)^{1/2}} = \frac{0.3}{0.06} = \left(\frac{2R}{l}\right)^{1/4}$$

whence

$$R \simeq 300l \simeq 600 \text{ meters}$$

so that the assumption $R \gg l$ is valid. The minimum beam spot size ω_0 is found, through (4.3-2) and (4.3-8), to be

$$\omega_0 = 0.9985\omega_{1/2} \simeq 0.3 \text{ cm}$$

Thus, to increase the mirror spot size from its minimum (confocal) value of 0.084 cm to 0.3 cm, we must use exceedingly plane mirrors ($R = 600$ meters). This also shows that even small mirror curvatures (that is, large R) give rise to "narrow" beams.

The numerical example we have worked out applies equally well to the case in which a plane mirror is placed at $z = 0$. The beam pattern is equal to that existing in the corresponding half of the symmetric resonator in the example, so the spot size on the planar reflector is ω_0.

4.4 Mode Stability Criteria

The ability of an optical resonator to support low (diffraction) loss[4] modes depends on the mirrors' separation l and their radii of curvature R_1 and R_2. To illustrate this point, consider first the symmetric resonator with $R_2 = R_1 = R$.

The ratio of the mirror spot size at a given l/R to its minimum confocal ($l/R = 1$) value, given by the ratio of (4.3-10) to (4.3-12), is

$$\frac{\omega_{1,2}}{\omega_{\text{conf}}} = \left[\frac{1}{(l/R)[2 - (l/R)]}\right]^{1/4} \tag{4.4-1}$$

This ratio is plotted in Figure 4-8. For $l/R = 0$ (plane-parallel mirrors) and for $l/R = 2$ (two concentric mirrors), the spot size becomes infinite.

---

[4] By diffraction loss we refer to the fact that due to the beam spread (see Equation 3.2-18), a fraction of the Gaussian beam energy "misses" the mirror and is not reflected and is thus lost.

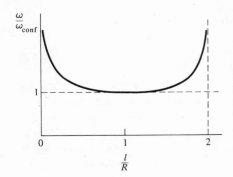

Figure 4-8 Ratio of beam spot size at the mirrors of a symmetrical resonator to its confocal ($l/R = 1$) value.

It is clear that the diffraction losses for these cases are very high, since most of the beam energy "spills over" the reflector edges. Since, according to Table 2.1, the reflection of a Gaussian beam from a mirror with a radius of curvature R is formally equivalent to its transmission through a lens with a focal length $f = R/2$, the problem of the existence of stable confined optical modes in a resonator is formally the same as that of the existence of stable solutions for the propagation of a Gaussian beam in a biperiodic lens sequence, as shown in Figure 4-9. This problem was considered in Section 3.3 and led to the stability condition (3.3-9).

If, in (3.3-9), we replace f_1 by $R_1/2$ and f_2 by $R_2/2$,[5] we obtain the

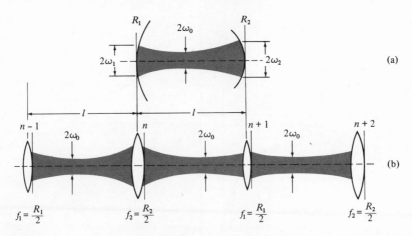

Figure 4-9 (**a**) Asymmetric resonator ($R_1 \neq R_2$) with mirror curvatures R_1 and R_2. (**b**) Biperiodic lens system (lens waveguide) equivalent to resonator shown in (**a**).

---

[5] This causes the sign convention of R_1 and R_2 to be different from that used in the preceding sections. The sign of R is the same as that of the focal length of the equivalent lens. This makes R_1 (or R_2) positive when the center of curvature of mirror 1 (or 2) is in the direction of mirror 2 (or 1), and negative otherwise.

stability condition for optical resonators

$$0 \leqslant \left(1 - \frac{l}{R_1}\right)\left(1 - \frac{l}{R_2}\right) \leqslant 1 \qquad \textbf{(4.4-2)}$$

A convenient representation of the stability condition (4.4-2) is by means of the diagram [7] shown in Figure 4-10. From this diagram, for example, it can be seen that the symmetric concentric ($R_1 = R_2 = l/2$), confocal ($R_1 = R_2 = l$), and the plane-parallel ($R_1 = R_2 = \infty$) resonators are all on the verge of instability and thus may become extremely lossy by small deviations of the parameters in the direction of instability.

4.5   The Resonance Frequencies

In Section 4.3 we noted in passing that at resonance the phase delay kl due to a single traversal of the cavity length is some multiple of π. This requirement can be justified if we consider the idealized problem of forming

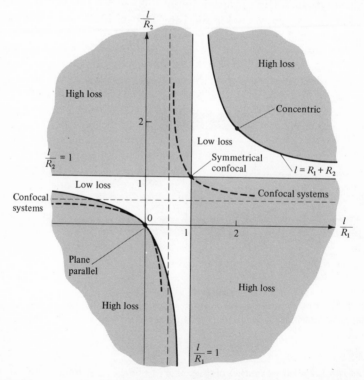

Figure 4-10   Stability diagram of optical resonator. Shaded (high-loss) areas are those in which the stability condition $0 \leq (1 - l/R_1)(1 - l/R_2) \leq 1$ is violated and the clear (low-loss) areas are those in which it is fulfilled. The sign convention for R_1 and R_2 is discussed in Footnote 5. (After Reference [7].)

a resonator by exciting a plane transverse electromagnetic wave between two perfectly conducting plane parallel plates separated by l. The total field is then the sum of the positive and negative traveling waves according to

$$e(z, t) = A[\cos(\omega t - kz) - \cos(\omega t + kz)]$$

where the position of one of the end plates is chosen at $z = 0$ so that $e(0, t) = 0$. We can write $e(z, t)$, using standard trigonometric identities, as a standing wave of the form

$$e(z, t) = 2A \sin kz \sin \omega t \qquad \text{(4.5-1)}$$

from which it becomes clear that we can only satisfy the boundary condition $e(l, t) = 0$ at the second reflector $(z = l)$ by choosing

$$kl = q\pi \qquad \text{(4.5-2)}$$

where q is some integer. To illustrate the resonance condition (4.5-2) from a different point of view, consider the incidence of a plane wave containing many frequency components on a resonator with slightly transmissive mirrors. It is clear that only at those frequencies for which condition (4.5-2) is satisfied (for some q) will the amplitudes at an arbitrary plane z, corresponding to successive reflections, add up in phase so as to give an appreciable total field. At frequencies where this condition is not satisfied, successive reflections do not add up in phase and the field remains small. This is the fundamental reason why a resonator acts as a filter in suppressing the fields at all frequencies except those near its resonances.

If we consider a resonator with reflectors at z_2 and $-z_1$, Equation (4.5-2) becomes

$$\theta(z_2) - \theta(z_1) = q\pi$$

where $\theta(z)$ is the phase at point z on the resonator axis. Using (3.6-2) for θ, the foregoing equation becomes

$$kl - (m + n + 1)\left[\tan^{-1}\frac{z_2}{z_0} - \tan^{-1}\frac{z_1}{z_0}\right] = q\pi \qquad \text{(4.5-3)}$$

where $l = z_2 - z_1$ is the resonator length. For a given transverse mode—that is, given m and n—we obtain

$$k_{q+1} - k_q = \frac{\pi}{l}$$

or using $k = 2\pi\nu/(c_0/n)$,

$$\nu_{q+1} - \nu_q = \frac{c_0}{2nl} \qquad \nu_q = \frac{qc_0}{2nl} \qquad \text{(4.5-4)}$$

for the intermode frequency spacing.

Let us consider, next, the effect of varying the transverse mode indices m and n in a mode with a fixed q. We notice from (4.5-3) that the resonant frequencies depend on the sum $(m + n)$ and not on m and n separately, so for a given q all the modes with the same value of $m + n$ are degenerate (that is, they have the same resonance frequencies). Considering (4.5-3) at two different values of $m + n$ gives

$$k_1l - (m + n + 1)_1 \left[\tan^{-1} \frac{z_2}{z_0} - \tan^{-1} \frac{z_1}{z_0} \right] = q\pi$$

$$k_2l - (m + n + 1)_2 \left[\tan^{-1} \frac{z_2}{z_0} - \tan^{-1} \frac{z_1}{z_0} \right] = q\pi$$

and, by subtraction,

$$(k_1 - k_2)l = [(m + n + 1)_1 - (m + n + 1)_2] \left(\tan^{-1} \frac{z_2}{z_0} + \tan^{-1} \frac{z_1}{z_0} \right)$$

$$\tag{4.5-5}$$

and, using $k = 2\pi n\nu/c_0$,

$$\Delta\nu = \frac{c_0}{2\pi nl} \Delta(m + n) \left[\tan^{-1} \frac{z_2}{z_0} - \tan^{-1} \frac{z_1}{z_0} \right] \tag{4.5-6}$$

for the change $\Delta\nu$ in the resonance frequency caused by a change $\Delta(m + n)$ in the sum $(m + n)$. As an example, in the case of a confocal resonator $(R = l)$ we have, according to (4.3-8), $z_2 = -z_1 = z_0$; therefore, $\tan^{-1}(z_2/z_0) = -\tan^{-1}(z_1/z_0) = \pi/4$, and (4.5-6) becomes

$$\Delta\nu_{\text{conf}} = \frac{1}{2} [\Delta(m + n)] \frac{c_0}{2nl} \tag{4.5-7}$$

Comparing (4.5-7) to (4.5-4) we find that in the confocal resonator the resonance frequencies of the transverse modes resulting from changing m and n either coincide or fall halfway between those that result from a change of the longitudinal mode index q. This situation is depicted in Figure 4-11.

To see what happens to the transverse resonance frequencies (that is, those due to a variation of m and n) in a nonconfocal resonator, we may consider the nearly planar resonator in which $|z_1|$ and z_2 are small compared

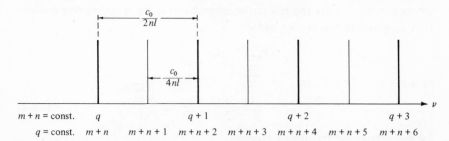

Figure 4-11   Position of resonance frequencies of a confocal $(l = R)$ optical resonator as a function of the mode indices m, n, and q.

to z_0 (that is, $l \ll R_1$ and R_2). In this case, Equation (4.5-6) becomes

$$\Delta \nu \simeq \frac{c_0}{2\pi n z_0} \Delta(m + n) \tag{4.5-8}$$

where the n inside the parentheses is an integer, not to be confused with the index of refraction n appearing in the denominator. The mode grouping for this case is illustrated in Figure 4-12.

The situation depicted in Figure 4-12 is highly objectionable if the resonator is to be used as a scanning interferometer in the manner described in Section 4.2. The reason is that in reconstructing the spectral profile of the unknown signal, an ambiguity is caused by the simultaneous transmission at more than one frequency. This ambiguity is resolved by using a confocal etalon with a mode spacing as shown in Figure 4-11 and by choosing l to be small enough that the intermode spacing $c_0/4nl$ exceeds the width of the spectral region that is scanned.

4.6   Losses in Optical Resonators

An understanding of the mechanisms by which electromagnetic energy is dissipated in optical resonators and the ability to control them are of major importance in understanding and operating a variety of optical devices. For historical reasons as well as for reasons of convenience, these losses are often characterized by a number of different parameters. Even this book (where an attempt at methodology has been made) has used the concepts of finesse, photon lifetime, and quality factor Q to describe losses in resonators. Let us see how these quantities are related to each other.

The decay lifetime (photon lifetime) t_c of a cavity mode is defined by means of the equation

$$\frac{d\mathcal{E}}{dt} = -\frac{\mathcal{E}}{t_c} \tag{4.6-1}$$

where $\mathcal{E}$ is the energy stored in the mode. If the fractional (intensity) loss per pass is L and the length of the resonator is l, then the fractional loss

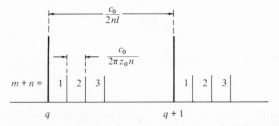

Figure 4-12   Resonant frequencies of a near-planar $(R \gg l)$ optical resonator as a function of the mode indices m, n, and q.

per unit time is $c_0 L/nl$; therefore,

$$\frac{d\mathcal{E}}{dt} = -\frac{c_0 L}{nl} \mathcal{E}$$

and, from (4.6-1),

$$t_c = \frac{nl}{c_0 L} \tag{4.6-2}$$

In cases where the loss is primarily due to the finite mirror transmission $T = 1 - R$ (where R is the mirror reflectivity, assumed to be the same for both mirrors), we have $L = (1 - R)$. Therefore,

$$t_c = \frac{nl}{c_0(1 - R)} \tag{4.6-3}$$

The quality factor was defined in (4.0-1) by the relation

$$Q = \frac{\omega \mathcal{E}}{P} = -\frac{\omega \mathcal{E}}{d\mathcal{E}/dt} \tag{4.6-4}$$

where $\mathcal{E}$ is the stored energy and $P = -d\mathcal{E}/dt$ is the rate of energy dissipation. By comparing (4.6-4) with (4.6-1) we obtain

$$Q = \omega t_c \tag{4.6-5}$$

In this context we may recall [see (4.2-6)] that the full width at the half-power points of the Lorentzian response curve of a resonator is

$$\Delta \nu_{1/2} = \frac{\nu}{Q} = \frac{1}{2\pi t_c} \approx \frac{c_0(1 - R)}{2\pi nl} \tag{4.6-6}$$

where the approximation is valid for $\theta \simeq 0°$ and $R \simeq 1$.

In our study of the Fabry–Perot etalon we found it convenient to characterize its resolution by means of the finesse defined by (4.2-5) as

$$F = \frac{\pi \sqrt{R}}{1 - R} = \frac{c_0}{2nl\, \Delta \nu_{1/2}} \tag{4.6-7}$$

where the first equality holds only when the losses are predominantly due to transmission.

From (4.6-6) and (4.6-7) we obtain

$$F = \frac{\lambda Q}{2l} = \frac{\pi c_0 t_c}{nl} \tag{4.6-8}$$

The most common loss mechanisms in optical resonators are the following:

1. *Loss resulting from nonperfect reflection.* Reflection loss is unavoidable, since without some transmission no power flow is possible. In addition, no mirror is ideal; and even when mirrors are made to yield the highest possible reflectivities, some residual absorption and scattering reduce the reflectivity to somewhat less than 100 percent. This loss was shown to lead to a cavity decay time t_c as in (4.6-3).

2. *Absorption and scattering in the laser medium.* Transitions from some of the atomic levels that are populated in the process of pumping to higher-lying levels constitute a loss mechanism in optical resonators when they are used as laser oscillators. Scattering from inhomogeneities and imperfections is especially serious in solid-state laser media.

3. *Diffraction losses.* From Equation (4.3-1) or from Figures 3-3 and 3-4, we find that the energy of propagating-beam modes extends to considerable distance from the axis. When a resonator is formed by "trapping" a propagating beam between two reflectors, it is clear that for finite-dimension reflectors some of the beam energy will not be intercepted by the mirrors and will therefore be lost. For a given set of mirrors this loss will be greater the higher the transverse mode indices m, n, since in this case the energy extends farther. This fact is used to prevent the oscillation of higher-order modes by inserting apertures into the laser resonator whose opening is large enough to allow most of the fundamental $(0, 0, q)$ mode energy through, but small enough to increase substantially the losses of the higher-order modes. Figure 4-13 shows the diffraction losses of a number of

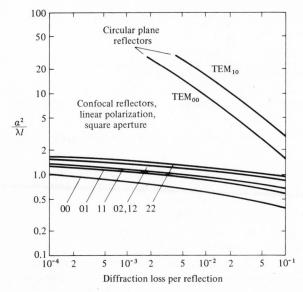

Figure 4-13 Diffraction losses for a plane-parallel and several low-order confocal resonators; a is the mirror radius and l is their spacing. The pairs of numbers under the arrows refer to the transverse-mode indices m, n. (After Reference [6].)

low-order confocal resonators. Of special interest is the dramatic decrease of the diffraction losses that results from the use of spherical reflectors instead of the plane-parallel ones.

■ PROBLEMS

4-1 Plot I_r/I_i vs. δ of a Fabry–Perot etalon with $R = 0.9$.

4-2 Show that if a Fabry–Perot etalon has a fractional intensity loss per pass of $(1 - A)$, its peak transmission is given as $(1 - R)^2 A/(1 - RA)^2$.

4-3 Starting with the definition (4.2-6)

$$F \equiv \frac{\nu_{m+1} - \nu_m}{\Delta\nu_{1/2}}$$

for the finesse of a Fabry–Perot etalon and using semiquantitative arguments, show why in the case where the root-mean-square surface deviation from perfect flatness is approximately λ/N, the finesse cannot exceed $F \simeq N/2$. (*Hint:* Consider the spreading of the transmission peak due to a small number of etalons of nearly equal length transmitting in parallel.)

4-4 Show that the angular spread of a beam that is incident normally on a plane-parallel Fabry–Perot etalon must not exceed

$$\theta_{1/2} = \sqrt{\frac{2\lambda_0}{nlF}}$$

if its peak transmission is not to deviate substantially from unity.

4-5 Complete the derivation of Equations (4.1-4), (4.1-5), (4.1-6), and (4.1-7).

4-6 Consider a diverging monochromatic beam that is incident on a plane-parallel Fabry–Perot etalon.
a. Obtain an expression for the various angles along which the output energy is propagating. [*Hint:* These correspond to the different values of θ in (4.1-8) that result from changing m.]
b. Let the output beam in (a) be incident on a lens with a focal length f. Show that the energy distribution in the focal plane consists of a series of circles, each corresponding to a different value of m. Obtain an expression for the radii of the circles.
c. Consider the effect in (b) of having simultaneously two frequencies ν_1 and ν_2 present in the input beam. Derive an expression for the separation

of the respective circles in the focal plane. Show that the smallest separation $\nu_1 - \nu_2$ that can be resolved by this technique is given by $(\Delta\nu)_{\min} \sim c_0/2nlF$.

4-7 **a.** Derive the phase shift between the incident and transmitted field amplitudes in a Fabry–Perot etalon as a function δ. Sketch it qualitatively for a number of different reflectivities.

b. Assume that the optical length of an etalon with $R = 0.9$ and $\theta = 0°$ is adjusted so that its transmission is a maximum and then modulated about this point according to

$$\Delta(nl) = \frac{\lambda}{100} \cos \omega_m t$$

Show that, to first-order, the output is phase-modulated. What is the modulation index? [For a definition of the modulation index δ see (9.4-3).]

4-8 Show that the number of modes per unit frequency in a resonator whose dimensions are large compared to the wavelength is given by

$$N = \frac{8\pi\nu^2 V}{c^3} \tag{1}$$

where c is the velocity of light and V is the volume of the resonator. (*Hint:* Assume a cube resonator with sides equal to L having perfectly conducting walls.) Taking the modes' fields as proportional to

$$\sin k_x x \, \sin k_y y \, \sin k_z z$$

show that in order for the fields to be zero at the boundaries, the conditions

$$k_x = \frac{2\pi l}{L} \qquad k_y = \frac{2\pi m}{L} \qquad k_z = \frac{2\pi n}{L}$$

where l, m, and n are any (positive) integers, must be satisfied. Each new combination of l, m, and n specifies a mode. Show that Equation (1) follows from the foregoing considerations and the fact that

$$k^2 = \frac{4\pi^2\nu^2}{c^2} = k_x{}^2 + k_y{}^2 + k_z{}^2$$

so each frequency ν defines a sphere in the space k_x, k_y, k_z.

4-9 Calculate the fraction of the power of a fundamental ($m = n = 0$) Gaussian beam that passes through an aperture with a radius equal to the beam spot size.

■ REFERENCES

[1] Ramo, S., J. R. Whinnery, and T. Van Duzer, *Fields and Waves in Communication Electronics*. New York: Wiley, 1965.

[2] Yariv, A., *Quantum Electronics*. New York: Wiley, 1967, p. 86.

[3] Fabry, C., and A. Perot, "Théorie et applications d'une nouvelle méthode de spectroscopie interférentielle," *Ann. Chim. Phys.*, vol. 16, p. 115, 1899.

[4] Born, M., and E. Wolf, *Principles of Optics*, 3d Ed. New York: Pergamon, 1965, Chap. 7.

[5] Peterson, D. G., and A. Yariv, "Interferometry and laser control with Fabry–Perot etalons," *Appl. Opt.*, vol. 5, p. 985, 1966.

[6] Boyd, G. D., and J. P. Gordon, "Confocal multimode resonator for millimeter through optical wavelength masers," *Bell System Tech. J.*, vol. 40, p. 489, 1961.

[7] Boyd, G. D., and H. Kogelnik, "Generalized confocal resonator theory," *Bell System Tech. J.*, vol. 41, p. 1347, 1962.

Interaction of Radiation and Atomic Systems

5.0 Introduction

In this chapter we consider what happens to an electromagnetic wave propagating in an atomic medium. We are chiefly concerned with the possibility of growth (or attenuation) of the radiation resulting from its interaction with atoms. We also consider the changes in the velocity of propagation of light due to such interaction. The concepts derived in this chapter will be used in the next one in treating the laser oscillator.

5.1 Spontaneous Transitions between Atomic Levels—Homogeneous and Inhomogeneous Broadening

One of the basic results of the theory of quantum mechanics is that each physical system can be found, upon measurement, in only one of a predetermined set of energetic states—the so-called eigenstates of the system. With each of these states we associate an energy that corresponds to the total energy of the system when occupying the state. Some of the simpler systems, which are treated in any basic text on quantum mechanics, include the free electron, the hydrogen atom, and the harmonic oscillator. Examples of more complicated systems include the hydrogen molecule and the semiconducting crystal. With each state, the state i of the hydrogen atom say, we associate an eigenfunction [1]

$$\psi_i(\mathbf{r}, t) = u_i(\mathbf{r})e^{-iE_it/\hbar} \tag{5.1-1}$$

where $|u_i(\mathbf{r})|^2 \, dx \, dy \, dz$ gives the probability of finding the electron, once it is known to be in the state i, within the volume element $dx \, dy \, dz$, which is centered on the point $\mathbf{r}$. E_i is the state energy described above and $\hbar = h/2\pi$ where $h = 6.626 \times 10^{-34}$ joule-second is Planck's constant.

One of the main tasks of quantum mechanics is the determination of the eigenfunctions $u_i(\mathbf{r})$ and the corresponding energies E_i of various physical systems. In this book, however, we will accept the existence of these states, their energy levels, as well as a number of other related results whose justification is provided by the experimentally proved formalism of quantum mechanics. Some of these results are discussed in the following.

The concept of spontaneous emission. In Figure 5-1 we show a system of energy levels that are associated with a given physical system—an atom, say. Let us concentrate on two of these levels—1 and 2, for example. If the atom is known to be in state 2 at $t = 0$ there is a finite probability per unit time that it will undergo a transition to state 1, emitting in the process a photon of energy $h\nu = E_2 - E_1$. This process, occurring as it does without the inducement of a radiation field, is referred to as *spontaneous emission*.

Another equivalent way of thinking about spontaneous transitions, and one corresponding more closely to experimental situations, is the following: Consider a large number N_2 of identical atoms that are known to be in state 2 at $t = 0$. The number of these atoms undergoing spontaneous transition to state 1 per unit time is

$$-\frac{dN_2}{dt} = A_{21}N_2 \equiv \frac{N_2}{(t_{\text{spont}})_{21}} \tag{5.1-2}$$

where A_{21} is the spontaneous transition rate and $(t_{\text{spont}})_{21} \equiv A_{21}^{-1}$ is

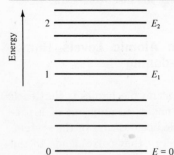

Figure 5-1 Some of the energy levels of an atomic system. Level 0, the ground state, is the lowest energy state. Levels 1 and 2 represent two excited states.

called the spontaneous lifetime associated with the transition $2 \to 1$. It follows from quantum mechanical considerations that spontaneous transitions take place from a given state only to states lying lower in energy, so no spontaneous transitions take place from 1 to 2. The rate A_{21} can be calculated using the eigenfunctions of states 2 and 1. In this book we *accept* the existence of spontaneous emission A_{21} and regard A_{21} as a parameter characterizing the transition $2 \to 1$ of the given physical system.[1]

The lineshape function—homogeneous and inhomogeneous broadening.
If one performs a spectral analysis of the radiation emitted by spontaneous $2 \to 1$ transitions, one finds that the radiation is not strictly monochromatic (that is, of one frequency) but occupies a finite frequency bandwidth. The function describing the distribution of emitted intensity versus the frequency ν is referred to as the lineshape function $g(\nu)$ (of the transition $2 \to 1$) and its arbitrary scale factor is usually chosen so that the function is normalized according to

$$\int_{-\infty}^{+\infty} g(\nu) \, d\nu = 1 \qquad \text{(5.1-3)}$$

We can consequently view $g(\nu) \, d\nu$ as the *a priori* probability that a given spontaneous emission from level 2 to level 1 will result in a photon whose frequency is between ν and $\nu + d\nu$.

Another method of determining $g(\nu)$ is to apply an electromagnetic field to the sample containing the atoms and then plot the amount of energy absorbed by $1 \to 2$ transitions as a function of the frequency. This function, when normalized according to (5.1-3) is again $g(\nu)$.

The fact that both the emission and the absorption are described by the same lineshape function $g(\nu)$ can be verified experimentally, and follows from basic quantum mechanical considerations. The proof is beyond the scope of this book, but we can perhaps make a plausibility argument using the following example. Consider an *RLC* circuit that is excited into oscillation by connecting it to a signal source of frequency $\nu_0 = 1/2\pi\sqrt{LC}$. The excitation is then discontinued and the transient decay of the oscillation is observed. It is a straightforward problem to show that the intensity spectrum of the decaying oscillation, which is analogous to spontaneous

---

[1] The quantum mechanical derivation gives [1]

$$A_{21} = \frac{2e^2\omega^3(x_{12}{}^2 + y_{12}{}^2 + z_{12}{}^2)}{3hc^3\epsilon}$$

for a class of transitions known as electric dipole transitions. The parameter ϵ is the dielectric constant at ω and

$$x_{12} = \int_{\substack{\text{all} \\ \text{space}}} u_1^*(\mathbf{r})xu_2(\mathbf{r}) \, d^3\mathbf{r}$$

where x, y, and z are the coordinates of the electron.

emission since the total energy is decreasing, is the same as a plot of the absorption power vs. frequency of the same circuit; this last process being equivalent to induced absorption in the atomic system. It will be left as an exercise to show that in the case of the RLC circuit the spectrum characterizing the decay or absorption is proportional to

$$f(\nu) = \frac{1}{(\nu - \nu_0)^2 + (\nu_0/2Q)^2} \tag{5.1-4}$$

where $Q = 2\pi\nu_0 CR$ is the quality factor of the circuit.

The formal equivalence between an atomic transition and an oscillator goes even further than this RLC circuit example indicates. Further in this chapter we will use it extensively to describe the interaction between an atomic system and an electromagnetic field.

Homogeneous and inhomogeneous broadening [2]. One of the possible causes for the frequency spread of spontaneous emission is the finite lifetime τ of the emitting state. If we consider the emission from the excited state as that corresponding to a damped oscillator and choose the decay time of the oscillator as τ we can take the radiated field as

$$e(t) = E_0 e^{-t/\tau} \cos \omega_0 t$$
$$= \frac{E_0}{2} [e^{i(\omega_0 + i\sigma/2)t} + e^{-i(\omega_0 - i\sigma/2)t}] \tag{5.1-5}$$

where $\sigma/2 = \tau^{-1}$ is the decay rate. The Fourier transform of $e(t)$ is

$$E(\omega) = \int_0^{+\infty} e(t)e^{-i\omega t}\, dt$$
$$= \frac{E_0}{2}\left[\frac{i}{(\omega_0 - \omega + i\sigma/2)} - \frac{i}{(\omega_0 + \omega + i\sigma/2)}\right] \tag{5.1-6}$$

where the lower limit of integration is taken as $t = 0$ (instead of $t = -\infty$) to correspond with the start of our observation period. The spectral density of the spontaneous emission is proportional to $|E(\omega)|^2$. If we limit our attention to the vicinity of the resonant frequency $\omega \simeq \omega_0$, we obtain

$$|E(\omega)|^2 \propto \frac{1}{(\omega - \omega_0)^2 + (\sigma/2)^2} \tag{5.1-7}$$

which is of the same form as (5.1-4).

Curves with the functional dependence of (5.1-7) are called Lorentzian. They occur often in physics and engineering, since, as shown, they characterize the response of damped resonant systems.

The separation $\Delta\nu$ between the two frequencies at which the Lorentzian is down to half its peak value is referred to as the linewidth and is given by

$$\Delta\nu = \frac{\sigma}{2\pi} = \frac{1}{\pi\tau} \tag{5.1-8}$$

Rewriting (5.1-7) in terms of $\Delta\nu$ and, at the same time, normalizing it according to (5.1-3), we obtain the normalized Lorentzian lineshape function

$$g(\nu) = \frac{\Delta\nu}{2\pi[(\nu - \nu_0)^2 + (\Delta\nu/2)^2]}$$ (5.1-9)

The type of broadening (that is, the finite width of the emitted spectrum) described above is called *homogeneous broadening*. It is characterized by the fact that the spread of the response over a band $\sim\Delta\nu$ is characteristic of *each* atom in the sample. The function $g(\nu)$ thus describes the response of any of the atoms which are indistinguishable.

As mentioned above, homogeneous broadening is due most often to the finite interaction lifetime of the emitting or absorbing atoms. Some of the most common mechanisms are:

1. The spontaneous lifetime of the excited state.
2. Collision of an atom embedded in a crystal with a phonon. This may involve the emission or absorption of acoustic energy. Such a collision does not terminate the lifetime of the atom in its absorbing or emitting state. It does interrupt, however, the relative phase between the atomic oscillation (see Section 5.4) and that of the field, thus causing a broadening of the response according to (5.1-6) where τ now represents the mean uninterrupted interaction time.
3. Pressure broadening of atoms in a gas. At sufficiently high atomic densities the collisions between atoms become frequent enough that lifetime termination and phase interruption as in the preceding mechanism dominate the broadening mechanism.

There are, however, many physical situations in which the individual atoms are distinguishable, each having a slightly different transition frequency ν_0. If one observes, in this case, the spectrum of the spontaneous emission, its spectral distribution will reflect the spread in the individual transition frequencies and not the broadening due to the finite lifetime of the excited state. Two typical situations give rise to this type of broadening, referred to as *inhomogeneous*.

First of all, the energy levels, hence the transition frequencies, of ions present as impurities in a host crystal depend on the immediate crystalline surroundings. The ever-present random strain, as well as other types of crystal imperfections, cause the crystal surroundings to vary from one ion to the next, thus effecting a spread in the transition frequencies.

Second, the transition frequency ν of a gaseous atom (or molecule) is Doppler-shifted due to the finite velocity of the atom according to

$$\nu = \nu_0 + \frac{v_x}{c}\nu_0$$ (5.

where v_x is the component of the velocity along the direction conne the observer with the moving atom, c is the velocity of light in the me and ν_0 is the frequency corresponding to a stationary atom. The Maxwell velocity distribution function of a gas with atomic mass M which is at equilibrium at temperature T is [3]

$$f(v_x, v_y, v_z) = \left(\frac{M}{2\pi kT}\right)^{3/2} \exp\left[-\frac{M}{2kT}(v_x^2 + v_y^2 + v_z^2)\right] \quad \text{(5.1-11)}$$

$f(v_x, v_y, v_z)\, dv_x\, dv_y\, dv_z$ corresponds to the fraction of all the atoms whose x component of velocity is contained in the interval v_x to $v_x + dv_x$ while, simultaneously, their y and z components lie between v_y and $v_y + dv_y$, v_z and $v_z + dv_z$, respectively. Alternatively, we may view $f(v_x, v_y, v_z)\, dv_x\, dv_y\, dv_z$ as the *a priori* probability that the velocity vector $\mathbf{v}$ of any given atom terminates within the differential volume $dv_x\, dv_y\, dv_z$ centered on $\mathbf{v}$ in velocity space so that

$$\iiint\limits_{-\infty}^{\infty} f(v_x, v_y, v_z)\, dv_x\, dv_y\, dv_z = 1 \quad \text{(5.1-12)}$$

According to (5.1-10) the probability $g(\nu)\, d\nu$ that the transition frequency is between ν and $\nu + d\nu$ is equal to the probability that v_x will be found between $v_x = (\nu - \nu_0)(c/\nu_0)$ and $(\nu + d\nu - \nu_0)(c/\nu_0)$ irrespective of the values of v_y and v_z [since if $v_x = (\nu - \nu_0)(c/\nu_0)$, the Doppler-shifted frequency will be equal to ν regardless of v_y and v_z]. This probability is thus obtained by substituting $v_x = (\nu - \nu_0)c/\nu_0$ in $f(v_x, v_y, v_z)\, dv_x\, dv_y\, dv_z$, and then integrating over all values of v_y and v_z. The result is

$$g(\nu)\, d\nu = \left(\frac{M}{2\pi kT}\right)^{3/2} \int_{-\infty}^{\infty} \int_{-\infty}^{\infty} e^{-(M/2kT)(v_y^2 + v_z^2)}\, dv_y\, dv_z$$
$$\times\, e^{-(M/2kT)(c^2/\nu_0^2)(\nu - \nu_0)^2} \left(\frac{c}{\nu_0}\right) d\nu \quad \text{(5.1-13)}$$

Using the definite integral

$$\int_{-\infty}^{\infty} e^{-(M/2kT)v_z^2}\, dv_z = \left(\frac{2\pi kT}{M}\right)^{1/2}$$

we obtain, from (5.1-13),

$$g(\nu) = \frac{c}{\nu_0}\left(\frac{M}{2\pi kT}\right)^{1/2} e^{-(M/2kT)(c^2/\nu_0^2)(\nu - \nu_0)^2} \quad \text{(5.1-14)}$$

for the *normalized Doppler-broadened lineshape*. The functional dependence of $g(\nu)$ in (5.1-14) is referred to as Gaussian. The width of $g(\nu)$ in this case is taken as the frequency separation between the points where $g(\nu)$ is down to half its peak value. It is obtained from (5.1-14) as

$$\Delta\nu_D = 2\nu_0 \sqrt{\frac{2kT}{Mc^2}\ln 2} \quad \text{(5.1-15)}$$

where the subscript D stands for "Doppler." We can reexpress $g(\nu)$ in terms of $\Delta\nu_D$, obtaining

$$g(\nu) = \frac{2(\ln 2)^{1/2}}{\pi^{1/2}\,\Delta\nu_D}\, e^{-[4(\ln 2)(\nu-\nu_0)^2/\Delta\nu_D^2]} \approx \frac{1}{\Delta\nu_D} \qquad \textbf{(5.1-16)}$$

In Figure 5-2 we show, as an example of a lineshape function, the spontaneous emission spectrum of Nd^{3+} when present as an impurity ion in a $CaWO_4$ lattice. The spectrum consists of a number of transitions, which are partially overlapping.

Numerical example—the Doppler linewidth of Ne.   Consider the 6328 Å transition in Ne, which is used in the popular He–Ne laser. Using the atomic mass 20 for neon in (5.1-15) and taking $T = 300°K$, we obtain

$$\Delta\nu_D \simeq 1.5 \times 10^9 \text{ Hz}$$

for the Doppler linewidth.

5.2 Induced Transitions

In the presence of an electromagnetic field of frequency $\nu \sim (E_2 - E_1)/h$ an atom whose energy levels are shown in Figure 5-1 can undergo a transition from state 1 to 2, *absorbing* in the process a quantum of excitation (photon) with energy $h\nu$ from the field. If the atom happens to occupy state 2 at the moment when it is first subjected to the electromagnetic

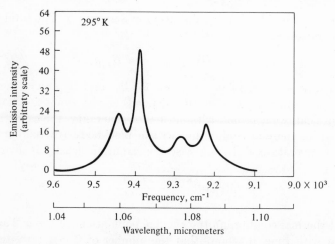

Figure 5-2   Emission spectrum of $Nd^{3+}:CaWO_4$ in the vicinity of the 1.06-μm laser transition. The main peak responds to the laser transition. (After Reference [4].)

field, it will make a downward transition to state 1, *emitting* a photon of energy $h\nu$.

What distinguishes the process of induced transition from the spontaneous one described in the last section is the fact that the induced rate for $2 \rightarrow 1$ and $1 \rightarrow 2$ transitions is *equal,* whereas the spontaneous $1 \rightarrow 2$ (that is, the one in which the atomic energy increases) transition rate is zero. Another fundamental difference—one that, again, follows from quantum mechanical considerations—is that the induced rate is *proportional* to the *intensity* of the electromagnetic field, whereas the spontaneous rate is independent of it. The relationship between the induced transition rate and the (inducing) field intensity is of fundamental importance in treating the interaction of atomic systems with electromagnetic fields. Its derivation follows.

Consider first the interaction of an assembly of identical atoms with a radiation field whose energy density is distributed uniformly in frequency in the vicinity of the transition frequency. Let the energy density per unit frequency be $\rho(\nu)$. We assume that the induced transition rates per atom from $2 \rightarrow 1$ and $1 \rightarrow 2$ are both proportional to $\rho(\nu)$ and take them as

$$(W'_{21})_{\text{induced}} = B_{21}\rho(\nu)$$
$$(W'_{12})_{\text{induced}} = B_{12}\rho(\nu)$$

(5.2-1)

where B_{21} and B_{12} are constants to be determined. The total downward $(2 \rightarrow 1)$ transition rate is the sum of the induced and spontaneous contributions

$$W'_{21} = B_{21}\rho(\nu) + A_{21}$$

(5.2-2)

The spontaneous rate A_{21} was discussed in Section 5.1. The total upward $(1 \rightarrow 2)$ transition rate is

$$W'_{12} = (W'_{12})_{\text{induced}} = B_{12}\rho(\nu)$$

(5.2-3)

Our first task is to obtain an expression for B_{12} and B_{21}. Since the magnitude of the coefficients B_{21} and B_{12} depends on the atoms and not on the radiation field, we consider, without loss of generality, the case where the atoms are in thermal equilibrium with a blackbody (thermal) radiation field at temperature T. In this case the radiation density is given by [5]

$$\rho(\nu) = \frac{8\pi h\nu^3}{c^3} \frac{1}{e^{h\nu/kT} - 1}$$

(5.2-4)

Since at thermal equilibrium the average populations of levels 2 and 1 are constant with time, it follows that the number of $2 \rightarrow 1$ transitions in a given time interval is equal to the number of $1 \rightarrow 2$ transitions; that is,

$$N_2 W'_{21} = N_1 W'_{12}$$

(5.2-5)

where N_1 and N_2 are the population densities of level 1 and 2, respectively. Using (5.2-2) and (5.2-3) in (5.2-5), we obtain

$$N_2[B_{21}\rho(\nu) + A_{21}] = N_1 B_{12}\rho(\nu)$$

and, substituting for $\rho(\nu)$ from (5.2-4),

$$N_2\left[B_{21}\frac{8\pi h\nu^3}{c^3(e^{h\nu/kT} - 1)} + A_{21}\right] = N_1\left[B_{12}\frac{8\pi h\nu^3}{c^3(e^{h\nu/kT} - 1)}\right] \qquad \textbf{(5.2-6)}$$

Since the atoms are in thermal equilibrium, the ratio N_2/N_1 is given by the Boltzmann factor [5] as

$$\frac{N_2}{N_1} = e^{-h\nu/kT} \qquad \textbf{(5.2-7)}$$

Equating (N_2/N_1) as given by (5.2-6) to (5.2-7) gives

$$\frac{8\pi h\nu^3}{c^3(e^{h\nu/kT} - 1)} = \frac{A_{21}}{B_{12}e^{h\nu/kT} - B_{21}} \qquad \textbf{(5.2-8)}$$

The last equality can be satisfied only when

$$B_{12} = B_{21} \qquad \textbf{(5.2-9)}$$

and simultaneously

$$\frac{A_{21}}{B_{21}} = \frac{8\pi h\nu^3}{c^3} \qquad \textbf{(5.2-10)}$$

The last two equations were first given by Einstein [6]. We can, using (5.2-10) rewrite the induced transition rate (5.2-1) as

$$W_i' = \frac{A_{21}c^3}{8\pi h\nu^3}\rho(\nu) = \frac{c^3}{8\pi h\nu^3 t_{\text{spont}}}\rho(\nu) \qquad \textbf{(5.2-11)}$$

where, because of (5.2-9) the distinction between $2 \to 1$ and $1 \to 2$ induced transition rates is superfluous.

Equation (5.2-11) gives the transition rate per atom due to a field with a uniform (white) spectrum with energy density per unit frequency $\rho(\nu)$. In quantum electronics our main concern is in the transition rates that are induced by a monochromatic (that is, single-frequency) field of frequency ν. Let us denote this transition rate as $W_i(\nu)$. We have established in Section 5.1 that the strength of interaction of a monochromatic field of frequency ν with an atomic transition is proportional to the lineshape function $g(\nu)$, so $W_i(\nu) \propto g(\nu)$. Furthermore, we would expect $W_i(\nu)$ to go over into W_i' as given by (5.2-11) if the spectral width of the radiation field is gradually increased from zero to a point at which it becomes large compared to the transition linewidth. These two requirements are satisfied if we take $W_i(\nu)$ as

$$W_i(\nu) = \frac{c^3 \rho_\nu}{8\pi h\nu^3 t_{\text{spont}}} g(\nu) \qquad \textbf{(5.2-12)}$$

where ρ_ν is the energy density (joules per cubic meter) of the electromagnetic field inducing the transitions. To show that $W_i(\nu)$ as given by (5.2-12) indeed goes over smoothly into (5.2-11) as the spectrum of the field broadens, we may consider the broad spectrum field as made up of a large number of closely spaced monochromatic components at ν_k with random phases and then by adding the individual transition rates obtained from (5.2-12)

$$W_i' = \sum_{\nu_k} W_i(\nu_k) = \frac{c^3}{8\pi h t_{\text{spont}}} \sum_k \frac{\rho_{\nu_k}}{\nu_k^3} g(\nu_k) \tag{5.2-13}$$

where ρ_{ν_k} is the energy density of the field component oscillating at ν_k. We can replace the summation of (5.2-13) by an integral if we replace ρ_{ν_k} by $\rho(\nu)\, d\nu$ where $\rho(\nu)$ is the energy density per unit frequency; thus, (5.2-13) becomes

$$W_i' = \frac{c^3}{8\pi h t_{\text{spont}}} \int_{-\infty}^{+\infty} \frac{\rho(\nu) g(\nu)\, d\nu}{\nu^3} \tag{5.2-14}$$

In situations where $\rho(\nu)$ is sufficiently broad compared with $g(\nu)$, and thus the variation of $\rho(\nu)/\nu^3$ over the region of interest [where $g(\nu)$ is appreciable] can be neglected, we can pull $\rho(\nu)/\nu^3$ outside the integral sign, obtaining

$$W_i' = \frac{c^3}{8\pi h \nu^3 t_{\text{spont}}} \rho(\nu)$$

where we used the normalization condition

$$\int_{-\infty}^{+\infty} g(\nu)\, d\nu = 1$$

This agrees with (5.2-11).

Returning to our central result, Equation (5.2-12), we can rewrite it in terms of the intensity $I_\nu = c\rho_\nu$ (watts per square meter) of the optical wave as

$$W_i(\nu) = \frac{A_{21} c^2 I_\nu}{8\pi h \nu^3} g(\nu) = \frac{\lambda^2 I_\nu}{8\pi h \nu t_{\text{spont}}} g(\nu) \tag{5.2-15}$$

where c is the velocity of propagation of light in the medium and $t_{\text{spont}} \equiv 1/A_{21}$.

5.3   Absorption and Amplification

Consider the case of a monochromatic plane wave of frequency ν and intensity I_ν propagating through an atomic medium with N_2 atoms per unit volume in level 2 and N_1 in level 1. According to (5.2-15) there will occur $N_2 W_i$ induced transitions per unit time per unit volume from level 2 to level 1 and $N_1 W_i$ transitions from 1 to 2. The net power generated within a unit volume is thus

$$\frac{dI}{dz} = \frac{P(z)}{\text{volume}} = (N_2 - N_1)W_i h\nu$$

This radiation is added coherently (that is, with a definite phase relationship) to that of the traveling wave so that it is equal, in the absence of any dissipation mechanisms, to the increase in the intensity per unit length, or, using (5.2-15),

$$\frac{dI_\nu}{dz} = (N_2 - N_1)\frac{c^2 g(\nu)}{8\pi\nu^2 t_{\text{spont}}} I_\nu \tag{5.3-1}$$

The solution of (5.3-1) is

$$I_\nu(z) = I_\nu(0)e^{\gamma(\nu)z} \tag{5.3-2}$$

where

$$\gamma(\nu) = (N_2 - N_1)\frac{c^2}{8\pi\nu^2 t_{\text{spont}}} g(\nu) \tag{5.3-3}$$

that is, the intensity grows exponentially when the population is inverted $(N_2 > N_1)$ or is attenuated when $N_2 < N_1$. The first case corresponds to laser-type amplification, whereas the second case is the one encountered in atomic systems at thermal equilibrium. The two situations are depicted in Figure 5-3. We recall that at thermal equilibrium

$$\frac{N_2}{N_1} = e^{-h\nu/kT} \tag{5.3-4}$$

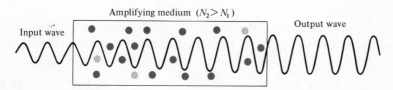

Amplifying medium $(N_2 > N_1)$

Input wave   Output wave

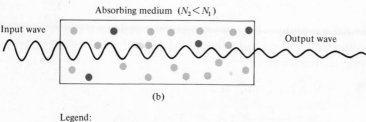

Absorbing medium $(N_2 < N_1)$

Input wave   Output wave

(b)

Legend:

● Atom in upper
   State 2

● Atom in lower
   State 1

Figure 5-3 Amplification of a traveling electromagnetic wave in (a) an inverted population $(N_2 > N_1)$, and (b) its attenuation in an absorbing $(N_2 < N_1)$ medium.

so that systems at thermal equilibrium are always absorbing. The inversion condition $N_2 > N_1$ can still be represented by (5.3-4), provided we take T as negative. As a matter of fact, the condition $N_2 > N_1$ is often referred to as one of "negative temperature"—the "temperature" in this case serving as an indicator of the population ratio, in accordance with (5.3-4).

The absorption, or amplification, of electromagnetic radiation by an atomic transition can be described not only by means of the exponential gain constant $\gamma(\nu)$ but also, alternatively, in terms of the imaginary part of the electric susceptibility $\chi''(\nu)$ of the propagation medium. According to (1.2-19) the density of absorbed power is

$$\frac{\overline{\text{Power}}}{\text{Volume}} = \frac{\omega \epsilon_0 \chi''(\nu)}{2} |E|^2 \qquad \textbf{(5.3-5)}$$

where, since we are concerned here only with electric susceptibilities, we replace $\chi_e(\nu)$ by the symbol $\chi(\nu)$. This last result must agree with a derivation using the concept of the induced transition rate $W_i(\nu)$ according to which

$$\frac{\overline{\text{Power}}}{\text{Volume}} = (N_1 - N_2) W_i(\nu) h\nu \qquad \textbf{(5.3-6)}$$

Equating (5.3-5) to (5.3-6), substituting (5.2-15) for $W_i(\nu)$, and using the relation $I_\nu = c\epsilon |E|^2/2$ [see (1.3-26)], we obtain

$$\chi''(\nu) = \frac{(N_1 - N_2)\lambda^3 n^2}{16\pi^2 t_{\text{spont}}} g(\nu) \qquad \textbf{(5.3-7)}$$

where $n^2 = \epsilon/\epsilon_0$ and λ is the wavelength in the medium. In the case of a Lorentzian lineshape function $g(\nu)$, we use (5.1-9) to rewrite the last result as

$$\chi''(v) = \frac{(N_1 - N_2)\lambda^3 n^2}{8\pi^3 t_{\text{spont}} \Delta\nu} \frac{1}{1 + \dfrac{4(\nu - \nu_0)^2}{(\Delta\nu)^2}} \qquad \textbf{(5.3-8)}$$

Numerical example.   Let us estimate the exponential gain constant at line center of a ruby (Al_2O_3 doped with Cr^{3+} ions) crystal having the following characteristics:

$$N_2 - N_1 = 5 \times 10^{18}/\text{cm}^3$$

$$\Delta\nu \simeq \frac{1}{g(\nu_0)} = 2 \times 10^{11} \text{ Hz at } 300°\text{K}$$

$$t_{\text{spont}} = 3 \times 10^{-3} \text{ second}$$

$$\nu = 4.326 \times 10^{14} \text{ Hz}$$

$$c \text{ (in ruby)} \simeq 2 \times 10^{10} \text{ cm/s} \quad (n = 1.5)$$

Using these values in (5.3-3) gives

$$\gamma(\nu) \simeq 7 \times 10^{-2} \text{ cm}^{-1}$$

Thus, the intensity of a wave with a frequency corresponding to the center of the transition is amplified by approximately 7 percent per cm in its passage through a ruby rod with the foregoing characteristics.

5.4   The Electron Oscillator Model of an Atomic Transition

The interaction of an electromagnetic field with an atomic transition is accompanied not only by absorption (or emission) of energy, but also by a dispersive effect in which the phase velocity of the incident wave depends on the frequency. The reason is that when the frequency ω of the wave is near that of the atomic transition, the atoms acquire large dipole moments that oscillate at ω, and the total field is now the sum of the incident and the field radiated by the dipoles. Since the radiated field is not necessarily in phase with the incident one, the effect is to change the phase velocity $(\mu\epsilon)^{-1/2}$ of the incident wave or, equivalently, to change the real part of the dielectric constant ϵ.

In treating this problem analytically we need to solve first for the dipole moment of an atom that is induced by an incident field. This problem is usually handled by the sophisticated quantum mechanical formalism of the density matrix [7]. We will employ, instead, the electron oscillator model for the atomic transition. According to this model which has been used by atomic physicists before the advent of quantum mechanics, we account for the dipole moment induced in a single atom by replacing the atom with an electron oscillating in a harmonic potential well [8]. The resonance frequency and absorption width of the electronic oscillator are chosen to agree with those of the real transition. We will also find it necessary to introduce an additional parameter, the so-called "oscillator strength," which characterizes the strength of the interaction between the oscillator and the field so that the calculated absorption (or emission) strength agrees with the experimental value.

The equation of motion of the one-dimensional electronic oscillator is

$$\frac{d^2x(t)}{dt^2} + \sigma\,\frac{dx(t)}{dt} + \frac{k}{m}\,x(t) = -\,\frac{e}{m}\,e(t) \qquad \textbf{(5.4-1)}$$

where $x(t)$ is the deviation of the electron from its equilibrium position, σ is the damping coefficient, kx is the restoring force, $e(t)$ is the instantaneous electric field, and the electronic charge is $-e$. Taking the electric field $e(t)$ and the deviation $x(t)$ as

$$e(t) = \text{Re}\,[Ee^{i\omega t}]$$
$$x(t) = \text{Re}\,[X(\omega)e^{i\omega t}] \qquad \textbf{(5.4-2)}$$

respectively, and defining the resonant frequency by

$$\omega_0 \equiv \sqrt{\frac{k}{m}} \tag{5.4-3}$$

Equation (5.4-1) becomes

$$(\omega_0{}^2 - \omega^2)X + i\omega\sigma X = -\frac{e}{m}E \tag{5.4-4}$$

so that the deviation amplitude is given by

$$X(\omega) = \frac{-(e/m)E}{\omega_0{}^2 - \omega^2 + i\omega\sigma} \tag{5.4-5}$$

We are interested primarily in the response at frequencies near resonance. Thus, if we put $\omega \simeq \omega_0$, (5.4-5) becomes

$$X(\omega \simeq \omega_0) = \frac{-(e/m)E}{2\omega_0(\omega_0 - \omega) + i\omega_0\sigma}$$

The dipole moment of a single electron is

$$\mu(t) = -ex(t)$$

Therefore, in the case of N oscillators per unit volume there results a polarization (dipole moment per unit volume)

$$p(t) = \mathrm{Re}\,[P(\omega)e^{i\omega t}] \tag{5.4-6}$$

where the complex polarization $P(\omega)$ is given by

$$P(\omega) = -NeX(\omega) = \frac{Ne^2/m}{2\omega_0(\omega_0 - \omega) + i\omega_0\sigma}E$$

$$= \frac{-i(Ne^2/m\omega_0\sigma)}{1 + i[2(\omega - \omega_0)/\sigma]}E \tag{5.4-7}$$

The electronic susceptibility $\chi(\omega)$ is defined as the ratio of the complex amplitude of the induced polarization to that of the inducing field (multiplied by ϵ_0)

$$P(\omega) = \epsilon_0\chi(\omega)E \tag{5.4-8}$$

and is consequently a complex number. If we separate $\chi(\omega)$ into its real and imaginary components according to

$$\chi(\omega) = \chi'(\omega) - i\chi''(\omega) \tag{5.4-9}$$

we obtain, from (5.4-6), (5.4-8), and (5.4-9),

$$p(t) = \mathrm{Re}\,[\epsilon_0\chi(\omega)Ee^{i\omega t}]$$
$$= \epsilon_0 E\chi'(\omega)\cos\omega t + \epsilon_0 E\chi''(\omega)\sin\omega t \tag{5.4-10}$$

Therefore, $\chi'(\omega)$ and $\chi''(\omega)$ are associated, respectively, with the in-phase and quadrature components of the polarization.

From (5.4-7) and (5.4-8) it follows that

$$\chi(\omega) = -i\left(\frac{Ne^2}{m\omega_0\sigma\epsilon_0}\right)\frac{1}{1 + 2i(\omega - \omega_0)/\sigma} \qquad \text{(5.4-11)}$$

and thus

$$\chi'(\omega) = \left(\frac{Ne^2}{m\omega_0\sigma\epsilon_0}\right)\frac{2(\omega_0 - \omega)/\sigma}{1 + 4(\omega - \omega_0)^2/\sigma^2} \qquad \text{(5.4-12)}$$

$$\chi''(\omega) = \left(\frac{Ne^2}{m\omega_0\sigma\epsilon_0}\right)\frac{1}{1 + 4(\omega - \omega_0)^2/\sigma^2} \qquad \text{(5.4-13)}$$

Expressing $\chi(\omega)$ in terms of $\nu = \omega/2\pi$ and introducing $\Delta\nu = \sigma/2\pi$, the frequency separation between the two points where $\chi''(\nu)$ is down to half its peak intensity, we obtain

$$\chi''(\nu) = \left(\frac{Ne^2}{16\pi^2 m\nu_0\epsilon_0}\right)\frac{\Delta\nu}{(\Delta\nu/2)^2 + (\nu - \nu_0)^2} \qquad \text{(5.4-14)}$$

$$\chi'(\nu) = \frac{2(\nu_0 - \nu)}{\Delta\nu}\chi''(\nu) = \left(\frac{Ne^2}{8\pi^2 m\nu_0\epsilon_0}\right)\frac{(\nu_0 - \nu)}{(\Delta\nu/2)^2 + (\nu - \nu_0)^2} \qquad \text{(5.4-15)}$$

By comparing (5.4-14) with (5.1-9), we find that $\chi''(\nu)$ has a Lorentzian shape. The Lorentzian was found in Section 5.1 to represent the absorption as a function of frequency of an RLC oscillator, so it should not come as a surprise to find, in the next section, that the power absorption of the electronic oscillator is also proportional to $\chi''(\nu)$.

A normalized plot of $\chi'(\nu)$ and $\chi''(\nu)$ is shown in Figure 5-4. The most noteworthy features of the plot are that the extrema of $\chi'(\nu)$ occur at the half-power frequencies and the effects of dispersion $\chi'(\nu)$ are also "felt" at frequencies at which the absorption $\chi''(\nu)$ is negligible; and that the magnitude of $\chi'(\nu)$ at its extrema is half the peak value of $\chi''(\nu)$.

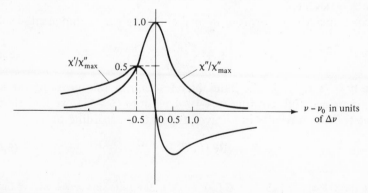

Figure 5-4   A plot of the real (χ') and imaginary (χ'') parts of the electronic susceptibility.

The significance of $\chi(v)$.   According to (1.2-3), the electric displacement vector is defined by

$$\mathbf{D} = \epsilon_0\mathbf{E} + \mathbf{P} + \mathbf{P}_{\text{transition}} = \epsilon\mathbf{E} + \epsilon_0\chi\mathbf{E}$$

where the complex notation is used and the polarization is separated into a resonant component $\mathbf{P}_{\text{transition}}$ due to the specific atomic transition and a nonresonant component $\mathbf{P}$ that accounts for all the other contributions to the polarization. We can rewrite the last equation as

$$\mathbf{D} = \epsilon\left[1 + \frac{\epsilon_0}{\epsilon}\chi(\omega)\right]\mathbf{E} = \epsilon'(\omega)\mathbf{E} \tag{5.4-16}$$

so that the complex dielectric constant becomes

$$\epsilon'(\omega) = \epsilon\left[1 + \frac{\epsilon_0}{\epsilon}\chi(\omega)\right] \tag{5.4-17}$$

We have thus accounted for the effect of the atomic transition by modifying ϵ according to (5.4-17). Having derived $\chi(\omega)$, using detailed atomic information, we can ignore its physical origin and proceed to treat the wave propagation in the medium with ϵ' given by (5.4-17), using Maxwell's equations.

As an example of this point of view we consider the propagation of a plane electromagnetic wave in a medium with a dielectric constant $\epsilon'(\omega)$. According to (1.3-17), the wave has the form of

$$e(z, t) = \text{Re}\,[Ee^{i(\omega t - k'z)}] \tag{5.4-18}$$

where, using (1.3-13) and (5.4-17) and assuming $(\epsilon_0/\epsilon)|\chi| \ll 1$, we obtain

$$k' = \omega\sqrt{\mu\epsilon'} \simeq k\left[1 + \frac{\epsilon_0}{2\epsilon}\chi\right]$$

where $k = \omega\sqrt{\mu\epsilon}$.

Expressing $\chi(v)$ in terms of its real and imaginary components leads to

$$k' = k\left[1 + \frac{\chi'(v)}{2n^2}\right] - i\frac{k\chi''(v)}{2n^2} \tag{5.4-19}$$

where $n = (\epsilon/\epsilon_0)^{1/2}$ is the index of refraction in the medium[2] far away from resonance. Substituting (5.4-19) back into (5.4-18), we find that the atomic transition results in a wave propagating according to

$$e(z, t) = \text{Re}\,[Ee^{i\omega t - i(k + \Delta k)z}e^{(\gamma/2)z}] \tag{5.4-20}$$

---

[2] Since the velocity of light is $c = (\mu\epsilon)^{-1/2}$, n is the ratio of the velocity of light in vacuum to that in the medium at frequencies sufficiently removed from resonance that the effect of the specific atomic transition can be ignored.

The result of the atomic polarization is thus to change the phase delay per unit length from k to $k + \Delta k$, where

$$\Delta k = \frac{k\chi'(\nu)}{2n^2} \tag{5.4-21}$$

as well as to cause the amplitude to vary exponentially with distance according to $e^{(\gamma/2)z}$, where

$$\gamma(\nu) = -\frac{k\chi''(\nu)}{n^2} \tag{5.4-22}$$

It is quite instructive to rederive (5.4-22) using a different approach. According to (1.2-13), the average power absorbed per unit volume from an electromagnetic field with an x component only is

$$\overline{\frac{\text{Power}}{\text{Volume}}} = \overline{e_x(t)\frac{dp_x(t)}{dt}} = \tfrac{1}{2}\,\text{Re}\,[E(i\omega P)^*] \tag{5.4-23}$$

where E and P are the complex electric field and polarization in the x direction, respectively, and horizontal bars denote time-averaging. Using (5.4-8) and (5.4-9) in (5.4-23), we obtain

$$\overline{\frac{\text{Power}}{\text{Volume}}} = \frac{\omega\epsilon_0}{2}\chi''|E|^2 \tag{5.4-24}$$

The absorption of energy at a rate given by (5.4-24) must lead to an attenuation of the wave intensity I, according to

$$I(z) = I_0 e^{\gamma(\nu)z} \tag{5.4-25}$$

where

$$\gamma(\nu) = I^{-1}\frac{dI}{dz} \tag{5.4-26}$$

Conservation of energy thus requires that

$$\frac{dI}{dz} = -(\text{power absorbed per unit volume}) = -\frac{\omega\epsilon_0}{2}\chi''|E|^2$$

Using the last result in (5.4-26), as well as relation (1.3-26),

$$I = \frac{c\epsilon}{2}|E|^2$$

where $c = \omega/k$ is the velocity of light in the medium, gives

$$\gamma(\nu) = -\frac{k\chi''(\nu)}{n^2}$$

in agreement with (5.4-22).

5.5   Atomic Susceptibility

In (5.4-14) and (5.4-15) we derived an expression for the electric susceptibility $\chi(\nu)$ of a medium made up of idealized electron oscillators. This expression cannot be used to represent the susceptibility of an actual atomic transition. This can be seen by comparing the classical expression for $\chi''(\nu)$ as given by (5.4-14) to the quantum mechanical expression

$$\chi''(\nu) = \frac{(N_1 - N_2)\lambda^3 n^2}{8\pi^3 t_{\text{spont}}\Delta\nu} \frac{1}{1 + [4(\nu - \nu_0)^2/(\Delta\nu)^2]} \tag{5.5-1}$$

which was derived in Section 5.3. We find that in the case of the electron oscillator, $\chi''(\nu) > 0$, so power can only be absorbed from the field. In the quantum mechanical model, on the other hand, the sign of $\chi''(\nu)$ is the same as that of $(N_1 - N_2)$ so, for $N_2 > N_1$, power is actually added to the field. The quantum mechanical derivation also shows that the absorption (or emission) strength is inversely proportional to t_{spont}, which is characteristic of a given transition.

We accept the quantum mechanical expression for $\chi''(\nu)$ given by (5.5-1) as a correct representation of the absorption due to an atomic transition. We justify this choice by its agreement with experiment. We use the classical analysis, however, to obtain a relationship between $\chi'(\nu)$ and $\chi''(\nu)$, assuming that such a relationship is correct in spite of the objections raised previously.[3] From (5.4-15) and (5.5-1) we obtain

$$\chi'(\nu) = \frac{2(\nu_0 - \nu)}{\Delta\nu} \chi''(\nu)$$

$$= \frac{(N_1 - N_2)\lambda^3 n^2}{4\pi^3(\Delta\nu)^2 t_{\text{spont}}} \frac{(\nu_0 - \nu)}{1 + [4(\nu - \nu_0)^2/(\Delta\nu)^2]} \tag{5.5-2}$$

This expression will be used to represent the dispersion of a homogeneously broadened transition with a Lorentzian lineshape.

5.6   Gain Saturation in Homogeneous Laser Media

In Section 5.3 we derived an expression (5.3-3) for the exponential gain constant due to a population inversion. It is given by

$$\gamma(\nu) = (N_2 - N_1) \frac{c^2}{8\pi\nu^2 t_{\text{spont}}} g(\nu) \tag{5.6-1}$$

---

[3] That this assumption is correct can be shown using the Kramers–Kronig relation (See Problem 5-3 and Reference [1], p. 130). Physically, this is attributable to the fact that both $\chi'(\nu)$ and $\chi''(\nu)$, as deduced from the electron oscillator model, are off by the same factor, so the ratio $\chi''(\nu)/\chi'(\nu)$ is correct.

where N_2 and N_1 are the population densities of the two atomic levels involved in the induced transition. There is nothing in (5.6-1) to indicate what causes the inversion ($N_2 - N_1$), and this quantity can be considered as a parameter of the system. In practice the inversion is caused by a "pumping" agent, hereafter referred to as the pump, which can take various forms such as the electric current in injection lasers, the flashlamp light in pulsed ruby lasers, or the energetic electrons in plasma-discharge gas lasers.

Consider next the situation prevailing at some point *inside* a laser medium in the presence of an optical wave. The pump establishes a population inversion, which in the absence of any optical field has a value ΔN^0. The presence of the optical field induces $2 \to 1$ and $1 \to 2$ transitions. Since $N_2 > N_1$ and the induced rates for $2 \to 1$ and $1 \to 2$ transitions are equal, it follows that more atoms are induced to undergo a transition from level 2 to level 1 than in the opposite direction and that, consequently, the new equilibrium population inversion is smaller than ΔN^0.

The reduction in the population inversion and hence of the gain constant brought about by the presence of an electromagnetic field is called gain saturation. Its understanding is of fundamental importance in quantum electronics. As an example, which will be treated in the next chapter, we may point out that gain saturation is the mechanism which reduces the gain inside laser oscillators to a point where it just balances the losses so that steady oscillation can result.

In Figure 5-5 we show the ground state 0 as well as the two laser levels 2 and 1 of a four-level laser system. The density of atoms pumped per unit time into level 2 is taken as R_2, and that pumped into 1 is R_1. Pumping into 1 is, of course, undesirable since it leads to a reduction of the inversion. In many practical situations it cannot be avoided. The actual decay life-

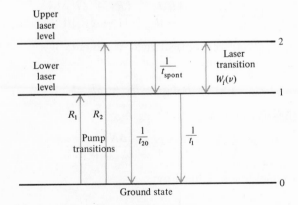

Figure 5-5 Energy levels and transition rates of a four-level laser system (the fourth level, which is involved in the original excitation by the pump, is not shown and the pumping is shown as proceeding directly into levels 1 and 2). The total lifetime of level 2 is t_2, where $1/t_2 = 1/t_{\text{spont}} + 1/t_{20}$.

time of atoms in level 2 at the absence of any radiation field is taken as t_2. This decay rate has a contribution t_{spont}^{-1} which is due to spontaneous (photon emitting) $2 \to 1$ transitions as well as to additional nonradiative relaxation from 2 to 1. The lifetime of atoms in level 1 is t_1. The induced rate for $2 \to 1$ and $1 \to 2$ transitions due to a radiation field at frequency ν is denoted by $W_i(\nu)$ and, according to (5.2-15), is given by

$$W_i(\nu) = \frac{\lambda^2 g(\nu)}{8\pi h \nu t_{\text{spont}}} I_\nu \tag{5.6-2}$$

where $g(\nu)$ is the normalized lineshape of the transition and I_ν is the intensity (watts per square meter) of the optical field.

The equations describing the populations of level 2 and 1 in the combined presence of a radiation field at ν and a pump are:

$$\frac{dN_2}{dt} = R_2 - \frac{N_2}{t_2} - (N_2 - N_1)W_i(\nu) \tag{5.6-3}$$

$$\frac{dN_1}{dt} = R_1 - \frac{N_1}{t_1} + \frac{N_2}{t_{\text{spont}}} + (N_2 - N_1)W_i(\nu) \tag{5.6-4}$$

N_2 and N_1 are the population densities (m^{-3}) of levels 2 and 1 respectively. R_2 and R_1 are the pumping rates ($m^{-3} - \text{s}^{-1}$) into these levels. N_2/t_2 is the change per unit time in the population of 2 due to decay out of level 2 to all levels. This includes spontaneous transitions to 1 but *not* induced transitions. The rate for the latter is $N_2 W_i(\nu)$ so that the net change in N_2 due to induced transitions is given by the last term of (5.6-3). At steady state the populations are constant with time, so putting $d/dt = 0$ in the two preceding equations, we can solve for N_1, N_2, and obtain[4]

$$N_2 - N_1 = \frac{[R_2 t_2 - (R_1 + \delta R_2)t_1]}{1 + [t_2 + (1 - \delta)t_1]W_i(\nu)} \tag{5.6-5}$$

where $\delta = t_2/t_{\text{spont}}$. If the optical field is absent, $W_i(\nu) = 0$, and the inversion density is given by

$$\Delta N^0 = R_2 t_2 - (R_1 + \delta R_2)t_1 \tag{5.6-6}$$

we can use (5.6-6) to rewrite (5.6-5) as

$$N_2 - N_1 = \frac{\Delta N^0}{1 + \phi t_{\text{spont}} W_i(\nu)} \tag{5.6-7}$$

where the parameter ϕ is defined by

$$\phi = \delta \left[1 + (1 - \delta) \frac{t_1}{t_2} \right]$$

---

[4] Levels 1 and 2 assumed to be high enough (in energy) that the role of thermal processes in populating them can be neglected.

We note that in efficient laser systems $t_2 \simeq t_{\text{spont}}$, so $\delta \simeq 1$, and that $t_1 \ll t_2$, so $\phi \simeq 1$. Substituting (5.6-2) for $W_i(\nu)$ the last equation becomes

$$N_2 - N_1 = \frac{\Delta N^0}{1 + [\phi\lambda^2 g(\nu)/8\pi h\nu]I_\nu} = \frac{\Delta N^0}{1 + [I_\nu/I_s(\nu)]} \qquad \textbf{(5.6-8)}$$

where $I_s(\nu)$, the saturation intensity, is given by

$$I_s(\nu) = \frac{8\pi h\nu}{\phi\lambda^2 g(\nu)} \qquad \textbf{(5.6-9)}$$

and corresponds to the intensity level (watts per square meter) that causes the inversion to drop to one half of its nonsaturated value (ΔN^0). By using (5.6-8) in the gain expression (5.6-1), we obtain our final result

$$\begin{aligned}
\gamma(\nu) &= \frac{1}{1 + [I_\nu/I_s(\nu)]} \frac{\Delta N^0 \lambda^2}{8\pi t_{\text{spont}}} g(\nu) \\
&= \frac{\gamma_0(\nu)}{1 + [I_\nu/I_s(\nu)]}
\end{aligned} \qquad \textbf{(5.6-10)}$$

which shows the dependence of the gain constant on the optical intensity.

In closing we recall that (5.6-10) applies to a homogeneous laser system. This is due to the fact that in the rate equations (5.6-3) and (5.6-4) we considered all the atoms as equivalent and, consequently, exercising the same transition rates. This assumption is no longer valid in inhomogeneous laser systems. This case is treated in the next section.

5.7   Gain Saturation in Inhomogeneous Laser Media

In Section 5.6 we considered the reduction in optical gain—that is, saturation—due to the optical field in a homogeneous laser medium. In this section we treat the problem of gain saturation in inhomogeneous systems.

According to the discussion of Section 5.1, in an inhomogeneous atomic system the individual atoms are distinguishable, with each atom having a unique transition frequency $(E_2 - E_1)/h$. We can thus imagine the inhomogeneous medium as made up of classes of atoms each designated by a continuous variable ξ.[5] Furthermore, we define a function $p(\xi)$ so that the *a priori* probability that an atom has its ξ parameter between ξ and $\xi + d\xi$ is $p(\xi)\, d\xi$. It follows that

$$\int_{-\infty}^{\infty} p(\xi)\, d\xi = 1 \qquad \textbf{(5.7-1)}$$

since any atom has a unit probability of having its ξ value between $-\infty$ and ∞.

---

[5] The variable ξ can, as an example, correspond to the center frequency of the lineshape function $g^\xi(\nu)$ of atoms in group ξ.

pressure

The atoms within a given class ξ are considered as homogeneously broadened, having a lineshape function $g^\xi(\nu)$ that is normalized so that

$$\int_{-\infty}^{\infty} g^\xi(\nu)\, d\nu = 1 \tag{5.7-2}$$

In Section 5.1 we defined the transition lineshape $g(\nu)$ by taking $g(\nu)\, d\nu$ to represent the *a priori* probability that a spontaneous emission will result in a photon whose frequency is between ν and $\nu + d\nu$. Using this definition we obtain

$$g(\nu)\, d\nu = \left[\int_{-\infty}^{\infty} p(\xi) g^\xi(\nu)\, d\xi \right] d\nu \tag{5.7-3}$$

$\quad = \sum_{\xi} g^\xi(\nu)\, d\nu$

which is a statement of the fact that the probability of emitting a photon of frequency between ν and $\nu + d\nu$ is equal to the probability $g^\xi(\nu)\, d\nu$ of this occurrence, given that the atom belongs to class ξ, summed up over all the classes.

Next we proceed to find the contribution to the inversion which is due to a single class ξ. The equations of motion [9] are

$$\frac{dN_2^\xi}{dt} = R_2 p(\xi) - \frac{N_2^\xi}{t_2} - [N_2^\xi - N_1^\xi] W_i^\xi(\nu)$$

$$\frac{dN_1^\xi}{dt} = R_1 p(\xi) - \frac{N_1^\xi}{t_1} + \frac{N_2^\xi}{t_{\text{spont}}} + [N_2^\xi - N_1^\xi] W_i^\xi(\nu) \tag{5.7-4}$$

and are similar to (5.6-3) and (5.6-4), except that N_2^ξ and N_1^ξ refer to the upper and lower level densities of atoms in class ξ only. The pumping rate (atoms/m^3-sec) into levels 2 and 1 is taken to be proportional to the probability of finding an atom in class ξ and is given by $R_2 p(\xi)$ and $R_1 p(\xi)$, respectively. The total pumping rate into level 2 is, as in Section 5.6, R_2 since

$$\int_{-\infty}^{\infty} R_2 p(\xi)\, d\xi = R_2 \int_{-\infty}^{\infty} p(\xi)\, d\xi = R_2$$

where we made use of (5.7-1). The induced transition rate $W_i^\xi(\nu)$ is given, according to (5.2-15), by

$$W_i^\xi(\nu) = \frac{\lambda^2}{8\pi h \nu t_{\text{spont}}}\, g^\xi(\nu) I_\nu \tag{5.7-5}$$

which is of a form identical to (5.6-2) except that $g^\xi(\nu)$ refers to the lineshape function of atoms in class ξ. The steady-state $d/dt = 0$ solution of (5.7-4) yields

$$N_2^\xi - N_1^\xi = \frac{\Delta N^0 p(\xi)}{1 + \phi t_{\text{spont}} W_i^\xi(\nu)} \tag{5.7-6}$$

where ΔN^0 and ϕ have the same significance as in Section 5.6. The total power emitted by induced transitions per unit volume by atoms in class ξ

is thus

$$\frac{P^{\xi}(\nu)}{V} = (N_2^{\xi} - N_1^{\xi})h\nu W_i^{\xi}(\nu) = \frac{\Delta N^0 p(\xi)h\nu}{[1/W_i^{\xi}(\nu)] + \phi t_{\text{spont}}} \qquad (5.7\text{-}7)$$

where the spontaneous lifetime is assumed the same for all the groups ξ.

Summing (5.7-7) over all the classes, we obtain an expression for the total power at ν per unit volume emitted by the atoms

$$\frac{P(\nu)}{V} = \frac{\Delta N^0 h\nu}{t_{\text{spont}}} \int_{-\infty}^{\infty} \frac{p(\xi)\,d\xi}{[1/W_i(\nu)t_{\text{spont}}] + \phi} \qquad (5.7\text{-}8)$$

which, by the use of (5.7-5), can be rewritten as

$$\frac{P(\nu)}{V} = \frac{\Delta N^0 h\nu}{t_{\text{spont}}} \int_{-\infty}^{\infty} \frac{p(\xi)\,d\xi}{[8\pi h\nu/\lambda^2 I_\nu g^{\xi}(\nu)] + \phi} \qquad (5.7\text{-}9)$$

The stimulated emission of power causes the intensity of the traveling optical wave to increase with distance z according to $I_\nu = I_\nu(0)\exp[\gamma(\nu)z]$, where

$$\gamma(\nu) = \frac{dI_\nu}{dz}\bigg/ I_\nu = \frac{P(\nu)}{V}\bigg/ I_\nu$$

$$= \frac{\Delta N^0 \lambda^2}{8\pi t_{\text{spont}}} \int_{-\infty}^{\infty} \frac{p(\nu_\xi)\,d\nu_\xi}{[1/g^{\xi}(\nu)] + (\phi\lambda^2 I_\nu/8\pi h\nu)} \qquad (5.7\text{-}10)$$

where we replaced $p(\xi)\,d\xi$ by $p(\nu_\xi)\,d\nu_\xi$.

This is our basic result.

As a first check on (5.7-10), we shall consider the case in which $I_\nu \ll 8\pi h\nu/\phi\lambda^2 g^{\xi}(\nu)$ and therefore the effects of saturation can be ignored. Using (5.7-3) in (5.7-10), we obtain

$$\gamma(\nu) = \frac{\Delta N^0 \lambda^2}{8\pi t_{\text{spont}}} g(\nu)$$

which is the same as (5.3-3). This shows that in the absence of saturation the expressions for the gain of a homogeneous and an inhomogeneous atomic system are identical.

Our main interest in this treatment is in deriving the saturated gain constant for an inhomogeneously broadened atomic transition. If we assume that in each class ξ all the atoms are identical (homogeneous broadening), we can use (5.1-9) for the lineshape function $g^{\xi}(\nu)$, and therefore,

$$g^{\xi}(\nu) = \frac{\Delta\nu}{2\pi[(\Delta\nu/2)^2 + (\nu - \nu_\xi)^2]} \qquad (5.7\text{-}11)$$

where $\Delta\nu$ is called the homogeneous linewidth of the inhomogeneous line. Atoms with transition frequencies that are clustered within $\Delta\nu$ from each other can be considered as indistinguishable. The term "homogeneous packet" is often used to describe them. Using (5.7-11) in (5.7-10) leads to

$$\gamma(\nu) = \frac{\Delta N^0 \lambda^2 \Delta\nu}{16\pi^2 t_{\text{spont}}} \int_{-\infty}^{\infty} \frac{p(\nu_\xi)\, d\nu_\xi}{(\nu - \nu_\xi)^2 + (\Delta\nu/2)^2 + (\phi\lambda^2 I_\nu \Delta\nu/16\pi^2 h\nu)} \quad \text{(5.7-12)}$$

In the extreme inhomogeneous case, the width of $p(\nu_\xi)$ is by definition very much larger than the remainder of the integrand in (5.7-12) and thus it is essentially a constant over the region in which the integrand is a maximum. In this case we can pull $p(\nu_\xi)_{\nu_\xi = \nu} = p(\nu)$ outside the integral sign in (5.7-12), obtaining

$$\gamma(\nu) = \frac{\Delta N^0 \lambda^2 \Delta\nu}{16\pi^2 t_{\text{spont}}} p(\nu)$$

$$\times \int_{-\infty}^{\infty} \frac{d\nu_\xi}{(\nu - \nu_\xi)^2 + (\Delta\nu/2)^2 + (\phi\lambda^2 \Delta\nu I_\nu/16\pi^2 h\nu)} \quad \text{(5.7-13)}$$

Using the definite integral

$$\int_{-\infty}^{\infty} \frac{dx}{x^2 + a^2} = \frac{\pi}{a}$$

to evaluate (5.7-13), we obtain

$$\gamma(\nu) = \frac{\Delta N^0 \lambda^2 p(\nu)}{8\pi t_{\text{spont}}} \frac{1}{\sqrt{1 + (\phi\lambda^2 I_\nu/4\pi^2 h\nu\Delta\nu)}} \quad \text{(5.7-14)}$$

$$= \gamma_0(\nu) \frac{1}{\sqrt{1 + (I_\nu/I_s)}} \quad \text{(5.7-15)}$$

where $I_s = 4\pi^2 h\nu\Delta\nu/\phi\lambda^2$ is the saturation intensity. A comparison of (5.7-15) with (5.7-10) shows that, because of the square root, the saturation—that is, decrease in gain—sets in more slowly as the intensity I_ν is increased.

■ PROBLEMS

5-1 Consider a parallel RLC circuit, which is connected to a signal generator so that the voltage across it is

$$v(t) = V_0 \cos 2\pi\nu t$$

At $t = 0$ the circuit is disconnected from the signal generator.
a. What is the voltage $v(t)$ for $t > 0$?
b. Find the Fourier transform $V(\omega)$ of $v(t)$. Show that in the high-Q case (where $Q = 2\pi\nu_0 RC$) and for frequencies $\nu \simeq \nu_0 \equiv 1/2\pi\sqrt{LC}$,

$$|V(\nu)|^2 \propto \frac{1}{(\nu - \nu_0)^2 + (\nu_0/2Q)^2}$$

c. Obtain the expression for the amount of average power $P(\nu)$ absorbed by the RLC circuit from a signal generator with an output current

$$i(t) = I_0 \cos 2\pi\nu t$$

Show that the expression for $P(\nu)$ is proportional to that of $|V(\nu)|^2$ obtained in (b).

5-2 Calculate the maximum absorption coefficient for the R_1 transition in pink ruby with a Cr^{3+} concentration of 2×10^{19} cm^{-3}. Assume that $t_{spont} = 3 \times 10^{-3}$ second and $\Delta\nu = 11$ cm^{-1}. Compare the result to the absorption data of Figure 7-4.

5-3 Show that (5.5-1) and (5.5-2) are derivable from each other using the Kramers–Kronig relationship. For a discussion of this relation see, for example, Reference [1], page 130.

■ **REFERENCES**

[1] See, for example, A. Yariv, *Quantum Electronics*. New York: Wiley, 1957.

[2] Portis, A. M., "Electronic structure of F centers: Saturation of the electron skin resonance," *Phys. Rev.*, vol. 91, p. 1071, 1953.

[3] See, for example, R. Kubo, *Statistical Mechanics*. Amsterdam: North Holland, 1964, p. 31.

[4] Johnson, L. F., "Optically pumped pulsed crystal lasers other than ruby," in *Lasers*, vol. 1, A. K. Levine, ed. New York: Marcel Dekker, Inc., 1966, p. 137.

[5] Kittel, C., *Elementary Statistical Physics*. New York: Wiley, 1958, p. 197.

[6] Einstein, A., "Zur Quantentheorie der Strahlung," *Phys. Z.*, vol. 18, pp. 121–128, March 1917.

[7] See, for example, R. H. Pantell and H. E. Puthoff, *Fundamentals of Quantum Electronics*. New York: Wiley, 1969, p. 31.

[8] Ditchburn, R. W., *Light*. New York: Interscience, 1963, Chap. 15.

[9] Gordon, J. P., unpublished memorandum, Bell Telephone Laboratories.

[10] *Lasers and Light—Readings from Scientific American*. San Francisco: Freeman, 1969.

[11] Mitchell, A. C. G., and M. W. Zemansky, *Resonance Radiation and Excited Atoms*. New York: Cambridge, 1961.

CHAPTER

6

Theory of Laser Oscillation

6.0 Introduction

In Chapter 5 we found that an atomic medium with an inverted population $(N_2 > N_1)$ is capable of amplifying an electromagnetic wave if the latter's frequency falls within the transition lineshape. Consider next the case in which the laser medium is placed inside an optical resonator. As the electromagnetic wave bounces back and forth between the two reflectors it passes through the laser medium and is amplified. If the amplification exceeds the losses caused by imperfect reflection in the mirrors and scattering in the laser medium, the field energy stored in the resonator will increase with time. This causes the amplification constant to decrease as a result of gain saturation [see Equation (5.6-10) and the discussion surrounding it.] The oscillation level will keep increasing until the saturated gain per pass just equals the losses. At this point the net gain per pass is unity and no further increase in the radiation intensity is possible—that is, steady-state oscillation ~~obtains~~. is obtained.

In this chapter we will derive the start-oscillation inversion needed to sustain laser oscillation, beginning with the theory of the Fabry–Perot

98

etalon. We will also obtain an expression for the oscillation frequency of the laser oscillator and show how it is affected by the dispersion of the atomic medium. We will conclude by considering the problem of optimum output coupling and laser pulses.

6.1 The Fabry–Perot Laser

A laser oscillator is basically a Fabry–Perot etalon, as studied in detail in Chapter 4, in which the space between the two mirrors contains an amplifying medium with an inverted atomic population. We can account for the inverted population by using (5.4-19). Taking the propagation constant of the medium as

$$k'(\omega) = k + k \frac{\chi'(\omega)}{2n^2} - ik \frac{\chi''(\omega)}{2n^2} - i \frac{\alpha}{2} \qquad \textbf{(6.1-1)}$$

where $k - i\alpha/2$ is the propagation constant of the medium at frequencies well removed from that of the laser transition, $\chi(\omega) = \chi'(\omega) - i\chi''(\omega)$ is the complex dielectric susceptibility due to the laser transition and is given by (5.5-1) and (5.5-2). Since α accounts for the distributed passive losses of the medium,[1] the intensity loss factor per pass is exp $(-\alpha l)$.

Figure 6-1 shows a plane wave of (complex) amplitude E_i which is incident on the left mirror of a Fabry–Perot etalon containing a laser medium. The ratio of transmitted to incident fields at the left mirror is taken as t_1 and that at the right mirror as t_2. The ratios of reflected to

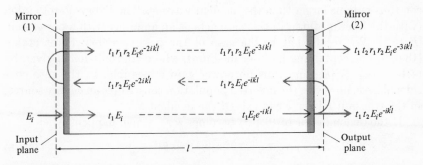

Figure 6-1 Model used to analyze a laser oscillator. A laser medium (that is, one with an inverted atomic population) with a complex propagation constant $k'(\omega)$ is placed between two reflecting mirrors.

---

[1] In addition to and in the presence of the gain attributable to the inverted laser transition, the medium may possess a residual attenuation due to a variety of mechanisms, such as scattering at imperfections, absorption by excited atomic levels, and others. The attenuation resulting from all of these mechanisms is lumped into the distributed loss constant α.

incident fields inside the laser medium at the left and right boundaries are r_1 and r_2, respectively.

The propagation factor corresponding to a single transit is $\exp(-ik'l)$ where k' is given by (6.1-1) and l is the length of the etalon.

Adding the partial waves at the output to get the total outgoing wave E_t we obtain

$$E_t = t_1 t_2 E_i e^{-ik'l}[1 + r_1 r_2 e^{-i2k'l} + r_1^2 r_2^2 e^{-i4k'l} + \cdots]$$

which is a geometric progression with a sum

$$E_t = t_1 t_2 E_i e^{-ik'l} \sum_{n=0}^{\infty} r_1^n r_2^n e^{-ik'l(2n)}$$

$$E_t = E_i \left[\frac{t_1 t_2 e^{-ik'l}}{1 - r_1 r_2 e^{-i2k'l}} \right]$$

$$= E_i \left[\frac{t_1 t_2 e^{-i(k+\Delta k)l} e^{(\gamma-\alpha)l/2}}{1 - r_1 r_2 e^{-2i(k+\Delta k)l} e^{(\gamma-\alpha)l}} \right] \qquad \textbf{(6.1-2)}$$

where we used (5.3-3), (6.1-1), and the relation $k' = k + \Delta k + i(\gamma - \alpha)/2$ with

$$\Delta k = k \frac{\chi'(\omega)}{2n^2} \qquad \textbf{(6.1-3)}$$

$$\gamma = -k \frac{\chi''(\omega)}{n^2}$$

$$= (N_2 - N_1) \frac{c^2}{8\pi \nu^2 t_{\text{spont}}} g(\nu) \qquad \textbf{(6.1-4)}$$

If the atomic transition is inverted ($N_2 > N_1$), then $\gamma > 0$ and the denominator of (6.1-2) can become very small. The transmitted wave E_t can thus become larger than the incident wave E_i. The Fabry–Perot etalon (with the laser medium) in this case acts as an amplifier with a power gain $|E_t/E_i|^2$. We recall that in the case of the passive Fabry–Perot etalon (that is, one containing no laser medium), whose transmission is given by (4.1-7), $|E_t| \leqslant |E_i|$ and thus no power gain is possible. In the case considered here, however, the inverted population constitutes an energy source, so the transmitted wave can exceed the incident one.

If the denominator of (6.1-2) becomes zero, which happens when

$$r_1 r_2 e^{-2i[k+\Delta k(\omega)]l} e^{[\gamma(\omega)-\alpha]l} = 1 \qquad \textbf{(6.1-5)}$$

then the ratio E_t/E_i becomes infinite. This corresponds to a finite transmitted wave E_t with a *zero* incident wave ($E_i = 0$)—that is, to *oscillation*. Physically, condition (6.1-5) represents the case in which a wave making a complete round trip inside the resonator returns to the starting plane with the *same amplitude* and, except for some integral multiple of 2π, with the *same phase*. Separating the oscillation condition (6.1-5) into the amplitude and phase requirements gives

$$r_1 r_2 e^{[\gamma_t(\omega)-\alpha]l} = 1 \qquad \textbf{(6.1-6)}$$

for the threshold gain constant $\gamma_t(\omega)$ and

$$2[k + \Delta k(\omega)]l = 2\pi m \qquad m = 1, 2, 3, \cdots \qquad \textbf{(6.1-7)}$$

for the phase condition. The amplitude condition (6.1-6) can be written as

$$\gamma_t(\omega) = \alpha - \frac{1}{l} \ln r_1 r_2 \qquad \textbf{(6.1-8)}$$

which, using (6.1-4), becomes

$$N_t \equiv (N_2 - N_1)_t = \frac{8\pi t_{\text{spont}}}{g(\nu)\lambda^2}\left(\alpha - \frac{1}{l} \ln r_1 r_2\right) \qquad \textbf{(6.1-9)}$$

This is the population inversion density at threshold.[2] It is often stated in a different form.[3]

Numerical example—population inversion. To get an order of magnitude estimate of the critical population inversion $(N_2 - N_1)_t$ we use data typical of a 6328 Å He–Ne laser (which is discussed in Section 7.5). The appropriate constants are

$$\lambda_0 = 6.328 \times 10^{-5} \text{ cm} \qquad t_{spon} = ?$$

$$c = 3 \times 10^{10} \text{ cm/s}$$

$$l = 10 \text{ cm}$$

$$1/g(\nu_0) \simeq \Delta\nu \simeq 10^9 \text{ Hz}$$

(The last figure is the Doppler broadened width of the laser transition.)

---

[2] It was derived originally by Schawlow and Townes in their classic paper showing the feasibility of lasers; see Reference [1].

[3] Consider the case in which the mirror losses and the distributed losses are all small, and therefore $r_1^2 \simeq 1$, $r_2^2 \simeq 1$ and $\exp(-\alpha l) \simeq 1$. A wave starting with a unit intensity will return after one round trip with an intensity $R_1 R_2 \exp(-2\alpha l)$, where $R_1 \equiv r_1^2$ and $R_2 \equiv r_2^2$ are the mirrors' reflectivities. The fractional intensity loss per round trip is thus $1 - R_1 R_2 \exp(-2\alpha l)$. Since this loss occurs in a time $2l/c$, it corresponds to an exponential decay time constant t_c (of the intensity) given by

$$\frac{1}{t_c} = \frac{(1 - R_1 R_2 e^{-2\alpha l})c}{2l}$$

Therefore, the energy $\mathcal{E}$ stored in the passive resonator decays as $d\mathcal{E}/dt = -\mathcal{E}/t_c$. Since $R_1 R_2 e^{-2\alpha l} \simeq 1$, we can use the relation $1 - x \simeq -\ln x$, $x \simeq 1$, to write $1/t_c$ as

$$\frac{1}{t_c} \simeq c\left[\alpha - \frac{1}{l} \ln r_1 r_2\right] \qquad (6.1\text{-}10)$$

and the threshold condition (6.1-9) becomes

$$N_t \equiv (N_2 - N_1)_t = \frac{8\pi\nu^2 t_{\text{spont}}}{c^3 t_c g(\nu)} \qquad (6.1\text{-}11)$$

where $N \equiv N_2 - N_1$ and the subscript t signifies threshold.

The cavity decay time t_c is calculated from (6.1-10) assuming $\alpha = 0$ and $R_1 = R_2 = 0.98$. Since $R_1 = R_2 \simeq 1$, we can use the approximation $-\ln x = 1 - x$, $x \simeq 1$, to write

$$R \equiv R_1 \equiv R_2 \; ; \quad t_c \simeq \frac{l}{c(1 - R)} = 2 \times 10^{-8} \text{ second}$$

Using the foregoing data in (6.1-11), we obtain

$$N_t \simeq 10^9 \text{ cm}^{-3}$$

6.2   The Oscillation Frequency

The phase part of the start oscillation condition as given by (6.1-7) is satisfied at an infinite set of frequencies, which correspond to the different value of the integer m. If, in addition, the gain condition (6.1-6) is satisfied at one or more of these frequencies, the laser will oscillate at this frequency.

To solve for the oscillation frequency we use (6.1-3) to rewrite (6.1-7) as

$$kl\left[1 + \frac{\chi'(\omega)}{2n^2}\right] = m\pi \tag{6.2-1}$$

Introducing

$$\nu_m = \frac{mc}{2l} \tag{6.2-2}$$

so that it corresponds to the mth resonance frequency of the passive $[N_2 - N_1 = 0]$ resonator and, using relations (5.4-15) and (5.4-22)

$$\chi'(\omega) = \frac{2(\nu_0 - \nu)}{\Delta\nu} \chi''(\omega)$$

$$\gamma(\omega) = -\frac{k\chi''(\omega)}{n^2}$$

we obtain from (6.2-1)

$$\nu\left[1 - \left(\frac{\nu_0 - \nu}{\Delta\nu}\right)\frac{\gamma(\nu)}{k}\right] = \nu_m \tag{6.2-3}$$

where ν_0 is the center frequency of the atomic lineshape function. Let us assume that the laser length is adjusted so that one of its resonance frequencies ν_m is very near ν_0. We anticipate that the oscillation frequency ν will also be close to ν_0 and take advantage of the fact that when $\nu \simeq \nu_0$ the gain constant $\gamma(\nu)$ is a slowly varying function of ν; see Figure 5-4 for $\chi''(\nu)$, which is proportional to $\gamma(\nu)$. We can consequently replace $\gamma(\nu)$ in (6.2-3) by $\gamma(\nu_m)$, obtaining

$$\nu = \nu_m - (\nu_m - \nu_0)\frac{\gamma(\nu_m)c}{2\pi \Delta\nu} \tag{6.2-4}$$

as the solution for the oscillation frequency ν.

We can recast (6.2-4) in a slightly different, and easier to use, form by starting with the gain threshold condition (6.1-6). Taking, for simplicity $r_1 = r_2 = \sqrt{R}$ and assuming that $R \simeq 1$ and $\alpha = 0$, we can write (6.1-6) as[4]

$$\gamma_t(\nu) \simeq \frac{1 - R}{l}$$

We also take advantage of the relation

$$\Delta\nu_{1/2} \simeq \frac{c(1 - R)}{2\pi l}$$

which relates the passive resonator linewidth $\Delta\nu_{1/2}$ to R [this relation was given in (4.6-6)], and rewrite (6.2-4) as

$$\nu = \nu_m - (\nu_m - \nu_0)\frac{\Delta\nu_{1/2}}{\Delta\nu} \tag{6.2-5}$$

A study of (6.2-5) shows that if the passive cavity resonance ν_m coincides with the atomic line center—that is, $\nu_m = \nu_0$—oscillation takes place at $\nu = \nu_0$. If $\nu_m \neq \nu_0$, oscillation takes place near ν_m but is shifted slightly toward ν_0. This phenomenon is referred to as *"frequency pulling."*

6.3 Three- and Four-Level Lasers

Lasers are commonly classified into the so-called "three-level" or "four-level" lasers. An idealized model of a four-level laser is shown in Figure 6-2. The feature characterizing this laser is that the separation E_1 of the

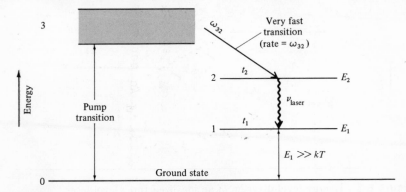

Figure 6-2 Energy-level diagram of an idealized four-level laser.

---

[4] This result can be obtained by putting $R = 1 - \Delta$, where $\Delta \ll 1$. Equation (6.1-6) becomes $1 + \gamma_t l \simeq 1 + \Delta \Rightarrow \gamma_t \simeq \Delta/l = (1 - R)/l$.

terminal laser level from the ground state is large enough that at the temperature T at which the laser is operated, $E_1 \gg kT$. This guarantees that the thermal equilibrium population of level 1 can be neglected. If, in addition, the lifetime t_1 of atoms in level 1 is short compared to t_2, we can neglect N_1 compared to N_2 and the threshold condition (6.1-11) is satisfied when

$$N_2 \simeq N_t \qquad \text{(6.3-1)}$$

Therefore, laser oscillation begins when the upper laser level acquires, by pumping, a population density equal to the threshold value N_t.

A three-level laser is one in which the lower laser level is either the ground state or a level whose separation E_1 from the ground state is small compared to kT, so that at thermal equilibrium a substantial fraction of the total population occupies this level. An idealized three-level laser system is shown in Figure 6-3.

At a pumping level that is strong enough to create a population $N_2 = N_1 = N_0/2$ in the upper laser level,[5] the optical gain γ is zero, since $\gamma \propto N_2 - N_1 = 0$. To satisfy the oscillation condition the pumping rate has to be further increased until

$$N_2 = \frac{N_0}{2} + \frac{N_t}{2}$$

and (6.3-2)

$$N_1 = \frac{N_0}{2} - \frac{N_t}{2}$$

so $N_2 - N_1 = N_t$. Since in most laser systems $N_0 \gg N_t$, we find by comparing (6.3-1) to (6.3-2) that the pump rate at threshold in a three-level

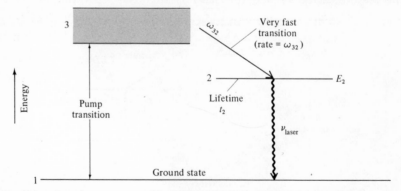

Figure 6-3   Energy-level diagram of an idealized three-level laser.

---

[5] Here we assume that because of the very fast transition rate ω_{32} out of level 3, the population of this level is negligible and $N_1 + N_2 = N_0$, where N_0 is the density of the active atoms.

laser must exceed that of a four-level laser—all other factors being equal—by

$$\frac{(N_2)_{3\text{-level}}}{(N_2)_{4\text{-level}}} \sim \frac{N_0}{2N_t}$$

In the numerical example given in the next chapter we will find that in the case of the ruby laser this factor is ~ 100.

The need to maintain about $N_0/2$ atoms in the upper level of a three-level laser calls for a *minimum* expenditure of power of

$$(P_s)_{3\text{-level}} = \frac{N_0 h\nu V}{2t_2} \tag{6.3-3}$$

and of

$$(P_s)_{4\text{-level}} = \frac{N_t h\nu V}{t_2} \tag{6.3-4}$$

in a four-level laser. V is the volume. The last two expressions are derived by multiplying the decay rate (atoms per second) from the upper level at threshold, which is $N_0 V/2t_2$ and $N_t V/t_2$ in the two cases, by the energy $h\nu$ per transition. If the decay rate per atom t_2^{-1} (seconds^{-1}) from the upper level is due to spontaneous emission only, we can replace t_2 by t_{spont}. P_s is then equal to the power emitted through fluorescence by atoms within the (mode) volume V at threshold. We will refer to it as the *critical fluorescence* power. In the case of the four-level laser we use (6.1-11) for N_t and, putting $t_2 = t_{\text{spont}}$, obtain

$$(P_s)_{4\text{-level}} = \frac{N_t h\nu V}{t_{\text{spont}}} = \frac{8\pi h \Delta\nu V}{\lambda^3 t_c} \tag{6.3-5}$$

where $\Delta\nu = 1/g(\nu_0)$ is the width of the laser transition lineshape.

Numerical example—critical fluorescence power of an Nd^{3+}:glass laser.
The critical fluorescence power of an Nd^{3+}:glass laser is calculated using the following data:

$l = 10$ cm

$V = 10$ cm^3

$\lambda_0 = 1.06 \times 10^{-6}$ meter

$R = $ (mirror reflectivity) $= 0.95$

$n \simeq 1.5$

$t_c \simeq \dfrac{nl}{(1 - R)c_0} = 10^{-8}$ second

$\Delta\nu = 3 \times 10^{12}$ Hz

The Nd^{3+}:glass is a four-level laser system (see Figure 7-11), since level 1 is about 2,000 cm^{-1} above the ground state so that at room temperature

$E_1 \approx 10kT$. We can thus use (6.3-5), obtaining $N_t = 8.5 \times 10^{15}$ cm^{-3} and

$$P_s \simeq 150 \text{ watts}$$

6.4   Power in Laser Oscillators

In Section 6.1 we derived an expression for the threshold population inversion N_t at which the laser gain becomes equal to the losses. We would expect that as the pumping intensity is increased beyond the point at which $N_2 - N_1 = N_t$ the laser will break into oscillation and emit power. In this section we obtain the expression relating the laser power output to the pumping intensity. We also treat the problem of optimum coupling—that is, of the mirror transmission that results in the maximum power output.

The rate equations.   Consider an ideal four-level laser such as the one shown in Figure 6-2. We take $E_1 \gg kT$ so that the thermal population of the lower laser level 1 can be neglected. We assume that the critical inversion density N_t is very small compared to the ground-state population, so during oscillation the latter is hardly affected. We can consequently characterize the pumping intensity by R_2 and R_1, the density of atoms pumped per second into levels 2 and 1, respectively. Process R_1, which populates the lower level 1, causes a reduction of the gain and is thus detrimental to the laser operation. In many laser systems, such as discharge gas lasers, considerable pumping into the lower laser level is unavoidable, and therefore a realistic analysis of such systems must take R_1 into consideration.

The rate equations that describe the populations of levels 1 and 2 become

$$\frac{dN_2}{dt} = -N_2\omega_{21} - W_i(N_2 - N_1) + R_2 \qquad \text{(6.4-1)}$$

$$\frac{dN_1}{dt} = -N_1\omega_{10} + N_2\omega_{21} + W_i(N_2 - N_1) + R_1 \qquad \text{(6.4-2)}$$

ω_{ij} is the decay rate per atom from level i to j; thus the density of atoms per second undergoing decay from i to j is $N_i\omega_{ij}$. If the decay rate is due entirely to spontaneous transitions, then ω_{ij} is equal to the Einstein A_{ij} coefficient introduced in Section 5.1. W_i is the probability per unit time that an atom in level 2 will undergo an *induced* (stimulated) transition to level 1 (or vice versa). W_i, given by (5.2-15), is proportional to the energy density of the radiation field inside the cavity.

Implied in the foregoing rate equations is the fact that we are dealing with a homogeneously broadened system. In an inhomogeneously broadened atomic transition, atoms with different transition frequencies $(E_2 - E_1)/h$ experience different induced transition rates and a single parameter W_i is not sufficient to characterize them.

In a steady-state situation we have $\dot{N}_1 = \dot{N}_2 = 0$. In this case we can solve (6.4-1) and (6.4-2) for N_1 and N_2, obtaining

$$N_2 - N_1 = \frac{R_2\{1 - (\omega_{21}/\omega_{10})[1 + (R_1/R_2)]\}}{W_i + \omega_{21}} \tag{6.4-3}$$

A necessary condition for population inversion in our model is thus $\omega_{21} < \omega_{10}$, which is equivalent to requiring that the lifetime of the upper laser level ω_{21}^{-1} exceed that of the lower one. The effectiveness of the pumping is, according to (6.4-3), reduced by the finite pumping rate R_1 and lifetime ω_{10}^{-1} of level 1 to an effective value

$$R = R_2\left[1 - \frac{\omega_{21}}{\omega_{10}}\left(1 + \frac{R_1}{R_2}\right)\right] \tag{6.4-4}$$

so (6.4-3) can be written as

$$\dot{N}_2 - N_1 = \frac{R}{W_i + \omega_{21}} \tag{6.4-5}$$

Below the oscillation threshold the induced transition rate W_i is zero (since the oscillation energy density is zero) and $N_2 - N_1$ is, according to (6.4-5), proportional to the pumping rate R. This state of affairs continues until $R = N_t\omega_{21}$, at which point $N_2 - N_1$ reaches the threshold value [see (6.1-11)]

$$N_t = \frac{8\pi\nu^2 t_{\text{spont}}}{c^3 t_c g(0)} = \frac{8\pi\nu^2 t_{\text{spont}}\Delta\nu}{c^3 t_c} \tag{6.4-6}$$

This is the point at which the gain due to the inversion is large enough to make up *exactly* for the cavity losses (the criterion that was used to derive N_t). Further increase of $N_2 - N_1$ with pumping is impossible in a *steady-state situation*, since it would result in a rate of induced (energy) emission that exceeds the losses so that the field energy stored in the resonator will increase with time in violation of the steady-state assumption.

This argument suggests that, under steady-state conditions, $N_2 - N_1$ must remain equal to N_t regardless of the amount by which the threshold pumping rate is exceeded. An examination of (6.4-5) shows that this is possible, provided W_i is allowed to increase once R exceeds its threshold value $\omega_{21}N_t$, so that the equality

$$N_t = \frac{R}{W_i + \omega_{21}} \tag{6.4-7}$$

is satisfied. Since, according to (5.2-15), W_i is proportional to the energy density in the resonator, Equation (6.4-7) relates the electromagnetic energy stored in the resonator to the pumping rate R. To derive this relationship we first solve (6.4-7) for W_i, obtaining

$$W_i = \frac{R}{N_t} - \omega_{21} \qquad R \gg N_t\omega_{21} \tag{6.4-8}$$

The total power generated by stimulated emission is

$$P_e = (N_t V)W_i h\nu \tag{6.4-9}$$

where V is the volume of the oscillating mode. Using (6.4-8) in (6.4-9) gives

$$\frac{P_e}{Vh\nu} = N_t\omega_{21}\left[\frac{R}{N_t\omega_{21}} - 1\right] \qquad R \gg N_t\omega_{21} \tag{6.4-10}$$

This expression may be recast in a slightly different form, which we will find useful later on. We use expression (6.4-6) for N_t and, recalling that in our idealized model $\omega_{21}^{-1} = t_{\text{spont}}$, obtain

$$\frac{P_e}{Vh\nu} = N_t\omega_{21}\left[\frac{R}{(p/t_c)} - 1\right] \qquad R \gg \frac{p}{t_c} \tag{6.4-11}$$

where

$$p = \frac{8\pi\nu^2}{c^3 g(0)} = \frac{8\pi\nu^2\Delta\nu}{c^3} \tag{6.4-12}$$

According to (4.0-7), p corresponds to the density (meters^{-3}) of radiation modes whose resonance frequencies fall within the atomic transition linewidth $\Delta\nu$—that is, the density of radiation modes that are capable of interacting with the transition.

Returning to the expression for the power output of a laser oscillator (6.4-11), we find that the term $R/(p/t_c)$ is the factor by which the pumping rate R exceeds its threshold value p/t_c. In addition, in an ideal laser system, $\omega_{21} = t_{\text{spont}}^{-1}$, so we can identify $N_t\omega_{21}h\nu V$ with the power P_s emitted by the spontaneous emission at threshold, which is defined by (6.3-5). We can consequently rewrite (6.4-11) as

$$P_e = P_s\left(\frac{R}{R_t} - 1\right) \tag{6.4-13}$$

The main attraction of (6.4-13) is in the fact that, in addition to providing an extremely simple expression for the power emitted by the laser atoms, it shows that for each increment of pumping, measured relative to the threshold value, the power increases by P_s. An experimental plot showing the linear relation predicted by (6.4-13) is shown in Figure 6-4.

In the numerical example of Section 6.3, which was based on an Nd^{3+}:glass laser, we obtained $P_s = 150$ watts. We may expect on this basis that the power from this laser for, say $(R/R_t) \simeq 2$ (that is, twice above threshold) will be of the order of 300 watts.

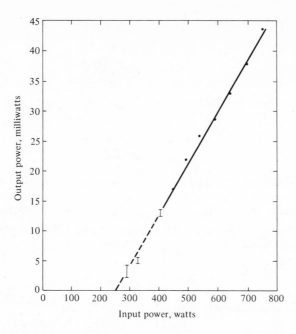

Figure 6-4   Plot of output power versus electric power input to a xenon lamp in a CW 0.1 percent $CaF_2:U^{3+}$ laser. Mirror transmittance at 2.61 μm and 77°K is 0.2 percent. (After Reference [2].)

6.5   Optimum Output Coupling in Laser Oscillators

The total loss encountered by the oscillating laser mode can conveniently be attributed to two different sources: (a) the inevitable residual loss due to absorption and scattering in the laser material, in the mirrors, as well as diffraction losses in the finite diameter reflectors; (b) the (useful) loss due to coupling of output power through the partially transmissive reflector. It is obvious that loss (a) should be made as small as possible since it raises the oscillation threshold without contributing to the output power. The problem of the coupling loss (b), however, is more subtle. At zero coupling (that is, both mirrors have zero transmission) the threshold will be at its minimum value and the power P_e emitted by the atoms will be maximum. But since none of this power is available as output, this is not a useful state of affairs. If, on the other hand, we keep increasing the coupling loss, the increasing threshold pumping will at some point exceed the actual pumping level. When this happens, oscillation will cease and the power output will again be zero. Between these two extremes there exists an optimum value of coupling (that is, mirror transmission) at which the power output is a maximum.

The expression for the population inversion was shown in (6.4-5) to have the form

$$N_2 - N_1 = \frac{R/\omega_{21}}{1 + (W_i/\omega_{21})} \tag{6.5-1}$$

Since the exponential gain constant $\gamma(\nu)$ is, according to (5.3-3), proportional to $N_2 - N_1$, we can use (6.5-1) to write it as

$$\gamma = \frac{\gamma_0}{1 + (W_i/\omega_{21})} \tag{6.5-2}$$

where γ_0 is the unsaturated $(W_i = 0)$ gain constant (that is, the gain exercised by a very weak field, so that $W_i \ll \omega_{21}$). We can use (6.4-9) to express W_i in (6.5-2) in terms of the total emitted power P_e and then, in the resulting expression, replace $N_t V h\nu\omega_{21}$ by P_s. [This is consistent with (6.3-5) in cases where $\omega_{21} = t_{\text{spont}}^{-1}$.] The result is

$$\gamma = \frac{\gamma_0}{1 + (P_e/P_s)} \tag{6.5-3}$$

The oscillation condition (6.1-6) can be written as

$$e^{\gamma_t l}(1 - L) = 1 \tag{6.5-4}$$

where $L = 1 - r_1 r_2 \exp{(-\alpha l)}$ is the fraction of the intensity lost per pass. In the case of small losses $(L \ll 1)$, Equation (6.5-4) can be written as

$$\gamma_t l = L \tag{6.5-5}$$

According to the discussion in the introduction to this chapter, once the oscillation threshold is exceeded, the actual gain γ exercised by the laser oscillation is clamped at the threshold value γ_t regardless of the pumping. We can thus replace γ by γ_t in (6.5-3) and, solving for P_e, obtain

$$P_e = P_s \left(\frac{g_0}{L} - 1\right) \tag{6.5-6}$$

where $g_0 = \gamma_0 l$ (that is, the unsaturated gain per pass in nepers). P_e, we recall, is the *total* power given off by the atoms due to stimulated emission. The total loss per pass L can be expressed as the sum of the residual (unavoidable) loss L_i and the useful mirror transmission[6] T, so

$$L = L_i + T \tag{6.5-7}$$

The fraction of the total power P_e that is coupled out of the laser as useful output is thus $T/(T + L_i)$. Therefore, using (6.5-6) we can write the

---

[6] For the sake of simplicity we can imagine one mirror as being perfectly reflecting, whereas the second (output) mirror has a transmittance T.

(useful) power output as

$$P_o = P_s \left(\frac{g_0}{L_i + T} - 1 \right) \frac{T}{T + L_i} \qquad \text{(6.5-8)}$$

Replacing P_s in (6.5-8) by the right side of (6.3-5), and recalling from (4.6-2) that for small losses

$$t_c = \frac{l}{(L_i + T)c} = \frac{l}{Lc} \qquad \text{(6.5-9)}$$

Equation (6.5-8) becomes

$$P_o = \left(\frac{8\pi hc\Delta\nu A}{\lambda^3} \right) T \left(\frac{g_0}{L_i + T} - 1 \right) \qquad \text{(6.5-10)}$$

where $A = V/l$ is the cross-sectional area of the mode (assumed constant). Maximizing P_0 with respect to T by setting $\partial P_0/\partial T = 0$ yields

$$T_{\text{opt}} = -L_i + \sqrt{g_0 L_i} \qquad \text{(6.5-11)}$$

as the condition for the mirror transmission that yields the maximum power output.

The expression for the power output at optimum coupling is obtained by substituting (6.5-11) for T in (6.5-10). The result is

$$\begin{aligned} (P_o)_{\text{opt}} &= \left(\frac{8\pi hc\Delta\nu A}{\lambda^3} \right) (\sqrt{g_0} - \sqrt{L_i})^2 \\ &\equiv S(\sqrt{g_0} - \sqrt{L_i})^2 \qquad \text{(6.5-12)} \end{aligned}$$

where the parameter S is defined by (6.5-12) and is independent of the excitation level (pumping) or losses.

Theoretical plots of (6.5-10) with L_i as a parameter are shown in Figure 6-5. Also shown are experimental data points obtained in a He–Ne

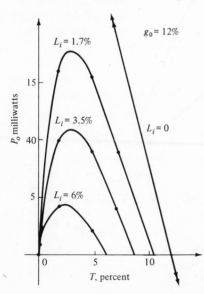

Figure 6-5 Useful power output (P_o) versus mirror transmission T for various values of internal loss L_i in an He-Ne 6328 Å laser. (After Laures, *Phys. Letters*, vol. 10, p. 61, 1964.)

6328 Å laser. Note that the value of g_0 is given by the intercept of the $L_i = 0$ curve and is equal to 12 percent. The existence of an optimum coupling resulting in a maximum power output for each L_i is evident.

It is instructive to consider what happens to the energy $\mathcal{E}$ stored in the laser resonator as the coupling T is varied. A little thinking will convince us that $\mathcal{E}$ is proportional to P_o/T.[7] A plot of P_o (taken from Figure 6-5) and $\mathcal{E} \propto P_o/T$ as a function of the coupling T is shown in Figure 6-6. As we may expect, $\mathcal{E}$ is a monotonically decreasing function of T.

6.6 Multimode Laser Oscillation and Mode Locking

In this section we contemplate the effect of homogeneous or inhomogeneous broadening (in the sense described in Section 5.1) on the laser oscillation.

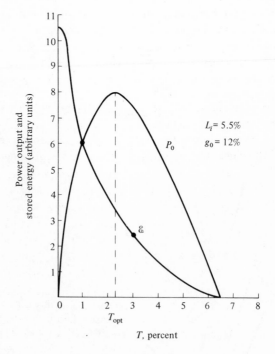

Figure 6-6 Power output P_o and stored energy $\mathcal{E}$ plotted against mirror transmission T.

---

[7] The internal one-way power P_i incident on the mirrors is related, by definition, to P_o by $P_o = P_iT$. The total energy $\mathcal{E}$ is proportional to P_i.

We start by reminding ourselves of some basic results pertinent to this discussion:

1. The actual gain constant prevailing inside a laser oscillator *at the oscillation frequency ν* is clamped, at steady state, at a value

$$\gamma_t(\nu) = \alpha - \frac{1}{l} \ln r_1 r_2 \qquad \text{(6.1-8)}$$

2. The gain constant of a distributed laser medium is

$$\gamma(\nu) = (N_2 - N_1) \frac{c^2}{8\pi\nu^2 t_{\text{spont}}} g(\nu) \qquad \text{(5.3-3)}$$

3. The optical resonator can support oscillations, provided sufficient gain is provided to overcome losses, at frequencies[8] ν_q separated by

$$\nu_{q+1} - \nu_q = \frac{c}{2l} \qquad \text{(4.5-4)}$$

where $c = c_0/n$.

Now consider what happens to the gain constant $\gamma(\nu)$ inside a laser oscillator as the pumping is increased from some value below threshold. Operationally, we can imagine an extremely weak wave of frequency ν launched into the laser medium and then measuring the gain constant $\gamma(\nu)$ as "seen" by this signal as ν is varied.

We treat first the case of a homogeneous laser. Below threshold the inversion $N_2 - N_1$ is proportional to the pumping rate and $\gamma(\nu)$, which is given by (5.3-3), is proportional to $g(\nu)$. This situation is illustrated by curve A in Figure 6-7(a). The spectrum (4.5-4) of the passive resonances is shown in Figure 6-7(b). As the pumping rate is increased, the point is reached at which the gain per pass at the center resonance frequency ν_0 is equal to the average loss per pass. This is shown in curve B. At this point, oscillation at ν_0 starts. An increase in the pumping cannot increase the inversion since this will cause $\gamma(\nu_0)$ to increase beyond its clamped value as given by Equation (6.1-8). Since the spectral lineshape function $g(\nu)$ describes the response of each individual atom, all the atoms being identical, it follows that the gain profile $\gamma(\nu)$ above threshold as in curve C is identical to that at the threshold B.[9] The gain at other frequencies— such as ν_{-1}, ν_1, ν_{-2}, ν_2, and so forth—remains below the threshold value so that the ideal homogeneously broadened laser can oscillate only at a single frequency.

---

[8] The high-order transverse modes discussed in Section 4.5 are ignored here.

[9] Further increase in pumping, and the resulting increase in optical intensity, will eventually cause a broadening of $\gamma(\nu)$ due to the shortening of the lifetime by induced emission.

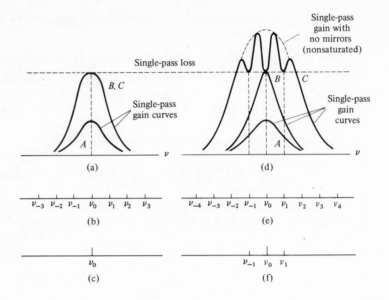

Figure 6-7   (a) Single-pass gain curves for a homogeneous atomic system (*A*—below threshold; *B*—at threshold; *C*—well above threshold). (b) Mode spectrum of optical resonator. (c) Oscillation spectrum (only one mode oscillates). (d) Single-pass gain curves for an inhomogeneous atomic system (*A*—below threshold; *B*—at threshold; *C*—well above threshold). (e) Mode spectrum of optical resonator. (f) Oscillation spectrum for pumping level *C*, showing three oscillating modes.

In the extreme inhomogeneous case, the individual atoms can be considered as being all different from one another and as acting independently. The lineshape function $g(\nu)$ reflects the distribution of the transition frequencies of the individual atoms. The gain profile $\gamma(\nu)$ below threshold is proportional to $g(\nu)$ and its behavior is similar to that of the homogeneous case. Once threshold is reached as in curve *B*, the gain at ν_0 remains clamped at the threshold value. There is no reason, however, why the gain at other frequencies should not increase with further pumping. This gain is due to atoms that do not communicate with those contributing to the gain at ν_0. Further pumping will thus lead to oscillation at additional longitudinal-mode frequencies as shown in curve *C*. Since the gain at each oscillating frequency is clamped, the gain profile curve acquires depressions at the oscillation frequencies. This phenomenon is referred to as "hole burning" [7].

A plot of the output frequency spectrum showing the multimode oscillation of a He–Ne 0.6328-μm laser is shown in Figure 6-8.

Mode locking.   We have argued above that in an inhomogeneously broadened laser, oscillation can take place at a number of frequencies, which are

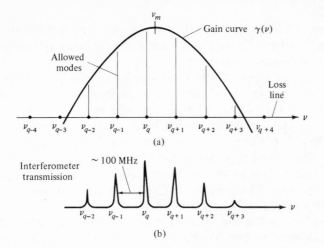

Figure 6-8 (a) Inhomogeneously broadened Doppler gain curve of the 6328 Å Ne transition and position of allowed longitudinal-mode frequencies. (b) Intensity versus frequency profile of an oscillating He-Ne laser. Six modes have sufficient gain to oscillate (After Reference [8].)

separated by

$$\omega_q - \omega_{q-1} = \frac{\pi c}{l} \equiv \omega$$

Now consider the total optical electric field resulting from such multimode oscillation at some arbitrary point, say one of the mirrors, in the optical resonator. It can be taken, using complex notation, as

$$e(t) = \sum_n E_n e^{i[(\omega_o + n\omega)t + \phi_n]} \tag{6.6-1}$$

where the summation is extended over the oscillating modes and ω_0 is chosen, arbitrarily, as a reference frequency. ϕ_n is the phase of the nth mode. One property of (6.6-1) is that $e(t)$ is periodic in $T \equiv 2\pi/\omega = 2l/c$, which is the round-trip transit time inside the resonator.

$$e(t + T) = \sum_n E_n \exp\left\{i\left[(\omega_0 + n\omega)\left(t + \frac{2\pi}{\omega}\right) + \phi_n\right]\right\}$$

$$= \sum_n E_n \exp\{i[(\omega_0 + n\omega)t + \phi_n]\} \exp\left\{i\left[2\pi\left(\frac{\omega_0}{\omega} + n\right)\right]\right\}$$

$$= e(t) \tag{6.6-2}$$

Since ω_0/ω is an integer ($\omega_0 = m\pi c/l$)

$$\exp\left[2\pi i\left(\frac{\omega_0}{\omega} + n\right)\right] = 1$$

Note that the periodic property of $e(t)$ depends on the fact that the phases ϕ_n are fixed. In typical lasers the phases ϕ_n are likely to vary randomly with time. This causes the intensity of the laser output to fluctuate randomly[10] and greatly reduces its usefulness for many applications where temporal coherence is important.

Two ways in which this problem can be attacked are: First, make it possible for the laser to oscillate at a single frequency only so that mode interference is eliminated. This can be achieved in a variety of ways, including shortening the resonator length l, thus increasing the mode spacing ($\omega = \pi c/l$) to a point where only one mode has sufficient gain to oscillate. The second approach is to force the modes ϕ_n to maintain their relative values. This is the so-called "mode locking" technique, which (as shown previously) causes the oscillation intensity to consist of a periodic train with a period of $T = 2l/c = 2\pi/\omega$.

One of the most useful forms of mode locking results when the phases ϕ_n are made equal to zero. To simplify the analysis of this case assume that there are N oscillating modes with equal amplitudes. Taking $E_n = 1$ and $\phi_n = 0$ in (6.6-1) gives

$$e(t) = \sum_{-(N-1)/2}^{(N-1)/2} e^{i(\omega_o + n\omega)t} \tag{6.6-3}$$

$$= e^{i\omega_o t} \frac{\sin(N\omega t/2)}{\sin(\omega t/2)} \tag{6.6-4}$$

The average laser power output is proportional to $e(t)e^*(t)$ and is given by[11]

$$P(t) \propto \frac{\sin^2(N\omega t/2)}{\sin^2(\omega t/2)} \tag{6.6-5}$$

Some of the analytic properties of $P(t)$ are immediately apparent:

1. The power is emitted in a form of a train of pulses with a period $T = 2\pi/\omega = 2l/c$.

2. The peak power, $P(sT)$ (for $s = 1, 2, 3, \cdots$), is equal to N times the average power, where N is the number of modes locked together.

3. The peak field amplitude is equal to N times the amplitude of a single mode.

4. The individual pulse width, defined as the time from the peak to the first zero is $\tau = T/N$. The number of oscillating modes can be estimated by $N \simeq \Delta\omega/\omega$—that is, the ratio of the transition

---

[10] It should be noted that this fluctuation takes place because of random interference between modes and not because of intensity fluctuations of individual modes.

[11] The averaging is performed over a time that is long compared with the optical period $2\pi/\omega_0$ but short compared with the modulation period $2\pi/\omega$.

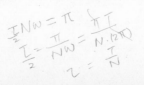

lineshape width $\Delta\omega$ to the frequency spacing ω between modes. Using this relation, as well as $T = 2\pi/\omega$ in $\tau = T/N$, we obtain

$$\tau \sim \frac{2\pi}{\Delta\omega} = \frac{1}{\Delta\nu} \tag{6.6-6}$$

Thus the length of the mode-locked pulses is approximately the inverse of the gain linewidth.

A theoretical plot of $\sqrt{P(t)}$ as given by (6.6-5) for the case of five modes ($N = 5$) is shown in Figure 6-9. The ordinate may also be considered as being proportional to the instantaneous field amplitude.

The foregoing discussion was limited to the consideration of mode locking as a function of time. It is clear, however, that since the solution of Maxwell's equation in the cavity involves traveling waves (a standing wave can be considered as the sum of two waves traveling in opposite directions), mode locking causes the oscillation energy of the laser to be condensed into a packet that travels back and forth between the mirrors with the velocity of light c. The pulsation period $T = 2l/c$ corresponds simply to the time interval between two successive arrivals of the pulse at the mirror. The spatial length of the pulse L_p must correspond to its time duration multiplied by its velocity c. Using $\tau = T/N$ we obtain

$$L_p \sim c\tau = \frac{cT}{N} = \frac{2\pi c}{\omega N} = \frac{2l}{N} \tag{6.6-7}$$

We can verify the last result by taking the basic resonator mode as being proportional to $\sin k_n x \sin \omega_n t$; the total optical field is then

$$e(z, t) = \sum_{n=-(N-1)/2}^{(N-1)/2} \sin\left[\frac{(m + n)\pi}{l} z\right] \sin\left[(m + n)\frac{\pi c}{l} t\right] \tag{6.6-8}$$

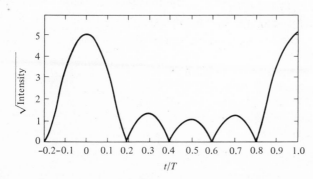

Figure 6-9   Theoretical plot of optical field amplitude [$\sqrt{P(t)} \propto \sin(N\omega t/2)/\sin(\omega t/2)$] resulting from phase locking of five ($N = 5$) equal-amplitude modes separated from each other by a frequency interval $\omega = 2\pi/T$.

where, using (4.5-4), $\omega_n = (m + n)(\pi c/l)$, $k_n = \omega_n/c$, and m is the integer corresponding to the central mode. We can rewrite (6.6-8) as

$$e(z, t) = \frac{1}{2} \sum_{n=-(N-1)/2}^{(N-1)/2} \left\{ \cos\left[(m + n)\frac{\pi}{l}(z - ct)\right] \right.$$
$$\left. - \cos\left[(m + n)\frac{\pi}{l}(z + ct)\right]\right\} \quad \textbf{(6.6-9)}$$

which can be shown to have the spatial and temporal properties described previously. Figure 6-10 shows a spatial plot of (6.6-9) at time t.

Methods of mode locking. In the preceding discussion we considered the consequences of fixing the phases of the longitudinal modes of a laser-mode locking. Mode locking can be achieved by modulating the losses (or gain) of the laser at a radian frequency $\omega = \pi c/l$, which is equal to the intermode frequency spacing. The theoretical proof of mode locking by loss modulation (References [2], [9], and [10]) is rather formal, but a good plausibility argument can be made as follows: As a form of loss modulation consider a thin shutter inserted inside the laser resonator. Let the shutter be closed (high optical loss) most of the time except for brief periodic openings for a duration of τ_{open} every $T = 2\pi/\omega$ seconds. This situation is illustrated by Figure 6-11. A single laser mode will not oscillate in this case because of the high losses (we assume that τ_{open} is too short to allow the oscillation to build up during each opening). The same applies to multimode oscillation with arbitrary phases. There is one exception, however. If the phases were locked as in (6.6-3), the energy distribution inside the resonator would correspond to that shown in Figure 6-10 and would consist of a narrow $(L_p \simeq 2l/N)$ traveling pulse. If this pulse should arrive at the shutter's position when it is open and if the pulse (temporal) length τ is short compared to the opening time τ_{open}, the mode-locked pulse will be "unaware" of the shutter's existence and, consequently, *will not be attenuated by it.* We

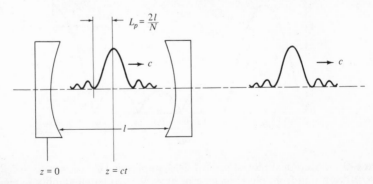

Figure 6-10 Traveling pulse of energy resulting from the mode locking of N laser modes; based on Equation (6.6-9).

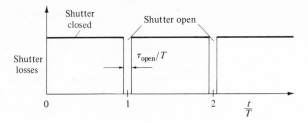

Figure 6-11   Periodic losses introduced by a shutter to induce mode locking. The presence of these losses favors the choice of mode phases that results in a pulse passing through the shutter during open intervals—that is, mode locking.

may thus reach the conclusion that loss modulation causes mode locking through some kind of "survival of the fittest" mechanism. In reality the periodic shutter chops off any intensity tails acquired by the mode-locked pulses due to a "wandering" of the phases from their ideal ($\phi_n = 0$) values. This has the effect of continuously restoring the phases.

An experimental setup used to mode-lock a He–Ne laser is shown in Figure 6-12; the periodic loss [11] is introduced by Bragg diffraction (see Sections 12.2 and 12.3) of a portion of the laser intensity from a standing acoustic wave. The loss, which is proportional to the acoustic intensity, is thus modulated at twice the acoustic frequency.

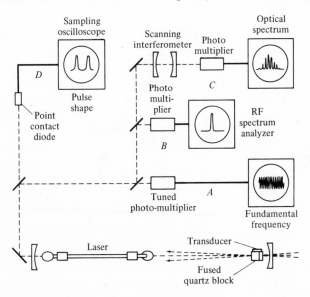

Figure 6-12   Experimental setup for laser mode locking by acoustic (Bragg) loss modulation. Parts A, B, C, and D of the experimental setup are designed to display the fundamental component of the intensity modulation, the power spectrum of the intensity modulation, the power spectrum of the optical field $e(t)$, and the optical intensity, respectively. (After Reference [12].)

Figure 6-13 shows the pulses resulting from mode locking an Nd^{3+}:YAG laser.

Mode locking occurs spontaneously in some lasers if the optical path contains a saturable absorber (an absorber whose opacity decreases with increasing optical intensity). This method is used to induce mode locking in the high-power-pulsed solid-state lasers; see References [13]–[15].

Table 6-1 lists some of the lasers commonly used in mode locking and the observed pulse durations.

Table 6-1   SOME LASER SYSTEMS, THEIR GAIN LINEWIDTH $\Delta\nu$, AND THE LENGTH OF THEIR PULSES IN THE MODE-LOCKED OPERATION

LASER MEDIUM	$\Delta\nu$, Hz	$(\Delta\nu)^{-1}$, SECONDS	OBSERVED PULSE DURATION, SECONDS
He–Ne (0.6328 μm) CW	~1.5×10^9	6.66×10^{-10}	~6×10^{-10}
Nd:YAG (1.06 μm) CW	~1.2×10^{10}	8.34×10^{-11}	~7.6×10^{-11}
Ruby (0.6934 μm) pulsed	6×10^{10}	1.66×10^{-11}	~1.2×10^{-11}
Nd^{3+}:glass pulsed	3×10^{12}	3.33×10^{-13}	~4×10^{-13}

6.7 Giant Pulse (Q-switched) Lasers

The technique of "Q-switching" is used to obtain intense and short bursts of oscillation from lasers; see References [16]–[18]. The quality factor Q of the optical resonator is degraded (lowered) by some means during the pumping so that the gain (that is, inversion $N_2 - N_1$) can build up to a very high value without oscillation. (The spoiling of the Q raises the threshold inversion to a value higher than that obtained by pumping.) When the inversion reaches its peak, the Q is restored suddenly to its (ordinary) high value. The gain (per pass) in the laser medium is now well above threshold. This causes an extremely rapid buildup of the oscillation and a simultaneous exhaustion of the inversion by stimulated $2 \rightarrow 1$ transitions. This process converts most of the energy that was stored by atoms pumped into the upper laser level into photons, which are now

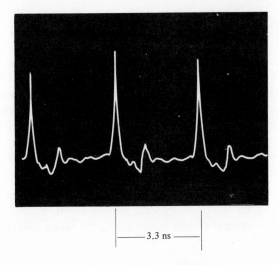

—— 3.3 ns ——

Figure 6-13   Power output as a function of time of a mode-locked Nd^{3+}:YAG laser. Width of pulse in display is limited by the detector. (After Reference [12].)

inside the optical resonator. These proceed to bounce back and forth between the reflectors with a fraction $(1 - R)$ "escaping" from the resonator each time. This causes a decay of the pulse with a characteristic time constant (the "photon lifetime") given in (4.6-3) as

$$t_c \simeq \frac{l}{c(1 - R)}$$

Both experiment and theory indicate that the total evolution of giant laser pulse as described above is typically completed in $\sim 2 \times 10^{-8}$ second. We will consequently neglect the effect of population relaxation and pumping that take place during the pulse. We will also assume that the switching of the Q from the low to the high value is accomplished instantaneously.

The laser is characterized by the following variables: ϕ; the total number of photons in the optical resonator, $n \equiv (N_2 - N_1)V$; the total inversion; and t_c, the decay time constant for photons in the *passive* resonator. The exponential gain constant γ is proportional to n. The radiation intensity I thus grows with distance as $I(z) = I_0 \exp(\gamma z)$ and $dI/dz = \gamma I$. An observer traveling with the wave velocity will see it grow at a rate

$$\frac{dI}{dt} = \frac{dI}{dz}\frac{dz}{dt} = \gamma c I$$

and thus the temporal exponential growth constant is γc. If the laser rod is of length L while the resonator length is l, then only a fraction L/l of the photons is undergoing amplification at any one time and the average growth constant is $\gamma c(L/l)$. We can thus write

$$\frac{d\phi}{dt} = \phi\left(\frac{\gamma cL}{l} - \frac{1}{t_c}\right) \tag{6.7-1}$$

where $-\phi/t_c$ is the decrease in the number of resonator photons per unit time due to incidental resonator losses and to the output coupling. Defining a dimensionless time by $\tau = t/t_c$ we obtain, upon multiplying (6.7-1) by t_c,

$$\frac{d\phi}{d\tau} = \phi\left[\left(\frac{\gamma}{l/cLt_c}\right) - 1\right] = \phi\left[\frac{\gamma}{\gamma_t} - 1\right]$$

where $\gamma_t = (l/cLt_c)$ is the minimum value of the gain constant at which oscillation (that is, $d\phi/d\tau = 0$) can be sustained. Since, according to (5.3-3) γ is proportional to the inversion n, the last equation can also be written as

$$\frac{d\phi}{d\tau} = \phi\left[\frac{n}{n_t} - 1\right] \tag{6.7-2}$$

where $n_t = N_t V$ is the total inversion at threshold as given by (6.1-9).

The term $\phi(n/n_t)$ in (6.7-2) gives the number of photons generated by induced emission per unit of normalized time. Since each generated photon results from a single transition, it corresponds to a decrease of $\Delta n = -2$ in the total inversion. We can thus write directly

$$\frac{dn}{d\tau} = -2\phi\frac{n}{n_t} \tag{6.7-3}$$

The coupled pair of equations, (6.7-2) and (6.7-3), describes the evolution of ϕ and n. It can be solved easily by numerical techniques. Before we proceed to give the results of such calculation we will consider some of the consequences that can be deduced analytically.

Dividing (6.7-2) by (6.7-3) results in

$$\frac{d\phi}{dn} = \frac{n_t}{2n} - \frac{1}{2}$$

and, by integration,

$$\phi - \phi_i = \frac{1}{2}\left[n_t \ln\frac{n}{n_i} - (n - n_i)\right]$$

Assuming that ϕ_i, the initial number of photons in the cavity, is negligible, we obtain

$$\phi = \frac{1}{2}\left[n_t \ln\frac{n}{n_i} - (n - n_i)\right] \tag{6.7-4}$$

for the relation between the number of photons ϕ and the inversion n at any moment. At $t \gg t_c$ the photon density ϕ will be zero so that setting $\phi = 0$ in (6.7-4) results in the following expression for the final inversion n_f:

$$\frac{n_f}{n_i} = \exp\left[\frac{n_f - n_i}{n_t}\right]$$ **(6.7-5)**

This equation is of the form $(x/a) = \exp(x - a)$, where $x = n_f/n_t$ and $a = n_i/n_t$, so that it can be solved graphically (or numerically) for n_f/n_i as a function of n_i/n_t.[12] The result is shown in Figure 6-14. We notice that the fraction of the energy originally stored in the inversion which is converted into laser oscillation energy is $(n_i - n_f)/n_f$ and that it tends to unity as n_i/n_t increases.

The instantaneous power output of the laser is given by $P = \phi h\nu/t_c$, or, using (6.7-4), by

$$P = \frac{h\nu}{2t_c}\left[n_t \ln \frac{n}{n_i} - (n - n_i)\right]$$ **(6.7-6)**

Of special interest to us is the peak power output. Setting $\partial P/\partial\phi = 0$ we find that maximum power occurs when $n = n_t$. Putting $n = n_t$ in (6.7-6)

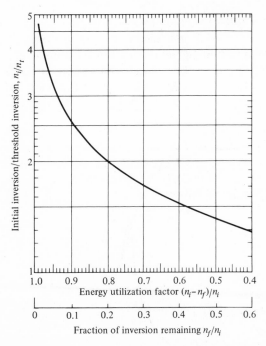

Figure 6-14   Energy utilization factor $(n_i - n_f)/n_i$ and inversion remaining after the giant pulse. (After Reference [19].)

---

[12] This can be done by assuming a value of a and finding the corresponding x at which the plots of x/a and $\exp(x - a)$ intersect.

gives

$$P_p = \frac{h\nu}{2t_c}\left[n_t \ln \frac{n_t}{n_i} - (n_t - n_i)\right] \tag{6.7-7}$$

for the peak power. If the initial inversion is well in excess of the (high-Q) threshold value (that is, $n_i \gg n_t$), we obtain from (6.7-7)

$$(P_p)_{n_i \gg n_t} \simeq \frac{n_i h\nu}{2t_c} \tag{6.7-8}$$

Since the power P at any moment is related to the number of photons ϕ by $P = \phi h\nu/t_c$ it follows from (6.7-8) that the maximum number of stored photons inside the resonator is $n_i/2$. This can be explained by the fact that if $n_i \gg n_t$, the buildup of the pulse to its peak value occurs in a time short compared to t_c so that at the peak of the pulse, when $n = n_t$, most of the photons that were generated by stimulated emission are still present in the resonator. Moreover, since $n_i \gg n_t$, the number of these photons $(n_i - n_t)/2$ is very nearly $n_i/2$.

A typical numerical solution of (6.7-2) and (6.7-3) is given in Figure 6-15.

To initiate the pulse we need, according to (6.7-2) and (6.7-3), to have $\phi_i \neq 0$. Otherwise the solution is trivial ($\phi = 0$, $n = n_i$). The appropriate value of ϕ_i is usually estimated on the basis of the number of spontaneously emitted photons within the acceptance solid angle of the laser mode at $t = 0$. We also notice, as discussed above, that the photon density, hence

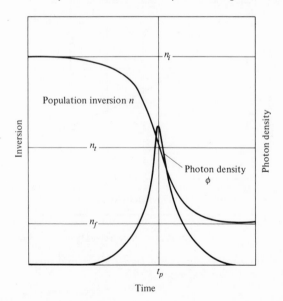

Figure 6-15   Inversion and photon density during a giant pulse. (After Reference [19].)

the power, reaches a peak when $n = n_t$. The energy stored in the cavity ($\propto \phi$) at this point is maximum, so stimulated transitions from the upper to the lower laser levels continue to reduce the inversion to a final value $n_f < n_t$.

Numerical solutions of (6.7-2) and (6.7-3) corresponding to different initial inversions n_i/n_t are shown in Figure 6-16. We notice that for $n_i \gg n_t$ the rise time becomes short compared to t_c but the fall time approaches a value nearly equal to t_c. The reason is that the process of stimulated emission is essentially over at the peak of the pulse ($\tau = 0$)

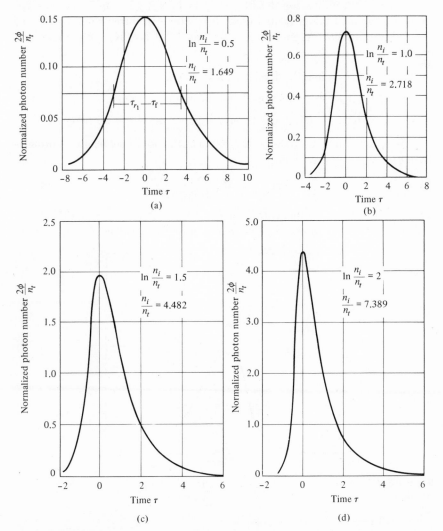

Figure 6-16 Photon number vs. time in central region of giant pulse. Time is measured in units of photon lifetime. (After Reference [19].)

and the observed output is due to the free decay of the photons in the resonator.

In Figure 6-17 we show an actual oscilloscope trace of a giant pulse. Giant laser pulses are used extensively in applications which depend on their extremely high peak powers and short duration. These applications include experiments in nonlinear optics, ranging, material machining and drilling, initiation of chemical reactions, and plasma diagnostics.

Numerical example—giant pulse ruby laser.   Consider the case of pink ruby with a chromium ion density of $N = 1.58 \times 10^{19}$ cm^{-3}. Its absorption coefficient is taken from Figure 7-4, where it corresponds to that of the R_1 line at 6943 Å, and is $\alpha \simeq 0.2$ cm^{-1} (at 300°K). Other assumed characteristics are:

$$l = \text{length of ruby rod} = 10 \text{ cm}$$

$$A = \text{cross-sectional area of mode} = 1 \text{ cm}^2$$

$$(1 - R) = \text{fractional intensity loss per pass}[13] = 20 \text{ percent}$$

Since, according to (5.3-3), the exponential loss coefficient is proportional to $N_1 - N_2$, we have

$$\alpha \, (\text{cm}^{-1}) = 0.2 \, \frac{N_1 - N_2}{1.58 \times 10^{19}} \qquad \textbf{(6.7-9)}$$

Thus, at room temperature, when $N_1 - N_2 = 1.58 \times 10^{19}$ cm^{-3}, $\alpha = 0.2$ cm^{-1} as observed. The expression for gain coefficient follow

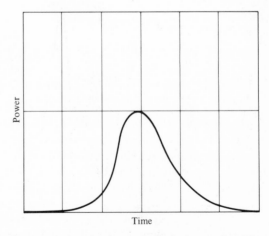

Figure 6-17   A scope trace of a fast-switched giant pulse. Time scale is 20 ns per division.

---

[13] We express the loss in terms of an effective reflectivity even though it is due to a number of factors, as discussed in Section 4.6.

directly from (6.7-9):

$$\gamma \ (\text{cm}^{-1}) = 0.2 \, \frac{N_2 - N_1}{1.58 \times 10^{19}} = 0.2 \, \frac{n}{1.58 \times 10^{19} V} \qquad \text{(6.7-10)}$$

where n is the total inversion in cm^{-3} and $V = AL$ is the crystal volume in cm^3.

Threshold is achieved when the net gain per pass is unity. This happens when

$$e^{\gamma_t l} R = 1 \qquad \text{or} \qquad \gamma_t = -\frac{1}{l} \ln R \qquad \text{(6.7-11)}$$

where the subscript t indicates the threshold condition.

Using (6.7-10) in the threshold condition (6.7-11) plus the appropriate data from above gives

$$n_t = 1.8 \times 10^{18} \qquad \text{(6.7-12)}$$

Assuming that the initial inversion is $n_i = 5n_t = 10^{18} V$ we find from (6.7-8) that the peak power is approximately

$$P_p = \frac{n_i h\nu}{2t_c} \qquad \text{(6.7-13)}$$

where $t_c = l/c(1 - R) \simeq 2.5 \times 10^{-9}$ second.

Substituting the foregoing data in (6.7-8) gives

$$P_p = 5.1 \times 10^7 \text{ watts}$$

The total pulse energy is

$$\mathcal{E} \sim \frac{n_i h\nu}{2} \sim 0.13 \text{ joule}$$

while the pulse duration (see Figure 6-16) $\simeq 3t_c \simeq 7.5 \times 10^{-9}$ second.

Methods of Q-switching. Some of the schemes used in Q-switching are:

1. Mounting one of the two end reflectors on a rotating shaft so that the optical losses are extremely high except for the brief interval in each rotation cycle in which the mirrors are nearly parallel.

2. The inclusion of a saturable absorber (bleachable dye) in the optical resonator; see References [13]–[15]. The absorber whose opacity decreases (saturates) with increasing optical intensity prevents rapid inversion depletion due to buildup of oscillation by presenting a high loss to the early stages of oscillation during which the slowly increasing intensity is not high enough to saturate the absorption. As the intensity increases the loss decreases, and the effect is similar, but not as abrupt, as that of a sudden increase of Q.

3. The use of an electrooptic crystal (or liquid Kerr cell) as a voltage-controlled gate inside the optical resonator. It provides a

more precise control over the losses (Q) than schemes 1 and 2. Its operation is illustrated by Figure 6-18 and is discussed in some detail in the following. The control of the phase delay in the electro-optic crystal by the applied voltage is discussed in detail in Chapter 9.

During the pumping of the laser by the light from a flashlamp, a voltage is applied to the electrooptic crystal of such magnitude as to introduce a $\pi/2$ relative phase shift (retardation) between the two mutually orthogonal components (x' and y') that make up the linearly polarized (x) laser field. On exiting from the electrooptic crystal at point f the light traveling to the right is circularly polarized. After reflection from the right mirror the light passes once more through the crystal. The additional retardation of $\pi/2$ adds to the earlier one to give a total retardation of π thus causing the emerging beam at d to be linearly polarized along y and consequently to be blocked by the polarizer.

It follows that with the voltage on, the losses are high, so oscillation is prevented. The Q-switching is timed to coincide with the point at which the inversion reaches its peak and is achieved by a removal of the voltage applied to the electrooptic crystal. This reduces the retardation to zero so that state of polarization of the wave passing through the crystal is unaffected and the Q regains its high value associated with the ordinary losses of the system.

6.8 Hole-Burning and the Lamb Dip in Doppler Broadened Gas Lasers

In this section we concern ourselves with some of the consequences of Doppler broadening in low pressure gas lasers.

Consider an atom with a transition frequency $\nu_0 = (E_2 - E_1)/h$ where 2 and 1 refer to the upper and lower laser levels, respectively. Let the component of the velocity of the atom parallel to the wave propagation direction be v. This component, thus, has the value

$$v = \frac{\mathbf{v}_{\text{atom}} \cdot \mathbf{k}}{k} \tag{6.8-1}$$

where the electromagnetic wave is described by

$$\mathbf{E} = \mathbf{E}e^{i(2\pi\nu t - \mathbf{k}\cdot\mathbf{r})} \tag{6.8-2}$$

An atom moving with a constant velocity $\mathbf{v}$, so that $\mathbf{r} = \mathbf{v}t + \mathbf{r}_0$, will exercise a field

$$\mathbf{E}_{\text{atom}} = \mathbf{E}e^{i[2\pi\nu t - \mathbf{k}\cdot(\mathbf{r}_0 + \mathbf{v}t)]}$$

$$= \mathbf{E}e^{i[(2\pi\nu - \mathbf{v}\cdot\mathbf{k})t - \mathbf{k}\cdot\mathbf{r}_0]} \tag{6.8-3}$$

and will thus "see" a Doppler shifted frequency

$$\nu_D = \nu - \frac{\mathbf{v} \cdot \mathbf{k}}{2\pi} = \nu - \frac{v}{c}\nu \qquad \textbf{(6.8-4)}$$

where in the second equality we used the relation $k = 2\pi\nu/c$ and Equation (6.8-1).

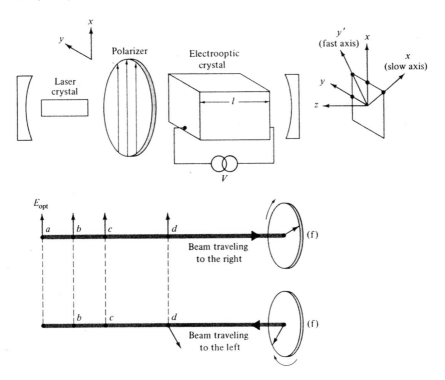

For beam traveling to right:

At point d,

$$\left. \begin{array}{l} E_x' = \dfrac{E}{\sqrt{2}}\cos\omega t \\[2ex] E_y' = \dfrac{E}{\sqrt{2}}\cos\omega t \end{array} \right\}$$ The optical field is linearly polarized with its electric field vector parallel to x

At point f,

$$\left. \begin{array}{l} E_x' = \dfrac{E}{\sqrt{2}}\cos\left(\omega t + kl + \dfrac{\pi}{2}\right) \\[2ex] E_y' = \dfrac{E}{\sqrt{2}}\cos(\omega t + kl) \end{array} \right\}$$ Circularly polarized

For beam traveling to left:

At point f,

$$\left. \begin{array}{l} E_x' = -\dfrac{E}{\sqrt{2}}\cos\left(\omega t + kl + \dfrac{\pi}{2}\right) \\[2ex] E_y' = -\dfrac{E}{\sqrt{2}}\cos(\omega t + kl) \end{array} \right\}$$ Circularly polarized

At point d,

$$\left. \begin{array}{l} E_x' = -\dfrac{E}{\sqrt{2}}\cos(\omega t + 2kl + \pi) \\[2ex] E_y' = -\dfrac{E}{\sqrt{2}}\cos(\omega t + 2kl) \end{array} \right\}$$ Linearly polarized along y

Figure 6-18   Electrooptic crystal used as voltage-controlled gate in Q-switching a laser.

The condition for the maximum strength of interaction (that is, emission or absorption) between the moving atom and the wave is that the apparent (Doppler) frequency ν_D "seen" by the atom be equal to the atomic resonant frequency ν_0

$$\nu_0 = \nu - \frac{v}{c}\nu \qquad (6.8\text{-}5)$$

or reversing the argument, a wave of frequency ν moving through an ensemble of atoms will "seek out" and interact most strongly with those atoms whose velocity component v satisfies

$$\nu = \frac{\nu_0}{1 - \dfrac{v}{c}} \approx \nu_0\left(1 + \frac{v}{c}\right) \qquad (6.8\text{-}6)$$

where the approximation is valid for $v \ll c$.

Now consider a gas laser oscillating at a single frequency ν where, for the sake of definiteness, we take $\nu > \nu_0$. The standing wave electromagnetic field at ν inside the laser resonator consists of two waves traveling in opposite directions. Consider, first, the wave traveling in the positive x direction (the resonator axis is taken parallel to the x axis). Since $\nu > \nu_0$ the wave interacts, according to Equation (6.8-6) with atoms having $v > 0$, that is, atoms with

$$v_x = +\frac{c}{\nu_0}(\nu - \nu_0) \qquad (6.8\text{-}7)$$

The wave traveling in the opposite direction $(-x)$ must also interact with atoms moving in the same direction so that the Doppler shifted frequency is reduced from ν to ν_0. These are atoms with

$$v_x = -\frac{c}{\nu_0}(\nu - \nu_0) \qquad (6.8\text{-}8)$$

We conclude that due to the standing wave nature of the field inside a conventional two-mirror laser oscillator, a given frequency of oscillation interacts with two velocity classes of atoms.

Consider, next, a four-level gas laser oscillating at a frequency $\nu > \nu_0$. At negligibly low levels of oscillation and at low gas pressure, the velocity distribution function of atoms in the upper laser level is given, according to Equation (5.1-11), by

$$f(v_x) \propto e^{-Mv_x^2/2kT} \qquad (6.8\text{-}9)$$

where $f(v_x)\,dv_x$ is proportional to the number of atoms (in the upper laser level) with x component of velocity between v_x and $v_x + dv_x$. As the oscillation level is increased, say by reducing the laser losses, we expect the number of atoms in the upper laser level, with x velocities near $v_x = \pm(c/\nu)(\nu - \nu_0)$, to decrease from their equilibrium value as given by Equation (6.8-9). This is due to the fact that these atoms undergo stimulated downward transitions from level 2 to 1, thus reducing the number of atoms in level 2. The velocity distribution function under conditions of oscillation has consequently two depressions as shown schematically in Figure 6-19.

If the oscillation frequency ν is equal to ν_0, only a single "hole" exists in the velocity distribution function of the inverted atoms. This "hole" is centered on $v_x = 0$. We may, thus, expect the power output of a laser oscillating at $\nu = \nu_0$ to be less than that of a laser in which ν is tuned slightly to one side or the other of ν_0 (this tuning can be achieved by moving one of the laser mirrors). This power dip first predicted by Lamb [20] is indeed observed in gas lasers [21]. An experimental plot of the power versus frequency in a He–Ne 1.15-μm laser is shown in Figure 6-20. The phenomenon is referred to as the "Lamb dip" and is used in frequency stabilization schemes of gas lasers [22].

6.9 Relaxation Oscillation in Lasers

Relaxation oscillation of the intensity has been observed in most types of lasers [23] [24]. This oscillation takes place characteristically with a period which is considerably longer than the cavity decay time t_c (see Section 4.6) or the resonator round trip time $2l/c$. Typical values range between $0.1\,\mu$s to $10\,\mu$s.

The basic physical mechanism is an interplay between the oscillation field in the resonator and the atomic inversion. An increase in the field

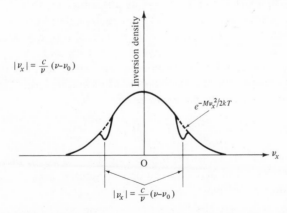

Figure 6-19 The distribution of inverted atoms as a function of v_x. The dashed curve which is proportional to exp $(-Mv_x{}^2/2kT)$ corresponds to the case of zero field intensity. The solid curve corresponds to a standing wave field at

$$\nu = \frac{\nu_o}{1 - \dfrac{v_x}{c}} \quad \text{or one at } \nu = \frac{\nu_o}{1 + \dfrac{v_x}{c}}$$

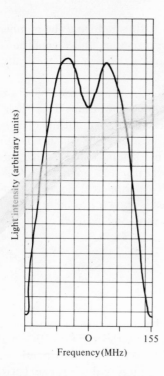

Light intensity (arbitrary units)

O   155

Frequency (MHz)

Figure 6-20 The power output as a function of the frequency of a single mode 1.15 μm He-Ne laser using the 20 Ne isotope. (After Reference [21].)

intensity causes a reduction in the inversion due to the increased rate of stimulated transitions. This causes a reduction in the gain which in turn tends to decrease the field intensity.

In the mathematical modeling of this phenomenon, we assume an ideal homogeneously broadened four-level laser such as described in Section 6.4. We also assume that the lower level population is negligible (that is, $W_i \ll \omega_{10} \gg \omega_{21}$) and take the inversion density $N \equiv N_2 - N_1 = N_2$. The pumping rate into level 2 (atoms/s $- m^3$) is R and the lifetime, due to all causes except stimulated emission, of atoms in level 2 is τ. Taking the induced transition rate per atom as W_i we have

$$\frac{dN}{dt} = R - W_i N - \frac{N}{\tau} \qquad \textbf{(6.9-1)}$$

The transition rate W_i is, according to Equation (5.2-15), proportional to the field intensity I and hence to the photon density q in the optical resonator. We can, consequently, rewrite Equation (6.9-1) as

$$\frac{dN}{dt} = R - qBN - \frac{N}{\tau} \qquad \textbf{(6.9-2)}$$

where B is a proportionality constant defined by $W_i \equiv Bq$. Since qBN is also the rate (s$^{-1} - m^{-3}$) at which photons are generated, we have

$$\frac{dq}{dt} = qBN - \frac{q}{t_c} \qquad \textbf{(6.9-3)}$$

where t_c is the decay time constant for photons in the optical resonator as discussed in Sections 4.6 and 6.1. Equations (6.9-2) and (6.9-3) describe the interplay between the photon density q and the inversion N [25].

First we notice that in equilibrium, $dq/dt = dN/dt = 0$, the following relations are satisfied

$$N_0 = \frac{1}{Bt_c}$$

$$q_0 = \frac{RBt_c - \dfrac{1}{\tau}}{B} \tag{6.9-4}$$

From Equation (6.9-4) it follows that when $R = (Bt_c\tau)^{-1}$, $q_0 = 0$. We denote this threshold pumping rate by R_t and define the pumping factor $r \equiv R/R_t$[14] so that the second of Equation (6.9-4) can also be written as

$$q_0 = \frac{(r-1)}{B\tau} \tag{6.9-5}$$

Next, we consider the behavior of small perturbations from equilibrium. We take

$$N(t) = N_0 + N_1(t), \qquad N_1 \ll N_0$$

and

$$q(t) = q_0 + q_1(t), \qquad q_1 \ll q_0$$

Substituting these relations in Equations (6.9-2) and (6.9-3), and making use of Equation (6.9-4) we obtain

$$\frac{dN_1}{dt} = -RBt_cN_1 - \frac{q_1}{t_c} \tag{6.9-6}$$

$$\frac{dq_1}{dt} = \left(RBt_c - \frac{1}{\tau}\right)N_1 \tag{6.9-7}$$

Taking the derivative of Equation (6.9-7), substituting Equation (6.9-6) for dN_1/dt and using Equation (6.9-4) leads to

$$\frac{d^2q_1}{dt^2} + RBt_c\frac{dq_1}{dt} + \left(RB - \frac{1}{\tau t_c}\right)q_1 = 0 \tag{6.9-8}$$

or in terms of the pumping factor $r = RBt_c\tau$ introduced above,

$$\frac{d^2q_1}{dt^2} + \frac{r}{\tau}\frac{dq_1}{dt} + \frac{1}{\tau t_c}(r-1)q_1 = 0 \tag{6.9-9}$$

This is the differential equation describing a damped harmonic oscillator so that assuming a solution $q \propto e^{pt}$ we obtain

$$p^2 + \frac{r}{\tau}p + \frac{1}{\tau t_c}(r-1) = 0$$

---

[14] r is equal to the ratio of the unsaturated ($q = 0$) gain to the saturated gain (the saturated gain is the actual gain "seen" by the laser field and is equal to the loss).

with the solutions

$$p(\pm) = -\alpha \pm i\omega_m$$

$$\alpha = \frac{r}{2\tau}, \qquad \omega_m = \sqrt{\frac{1}{t_c\tau}(r-1) - \left(\frac{r}{2\tau}\right)^2}$$

(6.9-10)

$$\approx \sqrt{\frac{1}{t_c\tau}(r-1)} \qquad \frac{1}{t_c\tau}(r-1) \gg \left(\frac{r}{2\tau}\right)^2$$

so that $q_1(t) \propto e^{-\alpha t} \cos \omega_m t$. The predicted perturbation in the power output (which is proportional to the number of photons q) is, thus, a damped sinusoid with the damping rate α and the oscillation frequency ω_m increasing with excess pumping.

While some lasers display the damped sinusoidal perturbation of intensity described above, in many other laser systems the perturbation is undamped. An example of the first is illustrated in Figure 6-21 which shows the output of a $CaWO_4$:Nd^{3+} laser.

Numerical example—relaxation oscillation. Considering the case shown in Figure 6-21 with the following parameters

$$\tau = 1.6 \times 10^{-4} \text{ second}$$

$$t_c \simeq 10^{-8} \text{ second}$$

$$r \simeq 2$$

which using Equation (6.9-10) gives $T_m \equiv 2\pi/\omega_m \approx 8 \times 10^{-6}$ second.

The undamped relaxation oscillation observed in many cases can be understood, at least qualitatively, by considering Equation (6.9-9). As it stands, the equation is identical in form to that describing a damped nondriven harmonic oscillator or equivalently, a resonant RLC circuit.[15] Persistent, that is, nondamped, oscillation is possible when the "oscillator"

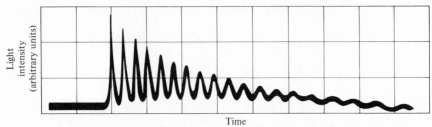

Time

Figure 6-21 Intensity Relaxation Oscillation in a $CaWO_4$:Nd^{3+} laser at 1.06 μm. Horizontal scale = 20 μsec/division. (After Reference [26].)

---

[15] The differential equation describing an oscillator is given in (5.4–1).

is driven. In this case, the driving function will replace the zero on the right side of Equation (6.9-9). One such driving mechanism may be due to time variation in the pumping rate R. In this case, we may take the pumping in the form

$$R = R_0 + R_1(t) \qquad \text{(6.9-11)}$$

where R_0 is the average pumping and $R_1(t)$ is the deviation.

Retracing the steps leading to Equation (6.9-6) but using Equation (6.9-11), we find that the inversion equation is now

$$\frac{dN_1}{dt} = R_1 - R_0 B t_c N_1 - \frac{q_1}{t_c}$$

and that Equation (6.9-9) takes the form

$$\frac{d^2 q_1}{dt^2} + \frac{r}{\tau} \frac{dq_1}{dt} + \frac{1}{\tau t_c} (r - 1) q_1 = -\frac{1}{\tau} (r - 1) R_1 \qquad \text{(6.9-12)}$$

Taking the Fourier transform of both sides of Equation (6.9-12), defining $Q(\omega)$ and $R(\omega)$ as the transforms of $q(t)$ and $R_1(t)$, respectively, and then solving for $Q(\omega)$, gives

$$Q(\omega) = \frac{\dfrac{1}{\tau}(r - 1) R(\omega)}{\omega^2 - i \dfrac{r}{\tau} \omega - \dfrac{1}{\tau t_c}(r - 1)} \qquad \text{(6.9-13)}$$

$$= \frac{\dfrac{1}{\tau}(r - 1) R(\omega)}{(\omega - \omega_m - i\alpha)(\omega + \omega_m - i\alpha)}$$

$$\omega_m = \sqrt{\frac{1}{t_c \tau}(r - 1) - \left(\frac{r}{2\tau}\right)^2} \qquad \text{(6.9-14)}$$

$$\approx \sqrt{\frac{1}{t_c \tau}(r - 1)}, \qquad \frac{1}{t_c \tau}(r - 1) \gg \left(\frac{r}{2\tau}\right)^2$$

$$\alpha = \frac{r}{2\tau} \qquad \text{(6.9-15)}$$

where we notice that ω_m and α correspond to the oscillation frequency and damping rate, respectively, of the transient case as given by Equation (6.9-10). If we assume that the spectrum $R(\omega)$ of the driving function $R(t)$ is uniform (that is, like "white" noise) near $\omega \approx \omega_m$, we may expect the intensity spectrum $Q(\omega)$ to have a peak near $\omega = \omega_m$ with a width $\Delta\omega \approx 2\alpha \equiv r/\tau$. In addition, if $\Delta\omega \ll \omega_m$ we may expect the intensity fluctuation

$q(t)$ as observed in the time domain to be modulated at a frequency ω_m [16] since for frequencies $\omega \approx \omega_m$ $Q(\omega)$ is a maximum.

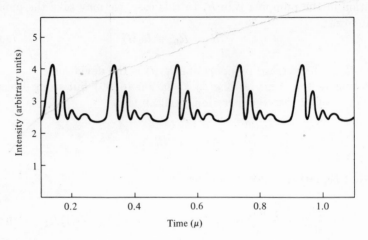

Figure 6-22 Intensity relaxation oscillation in a xenon 3.51 μm laser.

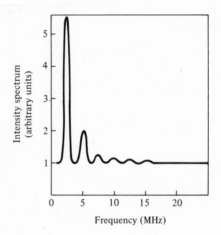

Figure 6-23 The intensity fluctuation spectrum of the laser output shown in Figure 6-22.

---

[16] To verify this statement, assume that $R(t)$ is approximated by a superposition of uncorrelated sinusoids $R(t) \propto \sum_n a_n e^{i\omega_n t}$ and using $R(\omega) \propto \int_{-\infty}^{\infty} R(t) e^{-i\omega t} dt$, we get $R(\omega) \propto \sum_n a_n \delta(\omega - \omega_n)$. From the inverse transform relation $q(t) \propto \int_{-\infty}^{\infty} Q(\omega) e^{i\omega t} d\omega$ and Equation (6.9-13), we get

$$q(t) \propto \sum_n \frac{a_n e^{i\omega_n t}}{[\omega_n - \omega_m - i\alpha][\omega_n + \omega_m - i\alpha]}$$

so that in the limit $\omega_m \gg \alpha$, $q(t)$ is a quasi-sinusoidal oscillation with a frequency ω_m.

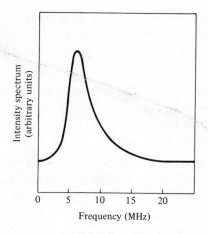

Figure 6-24 Same as Figure 6-23 except at increased pumping.

These conclusions are verified in experiments on different laser systems. In Figure 6-22 we show the intensity fluctuations of a xenon 3.51-μm laser. The repetition frequency is 2.5×10^6 Hz. A spectral analysis of the intensity yielding $Q(\omega)$ is shown in Figure 6-23. It consists of a narrow peak centered on $\omega_m = 2.5 \times 10^6$ Hz. An increase in the pumping strength is seen (Figure 6-24) to cause a broadening of the spectrum as well as a shift to higher frequencies consistent with the discussion following (6.9–15).

■ PROBLEMS

6-1 Show that the effect of frequency pulling by the atomic medium is to reduce the intermode frequency separation from $c/2l$ to

$$\frac{c}{2l}\left(1 - \frac{\gamma c}{2\pi\Delta\nu}\right)$$

where the symbols are defined in Section 6.2. Calculate the reduction for the case of a laser with $\Delta\nu = 10^9$ Hz, $\gamma = 4 \times 10^{-2}$ meter^{-1}, and $l = 100$ cm.

6-2 Derive Equation (6.4-3).

6-3 Derive the optimum coupling condition (6.5-11).

6-4 Calculate the saturation power P_s of the He–Ne laser operating at 6328 Å. Assume $V = 2$ cm^3, $L = 1$ percent per pass, and $\Delta\nu = 1.5 \times 10^9$ Hz.

6-5 Calculate the critical inversion density N_t of the He–Ne laser described in Problem 6-4.

6-6   Derive an expression for the finesse of a Fabry–Perot etalon containing an inverted population medium. Assume that $r_1{}^2 = r_2{}^2 \simeq 1$ and that the inversion is insufficient to result in oscillation. Compare the finesse to that of a passive Fabry–Perot etalon.

6-7   Derive an expression for the maximum gain–bandwidth product of a Fabry–Perot regenerative amplifier. Define the bandwidth as the frequency region in which the intensity gain $(E_t E_t^*)/(E_i E_i^*)$ exceeds half its peak value. Assume that $\nu_0 = \nu_m$.

6-8   **a.**   Derive Equation (6.6-4).
b.   Show that if in (6.6-3) the phases are taken as $\phi_n = n\phi$, where ϕ is some constant, instead of $\phi_n = 0$, the result is merely one of delaying the pulses by $-\phi/\omega$.

6-9   **a.**   Describe qualitatively what one may expect to see in parts A, B, C, and D of the mode-locking experiment sketched in Figure 6-12. (The reader may find it useful to read first the section on photomultipliers in Chapter 11.)
b.   What is the effect of mode locking on the intensity of the beat signal (at $\omega = \pi c/l$) displayed by the RF spectrum analyzer in B. Assume N equal amplitude modes spaced by ω whose phases before mode locking are random. (*Answer:* Mode locking increases the beat signal power by N.)
c.   Show that a standing wave at $\nu_0 + \delta$ (ν_0 is the center frequency of the Doppler broadened lineshape function) in a gas laser will burn the same two holes in the velocity distribution function (see Figure 6-19) as a field at $\nu_0 - \delta$.
d.   Can two traveling waves, one at $\nu_0 + \delta$ the other at $\nu_0 - \delta$, interact with the same class of atoms? If the answer is yes, under what conditions?

■ R E F E R E N C E S

[1]   Schawlow, A. L., and C. H. Townes, "Infrared and optical masers," *Phys. Rev.*, vol. 112, p. 1940, 1958.

[2]   Yariv, A., *Quantum Electronics*. New York: Wiley, 1967.

[3]   Smith, W. V., and P. P. Sorokin, *The Laser*. New York: McGraw-Hill, 1966.

[4]   Lengyel, B. A., *Introduction to Laser Physics*. New York: Wiley, 1966.

[5]   Birnbaum, G., *Optical Masers*. New York: Academic Press, 1964.

[6]   *Lasers and Light—Readings from Scientific American*. San Francisco: Freeman, 1969.

[7]   Bennett, W. R., Jr., "Gaseous optical masers," in *Appl. Opt. Suppl. 1, Optical Masers*, 1962, p. 24.

[8] Fork, R. L., D. R. Herriott, and H. Kogelnik, "A scanning spherical mirror interferometer for spectral analysis of laser radiation," *Appl. Optics*, vol. 3, p. 1471, 1964.

[9] DiDomenico, M., Jr., "Small signal analysis of internal modulation of lasers," *J. Appl. Phys.*, vol. 35, p. 2870, 1964.

[10] Yariv, A., "Internal modulation in multimode laser oscillators," *J. Appl. Phys.*, vol. 36, p. 388, 1965.

[11] Hargrove, L. E., R. L. Fork, and M. A. Pollack, "Locking of He–Ne laser modes induced by synchronous intracavity modulation," *Appl. Phys. Letters*, vol. 5, p. 4, 1964.

[12] DiDomenico, M., Jr., J. E. Geusic, H. M. Marcos, and R. G. Smith, "Generation of ultrashort optical pulses by mode locking the Nd^{3+}:YAG laser," *Appl. Phys. Letters*, vol. 8, p. 180, 1966.

[13] Mocker, H., and R. J. Collins, "Mode competition and self-locking effects in a Q-switched ruby laser," *Appl. Phys. Letters*, vol. 7, p. 270, 1965.

[14] DeMaria, A. J., "Picosecond laser pulses," Proc. IEEE, vol. 57, p. 3, 1969.

[15] DeMaria, A. J., "Mode locking," *Electronics*, Sept. 16, 1968, p. 112.

[16] Hellwarth, R. W., "Control of fluorescent pulsations," in *Advances in Quantum Electronics*, J. R. Singer, ed: New York: Columbia University Press, 1961, p. 334.

[17] McClung, F. J., and R. W. Hellwarth, *J. Appl. Phys.*, vol. 33, p. 828, 1962.

[18] Hellwarth, R. W., "*Q* modulation of lasers," in *Lasers*, vol. 1, A. K. Levine, ed. New York: Marcel Dekker, Inc., 1966, p. 253.

[19] Wagner, W. G., and B. A. Lengyel, "Evolution of the giant pulse in a laser," *J. Appl. Phys.*, vol. 34, p. 2042, 1963.

[20] Lamb, W. E., Jr., "Theory of an optical maser," *Phys. Rev.*, vol. 134, *A1429* (1964).

[21] Szöke, A., and A. Javan, "Isotope shift and saturation behavior of the 1.15μ transition of neon," *Phys. Rev. Letters*, vol. 10, *512* (1963).

[22] Bloom, A., *Gas Lasers*. New York: Wiley, 1963, p. 93.

[23] Collins, R. J., D. F. Nelson, A. L. Schawlow, W. Bond, C. G. B. Garrett, and W. Kaiser, *Phys. Rev. Letters*, *303* (1960).

[24] For additional references on relaxation oscillation the reader should consult
   (a) Birnbaum, G., *Optical Masers*. New York: Academic Press, 1964, p. 191.
   (b) Evtuhov, V., "Pulsed ruby lasers," in *Lasers*, edited by A. K. Levine. New York: M. Dekker, Inc., 1966, p. 76.

[25]   The explanation of "spiking" in terms of these equations is due to:
(a)   Dunsmuir, R., in *J. Elec. Control,* vol. 10, *453* (1961).
(b)   Statz, H., and G. de Mars, *Quantum Electronics.* New York: Columbia University Press, 1960, p. 530.

[26]   Johnson, L. F., in *Lasers,* edited by A. K. Levine. New York: M. Dekker, Inc., 1966, p. 174.

[27]   Casperson, L., and A. Yariv, "Relaxation oscillation in a xenon 3.51μm laser," *J. Quantum Electronics,* 1971.

7

Some Specific Laser Systems

7.0 Introduction

The pumping of the atoms into the upper laser level is accomplished in a variety of ways, depending on the type of laser. In this chapter we will review some of the more common laser systems and in the process describe their pumping mechanisms. The laser systems described include: ruby, Nd^{3+}:YAG, Nd^{3+}:glass, He–Ne, CO_2, Ar^+, and the GaAs semiconductor junction laser.

7.1 Pumping and Laser Efficiency

Figure 7-1 shows the pumping–oscillation cycle of some (hypothetical) representative laser. The pumping agency elevates the atoms into some excited state 3 from which they relax into the upper laser level 2. The stimulated laser transition takes place between levels 2 and 1 and results in the emission of a photon of frequency ν_{21}.

It is evident from this figure that the minimum energy input per output photon is $h\nu_{30}$, so the power efficiency of the laser cannot exceed

$$\eta_{\text{atomic}} = \frac{\nu_{21}}{\nu_{30}} \qquad \text{(7.1-1)}$$

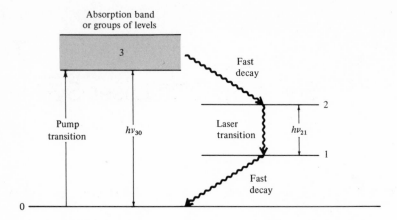

Figure 7-1   Pumping–oscillation cycle of a typical laser.

to which quantity we will refer as the "atomic quantum efficiency." The overall laser efficiency depends on the fraction of the total pump power which is effective in transferring atoms into level 3 and on the pumping quantum efficiency defined as the fraction of the atoms which, once in 3, make a transition to 2. The product of the last two factors, which constitutes an upper limit on the efficiency of optically pumped lasers, ranges from about 1 percent for solid-state lasers such as Nd^{3+}:YAG to about 30 percent in the CO_2 laser and to near unity in the GaAs junction laser. We shall discuss these factors when we get down to some specific laser systems. We may note, however, that according to (7.1-1), in an efficient laser system ν_{21} and ν_{30} must be of the same order of magnitude, so the laser transition should involve low-lying levels.

7.2   The Ruby Laser

The first material in which laser action was demonstrated [1] and still one of the most useful laser materials is ruby, whose output is at $\lambda_0 = 0.6943\ \mu$m. The active laser particles are Cr^{3+} ions present as impurities in Al_2O_3 crystal. Typical Cr^{3+} concentrations are ~0.05 percent by weight. The pertinent energy level diagram is shown in Figure 7-2.

The pumping of ruby is performed usually by subjecting it to the light of intense flashlamps (quite similar to the types used in flash photography). A portion of this light which corresponds in frequency to the two absorption bands $^4F_2$ and $^4F_1$ is absorbed, thereby causing Cr^{3+} ions to be transferred into these levels. The ions proceed to decay, within an average time of $\omega_{32}^{-1} \simeq 5 \times 10^{-8}$ seconds [2], into the upper laser level ^2E. The level ^2E is composed of two separate levels $2\overline{A}$ and $\overline{E}$ separated by

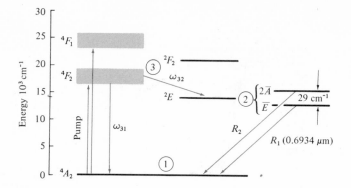

Figure 7-2 Energy levels pertinent to the operation of a ruby laser. (After Reference [2].)

29 cm^{-1}.[1] The lower of these two, $\overline{E}$, is the upper laser level. The lower laser level is the ground state, and thus, according to the discussion of Section 6.3, ruby is a three-level laser. The lifetime of atoms in the upper laser level $\overline{E}$ is $t_2 \simeq 3 \times 10^{-3}$ second. Each decay results in the (spontaneous) emission of a photon, so $t_2 \simeq t_{spont}$.

An absorption spectrum of a typical ruby with two orientations of the optical field relative to the c (optic) axis is shown in Figure 7-3. The two main peaks correspond to absorption into the useful $^4F_1$ and $^4F_2$ bands, which are responsible for the characteristic (ruby) color.

The ordinate is labeled in terms of the absorption coefficient and in terms of the transition cross section σ which may be defined as the absorption coefficient per unit inversion per unit volume and has consequently the dimension of area. According to this definition, $\alpha(\nu)$ is given by

$$\alpha(\nu) = (N_1 - N_2)\sigma(\nu) \tag{7.2-1}$$

A more detailed plot of the absorption near the laser emission wavelength is shown in Figure 7-4. The width $\Delta\nu$ of the laser transition as a function of temperature is shown in Figure 7-5. At room temperature, $\Delta\nu = 11$ cm^{-1}.

We can use ruby to illustrate some of the considerations involved in optical pumping of solid-state lasers. Figure 7-6 shows a typical setup of an optically pumped laser, such as ruby. The helical flashlamp surrounds the ruby rod. The flash excitation is provided by the discharge of the charge stored in a capacitor bank across the lamp.

The typical flash output consists of a pulse of light of duration $t_{flash} \simeq 5 \times 10^{-4}$ second. Let us, for the sake of simplicity, assume that the flash pulse is rectangular in time and of duration t_{flash}, and that it results in an

---

[1] The unit 1 cm^{-1} (one wavenumber) is the frequency corresponding to $\lambda_0 = 1$ cm, so 1 cm^{-1} is equivalent to $\nu = 3 \times 10^{10}$ Hz. It is also used as a measure of energy where 1 cm^{-1} corresponds to the energy $h\nu$ of a photon with $\nu = 3 \times 10^{10}$ Hz.

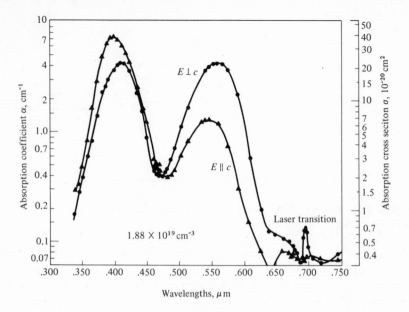

Figure 7-3 Absorption coefficient and absorption cross section as functions of wavelength for $E \parallel c$ and $E \perp c$. The 300°K data were derived from transmittance measurements on pink ruby with an average Cr ion concentration of 1.88×10^{19} cm^{-3}. (After Reference [3].)

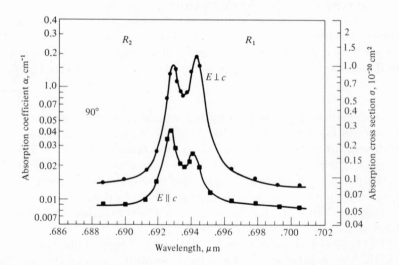

Figure 7-4 Absorption coefficient and absorption cross section as functions of wavelength for $E \parallel c$ and $E \perp c$. Sample was a pink ruby laser rod having a 90° c-axis orientation with respect to the rod axis and a Cr concentration of 1.58×10^{19} cm^{-3}. (After Reference [3].)

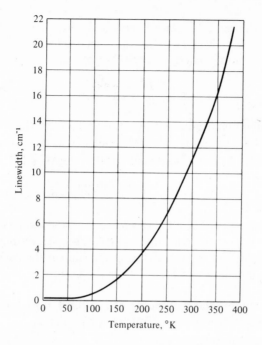

Figure 7-5 Line width of the R_1 line of ruby as a function of temperature. (After Reference [4].)

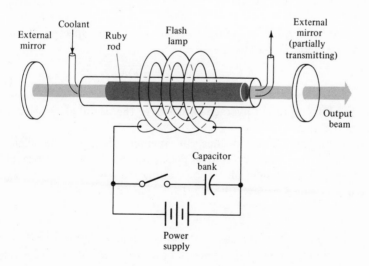

Figure 7-6 Typical setup of a pulsed ruby laser using flashlamp pumping and external mirrors.

optical flux at the crystal surface having $s(\nu)$ watts per unit area per unit frequency at the frequency ν. If the absorption coefficient of the crystal is $\alpha(\nu)$, then the amount of energy absorbed by the crystal per unit volume is[2]

$$t_{\text{flash}} \int_0^\infty s(\nu)\alpha(\nu)\, d\nu$$

If the absorption quantum efficiency (the probability that the absorption of a pump photon at ν results in transferring one atom into the upper laser level) is $\eta(\nu)$, the number of atoms pumped into level 2 per unit volume is

$$N_2 = t_{\text{flash}} \int_0^\infty \frac{s(\nu)\alpha(\nu)\eta(\nu)}{h\nu}\, d\nu \qquad (7.2\text{-}2)$$

Since the lifetime $t_2 = 3 \times 10^{-3}$ second of atoms in level 2 is considerably longer than the flash duration ($\sim 5 \times 10^{-4}$ second) we may neglect the spontaneous decay out of level 2 during the time of the flash pulse, so N_2 represents the population of level 2 after the flash.

Numerical example—flash pumping of a pulsed ruby laser. ·Consider the case of a ruby laser with the following parameters:

$$N_0 = 2 \times 10^{19} \text{ atoms/cm}^3$$

$$t_2 = t_{\text{spont}} = 3 \times 10^{-3} \text{ second}$$

$$t_{\text{flash}} = 5 \times 10^{-4} \text{ second}$$

If the useful absorption is limited to relatively narrow spectral regions, we may approximate (7.2-1) by

$$N_2 = \frac{t_{\text{flash}}\overline{s(\nu)}\,\overline{\alpha(\nu)}\,\overline{\eta(\nu)}\,\overline{\Delta\nu}}{h\overline{\nu}} \qquad (7.2\text{-}3)$$

where the bars represent average values over the useful absorption region whose width is $\overline{\Delta\nu}$.

From Figure 7-3 we deduce an average absorption coefficient of $\overline{\alpha(\nu)} \simeq 1 \text{ cm}^{-1}$ over the two central peaks. Since ruby is a three-level laser the upper level population is, according to (6.3-2), $N_2 \simeq N_0/2 = 10^{19} \text{ cm}^{-3}$. Using $\overline{\nu} \simeq 5 \times 10^{14}$ Hz, Equation (7.2-3) yields

$$\overline{s}\,\overline{\Delta\nu}\,t_{\text{flash}} \simeq 3 \text{ J/cm}^2$$

for the pump energy in the useful absorption region that must fall on each square centimeter of crystal surface in order to obtain threshold inversion. To calculate the total lamp energy that is incident on the crystal we need

---

[2] We assume that the total absorption in passing the crystal is small, so $s(\nu)$ is taken to be independent of the distance through the crystal.

to know the spectral characteristics of the lamp output. Typical data of this sort are shown in Figure 7-7. The mercury-discharge lamp is seen to contain considerable output in the useful absorption regions (near 4000 Å and 5500 Å) of ruby. If we estimate the useful fraction of the lamp output at 10 percent, the fraction of the lamp light actually incident on the crystal as 20 percent, and the conversion of electrical-to-optical energy as 50 percent, we find the threshold electric energy input to the flashlamp per square centimeter of laser surface is

$$\frac{3}{0.1 \times 0.2 \times 0.5} = 300 \text{ J/cm}^2$$

These are, admittedly, extremely crude calculations. They are included not only to illustrate the order of magnitude numbers involved in laser pumping, but also as an example of the quick and rough estimates needed to discriminate between feasible ideas and "pie in the sky" schemes.

7.3 The Nd³⁺:YAG Laser

One of the most important laser systems is that using trivalent neodymium ions (Nd^{3+}) which are present as impurities in yttrium aluminum garnet (YAG = $Y_3Al_5O_{12}$); see References [6] and [7]. The laser emission occurs at $\lambda_0 = 1.0641 \ \mu m$ at room temperature. The relevant energy levels are

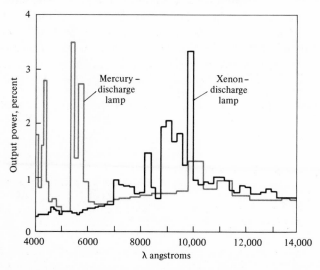

Figure 7-7 Spectral output characteristics of two commercial high-pressure lamps. Output is plotted as a fraction of electrical input to lamp over certain wavelength intervals (mostly 200 Å) between 0.4 and 1.4 μm. (After Reference [5].)

shown in Figure 7-8. The lower laser level is at $E_2 \simeq 2111$ cm^{-1} from the ground state so that at room temperature its population is down by a factor of $\exp(-E_2/kT) \simeq e^{-10}$ from that of the ground state and can be neglected. The Nd^{3+}:YAG thus fits our definition (see Section 6.3) of a four-level laser.

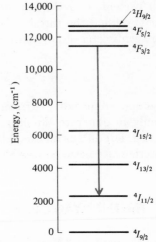

Figure 7-8 Energy-level diagram of Nd^{3+} in YAG. (After Reference [6].)

The spontaneous emission spectrum of the laser transition is shown in Figure 7-9. The width of the gain linewidth at room temperature is $\Delta \nu \simeq 6$ cm^{-1}. The spontaneous lifetime for the laser transition has been measured [7] as $t_{\text{spont}} = 5.5 \times 10^{-4}$ second. The room-temperature cross section at the center of the laser transition is $\sigma = 9 \times 10^{-19}$ cm^2. If we compare this number to $\sigma = 1.22 \times 10^{-20}$ cm^2 in ruby (see Figure 7-4), we expect that at a given inversion the optical gain constant γ in

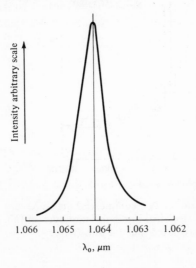

Figure 7-9 Spontaneous-emission spectrum of Nd^{3+} in YAG near the laser transition at $\lambda_0 = 1.064\ \mu$m. (After Reference [7].)

Nd^{3+}:YAG is approximately 75 times that of ruby. This causes the oscillation threshold to be very low and explains the easy continuous (CW) operation of this laser compared to ruby.

The absorption responsible for populating the upper laser level takes place in a number of bands between 13,000 and 25,000 cm^{-1}.

Numerical example—threshold of an Nd^{3+}:YAG laser

(a) *Pulsed threshold*. First we estimate the energy needed to excite a typical Nd^{3+}:YAG laser on a pulse basis so that we can compare it with that of ruby. We use the following data:

$$
\left.\begin{array}{l}
l = 20 \text{ cm (length optical resonator)}\\
L = 4 \text{ percent } (= \text{ loss per pass})\\
n = 1.5
\end{array}\right\} t_c = \frac{l}{Lc} = 1.65 \times 10^{-8} \text{ second}
$$

$\Delta\nu = 6 \text{ cm}^{-1} \ (= 6 \times 3 \times 10^{10} \text{ Hz}) \qquad \lambda\nu = c$

$t_{\text{spont}} = 5.5 \times 10^{-4} \text{ second} \qquad\qquad \nu = \frac{c}{\lambda}$

$\lambda = \lambda_0/n = \dfrac{1.06}{1.5} \times 10^{-4} \text{ cm}$

Using the foregoing data in (6.1-11) gives

$$
N_t = \frac{8\pi t_{\text{spont}}\Delta\nu}{ct_c\lambda^2} \simeq 1.2 \times 10^{15} \text{ cm}^{-3}
$$

Assuming that 5 percent of the exciting light energy falls within the useful absorption bands, that 5 percent of this light is actually absorbed by the crystal, that the average ratio of laser frequency to the pump frequency is 0.5, and that the lamp efficiency (optical output/electrical input) is 0.5, we obtain

$$
\mathcal{E}_{\text{lamp}} = \frac{N_t h\nu_{\text{laser}}}{5 \times 10^{-2} \times 5 \times 10^{-2} \times 0.5 \times 0.5} \simeq 0.4 \text{ J/cm}^3
$$

for the energy input to the lamp at threshold.

It is interesting to compare this last number to the figure of 300 joules per square centimeter of surface area obtained in the ruby example of Section 7.2. For reasonable dimension crystals (say, length = 5 cm, $r = 2$ mm) we obtain $\mathcal{E}_{\text{lamp}} = 0.25$ J. We expect the ruby threshold to exceed that of Nd^{3+}:YAG by three orders of magnitude, which is indeed the case.

(b) *Continuous Operation*. The critical fluorescence power—that is, the actual power given off by spontaneous emission just below threshold

—is given by (6.3-4) as

$$\left(\frac{P_s}{V}\right) = \frac{N_t h\nu}{t_{\text{spont}}} \simeq 0.4 \text{ W/cm}^3$$

Taking the crystal diameter as 0.25 cm and its length as 3 cm and using the same efficiency factors assumed in the first part of this example, we can estimate the power input to the lamp at threshold as

$$P_{(\text{to lamp})} = \frac{0.4 \times (\pi/4) \times (0.25)^2 \times 3}{5 \times 10^{-2} \times 5 \times 10^{-2} \times 0.5 \times 0.5} \simeq 100 \text{ watts}$$

which is in reasonable agreement with experimental values [6].

A typical arrangement used in continuous solid state lasers is shown in Figure 7-10. The highly polished elliptic cylinder is used to concentrate the light from the lamp, which is placed along one focal axis, onto the laser rod, which occupies the other axis. This configuration guarantees that most of the light emitted by the lamp passes through the laser rod. The reflecting mirrors are placed outside the cylinder.

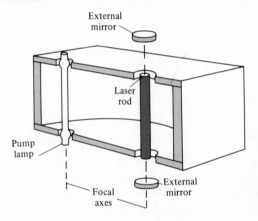

Figure 7-10 Typical continuous solid-state laser arrangement employing an elliptic cylinder housing for concentrating lamp light onto laser.

7.4 The Neodymium-Glass Laser

One of the most useful laser systems is that which results when the Nd^{3+} ion is present as an impurity atom in glass [8].

The energy levels involved in the laser transition in a typical glass are shown in Figure 7-11. The laser emission wavelength is at $\lambda_0 = 1.059 \,\mu m$ and the lower level is approximately 1950 cm^{-1} above the ground state. As in the case of Nd^{3+}:YAG described in Section 7.3, we have here a four-level laser, since the thermal population of the lower laser level is

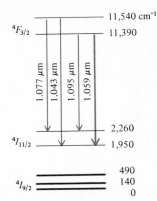

11,540 cm⁻¹

$^4F_{3/2}$ ——————— 11,390

1.077 μm 1.043 μm 1.095 μm 1.059 μm

2,260

$^4I_{11/2}$ ——————— 1,950

490
140
0

$^4I_{9/2}$

Figure 7-11 Energy-level diagram for the ground state and the states involved in laser emission at 1.059 μm for Nd^{3+} in a rubidium potassium barium silicate glass. (After Reference [8].)

negligible. The fluorescent emission near $\lambda_0 = 1.06$ μm is shown in Figure 7-12. The fluorescent linewidth can be measured off directly and ranges, for the glasses shown, around 300 cm⁻¹. This width is approximately a factor of 50 larger than that of Nd^{3+} in YAG. This is due to the amorphous structure of glass, which causes different Nd^{3+} ions to "see" slightly different surroundings. This causes their energy splittings to vary slightly. Different ions consequently radiate at slightly different frequencies, causing a broadening of the spontaneous emission spectrum. The absorption bands responsible for pumping the laser level are shown in Figure 7-13. The probability that the absorption of a photon in any of these bands will result in pumping an atom to the upper laser level (that is, the absorption quantum efficiency) has been estimated [8] at about 0.4.

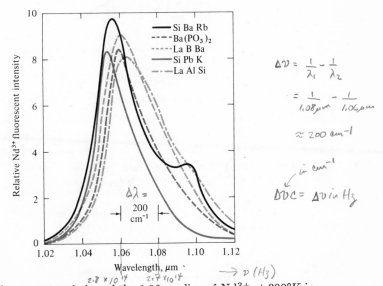

Figure 7-12 Fluorescent emission of the 1.06-μm line of Nd^{3+} at 300°K in various glass bases. (After Reference [8].)

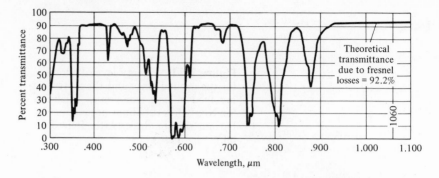

Figure 7-13 Nd^{3+} absorption spectrum for a sample of glass 6.4 mm thick with the composition 66 wt % SiO_2, 5 wt. % Nd_2O_3, 16 wt. % Na_2O, 5 wt. % BaO, 2 wt. % Al_2O_3, and 1 wt. % Sb_2O_3. (After Reference [8].)

The lifetime t_2 of the upper laser level depends on the host glass and on the Nd^{3+} concentration. This variation in two glass series is shown in Figure 7-14.

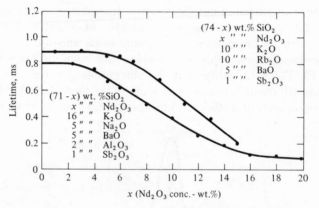

Figure 7-14   Lifetime as function of concentration for two glass series. (After Reference [8].)

Numerical example—thresholds for CW and pulsed operation of Nd^{3+}:glass lasers. Let us estimate first the threshold for continuous (CW) laser action in a Nd^{3+} glass laser using the following data:

$$\Delta\nu = 200 \text{ cm}^{-1} \text{ (see Figure 7-12)}$$

$$n = 1.5$$

$$t_{\text{spont}} \simeq t_2 = 3 \times 10^{-4} \text{ second}$$

$$\left. \begin{aligned} l &= \text{length of resonator} = 20 \text{ cm} \\ L &= \text{loss per pass} = 2 \text{ percent} \end{aligned} \right\} t_c \simeq \frac{l}{Lc} = 3.3 \times 10^{-8} \text{ second}$$

Using (6.1-11) we obtain

$$N_t = \frac{8\pi t_{\text{spont}}\Delta\nu}{ct_c\lambda^2} = 6 \times 10^{15} \text{ atoms/cm}^3$$

for the critical inversion. The fluorescence power at threshold P_s is thus [see Equation (6.3-5)]

$$P_s = \frac{N_t h\nu V}{t_{\text{spont}}} = 4.8 \text{ watts}$$

in a crystal volume $V = 1 \text{ cm}^3$.

We assume (a) that only 10 percent of the pump light lies within the useful absorption bands; (b) that because of the optical coupling inefficiency and the relative transparency of the crystal only 10 percent of the energy leaving the lamp within the absorption bands is actually absorbed; (c) that the absorption quantum efficiency is 40 percent; and (d) that the average pumping frequency is twice that of the emitted radiation. The lamp output at threshold is thus

$$\frac{2 \times 4.8}{0.1 \times 0.1 \times 0.4} = 2400 \text{ watts}$$

If the efficiency of the lamp in converting electrical to optical energy is about 50 percent, we find that continuous operation of the laser requires about 5 kW of power. This number is to be contrasted with a threshold of approximately 100 watts for the Nd:YAG laser, which helps explain why Nd:glass lasers are not operated continuously.

If we consider the pulsed operation of a Nd:glass laser by flash excitation we have to estimate the minimum energy needed to pump the laser at threshold. Let us assume here that the losses (attributable mostly to the output mirror transmittance) are $L = 20$ percent.[3] A recalculation of N_t gives

$$N_t = 6 \times 10^{16} \text{ atoms/cm}^3$$

The minimum energy needed to pump N_t atoms into level 2 is then

$$\frac{\mathcal{E}_{\min}}{V} = N_t(h\nu) = 2 \times 10^{-2} \text{ J/cm}^3$$

Assuming a crystal volume $V = 10 \text{ cm}^3$ and the same efficiency factors used in the CW example above, we find that the input energy to the flash-lamp at threshold $\simeq 2 \times 2 \times 10^{-2} \times 10/0.1 \times 0.1 \times 0.4 = 100$ J. Typical Nd^{3+}:glass lasers with characteristics similar to those used in this example are found to require an input of about 150–300 joules at threshold.

---

[3] Because of the higher pumping rate available with flash pumping, optimum coupling (see Section 6.5) calls for larger mirror transmittances compared to the CW case.

7.5   The He-Ne Laser

The first CW laser, as well as the first gas laser, was one in which a transition between the $2S$ and the $2p$ levels in atomic Ne resulted in the emission of 1.15 μm radiation [9]. Since then transitions in Ne were used to obtain laser oscillation at $\lambda_0 = 0.6328$ μm [10] and at $\lambda_0 = 3.39$ μm. The operation of this laser can be explained with the aid of Figure 7-15. A dc (or rf) discharge is established in the gas mixture containing typically, 1.0 mm Hg of He and 0.1 mm of Ne. The energetic electrons in the discharge excite helium atoms into a variety of excited states. In the normal cascade of these excited atoms down to the ground state, many collect in the long-lived metastable states 2^3S and 2^1S whose lifetimes are 10^{-4} second and 5×10^{-6} second, respectively. Since these long-lived (metastable) levels nearly coincide in energy with the $2S$ and $3S$ levels of Ne they can excite Ne atoms into these two excited states. This excitation takes place when an excited He atom collides with a Ne atom in the ground state and ex-

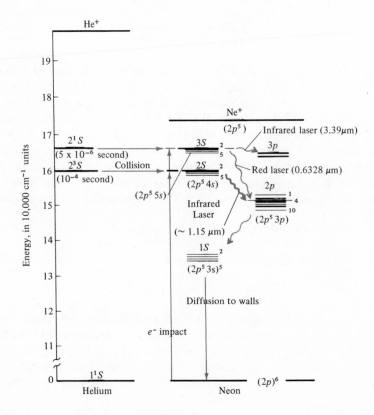

Figure 7-15   He-Ne energy levels. The dominant excitation paths for the red and infrared laser–maser transitions are shown. (After Reference [11].)

changes energy with it. The small difference in energy ($\sim$400 cm^{-1} in the case of the $2S$ level) is taken up by the kinetic energy of the atoms after the collision. This is the main pumping mechanism in the He–Ne system.

1. *The 0.6328 μm oscillation.* The upper level is one of the Ne $3S$ levels, whereas the terminal level belongs to the $2p$ group. The terminal ($2p$) level decays radiatively with a time constant of about 10^{-8} second into the long-lived $1S$ state. This time is much shorter than the 10^{-7} second lifetime of the upper laser level $3S$. The condition $t_1 < t_2$ for population inversion in the $3S$–$2p$ transition (see Section 6.4) is thus fulfilled.

Another important point involves the level $1S$. Because of its long life it tends to collect atoms reaching it by radiative decay from the lower laser level $2p$. Atoms in $1S$ collide with discharge electrons and are excited back into the lower laser level $2p$. This reduces the inversion. Atoms in the $1S$ states relax back to the ground state mostly in collisions with the wall of the discharge tube. For this reason the gain in the 0.6328 μm transition is found to increase with decreasing tube diameter.

2. *The 1.15 μm oscillation.* The upper laser level $2S$ is pumped by resonant (that is, energy-conserving) collisions with the metastable 2^3S He level. It uses the same lower level as the 0.6328 μm transition and, consequently, also depends on wall collisions to depopulate the $1S$ Ne level.

3. *The 3.39 μm oscillation.* This involves a $3S$–$3p$ transition and thus uses the same upper level as the 0.6328 μm oscillation. It is remarkable for the fact that it provides a small-signal[4] optical gain of about 50 dB/m. This large gain reflects partly the inverse dependence of γ on ν^2 [see Equation (5.3-3)] as well as the short lifetime of the $3p$ level, which allows the buildup of a large inversion.

Because of the high gain in this transition, oscillation would normally occur at 3.39 μm rather than at 0.6328 μm. The reason is that the threshold condition will be reached first at 3.39 μm and, once that happens, the gain "clamping" will prevent any further buildup of the population of $3S$. The 0.6328 μm lasers overcome this problem by introducing into the optical path elements, such as glass or quartz Brewster windows, which absorb strongly at 3.39 μm but not at 0.6328 μm. This raises the threshold pumping level for the 3.39 μm oscillation above that of the 0.6328 μm oscillation.

---

[4] This is not the actual gain that exists inside the laser resonator, but the one-pass gain exercised by a very small input wave propagating through the discharge. In the laser the gain per pass is reduced by saturation until it equals the loss per pass.

A typical gas laser setup is illustrated by Figure 7-16. The gas envelope windows are tilted at Brewster's angle θ_B, so radiation with the electric field vector in the plane of the paper suffers no reflection losses at the windows. This causes the output radiation to be polarized in the sense shown, since the orthogonal polarization (the E vector out of the plane of the paper) undergoes reflection losses at the windows and, consequently, has a higher threshold.

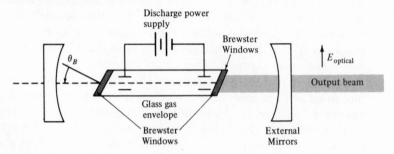

Figure 7-16   Typical gas laser.

7.6   The Carbon Dioxide Laser

The lasers described so far in this chapter depend on electronic transitions between states in which the electronic orbitals (that is, charge distributions around the atomic nucleus) are different. As an example, consider the red (0.6328 μm) transition in Ne shown in Figure 7-15. It involves levels $2p^55s$ and $2p^53p$ so that in making a transition from the upper to the lower laser level one of the six outer electrons changes from a hydrogen-like state $5s$ (that is, $n = 5$, $l = 0$) to one in which $n = 3$ and $l = 1$.

The CO_2 laser [12] is representative of the so-called molecular lasers in which the energy levels of concern involve the internal vibration of the molecules—that is, the relative motion of the constituent atoms. The atomic electrons remain in their lowest energetic states and their degree of excitation is not affected.

As an illustration, consider the simple case of the nitrogen molecule. The molecular vibration involves the relative motion of the two atoms with respect to each other. This vibration takes place at a characteristic frequency of $\nu_0 = 2326$ cm^{-1} which depends on the molecular mass as well as the elastic restoring force between the atoms [13]. According to basic quantum mechanics the degrees of vibrational excitation are discrete (that is, quantized) and the energy of the molecule can take on the values $h\nu_0 (v + \frac{1}{2})$, where $v = 0, 1, 2, 3, \cdots$. The energy-level diagram of N_2 (in its lowest electronic state) would then ideally consist of an equally spaced set of levels with a spacing of $h\nu_0$. The ground state ($v = 0$) and the first excited state ($v = 1$) are shown on the right side of Figure 7-17.

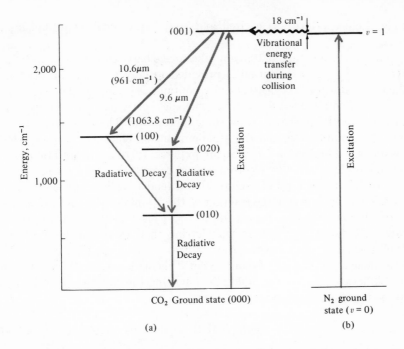

Figure 7-17 (a) Some of the low-lying vibrational levels of the carbon dioxide (CO_2) molecule, including the upper and lower levels for the 10.6-μm and 9.6-μm laser transitions. (b) Ground state ($v = 0$) and first excited state ($v = 1$) of the nitrogen molecule, which plays an important role in the selective excitation of the (001) CO_2 level.

The CO_2 molecule presents a more complicated case. Since it consists of three atoms, it can execute three basic internal vibrations, the so-called normal modes of vibration. These are shown in Figure 7-18. In (a) the molecule is at rest. In (b) the atoms vibrate along the internuclear axis in a symmetric manner. In (c) the molecules vibrate symmetrically along an axis perpendicular to the internuclear axis—the bending mode. In (d) the atoms vibrate asymmetrically along the internuclear axis. This mode is referred to as the asymmetric stretching mode. In the first approximation one can assume that the three normal modes are independent of each other, so the state of the CO_2 molecule can be described by a set of three integers (v_1, v_2, v_3), which correspond respectively to the degree of excitation of the three modes described. The total energy of the molecule is thus

$$E(v_1, v_2, v_3) = h\nu_1(v_1 + \tfrac{1}{2}) + h\nu_2(v_2 + \tfrac{1}{2}) + h\nu_3(v_3 + \tfrac{1}{2}) \qquad \textbf{(7.6-1)}$$

where ν_1, ν_2, and ν_3 are the frequencies of the symmetric stretch, bending, and asymmetric stretch modes, respectively.

Some of the low vibrational levels of CO_2 are shown in Figure 7-17. The upper laser level (001) is thus one in which only the asymmetric stretch mode, Figure 7-18(d), is excited and contains a single quantum $h\nu_3$ of energy.

The laser transition at 10.6 μm takes place between the (001) and (100) levels of CO_2. The excitation is provided usually in a plasma discharge which, in addition to CO_2, typically contains N_2 and He. The CO_2 laser possesses a high overall working efficiency of about 30 percent. This efficiency results primarily from three factors: (a) The laser levels are all near the ground state, and the atomic quantum efficiency ν_{21}/ν_{30}, which was discussed in Section 7.1, is about 45 percent; (b) a large fraction of the CO_2 molecules excited by electron impact cascade down the energy ladder from their original level of excitation and tend to collect in the long-lived (001) level; (c) a very large fraction of the N_2 molecules that are excited by the discharge tend to collect in the $v = 1$ level. Collisions with ground-state CO_2 molecules result in transferring their excitation to the latter, thereby exciting them to the (001) state as shown in Figure 7-17. The slight deficiency in energy (about 18 cm^{-1}) is made up by a decrease of the total kinetic energy of the molecules following the collision. This collision can be represented by

$$(v = 1) + (000) + \text{K.E.} = (v = 0) + (001) \qquad \textbf{(7.6-2)}$$

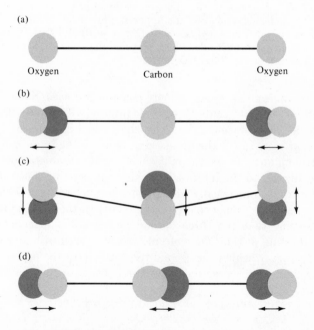

Figure 7-18 (a) Unexcited CO_2 molecule. (b), (c), and (d) The three normal modes of vibration of the CO_2 molecule. (After Reference [14].)

and has a sufficiently high cross section[5] that at the pressures and temperatures involved in the operation of a CO_2 laser most of the N_2 molecules in the $v = 1$ lose their excitation energy by this process.

Carbon dioxide lasers are not only efficient but can emit large amounts of power. Laboratory size lasers with discharge envelopes of a few feet in length can yield an output of a few kilowatts. This is due not only to the very *selective* excitation of the low-lying upper laser level, but also to the fact that once a molecule is stimulated to emit a photon it returns quickly to the ground state, where it can be used again. This is accomplished mostly through collisions with other molecules—such as that of He, which is added to the gas mixture.

7.7 The Ar⁺ Laser

Transitions between highly excited states of the singly ionized argon atom can be used to obtain oscillation at a number of visible (or near visible) wavelengths between $0.35\,\mu m$ and $0.52\,\mu m$; see References [15] and [16]. The Ar⁺ laser is consequently one of the most important lasers in use today. The pertinent energy level scheme is shown in Figure 7-19. The most prominent transition is the one at 4880 Å.

The Ar⁺ laser can be operated in a pure Ar discharge that contains no other gases. The excitation mechanism involves collisions with energetic

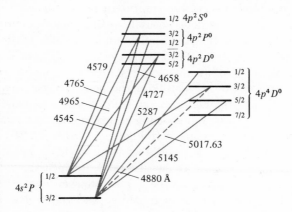

Figure 7-19 Energy level of Ar⁺ and nine laser transitions. (After Reference [15].)

---

[5] The cross section σ was defined in Section 7.2. In the present context it follows directly from that definition that the number of collisions of the type described by (7.6-2) per unit volume per unit time is equal to $N(v = 1)N(000)\sigma\bar{v}$ where $N(v = 1)$ and $N(000)$ are the densities of molecules in the states $v = 1$ of N_2 and (000) of CO_2, respectively. $\bar{v}$ is the (mean) relative velocity of the colliding molecules.

($\sim$4–5 eV) electrons. Since the mean electron energy is small compared to the energy of the upper laser level ($\sim$20 eV above the ground state of the ion), it is clear that pumping is achieved by multiple collisions of Ar^+ ground-state ions with electrons followed by a number of cascading paths. The details of the collision and cascading processes are not clearly understood.

7.8 Semiconductor Junction Lasers[6]

In a semiconductor laser (see References [17]–[19]) the induced transitions take place in a p-n junction between occupied electron states in the conduction band and empty states in the valence band. One main difference between the semiconductor laser and the other lasers (atomic, molecular) considered in this chapter is that the transition takes place between states that are distributed in energy rather than between two well-defined energy levels.

The distribution of the electron states in a semiconductor is shown in Figure 7-20. The small dots in (a) indicate the position in energy of allowed electron states as a function of the propagation constant k of the electron for both the conduction and valence bands. In Figure 7-20(b) is shown an intrinsic (undoped) semiconductor at a very low temperature. All the states in the valence band are filled with electrons (heavy black dots), whereas those in the conduction band are empty. In (c) we show what happens when the semiconductor is doped heavily with a donor impurity. All the valence band states as well as the conduction band states up to some level E_F, the Fermi energy,[7] are filled with electrons. This is the so-called degenerate n-type semiconductor. A heavy p-type doping density with an acceptor impurity causes a lowering of the boundary between filled and empty states—that is, the Fermi energy—into the valence band, so all the conduction band states as well as states near the top of the valence band are now empty. A feature common to Figures 7-20(b), (c), and (d) is that all the electron states up to the Fermi level E_F are filled, but those above it are empty. In (e) we show a new situation, in which the valence-band occupation is like that of the p-type degenerate semiconductor shown in (d), whereas the conduction band resembles the n-type degenerate case shown in (c). We have here a *doubly degenerate* semiconductor, which must be characterized with two Fermi energies E_{Fv} and E_{Fc} as shown. This situation can exist only under nonthermal equilibrium conditions. One

---

[6] A familiarity with the basic concepts of semiconductor energy bands and p-n junction theory is assumed. A good treatment can be found in Reference [20].

[7] At zero temperature the Fermi energy separates the occupied electron states that lie below it from the empty states above it.

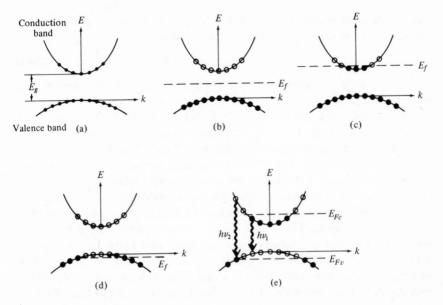

Figure 7-20   (a) Position of energy levels (small dots) of electrons in a direct semiconductor (such as GaAs) as a function of the electron propagation constant k. (b) An intrinsic semiconductor at 0°K. (c) An n-type degenerate semiconductor. (d) A p-type degenerate semiconductor. (e) A doubly degenerate semiconductor.

example of double degeneracy is the case of an intrinsic semiconductor that is illuminated with light of frequency $\nu > E_g/h$. Absorption of this light proceeds by lifting electrons from the valence to the conduction band, leaving unoccupied states behind them. Since relaxation processes within each band are very fast compared with those between bands, the electrons within each band proceed to seek the lowest possible energies, which results in a distribution such as shown in Figure 7-20(e). Of course, if the light is turned off, all the electrons will relax back to the valence band and the electron distribution will return to that depicted by (b). Another example of a doubly degenerate distribution will be described below in connection with the p-n junction laser.

Now consider what happens to a wave propagating through a semiconductor at some frequency ν. The electrons can be induced by the radiation field to make transitions into *empty* states only. In Figure 7-20(b), (c), and (d), the empty states are always above the filled ones, so energy can only be absorbed from the wave. This no longer applies in the case of the doubly degenerate semiconductor (e). Frequencies ν such that $E_g < h\nu < E_{Fc} - E_{Fv}$ can induce only *downward* transitions from occupied conduction-band states to empty valence-band states. One such frequency ν_1 is shown in the figure. These frequencies cause the electrons to give up their energy and are thus amplified. Frequencies $\nu > (E_{Fc} - E_{Fv})/h$, such as ν_2, are absorbed. The condition for amplification is thus

$$E_{Fc} - E_{Fv} > h\nu > Eg \qquad (7.8\text{-}1)$$

A more formal derivation shows condition (7.8-1) to be valid at any temperature [21].

The p and n regions in a p-n junction laser are both degenerate. The position of the energy bands and electron occupation across the junction with no applied bias are shown in Figure 7-21(a). The Fermi energy has the same value all the way across the sample as appropriate to thermal equilibrium. Figure 7-21(b) shows what happens when a forward bias voltage V_{appl} that is nearly equal to the energy-gap voltage (E_g/e) is applied. The Fermi level in the n region is raised by eV_{appl} with respect to that in the p region. There now exists a narrow zone, called the active region, that contains both electrons and holes and is doubly degenerate. Electromagnetic radiation of frequency $E_g/h < \nu < (E_{Fc} - E_{Fv})/h$ propagating through this region is amplified. The thickness t of the active region can be approximated by the diffusion distance of electrons that are

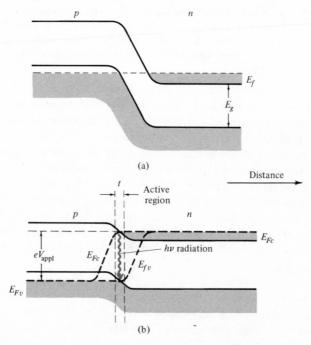

Figure 7-21   Degenerate p-n junction at (**a**) zero applied bias and (**b**) at a forward bias voltage $V_{\text{appl}} \simeq E_g/e$. The region containing both electrons and holes is called the active region. The oscillatory arrow indicates a recombination of an electron with a hole in the active region, leading to an emission of a photon with energy $h\nu$.

injected into a degenerate p region (that is, the mean distance traversed by the electrons before making a transition to an empty state in the valence band—the last event being referred to as an electron–hole recombination). This distance is given by $\sqrt{D\tau}$, where D is the diffusion coefficient and τ is the recombination time [20]. In GaAs, $D = 10 \text{ cm}^2/\text{s}$ and $\tau \simeq 10^{-9}$ second, so $t \sim 10^{-4}$ cm.

A typical GaAs laser whose emission is near $0.84\,\mu\text{m}$ is shown in Figure 7-22. It is fabricated starting with a degenerate n-type semiconductor containing about 10^{18} tellurium (donor) atoms per cubic centimeter. The p region of the junction is obtained by diffusing an acceptor impurity such as Zn starting with a surface concentration of $\sim 10^{20}\text{ cm}^{-3}$. Two end surfaces, normal to the junction plane, are polished (or cleaved) and serve as the laser reflectors.

Spontaneous recombination. The effect of applying a large $(\sim E_g/e)$ forward bias voltage has been shown in Figure 7-21 to create a situation in which a large density of conduction-band electrons are present in a region—the socalled "active region"—that also contains a large number of unfilled valence-band states (holes). As in the case of the excited atoms discussed in Section 5.1, there is a finite probability per unit time that an electron in the conduction band in the active region will undergo a spontaneous transition to the valence band, giving off one photon in the process. This process results in the simultaneous annihilation of a conduction-band electron and an unfilled state (hole) in the valence band. It is referred to, consequently, as electron–hole recombination. The mean lifetime of an electron in the active region is the inverse of the spontaneous transition probability per unit time and is called the recombination lifetime.

The recombination radiation spectrum of an InSb junction is shown in Figure 7-23.

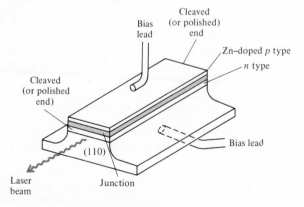

Figure 7-22 Typical p-n junction laser made of GaAs. Two parallel (110) faces are cleaved and serve as reflectors.

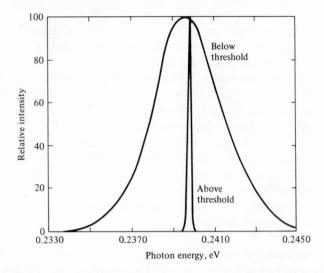

Figure 7-23   Infrared-emission spectra of a forward-biased InSb diode at 1.7°K below and above threshold. The broad spectrum corresponds to 300 mA and the narrow line to 400 mA. Width of line above threshold is limited by resolution of spectrometer. (After Reference [26].)

Amplification and oscillation in *p-n* junctions.   In considering the problem of the amplification of electromagnetic radiation in *p-n* junctions we encounter a new situation. The inverted population of electrons is localized to within a distance $t \sim 1$ μm of the junction center (the active region). The electromagnetic mode, on the other hand, is confined to a larger distance d.[8] The situation is depicted in Figure 7-24. Experiments reveal that, in GaAs, $d \simeq 2$–5 μm and is thus larger than the active region thickness t.

Consider a crystal such as that shown in Figure 7-24, of a length l and a width in the y direction of w. Let us assume, for a moment, that $d = t$, and thus the inverted population is distributed more or less uniformly over the mode volume $V = dlw$.

This situation is identical to those considered in Section 5.3, so we can take the expression for the exponential gain constant, following (5.3-3), as

$$\gamma(\nu) = \frac{c^2 (n_2 - n_1)/dlw}{8\pi\nu^2 t_{\text{recombination}}} g(\nu) \qquad \textbf{(7.8-2)}$$

where n_2 and n_1 are, respectively, the *total* number of inverted electrons, $g(\nu)$ is the natural lineshape function of the spontaneous emission of the

---

[8] The transverse confinement of the mode is due to the fact that near the junction mid-plane the index of refraction decreases as a function of the distance from the center. This type of index variation is known to give rise to the so-called dielectric waveguide modes, which can be confined to small distances; see References [22]–[24].

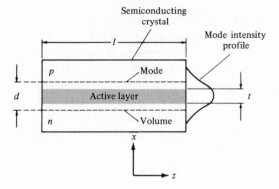

Figure 7-24 Schematic diagram showing active layer and transverse (x) distribution of the laser mode.

junction, and $t_{\text{recombination}}$ is the lifetime of a conduction electron in the p region before making a spontaneous transition to an empty state in the valence band.

Next consider what happens to $\gamma(\nu)$ if the mode height d is made larger than t, as is the case in junction lasers. If the total mode power (watts) is kept a constant, the radiation intensity I (watts per square meter) as seen by the inverted electrons in the active region decreases. This causes, according to (5.2-15), a decrease in the induced transition rate W_i per electron, so the total power $W_i(n_2 - n_1)h\nu$ emitted by the electrons decreases. It follows, then, that when $d > t$ the gain constant $\gamma(\nu)$ is inversely proportional to d and is given by (7.8-2). Similar reasoning shows that if $d < t$ we need to replace d in (7.8-2) by t. This is the case in most other types of lasers in which the active region—that is, the region containing the inverted atomic population—is larger than that occupied by the electromagnetic mode.

The magnitude of the inversion $(n_2 - n_1)$ is not easily determined in an injection laser. It is possible, however, to relate it to the current through the diode. Assuming a low enough temperature that $n_1 = 0$, the total number of electrons injected into the diode in a given time interval must be equal in equilibrium to the number of spontaneous recombinations occurring during the same time

$$\frac{n_2}{t_{\text{recombination}}} = \frac{I\eta_i}{e} \qquad \textbf{(7.8-3)}$$

where η_i, the internal quantum efficiency, is the fraction of the injected carriers (electrons or holes) that recombine radiatively and e is the electron charge. Using (7.8-3) in (7.8-2), putting $n_1 = 0$, and recalling that $lw = A$ is the junction area, we get

$$\gamma(\nu) = \frac{c^2 g(\nu)\eta_i}{8\pi\nu^2 ed}\left(\frac{I}{A}\right) \qquad \textbf{(7.8-4)}$$

so that I/A (amperes per square meter) is the current density.

The threshold condition.   Before deriving the start-oscillation condition of the injection laser we need to understand the origin of the optical losses. According to Figure 7-24, only a portion of the mode energy travels within the active region where it is amplified. Most of the energy propagates through the p and n regions and undergoes attenuation, which is characteristic of these regions.[9] We denote the distributed loss constant of the laser mode as α.[10] The other source of mode loss is the transmission through the end reflectors. Taking the reflectivity of the mirrors as R, the threshold condition (6.1-6) becomes

$$e^{(\gamma_t - \alpha)l} R = 1 \qquad (7.8\text{-}5)$$

where the subscript t denotes threshold. Taking the logarithm of the last equation and using (7.8-4) we obtain

$$\frac{I_t}{A} = \frac{8\pi\nu^2 ed\Delta\nu}{c^2\eta_i}\left(\alpha - \frac{1}{l}\ln R\right) \qquad (7.8\text{-}6)$$

for the current density at threshold, where $\Delta\nu$, the transition linewidth, is defined by $\Delta\nu = g(\nu_0)^{-1}$. We note that the threshold current is proportional to the mode confinement distance d.

Numerical example—threshold current of a GaAs junction laser.   Let us estimate the threshold injection current of a GaAs junction laser with the following characteristics:

$$\Delta\nu = 200\ \text{cm}^{-1}$$

$$\eta_i \simeq 1$$

$$\left(\alpha - \frac{1}{l}\ln R\right) = 20\ \text{cm}^{-1}$$

$$\lambda_0 = 0.84\ \mu\text{m}$$

$$n = 3.35$$

$$d = 2\ \mu\text{m}$$

Using these data in (7.8-6) gives

$$\frac{I_t}{A} \simeq 150\ \text{A/cm}^2$$

a value quite near that measured at low temperatures in GaAs injection lasers.

---

[9] This attenuation is due mostly to the presence of free carriers (electrons in the n, and holes in the p regions), which are accelerated by the optical field and dissipate energy through collisions [25].

[10] See Problem 7.1.

Table 7-1 contains a list of semiconductor junction lasers and their operating wavelengths.

Table 7-1 OSCILLATION WAVELENGTH AND OPERATING TEM-
PERATURE OF A NUMBER OF SEMICONDUCTOR p-n
JUNCTION LASERS

MATERIAL	OSCILLATION WAVELENGTH, MICROMETERS		REFERENCES
GaAs	0.837 (4.2°K)	0.843 (77°K)	[17]–[19]
InP		0.907 (77°K)	[27]
InAs		3.1 (77°K)	[28], [29]
InSb	5.26 (10°K)		[30]
PbSe	8.5 (4.2°K)		[31]
PbTe	6.5 (12°K)		[32]
Ga(As$_x$P$_{1-x}$)	0.65–0.84		[33]
(Ga$_x$In$_{1-x}$)As	0.84–3.5		[34]
In(As$_x$P$_{1-x}$)	0.91–3.5		[35]
GaSb		1.6 (77°K)	[36]
Pb$_{1-x}$Sn$_x$Te	9.5–28 (~12°K)		[37]

$$x = 0.15 \quad x = 0.27$$

Power output of injection lasers. The considerations of saturation and power output in an injection laser are basically the same as that of conventional lasers, which were described in Section 6.4. As the injection current is increased above the threshold value (7.8-6), the laser oscillation intensity builds up. The resulting stimulated emission shortens the lifetime of the inverted carriers to the point where the magnitude of the inversion is clamped at its threshold value. Taking the probability that an injected carrier recombines radiatively within the active region as η_i (this is the internal quantum efficiency defined in Section 7.8), we can write the following expression for the power emitted by stimulated emission:

$$P_e = \frac{(I - I_t)\eta_i}{e} h\nu \qquad \textbf{(7.8-7)}$$

Part of this power is dissipated inside the laser resonator, and the rest is coupled out through the end reflectors. These two powers are, according to (7.8-6), proportional to α and to $-l^{-1} \ln R$, respectively. We can thus write the output power as

$$P_o = \frac{(I - I_t)\eta_i h\nu}{e} \left(\frac{(1/l) \ln (1/R)}{\alpha + (1/l) \ln (1/R)} \right) \qquad \textbf{(7.8-8)}$$

The external differential quantum efficiency η_{ex} is defined as the ratio of the photon output rate that results from an increase in the injection rate (carriers per second) to the increase in the injection rate:

$$\eta_{\text{ex}} = \frac{d(P_o/h\nu)}{d[(I - I_t)/e]} \tag{7.8-9}$$

Using (7.8-8) we obtain

$$\eta_{\text{ex}}^{-1} = \eta_i^{-1} \frac{\alpha l + \ln(1/R)}{\ln(1/R)}$$

$$= \eta_i^{-1} \left[\frac{\alpha l}{\ln(1/R)} + 1 \right] \tag{7.8-10}$$

This relation is used to determine η_i from the experimentally measured dependence of η_{ex} on l. At 77°K, η_i in GaAs $\simeq 0.7$–1.

Power efficiency of injection lasers.   If the voltage applied to a diode is V_{appl}, the electric power input is $V_{\text{appl}}I$. The efficiency of the laser in converting electrical input to laser output is thus

$$\eta = \frac{P_o}{VI} = \eta_i \frac{(I - I_t)}{I} \left(\frac{h\nu}{eV_{\text{appl}}} \right) \frac{\ln(1/R)}{\alpha l + \ln(1/R)} \tag{7.8-11}$$

From Figure 7-21, $eV_{\text{appl}} \simeq h\nu$ (in practice the small voltage drop in the diode bulk resistance makes eV_{appl} slightly larger than $h\nu$); therefore, well above threshold ($I \gg I_t$), where optimum coupling (see Section 6.5) dictates that $(1/l) \ln(1/R) \gg \alpha$, η approaches η_i. Since η_i in most lasers is high (0.7–1 in GaAs), the injection laser possesses the highest power efficiency of all the laser types.

7.9 Organic-Dye Lasers

Many organic dyes (that is, organic compounds that absorb strongly in certain visible-wavelength regions) also exhibit efficient luminescence, which often spans a large wavelength region in the visible portion of the spectrum. This last property makes it possible to obtain an appreciable tuning range from dye lasers; see References [38]–[40].

A schematic representation of an organic dye molecule (such as rhodamine 6G, for example) is shown in Figure 7-25.

State S_0 is the ground state. S_1, S_2, T_1, and T_2 are excited electronic states—that is, states in which one ground-state electron is elevated to an excited orbit. Typical energy separation, such as S_0–S_1 is about 20,000 cm^{-1}. In a singlet (S) state, the magnetic spin of the excited electron is antiparallel to the spin of the remaining molecule. In a triplet (T) state, the spins are parallel. Singlet → triplet, or triplet → singlet transitions thus involve a spin flip and are far less likely than transitions between two singlet or between two triplet states.

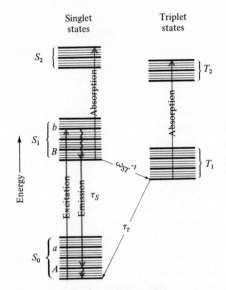

Figure 7-25 Schematic representation of the energy levels of an organic dye molecule. The heavy horizontal lines represent vibrational states and the lighter lines represent the rotational fine structure. Excitation and laser emission are represented by the transitions $A \rightarrow b$ and $B \rightarrow a$, respectively.

Transitions between two singlet states or between two triplet states, which are spin-allowed (that is, they do not involve a spin flip), give rise to intense absorption and fluorescence. The characteristic color of organic dyes is due to the $S_0 \rightarrow S_1$ absorption.

The singlet and triplet states, in turn, are split further into vibrational levels shown as heavy horizontal lines in Figure 7-25. These correspond to the quantized vibrational states of the organic molecule, as discussed in detail in Section 7.6. Typical energy separation between two adjacent vibrational levels within a given singlet or triplet state is about 1500 cm^{-1}. The fine splitting shown corresponds to rotational levels[11] whose spacing is about 15 cm^{-1}.

In the process of pumping the laser, the molecule is first excited, by absorbing a pump photon, into a rotational–vibrational state b within S_1. This is followed by a very fast decay to the bottom of the S_1 state, with the excess energy taken up by the vibrational and rotational energy of the molecules. Most of the excited molecules will then decay spontaneously to state a, emitting a photon of energy $\nu = (E_B - E_a)/h$. The lifetime for this process is τ_S.

There is, however, a small probability, approximately $\omega_{ST}\tau_S$, that an excited molecule will decay instead to the triplet state T_1, where ω_{ST} is the rate per molecule for undergoing an $S_1 \rightarrow T_1$ transition. Since this is a spin-forbidden transition, its rate is usually much smaller than the spontaneous decay rate τ_S^{-1}, so that $\omega_{ST}\tau_S \ll 1$. The lifetime τ_T for decay of T_1 to the ground state is relatively long (since this too is a spin-forbidden

---

[11] A transition between two adjacent rotational levels involves a change in the total angular momentum of the molecule about some axis.

transition) and may vary from 10^{-7} to 10^{-3} second, depending on the experimental conditions [41]. Owing to its relatively long lifetime, the triplet state T_1 acts as a trap for excited molecules. The absorption of molecules due to a $T_1 \rightarrow T_2$ transition is spin-allowed and is therefore very strong. If the wavelength region of this absorption coincides with that of the laser emission [at $\nu \simeq (E_B - E_a)/h$], an accumulation of molecules in T_1 increases the laser losses and at some critical value quenches the laser ocillation. For this reason, many organic-dye lasers operate only on a pulsed basis. In these cases fast-rise-time pump pulses—often derived from another laser [39]—cause a buildup of the S_1 population with oscillation taking place until an appreciable buildup of the T_1 population occurs.

Another basic property of molecules is that the peak of the absorption spectrum usually occurs at shorter wavelengths than the peak of the corresponding emission spectrum. This is illustrated in Figure 7-25—and also in Figure 7-26, which shows the absorption and emission spectra of rhodamine 6G which when dissolved in H_2O is used as a CW laser medium [43]. Laser oscillation occurring near the peak of the emission curve is thus absorbed weakly. But for this fortunate circumstance, laser action involving electronic transitions in molecules would not be possible.

Typical excitation and oscillation waveforms of a dye laser are shown in Figure 7-27. The possibility quenching of the laser action by triplet state absorption is evident.

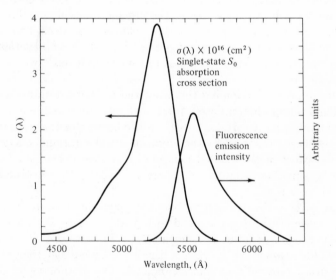

Figure 7-26 Singlet-state absorption and fluorescence spectra of rhodamine 6G obtained from measurements with a 10^{-4} molar ethanol solution of the dye. (After Reference [41].)

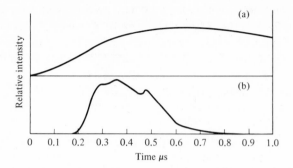

Figure 7-27 (**a**) Flashlamp pulse produced by a linear xenon flashlamp in a low-inductance circuit. (**b**) Laser pulse from a 10^{-3} molar solution of rhodamine 6G in methanol (After Reference [40].)

A list of some common laser dyes is given in Table 7-2.

The broad fluorescence spectrum of the organic dyes suggests a broad tunability range for lasers using them as the active material. The spectrum in Figure 7-26, as an example, corresponds to a width of $\Delta\nu \simeq 1000$ cm^{-1}. One elegant solution for realizing this tuning range consists of replacing one of the laser mirrors with a diffraction grating, as shown in Figure 7-28. A diffraction grating has the property that (for a given order) an incident beam will be reflected back *exactly* along the direction of incidence, provided

$$2d \cos \theta = m\lambda \qquad m = 1, 2, \cdots \tag{7.9-1}$$

where d is the ruling distance, θ is the angle between the propagation direction and its projection on the grating surface, λ is the optical wavelength and m is the order of diffraction. This type of operation of a grating is usually referred to as the Littrow arrangement. When a grating is used as one of the laser mirrors, it is clear that the oscillation wavelength will be that which satisfies Equation (7.9-1), since other wavelengths are not reflected along the axis of the optical resonator and will consequently "see"

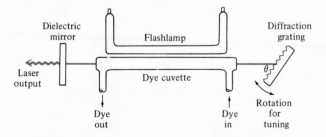

Figure 7-28 A typical dye laser experimental setup employing a linear flashlamp and a wavelength-selecting diffraction-grating reflector.

Table 7-2 MOLECULAR STRUCTURE, LASER WAVELENGTH, AND SOLVENTS FOR SOME LASER DYES (AFTER REFERENCE [41])

Dye	Structure	Solvent	Wavelength
Acridine red	$(H_3C)NH$ ... $\{NH(CH_3)\}\,Cl^-$	EtOH	Red 600–630 nm
Puronin B	$(C_2H_5)_2N$ ... $\{NH(C_2H_5)_2\}\,Cl^-$	MeOH H_2O	Yellow
Rhodamine 6G	C_2H_5HN ... $\{NHC_2H_5\}\,Cl^-$, H_3C, CH_3, $COOC_2H_3$	EtOH MeOH H_2O DMSO Polymethyl-methacrylate	Yellow 570–610 nm
Rhodamine B	$(C_2H_5)_2N$ ... $\{N(C_2H_5)_2\}\,Cl^-$, $COOH$	EtOH MeOH Polymethyl-methacrylate	Red 605–635 nm
Na-fluorescein	NaO ... O, $COONa$	EtOH H_2O	Green 530–560 nm
2, 7-Dichloro-fluorescein	HO ... O, Cl, Cl, $COOH$	EtOH	Green 530–560nm
7-Hydroxycoumarin	... OH	H_2O (pH ~ 9)	Blue 450–470 nm
4-Methylumbelliferone	... OH, CH_3	H_2O (pH ~ 9)	Blue 450–470 nm
Esculin	... OH, $HC-C-C-C-C-CH_2OH$ $OH\ H\ OH$	H_2O (pH ~ 9)	Blue 450–470 nm
7-Diethylamino-4-Methylcoumarin	... $N\,^{C_2H_5}_{C_2H_5}$, CH_5	EtOH	Blue
Acetamidopyrene-trisulfonate	NaO_3S, SO_3Na, NaO_3S, $N\,^{COCH_3}_{H}$	MeOH H_2O	Green-Yellow
Pyrylium salt	BF_4, H_3CO ... O^+ ... OCH_3	MeOH	Green

a very lossy (low-Q) resonator. The tuning (wavelength selection) is thus achieved by a rotation of the grating. It follows also that any other means of introducing a controlled, wavelength-dependent loss into the optical resonator can be used for tuning the output.

■ PROBLEMS

7-1 Show how the distributed loss constant α of an injection laser can be determined from two measurements of the threshold current taken at two different values of mirror reflectivity R.

7-2 Show that if the mode thickness d of an injection laser is smaller than t, the thickness of the active region, the gain constant is given by (7.8-2) with d replaced by t.

7-3 Derive the expression relating the absorption cross section for a given transition to the spontaneous lifetime.

7-4 Derive condition (7.9-1) for the Littrow arrangement of a diffraction grating for which the reflection is parallel to the direction of incidence.

7-5 a. Estimate the exponential gain coefficient $\gamma(\nu_0)$ of a 10^{-4} molar solution of rhodamine 6G in ethanol by assuming the peak emission cross section to be comparable to the peak absorption cross section. Use the data of Figure 7-26.
b. Estimate the spontaneous lifetime for an $S_1 \rightarrow S_0$ transition.
c. Estimate the CW pump power threshold assuming 50 percent absorption of pump and 100 percent pumping quantum efficiency.

■ REFERENCES

[1] Maiman, T. H., "Stimulated optical radiation in ruby masers," Nature, vol. 187, p. 493, 1960.

[2] Maiman, T. H., "Optical and microwave-optical experiments in ruby," *Phys. Rev. Letters*, vol. 4, p. 564, 1960.

[3] Cronemeyer, D. C., "Optical absorption characteristics of pink ruby," *J. Opt. Soc. Am.*, vol. 56, p. 1703, 1966.

[4] Schawlow, A. L., "Fine structure and properties of chromium fluorescence," in *Advances in Quantum Electronics*, J. R. Singer, ed. New York: Columbia University Press, p. 53, 1961.

[5] Yariv, A., "Energy and power considerations in injection and optically pumped lasers," *Proc. IEEE*, vol. 51, p. 1723, 1963.

[6] Geusic, J. E., H. M. Marcos, and L. G. Van Uitert, "Laser oscillations in Nd-doped yttrium aluminum, yttrium gallium and gado-
linium garnets," *Appl. Phys. Letters*, vol. 4, p. 182, 1964.

[7] Kushida, T., H. M. Marcos, and J. E. Geusic, "Laser transition cross
section and fluorescence branching ratio for Nd^{3+} in yttrium aluminum garnet," *Phys. Rev.*, vol. 167, p. 1289, 1968.

[8] Snitzer, E., and C. G. Young, "Glass lasers," in *Lasers*, vol. 2, A. K.
Levine, ed. New York: Marcel Dekker, Inc., p. 191, 1968.

[9] Javan, A., W. R. Bennett, Jr., and D. R. Herriott, "Population inversion and continuous optical maser oscillation in a gas discharge
containing a He–Ne mixture," *Phys. Rev. Letters*, vol. 6, p. 106, 1961.

[10] White, A. D., and J. D. Rigden, "Simultaneous gas maser action in
the visible and infrared," *Proc. IRE*, vol. 50, p. 2366, 1962.

[11] Bennett, W. R., "Gaseous optical masers," *Appl. Optics, Suppl. 1,
Optical Masers*, p. 24, 1962.

[12] Patel, C. K. N., "Interpretation of CO_2 optical maser experiments,"
Phys. Rev. Letters, vol. 12, p. 588, 1964; also, "Continuous-wave laser
action on vibrational rotational transitions of CO_2," *Phys. Rev.*, vol.
136, p. A1187, 1964.

[13] Herzberg, G. H., *Spectra of Diatomic Molecules*. Princeton, N.J.:
Van Nostrand, 1963.

[14] Patel, C. K. N., "High power CO_2 lasers," *Sci. Am.*, vol. 219, p. 22,
Aug. 1968.

[15] Bridges, W. B., "Laser oscillation in singly ionized argon in the
visible spectrum," *Appl. Phys. Letters*, vol. 4, p. 128, 1964.

[16] Gordon, E. I., E. F. Labuda, and W. B. Bridges, "Continuous visible
laser action in singly ionized argon, krypton and xenon," *Appl. Phys.
Letters*, vol. 4, p. 178, 1964.

[17] Hall, R. N., G. E. Fenner, J. D. Kingsley, T. J. Soltys, and R. O.
Carlson, "Coherent light emission from GaAs junctions," *Phys. Rev.
Letters*, vol. 9, pp. 366–367, 1962.

[18] Nathan, M. I., W. P. Dumke, G. Burns, F. H. Dills, and G. Lasher,
"Stimulated emission of radiation from GaAs *p-n* junctions," *Appl.
Phys. Letters*, vol. 1, pp. 62–64, 1962.

[19] Quist, T. M., R. J. Keyes, W. E. Krag, B. Lax, A. L. McWhorter,
R. H. Rediker, and H. J. Zeiger, "Semiconductor maser of GaAs,"
Appl. Phys. Letters, vol. 1, p. 91, 1962.

[20] Kittel, C., *Introduction to Solid State Physics*, 3d ed. New York:
Wiley, 1967.

[21] Bernard, M. G., and G. Duraffourg, "Laser conditions in semiconductors," *Phys. Status Solidi*, vol. 1, p. 699, 1961.

[22] Yariv, A., and R. C. C. Leite, "Dielectric waveguide mode of light propagation in *p-n* junctions," *Appl. Phys. Letters*, vol. 2, p. 55, 1963.

[23] Anderson, W. W., "Mode confinement in junction lasers," *IEEE J. Quantum Electron.*, vol. QE-1, p. 228, 1965.

[24] Stern, F., in *Radiative Recombinations in Semiconductors* (Proc. 7th Int. Conf. on the Physics of Semiconductors). New York: Academic Press, and Paris: Dunod, p. 165, 1964.

[25] See, for example, R. A. Smith, *Semiconductors*. New York: Cambridge, p. 216, 1959.

[26] Phelan, R. J., A. R. Calawa, R. H. Rediker, R. J. Keyes, and B. Lax, "Infrared InSb laser diode in high magnetic fields," *Appl. Phys. Letters*, vol. 3, p. 143, 1963.

[27] Weiser, K., and R. S. Levitt, "Radiative recombination from indium phosphide in *p-n* junctions," *Bull. Am. Phys. Soc.*, vol. 8, p. 29, 1963.

[28] Melngailis, I., "Maser action in InAs diodes," *Appl. Phys. Letters*, vol. 2, p. 176, 1963.

[29] Melngailis, I., and R. H. Rediker, "Properties of InAs lasers," *J. Appl. Phys.*, vol. 37, p. 899, 1966.

[30] Phelan, R. J., A. R. Calawa, R. H. Rediker, R. J. Keyes, and B. Lax, "Infrared InSb laser in high magnetic fields," *Appl. Phys. Letters*, vol. 3, p. 143, 1963.

[31] Butler, J. F., A. R. Calawa, R. J. Phelan, Jr., A. J. Strauss, and R. H. Rediker, "PbSe diode laser," *Solid State Commun.*, vol. 2, p. 303, 1964.

[32] Butler, J. F., A. R. Calawa, R. J. Phelan, Jr., T. C. Harman, A. J. Strauss, and R. H. Rediker, "PbTe diode laser," *Appl. Phys. Letters*, vol. 5, p. 75, 1964.

[33] Holnyak, N., Jr., and S. F. Bevacqua, "Coherent (visible) light emission from $Ga(As_{1-x}P_x)$ junctions," *Appl. Phys. Letters*, vol. 1, p. 82, 1962.

[34] Melngailis, I., A. J. Strauss, and R. H. Rediker, "Semiconductor diode masers of $(In_xGa_{1-x})As$," *Proc. IEEE*, vol. 51, p. 1154, 1963.

[35] Alexander, F. B., V. R. Bird, D. R. Carpenter, G. W. Manley, P. S. McDermott, J. R. Peloke, H. F. Quinn, R. J. Riley, and L. R. Yetter, "Spontaneous and stimulated infrared emission from indium phosphide arsenide diodes," *Appl. Phys. Letters*, vol. 4, p. 13, 1964.

[36] Calawa, A. R., and I. Melngailis, "Infrared radiation from GaSb diodes," *Bull. Am. Phys. Soc.*, vol. 8, p. 29, 1963.

[37] Butler, J. F., and T. C. Harman, "Long wavelength infrared $Pb_{1-x}Sn_xTe$ diode lasers," *Appl. Phys. Letters*, vol. 12, p. 347, 1968.

[38] Stockman, D. L., W. R. Mallory, and K. F. Tittel, "Stimulated emission in aromatic organic compounds," *Proc. IEEE*, vol. 52, p. 318, 1964.

[39] Sorokin, P. P., and J. R. Lankard, "Stimulated emission observed from an organic dye, chloroaluminum phtalocyanine," *IBM J. Res. Develop.*, vol. 10, p. 162, 1966.

[40] Schafer, F. P., W. Schmidt, and J. Volze, "Organic dye solution laser," *Appl. Phys. Letters*, vol. 9, p. 306, 1966.

[41] Snavely, B. B., "Flashlamp-excited dye lasers," *Proc. IEEE*, vol. 57, p. 1374, 1969.

[42] Soffer, B. H., and B. B. McFarland, "Continuously tunable, narrow band organic dye lasers," *Appl. Phys. Letters*, vol. 10, p. 266, 1967.

[43] Peterson, O. G., Tuccio, S. A., and B. B. Snavely, "CW operation of an organic dye laser," *Appl. Phys. Letters*, vol. 17, 1970.

Second-Harmonic Generation and Parametric Oscillation

8.0 Introduction

In Chapter 1 we considered the propagation of electromagnetic radiation in linear media in which the polarization is proportional to the electric field that induces it. In this chapter we consider some of the consequences of the nonlinear dielectric properties of certain classes of crystals in which, in addition to the linear response, a field produces a polarization proportional to the square of the field.

The nonlinear response can give rise to exchange of energy between a number of electromagnetic fields of different frequencies. Two of the most important applications of this phenomenon are: (1) second-harmonic generation in which part of the energy of an optical wave of frequency ω propagating through a crystal is converted to that of a wave at 2ω; (2) parametric oscillation in which a strong pump wave at ω_3 causes the simultaneous generation in a nonlinear crystal of radiation at ω_1 and ω_2, where $\omega_3 = \omega_1 + \omega_2$. These will be treated in detail in this chapter.

8.1   On the Physical Origin of Nonlinear Polarization

The optical polarization of dielectric crystals is due mostly to the outer, loosely bound valence electrons that are displaced by the optical field. Denoting the electron deviation from the equilibrium position by x and the density of electrons by N, the polarization p is given by

$$p(t) = -Nex(t)$$

In symmetric crystals the potential energy of an electron must reflect the crystal symmetry, so that, using a one-dimensional analog, it can be written as

$$V(x) = \frac{m}{2} \omega_0{}^2 x^2 + \frac{m}{4} Bx^4 + \cdots \qquad \text{(8.1-1)}$$

where $\omega_0{}^2$ and B are constants[1] and m is the electron mass. Because of the symmetry $V(x)$ contains only even powers of x, so $V(-x) = V(x)$. The restoring force on an electron is

$$F = -\frac{\partial V}{\partial x} = -m\omega_0{}^2 x - mBx^3 \qquad \text{(8.1-2)}$$

and is zero at the equilibrium position $x = 0$.

The linear polarization of crystals in which the polarization is proportional to the electric field is accounted for by the first term in (8.1-1). To see this, consider a "low" frequency electric field $E(t)$—that is, a field whose Fourier components are at frequencies small compared to ω_0. The excursion $x(t)$ caused by this field is found by equating the total force on the electron to zero[2]

$$-eE(t) - m\omega_0{}^2 x(t) = 0$$

so that

$$x(t) = -\frac{e}{m\omega_0{}^2} E(t) \qquad \text{(8.1-3)}$$

thus resulting in a polarization which is instantaneously proportional to the field.

Now in an asymmetric crystal in which the condition $V(x) = V(-x)$ is no longer fulfilled, the potential function can contain odd powers, and thus

$$V(x) = \frac{m\omega_0{}^2}{2} x^2 + \frac{m}{3} Dx^3 + \cdots \qquad \text{(8.1-4)}$$

---

[1] The constant ω_0 was found in Section 5.4 to correspond to the resonance frequency of the electronic oscillator.

[2] The "low" frequency assumption makes it possible to neglect the acceleration term $m\, d^2x/dt^2$ in the force equation.

which corresponds to a restoring force on the electron

$$F = -\frac{\partial V(x)}{\partial x} = -(m\omega_0{}^2 x + mDx^2 + \cdots) \qquad \textbf{(8.1-5)}$$

An examination of (8.1-5) reveals that a positive excursion ($x > 0$) results in a larger restoring force, assuming $D > 0$, than does the same excursion in the opposite direction. It follows immediately that if the electric force on the electron is positive ($E < 0$), the induced polarization is smaller than when the field direction is reversed. This situation is depicted in Figure 8-1.

Next consider an alternating electric field at an (optical) frequency ω applied to the crystal. In a linear crystal the induced polarization will be proportional, at any moment, to the field, resulting in a polarization oscillating at ω as shown in Figure 8-2(a). In a nonlinear crystal we can use Figure 8-1(b) to obtain the induced polarization corresponding to a given field and then plot it (vertically) as in Figure 8-2(b). The result is

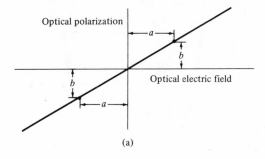

(a)

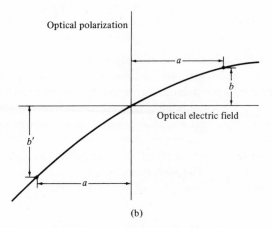

(b)

Figure 8-1 Relation between induced polarization and the electric field causing it; (**a**) in a linear dielectric and (**b**) in a crystal lacking inversion symmetry.

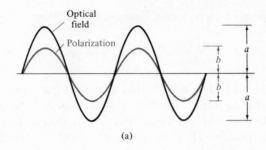

(a)

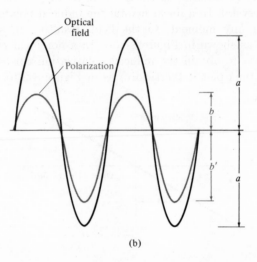

(b)

Figure 8-2   An applied sinusoidal electric field and the resulting polarization;
(a) in a linear crystal and (b) in a crystal lacking inversion symmetry.

a polarization wave in which the stiffer restoring force at $x > 0$ results in
positive peaks (b), which are smaller than the negative ones (b'). A Fourier
analysis of the nonlinear polarization wave in Figure 8-2(b) shows that it
contains the second harmonic of ω as well as an average (dc) term. The
average, fundamental, and second-harmonic components are plotted in
Figure 8-3.

   To relate the nonlinear polarization formally to the inducing field, we
use Equation (8.1-5) for the restoring force and take the driving electric
field as $E^{(\omega)} \cos \omega t$. The equation of motion of the electron $F = m\ddot{x}$ is
then

$$\frac{d^2x(t)}{dt^2} + \sigma\,\frac{dx(t)}{dt} + \omega_0{}^2 x(t) + Dx^2(t) = -\frac{eE^{(\omega)}}{2m}\,(e^{i\omega t} + e^{-i\omega t}) \qquad \textbf{(8.1-6)}$$

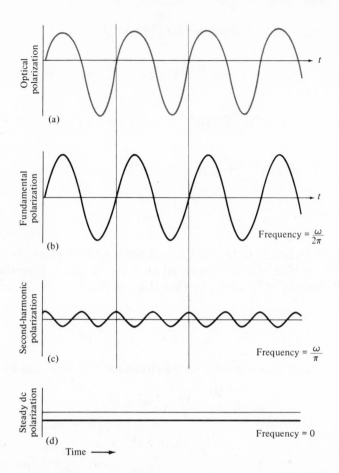

Figure 8-3   Analysis of the nonlinear polarization wave (**a**) of Figure 8.2(b) shows that it contains components oscillating at (**b**) the same frequency (ω) as the wave inducing it, (**c**) twice that frequency (2ω), and (**d**) an average (dc) negative component.

where, as in (5.4-1), we account for the losses by a frictional force $-m\sigma\dot{x}$. An inspection of (8.1-6) shows that the term Dx^2 gives rise to a component oscillating at 2ω, so we assume the solution for $x(t)$ in the form[3]

$$x(t) = \tfrac{1}{2}(q_1 e^{i\omega t} + q_2 e^{2i\omega t} + \text{c.c.}) \tag{8.1-7}$$

where c.c. stands for "complex conjugate."

---

[3] Here we must use the real form of $x(t)$ instead of the complex one since, as discussed in Section 1.1, the differential equation involves x^2.

Substituting the last expression into (8.1-6) gives

$$-\frac{\omega^2}{2}(q_1 e^{i\omega t} + \text{c.c.}) - 2\omega^2(q_2 e^{2i\omega t} + \text{c.c.}) + \frac{i\omega\sigma}{2}(q_1 e^{i\omega t} - \text{c.c.})$$

$$+ i\omega\sigma(q_2 e^{2i\omega t} - \text{c.c.}) + \frac{{\omega_0}^2}{2}(q_1 e^{i\omega t} + q_2 e^{2i\omega t} + \text{c.c.})$$

$$+ \frac{D}{4}({q_1}^2 e^{2i\omega t} + {q_2}^2 e^{4i\omega t} + q_1 q_1^* + 2q_1 q_2 e^{3i\omega t}$$

$$+ 2q_1 q_2^* e^{-i\omega t} + q_2 q_2^* + \text{c.c.}) = \frac{-eE^{(\omega)}}{2m}(e^{i\omega t} + \text{c.c.}) \qquad \textbf{(8.1-8)}$$

If Equation (8.1-8) is to be valid for all times t, the coefficients of $e^{\pm i\omega t}$ and $e^{\pm 2i\omega t}$ on both sides of the equation must be equal. Equating first the coefficients of $e^{i\omega t}$, assuming that $|Dq_2| \ll [({\omega_0}^2 - \omega^2)^2 + \omega^2\sigma^2]^{1/2}$, gives

$$q_1 = -\frac{eE^{(\omega)}}{m}\frac{1}{({\omega_0}^2 - \omega^2) + i\omega\sigma} \qquad \textbf{(8.1-9)}$$

The polarization at ω is related to the electronic deviation at ω by

$$p^{(\omega)}(t) = -\frac{Ne}{2}(q_1 e^{i\omega t} + \text{c.c.})$$

$$\equiv \frac{\epsilon_0}{2}[\chi(\omega)E^{(\omega)}e^{i\omega t} + \text{c.c.}] \qquad \textbf{(8.1-10)}$$

where $\chi(\omega)$ is thus the linear susceptibility defined by Equation (5.4-8). By using (8.1-9) in (8.1-10) and solving for $\chi(\omega)$, we obtain

$$\chi(\omega) = \frac{Ne^2}{m\epsilon_0[({\omega_0}^2 - \omega^2) + i\omega\sigma]} \qquad \textbf{(8.1-11)}$$

We now proceed to solve for the amplitude q_2 of the electronic motion at 2ω. Equating the coefficients of $e^{2i\omega t}$ on both sides of (8.1-8) leads to

$$q_2(-4\omega^2 + 2i\omega\sigma + {\omega_0}^2) = -\tfrac{1}{2}D{q_1}^2$$

and, after substituting the solution (8.1-9) for q_1, we obtain

$$q_2 = \frac{-De^2[E^{(\omega)}]^2}{2m^2[({\omega_0}^2 - \omega^2) + i\omega\sigma]^2[{\omega_0}^2 - 4\omega^2 + 2i\omega\sigma]} \qquad \textbf{(8.1-12)}$$

In a manner similar to (8.1-10), the nonlinear polarization at 2ω is

$$p^{(2\omega)}(t) = -\frac{Ne}{2}(q_2 e^{2i\omega t} + \text{c.c.})$$

$$\equiv \tfrac{1}{2}\{d^{(2\omega)}[E^{(\omega)}]^2 e^{2i\omega t} + \text{c.c.}\} \tag{8.1-13}$$

The second of equations (8.1-13) defines the *nonlinear optical coefficient* $d^{(2\omega)}$. If we denote the complex amplitude of the polarization as $P^{(2\omega)}$ we have, from (8.1-13),

$$p^{(2\omega)}(t) = \tfrac{1}{2}[P^{(2\omega)} e^{2i\omega t} + \text{c.c.}]$$

and $\tag{8.1-14}$

$$P^{(2\omega)} = d^{(2\omega)} E^{(\omega)} E^{(\omega)}$$

that is, $d^{(2\omega)}$ is the ratio of the (complex) amplitude of the polarization at 2ω to the square of the fundamental amplitude. Substituting (8.1-12) for q_2 in (8.1-13), then solving for $d^{(2\omega)}$, results in

$$d^{(2\omega)} = \frac{-DNe^3}{2m^2[(\omega_0{}^2 - \omega^2) + i\omega\sigma]^2[\omega_0{}^2 - 4\omega^2 + 2i\omega\sigma)]} \tag{8.1-15}$$

Using (8.1-11) we can rewrite (8.1-15) as

$$d^{(2\omega)} = \frac{mD[\chi^{(\omega)}]^2 \chi^{(2\omega)} \epsilon_0{}^3}{2N^2 e^3} \tag{8.1-16}$$

Equation (8.1-16) is of importance since it relates the nonlinear optical coefficient d to the linear optical susceptibilities χ and to the anharmonic coefficient D. Estimates based on this relation are quite successful in predicting the size of the coefficient d in a large variety of crystals; see References [1] and [2].

Relation (8.1-14) is scalar. In reality the second harmonic polarization along, say, the x direction, is related to the electric field at ω by

$$\begin{aligned} P_x^{(2\omega)} = {} & d_{xxx}^{(2\omega)} E_x^{(\omega)} E_x^{(\omega)} + d_{xyy}^{(2\omega)} E_y^{(\omega)} E_y^{(\omega)} + d_{xzz}^{(2\omega)} E_z^{(\omega)} E_z^{(\omega)} \\ & + 2d_{xzy}^{(2\omega)} E_z^{(\omega)} E_y^{(\omega)} + 2d_{xzx}^{(2\omega)} E_z^{(\omega)} E_x^{(\omega)} + 2d_{xxy}^{(2\omega)} E_x^{(\omega)} E_y^{(\omega)} \end{aligned} \tag{8.1-17}$$

Similar relations give $P_y{}^{(2\omega)}$ and $P_z{}^{(2\omega)}$. Considerations of crystal symmetry reduce the number of nonvanishing $d_{ijk}{}^{(2\omega)}$ coefficients—or, in certain cases to be discussed in the following, cause them to vanish altogether. Table 8-1 lists the nonlinear coefficients of a number of crystals.

Crystals are usually divided into two main groups, depending on

Table 8-1 THE NONLINEAR OPTICAL COEFFICIENTS OF A NUMBER OF CRYSTALS*

CRYSTAL	$d_{ijk}^{(2\omega)}$ IN UNITS OF $1/9 \times 10^{-22}$ (mks)
LiIO$_3$	$d_{31} = 0.46 \pm 0.1$
NH$_4$H$_2$PO$_4$	$d_{36} = d_{312} = 0.45$
(ADP)	$d_{14} = d_{123} = 0.45 \pm 0.02$
KH$_2$PO$_4$	$d_{36} = d_{312} = 0.45 \pm 0.03$
(KDP)	$d_{14} = d_{123} = 0.45 \pm 0.03$
KD$_2$PO$_4$	$d_{36} = d_{312} = 0.42 \pm 0.02$
	$d_{14} = d_{123} = 0.42 \pm 0.02$
KH$_2$ASO$_4$	$.d_{36} = d_{312} = 0.48 \pm 0.03$
	$d_{14} = d_{123} = 0.51 \pm 0.03$
Quartz	$d_{11} = d_{111} = 0.37 \pm 0.02$
AlPO$_4$	$d_{11} = d_{111} = 0.38 \pm 0.03$
ZnO	$d_{33} = d_{333} = 6.5 \pm 0.2$
	$d_{31} = d_{311} = 1.95 \pm 0.2$
	$d_{15} = d_{113} = 2.1 \pm 0.2$
CdS	$d_{33} = d_{333} = 28.6 \pm 2$
	$d_{31} = d_{311} = 14.5 \pm 1$
	$d_{15} = d_{113} = 16 \pm 3$
GaP	$d_{14} = d_{123} = 80 \pm 14$
GaAs	$d_{14} = d_{123} = 107 \pm 30$
BaTiO$_3$	$d_{33} = d_{333} = 6.4 \pm 0.5$
	$d_{31} = d_{311} = 18 \pm 2$
	$d_{15} = d_{113} = 17 \pm 2$
LiNbO$_3$	$d_{31} = d_{311} = 4.76 \pm 0.5$
	$d_{22} = d_{222} = 2.3 \pm 1.0$
Te	$d_{11} = d_{111} = 730 \pm 230$
Se	$d_{11} = d_{111} = 130 \pm 30$
Ba$_2$NaNb$_5$O$_{15}$	$d_{33} = d_{333} = 10.4 \pm 0.7$
	$d_{32} = d_{322} = 7.4 \pm 0.7$
Ag$_3$AsS$_3$	$d_{22} = d_{222} = 225$
(Proustite)	$d_{36} = d_{312} = 135$

* These coefficients are defined by (8.1-17) with $1 = x$, $2 = y$, $3 = z$.

whether the crystal structure remains unchanged upon inversion (that is, replacing the coordinate **r** by $-$**r**) or not. Crystals belonging to the first group are called centrosymmetric, whereas crystals of the second group are called noncentrosymmetric [3]. In Figure 8-4 we show the crystal structure of NaCl, a centrosymmetric crystal; an example of a crystal lacking inversion symmetry (noncentrosymmetric) is provided by crystals of the ZnS (zinc blende) class such as GaAs, CdTe, and others. The crystal structure of ZnS is shown in Figure 8-5. The lack of inversion symmetry is evident in the projection of the atomic positions given by Figure 8-6.

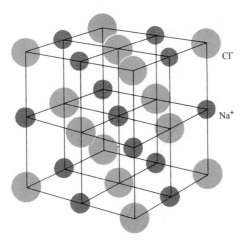

Figure 8-4 The crystal structure of NaCl. The crystal is centrosymmetric, since an inversion of any ion about the central Na^+ ion, as an example, leaves the crystal structure unchanged.

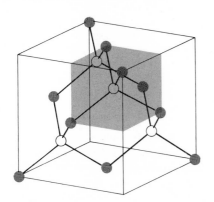

Figure 8-5 The crystal structure of cubic zinc sulfide.

Figure 8-6 The atomic positions in the unit cell of ZnS projected on a cube face. The fractions denote height above base in units of a cube edge. The dark spheres correspond to zinc (or sulfur) atoms and are situated on a face-centered cubic (fcc) lattice, and the white spheres correspond to sulfur (or zinc) atoms and are situated on another fcc lattice displayed by $(\frac{1}{4}, \frac{1}{4}, \frac{1}{4})$ from the first one. Note the lack of inversion symmetry.

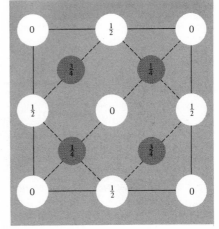

In crystals possessing an inversion symmetry all the nonlinear optical coefficients $d_{ijk}^{(2\omega)}$ must be zero. This follows directly from the relation

$$P_i^{(2\omega)} = \sum_{j,k=x,y,z} d_{ijk}^{(2\omega)} E_j^{(\omega)} E_k^{(\omega)} \qquad \textbf{(8.1-18)}$$

which is a compact notation for relation (8.1-17). Let us reverse the direction of the electric field so that in (8.1-18) $E_j^{(\omega)}$ becomes $-E_j^{(\omega)}$ and $E_k^{(\omega)}$ becomes $-E_k^{(\omega)}$. Since the crystal is centrosymmetric, the reversed field "sees" a crystal identical to the original one so that the polarization produced by it must bear the same relationship to the field as originally; that is, the new polarization is $-P_i^{(2\omega)}$. Since the new polarization and the electric field causing it are still related by (8.1-18), we have

$$-P_i^{(2\omega)} = \sum_{j,k} d_{ijk}^{(2\omega)} (-E_j^{(\omega)})(-E_k^{(\omega)}) \qquad \textbf{(8.1-19)}$$

Equations (8.1-18) and (8.1-19) can hold simultaneously only if the coefficients $d_{ijk}^{(2\omega)}$ are all zero. We may thus summarize: *In crystals possessing an inversion symmetry there is no second-harmonic generation.*

In the following work we will ignore the vector nature of the optical nonlinearity and use the scalar form (8.1-14).

8.2   The Formalism of Wave Propagation in Nonlinear Media

In this section we derive the equations governing the propagation of electromagnetic waves in nonlinear media. These equations will then be used to describe second-harmonic generation and parametric oscillation.

The starting point is Maxwell's equations (1.2-1), (1.2-2):

$$\mathbf{\nabla} \times \mathbf{h} = \mathbf{i} + \frac{\partial \mathbf{d}}{\partial t}$$

$$\mathbf{\nabla} \times \mathbf{e} = -\mu_0 \frac{\partial \mathbf{h}}{\partial t} \qquad \textbf{(8.2-1)}$$

and

$$\mathbf{d} = \epsilon_0 \mathbf{e} + \mathbf{p}$$

$$\mathbf{i} = \sigma \mathbf{e} \qquad \textbf{(8.2-2)}$$

where σ is the conductivity. If we separate the total polarization $\mathbf{p}$ into its linear and nonlinear portions according to

$$\mathbf{p} = \epsilon_0 \chi_e \mathbf{e} + \mathbf{p}_{NL} \qquad \textbf{(8.2-3)}$$

the first of equations (8.2-1) becomes

$$\mathbf{\nabla} \times \mathbf{h} = \sigma \mathbf{e} + \epsilon \frac{\partial \mathbf{e}}{\partial t} + \frac{\partial}{\partial t} \mathbf{p}_{NL} \qquad \textbf{(8.2-4)}$$

with $\epsilon \equiv \epsilon_0(1 + \chi_e)$. Taking the curl of both sides of the second of (8.2-1), using the vector identity

$$\nabla \times \nabla \times \mathbf{e} = \nabla\nabla \cdot \mathbf{e} - \nabla^2\mathbf{e},$$

From equation (8.2-4) and taking $\nabla \cdot \mathbf{e} = 0$, we get

$$\nabla^2\mathbf{e} = \mu_0\sigma \frac{\partial \mathbf{e}}{\partial t} + \mu_0\epsilon \frac{\partial^2\mathbf{e}}{\partial t^2} + \mu_0 \frac{\partial^2}{\partial t^2}\mathbf{p}_{NL} \qquad \text{(8.2-5)}$$

Next we go over to a scalar notation and, using (8.1-14), replace p_{NL} by de^2; therefore, (8.2-5) becomes

$$\nabla^2 e = \mu_0\sigma \frac{\partial e}{\partial t} + \mu_0\epsilon \frac{\partial^2 e}{\partial t^2} + \mu_0 d \frac{\partial^2 e^2}{\partial t^2} \qquad \text{(8.2-6)}$$

where we assumed, for simplicity, that $\mathbf{p}_{NL}$ is parallel to $\mathbf{e}$. Let us limit our consideration to a field made up of three plane waves propagating in the z direction with frequencies ω_1, ω_2, and ω_3 according to

$$e^{(\omega_1)}(z, t) = \tfrac{1}{2}[E_1(z)e^{i(\omega_1 t - k_1 z)} + \text{c.c.}]$$

$$e^{(\omega_2)}(z, t) = \tfrac{1}{2}[E_2(z)e^{i(\omega_2 t - k_2 z)} + \text{c.c.}] \qquad \text{(8.2-7)}$$

$$e^{(\omega_3)}(z, t) = \tfrac{1}{2}[E_3(z)e^{i(\omega_3 t - k_3 z)} + \text{c.c.}]$$

Then the total instantaneous field is

$$e = e^{(\omega_1)}(z, t) + e^{(\omega_2)}(z, t) + e^{(\omega_3)}(z, t) \qquad \text{(8.2-8)}$$

Next we substitute (8.2-8), using (8.2-7), into the wave equation (8.2-6) and separate the resulting equation into three equations, each containing only terms oscillating at one of the three frequencies. The last term in (8.2-6) will give rise to terms such as

$$\mu_0 d \frac{\partial^2}{\partial t^2} E_1 E_2 e^{i[(\omega_1 + \omega_2)t - (k_1 + k_2)z]}$$

or

$$\mu_0 d \frac{\partial^2}{\partial t^2} E_3 E_2^* e^{i[(\omega_3 - \omega_2)t - (k_3 - k_2)z]}$$

These oscillate at the new frequencies $(\omega_1 + \omega_2)$ and $(\omega_3 - \omega_2)$ and, in general being nonsynchronous, will not be able to drive the oscillation at ω_1, ω_2, or ω_3. An exception to the last statement is the case when

$$\omega_3 = \omega_1 + \omega_2 \qquad \text{(8.2-9)}$$

In this case the term

$$\mu_0 d \frac{\partial^2}{\partial t^2} E_1 E_2 e^{i[(\omega_1 + \omega_2)t - (k_1 + k_2)z]}$$

oscillates at $\omega_1 + \omega_2 = \omega_3$ and can thus act as a source for the wave at ω_3. In physical terms, we have power flow from the fields at ω_1 and ω_2

into that at ω_3, or vice versa. Assuming that (8.2-9) holds, we return to (8.2-6) and, writing it for the oscillation at ω_1, obtain

$$\nabla^2 e^{(\omega_1)} = \mu_0 \sigma_1 \frac{\partial e^{(\omega_1)}}{\partial t} + \mu_0 \epsilon \frac{\partial^2 e^{(\omega_1)}}{\partial t^2} + \mu_0 d \frac{\partial^2}{\partial t^2}$$

$$\times \left[\frac{E_3(z) E_2^*(z)}{4} e^{i[(\omega_3 - \omega_2)t - (k_3 - k_2)z]} + \text{c.c.} \right] \quad \textbf{(8.2-10)}$$

Next we observe that, in view of (8.2-7),

$$\nabla^2 e^{(\omega_1)} = \frac{1}{2} \frac{\partial^2}{\partial z^2} [E_1(z) e^{i(\omega_1 t - k_1 z)} + \text{c.c.}]$$

$$= -\frac{1}{2} \left[k_1{}^2 E_1(z) + 2i k_1 \frac{dE_1(z)}{dz} \right] e^{i(\omega_1 t - k_1 z)} + \text{c.c.}$$

where we assumed that

$$\left| k_1 \frac{dE_1(z)}{dz} \right| \gg \left| \frac{d^2 E_1(z)}{dz^2} \right| \quad \textbf{(8.2-11)}$$

If we use (8.2-9) and the last result in (8.2-10), and take $\partial/\partial t = i\omega_i$, we obtain

$$-\frac{1}{2} \left[k_1{}^2 E_1(z) + 2i k_1 \frac{dE_1(z)}{dz} \right] e^{i(\omega_1 t - k_1 z)} + \text{c.c.}$$

$$= [i\omega_1 \mu_0 \sigma_1 - \omega_1{}^2 \mu_0 \epsilon] \left[\frac{E_1(z)}{2} e^{i(\omega_1 t - k_1 z)} + \text{c.c.} \right]$$

$$- \left[\frac{\omega_1{}^2 \mu_0 d}{4} E_3(z) E_2^*(z) e^{i[\omega_1 t - (k_3 - k_2)z]} + \text{c.c.} \right] \quad \textbf{(8.2-12)}$$

Recognizing that $k_1{}^2 = \omega_1{}^2 \mu_0 \epsilon$, we can rewrite (8.2-12) after multiplying all the terms by

$$\frac{i}{k_1} \exp(-i\omega_1 t + i k_1 z)$$

as

$$\frac{dE_1}{dz} = -\frac{\sigma_1}{2} \sqrt{\frac{\mu_0}{\epsilon_1}} E_1 - \frac{i\omega_1}{2} \sqrt{\frac{\mu_0}{\epsilon_1}} dE_3 E_2^* e^{-i(k_3 - k_2 - k_1)z}$$

and, similarly,

$$\frac{dE_2^*}{dz} = -\frac{\sigma_2}{2} \sqrt{\frac{\mu_0}{\epsilon_2}} E_2^* + \frac{i\omega_2}{2} \sqrt{\frac{\mu_0}{\epsilon_2}} dE_1 E_3^* e^{-i(k_1 - k_3 + k_2)z}$$

$$\frac{dE_3}{dz} = -\frac{\sigma_3}{2} \sqrt{\frac{\mu_0}{\epsilon_3}} E_3 - \frac{i\omega_3}{2} \sqrt{\frac{\mu_0}{\epsilon_3}} dE_1 E_2 e^{-i(k_1 + k_2 - k_3)z}$$

$$\textbf{(8.2-13)}$$

for the fields at ω_2 and ω_3. These are the basic equations describing nonlinear parametric interactions [4]. We notice that they are coupled to each other via the nonlinear constant d.

8.3 Optical Second-Harmonic Generation

The first experiment in nonlinear optics [5] consisted of generating the second harmonic ($\lambda = 0.3470\,\mu\text{m}$) of a ruby laser beam ($\lambda = 0.694\,\mu\text{m}$) that was focused on a quartz crystal. The experimental arrangement is depicted in Figure 8-7. The conversion efficiency of this first experiment ($\sim 10^{-8}$) was improved by methods to be described below to a point where about 30 percent conversion has been observed in a single pass through a few centimeters length of a nonlinear crystal. This technique is finding important applications in generating short-wave radiation from longer-wave lasers.

In the case of second-harmonic generation, two of the three fields that figure in (8.2-13) are of the same frequency. We may thus put $\omega_1 = \omega_2 = \omega$, for which case the first two equations are the complex conjugate of one another and we need to consider only one of them. We take the input field at ω to correspond to E_1 in (8.2-13) and the second-harmonic field to E_3, and we put $\omega_3 = \omega_1 + \omega_2 = 2\omega$, neglecting the absorption, so $\sigma_{1,2,3} = 0$. The last equation becomes

$$\frac{dE^{(2\omega)}}{dz} = -i\omega\sqrt{\frac{\mu_0}{\epsilon}}\,d[E^{(\omega)}(z)]^2 e^{i(\Delta k)z} \qquad \textbf{(8.3-1)}$$

where

$$\Delta k \equiv k_3 - 2k_1 = k^{(2\omega)} - 2k^{(\omega)} \qquad \textbf{(8.3-2)}$$

To simplify the analysis further, we may assume that the depletion of the input wave at ω due to conversion of its power to 2ω is negligible. Under those conditions, which apply in the majority of the experimental situations, we can take $E^{(\omega)}(z) = \text{constant}$ in (8.3-1) and neglect its dependence on z. Assuming no input at 2ω—that is, $E^{(2\omega)}(0) = 0$—we obtain from

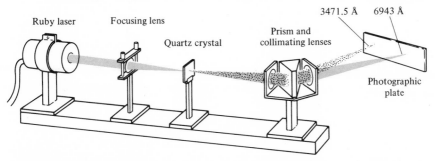

Figure 8-7 Arrangement used in first experimental demonstration of second-harmonic generation [5]. Ruby laser beam at $\lambda_0 = 0.694\,\mu\text{m}$ is focused on a quartz crystal, causing generation of a (weak) beam at $\lambda_0/2 = 0.347\,\mu\text{m}$. The two beams are then separated by a prism and detected on a photographic plate.

(8.3-1) by integration the output field at the end of a crystal of length l:

$$E^{(2\omega)}(l) = -i\omega \sqrt{\frac{\mu_0}{\epsilon}} \, d[E^{(\omega)}]^2 \, \frac{e^{i\Delta k l} - 1}{i\Delta k}$$

The output intensity is proportional to

$$E^{(2\omega)}(l)E^{(2\omega)*}(l) = \left(\frac{\mu_0}{\epsilon_0}\right) \frac{\omega^2 d^2}{n^2} [E^{(\omega)}]^4 l^2 \frac{\sin^2 (\Delta k l/2)}{(\Delta k l/2)^2} \qquad \textbf{(8.3-3)}$$

Here we used $\epsilon/\epsilon_0 = n^2$, where n is the index of refraction. If the input beam is confined to a cross section $A(m^2)$, then, according to (1.3-25), the power per unit area (intensity) is related to the field by

$$I \equiv \frac{P_{2\omega}}{A} = \frac{1}{2} \sqrt{\frac{\epsilon}{\mu_0}} [E^{(2\omega)}]^2 \qquad \textbf{(8.3-4)}$$

and (8.3-3) can be written as

$$\eta_{SHG} \equiv \frac{P_{2\omega}}{P_\omega} = 2 \left(\frac{\mu_0}{\epsilon_0}\right)^{3/2} \frac{\omega^2 d^2 l^2}{n^3} \frac{\sin^2 (\Delta k l/2)}{(\Delta k l/2)^2} \frac{P_\omega}{A} \quad -Int^{en} \qquad \textbf{(8.3-5)}$$

for the conversion efficiency from ω to 2ω. We notice that the conversion efficiency is proportional to the intensity P_ω/A of the fundamental beam.

Phase-matching in second-harmonic generation.   According to (8.3-5), a prerequisite for efficient second-harmonic generation is that $\Delta k = 0$—or, using (8.3-2),

$$k^{(2\omega)} = 2k^{(\omega)} \qquad \textbf{(8.3-6)}$$

If $\Delta k \neq 0$, the second-harmonic power generated at some plane, say z_1, having propagated to some other plane (z_2), is not in phase with the second-harmonic wave generated at z_2. This results in the interference described by the factor

$$\frac{\sin^2 (\Delta k l/2)}{(\Delta k l/2)^2}$$

in (8.3-5). Two adjacent peaks of this spatial interference pattern are separated by the so-called "coherence length"

$$l_c = \frac{2\pi}{\Delta k} = \frac{2\pi}{k^{(2\omega)} - 2k^{(\omega)}} \qquad \textbf{(8.3-7)}$$

The coherence length l_c is thus a *measure* of the *maximum crystal length that is useful in producing the second-harmonic power.* Under ordinary circumstances it may be no larger than 10^{-2} cm. This is because the index of refraction n_ω normally increases with ω so Δk is given by

$$\Delta k = k^{(2\omega)} - 2k^{(\omega)} = \frac{2\omega}{c_0} [n^{2\omega} - n^\omega] \qquad \textbf{(8.3-8)}$$

where we used the relation $k^{(\omega)} = \omega n^\omega / c_0$. The coherence length is thus

$$l_c = \frac{\pi c_0}{\omega[n^{2\omega} - n^\omega]} = \frac{\lambda_0}{2[n^{2\omega} - n^\omega]} \tag{8.3-9}$$

where λ_0 is the free-space wavelength of the fundamental beam. If we take a typical value of $\lambda_0 = 1\,\mu m$ and $n(2\omega) - n(\omega) \simeq 10^{-2}$, we get $l_c \simeq 100\,\mu m$. If l_c were to increase from $100\,\mu m$ to 2 cm, as an example, according to (8.3-5) the second-harmonic power would go up by a factor of 4×10^4.

The technique that is used widely (see References [6] and [7]) to satisfy the *phase-matching* requirement $\Delta k = 0$ takes advantage of the natural birefringence of anisotropic crystals, which was discussed in Section 1.4. Using the relation $k^{(\omega)} = \omega\sqrt{\mu\epsilon_0}n^\omega$, Equation (8.3-6) becomes

$$n^{2\omega} = n^\omega \tag{8.3-10}$$

so the indices of refraction at the fundamental and second-harmonic frequencies must be equal. In normally dispersive materials the index of the ordinary wave or the extraordinary wave along a given direction increases with ω, as can be seen from Table 8-2. This makes it impossible to satisfy (8.3-10) when both the ω and 2ω beams are of the same type— that is, when both are extraordinary or ordinary. We can, however, under certain circumstances, satisfy (8.3-10) by making the two waves be of

Table 8-2 INDEX OF REFRACTION DISPERSION DATA OF KH_2PO_4. (AFTER REFERENCE [8])

WAVELENGTH, μm	INDEX	
	n_o (ORDINARY RAY)	n_e (EXTRAORDINARY RAY)
0.2000	1.622630	1.563913
0.3000	1.545570	1.498153
0.4000	1.524481	1.480244
0.5000	1.514928	1.472486
0.6000	1.509274	1.468267
0.7000	1.505235	1.465601
0.8000	1.501924	1.463708
0.9000	1.498930	1.462234
1.0000	1.496044	1.460993
1.1000	1.493147	1.459884
1.2000	1.490169	1.458845
1.3000	1.487064	1.457838
1.4000	1.483803	1.456838
1.5000	1.480363	1.455829
1.6000	1.476729	1.454797
1.7000	1.472890	1.453735
1.8000	1.468834	1.452636
1.9000	1.464555	1.451495
2.0000	1.460044	1.450308

different type. To illustrate the point, consider the dependence of the index of refraction of the extraordinary wave in a uniaxial crystal on the angle θ between the propagation direction and the crystal optic (z) axis. It is given by (1.4-12) as

$$\frac{1}{n_e{}^2(\theta)} = \frac{\cos^2 \theta}{n_o{}^2} + \frac{\sin^2 \theta}{n_e{}^2} \qquad \text{(8.3-11)}$$

If $n_e{}^{2\omega} < n_o{}^{\omega}$, there exists an angle θ_m at which $n_e{}^{2\omega}(\theta_m) = n_o{}^{\omega}$; so if the fundamental beam (at ω) is launched along θ_m as an ordinary ray, the second-harmonic beam will be generated along the *same direction* as an extraordinary ray. The situation is illustrated by Figure 8-8. The angle θ_m is determined by the intersection between the sphere (shown as a circle in the figure) correspondending to the index surface of the ordinary beam at ω with the index surface of the extraordinary ray which gives $n_e{}^{2\omega}(\theta)$. The angle θ_m for negative uniaxial crystals—that is, crystals in which $n_e{}^{\omega} < n_o{}^{\omega}$—is that satisfying $n_e{}^{2\omega}(\theta_m) = n_o{}^{\omega}$ or, using (8.3-11),

$$\frac{\cos^2 \theta_m}{(n_o{}^{2\omega})^2} + \frac{\sin^2 \theta_m}{(n_e{}^{2\omega})^2} = \frac{1}{(n_o{}^{\omega})^2} \qquad \text{(8.3-12)}$$

and, solving for θ_m,

$$\sin^2 \theta_m = \frac{(n_o{}^{\omega})^{-2} - (n_o{}^{2\omega})^{-2}}{(n_e{}^{2\omega})^{-2} - (n_o{}^{2\omega})^{-2}} \qquad \text{(8.3-13)}$$

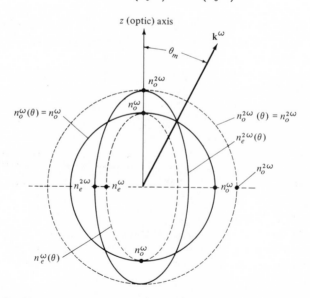

Figure 8-8   Normal (index) surfaces for the ordinary and extraordinary rays in a negative ($n_e < n_o$) uniaxial crystal. If $n_e{}^{2\omega} < n_o{}^{\omega}$, the condition $n_e{}^{2\omega}(\theta) = n_o{}^{\omega}$ is satisfied at $\theta = \theta_m$. The eccentricities shown are vastly exaggerated.

Numerical example—second-harmonic generation. Consider the problem of second-harmonic generation using the output of a pulsed ruby laser ($\lambda_0 = 0.6940 \, \mu\text{m}$) in a KH_2PO_4 crystal (KDP) under the following conditions:

$$l = 1 \text{ cm}$$

$$P_\omega/A = 10^8 \text{ W/cm}^2$$

The appropriate d coefficient is, according to Table 8-1, $d = 5 \times 10^{-24}$ mks units. Using these data in (8.3-5) and assuming $\Delta k = 0$ gives a conversion efficiency of

$$\frac{P_{(\lambda_0 = 0.347\mu\text{m})}}{P_{(\lambda_0 = 0.694\mu\text{m})}} \simeq 15 \text{ percent}$$

The angle θ_m between the z axis and the direction of propagation for which $\Delta k = 0$ is given by (8.3-13). The appropriate indices are taken from Table 8-2, and are

$$n_e(\lambda_0 = 0.694 \, \mu\text{m}) = 1.465 \qquad n_e(\lambda_0 = 0.347 \, \mu\text{m}) = 1.487$$

$$n_o(\lambda_0 = 0.694 \, \mu\text{m}) = 1.505 \qquad n_o(\lambda_0 = 0.347 \, \mu\text{m}) = 1.534$$

Substituting of the foregoing data into (8.3-13) gives

$$\theta_m = 50.4°$$

To obtain phase-matching along this direction, the fundamental beam in the crystal must be polarized as appropriate to an ordinary ray in accordance with the discussion following (8.3-11).

We conclude from this example that very large intensities are needed to obtain high-efficiency second-harmonic generation. This efficiency will, according to (8.3-5), increase as the square of the nonlinear optical coefficient d and will consequently improve as new materials are developed. Another approach is to take advantage of the dependence of η_{SHG} on P_ω/A and to place the nonlinear crystal inside the laser resonator where the energy flux P_ω/A can be made very large.[4] This approach has been used successfully [9] and it will be discussed in considerable detail further in this chapter.

Experimental verification of phase-matching. According to (8.3-5) if the phase-matching condition $\Delta k = 0$ is violated, the output power is reduced by a factor

$$F = \frac{\sin^2 (\Delta k l/2)}{(\Delta k l/2)^2} \tag{8.3-14}$$

---

[4] The one-way power flow inside the optical resonator P_i is related to the power output P_e as $P_i = P_e/(1 - R)$, where R is the reflectivity.

from its (maximum) phase-matched value. The phase mismatch $\Delta k l/2$ is given according to (8.3-8) by

$$\frac{\Delta k l}{2} = \frac{\omega l}{c_0} [n_e{}^{2\omega}(\theta) - n_o{}^\omega] \tag{8.3-15}$$

and is thus a function of θ. If we use (8.3-11) to expand $n_e{}^{2\omega}(\theta)$ as a Taylor series near $\theta \simeq \theta_m$, retain the first two terms only, and assume perfect phase-matching at $\theta = \theta_m$ so $n_e{}^{2\omega}(\theta_m) = n_o{}^\omega$, we obtain

$$\Delta k(\theta) l = -\frac{2\omega l}{c_0} \sin(2\theta_m) \frac{(n_e{}^{2\omega})^{-2} - (n_o{}^{2\omega})^{-2}}{2(n_o{}^\omega)^{-3}} (\theta - \theta_m) \tag{8.3-16}$$

$$\equiv 2\beta(\theta - \theta_m)$$

where β, as defined by (8.3-16), is a constant depending on $n_e{}^{2\omega}$, $n_o{}^{2\omega}$, $n_o{}^\omega$, ω, and l. If we plot the output power at 2ω as a function of θ we would expect, according to (8.3-5) and (8.3-16), to find it varying as

$$P_{2\omega}(\theta) \propto \frac{\sin^2[\beta(\theta - \theta_m)]}{[\beta(\theta - \theta_m)]^2} \tag{8.3-17}$$

Figure 8-9 shows an experimental plot of $P_{2\omega}(\theta)$ as well as a plot of (8.3-17).

8.4 Second-Harmonic Generation Inside the Laser Resonator

According to the numerical example of Section 8.3 we need to use large power densities at the fundamental frequency ω to obtain appreciable conversion from ω to 2ω in typical nonlinear optical crystals. These power densities are not usually available from continuous (CW) lasers. The situation is altered, however, if the nonlinear crystal is placed within the laser resonator. The intensity (one-way power per unit area in watts per

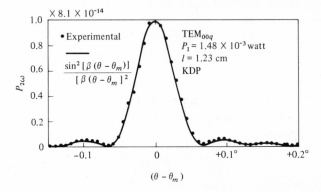

Figure 8-9 Variation of the second-harmonic power $P_{2\omega}$ with the angular departure $(\theta - \theta_m)$ from the phase-matching angle. (After Reference [10].)

square meter) inside the resonator exceeds its value outside a mirror by $(1 - R)^{-1}$, where R is the mirror reflectivity. If $R \simeq 1$, the enhancement is very large and since the second-harmonic conversion efficiency is, according to (8.3-5), proportional to the intensity, we may expect a far more efficient conversion inside the resonator. We will show below that under the proper conditions we can extract the *total available power* of the laser at 2ω instead of at ω and in that sense obtain 100 percent conversion efficiency. In order to appreciate the last statement, consider as an example the case of a (CW) laser in which the maximum power output, at a given pumping rate, is available when the output mirror has a (optimal) transmission of 5 percent.

The output mirror is next replaced with one having 100 percent reflection at ω and a nonlinear crystal is placed inside the laser resonator. If with the crystal inside the conversion efficiency from ω to 2ω in a *single pass* is 5 percent, the laser is loaded optimally as in the previous case except that the coupling is attributable to loss of power caused by second-harmonic generation instead of by the output mirror. It follows that the power generated at 2ω is the same as that coupled previously through the mirror and that the total available power of a laser can thus be converted to the second harmonic.

An experimental setup similar to the one used in the first internal second-harmonic generation experiment [9] is shown in Figure 8-10. The Nd^{3+}:YAG laser (see Chapter 7 for a description of this laser) emits a (fundamental) wave at $\lambda_0 = 1.06\,\mu m$. The mirrors are, as nearly as possible, totally reflecting at $\lambda_0 = 1.06\,\mu m$. A Ba_2NaNbO_{15} crystal is used to generate the second harmonic at $\lambda_0 = 0.53\,\mu m$. The latter is coupled through the mirror—which, ideally, transmits all the radiation at this wavelength.

In the mathematical treatment of internal second-harmonic generation that follows we use the results of the analysis of optimum power coupling in laser oscillators of Section 6.5.

The mirror transmission T_{opt} that results in the maximum power output from a laser oscillator is given by (6.5-11) as

$$T_{opt} = \sqrt{g_0 L_i} - L_i \qquad \qquad \textbf{(8.4-1)}$$

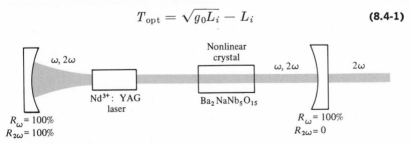

Figure 8-10 Typical setup for second-harmonic conversion inside a laser resonator. (After Reference [9].)

where L_i is the residual (that is, unavoidable) fractional intensity loss per pass and g_0 is the fractional unsaturated gain per pass.[5] The useful power output under optimum coupling is

$$P_o = S(\sqrt{g_0} - \sqrt{L_i})^2 \qquad (8.4\text{-}2)$$

where the saturation power of the laser transition S was given by (6.5-12) as[6]

$$S = \frac{8\pi hc\Delta\nu A}{\lambda^3} \qquad (8.4\text{-}3)$$

In the present problem the conversion from ω to 2ω can be considered, as far as the ω oscillation is concerned, just as another loss mechanism. We may think of it as due to a mirror with a transmission T' taken as equal to the conversion efficiency (from ω to 2ω) per pass, which, according to (8.3-5), is

$$T' \equiv \frac{P_{2\omega}}{P_\omega} = 2\left(\frac{\mu_0}{\epsilon_0}\right)^{3/2} \frac{\omega^2 d^2 l^2}{n^3}\left[\frac{\sin^2\,(\Delta kl/2)}{(\Delta kl/2)^2}\right]\frac{P_\omega}{A} \qquad (8.4\text{-}4)$$

where d is the crystal nonlinear coefficient, l its length, A its cross-sectional area, Δk the wave-vector mismatch, and P_ω the one-way traveling power *inside* the laser. We can rewrite T' in the form

$$T' = \kappa P_\omega \qquad (8.4\text{-}5)$$

where the value of the constant κ is evident from Equation (8.4-4). The equivalent mirror transmission T' is thus proportional to the power.

Using the last result in (8.4-1) we find immediately that at optimum conversion the product κP_ω must have the value

$$(\kappa P_\omega)_{\text{opt}} = \sqrt{g_0 L_i} - L_i \qquad (8.4\text{-}6)$$

The total loss per pass seen by the fundamental beam is the sum of the conversion loss (κP_ω) and the residual losses, which, under optimum coupling, becomes

$$L_{\text{opt}} = L_i + (\kappa P_\omega)_{\text{opt}} = \sqrt{g_0 L_i} \qquad (8.4\text{-}7)$$

Our next problem is to find the internal power P_ω at optimum coupling so that using (8.4-4) we may calculate the second-harmonic power. We start with the expression (6.5-6) for the total power P_e extracted from the

---

[5] We may recall here that the residual losses include all loss mechanisms except those representing useful power coupling. The unsaturated gain g_0 is that exercised by a very weak wave and represents the maximum available gain at a given pumping strength.

[6] S/A is, according to (5.6-9) (and putting $g(\nu)^{-1} = \Delta\nu$ and $\phi = 1$) the optical intensity (watts per square meter) that reduces the inversion, hence the gain, to one half its zero intensity (unsaturated) value.

laser atoms and replace the loss L by its optimum value (8.4-7) to obtain

$$(P_e)_{\text{opt}} = P_s\left[\frac{g_0}{L_{\text{opt}}} - 1\right] = P_s\left[\sqrt{\frac{g_0}{L_i}} - 1\right]$$

$$= \frac{8\pi h\Delta\nu V}{\lambda^3 (t_c)_{\text{opt}}}\left[\sqrt{\frac{g_0}{L_i}} - 1\right] = L_{\text{opt}}S\left[\sqrt{\frac{g_0}{L_i}} - 1\right] \qquad \textbf{(8.4-8)}$$

where to get the last equality we used relation (4.6-2)

$$t_c = \frac{l}{cL}$$

to relate the resonator decay time t_c to the loss per pass L. The fraction of the total power P_e emitted by the atoms that is available as useful output is T'/L. This power is also given by the product $P_\omega T'$ of the one-way internal power P_ω and the fraction T' of this power that is converted per pass. Equating these two forms gives

$$P_\omega = \frac{P_e}{L}$$

and using (8.4-8) we get

$$(P_\omega)_{\text{opt}} = S\left[\sqrt{\frac{g_0}{L_i}} - 1\right] \qquad \textbf{(8.4-9)}$$

for the one-way fundamental power inside the laser under optimum coupling conditions. The amount of second-harmonic power generated under optimum coupling is

$$(P_{2\omega})_{\text{opt}} = (\kappa P_\omega)_{\text{opt}}(P_\omega)_{\text{opt}}$$

which, through the use of (8.4-6) and (8.4-9), results in

$$(P_{2\omega})_{\text{opt}} = S(\sqrt{g_0} - \sqrt{L_i})^2 \qquad \textbf{(8.4-10)}$$

This is the same expression as the one previously obtained in (6.5-12) for the maximum available power output from a laser oscillator.

The nonlinear coupling constant κ was defined by (8.4-4) and (8.4-5) as

$$\kappa = 2\left(\frac{\mu_0}{\epsilon_0}\right)^{3/2}\frac{\omega^2 d^2 l^2}{n^3 A}\left[\frac{\sin^2(\Delta kl/2)}{(\Delta kl/2)^2}\right] \qquad \textbf{(8.4-11)}$$

Its value under optimum coupling can be derived from (8.4-6) and (8.4-9) and is

$$\kappa_{\text{opt}} = \frac{(\kappa P_\omega)_{\text{opt}}}{(P_\omega)_{\text{opt}}} = \frac{L_i}{S} \qquad \textbf{(8.4-12)}$$

and is thus *independent of the pumping strength*.[7] It follows that once κ is adjusted to its optimum value L_i/S, it remains optimal at any pumping

---

[7] We recall here that the pumping strength in our analysis is represented by the unsaturated gain g_0.

level. This is quite different from the case of optimum coupling in ordinary lasers, in which optimum mirror transmission was found [see (6.5-11)] to depend on the pumping strength.

In closing we may note that apart from its dependence on the crystal length l, the nonlinear coefficient d, and the beam cross section A, κ depends also on the phase mismatch Δkl. Since Δk was shown in (8.3-15) to depend on the direction of propagation in the crystal, we can use the crystal orientation as a means of varying κ.

Numerical example—internal second-harmonic generation. Consider the problem of designing an internal second harmonic generator of the type illustrated in Figure 8-10. The Nd^{3+}:YAG laser is assumed to have the following characteristics:

$\lambda_0 = 1.06\,\mu m = 1.06 \times 10^{-6}$ meter

$\Delta \nu = 1.35 \times 10^{11}$ Hz

Beam diameter (averaged over entire resonator length) $= 2$ mm

$L_i =$ internal loss per pass $= 2 \times 10^{-2}$

$n = 1.5$

The crystal used for second-harmonic generation is $BaNaNb_5O_{15}$, whose second-harmonic coefficient (see Table 8-1) is $d \simeq 1.1 \times 10^{-22}$ MKS units.

Our problem is to calculate the length l of the nonlinear crystal that results in a full conversion of the optimally available fundamental power into the second harmonic at $\lambda_0 = 0.53\,\mu m$. The crystal is assumed to be oriented at the phase-matching condition, so $\Delta k = k^{2\omega} - 2k^{\omega} = 0$.

The optimum coupling parameter is given by (8.4-12) as $\kappa_{opt} = L_i/S$, where S is the saturation power parameter defined by (8.4-3). Using the foregoing data in (8.4-3) gives

$$S = 8 \text{ watts}$$

which, taking $L_i = 2 \times 10^{-2}$, yields

$$\kappa_{opt} = 2.5 \times 10^{-3}$$

Next we use the definition (8.4-11)

$$\kappa = 2\left(\frac{\mu_0}{\epsilon_0}\right)^{3/2} \frac{\omega^2 d^2 l^2}{n^3 A}$$

where we put $\Delta k = 0$ and take the beam diameter at the crystal as $50\,\mu m$. (The crystal can be placed near a beam waist so the diameter is a minimum.) Equating the last expression to $\kappa_{opt} = 2.5 \times 10^{-3}$ using the numerical data given above, and solving for the crystal length, results in

$$l_{opt} = 0.185 \text{ cm}$$

8.5 Photon Model of Second-Harmonic Generation

A very useful point of view and one that follows directly from the quantum
mechanical analysis of nonlinear optical processes [11] is based on the
photon model illustrated in Figure 8-11. According to this picture, the
basic process of second-harmonic generation can be viewed as an annihilation of two photons at ω and a simultaneous creation of a photon at 2ω.
Recalling that a photon has an energy $\hbar\omega$ and a momentum $\hbar\mathbf{k}$, it follows
that if the fundamental conversion process is to conserve momentum as
well as energy that

$$\mathbf{k}^{(2\omega)} = 2\mathbf{k}^{(\omega)} \tag{8.5-1}$$

which is a generalization to three dimensions of the condition $\Delta k = 0$
shown in Section 8.3 to lead to maximum second-harmonic generation.

8.6 Parametric Amplification and Oscillation

Optical parametric amplification in its simplest form involves the transfer
of power from a "pump" wave at ω_3 to waves at frequencies ω_1 and ω_2,
where $\omega_3 = \omega_1 + \omega_2$. It is fundamentally similar to the case of second-
harmonic generation treated in Section 8.3. The only difference is in the
direction of power flow. In second-harmonic generation, power is fed from
the low-frequency optical field at ω to the field at 2ω. In parametric

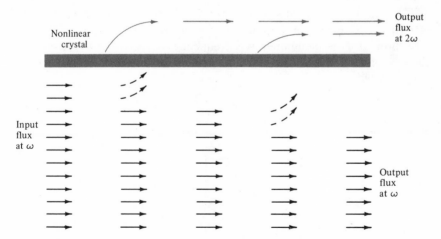

Figure 8-11 Schematic representation of the process of second-harmonic
generation. Input photons (each arrow represents one photon) at ω are
"annihilated" by the nonlinear crystal in pairs, with a new photon at 2ω being
created for each annihilated pair. (Note that in reality both ω and 2ω occupy
the same space inside the crystal.)

amplification, power flow is from the high-frequency field (ω_3) to the low-frequency fields at ω_1 and ω_2. In the special case where $\omega_1 = \omega_2$ we have the exact reverse of second-harmonic generation. This is the case of the so-called "degenerate parametric amplification."

Before we embark on a detailed analysis of the optical case it may be worthwhile to review some of the low-frequency beginnings of parametric oscillation.

Consider a classical nondriven oscillator whose equation of motion is given by

$$\frac{d^2v}{dt^2} + \kappa \frac{dv}{dt} + \omega_0{}^2 v = 0 \qquad (8.6\text{-}1)$$

The variable v may correspond to the excursion of a mass M, which is connected to a spring with a constant $\omega_0{}^2 M$, or to the voltage across a parallel RLC circuit, in which case $\omega_0{}^2 = (LC)^{-1}$ and $\kappa = (RC)^{-1}$. The solution of (8.6-1) is

$$v(t) = v(0) \exp\left[-\frac{\kappa t}{2}\right] \exp\left[\pm i \sqrt{\omega_0{}^2 - \frac{\kappa^2}{4}}\, t\right] \qquad (8.6\text{-}2)$$

that is, a damped sinusoid.

In 1883 Lord Rayleigh [12], investigating parasitic resonances in pipe organs, considered the consequences of the following equation

$$\frac{d^2v}{dt^2} + \kappa \frac{dv}{dt} + (\omega_0{}^2 + 2\alpha \sin \omega_p t)v = 0 \qquad (8.6\text{-}3)$$

This equation may describe an oscillator in which an energy storage parameter (mass or spring constant in the mechanical oscillator, L or C in the RLC oscillator) is modulated at a frequency ω_p. As an example consider the case of the RLC circuit shown in Figure 8-12, in which the capacitance is modulated according to

$$C = C_0\left(1 - \frac{\Delta C}{C_0} \sin \omega_p t\right) \qquad (8.6\text{-}4)$$

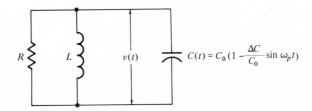

Figure 8-12   A degenerate parametric oscillator with a sinusoidally modulated capacitance.

The equation of the voltage across the RLC circuit is given by (8.6-1) with $\omega_0{}^2 = (LC)^{-1}$.

Using (8.6-4) and assuming $\Delta C \ll C_0$ (8.6-1) becomes

$$\frac{d^2 v}{dt^2} + \kappa \frac{dv}{dt} + \frac{1}{LC_0}\left(1 + \frac{\Delta C}{C_0}\sin \omega_p t\right)v = 0 \qquad \text{(8.6-5)}$$

which, if we make the identification

$$\omega_0{}^2 = \frac{1}{LC_0}, \qquad \alpha = \frac{\omega_0{}^2 \Delta C}{2 C_0} \qquad \text{(8.6-6)}$$

is identical to (8.6-3).

The most important feature of the parametrically driven oscillator described by (8.6-3) is that it is capable of *sustained oscillation* at ω_0. To show this let us assume a solution

$$v = a \cos\left[\omega t + \phi\right] \qquad \text{(8.6-7)}$$

Expanding $\sin \omega_p t$ in (8.6-3) in terms of exponentials, substituting (8.6-7), and neglecting nonsynchronous terms oscillating at $(\omega_p + \omega)$ leads to

$$(\omega_0{}^2 - \omega^2)e^{i(\omega t + \phi)} + i\omega\kappa e^{i(\omega t + \phi)} - i\alpha e^{i[(\omega_p - \omega)t - \phi]} = 0 \qquad \text{(8.6-8)}$$

From (8.6-8) it follows that steady-state oscillation is possible if

$$\omega_p = 2\omega \quad \text{(so that } \omega_p - \omega = \omega)$$

$$\omega = \omega_0 \qquad \phi = 0 \qquad \alpha = \omega\kappa$$

(8.6-9)

or, in words:

The pump frequency ω_p is twice the oscillation frequency ω_0. The oscillation phase[8] is $\phi = 0$ and the strength of the pumping α must satisfy $\alpha = \omega\kappa$. The last condition is referred to as the "start-oscillation" condition or "threshold condition," since it gives the pumping strength (α) needed to overcome the losses (κ) at the oscillation threshold. In the case of the RLC circuit, whose capacitance is pumped according to (8.6-4), the threshold oscillation condition $\alpha = \omega\kappa$ can be written with the aid of (8.6-6) as

$$\frac{\Delta C}{2C_0} = \frac{\kappa}{\omega_0} = \frac{1}{Q} \qquad \text{(8.6-10)}$$

where the quality factor $Q = \omega_0 RC$ is related to the decay rate κ by $\kappa = \omega_0/Q$.

In practice, if the capacitance of the circuit shown in Figure 8-12 is modulated so that condition (8.6-10) is satisfied, the circuit will break into

---

[8] The phase ϕ is relative to that of the pump oscillation as given by (8.6-4).

spontaneous oscillation at a frequency $\omega_0 = \omega_p/2$. This constitutes a transfer of energy from ω_p to $\omega_p/2$.

The physical nature of this transfer may become clearer if we consider the time behavior of the voltage $v(t)$, the charge $q(t)$, and the capacitance $C(t)$ as illustrated in Figure 8-13.

$C(t)$ is a parallel-plate capacitor whose capacitance is periodically varied. Assume first that $C(t)$ is varied as in Figure 8-10(a) by pulling the capacitor plates apart and pushing them together again $[C \propto$ (plate separation)$^{-1}]$. At the same time the circuit is caused to oscillate so that the charge $q(t)$ on the capacitor plates varies as in Figure 8-13(b). Now, according to Figure 8-13(a), when the charge on the plates is a maximum, the plates are pulled apart slightly. The charge cannot change instantaneously, but since work must be done (against the Coulomb attraction of the opposite charges on the capacitor plates) to separate the plates, energy is fed into the capacitor and appears as a sudden increase in the voltage ($v = q/C$, $\mathcal{E} = \frac{1}{2}q^2/C$), as in Figure 8-13(c). One quarter of a period later, the charge and thus the field between the plates is zero and the plates can be returned to their original position with no energy expenditure. At the end of half a cycle, the charge has reversed sign and is again a maximum, so the plates are pulled apart once more. This process is then repeated many times, causing the total voltage to increase twice in each oscillation cycle. In this way, energy at *twice* the resonant frequency is pumped into the circuit where it appears as an increase in energy of the resonant frequency.

There are two noteworthy features to this degenerate oscillator. First, the frequency of the pump *must* be very nearly twice the resonant frequency of the oscillator for gain to occur, in agreement with the previous conclusions; see (8.6-9). In addition, the phase of the pump relative to the charge on the capacitor plates must be chosen properly. Consider the case where $C(t) = C_0 \pm (\Delta C) \sin (2\omega_0 t)$, as in Figure 8-13(d). If we take the minus sign, which corresponds to the curve, then energy is continuously fed *into* the system as described above. If, however, the pumping phase is inverted (that is, the plus sign), then the capacitor plates are pushed together when the charge is a maximum, thus performing work, giving up energy, and decreasing the total voltage. Any initial oscillations that may be present will be damped out. The phase condition ($\phi = 0$) agrees with the second of Equations (8.6-9).

To make a connection between the lumped-circuit parametric oscillator and the optical nonlinearity discussed in (8.1-14) we show that the (time) modulation of a capacitance at some frequency ω_p which was shown to give rise to oscillation at $\omega_p/2$ is formally equivalent to applying a field at ω_p to a nonlinear dielectric in which the polarization p and the electric field e are related by

$$p = \epsilon_0 \chi e + de^2 \tag{8.6-11}$$

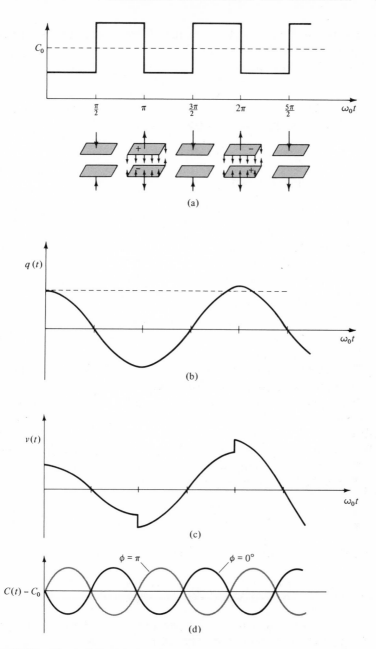

Figure 8-13 Physical model of a capacitively pumped parametric oscillator.
(**a**) Square-wave capacitance variation at twice the circuit oscillation
frequency. (Also shown is the motion of the capacitor plates, the charge, and
the forces on the plates.) (**b**) The charge on one of the capacitor plates. (**c**) The
voltage across the circuit. (**d**) Variation of the capacitance $C(t)$ at two phases
relative to that of the charge.

This can be done by considering a parallel-plate capacitance of area A and separation s which is filled with a medium whose polarization is given by (8.6-11). Using the relations[9]

$$d(t) = \epsilon_0 e(t) + p(t) = \epsilon e(t) \tag{8.6-12}$$

the dielectric constant ϵ can be written as

$$\epsilon = \epsilon_0(1 + \chi) + de$$

and the capacitance $C = \epsilon A/s$ as

$$C = \frac{\epsilon_0(1 + \chi)A}{s} + \frac{Ad}{s} e \tag{8.6-13}$$

If the electric field is given by

$$e = -E_0 \sin \omega_p t$$

the capacitance becomes

$$C = \frac{\epsilon_0(1 + \chi)A}{s} - \frac{AdE_0}{s} \sin \omega_p t \tag{8.6-14}$$

which is of a form identical to (8.6-4). It follows that the two points of view used to describe parametric processes—the one represented by (8.6-4), in which an energy-storage parameter is modulated, and that in which the electric (or magnetic) response is nonlinear, as in (8.6-11)—are equivalent.

We return now to the basic nonlinear parametric equations (8.2-13) to analyze the case of optical parametric amplification. We find it convenient to introduce a new field variable, defined by

$$A_l \equiv \sqrt{\frac{n_l}{\omega_l}} E_l \qquad l = 1, 2, 3 \tag{8.6-15}$$

so that the power flow per unit area at ω_l is given by

$$\frac{P_l}{A} = \frac{1}{2}\sqrt{\frac{\epsilon_0}{\mu_0}} n_l|E_l|^2 = \frac{1}{2}\sqrt{\frac{\epsilon_0}{\mu_0}} \omega_l|A_l|^2 \tag{8.6-16}$$

If we describe the power flow P_l/A per unit area in terms of the photon flux N_l (photons per square meter per second) we have

$$\frac{P_l}{A} = N_l\hbar\omega_l = \frac{1}{2}\sqrt{\frac{\epsilon_0}{\mu_0}} |A_l|^2\omega_l \tag{8.6-17}$$

---

[9] The electric displacement $d(t)$ should not be confused with the nonlinear constant d in (8.6-11).

so that $|A_l|^2$ is proportional to the photon flux at ω_l. The equations of motion (8.2-13) for the A_l variables become

$$\frac{dA_1}{dz} = -\frac{1}{2}\,\alpha_1 A_1 - \frac{i}{2}\,\lambda A_2^* A_3 e^{-i(\Delta k)z}$$

$$\frac{dA_2^*}{dz} = -\frac{1}{2}\,\alpha_2 A_2^* + \frac{i}{2}\,\lambda A_1 A_3^* e^{i(\Delta k)z} \qquad \textbf{(8.6-18)}$$

$$\frac{dA_3}{dz} = -\frac{1}{2}\,\alpha_3 A_3 - \frac{i}{2}\,\lambda A_1 A_2 e^{i(\Delta k)z}$$

where

$$\Delta k \equiv k_3 - (k_1 + k_2)$$

$$\lambda \equiv d\,\sqrt{\left(\frac{\mu_0}{\epsilon_0}\right)\frac{\omega_1\omega_2\omega_3}{n_1 n_2 n_3}} \qquad \textbf{(8.6-19)}$$

$$\alpha_l \equiv \sigma_l\,\sqrt{\frac{\mu_0}{\epsilon_l}} \qquad l = 1,\,2,\,3$$

The advantage of using the A_l instead of E_l is now apparent since, unlike (8.2-13), relations (8.6-18) involve a single coupling parameter λ.

We will now use (8.6-18) to solve for the field variables $A_1(z)$, $A_2(z)$, and $A_3(z)$ for the case in which three waves with amplitudes $A_1(0)$, $A_2(0)$, and $A_3(0)$ at frequencies ω_1, ω_2, and ω_3, respectively, are incident on a nonlinear crystal at $z = 0$. We take $\omega_3 = \omega_1 + \omega_2$, $\alpha_1 = \alpha_2 = \alpha_3 = 0$ (no losses), and $\Delta k = k_3 - k_1 - k_2 = 0$. In addition, we assume that $\omega_1|A_1(z)|^2$ and $\omega_2|A_2(z)|^2$ remain small compared to $\omega_3 A_3(0)^2$ throughout the interaction region. This last condition, in view of (8.6-17), is equivalent to assuming that the power drained off the "pump" (at ω_3) by the "signal" (ω_1) and idler (ω_2) is negligible compared to the input power at ω_3. This enables us to view $A_3(z)$ as a constant. With the assumptions stated above, equations (8.6-18) become

$$\frac{dA_1}{dz} = -\frac{ig}{2}\,A_2^* \qquad \frac{dA_2^*}{dz} = \frac{ig}{2}\,A_1 \qquad \textbf{(8.6-20)}$$

where

$$g \equiv \lambda A_3(0) = \sqrt{\left(\frac{\mu_0}{\epsilon_0}\right)\frac{\omega_1\omega_2}{n_1 n_2}}\,dE_3(0) \qquad \textbf{(8.6-21)}$$

The solution of the coupled equations (8.6-20) subject to the initial conditions $A_1(z = 0) = A_1(0)$, $A_2(z = 0) = A_2(0)$ is

$$A_1(z) = A_1(0)\cosh\frac{g}{2}\,z - iA_2^*(0)\sinh\frac{g}{2}\,z$$

$$A_2^*(z) = A_2^*(0)\cosh\frac{g}{2}\,z + iA_1(0)\sinh\frac{g}{2}\,z \qquad \textbf{(8.6-22)}$$

Equations (8.6-22) describe the growth of the signal and idler waves under phase-matching conditions. In the case of parametric amplification the input will consist of the pump (ω_3) wave and one of the other two fields, say ω_1. In this case $A_2(0) = 0$, and using the relation $N_i \propto A_i A_i^*$ for the photon flux we obtain from (8.6-22)

$$N_1(z) \propto A_1^*(z) A_1(z) = |A_1(0)|^2 \cosh^2 \frac{gz}{2} \underset{gz \gg 1}{\longrightarrow} \frac{|A_1(0)|^2}{4} e^{gz}$$

$$N_2(z) \propto A_2^*(z) A_2(z) = |A_1(0)|^2 \sinh^2 \frac{gz}{2} \underset{gz \gg 1}{\longrightarrow} \frac{|A_1(0)|^2}{4} e^{gz}$$

(8.6-23)

Thus, for $gz \gg 1$, the photon fluxes at ω_1 and ω_2 grow exponentially. If we limit our attention to the wave at ω_1, it undergoes an amplification by a factor

$$\frac{A_1^*(z) A_1(z)}{A_1^*(0) A_1(0)} \underset{gz \gg 1}{=} \tfrac{1}{4} e^{gz}$$

(8.6-24)

Numerical example—parametric amplification. The magnitude of the gain coefficient g available in a traveling-wave parametric interaction is estimated for the following case involving the use of a LiNbO$_3$ crystal.

$$d_{311} = 5 \times 10^{-23}$$

$$\nu_1 \cong \nu_2 = 3 \times 10^{14}$$

$$P_3 = (\text{pump power}) = 5 \times 10^6 \text{ W/cm}^2$$

$$n_1 \simeq n_2 = 2.2$$

Converting P_3 to $|E_3|^2$ with the use of (8.6-16), and then substituting in (8.6-21), yields

$$g = 0.7 \text{ cm}^{-1}$$

This shows that traveling-wave parametric amplification is not expected to lead to large values of gain except for extremely large pump-power densities. The main attraction of the parametric amplification just described is probably in giving rise to parametric oscillation, which will be described in Section 8.8.

8.7 Phase-Matching in Parametric Amplification

In the preceding section the analysis of parametric amplification assumed that the phase-matching condition

$$k_3 = k_1 + k_2$$

(8.7-1)

is satisfied. It is important to determine the consequences of violating this condition. We start with equations (8.6-18) taking the loss coefficients $\alpha_1 = \alpha_2 = 0$:

$$\frac{dA_1}{dz} = -i\frac{g}{2}\,A_2^*\,e^{-i(\Delta k)z}$$

$$\frac{dA_2^*}{dz} = +i\frac{g}{2}\,A_1\,e^{i(\Delta k)z}$$

(8.7-2)

The solution of (8.7-2) is facilitated by the substitution

$$A_1(z) = m_1 e^{[s-i(\Delta k/2)]z}$$

$$A_2^*(z) = m_2 e^{[s+i(\Delta k/2)]z}$$

(8.7-3)

where m_1 and m_2 are coefficients independent of z. The exponential growth constant s is to be determined. Substitution of (8.7-3) in (8.7-2) leads to

$$\left(s - i\frac{\Delta k}{2}\right)m_1 + i\frac{g}{2}\,m_2 = 0$$

$$-i\frac{g}{2}\,m_1 + \left(s + i\frac{\Delta k}{2}\right)m_2 = 0$$

(8.7-4)

By equating the determinant of the coefficients of m_1 and m_2 in (8.7-4) to zero we obtain the two solutions

$$s_\pm = \pm\tfrac{1}{2}\sqrt{g^2 - (\Delta k)^2} \equiv \pm b$$

(8.7-5)

The general solution of (8.7-2) is the sum of the two independent solutions

$$A_1(z) = m_1^+ e^{[s_+ - i(\Delta k/2)]z} + m_1^- e^{[s_- - i(\Delta k/2)]z}$$

$$A_2^*(z) = m_2^+ e^{[s_+ + i(\Delta k/2)]z} + m_2^- e^{[s_- - i(\Delta k/2)]z}$$

(8.7-6)

The coefficients m_1^+, m_1^-, m_2^+, m_2^- are next determined by requiring that at $z = 0$ the solution (8.7-6) agree with the input amplitudes $A_1(0)$ and $A_2^*(0)$. This leads straightforwardly to the result

$$A_1(z)e^{i(\Delta k/2)z} = A_1(0)\left[\cosh(bz) + \frac{i(\Delta k)}{2b}\sinh(bz)\right]$$
$$- i\frac{g}{2b}\,A_2^*(0)\sinh(bz)$$

(8.7-7)

$$A_2^*(z)e^{-i(\Delta k/2)z} = A_2^*(0)\left[\cosh(bz) - \frac{i(\Delta k)}{2b}\sinh(bz)\right]$$
$$+ i\frac{g}{2b}\,A_1(0)\sinh(bz)$$

The last result reduces, as it should, to (8.6-22) if we put $\Delta k = 0$.

The most noteworthy feature of Equations (8.7-5) and (8.7-7) is that the exponential gain coefficient b is a function of Δk and that unless

$$g \gtreqless \Delta k \qquad \text{(8.7-8)}$$

no sustained growth of the signal (A_1) and idler (A_2) waves is possible, since in this case the cosh and sinh functions in (8.7-7) become

$$\sin \{\tfrac{1}{2}[(\Delta k)^2 - g^2]^{1/2}z\}$$

$$\cos \{\tfrac{1}{2}[(\Delta k)^2 - g^2]^{1/2}z\}$$

respectively, and the energies at ω_1 and ω_2 oscillate as a function of the distance z.

The problem of phase-matching in parametric amplification is fundamentally the same as that in second-harmonic generation. Instead of satisfying the condition (8.3-6), $k^{2\omega} = 2k^\omega$, we have, according to (8.7-1), to satisfy the condition

$$k_3 = k_1 + k_2$$

This is done, as in second-harmonic generation, by using the dependence of the phase velocity of the extraordinary wave in axial crystals on the direction of propagation. In a negative uniaxial crystal ($n_e < n_0$) we can, as an example, choose the signal and idler waves as ordinary while the pump at ω_3 is applied as an extraordinary wave. Using (8.3-11) and the relation $k^\omega = (\omega/c)n^\omega$ the phase-matching condition (8.7-1) is satisfied when all three waves propagate at an angle θ_m to the z (optic) axis where

$$n_e{}^{\omega_3}(\theta_m) = \left[\left(\frac{\cos\theta_m}{n_0{}^{\omega_3}}\right)^2 + \left(\frac{\sin\theta_m}{n_e{}^{\omega_3}}\right)^2\right]^{-1/2} = \frac{\omega_1}{\omega_3}n_0{}^{\omega_1} + \frac{\omega_2}{\omega_3}n_0{}^{\omega_2} \qquad \text{(8.7-9)}$$

8.8 Parametric Oscillation[10]

In the two preceding sections we have demonstrated that a pump wave at ω_3 can cause a simultaneous amplification in a nonlinear medium of "signal" and "idler" waves at frequencies ω_1 and ω_2, respectively, where $\omega_3 = \omega_1 + \omega_2$. If the nonlinear crystal is placed within an optical resonator (as shown in Figure 8.11) that provides resonances for the signal or idler waves (or both), the parametric gain will, at some threshold pumping intensity, cause a simultaneous oscillation at the signal and idler frequencies. The threshold pumping corresponds to the point at which the parametric gain just balances the losses of the signal and idler waves. This is the physical basis of the optical parametric oscillator. Its practical importance

---

[10] See References [13]–[15].

derives from its ability to convert the power output of the pump laser to power at the signal and idler frequencies which, as will be shown below, can be tuned continuously over large ranges.

To analyze this situation we return to Equations (8.6-18). We take $\Delta k = 0$ and neglect the depletion of the pump waves, so $A_3(z) = A_3(0)$. The result is

$$\frac{dA_1}{dz} = -\frac{1}{2}\alpha_1 A_1 - i\frac{g}{2}A_2^*$$

$$\frac{dA_2^*}{dz} = -\frac{1}{2}\alpha_2 A_2^* + i\frac{g}{2}A_1$$

(8.8-1)

where, as in (8.6-21),

$$g \equiv \sqrt{\left(\frac{\mu_0}{\epsilon_0}\right)\frac{\omega_1\omega_2}{n_1 n_2}}\, dE_3(0)$$

$$\alpha_{1,2} \equiv \sigma_{1,2}\sqrt{\frac{\mu_0}{\epsilon_{1,2}}}$$

(8.8-2)

Equations (8.8-1) describe traveling-wave parametric interaction. We will use them to describe the interaction inside a resonator such as the one shown in Figure 8-14. This procedure seems plausible if we think of propagation inside an optical resonator as a folded optical path. The magnitude of the spatial distributed loss constants α_1 and α_2 must then be chosen so that they account for the actual losses in the resonator. The latter will include losses caused by the less than perfect reflection at the mirrors, as well as distributed loss in the nonlinear crystal and that due to diffraction.[11]

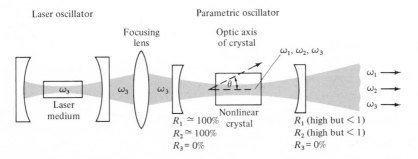

Figure 8-14   Schematic diagram of an optical parametric oscillator in which the laser output at ω_3 is used as the pump, giving rise to oscillations at ω_1 and ω_2 (where $\omega_3 = \omega_1 + \omega_2$) in an optical cavity that contains the nonlinear crystal and resonates at ω_1 and ω_2.

---

[11] The effective loss constant α_i is chosen so that $\exp(-\alpha_i l)$ is the total attenuation in intensity per resonator pass at ω_i, where l is the crystal length.

If the parametric gain is sufficiently high to overcome the losses, steady-state oscillation results. When this is the case,

$$\frac{dA_1}{dz} = \frac{dA_2^*}{dz} = 0 \qquad \text{(8.8-3)}$$

and thus the power gained via the parametric interaction just balances the losses.

Putting $d/dz = 0$ in (8.8-1) gives

$$-\frac{\alpha_1}{2} A_1 - i\frac{g}{2} A_2^* = 0$$

$$i\frac{g}{2} A_1 - \frac{\alpha_2}{2} A_2^* = 0 \qquad \text{(8.8-4)}$$

The condition for nontrivial solutions for A_1 and A_2^* is that the determinant at (8.8-4) vanish; that is,

$$\det \begin{vmatrix} -\dfrac{\alpha_1}{2} & -i\dfrac{g}{2} \\ i\dfrac{g}{2} & -\dfrac{\alpha_2}{2} \end{vmatrix} = 0$$

and, therefore,

$$g^2 = \alpha_1 \alpha_2 \qquad \text{(8.8-5)}$$

This is the *threshold condition* for *parametric oscillation*.

If we choose to express the mode losses at ω_1 and ω_2 by the quality factors Q_1 and Q_2, respectively, we have[12]

$$\alpha_i = \frac{\omega_i n_i}{Q_i c_0} \qquad \text{(8.8-6)}$$

By the use of (8.8-2), condition (8.8-5) can be written as

$$\frac{d(E_3)_t}{\sqrt{\epsilon_1 \epsilon_2}} = \frac{1}{\sqrt{Q_1 Q_2}} \qquad \text{(8.8-7)}$$

where $(E_3)_t$ is the value of E_3 at threshold. This relation can be shown to be formally analogous to that obtained in (8.6-10) for the lumped-circuit parametric oscillator. According to (8.6-14), $\Delta C/C_0 = dE/\epsilon$; therefore, apart from a factor of two, if we put $Q_1 = Q_2$ and $\epsilon_1 = \epsilon_2$, Equation (8.8-7) is the same as (8.6-10).

Another useful form of the threshold relation results from representing the quality factor Q in terms of the (effective) mirror reflectivities as in (4.6-3). If, furthermore, we express E_3 in terms of the power flow per unit area according to

$$E_3{}^2 = 2\frac{P_3}{A} \sqrt{\frac{\mu_0}{\epsilon_0 n_3{}^2}}$$

---

[12] This relation follows from recognizing that the temporal decay rate $\sigma = \omega/Q$ is related to α by $\sigma = \alpha c = \alpha c_0/n$.

we can rewrite (8.8-7) as

$$\left(\frac{P_3}{A}\right)_t = \frac{1}{2}\left(\frac{\epsilon_0}{\mu_0}\right)^{3/2} \frac{n_1 n_2 n_3 (1 - R_1)(1 - R_2)}{\omega_1 \omega_2 l_R^2 d^2} \tag{8.8-8}$$

where l_R is the length of the resonator.

Numerical example—parametric oscillation threshold. Let us estimate the threshold pump requirement P_3/A (watts per square centimeter) of a parametric oscillator of the kind shown in Figure 8-14, which utilizes an LiNbO$_3$ crystal. We use the following set of parameters:

$$(1 - R_1) = (1 - R_2) = 2 \times 10^{-2} \text{ (that is, total loss per}$$
$$\text{pass at } \omega_1 \text{ and } \omega_2 = 2 \text{ percent)}$$

$$(\lambda_0)_1 = (\lambda_0)_2 = 1 \ \mu\text{m}$$

$$l_R = 0.5 \text{ meter}$$

$$n_1 = n_2 = n_3 = 1.5$$

$$d_{311}(\text{LiNbO}_3) = 5 \times 10^{-23}$$

Substitution in (8.8-8) yields

$$\left(\frac{P_3}{A}\right)_t = 0.52 \text{ W/cm}^2$$

This is a modest amount of power so that the example helps us appreciate the attractiveness of optical parametric oscillation as a means for generating coherent optical frequency at new optical frequencies.

8.9 Frequency Tuning in Parametric Oscillation

We have shown above that the pair of signals (ω_1) and idler frequencies that are caused to oscillate by parametric pumping at ω_3 satisfy the condition $k_3 = k_1 + k_2$. Using $k_i = \omega_i n_i / C_0$ we can write it as

$$\omega_3 n_3 = \omega_1 n_1 + \omega_2 n_2 \tag{8.9-1}$$

In a crystal the indices of refraction generally depend as shown in Section 8-3, on the frequency, crystal orientation (if the wave is extraordinary), electric field (in electrooptic crystals), and on the temperature. If, as an example, we change the crystal orientation in the oscillator shown in Figure 8-14, the oscillation frequencies ω_1 and ω_2 will change so as to compensate for the change in indices, and thus condition (8.9-1) will be satisfied at the new frequencies.

To be specific, we consider the case of a parametric oscillator pumped by an extraordinary beam at a fixed frequency ω_3. The signal (ω_1) and idler (ω_2) are ordinary waves. At some crystal orientation θ_0 the oscillation takes place at frequencies ω_{10} and ω_{20}. Let the indices of refraction at ω_{10}, ω_{20}, and ω_{30} under those conditions be n_{10}, n_{20}, and n_{30}, respectively. We want to find the change in ω_1 and ω_2 due to a small change $\Delta\theta$ in the crystal orientation.

From (8.9-1) we have, at $\theta = \theta_0$,

$$\omega_3 n_{30} = \omega_{10} n_{10} + \omega_{20} n_{20} \tag{8.9-2}$$

After the crystal orientation has been changed from θ_0 to $\theta_0 + \Delta\theta$, the following changes occur:

$$n_{30} \rightarrow n_{30} + \Delta n_3$$

$$n_{10} \rightarrow n_{10} + \Delta n_1$$

$$n_{20} \rightarrow n_{20} + \Delta n_2$$

$$\omega_{10} \rightarrow \omega_{10} + \Delta\omega_1$$

Since $\omega_1 + \omega_2 = \omega_3 = $ constant,

$$\omega_{20} \rightarrow \omega_{20} + \Delta\omega_2 = \omega_{20} - \Delta\omega_1$$

that is, $\Delta\omega_2 = -\Delta\omega_1$. Since (8.9-1) must be satisfied at $\theta = \theta_0 + \Delta\theta$, we have

$$\omega_3(n_{30} + \Delta n_3) = (\omega_{10} + \Delta\omega_1)(n_{10} + \Delta n_1) + (\omega_{20} - \Delta\omega_1)(n_{20} + \Delta n_2)$$

Neglecting the second-order terms $\Delta n_1 \Delta\omega_1$ and $\Delta n_2 \Delta\omega_1$ and using (8.9-8), we obtain

$$\Delta\omega_1 \Big|_{\substack{\omega_1 \simeq \omega_{10} \\ \omega_2 \simeq \omega_{20}}} = \frac{\omega_3 \Delta n_3 - \omega_{10} \Delta n_1 - \omega_{20} \Delta n_2}{n_{10} - n_{20}} \tag{8.9-3}$$

According to our starting hypotheses the pump is an extraordinary ray; therefore, according to (1.4-12), it depends on the orientation θ, giving

$$\Delta n_3 = \frac{\partial n_3}{\partial \theta}\Big|_{\theta_0} \Delta\theta \tag{8.9-4}$$

The signal and idler are ordinary rays, so their indices depend on the frequencies but not on the direction. It follows that

$$\Delta n_1 = \frac{\partial n_1}{\partial \omega_1}\Big|_{\omega_{10}} \Delta\omega_1$$

$$\Delta n_2 = \frac{\partial n_2}{\partial \omega_2}\Big|_{\omega_{20}} \Delta\omega_2 \tag{8.9-5}$$

Using the last two equations in (8.9-9) results in

$$\frac{\partial \omega_1}{\partial \theta} = \frac{\omega_3(\partial n_3/\partial\theta)}{(n_{10} - n_{20}) + [\omega_{10}(\partial n_1/\partial\omega_1) - \omega_{20}(\partial n_2/\partial\omega_2)]} \tag{8.9-6}$$

for the rate of change of the oscillation frequency with respect to the crystal orientation. Using (1.4-12) and the relation $d(1/x^2) = -(2/x^3)\, dx$, we obtain

$$\frac{\partial n_3}{\partial \theta} = -\frac{n_3^{\,3}}{2} \sin (2\theta) \left[\left(\frac{1}{n_e^{\omega_3}} \right)^2 - \left(\frac{1}{n_o^{\omega_3}} \right)^2 \right]$$

which, when substituted in (8.9-12), gives

$$\frac{\partial \omega_1}{\partial \theta} = \frac{-\dfrac{1}{2}\, \omega_3 n_{30}^{\,3} \left[\left(\dfrac{1}{n_e^{\omega_3}} \right)^2 - \left(\dfrac{1}{n_o^{\omega_3}} \right)^2 \right] \sin (2\theta)}{(n_{10} - n_{20}) + \left(\omega_{10} \dfrac{\partial n_1}{\partial \omega_1} - \omega_{20} \dfrac{\partial n_2}{\partial \omega_2} \right)} \tag{8.9-7}$$

An experimental curve showing the dependence of the signal and idler frequencies on θ in $NH_4H_2PO_4$ (ADP) is shown in Figure 8-15. Also shown is a theoretical curve based on a quadratic approximation of (8.9-1), which was plotted using the dispersion (that is, n versus ω) data of ADP; see Reference [16].

Reasoning similar to that used to derive the angle-tuning expression (8.9-7) can be applied to determine the dependence of the oscillation

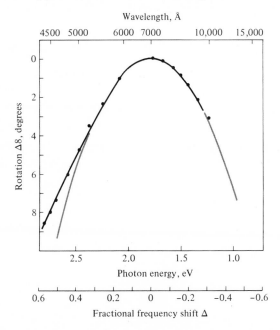

Figure 8-15   Dependence of the signal (ω_1) frequency on the angle between the pump propagation direction and the optic axis of the ADP crystal. The angle θ is measured with respect to the angle for which $\omega_1 = \omega_3/2$. $\Delta = (\omega_1 - \omega_3/2)/(\omega_3/2)$. (After Reference [16].)

frequency on temperature. Here we need to know the dependence of the various indices on temperature. This is discussed further in Problem 8-6. An experimental temperature-tuning curve is shown in Figure 8-16.

8.10 Power Output and Pump Saturation in Optical Parametric Oscillators

In the treatment of the laser oscillator in Section 6.5 we showed that in the steady state the gain could not exceed the threshold value regardless of the intensity of the pump. A closely related phenomenon exists in the case of parametric oscillation. The pump field E_3 gives rise to amplification of the signal and idler waves. When E_3 reaches its critical (threshold) value given by (8.8-7) the gain just equals the losses and the device is on the threshold of oscillation. If the pump field E_3 is increased beyond its threshold value the gain can no longer follow it and must be "clamped" at its threshold value. This follows from the fact that if the gain constant g exceeds its threshold value (8.8-5), a steady-state solution is no longer

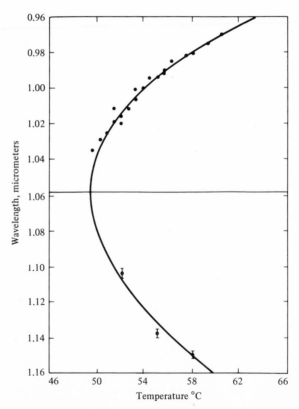

Figure 8-16 Signal and idler wavelength as a function of the temperature of the oscillator crystal. (After Reference [14].)

possible and the signal and idler intensities will increase with time. Since the gain g is proportional to the pump field E_3, it follows that above threshold the *pump field inside* the optical resonator must saturate at its level just prior to oscillation. As power is conserved it follows that any additional pump power input must be diverted into power at the signal and idler fields. Since $\omega_3 = \omega_1 + \omega_2$, it follows that for each input pump photon above threshold we generate one photon at the signal (ω_1) and one at the idler (ω_2) frequencies, so [17]

$$\frac{P_1}{\omega_1} = \frac{P_2}{\omega_2} = \frac{(P_3)_t}{\omega_3}\left[\frac{P_3}{(P_3)_t} - 1\right] \qquad \textbf{(8.10-1)}$$

The last argument shows that in principle the parametric oscillator can attain high efficiencies. This requires operation well above threshold, and thus $P_3/(P_3)_t \gg 1$. These considerations are borne out by actual experiments [18].

Figure 8-17 shows experimental confirmation of the phenomenon of

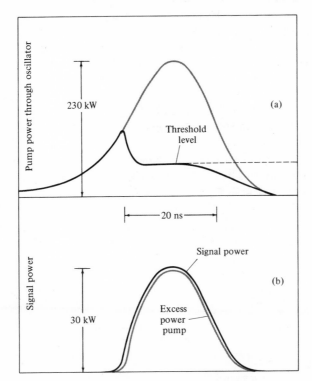

Figure 8-17   Power levels and pumping in a parametric oscillator.
(**a**) Waveforms of P_3, the pump power passing through the oscillator. The dashed waveform was obtained when the crystal was rotated so that oscillation did not occur; the solid waveform was obtained when oscillation took place.
(**b**) Signal power and excess pump power. The dashed waveform is the normalized difference between the waveforms in (**a**). (After Reference [18].)

pump saturation; see References [17] and [20]. After a transient buildup the pump intensity inside the resonator settles down to its threshold value.

Figure 8-17(b) shows that the signal power is proportional to the excess (above threshold) pump input power. This is in agreement with Equation (8.10-1).

8.11 Frequency Up-Conversion

Parametric interactions in a crystal can be used to convert a signal from a "low" frequency ω_1 to a "high" frequency ω_3 by mixing it with a strong laser beam at ω_2, where

$$\omega_1 + \omega_2 = \omega_3 \tag{8.11-1}$$

Using the quantum mechanical photon picture described in Section 8-5 we can consider the basic process taking place in frequency up-conversion as one in which a signal (ω_1) photon and a pump (ω_2) photon are annihilated while, simultaneously, one photon at ω_3 is generated; see References [11] and [21]–[24]. Since a photon energy is $\hbar\omega$, conservation of energy dictates that $\omega_3 = \omega_1 + \omega_2$ and, in a manner similar to (8.5-1), the conservation of momentum leads to the relationship

$$\mathbf{k}_3 = \mathbf{k}_1 + \mathbf{k}_2 \tag{8.11-2}$$

between the wave vectors at the three frequencies. This point of view also suggests that the number of output photons at ω_3 cannot exceed the input number of photons at ω_1.

The experimental situation is demonstrated by Figure 8-18. The ω_1 and ω_2 beams are combined in a partially transmissive mirror (or prism), so they traverse together (in near parallelism) the length l of a crystal possessing nonlinear optical characteristics.

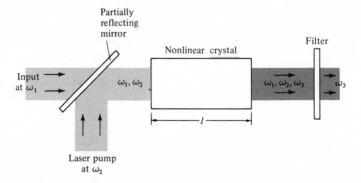

Figure 8-18 Parametric up-conversion in which a signal at ω_2 and a strong laser beam at ω_2 combine in a nonlinear crystal to generate a beam at the sum frequency $\omega_3 = \omega_1 + \omega_2$.

The analysis of frequency up-conversion starts with Equations (8.6-18). Assuming negligible depletion of the pump wave A_2 and no losses ($\alpha = 0$) at ω_1 and ω_3, we can write the first and third of these equations as

$$\frac{dA_1}{dz} = -i\frac{g}{2} A_3$$

$$\frac{dA_3}{dz} = -i\frac{g}{2} A_1$$

(8.11-3)

where, using (8.6-15) and (8.6-19) and choosing without loss of generality the pump phase as zero so that $A_2(0) = A_2^*(0)$,

$$g \equiv \sqrt{\frac{\omega_1\omega_3}{n_1 n_3} \left(\frac{\mu_0}{\epsilon_0}\right)} dE_2$$

(8.11-4)

where E_2 is the amplitude of the electric field of the pump laser. Taking the input waves with (complex) amplitudes $A_1(0)$ and $A_3(0)$, the general solution of (8.11-3) is

$$A_1(z) = A_1(0) \cos\left(\frac{g}{2} z\right) - iA_3(0) \sin\left(\frac{g}{2} z\right)$$

$$A_3(z) = A_3(0) \cos\left(\frac{g}{2} z\right) - iA_1(0) \sin\left(\frac{g}{2} z\right)$$

(8.11-5)

In the case of a single (low) frequency input at ω_1, we have $A_3(0) = 0$. In this case,

$$|A_1(z)|^2 = |A_1(0)|^2 \cos^2\left(\frac{g}{2} z\right)$$

$$|A_3(z)|^2 = |A_1(0)|^2 \sin^2\left(\frac{g}{2} z\right)$$

(8.11-6)

therefore,

$$|A_1(z)|^2 + |A_3(z)|^2 = |A_1(0)|^2$$

In the discussion following (8.6-17) we pointed out that $|A_l(z)|^2$ is proportional to the photon flux (photons per square meter per second) at ω_l. Using this fact we may interpret (8.11-6) as stating that the photon flux at ω_1 plus that at ω_3 at any plane z is a constant equal to the input ($z = 0$) flux at ω_1. If we rewrite (8.11-6) in terms of powers, we obtain

$$P_1(z) = P_1(0) \cos^2\left(\frac{g}{2} z\right)$$

$$P_3(z) = \frac{\omega_3}{\omega_1} P_1(0) \sin^2\left(\frac{g}{2} z\right)$$

(8.11-7)

In a crystal of length l, the conversion efficiency is thus

$$\frac{P_3(l)}{P_1(0)} = \frac{\omega_3}{\omega_1} \sin^2\left(\frac{g}{2} l\right)$$

(8.11-8)

and can have a maximum value of ω_3/ω_1, corresponding to the case in which all the input (ω_1) photons are converted to ω_3 photons.

In most practical situations the conversion efficiency is small (see the following numerical example) so using $\sin x \simeq x$ for $x \ll 1$, we get

$$\frac{P_3(l)}{P_1(0)} \simeq \frac{\omega_3}{\omega_1}\left(\frac{g^2 l^2}{4}\right)$$

which, by the use of (8.11-4) and (8.6-16), can be written as

$$\frac{P_3(l)}{P_1(0)} \simeq \frac{\omega_3{}^2 l^2 d^2}{2n_1 n_2 n_3}\left(\frac{\mu_0}{\epsilon_0}\right)^{3/2}\left(\frac{P_2}{A}\right) \tag{8.11-9}$$

where A is the cross-sectional area of the interaction region.

Numerical example—frequency up-conversion. The main practical interest in parametric frequency up-conversion stems from the fact that it offers a means of detecting infrared radiation (a region where detectors are either inefficient, very slow, or require cooling to cryogenic temperatures) by converting the frequency into the visible or near-visible part of the spectrum. The radiation can then be detected by means of efficient and fast detectors such as photomultipliers or photodiodes; see References [22]–[25].

As an example of this application, consider the problem of up-converting a 10.6-μm signal, originating in a CO_2 laser to 0.96 μm by mixing it with the 1.06-μm output of an Nd^{3+}:YAG laser. The nonlinear crystal chosen for this application has to have low losses at 1.06 μm and 10.6 μm, as well as at 0.96 μm. In addition, its birefringence has to be such as to make phase matching possible. The crystal proustite (Ag_3AsS_3) listed in Table 8-1 meets these requirements [25].

Using the data

$$\frac{P_{1.06\,\mu m}}{A} = 10^4 \text{ W/cm}^2 = 10^8 \text{ W/m}^2$$

$$l = 10^{-2} \text{ meter}$$

$n_1 \simeq n_2 \simeq n_3 = 2.6$ (an average number based on the data of
Reference [25])

$d_{\text{eff}} = 1.1 \times 10^{-21}$ (taken conservatively as a little less than half the value given in Table 8.1 for d_{22})

we obtain, from (8.11-9),

$$\frac{P_{\lambda=0.96\,\mu m}(l = 1 \text{ cm})}{P_{\lambda=10.6\,\mu m}(l = 0)} = 6 \times 10^{-2}$$

indicating a useful amount of conversion efficiency.

■ PROBLEMS

8-1 Show that if θ_m is the phase-matching angle for an ordinary wave at ω and an extraordinary wave at 2ω, then

$$\Delta k(\theta)l|_{\theta \simeq \theta_m} = -\frac{2\omega l}{c_0} \sin(2\theta_m) \frac{(n_e{}^{2\omega})^{-2} - (n_o{}^{2\omega})^{-2}}{2(n_o{}^{\omega})^{-3}} (\theta - \theta_m)$$

8-2 Derive the expression for the phase-matching angle of a parametric amplifier using KDP in which two of the waves are extraordinary while the third is ordinary. Which of the three waves (that is, signal, idler, or pump) would you choose as ordinary? Can this type of phase-matching be accomplished with $\omega_3 = 10,000 \text{ cm}^{-1}$, $\omega_1 = \omega_2 = 5000 \text{ cm}^{-1}$? If so, what is θ_m?

8-3 Show that Equations (8.6-22) are consistent with the fact that the increases in the photon flux at ω_1 and ω_2 are identical—that is, that $A_1^*(z)A_1(z) - A_1^*(0)A_1(0) = A_2^*(z)A_2(z) - A_2^*(0)A_2(0)$.

8-4 Complete the missing steps in the derivation of Equation (8.7-7).

8-5 Show that the voltage $v(t)$ across an open-circuited parallel RLC circuit obeys

$$\frac{d^2v}{dt^2} + \frac{1}{RC}\frac{dv}{dt} + \frac{1}{LC}v = 0$$

and is thus of the form of Equation (8.6-1).

8-6 Consider a parametric oscillator setup such as that shown in Figure 8.9. The crystal orientation angle is θ, its temperature is T, and the signal and idler frequencies are ω_{10} and ω_{20}, respectively, with $\omega_{10} + \omega_{20} = \omega_3$. Show that a small temperature change ΔT causes the signal frequency to change by

$$\Delta\omega_1 = \Delta T \times \left\{ \omega_3 \left[\cos^2\theta \left(\frac{n_e{}^{\omega_3}(\theta)}{n_o{}^{\omega_3}}\right)^3 \frac{\partial n_o{}^{\omega_3}}{\partial T} + \sin^2\theta \left(\frac{n_e{}^{\omega_3}(\theta)}{n_e{}^{\omega_3}}\right)^3 \frac{\partial n_e{}^{\omega_3}}{\partial T} \right] \right. $$
$$\left. - \omega_{10}\frac{\partial n_o{}^{\omega_1}}{\partial T} - \omega_{20}\frac{\partial n_o{}^{\omega_2}}{\partial T} \right\} \times \frac{1}{n_{10} - n_{20}}$$

The pump is taken as an extraordinary ray, whereas the signal and idler are ordinary. [*Hint:* The starting point is Equation (8.9-3), which is valid regardless of the nature of the perturbation.]

8-7 Using the published dispersion data of proustite (Reference [25]), calculate the maximum angular deviation of the input beam at ν_1 (from parallelism with the pump beam at ν_2) that results in a reduction by a factor of 2 in the conversion efficiency. [*Hint:* A proper choice must be made for the polarizations at ω_1, ω_2, and ω_3 so that phase-matching can be achieved along some angle.] The maximum angular deviation is that for which

$$\frac{\sin^2 [\Delta k(\theta)l/2]}{[\Delta k(\theta)l/2]^2} = \frac{1}{2}$$

where, at the phase-matching angle θ_m, $\Delta k(\theta_m) = 0$. Approximate the dispersion data by a Taylor-series expansion about the nominal ($\Delta k = 0$) frequencies.

8-8   Using the dispersion data of Reference [25], discuss what happens to phase-matching due to a deviation of the input frequency from the nominal ($\Delta k = 0$) ν_{10} value. Derive an expression for the spectral width of the output in the case where the input spectral density (power per unit frequency) in the vicinity of ν_{10} is uniform. [*Hint:* Use a Taylor-series expansion of the dispersion data about the phase-matching ($\Delta k = 0$) frequencies to obtain an expression for $\Delta k(\nu_3)$.] Define the output spectral width as twice the frequency deviation at which the output is half its maximum ($\Delta k = 0$) value.

■ REFERENCES

[1] Miller, R. C., "Optical second harmonic generation in piezoelectric crystals," *Appl. Phys. Letters*, vol. 5, p. 17, 1964.

[2] Garret, C. G. B., and F. N. H. Robinson, "Miller's phenomenological rule for computing nonlinear susceptibilities," *IEEE J. Quantum Electron.*, vol. QE-2, p. 328, 1966.

[3] See, for example, J. F. Nye, *Physical Properties of Crystals*. New York: Oxford, 1957.

[4] Armstrong, J. A., N. Bloembergen, J. Ducuing, and P. S. Pershan, "Interactions between light waves in a nonlinear dielectric," *Phys. Rev.*, vol. 127, p. 1918, 1962.

[5] Franken, P. A., A. E. Hill, C. W. Peters, and G. Weinreich, "Generation of optical harmonics," *Phys. Rev. Letters*, vol. 7, p. 118, 1961.

[6] Maker, P. D., R. W. Terhune, M. Nisenoff, and C. M. Savage, "Effects of dispersion and focusing on the production of optical harmonics," *Phys. Rev. Letters*, vol. 8, p. 21, 1962.

[7] Giordmaine, J. A., "Mixing of light beams in crystals," *Phys. Rev. Letters*, vol. 8, p. 19, 1962.

[8] Zernike, F., Jr., "Refractive indices of ammonium dihydrogen phosphate and potassium dihydrogen phosphate between 2000 Å and 1.5 μ," *J. Opt. Soc. Am.*, vol. 54, p. 1215, 1964.

[9] Geusic, J. E., H. J. Levinstein, S. Singh, R. G. Smith, and L. G. Van Uitert, "Continuous 0.53-μm solid-state source using $Ba_2NaNb_5O_{15}$," *IEEE J. Quantum Electron.*, vol. QE-4, p. 352, 1968.

[10] Ashkin, A., G. D. Boyd, and J. M. Dziedzic, "Observation of continuous second harmonic generation with gas lasers," *Phys. Rev. Letters*, vol. 11, p. 14, 1963.

[11] Yariv, A., *Quantum Electronics*. New York: Wiley, 1967.

[12] Lord, Rayleigh, "On maintained vibrations," *Phil. Mag.*, vol. 15, ser. 5, pt. I, p. 229, 1883.

[13] Parametric amplification was first demonstrated by C. C. Wang and G. W. Racette, "Measurement of parametric gain accompanying optical difference frequency generation," *Appl. Phys. Letters*, vol. 6, p. 169, 1965.

[14] The first demonstration of optical parametric oscillation is that of J. A. Giordmaine and R. C. Miller, "Tunable optical parametric oscillation in $LiNbO_3$ at optical frequencies," *Phys. Rev. Letters*, vol. 14, p. 973, 1965.

[15] Some of the early theoretical analyses of optical parametric oscillation are attributable to R. H. Kingston, "Parametric amplification and oscillation at optical frequencies," *Proc. IRE*, vol. 50, p. 472, 1962, and N. M. Kroll, "Parametric amplification in spatially extended media and applications to the design of tunable oscillators at optical frequencies," *Phys. Rev.*, vol. 127, p. 1207, 1962.

[16] Magde, D., and H. Mahr, "Study in ammonium dihydrogen phosphate of spontaneous parametric interaction tunable from 4400 to 16000 Å," *Phys. Rev. Letters*, vol. 18, p. 905, 1967.

[17] Yariv, A., and W. H. Louisell, "Theory of the optical parametric oscillator," *IEEE J. Quantum Electron.*, vol. QE-2, p. 418, 1966.

[18] Bjorkholm, J. E., "Efficient optical parametric oscillation using doubly and singly resonant cavities," *Appl. Phys. Letters*, vol. 13, p. 53, 1968.

[19] Kreuzer, L. B., "High-efficiency optical parametric oscillation and power limiting in $LiNbO_3$," *Appl. Phys. Letters*, vol. 13, p. 57, 1968.

[20] Siegman, A. E., "Nonlinear optical effects: An optical power limiter," *Appl. Opt.*, vol. 1, p. 739, 1962.

[21] Louisell, W. H., A. Yariv, and A. E. Siegman, "Quantum fluctuations and noise in parametric processes," *Phys. Rev.*, vol. 124, p. 1646, 1961.

[22] Johnson, F. M., and J. A. Durado, "Frequency up-conversion," *Laser Focus*, vol. 3, p. 31, 1967.

[23] Midwinter, J. E., and J. Warner, "Up-conversion of near infrared to visible radiation in lithium-meta-niobate," *J. Appl. Phys.*, vol. 38, p. 519, 1967.

[24] Warner, J., "Photomultiplier detection of 10.6 μ radiation using optical up-conversion in proustite," *Appl. Phys. Letters*, vol. 12, p. 222, 1968.

[25] Hulme, K. F., O. Jones, P. H. Davies, and M. V. Hobden, "Synthetic proustite (Ag_3AsS_3): A new material for optical mixing," *Appl. Phys. Letters*, vol. 10, p. 133, 1967.

9

The Modulation of Optical Radiation

9.0 Introduction

In Chapter 1 we treated the propagation of electromagnetic waves in anisotropic crystal media. It was shown how the properties of the propagating wave can be determined from the index ellipsoid surface.

In this chapter we consider the problem of propagation of optical radiation in crystals in the presence of an applied electric field. We find that in certain types of crystals it is possible to effect a change in the index of refraction which is proportional to the field. This is the linear electrooptic effect. It affords a convenient and widely used means of controlling the intensity or phase of the propagating radiation. This modulation is used in an ever expanding number of applications including: the impression of information onto optical beams, Q-switching of lasers (Sec. 6.7) for generation of giant optical pulses, mode locking, and optical beam deflection. Some of these applications will be discussed further in this chapter.

9.1   The Electrooptic Effect

In Chapter 1 we found that, given a direction in a crystal, in general two possible linearly polarized modes exist; the so-called rays of propagation. Each mode possesses a unique direction of polarization (that is, direction of **D**) and a corresponding index of refraction (that is, a velocity of propagation). The mutually orthogonal polarization directions and the indices of the two rays are found most easily by using the index ellipsoid

$$\frac{x^2}{n_x{}^2} + \frac{y^2}{n_y{}^2} + \frac{z^2}{n_z{}^2} = 1 \qquad (9.1\text{-}1)$$

where the directions x, y, and z are the principal dielectric axes—that is, the directions in the crystal along which **D** and **E** are parallel. The existence of two "ordinary" and "extraordinary" rays with different indices of refraction is called birefringence.

The linear electrooptic effect is the change in the indices of the ordinary and extraordinary rays that is caused by and is proportional to an applied electric field. This effect exists only in crystals that do not possess inversion symmetry.[1] This statement can be justified as follows: Assume that in a crystal possessing an inversion symmetry, the application of an electric field E along some direction causes a change $\Delta n_1 = sE$ in the index, where s is a constant characterizing the linear electrooptic effect. If the direction of the field is reversed, the change in the index is given by $\Delta n_2 = s(-E)$, but because of the inversion symmetry the two directions are physically equivalent, so $\Delta n_1 = \Delta n_2$. This requires that $s = -s$, which is possible only for $s = 0$, so no linear electrooptic effect can exist. The division of all crystal classes into those that do and those that do not possess an inversion symmetry is an elementary consideration in crystallography and this information is widely tabulated [1].

Since the propagation characteristics in crystals are fully described by means of the index ellipsoid (9.1-1), the effect of an electric field on the propagation is expressed most conveniently by giving the changes in the constants $1/n_x{}^2$, $1/n_y{}^2$, $1/n_z{}^2$ of the index ellipsoid.

Following convention [2], we take the equation of the index ellipsoid in the presence of an electric field as

$$\left(\frac{1}{n^2}\right)_1 x^2 + \left(\frac{1}{n^2}\right)_2 y^2 + \left(\frac{1}{n^2}\right)_3 z^2 + 2\left(\frac{1}{n^2}\right)_4 yz$$
$$+ 2\left(\frac{1}{n^2}\right)_5 xz + 2\left(\frac{1}{n^2}\right)_6 xy = 1 \qquad (9.1\text{-}2)$$

---

[1] If a crystal contains points such that inversion (replacing each atom at **r** by one at −**r**, with **r** being the position vector relative to the point) about any one of these points leaves the crystal structure invariant, the crystal is said to possess inversion symmetry.

If we choose x, y, and z to be parallel to the principal dielectric axes of the crystal, then with zero applied field, Equation (9.1-2) must reduce to (9.1-1); therefore,

$$\left(\frac{1}{n^2}\right)_1\bigg|_{E=0} = \frac{1}{n_x{}^2} \qquad \left(\frac{1}{n^2}\right)_2\bigg|_{E=0} = \frac{1}{n_y{}^2}$$

$$\left(\frac{1}{n^2}\right)_3\bigg|_{E=0} = \frac{1}{n_z{}^2} \qquad \left(\frac{1}{n^2}\right)_4\bigg|_{E=0} = \left(\frac{1}{n^2}\right)_5\bigg|_{E=0} = \left(\frac{1}{n^2}\right)_6\bigg|_{E=0} = 0$$

The linear change in the coefficients

$$\left(\frac{1}{n^2}\right)_i \quad i = 1, \cdots, 6$$

due to an arbitrary electric field $\mathbf{E}(E_x, E_y, E_z)$ is defined by

$$\Delta\left(\frac{1}{n^2}\right)_i = \sum_{j=1}^{3} r_{ij}E_j \qquad\qquad (9.1\text{-}3)$$

where in the summation over j we use the convention $1 = x$, $2 = y$, $3 = z$. Equation (9.1-3) can be expressed in a matrix form as

$$
\begin{vmatrix}
\Delta\left(\dfrac{1}{n^2}\right)_1 \\[2mm]
\Delta\left(\dfrac{1}{n^2}\right)_2 \\[2mm]
\Delta\left(\dfrac{1}{n^2}\right)_3 \\[2mm]
\Delta\left(\dfrac{1}{n^2}\right)_4 \\[2mm]
\Delta\left(\dfrac{1}{n^2}\right)_5 \\[2mm]
\Delta\left(\dfrac{1}{n^2}\right)_6
\end{vmatrix}
=
\begin{vmatrix}
r_{11} & r_{12} & r_{13} \\
r_{21} & r_{22} & r_{23} \\
r_{31} & r_{32} & r_{33} \\
r_{41} & r_{42} & r_{43} \\
r_{51} & r_{52} & r_{53} \\
r_{61} & r_{62} & r_{63}
\end{vmatrix}
\begin{vmatrix}
E_1 \\
E_2 \\
E_3
\end{vmatrix}
\qquad (9.1\text{-}4)
$$

where, using the rules for matrix multiplication, we have, for example,

$$\Delta\left(\frac{1}{n^2}\right)_6 = r_{61}E_1 + r_{62}E_2 + r_{63}E_3$$

The 6×3 matrix with elements r_{ij} is called the electrooptic tensor. We have shown in Section 9.1 that in crystals possessing an inversion symmetry (centrosymmetric), $r_{ij} = 0$. The form, but not the magnitude, of the tensor r_{ij} can be derived from symmetry considerations [1], which dictate which of the 18 r_{ij} coefficients are zero, as well as the relationships that exist between the remaining coefficients. In Table 9-1 we give the form of the electrooptic tensor for all the noncentrosymmetric crystal classes. The electrooptic coefficients of some crystals are given in Table 9-2.

Table 9-1   THE FORM OF THE ELECTROOPTIC TENSOR FOR ALL CRYSTAL SYMMETRY CLASSES

Symbols:

- zero element
- nonzero element

⦁⦁ equal nonzero elements

⦁○ equal nonzero elements, but opposite in sign

The symbol at the upper left corner of each tensor is the conventional symmetry group designation.

Centrosymmetric—All elements zero

Triclinic

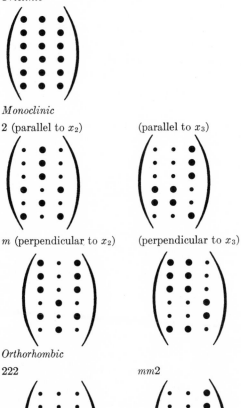

Monoclinic

2 (parallel to x_2)   (parallel to x_3)

m (perpendicular to x_2)   (perpendicular to x_3)

Orthorhombic

222   *mm2*

Tetragonal

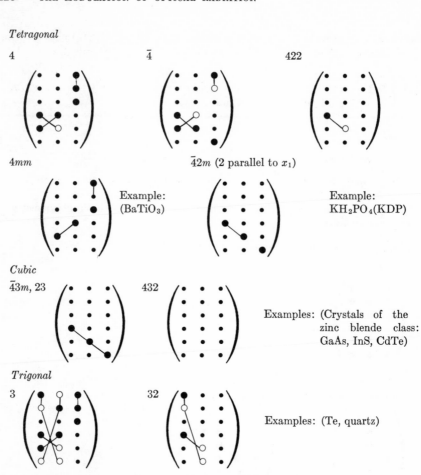

4                              $\bar{4}$ 422

4mm $\bar{4}2m$ (2 parallel to x_1)

Example: Example:
(BaTiO₃)   KH₂PO₄(KDP)

Cubic

$\bar{4}3m$, 23   432   Examples: (Crystals of the
                                      zinc blende class:
                                      GaAs, InS, CdTe)

Trigonal

3   32   Examples: (Te, quartz)

3m (m perpendicular to x_1)   3m(m perpendicular to x_2)
standard orientation

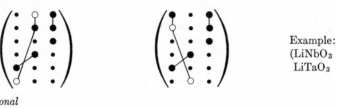

Example:
(LiNbO₃
LiTaO₃)

Hexagonal

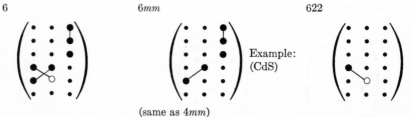

6   6mm   622

Example:
(CdS)

(same as 4mm)

$\bar{6}$ $\bar{6}m2$ (*m* perpendicular to x_1 standard orientation)

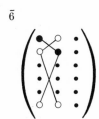   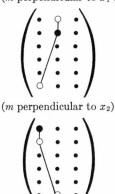

(*m* perpendicular to x_2)

Example: the electrooptic effect in KH$_2$PO$_4$.   Consider the specific example of a crystal of potassium dihydrogen phosphate (KH$_2$PO$_4$) also known as KDP. The crystal has a fourfold axis of symmetry,[2] which by strict convention is taken as the *z* (optic) axis, as well as two mutually orthogonal twofold axes of symmetry that lie in the plane normal to *z*. These are designated as the *x* and *y* axes. The symmetry group[3] of this crystal is $\bar{4}2m$. Using Table 9-1, we take the electrooptic tensor in the form of

$$r_{ij} = \begin{vmatrix} 0 & 0 & 0 \\ 0 & 0 & 0 \\ 0 & 0 & 0 \\ r_{41} & 0 & 0 \\ 0 & r_{41} & 0 \\ 0 & 0 & r_{63} \end{vmatrix} \qquad \textbf{(9.1-5)}$$

so the only nonvanishing elements are $r_{41} = r_{52}$ and r_{63}. Using (9.1-1), (9.1-4), and (9.1-5), we obtain the equation of the index ellipsoid in the presence of a field $\mathbf{E}(E_x, E_y, E_z)$ as

$$\frac{x^2}{n_o^2} + \frac{y^2}{n_o^2} + \frac{z^2}{n_e^2} + 2r_{41}E_x yz + 2r_{41}E_y xz + 2r_{63}E_z xy = 1 \qquad \textbf{(9.1-6)}$$

where the constants involved in the first three terms do not depend on the field and, since the crystal is uniaxial, are taken as $n_x = n_y = n_o$, $n_z = n_e$.

---

[2] That is, a rotation by $2\pi/4$ about this axis leaves the crystal structure invariant.
[3] The significance of the symmetry group symbols and a listing of most known crystals and their symmetry groups is to be found in any basic book on crystallography.

Table 9-2 SOME ELECTROOPTIC MATERIALS AND THEIR PROPERTIES [2]

MATERIAL	ROOM TEMPERATURE ELECTROOPTIC COEFFICIENTS IN UNITS OF 10^{-12} m/V	INDEX OF REFRACTION*	$n_0^3 r$, IN UNITS OF 10^{-12} m/V	ϵ/ϵ_0 (ROOM TEMPERATURE)	POINT-GROUP SYMMETRY
KDP (KH_2PO_4)	$r_{41} = 8.6$ $r_{63} = 10.6$	$n_o = 1.51$ $n_e = 1.47$	29 34	$\epsilon \parallel c = 20$ $\epsilon \perp c = 45$	$\bar{4}2m$
KD_2PO_4	$r_{63} = 23.6$	~ 1.50	80	$\epsilon \parallel c \sim 50$ at 24°C	$\bar{4}2m$
ADP ($NH_4H_2PO_4$)	$r_{41} = 28$ $r_{63} = 8.5$	$n_o = 1.52$ $n_e = 1.48$	95 27	$\epsilon \parallel c = 12$	$\bar{4}2m$
Quartz	$r_{41} = 0.2$ $r_{63} = 0.93$	$n_o = 1.54$ $n_e = 1.55$	0.7 3.4	$\epsilon \parallel c \sim 4.3$ $\epsilon \perp c \sim 4.3$	32
CuCl	$r_{41} = 6.1$	$n_o = 1.97$	47	7.5	$\bar{4}3m$
ZnS	$r_{41} = 2.0$	$n_o = 2.37$	27	~ 10	$\bar{4}3m$
GaAs	$r_{41} = 1.6$	$n_o = 3.34$	59	11.5	$\bar{4}3m$
ZnTe	$r_{41} = 3.9$	$n_o = 2.79$	85	7.3	$\bar{4}3m$
CdTe	$r_{41} = 6.8$	$n_o = 2.6$	120		$\bar{4}3m$
LiNbO$_3$	$r_{33} = 30.8$ $r_{13} = 8.6$ $r_{22} = 3.4$ $r_{42} = 28$	$n_o = 2.29$ $n_e = 2.20$	$n_e^3 r_{33} = 328$ $n_o^3 r_{22} = 37$ $\frac{1}{2}(n_e^3 r_{33} - n_o^3 r_{13}) = 112$	$\epsilon \perp c = 98$ $\epsilon \parallel c = 50$	$3m$
GaP	$r_{41} = 0.97$	$n_o = 3.31$	$n_o^3 r_{41} = 29$		$\bar{4}3m$
LiTaO$_3$ (30°C)	$r_{33} = 30.3$ $r_{13} = 5.7$	$n_o = 2.175$ $n_e = 2.180$	$n_e^3 r_{33} = 314$	$\epsilon \parallel c = 43$	$3m$
BaTiO$_3$ (30°C)	$r_{33} = 23$ $r_{13} = 8.0$ $r_{42} = 820$	$n_o = 2.437$ $n_e = 2.365$	$n_e^3 r_{33} = 334$	$\epsilon \perp c = 4300$ $\epsilon \parallel c = 106$	$4mm$

* Typical value near 5500 Å

We thus find that the application of an electric field causes the appearance of "mixed" terms in the equation of the index ellipsoid. These are the terms with xy, xz, and yz. This means that the major axes of the ellipsoid, with a field applied, are no longer parallel to the x, y, and z axes. It becomes necessary, then, to find the directions and magnitudes of the new axes, in the presence of **E**, so that we may determine the effect of the field on the propagation. To be specific we choose the direction of the applied field parallel to the z axis, so (9.1-6) becomes

$$\frac{x^2 + y^2}{n_o{}^2} + \frac{z^2}{n_e{}^2} + 2r_{63}E_z xy = 1 \tag{9.1-7}$$

The problem is one of finding a new coordinate system—x', y', z'—in which the equation of the ellipsoid (9.1-7) contains no mixed terms; that is, it is of the form

$$\frac{x'^2}{n_{x'}{}^2} + \frac{y'^2}{n_{y'}{}^2} + \frac{z'^2}{n_{z'}{}^2} = 1 \tag{9.1-8}$$

x', y', and z' are then the directions of the major axes of the ellipsoid in the presence of an external field applied parallel to z. The length of the major axes of the ellipsoid is, according to (9.1-8), $2n_{x'}$, $2n_{y'}$, and $2n_{z'}$ and these will, in general, depend on the applied field.

In the case of (9.1-7) it is clear from inspection that in order to put it in a diagonal form we need to choose a coordinate system x', y', z', where z' is parallel to z, and because of the symmetry of (9.1-7) in x and y, x' and y' are related to x and y by a 45° rotation, as shown in Figure 9-1. The transformation relations from x, y to x', y' are thus

$$x = x' \cos 45° - y' \sin 45°$$
$$y = x' \sin 45° + y' \cos 45°$$

which, upon substitution in (9.1-7), yield

$$\left(\frac{1}{n_o{}^2} + r_{63}E_z\right) x'^2 + \left(\frac{1}{n_o{}^2} - r_{63}E_z\right) y'^2 + \frac{z^2}{n_e{}^2} = 1 \tag{9.1-9}$$

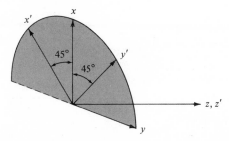

Figure 9-1 The x, y, and z axes of $\overline{4}2m$ crystals (such as KH$_2$PO$_4$) and the x', y', and z' axes, where z is the fourfold optic axis and x and y are the twofold axes of crystals with $\overline{4}2m$ symmetry.

Equation (9.1-9) shows that x', y', and z are indeed the principal axes of the ellipsoid when a field is applied along the z direction. According to (9.1-9), the length of the x' axis of the ellipsoid is $2n_{x'}$, where

$$\frac{1}{n_{x'}^2} = \frac{1}{n_o^2} + r_{63}E_z$$

which, assuming $r_{63}E_z \ll n_o^{-2}$ and using the differential relation $dn = -(n^3/2)\, d(1/n^2)$, gives

$$n_{x'} = n_o - \frac{n_o^3}{2} r_{63}E_z \tag{9.1-10}$$

and, similarly,

$$n_{y'} = n_o + \frac{n_o^3}{2} r_{63}E_z \tag{9.1-11}$$

$$n_z = n_e \tag{9.1-12}$$

9.2 Electrooptic Retardation

The index ellipsoid for KDP with **E** applied parallel to z is shown in Figure 9-2. If we consider propagation along the z direction, then according to the procedure described in Section 1.4 we need to determine the ellipse formed by the intersection of the plane $z = 0$ (in general, the plane that contains the origin and is normal to the propagation direction) and the ellipsoid. The equation of this ellipse is obtained from (9.1-9) by putting $z = 0$ and is

$$\left(\frac{1}{n_o^2} + r_{63}E_z\right) x'^2 + \left(\frac{1}{n_o^2} - r_{63}E_z\right) y'^2 = 1 \tag{9.2-1}$$

One quadrant of the ellipse is shown (crosshatched) in Figure 9-2, along with its minor and major axes, which in this case coincide with x' and y',

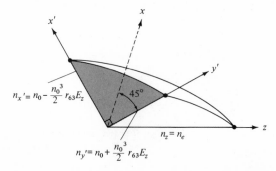

Figure 9-2 A section of the index ellipsoid of KDP, showing the principal dielectric axes x', y', and z due to an electric field applied along the z axis. The directions x' and y' are defined by Figure 9.1.

respectively. It follows from Section 1.4 that the two allowed directions of polarization are x' and y' and that their indices of refraction are $n_{x'}$ and $n_{y'}$, which are given by (9.1-10) and (9.1-11).

We are now in a position to take up the concept of retardation. We consider an optical field which is incident normally on the $x'y'$ plane with its **E** vector along the x direction. We can resolve the optical field at $z = 0$ (input plane) into two mutually orthogonal components polarized along x' and y'. The x' component propagates as

$$e_{x'} = A e^{i[\omega t - (\omega/c_0)n_{x'}z]}$$

which, using (9.1-10), becomes

$$e_{x'} = A e^{i\{\omega t - (\omega/c_0)[n_o - (n_o^3/2)r_{63}E_z]z\}} \tag{9.2-2}$$

while the y' component is given by

$$e_{y'} = A e^{i\{\omega t - (\omega/c_0)[n_o + (n_o^3/2)r_{63}E_z]z\}} \tag{9.2-3}$$

The phase difference at the output plane $z = l$ between the two components is called the *retardation*. It is given by the difference of the exponents in (9.2-2) and (9.2-3) and is equal to

$$\Gamma = \phi_{x'} - \phi_{y'} = \frac{\omega n_o^3 r_{63} V}{c_0} \tag{9.2-4}$$

where $V = E_z l$ and $\phi_{x'} = (\omega n_{x'}/c_0)l$.

Figure 9-3 shows $E_{x'}(z)$ and $E_{y'}(z)$ at some moment in time. Also shown are the curves traversed by the tip of the optical field vector at various points along the path. At $z = 0$, the retardation is $\Gamma = 0$ and the field is linearly polarized along x. At point e, $\Gamma = \pi/2$; thus, omitting a common phase factor, we have

$$e_{x'} = A \cos \omega t$$
$$e_{y'} = A \cos \left(\omega t - \frac{\pi}{2}\right) = A \sin \omega t \tag{9.2-5}$$

and the electric field vector is circularly polarized in the clockwise sense as shown in the figure. At point i, $\Gamma = \pi$ and thus

$$e_{x'} = A \cos \omega t$$
$$e_{y'} = A \cos (\omega t - \pi) = -A \cos \omega t$$

and the radiation is again linearly polarized, but this time along the y direction—that is, at 90° to its input direction of polarization.

The retardation as given by (9.2-4) can also be written as

$$\Gamma = \pi \frac{E_z l}{V_\pi} = \pi \frac{V}{V_\pi} \tag{9.2-6}$$

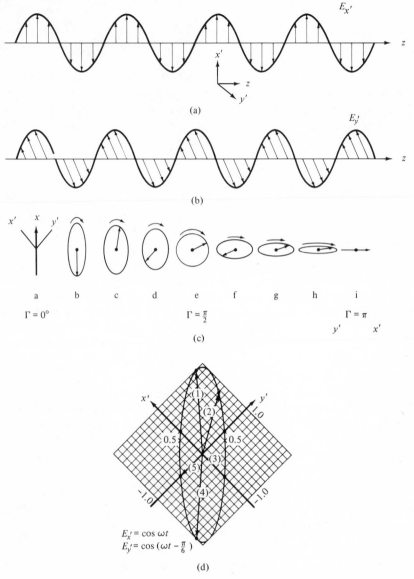

Figure 9-3 An optical field that is linearly polarized along x is incident on an electrooptic crystal having its electrically induced principal axes along x' and y'. (This is the case in KH_2PO_4 when an electric field is applied along its z axis.) (**a**) The component $e_{x'}$ at some time t as a function of the position z along the crystal. (**b**) $e_{y'}$ as a function of z at the same value of t as in (**a**). (**c**) The ellipses in the x'-y' plane traversed by the tip of the optical electric field at various points (a through i) along the crystal during one optical cycle. The arrow shows the instantaneous field vector at time t, while the curved arrow gives the sense in which the ellipse is traversed. (**d**) A plot of the polarization ellipse due to two orthogonal components $e_{x'} = \cos \omega t$ and $e_{y'} = \cos (\omega t - \pi/6)$. Also shown are the instantaneous field vectors at (1) $\omega t = 0^0$, (2) $\omega t = 60°$, (3) $\omega t = 120°$, (4) $\omega t = 210°$, and (5) $\omega t = 270°$.

where V_π, the voltage yielding a retardation $\Gamma = \pi$,[4] is

$$V_\pi = \frac{\lambda_0}{2n_o^3 r_{63}} \tag{9.2-7}$$

where $\lambda_0 = 2\pi c_0/\omega$ is the free space wavelength. Using, as an example, the value of r_{63} for ADP as given in Table 9-2, we obtain from (9.2-7)

$$(V_\pi)_{\text{ADP}} = 10{,}000 \text{ volts} \quad \text{at} \quad \lambda = 0.5 \,\mu\text{m}$$

9.3 Electrooptic Amplitude Modulation

An examination of Figure 9-3 reveals that the electrically induced bire-fringence causes a wave launched at $z = 0$ with its polarization along x to acquire a y polarization, which grows with distance at the expense of the x component until at point i, at which $\Gamma = \pi$, the polarization becomes parallel to y. If point i corresponds to the output plane of the crystal and if one inserts at this point a polarizer at right angles to the input polariza-tion—that is, one that allows only E_y to pass—then with the field on, the optical beam passes through unattenuated, whereas with the field off ($\Gamma = 0$), the output beam is blocked off completely by the crossed output polarizer. This control of the optical energy flow serves as the basis of the electrooptic amplitude modulation of light.

A typical arrangement of an electrooptic amplitude modulator is shown in Figure 9-4. It consists of an electrooptic crystal placed between two crossed polarizers, which, in turn, are at an angle of 45° with respect to

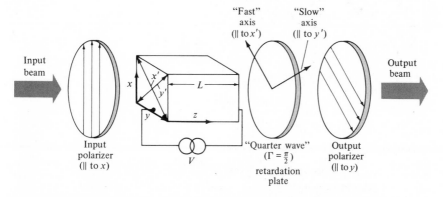

Figure 9-4 A typical electrooptic amplitude modulator. The total retardation Γ is the sum of the fixed retardation bias ($\Gamma_B = \pi/2$) introduced by the "quarter-wave" plate and that attributable to the electrooptic crystal.

---

[4] V_π is referred to as the "half-wave" voltage since, as can be seen in Figure 9.3(i), it causes the two waves that are polarized along x' and y' to acquire a relative spatial displacement of $\Delta z = \lambda/2$, where λ is the optical wavelength.

the electrically induced birefringent axes x' and y'. To be specific, we show how this arrangement is achieved using a KDP crystal. Also included in the optical path is a naturally birefringent crystal that introduces a fixed retardation, so the total retardation Γ is the sum of the retardation due to this crystal and the electrically induced one. The incident field is parallel to x at the input face of the crystal, thus having equal-in-phase components along x' and y' which we take as

$$e_{x'} = A \cos \omega t$$

$$e_{y'} = A \cos \omega t$$

or, using the complex amplitude notation,

$$E_{x'}(0) = A$$

$$E_{y'}(0) = A$$

The incident intensity is thus

$$I_i \propto \mathbf{E} \cdot \mathbf{E}^* = |E_{x'}(0)|^2 + |E_{y'}(0)|^2 = 2A^2 \qquad \textbf{(9.3-1)}$$

Upon emerging from the output face $z = l$, the x' and y' components have acquired, according to (9.2-4), a relative phase shift (retardation) of Γ radians, so we may take them as

$$E_{x'}(l) = A$$
$$E_{y'}(l) = Ae^{-i\Gamma} \qquad \textbf{(9.3-2)}$$

The total (complex) field emerging from the output polarizer is the sum of the y components of $E_{x'}(l)$ and $E_{y'}(l)$

$$(E_y)_o = \frac{A}{\sqrt{2}} (e^{-i\Gamma} - 1) \qquad \textbf{(9.3-3)}$$

which corresponds to an output intensity[5]

$$I_o \propto [(E_y)_o(E_y^*)_o]$$

$$= \frac{A^2}{2} [(e^{-i\Gamma} - 1)(e^{i\Gamma} - 1)] = 2A^2 \sin^2 \frac{\Gamma}{2}$$

where the proportionality constant is the same as in (9.3-1). The ratio of the output intensity to the input is thus

$$\frac{I_o}{I_i} = \sin^2 \frac{\Gamma}{2} = \sin^2 \left[\left(\frac{\pi}{2} \right) \frac{V}{V_\pi} \right] \qquad \textbf{(9.3-4)}$$

---

[5] We recall here that the time average of the product of two sinusoidal fields Re $[Be^{i\omega t}]$ and Re $[Ce^{i\omega t}]$ is equal to $\frac{1}{2}$ Re $[BC^*]$.

The second equality in (9.3-4) was obtained from (9.2-6). The transmission factor (I_o/I_i) is plotted in Figure 9-5 against the applied voltage.

The process of amplitude modulation of an optical signal is also illustrated in Figure 9-5. The modulator is usually biased[6] with a fixed retardation $\Gamma = \pi/2$ to the 50 percent transmission point. A small sinusoidal modulation voltage would then cause a nearly sinusoidal modulation of the transmitted intensity as shown.

To treat the situation depicted by Figure 9-5 mathematically, we take

$$\Gamma = \frac{\pi}{2} + \Gamma_m \sin \omega_m t \qquad (9.3\text{-}5)$$

where the retardation bias is taken as $\pi/2$, and Γ_m is related to the amplitude V_m of the modulation voltage $V_m \sin \omega_m t$ by (9.2-6); thus, $\Gamma_m = \pi(V_m/V_\pi)$.

Using (9.3-4) we obtain

$$\frac{I_o}{I_i} = \sin^2\left(\frac{\pi}{4} + \frac{\Gamma_m}{2} \sin \omega_m t\right) \qquad (9.3\text{-}6)$$

$$= \tfrac{1}{2}[1 + \sin (\Gamma_m \sin \omega_m t)] \qquad (9.3\text{-}7)$$

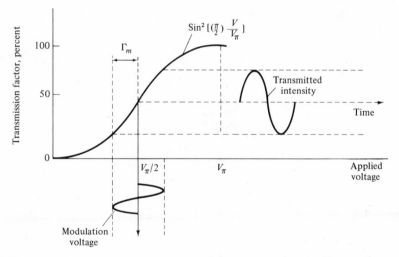

Figure 9-5   Transmission factor of a cross-polarized electrooptic modulator as a function of an applied voltage. The modulator is biased to the point $\Gamma = \pi/2$, which results in a 50 percent intensity transmission. A small applied sinusoidal voltage modulates the transmitted intensity about the bias point.

---

[6] This bias can be achieved by applying a voltage $V = V_\pi/2$ or, more conveniently, by using a naturally birefringent crystal as in Figure 9-4 to introduce a phase difference (retardation) of $\pi/2$ between the x' and y' components.

which, for $\Gamma_m \ll 1$, becomes

$$\frac{I_o}{I_i} \simeq \frac{1}{2}\left[1 + \Gamma_m \sin \omega_m t\right] \qquad \textbf{(9.3-8)}$$

so that the intensity modulation is a linear replica of the modulating voltage $V_m \sin \omega_m t$. If the condition $\Gamma_m \ll 1$ is not fulfilled, it follows from Figure 9-5 or from (9.3-7) that the intensity variation is distorted and will contain an appreciable amount of the higher (odd) harmonics. The dependence of the distortion on Γ_m is discussed further in Problem 9.11.

In Figure 9-6 we show how some information signal $f(t)$ (the electric output of a phonograph stylus in this case) can be impressed electrooptically as an amplitude modulation on a laser beam and subsequently be recovered by an optical detector. The details of the optical detection are considered in Chapter 11.

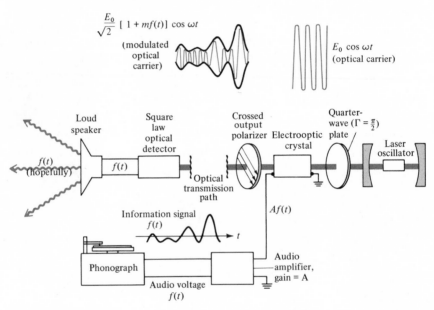

Figure 9-6   An optical communication link using an electrooptic modulator.

9.4   Phase Modulation of Light

In the preceding section we saw how the modulation of the state of polarization, from linear to elliptic, of an optical beam by means of the electrooptic effect can be converted, using polarizers, to intensity modulation. Here we consider the situation depicted by Figure 9-7, in which, instead of there being equal components along the induced birefringent axes (x' and y' in Figure 9-4), the incident beam is polarized parallel to one of them, x'

say. In this case the application of the electric field does not change the state of polarization, but merely changes the output phase by

$$\Delta\phi'_x = -\frac{\omega l}{c_0}\Delta n_{x'}$$

where, from (9.1-10),

$$\Delta\phi'_x = -\frac{\omega n_o{}^3 r_{63}}{2c_0} E_z l \tag{9.4-1}$$

If the bias field is sinusoidal and is taken as

$$E_z = E_m \sin\omega_m t \tag{9.4-2}$$

then an incident optical field which, at the input ($z = 0$) face of the crystal varies as $e_{\text{in}} = A\cos\omega t$, will emerge according to (9.2-2) as

$$e_{\text{out}} = A\cos\left[\omega t - \frac{\omega}{c_0}\left(n_o - \frac{n_o{}^3}{2}r_{63}E_m\sin\omega_m t\right)l\right]$$

where l is the length of the crystal. Dropping the constant phase factor, which is of no consequence here, we rewrite the last equation as

$$e_{\text{out}} = A\cos\left[\omega t + \delta\sin\omega_m t\right] \tag{9.4-3}$$

where

$$\delta = \frac{\omega n_o{}^3 r_{63}E_m l}{2c_0} = \frac{\pi n_o{}^3 r_{63}E_m l}{\lambda_0} \tag{9.4-4}$$

is referred to as the phase modulation index. The optical field is thus phase-modulated with a modulation index δ. Is we use the Bessel function identities

$$\cos(\delta\sin\omega_m t) = J_0(\delta) + 2J_2(\delta)\cos 2\omega_m t + 2J_4(\delta)\cos 4\omega_m t + \cdots$$

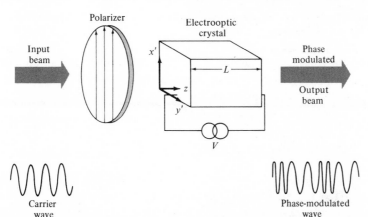

Figure 9-7 An electrooptic phase modulator. The crystal orientation and applied directions are appropriate to KDP. The optical polarization is parallel to an electrically induced principal dielectric axis (x').

and

$$\sin{(\delta \sin{\omega_m t})} = 2J_1(\delta)\sin{\omega_m t} + 2J_3(\delta)\sin{3\omega_m t} + \cdots \qquad \textbf{(9.4-5)}$$

we can rewrite (9.4-3) as

$$
\begin{aligned}
e_{\text{out}} = A[&J_0(\delta)\cos{\omega t} + J_1(\delta)\cos{(\omega + \omega_m)t} \\
&- J_1(\delta)\cos{(\omega - \omega_m)t} + J_2(\delta)\cos{(\omega + 2\omega_m)t} \\
&+ J_2(\delta)\cos{(\omega - 2\omega_m)t} + J_3(\delta)\cos{(\omega + 3\omega_m)t} \\
&- J_3(\delta)\cos{(\omega - 3\omega_m)t} + J_4(\delta)\cos{(\omega + 4\omega_m)t} \\
&- J_4(\delta)\cos{(\omega - 4\omega_m)t} + \cdots]
\end{aligned}
\qquad \textbf{(9.4-6)}
$$

which form gives the distribution of energy in the sidebands as a function of the modulation index δ. We note that, for $\delta = 0$, $J_0(0) = 1$ and $J_n(\delta) = 0$, $n \neq 0$. Another point of interest is that the phase modulation index δ as given by (9.4-4) is one half the retardation Γ as given by (9.2-4).

9.5   Transverse Electrooptic Modulators

In the examples of electrooptic retardation discussed in the two preceding sections, the electric field was applied along the direction of light propagation. This is the so-called longitudinal mode of modulation. A more desirable mode of operation is the transverse one, in which the field is applied normal to the direction of propagation. The reason is that in this case the field electrodes do not interfere with the optical beam, and the retardation, being proportional to the product of the field times the crystal length, can be increased by the use of longer crystals. In the longitudinal case the retardation, according to (9.2-4), is proportional to $E_z l = V$ and is independent of the crystal length l. Figures 9-1 and 9-2 suggest how transverse retardation can be obtained using a KDP crystal with the actual arrangement shown in Figure 9-8. The light propagates along y' and its polarization is in the x'–z plane at 45° from the z axis. The retardation, with a field applied along z, is, from (9.1-10) and (9.1-12),

$$
\begin{aligned}
\Gamma &= \phi_z - \phi_{x'} \\
&= \frac{\omega l}{c_0}\left[(n_o - n_e) - \frac{n_o^3}{2}r_{63}\left(\frac{V}{d}\right)\right]
\end{aligned}
\qquad \textbf{(9.5-1)}
$$

where d is the crystal dimension along the direction of the applied field. We note that Γ contains a term that does not depend on the applied voltage. This point will be discussed in Problem 9-2. A detailed example of transverse electrooptic modulation using $\bar{4}3m$, cubic zinc-blende type crystals is given in the Appendix.

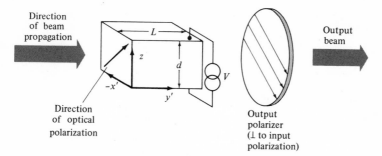

Figure 9-8 A transverse electrooptic amplitude modulator using a KH_2PO_4 (KDP) crystal in which the field is applied normal to the direction of propagation.

9.6 High-Frequency Modulation Considerations

In the examples considered in the three preceding sections, we derived expressions for the retardation caused by electric fields of low frequencies. In many practical situations the modulation signal is often at very high frequencies and, in order to utilize the wide frequency spectrum available with lasers, may occupy a large bandwidth. In this section we consider some of the basic factors limiting the highest usable modulation frequencies in a number of typical experimental situations.

Consider first the situation described by Figure 9-9. The electrooptic crystal is placed between two electrodes with a modulation field containing frequencies near $\omega_0/2\pi$ applied to it. R_s is the internal resistance of the modulation source and C represents the parallel-plate capacitance due to the electrooptic crystal. If $R_s > (\omega_0 c)^{-1}$, most of the modulation voltage drop is across R_s and is thus wasted, since it does not contribute to the retardation. This can be remedied by resonating the crystal capacitance with an inductance L, where $\omega_0{}^2 = (LC)^{-1}$, as shown in Figure 9-9. In addition, a shunting resistance R_L is used so that at $\omega = \omega_0$ the impedance

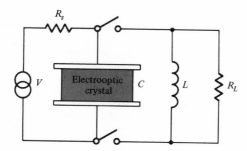

Figure 9-9 Equivalent circuit of an electrooptic modulation crystal in a parallel-plate configuration.

of the parallel RLC circuit is R_L, which is chosen to be larger than R_s so most of the modulation voltage appears across the crystal. The resonant circuit has a finite bandwidth—that is, its impedance is high only over a frequency interval $\Delta\omega/2\pi \simeq 1/2\pi R_L C$ (centered on ω_0). Therefore, the maximum modulation bandwidth (the frequency spectrum occupied by the modulation signal) must be less than

$$\frac{\Delta\omega}{2\pi} \simeq \frac{1}{2\pi R_L C} \tag{9.6-1}$$

if the modulation field is to be a faithful replica of the modulation signal.

In practice, the size of the modulation bandwith $\Delta\omega/2\pi$ is dictated by the specific application. In addition, one requires a certain peak retardation Γ_m. Using Equation (9.2-4) to relate Γ_m to the peak modulation voltage $V_m = (E_z)_m l$ we can show, with the aid of (9.6-1), that the power $V_m{}^2/2R_L$ needed in KDP-type crystals to obtain a peak retardation Γ_m is related to the modulation bandwidth $\Delta\nu = \Delta\omega/2\pi$ as

$$P = \frac{\Gamma_m{}^2\lambda_0{}^2 A \epsilon \, \Delta\nu}{4\pi l n_0{}^6 r_{63}{}^2} \tag{9.6-2}$$

where l is the length of the optical path in the crystal, A is the cross-sectional area of the crystal normal to l, and ϵ is the dielectric constant at the modulation frequency ω_0.

Transit-time limitations to high-frequency electrooptic modulation.

According to Equation (9.2-4) the electrooptic retardation due to a field E can be written as

$$\Gamma = aEl \tag{9.6-3}$$

where $a = n_0{}^3 r_{63}/c_0$ and l is the length of the optical path in the crystal. If the field E changes appreciably during the transit time $\tau_d = l/c$ of light through the crystal, we must replace (9.6-3) by

$$\Gamma(t) = a\int_0^l e(t') \, dz = ac\int_{t-\tau_d}^t e(t') \, dt' \tag{9.6-4}$$

where c is the velocity of light and $e(t')$ is the instantaneous electric field. In the second integral we replace integration over z by integration over time, recognizing that the portion of the wave which reaches the output face $z = l$ at time t entered the crystal at time $t - \tau_d$. We also assumed that at any given moment the field $e(t)$ has the same value throughout the crystal.

Taking $e(t')$ as a sinusoid

$$e(t') = E_m e^{i\omega_m t'}$$

we obtain from (9.6-4)

$$\Gamma(t) = acE_m \int_{t-\tau_d}^{t} e^{i\omega_m t'} \, dt'$$

$$= \Gamma_0 \left[\frac{1 - e^{-i\omega_m \tau_d}}{i\omega_m \tau_d} \right] e^{i\omega_m t} \tag{9.6-5}$$

where $\Gamma_0 = ac\tau_d E_m = alE_m$ is the peak retardation, which obtains when $\omega_m \tau_d \ll 1$. The factor

$$r = \frac{1 - e^{-i\omega_m \tau_d}}{i\omega_m \tau_d} \tag{9.6-6}$$

gives the decrease in peak retardation resulting from the finite transit time. For $r \simeq 1$ (that is, no reduction), the condition $\omega_m \tau_d \ll 1$ must be satisfied, so the transit time must be small compared to the shortest modulation period. The factor r is plotted in Figure 11-7.

If, somewhat arbitrarily, we take the highest useful modulation frequency as that for which $\omega_m \tau_d = \pi/2$ (at this point, according to Figure 11-17, $|r| = 0.9$) and we use the relation $\tau_d = ln/c_0$, we obtain

$$(\nu_m)_{\max} = \frac{c_0}{4ln} \tag{9.6-7}$$

which, using a KDP crystal ($n \simeq 1.5$) and a length $l = 1$ cm, yields $(\nu_m)_{\max} = 5 \times 10^9$ Hz.

Traveling-wave modulators.   One method that can, in principle, overcome the transit-time limitation, involves applying the modulation signal in the form of a traveling wave [3], as shown in Figure 9-10. If the optical and modulation field phase velocities are equal to each other, then a portion of an optical wavefront will exercise the same instantaneous

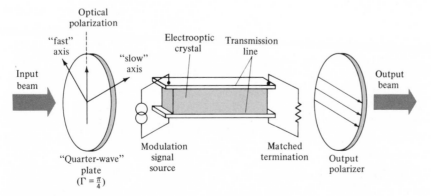

Figure 9-10   A traveling-wave electrooptic modulator.

electric field, which corresponds to the field it encounters at the entrance face, as it propagates through the crystal and the transit-time problem discussed above is eliminated. This form of modulation can be used only in the transverse geometry was discussed in the preceding section, since the RF field in most propagating structures is predominantly transverse.

Consider an element of the optical wavefront that *enters* the crystal at $z = 0$ at time t. The position z of this element at some later time t' is

$$z(t') = c(t' - t) \tag{9.6-8}$$

where $c = c_0/n$ is the optical phase velocity. The retardation exercised by this element is given similarly to (9.6-4) by

$$\Gamma(t) = ac \int_t^{t+\tau d} e[t', z(t')] \, dt' \tag{9.6-9}$$

where $e[t', z(t')]$ is the instantaneous modulation field as seen by an observer traveling with the phase front. Taking the traveling modulation field as

$$e(t', z) = E_m e^{i[\omega_m t' - k_m z]}$$

we obtain, using (9.6-8),

$$e[t', z(t')] = E_m e^{i[\omega_m t' - k_m c(t' - t)]} \tag{9.6-10}$$

Recalling that $k_m = \omega_m/c_m$, where c_m is the phase velocity of the modulation field, we substitute (9.6-10) in (9.6-9) and, carrying out the simple integration, obtain

$$\Gamma(t) = \Gamma_0 e^{i\omega_m t} \left[\frac{e^{i\omega_m \tau_d (1 - c/c_m)} - 1}{i\omega_m \tau_d (1 - c/c_m)} \right] \tag{9.6-11}$$

where $\Gamma_0 = alE_m = ac\tau_d E_m$ is the retardation that would result from a dc field equal to E_m.

The reduction factor

$$r = \frac{e^{i\omega_m \tau_d (1 - c/c_m)} - 1}{i\omega_m \tau_d (1 - c/c_m)} \tag{9.6-12}$$

is of the same form as that of the lumped-constant modulator (9.6-6) except that τ_d is replaced by $\tau_d(1 - c/c_m)$. If the two phase velocities are made equal so that $c = c_m$, then $r = 1$ and maximum retardation is obtained *regardless* of the crystal length.

The maximum useful modulation frequency is taken, as in the treatment leading to (9.6-7), as that for which $\omega_m \tau_d (1 - c/c_m) = \pi/2$, yielding

$$(\nu_m)_{\max} = \frac{c_0}{4ln(1 - c_0/nc_m)} \tag{9.6-13}$$

which, upon comparison with (9.6-7), shows an increase in the frequency limit or useful crystal length of $(1 - c_0/nc_m)^{-1}$. The problem of designing traveling wave electrooptic modulators is considered in References [4]–[6].

9.7 Electrooptic Beam Deflection

The electrooptic effect is also used to deflect light beams [7]. The operation of such a beam deflector is shown in Figure 9-11. Imagine an optical wavefront incident on a crystal in which the optical path length depends on the transverse position x. This could be achieved by having the velocity of propagation—that is, the index of refraction n—depend on x, as in Figure 9-11. Taking the index variation to be a linear function of x, the upper ray A "sees" an index $n + \Delta n$ and hence traverses the crystal in a time

$$T_A = \frac{l}{c_0} (n + \Delta n)$$

The lower portion of the wavefront (that is, ray B) "sees" an index n and has a transit time

$$T_B = \frac{l}{c_0} n$$

The difference in transit times results in a lag of ray A with respect to B of

$$\Delta y = \frac{c_0}{n} (T_A - T_B) = l \frac{\Delta n}{n}$$

which corresponds to a deflection of the beam-propagation axis, as measured inside the crystal, at the output face of

$$\theta' = -\frac{\Delta y}{D} = -\frac{l \, \Delta n}{Dn} = -\frac{l}{n} \frac{dn}{dx} \qquad \textbf{(9.7-1)}$$

where we replaced $\Delta n/D$ by dn/dx. The external deflection angle θ, measured with respect to the horizontal axis, is related to θ' by Snell's law

$$\frac{\sin \theta}{\sin \theta'} = n$$

which, using (9.7-1) and assuming $\sin \theta \simeq \theta \ll 1$ yields

$$\theta = \theta' n = -l \frac{\Delta n}{D} = -l \frac{dn}{dx} \qquad \textbf{(9.7-2)}$$

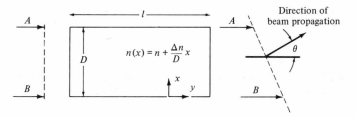

Figure 9-11 Schematic diagram of a beam deflector. The index of refraction varies linearly in the x direction as $n(x) = n_o + ax$. Ray B "gains" on ray A in passing through the crystal axis, thus causing a tilting of the wavefront by θ.

A simple realization of such a deflector using a KH_2PO_4 (KDP) crystal is shown in Figure 9-12. It consists of two KDP prisms with edges along the x', y', and z directions.[7] The two prisms have their z axes opposite to one another, but are otherwise similarly oriented. The electric field is applied parallel to the z direction and the light propagates in the y' direction with its polarization along x'. For this case the index of refraction "seen" by ray A, which propagates entirely in the upper prism, is given by (9.1-10) as

$$n_A = n_o - \frac{n_o{}^3}{2} r_{63} E_z$$

while in the lower prism the sign of the electric field with respect to the z axis is reversed so that

$$n_B = n_o + \frac{n_o{}^3}{2} r_{63} E_z$$

Using (9.7-2) with $\Delta n = n_A - n_B$ the deflection angle is given by

$$\theta = \frac{l}{D} n_o{}^3 r_{63} E_z \tag{9.7-3}$$

According to (3.2-18), every optical beam has a finite, far-field divergence angle which we call θ_{beam}. It is clear that a fundamental figure of merit for the deflector is not the angle of deflection θ that can be changed by a lens, but the factor N by which θ exceeds θ_{beam}. If one were, as an example, to focus the output beam, then N would correspond to the

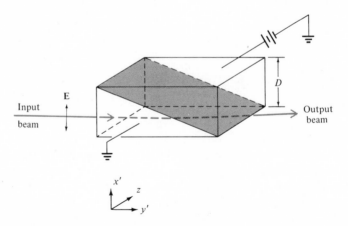

Figure 9-12 Double-prism KDP beam deflector. Upper and lower prisms have their z axes reversed with respect to each other. The deflection field is applied parallel to z.

---

[7] These are the principal axes of the index ellipsoid when an electric field is applied along the z direction as described in Section 9.1 and in the example of Section 9.5.

number of resolvable spots that can be displayed in the focal plane using fields with a magnitude up to E_z.

To get an expression for N we assume that the crystal is placed at the "waist" of a Gaussian (fundamental) beam with a spot size ω_0. According to (3.2-18) the far-field diffraction angle is

$$\theta_{\text{beam}} = \frac{\lambda}{\pi \omega_0}$$

Such a beam can be passed through a crystal with height $D = 2\omega_0$ so that, using (9.7-3), the number of resolvable spots is

$$N = \frac{\theta}{\theta_{\text{beam}}} = \frac{\pi l n_o{}^3 r_{63}}{2\lambda} E_z \qquad (9.7\text{-}4)$$

It follows directly from (9.7-4), the details being left as a problem, that an electric field that induces a birefringent retardation (in a distance l) $\Delta\Gamma = \pi$ will yield $N \simeq 1$. Therefore, fundamentally, the electrooptic extinction of a beam, which according to (9.3-4) requires $\Gamma = \pi$, is equivalent to a deflection by one spot diameter.

The deflection of optical beam by diffraction from a sound wave is discussed in Chapter 12.

■ PROBLEMS

9-1 Derive the equations of the nine ellipses traced by the optical field vector as shown in Figure 9-3(c), as a function of the retardation Γ.

9-2 Discuss the consequence of the field-independent retardation $(\omega L/c_0)(n_0 - n_e)$ in (9.5-1) on an amplitude modulator such as that shown in Figure 9.4.

9-3 Use the Bessel-function expansion of $\sin[a \sin x]$ to express (9.3-7) in terms of the harmonics of the modulation frequency ω_m. Plot the ratio of the third harmonic $(3\omega_m)$ of the output intensity to the fundamental as a function of Γ_m. What is the maximum allowed Γ_m if this ratio is not to exceed 10^{-2}? (*Answer:* $\Gamma_m < 0.5$).

9-4 Show that, if a phase-modulated optical wave is incident on a square-law detector, the output consists only of the even harmonics of the modulation frequency ω_m.

9-5 Using References [4] and [5], design a partially loaded KDP phase modulator that operates at $\nu_m = 10^9$ Hz and yields a peak phase excursion of $\delta = \pi/3$. What is the modulation power?

9-6 Derive the expression (similar to 9.6-2) for the modulation power of a transverse $\overline{4}3m$ crystal electrooptic modulator of the type described in the Appendix.

9-7 Derive an expression for the modulation power requirement (corresponding to Equation (9.6-2)) for a GaAs transverse modulator.

9-8 a. Show that if a ray propagates at an angle $\theta(\ll 1)$ to the z axis in the arrangement of Figure 9-4, it exercises a birefringent contribution to the retardation.

$$\Delta\Gamma_{\text{birefringent}} = \frac{\omega l}{2c_0} n_0 \left(\frac{n_0^2}{n_e^2} - 1\right) \theta^2$$

which corresponds to a change in index

$$n_0 - n_e(\theta) = \frac{n_0\theta^2}{2} \left(\frac{n_0^2}{n_e^2} - 1\right)$$

b. Derive an approximate expression for the maximum allowable beam spreading angle for which $\Delta\Gamma_{\text{birefringent}}$ does not interfere with the operation of the modulator. *Answer:*

$$\theta < \left[\lambda_0/4ln_0 \left(\frac{n_0^2}{n_e^2} - 1\right) \right]^{1/2}$$

■ REFERENCES

[1] See, for example, J. F. Nye, *Physical Properties of Crystals.* New York: Oxford, 1957, p. 123.

[2] See, for example, A. Yariv, *Quantum Electronics.* New York, Wiley, 1967, Chap. 18.

[3] Peters, L. C., "Gigacycle bandwidth coherent light traveling-wave phase modulators," *Proc. IEEE*, vol. 51, p. 147, 1963.

[4] Rigrod, W. W., and I. P. Kaminow, "Wide-band microwave light modulation," *Proc. IEEE*, vol. 51, p. 137, 1963.

[5] Kaminow, I. P., and J. Lin, "Propagation characteristics of partially loaded two-conductor transmission lines for broadband light modulators," *Proc. IEEE*, vol. 51, p. 132, 1963.

[6] White, R. M., and C. E. Enderby, "Electro-optical modulators employing intermittent interaction," *Proc. IEEE*, vol. 51, p. 214, 1963.

[7] Fowler, V. J., and J. Schlafer, "A survey of laser beam deflection techniques," *Proc. IEEE*, vol. 54, p. 1437, 1966.

Noise in Optical Detection and Generation

10.0 Introduction

In this chapter we study the problem of noise in two instances: first, in the detection of optical radiation and then in laser oscillators.

In optical detection, noise constitutes a *random fluctuation in the measurement*, thus limiting the accuracy with which we can determine very small optical intensities or very small increments in the intensity. These random fluctuations are what we mean when we use the word *noise* in this book.

In the case of laser oscillators, noise power caused by spontaneous power emission by atoms in the upper laser level mingles with the stimulated emission, thus giving it a finite spectral width.

In this book we concern ourselves with optical detectors utilizing light-generated charge carriers. These include the photomultiplier, the photoconductive detector, the *p-n* junction photodiode, and the avalanche photodiode. These detectors are the main ones used in the field of quantum electronics, because they combine high sensitivity with very short response times. Other types of detectors, such as bolometers, Golay cells, and thermocouples, whose operation depends on temperature changes induced by the absorbed radiation, will not be discussed in this book.[1]

Two types of noise will be discussed in detail. The first type is thermal (Johnson) noise, which represents noise power generated by thermally agitated charge carriers. The expression for this noise will be derived using the conventional thermodynamic treatment as well as by a statistical analysis of a particular model in which the physical origin of the noise is more apparent. The second type, shot noise (or generation-recombination noise in photoconductive detectors), is attributable to the random way in which electrons are emitted or generated. This noise exists even at zero temperature, where thermal agitation or generation of carriers can be neglected. In this case it results from the randomness with which carriers are generated by the *very signal which is measured*. This case of signal-generated shot noise is called quantum-limited detection, since the corresponding sensitivity is that allowed by the uncertainty principle in quantum mechanics. This point will be brought out in the next chapter.

10.1 Why Is Noise Bad?

To illustrate the point, consider the problem of measuring the amplitude V_S of a signal

$$v_s(t) = V_S \cos \omega t \tag{10.1-1}$$

in the presence of a noise[2]

$$v_N(t) = V_{NC}(t) \cos \omega t + V_{NS}(t) \sin \omega t \tag{10.1-2}$$

where $V_{NC}(t)$ and $V_{NS}(t)$ are random uncorrelated quantities [1].

The total (signal plus noise) field can be written using the complex notation as

$$V(t) = [V_S + V_{NC}(t) - iV_{NS}(t)]e^{i\omega t} \tag{10.1-3}$$

so that its instantaneous (complex) amplitude is given by

$$V_t = V_S + V_{NC}(t) - iV_{NS}(t) \tag{10.1-4}$$

and is illustrated in Figure 10-1.

Assuming for a moment that

$$\overline{V_{NC}^2(t)} = \overline{V_{NS}^2(t)} \ll V_S^2 \tag{10.1-5}$$

---

[1] The interested reader will find a good description of these devices in Reference [6].
[2] This form of writing the noise is especially useful when the noise spectrum is limited by filtering to a spectral width small compared to ω, so that $V_{NC}(t)$ and $V_{NS}(t)$ are slowly varying functions compared to $\cos \omega t$ and $\sin \omega t$.

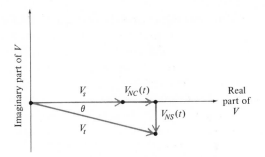

Figure 10-1 Phasor diagram, showing the signal (complex) amplitude V_s as well as the in-phase noise amplitude $V_{NC}(t)$ and the quadrature component $V_{NS}(t)$ at some time t. The total (signal plus noise) field amplitude is V_t.

where the horizontal bar indicates a long time average or an ensemble average,[3] we have

$$V_t \simeq V_S + V_{NC}(t) \qquad (10.1\text{-}6)$$

If our detecting system yields an output that is proportional to V_t, we may reasonably define the resolution limit—that is, the uncertainty in the measurement—as equal to $[\overline{(\Delta V_t)^2}]^{1/2}$, where

$$\overline{(\Delta V_t)^2} = \overline{(V_t - \overline{V}_t)^2} = \overline{V_t^2} - \overline{V}_t^2 \qquad (10.1\text{-}7)$$

which, using (10.1-6), gives

$$\overline{(\Delta V_t)^2} = \overline{V_{NC}^2} \qquad (10.1\text{-}8)$$

where we use the fact that $\overline{V}_t = V_S$ since $\overline{V_{NC}(t)} = 0$.[4] It follows from (10.1-8) that the rms (root mean square) fluctuation in the amplitude measurement, and hence the smallest increment of V_t that can be resolved is equal to $(\overline{V_{NC}^2})^{1/2}$.

The foregoing discussion concerned the ability of the measuring system to discriminate small signal increments. If we consider instead the problem

---

[3] The ensemble average $\overline{A(t)}$ of a quantity $A(t)$ is obtained by measuring A simultaneously at time t in a very large number of systems that, *to the best of our knowledge*, are identical. Mathematically,

$$\overline{A(t)} = \lim_{N \to \infty} \left[\frac{1}{N} \sum_{n=1}^{N} A_n(t) \right]$$

where $A_n(t)$ denotes the observation in the nth system. In a truly random phenomenon, the time averaging and ensemble averaging lead to the same result, so the ensemble average is independent of the time t in which it is performed.

[4] The reason for $\overline{V_{NC}(t)} = 0$ can be appreciated from Figure 10-1. $V_{NC}(t)$ has an equal probability of having a zero phase (as in the figure) as a phase of 180°, so averaging over a long time will yield zero.

of measuring small power levels, *we may reasonably define the minimum detectable power as that resulting in a signal power output from the detector which is equal to that of the noise.*[5] At this point the rms fluctuation in the (total) output becomes equal to the average output.

Our next task is thus naturally one of determining the amount of noise present in the physical situations which are of interest to us. Before tackling this task, however, we need to develop some mathematical tools for dealing with random processes.

10.2 Noise—Basic Definitions and Theorems [1]

A real function $v(t)$ and its Fourier transform $V(\omega)$ are related by

$$V(\omega) = \int_{-\infty}^{\infty} v(t)e^{-i\omega t}\, dt \qquad \textbf{(10.2-1)}$$

and

$$v(t) = \frac{1}{2\pi} \int_{-\infty}^{\infty} V(\omega)e^{i\omega t}\, d\omega \qquad \textbf{(10.2-2)}$$

In the process of measuring a signal $v(t)$ we are not in a position to use the infinite time interval needed, according to (10.2-1), to evaluate $V(\omega)$. If the time duration of the measurement is T we may consider the function $v(t)$ to be zero for $t \leqslant 0$ and $t \geqslant T$ and, instead of (10.2-1), get

$$V_T(\omega) = \int_{0}^{T} v(t)e^{-i\omega t}\, dt \qquad \textbf{(10.2-3)}$$

Since $v(t)$ is real, it follows that

$$V_T(\omega) = V_T^*(-\omega) \qquad \textbf{(10.2-4)}$$

T is usually called the resolution or integration time of the system.

Let us evaluate the average power P associated with $v(t)$. Taking the instantaneous power as $v^2(t)$,[6] we obtain

$$P = \frac{1}{T}\int_{0}^{T} v^2(t)\, dt = \frac{1}{2\pi T}\int_{0}^{T}\left\{v(t)\left[\int_{-\infty}^{\infty} V_T(\omega)e^{i\omega t}\, d\omega\right]\right\} dt \qquad \textbf{(10.2-5)}$$

---

[5] The minimum detectable signal power may be defined alternatively as the input power resulting in an output power twice as large as the output in the case of zero input.

[6] It may be convenient for this purpose to think of $v(t)$ as the voltage across a one-ohm resistance.

Interchanging the order of integration and using (10.2-3) and (10.2-4) leads to

$$P = \frac{1}{T} \int_0^T v^2(t)\, dt = \frac{1}{2\pi T} \int_{-\infty}^{\infty} |V_T(\omega)|^2\, d\omega \qquad \textbf{(10.2-6)}$$

$$= \frac{1}{\pi T} \int_0^{\infty} |V_T(\omega)|^2\, d\omega \qquad \textbf{(10.2-7)}$$

If we define the *spectral density function* $S_T(\omega)$ of $v(t)$ by

$$S_T(\omega) \equiv \frac{|V_T(\omega)|^2}{\pi T} \qquad \textbf{(10.2-8)}$$

then, according to Equation (10.2-7), $S_T(\omega)\, d\omega$ is the portion of the average power of $v(t)$ that is due to frequency components between ω and $\omega + d\omega$. According to this physical interpretation we may measure $S_T(\omega)$ by separating the spectrum of $v(t)$ into its various frequency classes as shown in Figure 10-2 and then measuring the power output $S_T(\omega_i)\, \Delta\omega_i$ of each of the filters [2].

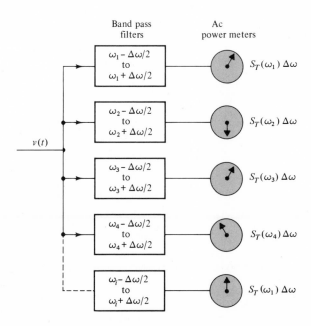

Figure 10-2 Diagram illustrating how the spectral density function $S_T(\omega)$ of a signal $v(t)$ can be obtained by measuring the power due to different frequency intervals.

10.3   The Spectral Density Function of a Train of Randomly Occurring Events

Consider a time-dependent random variable $i(t)$ made up of a very large number of individual events $f(t - t_i)$, which occur at random times t_i.[7] An observation of $i(t)$ during a period T will yield

$$i_T(t) = \sum_{i=1}^{N_T} f(t - t_i) \qquad 0 \leqslant t \leqslant T \tag{10.3-1}$$

where N_T is the total number of events occurring in T. Typical examples of a random function $i(t)$ are provided by the thermionic emission current emitted by a hot cathode (under temperature-limited conditions), or the electron current caused by photoemission from a surface. In these cases $f(t - t_i)$ represents the current resulting from a single electron emission occurring at t_i.

The Fourier transform of $i_T(t)$ is given according to (10.2-3) by

$$I_T(\omega) = \sum_{i=1}^{N_T} F_i(\omega) \tag{10.3-2}$$

where $F_i(\omega)$ is the Fourier transform[8] of $f(t - t_i)$

$$F_i(\omega) = \int_{-\infty}^{\infty} f(t - t_i)e^{-i\omega t}\,dt = e^{-i\omega t_i} \int_{-\infty}^{\infty} f(t)e^{-i\omega t}\,dt$$

$$= e^{-i\omega t_i}F(\omega) \tag{10.3-3}$$

From (10.3-2) and (10.3-3) we obtain

$$|I_T(\omega)|^2 = |F(\omega)|^2 \sum_{i=1}^{N_T} \sum_{j=1}^{N_T} e^{-i\omega(t_i - t_j)}$$

$$= |F(\omega)|^2 \left[N_T + \sum_{i \neq j}^{N_T} \sum_{j}^{N_T} e^{i\omega(t_j - t_i)} \right] \tag{10.3-4}$$

If we take the average of (10.3-4) over an ensemble of a very large number of physically identical systems, the second term on the right side of (10.3-4) can be neglected in comparison to N_T since the times t_i are random.

---

[7] This means that the *a priori* probability that a given event will occur in any time interval is distributed uniformly over the interval, or equivalently, that the probability $p(n)$ for n events to occur in an observation period T is given by the Poisson distribution function [2]

$$p(n) = \frac{[(\bar{n})^n e^{-\bar{n}}]}{n!}$$

where $\bar{n}$ is the average number of events occurring in T.

[8] We assume that the individual event $f(t - t_i)$ is over in a time short compared to the observation period T, so the integration limits can be taken as $-\infty$ to ∞ instead of 0 to T.

This results in

$$\overline{|I_T(\omega)|^2} = \overline{N}_T|F(\omega)|^2 \equiv \overline{N}T|F(\omega)|^2 \qquad \text{(10.3-5)}$$

where the horizontal bar denotes ensemble averaging, and where $\overline{N}$ is the average rate at which the events occur so that $\overline{N}_T = \overline{N}T$. The spectral density function $S_T(\omega)$ of the function $i_T(t)$ is given according to (10.2-8) and (10.3-5) as

$$S(\omega) = \frac{\overline{N}|F(\omega)|^2}{\pi} \qquad \text{(10.3-6)}$$

In practice, one uses more often the spectral density function $S(\nu)$ defined so that the average power due to frequencies between ν and $\nu + d\nu$ is equal to $S(\nu)\,d\nu$. It follows then, that $S(\nu)\,d\nu = S(\omega)\,d\omega$; thus, since $\omega = 2\pi\nu$,

$$S(\nu) = 2\overline{N}|F(2\pi\nu)|^2 \qquad \text{(10.3-7)}$$

The last result is known as Carson's theorem and its usefulness will be demonstrated in the following sections where we employ it in deriving the spectral density function associated with a number of different physical processes related to optical detection.

Equation (10.3-7) was derived for the case in which the individual events $f(t - t_i)$ were displaced in time but were, otherwise, identical. There are physical situations in which the individual events may depend on one or more additional parameters. Denoting the parameter (or group of parameters) as α we can clearly single out the subclass of events $f_\alpha(t - t_i)$ whose α is nearly the same and use (10.3-7) to obtain directly

$$S_\alpha(\nu) = 2\overline{N}(\alpha)|F_\alpha(2\pi\nu)|^2\Delta\alpha \qquad \text{(10.3-8)}$$

for the contribution of this subclass of events to $S(\nu)$. $F_\alpha(\omega)$ is the Fourier transform of $f_\alpha(t)$ and thus $\overline{N}(\alpha)\Delta\alpha$ is the average number of events per second whose α parameter falls between α and $\alpha + \Delta\alpha$.

$$\int_0^\infty \overline{N}(\alpha)\,d\alpha = \overline{N}$$

The probability distribution function for α is $p(\alpha) = \overline{N}(\alpha)/\overline{N}$; therefore,

$$\int_{-\infty}^\infty p(\alpha)\,d\alpha = \frac{1}{\overline{N}}\int_{-\infty}^\infty \overline{N}(\alpha)\,d\alpha = 1 \qquad \text{(10.3-9)}$$

Summing (10.3-8) over all classes α and weighting each class by the probability $p(\alpha)\Delta\alpha$ of its occurrence, we obtain

$$S(\nu) = \sum_\alpha S_\alpha(\nu) = 2\sum_\alpha \overline{N}(\alpha)|F_\alpha(2\pi\nu)|^2\Delta\alpha$$

$$= 2\overline{N}\sum_\alpha |F_\alpha(2\pi\nu)|^2 p(\alpha)\Delta\alpha \qquad \text{(10.3-10)}$$

$$= 2\overline{N}\int_{-\infty}^\infty |F_\alpha(2\pi\nu)|^2 p(\alpha)\,d\alpha = 2\overline{N}\overline{|F(2\pi\nu)|^2}$$

where the bar denotes averaging over α. Equation (10.3-10) is thus the extension of (10.3-7) to the case of events whose characterization involves, in addition to their time t_i, some added parameters. We will use it further in this chapter to derive the noise spectrum of photoconductive detectors in which α is the lifetime of the excited photocarriers.

10.4 Shot Noise [3]

Let us consider the spectral density function of current arising from random generation and flow of mobile charge carriers. This current is identified with "shot noise." To be specific, we consider the case illustrated in Figure 10-3, in which electrons are released at random into the vacuum from electrode A to be collected at electrode B, which is maintained at a slight positive potential relative to A.

The average rate $\overline{N}$ of electron emission from A is $\overline{N} = \overline{I}/e$, where $\overline{I}$ is the average current and the electronic charge is taken as $-e$. The current pulse due to a single electron as observed in the external circuit is

$$i_e(t) = \frac{ev(t)}{d} \tag{10.4-1}$$

where $v(t)$ is the instantaneous velocity and d is the separation between A and B. To prove (10.4-1), consider the case in which the moving electron is replaced by a thin sheet of a very large area and of total charge $-e$ moving between the plates, as illustrated in Figure 10-4.

It is a simple matter to show (see Problem 10-1), using the relation $\nabla \cdot \mathbf{E} = \rho/\epsilon$, that the charge induced by the moving sheet on the left electrode is

$$Q_1 = \frac{e(d - x)}{d} \tag{10.4-2}$$

and that on the right electrode is

$$Q_2 = \frac{ex}{d} \tag{10.4-3}$$

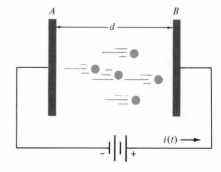

Figure 10-3   Random electron flow between two electrodes. This basic configuration is used in the derivation of shot noise.

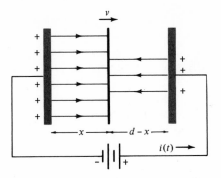

Figure 10-4 Induced charges and field lines due to a thin charge layer between the electrodes.

where x is the position of the charged sheet measured from the left electrode. The current in the external circuit due to a single electron is thus

$$i_e(t) = \frac{dQ_2}{dt} = \frac{e}{d}\frac{dx}{dt} = \frac{e}{d}\,v(t) \qquad (10.4\text{-}4)$$

in agreement with (10.4-1).

The Fourier transform of a single current pulse is

$$F(\omega) = \frac{e}{d}\int_0^{t_a} v(t)e^{-i\omega t}\,dt \qquad (10.4\text{-}5)$$

where t_a is the arrival time of an electron emitted at $t = 0$. If the transit time of an electron is sufficiently small that, at the frequency of interest ω,

$$\omega t_a \ll 1 \qquad (10.4\text{-}6)$$

we can replace $\exp(-i\omega t)$ in (10.4-5) by unity and obtain

$$F(\omega) = \frac{e}{d}\int_0^{t_a} \frac{dx}{dt}\,dt = e \qquad (10.4\text{-}7)$$

since $x(t_a)$ is, by definition, equal to d. Using (10.4-7) in (10.3-7) and recalling that $\overline{I} = e\overline{N}$ gives

$$S(\nu) = 2\overline{N}e^2 = 2e\overline{I} \qquad (10.4\text{-}8)$$

The power (in the sense of 10.2-5) in the frequency interval ν to $\nu + \Delta\nu$ associated with the current is, according to the discussion following Equation (10.2-8), given by $S(\nu)\,\Delta\nu$. It is convenient to represent this power by an *equivalent noise generator* at ν with a mean-square current amplitude

$$\overline{i_N^2}(\nu) \equiv S(\nu)\,\Delta\nu = 2e\overline{I}\Delta\nu \qquad (10.4\text{-}9)$$

The noise mechanism described above is referred to as shot noise.

It is interesting to note that e in (10.4-9) is the charge of the particle responsible for the current flow. If, hypothetically, these carriers had a charge of $2e$, then at the *same average current* $\overline{I}$ the shot noise power would double. Conversely, shot noise would disappear if the magnitude of an individual charge tended to zero. This is a reflection of the fact that shot noise is caused by fluctuations in the current that are due to the discreteness of the charge carriers and to the random electronic emission (for which the number of electrons emitted per unit time obey Poisson statistics [2]). The ratio of the fluctuations to the average current decreases with increasing number of events.[9]

Another point to remember is that, in spite of the appearance of $\overline{I}$ on the right side of (10.4-9), $i_N{}^2(\nu)$ represents an alternating current with frequencies near ν.

10.5 Johnson Noise

Johnson, or Nyquist, noise describes the fluctuations in the voltage across a dissipative circuit element; see References [4] and [5]. These fluctuations are most often caused by the thermal motion of the charge carriers.[10] The charge neutrality of an electrical resistance is satisfied when we consider the whole volume, but locally the random thermal motion of the carriers sets up fluctuating charge gradients and, correspondingly, a fluctuating (ac) voltage. If we now connect a second resistance across the first one, the thermally induced voltage described above will give rise to a current and hence to a power transfer to the second resistor.[11] This is the so-called Johnson noise, whose derivation follows.

Consider the case illustrated in Figure 10-5 of a transmission line connected between two similar resistances R, which are maintained at the same temperature T. We choose the resistance R to be equal to the characteristic impedance Z_0 of the lines, so that no reflection can take place at the ends. The transmission line can support traveling voltage waves of the form

$$v(t) = A \cos (\omega t \pm kz) \tag{10.5-1}$$

where $k = 2\pi/\lambda$ and the phase velocity is $c = \omega/k$.

---

[9] More precisely, for Poisson statistics we have [1]

$$\frac{[\overline{(\Delta N)^2}]^{1/2}}{\overline{N}} = \frac{1}{(\overline{N})^{1/2}}$$

where N is the number of events in an observation time, $\overline{N}$ is the average value of N, and $(\Delta N)^2 \equiv (N - \overline{N})^2$.

[10] We use the word "carriers" rather than "electrons" to include cases of ionic conduction or conduction by holes.

[11] The same argument applies to the second resistor, so at thermal equilibrium the net power leaving each resistor is zero.

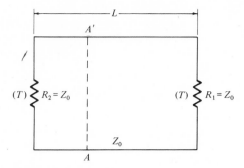

Figure 10-5   Lossless transmission line of characteristic impedance Z_0 connected between two matched loads ($R = Z_0$) at temperature T.

For simplicity we require that the allowed solutions be periodic in the distance L,[12] so if we extend the solution outside the limits $0 \leqslant z \leqslant L$ we obtain

$$v(t) = A \cos\left[\omega t \pm k(z + L)\right] = A \cos\left[\omega t \pm kz\right]$$

This condition is fulfilled when

$$kL = 2m\pi \qquad m = 1, 2, 3, \cdots \qquad \textbf{(10.5-2)}$$

Therefore, two adjacent modes differ in their value of k by

$$\Delta k = \frac{2\pi}{L} \qquad \textbf{(10.5-3)}$$

and the number of modes having their k values somewhere between zero and $+k$ is[13]

$$N_k = \frac{kL}{2\pi} \qquad \textbf{(10.5-4)}$$

or, using $k = 2\pi\nu/c$, we obtain

$$N(\nu) = \frac{\nu L}{c}$$

for the number of positively traveling modes having their frequencies between zero and ν.

The number of modes per unit frequency interval is

$$p(\nu) = \frac{dN(\nu)}{d\nu} = \frac{L}{c} \qquad \textbf{(10.5-5)}$$

---

[12] This, seemingly arbitrary, type of boundary condition is used extensively in similar situations in thermodynamics to derive the blackbody radiation density, or in solid-state physics to derive the density of electronic states in crystals.

[13] Negative k values correspond, according to (10.5-1), to waves traveling in the $-z$ direction. Our bookkeeping is thus limited to modes carrying power in the $+z$ direction.

Consider the power flowing in the $+z$ direction across some arbitrary plane, $A - A'$ say. It is clear that due to the lack of reflections this power must originate in R_2. Since the power is carried by the electromagnetic modes of the system, we have

$$\text{power} = (\text{energy/distance})(\text{velocity of energy})$$

We find, taking the velocity of light as c, that the power P due to frequencies between ν and $\nu + \Delta\nu$ is given by

$$P = \left(\frac{1}{L}\right)\left(\begin{array}{c}\text{number of modes between}\\ \nu \text{ and } \nu + \Delta\nu\end{array}\right)(\text{energy per mode})(c)$$

$$= \left(\frac{1}{L}\right)\left(\frac{L}{c}\,\Delta\nu\right)\left(\frac{h\nu}{e^{h\nu/kT} - 1}\right)(c)$$

or

$$P = \frac{h\nu\Delta\nu}{e^{h\nu/kT} - 1} \approx kT\Delta\nu \qquad (kT \gg h\nu) \tag{10.5-6}$$

where we used the fact that in thermal equilibrium the energy of a mode is given by [7]

$$\overline{E} = \frac{h\nu}{e^{h\nu/kT} - 1} \tag{10.5-7}$$

An equal amount of noise power is, of course, generated in the right resistor and is dissipated in the left one, so in thermal equilibrium the net power crossing any plane is zero.

The power given by (10.5-6) represents the maximum noise power available from the resistance, since it is delivered to a matched load. If the load connected across R has a resistance different from R the noise power delivered is less than that given by (10.5-6). The noise-power bookkeeping is done correctly if the resistance R appearing in a circuit is replaced by either one of the following two equivalent circuits: a noise generator in series with R with mean-square voltage amplitude

$$\overline{v_N}^2 = \frac{4h\nu R\Delta\nu}{e^{h\nu/kT} - 1} \underset{kT \gg h\nu}{\simeq} 4kTR\Delta\nu \tag{10.5-8}$$

or a noise current generator of mean square value

$$\overline{i_N}^2 = \frac{4h\nu\Delta\nu}{R(e^{h\nu/kT} - 1)} \underset{kT \gg h\nu}{\simeq} \frac{4kT\Delta\nu}{R} \tag{10.5-9}$$

in parallel with R. The noise representations of the resistor are shown in Figure 10-6. There are numerous other derivations of the formula for Johnson noise. For derivations using lumped-circuit concepts and an antenna example, the reader is referred to References [6] and [7], respectively.

Statistical derivation of Johnson noise.   The derivation of Johnson noise leading to (10.5-6) leans heavily on thermodynamic and statistical mechanics considerations. It may be instructive to obtain this result using a

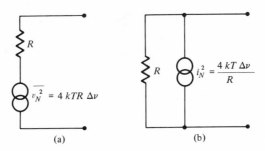

Figure 10-6   (a) Voltage and (b) current noise equivalent circuits of a resistance.

physical model for a resistance and applying the mathematical tools developed in this chapter. The model used is shown in Figure 10-7.

The resistor consists of a medium of volume $V = Ad$, which contains N free electrons per unit volume. In addition, there are N positively charged ions, which preserve the (average) charge neutrality. The electrons move about randomly with an average kinetic energy per electron of

$$\overline{E} = \tfrac{3}{2}kT = \tfrac{1}{2}m(\overline{v_x^2} + \overline{v_y^2} + \overline{v_z^2}) \tag{10.5-10}$$

where $\overline{v_x^2} = \overline{v_y^2} = \overline{v_z^2}$ refer to thermal averages. A variety of scattering mechanisms including electron–electron, electron–ion, and electron–phonon collisions act to interrupt the electron motion at an average rate of τ_0^{-1} times per second. τ_0 is thus the mean scattering time. These scattering mechanisms are responsible for the electrical resistance and give rise to a conductivity[14]

$$\sigma = \frac{Ne^2\tau_0}{m} \tag{10.5-11}$$

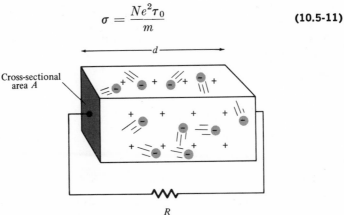

Figure 10-7   Model of a resistance used in deriving the Johnson-noise formula.

---

[14] The derivation of (10.5-11) can be found in any introductory book on solid-state physics.

where m is the mass of the electron.[15] The sample resistance is thus

$$R = \frac{d}{\sigma A} = \frac{md}{Ne^2\tau_0 A} \qquad \textbf{(10.5-12)}$$

We apply next the results of Section 10-3 to the problem and choose as our basic single event the current pulse $i_e(t)$ in the external circuit due to the motion of *one* electron between two successive scattering events. Using (10.4-1), we write

$$i_e(t) = \begin{cases} \dfrac{ev_x}{d} & 0 \leqslant t \leqslant \tau \\ 0 & \text{otherwise} \end{cases} \qquad \textbf{(10.5-13)}$$

where v_x is the x component of the velocity (assumed constant) and where τ is the scattering time of the electron under observation. Taking the Fourier transform of $i_e(t)$, we have

$$I_e(\omega, \tau, v_x) = \int_0^\tau i_e(t)e^{-i\omega t}\, dt = \frac{ev_x}{-i\omega d}[e^{-i\omega\tau} - 1] \qquad \textbf{(10.5-14)}$$

from which

$$|I_e(\omega, \tau, v_x)|^2 = \frac{e^2 v_x^2}{\omega^2 d^2}[2 - e^{i\omega\tau} - e^{-i\omega\tau}] \qquad \textbf{(10.5-15)}$$

According to (10.3-10) we need to average $|I_e(\omega, \tau, v_x)|^2$ over the parameters τ and v_x. We assume that τ and v_x are independent variables—that is, that the probability function

$$p(\alpha) = p(\tau, v_x) = g(\tau)f(v_x)$$

is the product of the individual probabilities [1]—and take $g(\tau)$ as[16]

$$g(\tau) = \frac{1}{\tau_0}e^{-\tau/\tau_0} \qquad \textbf{(10.5-16)}$$

---

[15] In a semiconductor we use the effective mass of the charge carrier.

[16] If the collision probability per carrier per unit times is $1/\tau_0$ and $q(t)$ is the probability that an electron *has not* collided by time t, we have:

$$q'(t) = -q(t)\frac{1}{\tau_0} \Rightarrow q(t) = e^{-t/\tau_0}$$

Taking $g(\tau)\, d\tau$ as the probability that a collision will occur between τ and $\tau + d\tau$, it follows that

$$q(t) = 1 - \int_0^t g(t')\, dt'$$

and thus

$$g(t) = -\frac{dq}{dt} = \frac{1}{\tau_0}e^{-t/\tau_0}$$

as in (10.5-16).

and, performing the averaging over τ, obtain

$$\overline{|I_e(\omega, v_x)|^2} = \int_0^\infty g(\tau) |I_e(\omega, v_x, \tau)|^2 \, d\tau = \frac{2e^2 v_x^2 \tau_0^2}{d^2(1 + \omega^2 \tau_0^2)} \qquad \textbf{(10.5-17)}$$

The second averaging over v_x^2 is particularly simple, since it results in the replacement of v_x^2 in (10.5-17) by its average $\overline{v_x^2}$, which, for a sample at thermal equilibrium, is given according to (10.5-10) by $\overline{v_x^2} = kT/m$. The final result is then

$$\overline{|I_e(\omega)|^2} = \frac{2e^2 \tau_0^2 kT}{md^2(1 + \omega^2 \tau_0^2)} \qquad \textbf{(10.5-18)}$$

The average number of scattering events per second $\overline{N}$ is equal to the total number of electrons NV divided by the mean scattering time τ_0

$$\overline{N} = \frac{NV}{\tau_0} \qquad \textbf{(10.5-19)}$$

thus, from (10.3-10), we obtain

$$S(\nu) = \frac{4NVe^2 \tau_0 kT}{md^2(1 + \omega^2 \tau_0^2)}$$

and, after using (10.5-12) and limiting ourselves as in (10.4-6) to frequencies where $\omega \tau_0 \ll 1$, we get

$$\overline{i_N^2}(\nu) \equiv S(\nu)\Delta\nu = \frac{4kT\Delta\nu}{R} \qquad \textbf{(10.5-20)}$$

in agreement with (10.5-9).

10.6 Spontaneous Emission Noise in Laser Oscillators

Another type of noise that plays an important role in quantum electronics is that of spontaneous emission in laser oscillators and amplifiers. As shown in Chapter 5, a necessary condition for laser amplification is that the atomic population of a pair of levels 1 and 2 be inverted. If $E_2 > E_1$, gain occurs when $N_2 > N_1$. Assume that an optical wave with frequency $\nu \simeq (E_2 - E_1)/h$ is propagating through an inverted population medium. This wave will grow coherently due to the effect of stimulated emission. In addition, its radiation will be contaminated by noise radiation caused by spontaneous emission from level 2 to level 1. Some of the radiation emitted by the spontaneous emission will propagate very nearly along the same direction as that of the stimulated emission and cannot be separated from it. This has two main consequences. First, the laser output has a finite spectral width. This effect is described in this section. Second, the signal-to-noise ratio achievable at the output of laser amplifiers [7] is limited because of the intermingling of spontaneous emission noise power with that of the amplified signal. (See Figure 10-8.)

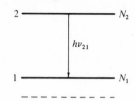

Figure 10-8 An atomic transition with $N_2 > N_1$ providing gain for laser oscillation.

Returning to the case of a laser oscillator, we represent it by an *RLC* circuit, as shown in Figure 10-9. The presence of the laser medium with negative loss (that is, gain) is accounted for by including a negative conductance $-G_m$ while the ordinary loss mechanisms described in Chapter 6 are represented by the positive conductance G_0. The noise generator associated with the losses G_0 is given according to (10.5-9) as

$$\overline{i_N{}^2} = \frac{4\hbar\omega G_0(\Delta\omega/2\pi)}{e^{\hbar\omega/kT} - 1}$$

where T is the actual temperature of the losses. Spontaneous emission is represented by a similar expression[17]

$$\left(\overline{i_N{}^2}\right)_{\substack{\text{spont.}\\\text{emission}}} = \frac{4\hbar\omega(-G_m)(\Delta\omega/2\pi)}{e^{\hbar\omega/kT_m} - 1} \tag{10.6-1}$$

where the term $(-G_m)$ represents negative losses and T_m is a temperature determined by the population ratio according to

$$\frac{N_2}{N_1} = e^{-\hbar\omega/kT_m} \tag{10.6-2}$$

Since $N_2 > N_1$, then $T_m < 0$, $(\overline{i_N{}^2})$ in (10.6-1) is positive definite.

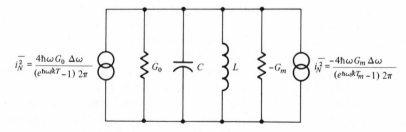

Figure 10-9 Equivalent circuit of a laser oscillator.

---

[17] The 2π factor appearing in the denominators of $\overline{i_N{}^2}$ is due to the fact that here we use $\overline{i_N{}^2}(\omega)$ instead of $\overline{i_N{}^2}(\nu)$ with

$$\overline{i_N{}^2}(\omega)\Delta\omega = \overline{i_N{}^2}(\nu)\Delta\nu$$

Although a detailed justification of (10.6-1) is outside the scope of the present treatment, a strong case for its plausibility can be made by noting that since $G_m \propto N_2 - N_1$, $\overline{(i_N{}^2)}$ in (10.6-1) can be written, using (10.6-2), as[18]

$$\overline{(i_N{}^2)}_{\substack{\text{spont.}\\\text{emission}}} \propto \frac{-4\hbar\omega\Delta\omega(N_2 - N_1)}{(N_1/N_2) - 1} = 4\hbar\omega\Delta\omega N_2 \qquad \textbf{(10.6-3)}$$

and is thus proportional to N_2. This makes sense, since spontaneous emission power is due to $2 \rightarrow 1$ transitions and should consequently be proportional to N_2.

Returning to the equivalent circuit, its quality factor Q is given by

$$Q^{-1} = \frac{G_0 - G_m}{\omega_0 C} = \frac{1}{Q_0} - \frac{1}{Q_m} \qquad \textbf{(10.6-4)}$$

where $\omega_0{}^2 = (LC)^{-1}$. The circuit impedance is

$$Z(\omega) = \frac{1}{(G_0 - G_m) + (1/i\omega L) + i\omega C}$$
$$= \frac{i\omega}{C} \frac{1}{(i\omega\omega_0/Q) + (\omega_0{}^2 - \omega^2)} \qquad \textbf{(10.6-5)}$$

so the voltage across this impedance due to a current source with a complex amplitude $I(\omega)$ is

$$V(\omega) = \frac{i}{C} \frac{I(\omega)}{[(\omega_0{}^2 - \omega^2)/\omega] + (i\omega_0/Q)} \qquad \textbf{(10.6-6)}$$

which, near $\omega = \omega_0$, becomes

$$\overline{|V(\omega)|^2} = \frac{1}{4C^2} \frac{\overline{|I(\omega)|^2}}{(\omega_0 - \omega)^2 + (\omega_0{}^2/4Q^2)} \qquad \textbf{(10.6-7)}$$

The current sources driving the resonant circuit are those shown in Figure 10-9; since they are not correlated, we may take $|I(\omega)|^2$ as the sum of their mean-square values

$$\overline{|I(\omega)|^2} = 4\hbar\omega \left[\frac{G_m N_2}{N_2 - N_1} + \frac{G_0}{e^{\hbar\omega/kT} - 1} \right] \frac{d\omega}{2\pi} \qquad \textbf{(10.6-8)}$$

[18] The proportionality of G_m to $N_2 - N_1$ can be justified by noting that in the equivalent circuit (Figure 10.9) the stimulated emission power is given by $v^2 G_m$ where v is the voltage. Using the field approach, this power is proportional to $E^2(N_2 - N_1)$ where E is the field amplitude. Since v is proportional to E, G_m is proportional to $N_2 - N_1$.

where in the first term inside the square brackets we used (10.6-2). In the optical region, $\lambda = 1\ \mu$m say, and for $T = 300°$K we have $\hbar\omega/kT \simeq 50$; thus, since near oscillation $G_m \simeq G_0$, we may neglect the thermal (Johnson) noise term in (10.6-8), thereby obtaining

$$\overline{|V(\omega)|^2}_{\omega \simeq \omega_0} = \frac{\hbar G_m}{2\pi C^2}\left(\frac{N_2}{N_2 - N_1}\right)\frac{\omega\,d\omega}{(\omega_0{}^2 - \omega^2) + (\omega_0{}^2/4Q^2)} \qquad \textbf{(10.6-9)}$$

Equation (10.6-9) represents the spectral distribution of the laser output. If we subject the output to high-resolution spectral analysis we should, according to (10.6-9), measure a linewidth

$$\Delta\omega = \frac{\omega_0}{Q} \qquad \textbf{(10.6-10)}$$

between the half-intensity points. The trouble is that, though correct, Equation (10.6-10) is not of much use in practice. The reason is that according to (10.6-4), Q is equal to the difference of two nearly equal quantities neither of which is known with high enough accuracy. We can avoid this difficulty by showing that Q is related to the laser power output, and thus $\Delta\omega$ may be expressed in terms of the power.

The total power extracted from the atoms comprising the laser is

$$\begin{aligned}
P &= G_0 \int_0^\infty \frac{|V(\omega)|^2}{d\omega}\,d\omega \\[2mm]
&= \frac{\hbar G_m G_0}{2\pi C^2}\left(\frac{N_2}{N_2 - N_1}\right)\int_0^\infty \frac{\omega\,d\omega}{(\omega_0{}^2 - \omega^2) + (\omega_0/2Q)^2}
\end{aligned} \qquad \textbf{(10.6-11)}$$

Since the integrand peaks sharply near $\omega \simeq \omega_0$, we may replace ω in the numerator of (10.6-11) by ω_0 and after integration obtain

$$P = \frac{\hbar G_m G_0 Q}{2C^2}\left(\frac{N_2}{N_2 - N_1}\right) \qquad \textbf{(10.6-12)}$$

which is the desired result linking P to Q. In a laser oscillator the gain very nearly equals the loss, or in our notation, $G_m \simeq G_0$. Using this result in (10.6-12), we obtain

$$Q = \frac{2C^2}{\hbar G_0{}^2}\left(\frac{N_2 - N_1}{N_2}\right)P$$

which, when substituted in (10.6-10), yields

$$\Delta\nu = \frac{\pi h \nu_0 (\Delta\nu_{1/2})^2}{P} \left(\frac{N_2}{N_2 - N_1} \right) \qquad \textbf{(10.6-13)}$$

where $\Delta\nu_{1/2}$ is the full width of the passive cavity resonance given as $\Delta\nu_{1/2} = \nu_0/Q_c = (1/2\pi)(G_0/C)$.

Numerical example. Consider a laser oscillator with the following characteristics

$\nu = 4.73 \times 10^{14}\,\text{Hz}$

$l = 100\,\text{cm}$

$\alpha = 1$ percent per pass

$P = 1\,\text{mW}$

$N_2 \gg N_1$

These numbers are typical of low-power laboratory He-Ne lasers. From (4.6-6) we get

$$\Delta\nu_{1/2} = \frac{1}{2\pi l_c} = \frac{c\alpha}{2\pi l} \simeq 5 \times 10^5$$

Using the foregoing data in (10.6-13) gives

$$\Delta\nu \simeq 10^{-3}\,\text{Hz}$$

for the spectral width of the laser output. We must emphasize, however, that $\Delta\nu$ as given by (10.6-13) represents a theoretical limit and does not necessarily correspond to the value commonly observed in the laboratory. The output of operational laser is broadened mostly by thermal and acoustic fluctuations in the optical resonator length, which cause the resonance frequencies to shift about rapidly. An experimental determination of the limiting $\Delta\nu$ requires great care in acoustic isolation and thermal stabilization; see References [11] and [12]. An observed value of $\Delta\nu \sim 10^3$ Hz reported in [11] in a 1-mW He-Ne laser is still limited by vibrations and thermal fluctuations.

Figure 10-10 shows the output spectrum of a $Pb_{0.88}Sn_{0.12}Te$ injection laser at 10.6 μm [13]. The narrowing of the spectrum from $\Delta\nu = 1.75$ MHz to $\Delta\nu = 0.75$ MHz is consistent with the inverse dependence on P predicted by Equation (10.6-13).

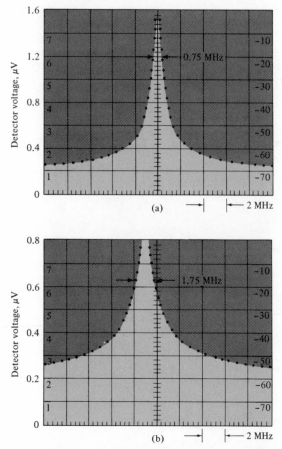

Figure 10-10 Spectrum analyzer display of beat note between low-power diode laser mode and P(16) transition of a CO_2 gas laser, corresponding to diode laser current of 865 mA in (**a**) and 845 mA in (**b**). Center frequency is 92 MHz. The dotted curves correspond to a Lorentzian lineshape, with the indicated half-power linewidths. (After Reference [13].)

■ PROBLEMS

10-1 Derive Equations (10.4-3) and (10.4-4). (*Hint:* Apply the relation

$$\int_s \mathbf{D} \cdot \mathbf{n} \, ds = \int_v \rho \, dv$$

to a differential volume containing the charge sheet.)

10-2 Derive the shot noise formula without making the restriction (10.4-6) $\omega t_a \ll 1$. Assume the carriers move between the electrodes at a constant velocity.

10-3   Derive Equation (10.5-11).

10-4   Complete the missing steps in the derivation of (10.5-20).

10-5   Estimate the scattering time τ_0 of carriers in copper at $T = 300°$K using a tabulated value for its conductivity. At what frequencies is the condition $\omega\tau_0 \ll 1$ violated?

10-6   Repeat Problem 10-5 for a material with a carrier density of 10^{22} cm^{-3} and $\sigma = 10^{-5}$ (ohm-cm)$^{-1}$.

10-7   What is the change $\Delta\nu$ in the resonant frequency of a laser whose cavity length changes by Δl?

10-8   a.   Estimate the frequency smearing $\Delta\nu$ of a laser in which fused-quartz rods are used to determine the length of the optical cavity in an environment where the temperature stability is $\pm 0.5°$K. [*Caution:* Do not forget the dependence of n on T.]

b.   What temperature stability is needed to reduce $\Delta\nu$ to less than 10^3 Hz?

10-9   Derive expression (10.5-9), $\overline{i_N^2}(\omega) = 4kT\Delta\nu/R$, for the Johnson noise by considering a high-Q parallel RLC circuit which is shunted by a current source of mean-square amplitude $\overline{i_N^2}(\omega)$. The magnitude of $\overline{i_N^2}(\omega)$ is to be chosen so that the resulting excitation of the circuit corresponds to a stored electromagnetic energy of kT. [*Hint:* Since the magnetic and electric energies are equal, then

$$kT = C\overline{v^2(t)} = C \int_0^\infty \frac{\overline{V_N^2}(\omega)}{d\omega} \, d\omega$$

where $\overline{V_N^2}(\omega) = \overline{i_N^2}(\omega)|Z(\omega)|^2$. Also assume that $\overline{i_N^2}(\omega)/\Delta\nu$ is independent of frequency.]

■ **REFERENCES**

[1]   The basic concepts of noise theory used in this chapter can be found, for example, in W. B. Davenport and W. L. Root, *An Introduction to the Theory of Random Signals and Noise.* New York: McGraw-Hill, 1958.

[2]   Bennett, W. R., "Methods of solving noise problems," *Proc. IRE,* vol. 44, p. 609, 1956.

[3]   The classic reference to this topic is: S. O. Rice, "Mathematical analysis of random noise," *Bell System Tech. J.,* vol. 23, p. 282, 1944; vol. 24, p. 46, 1945.

[4] Johnson, J. B., "Thermal agitation of electricity in conductors," *Phys. Rev.*, vol. 32, p. 97, 1928.

[5] Nyquist, H., "Thermal agitation of electric charge in conductors," *Phys. Rev.*, vol. 32, p. 110, 1928.

[6] Smith, R. A., F. A. Jones, and R. P. Chasmar, *The Detection and Measurement of Infrared Radiation*. New York: Oxford, 1968.

[7] Yariv, A., *Quantum Electronics*. New York: Wiley, 1967.

[8] Gordon, J. P., H. J. Zeiger, and C. H. Townes, "The maser—New type of microwave amplifier, frequency standard and spectrometer," *Phys. Rev.*, vol. 99, p. 1264, 1955.

[9] Gordon, E. I., "Optical maser oscillators and noise," *Bell System Tech. J.*, vol. 43, p. 507, 1964.

[10] Grivet, P. A., and A. Blaquiere, *Optical Masers*. New York: Polytechnic Press, 1963, p. 69.

[11] Jaseja, T. J., A. Javan, and C. H. Townes, "Frequency stability of He-Ne masers and measurements of length," *Phys. Rev. Letters*, vol. 10, p. 165, 1963.

[12] Egorov, Y. P., "Measurements of natural line width of the emission of a gas laser with coupled modes," *JETP Letters*, vol. 8, p. 320, 1968.

[13] Hinkley, E. D., and C. Freed, "Direct observation of the Lorentzian lineshape as limited by quantum phase noise in a laser above threshold," *Phys. Rev. Letters*, vol. 23, p. 277, 1969.

CHAPTER

11

The Detection of Optical Radiation

11.0 Introduction

The detection of optical radiation is often accomplished by converting the radiant energy into an electric signal whose intensity is measured by conventional techniques. Some of the physical mechanisms that may be involved in this conversion include

1. the generation of mobile charge carriers in solid-state photoconductive detectors,
2. changing through absorption the temperature of thermocouples, thus causing a change in the junction voltage, and
3. the release by the photoelectric effect of free electrons from photoemissive surfaces.

In this chapter we consider in some detail the operation of four of the most important detectors:

1. the photomultiplier,
2. the photoconductive detector,
3. the photodiode, and
4. the avalanche photodiode.

The limiting sensitivity of each is discussed and compared to the theoretical limit. We will find that by use of the heterodyne mode of detection the theoretical limit of sensitivity may be approached.

269

11.1   Optically Induced Transition Rates

A common feature of all the optical detection schemes discussed in this chapter is that the electric signal is proportional to the rate at which electrons are excited by the optical field. This excitation involves a transition of the electron from some initial bound state, say a, to a final state (or a group of states) b in which it is free to move and contribute to the current flow. For example, in an n-type photoconductive detector, state a corresponds to electrons in the filled valence band or localized donor impurity atoms, while state b corresponds to electrons in the conduction band. The two levels involved are shown schematically in Figure 11-1. A photon of energy $h\nu$ is absorbed in the process of exciting an electron from a "bound" state a to a "free" state b in which the electron can contribute to the current flow.

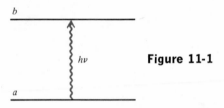

Figure 11-1

An important point to understand before proceeding with the analysis of different detection schemes is the manner of relating the transition rate per electron from state a to b to the intensity of the optical field. This rate is derived by quantum mechanical considerations.[1] In our case it can be stated in the following form: Given a nearly sinusoidal[2] optical field

$$e(t) = \tfrac{1}{2}[E(t)e^{i\omega_0 t} + E^*(t)e^{-i\omega_0 t}] \equiv \mathrm{Re}\,[V(t)] \qquad \textbf{(11.1-1)}$$

where $V(t) = E(t)\exp(i\omega_0 t)$,[3] the transition rate per electron induced by this field is proportional to $V(t)V^*(t)$. Denoting the transition rate as $W_{a\to b}$, we have

$$W_{a\to b} \propto V(t)V^*(t) \qquad \textbf{(11.1-2)}$$

We can easily show that $V(t)V^*(t)$ is equal to twice the average value of $e^2(t)$, where the averaging is performed over a few optical periods.

---

[1] More specifically, from first order time-dependent perturbation theory; see for example, Reference [1].

[2] By "nearly sinusoidal" we mean a field where $E(t)$ varies slowly compared to $\exp(i\omega_0 t)$ or, equivalently, where the Fourier spectrum of $E(t)$ occupies a bandwidth that is small compared to ω_0. Under these conditions the variation of the amplitude $E(t)$ during a few optical periods can be neglected.

[3] $V(t)$ is referred to as the "analytic signal" of $e(t)$. See Problem 1.1.

To illustrate the power of this seemingly simple result, consider the problem of determining the transition rate due to a field

$$e(t) = E_0 \cos (\omega_0(t) + \phi_0) + E_1 \cos (\omega_1 t + \phi_1) \qquad \textbf{(11.1-3)}$$

taking $\omega_1 - \omega_0 \equiv \omega \ll \omega_0$. We can rewrite (11.1-3) as

$$\begin{aligned} e(t) &= \mathrm{Re}\,(E_0 e^{i(\omega_0 t + \phi_0)} + E_1 e^{i(\omega_1 t + \phi_1)}) \\ &= \mathrm{Re}\,[(E_0 e^{i\phi_0} + E_1 e^{i(\omega t + \phi_1)})e^{i\omega_0 t}] \end{aligned} \qquad \textbf{(11.1-4)}$$

and, using (11.1-1), identify $V(t)$ as

$$V(t) = [E_0 e^{i\phi_0} + E_1 e^{i(\omega t + \phi_1)}]e^{i\omega_0 t}$$

thus, using (11.1-2), we obtain

$$\begin{aligned} W_{a \to b} &\propto (E_0 e^{i\phi_0} + E_1 e^{i(\omega t + \phi_1)})(E_0 e^{-i\phi_0} + E_1 e^{-i(\omega t + \phi_1)}) \\ &= E_0{}^2 + E_1{}^2 + 2E_0 E_1 \cos (\omega t + \phi_1 - \phi_0) \end{aligned} \qquad \textbf{(11.1-5)}$$

This shows that the transition rate has, in addition to a constant term $E_0{}^2 + E_1{}^2$, a component oscillating at the difference frequency ω with a phase equal to the difference of the two original phases. This coherent "beating" effect forms the basis of the heterodyne detection scheme, which is discussed in detail in Section 11.4.

11.2 The Photomultiplier

The photomultiplier, one of the most common optical detectors, is used to measure radiation in the near ultraviolet, visible, and near infrared regions of the spectrum. Because of its inherent high current amplification and low noise, the photomultiplier is one of the most sensitive instruments devised by man and under optimal operation—which involves long integration time, cooling of the photocathode, and pulse-height discrimination—has been used to detect power levels as low as about 10^{-19} watts [2].

A schematic diagram of a conventional photomultiplier is shown in Figure 11–2. It consists of a photocathode (C) and a series of electrodes, called dynodes, which are labeled 1 through 8. The dynodes are kept at progressively higher potentials with respect to the cathode, with a typical potential difference between adjacent dynodes of 100 volts. The last electrode (A), the anode, is used to collect the electrons. The whole assembly is contained within a vacuum envelope in order to reduce the possibility of electronic collisions with gas molecules.

The photocathode is the most crucial part of the photomultiplier, since it converts the incident optical radiation to electronic current and thus determines the wavelength-response characteristics of the detector and, as will be seen, its limiting sensitivity. The photocathode consists of materials with low surface work functions. Compounds involving Ag-O-Cs and

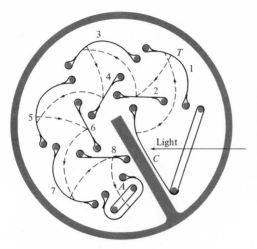

Figure 11-2   Photocathode and focusing dynode configuration of a typical commercial photo-multiplier. C = cathode; 1–8 = secondary-emission dynodes; A = collecting anode. (After Reference [3].)

Sb-Cs are often used; see References [2] and [3]. These compounds possess work functions as low as 1.5 eV as compared to 4.5 eV in typical metals. As can be seen in Figure 11-3, this makes it possible to detect photons with longer wavelengths. It follows from the figure that the low-frequency detection limit corresponds to $h\nu = \phi$. At present the lowest-work-function materials make possible photoemission at wavelengths as long as 1–1.1 μm.

Spectral response curves of a number of commercial photocathodes are shown in Figure 11-4. The quantum efficiency (or quantum yield as it is often called) is defined as the number of electrons released per incident photon.

The electrons that are emitted from the photocathode are focused electrostatically and accelerated toward the first dynode arriving with a kinetic energy of, typically, about 100 eV. Secondary emission from dynode surfaces causes a multiplication of the initial current. This process repeats itself at each dynode until the initial current emitted by the photocathode is amplified by a very large factor. If the average secondary emission multiplication at each dynode is δ (that is, δ secondary electrons for each incident one) and the number of dynodes is N, the total current multipli-

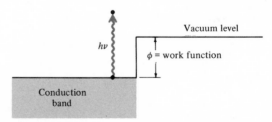

Figure 11-3   Photomultiplier photocathode. The vacuum level corresponds to the energy of an electron at rest an infinite distance from the cathode. The work function ϕ is the minimum energy required to lift an electron from the metal into the vacuum, so only photons with $h\nu > \phi$ can be detected.

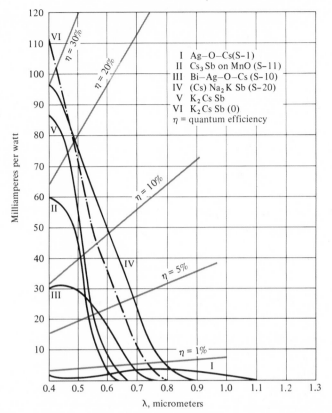

Figure 11-4 Photoresponse versus wavelength characteristics and quantum efficiency of a number of commercial photocathodes. (After Reference [3], p. 228.)

cation between the cathode and anode is

$$G = \delta^N$$

which for typical values[4] of $\delta = 5$ and $N = 9$ gives $G \simeq 2 \times 10^6$.

11.3 Noise Mechanisms in Photomultipliers

The random fluctuations observed in the photomultiplier output are due to:

1. Cathode shot noise, given according to (10.4-9) by

$$\overline{(i_{N1}{}^2)} = G^2 2e(\overline{i}_c + i_d)\Delta\nu \qquad \textbf{(11.3-1)}$$

---

[4] The value of δ depends on the voltage V between dynodes and values of $\delta \simeq 10$ can be obtained (for $V \simeq 400$ volts). In commercial tubes, values of $\delta \simeq 5$, achievable with $V \simeq 100$ volts, are commonly used.

where $\bar{i}_c$ is the average current emitted by the photocathode due to the signal power which is incident on it. The current i_d is the so-called "dark current," which is due to random thermal excitation of electrons from the surface as well as to excitation by cosmic rays and radioactive bombardment.

2.   Dynode shot noise, which is the shot noise due to the random nature of the secondary emission process at the dynodes. Since current originating at a dynode does not exercise the full gain of the tube, the contribution of all the dynodes to the total shot noise output is smaller by a factor of $\sim \delta^{-1}$ than that of the cathode; since $\delta \simeq 5$ it amounts to a small correction and will be ignored in the following.

3.   Johnson noise, which is the thermal noise associated with the output resistance R connected across the anode. Its magnitude is given by (10.5-9) as

$$\overline{(i_{N2}{}^2)} = \frac{4kT\Delta\nu}{R} \tag{11.3-2}$$

Minimum detectable power in photomultipliers—video detection.   Photomultipliers are used primarily in one of two ways. In the first, the optical wave to be detected is modulated at some low frequency ω_m before impinging on the photocathode. The signal consists then, of an output current oscillating at ω_m, which, as will be shown below, has an amplitude proportional to the optical intensity. This mode of operation is known as *video*, or straight, detection.

In the second mode of operation, the signal to be detected, whose optical frequency is ω_s, is combined at the photocathode with a much stronger optical wave of frequency $\omega_s + \omega$. The output signal is then a current at the offset frequency ω. This scheme, known as *heterodyne* detection, will be considered in detail in Section 11-4.

The optical signal in the case of video detection may be taken as

$$e_s(t) = E_s(1 + m \cos \omega_m t) \cos \omega_s t$$

$$= \mathrm{Re}\,[E_s(1 + m \cos \omega_m t)e^{i\omega_s t}] \tag{11.3-3}$$

where the factor $(1 + m \cos \omega_m t)$ represents amplitude modulation of the carrier.[5] The photocathode current is given, according to (11.1-2), by

$$i_c(t) \propto [E_s(1 + m \cos \omega_m t)]^2$$

$$= E_s{}^2\left[\left(1 + \frac{m^2}{2}\right) + 2m \cos \omega_m t + \frac{m^2}{2} \cos 2\omega_m t\right] \tag{11.3-4}$$

To determine the proportionality constant involved in (11.3-4), consider

---

[5] The amplitude modulation can be due to the information carried by the optical wave or, as an example, to chopping before detection.

the case of $m = 0$. The average photocathode current due to the signal is then[6]

$$\bar{i}_c = \frac{Pe\eta}{h\nu_s} \qquad (11.3\text{-}5)$$

where $\nu_s = \omega_s/2\pi$, P is the average optical power, and η (the quantum efficiency) is the average number of electrons emitted from the photocathode per incident photon. This number depends on the photon frequency, the photocathode surface, and in practice (see Figure 11-4) is found to approach 0.3. Using (11.3-5), we rewrite (11.3-4) as

$$i_c(t) = \frac{Pe\eta}{h\nu_s}\left[\left(1 + \frac{m^2}{2}\right) + 2m\cos\omega_m t + \frac{m^2}{2}\cos 2\omega_m t\right] \qquad (11.3\text{-}6)$$

The signal output current at ω_m is

$$i_s = \frac{GPe\eta}{h\nu_s}(2m)\cos\omega_m t \qquad (11.3\text{-}7)$$

If the output of the detector is limited by filtering to a bandwidth $\Delta\nu$ centered on ω_m, it contains a shot-noise current, which, according to (11.3-1), has a mean-squared amplitude

$$\overline{(i_{N1}{}^2)} = 2G^2e(\bar{i}_c + i_d)\Delta\nu \qquad (11.3\text{-}8)$$

where $\bar{i}_c$ is the average signal current and i_d is the dark current.

The noise and signal equivalent circuit is shown in Figure 11-5, where for the sake of definiteness we took the modulation index $m = 1$. R represents the output load of the photomultiplier. T_e is chosen so that the term $4kT_e\,\Delta\nu/R$ accounts for the thermal noise of R as well as for the noise generated by the amplifier that follows the photomultiplier.

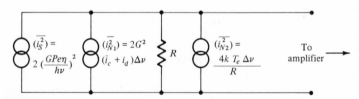

Figure 11-5   Equivalent circuit of a photomultiplier.

The signal-to-noise power ratio at the output is thus

$$\frac{S}{N} = \frac{\overline{i_s{}^2}}{\overline{(i_{N1}{}^2)} + \overline{(i_{N2}{}^2)}}$$

$$= \frac{2(Pe\eta/h\nu_s)^2 G^2}{2G^2e(\bar{i}_c + i_d)\Delta\nu + (4kT_e\Delta\nu/R)} \qquad (11.3\text{-}9)$$

---

[6] $P/h\nu_s$ is the rate of photon incidence on the photocathode; thus, if it takes $1/\eta$ photons to generate one electron, the average current is given by (11.3-5).

Due to the large current gain ($G \simeq 10^6$) the first term in the denominator of (11.3-9) which represents amplified cathode shot noise is much larger than the thermal and amplifier noise term $4kT_e \, \Delta\nu/R$. Neglecting the term $4kT_e \, \Delta\nu/R$, assuming $i_d \gg \bar{i}_c$, and setting $S/N = 1$, we can solve for the minimum detectable optical power.

$$P_{\min} = \frac{h\nu_s (i_d \Delta\nu)^{1/2}}{\eta e^{1/2}} \qquad \text{(11.3-10)}$$

Numerical example—sensitivity of photomultiplier. Consider a typical case of detecting an optical signal under the following conditions:

$$\nu_s = 6 \times 10^{14} \text{ Hz } (\lambda = 0.5 \, \mu\text{m})$$
$$\eta = 10 \text{ percent}$$
$$\Delta\nu = 1 \text{ Hz}$$
$$i_d = 10^{-15} \text{ ampere (a typical value of the dark photocathode current)}$$

Substitution in (11.3-10) gives

$$P_{\min} = 3 \times 10^{-16} \text{ watt}$$

The corresponding cathode signal current is $\bar{i}_c \sim 10^{-17}$ ampere, so the assumption $i_d \gg \bar{i}_c$ is justified.

Signal-limited shot noise. If one could, somehow, eliminate the dark current altogether, so that the only contribution to the average photocathode current is $\bar{i}_c$, that is that due to the optical signal, then, using (11.3-5) and (11.3-9) to solve self-consistently for $P_{\min}$,

$$P_{\min} \simeq \frac{h\nu_s \Delta\nu}{\eta} \qquad \text{(11.3-11)}$$

This corresponds to the quantum limit of optical detection. Its significance will be discussed in the next section. The practical achievement of this limit in video detection is nearly impossible since it depends on near total suppression of the dark current and other extraneous noise sources such as background radiation reaching the photocathode and causing shot noise.

The quantum detection limit (11.3-11) can, however, be achieved in the heterodyne mode of optical detection. This is discussed in the next section.

11.4   Heterodyne Detection with Photomultipliers

In the heterodyne mode of optical detection, the signal to be detected $E_s \cos \omega_s t$ is combined with a second optical field, referred to as the local-oscillator field, $E_L \cos (\omega_s + \omega)t$, shifted in frequency by ω ($\omega \ll \omega_s$). The total field incident on the photocathode is therefore given by

$$e(t) = \text{Re}\,[E_L e^{i(\omega_s + \omega)t} + E_s e^{i\omega_s t}] \equiv \text{Re}\,[V(t)] \qquad \textbf{(11.4-1)}$$

The local-oscillator field originates usually at a laser at the receiving end, so that it can be made very large compared to the signal to be detected. In the following we will assume that

$$E_L \gg E_s \qquad \textbf{(11.4-2)}$$

A schematic diagram of a heterodyne detection scheme is shown in Figure 11-6. The current emitted by the photocathode is given, according to (11.1-2) and (11.4-1), by

$$i_c(t) \propto V(t)V^*(t) = E_L{}^2 + E_s{}^2 + 2E_L E_s \cos \omega t$$

which, using (11.4-2) can be written as

$$i_c(t) \equiv aE_L{}^2 \left(1 + \frac{2E_s}{E_L} \cos \omega t\right) = aE_L{}^2 \left(1 + 2\sqrt{\frac{P_s}{P_L}} \cos \omega t\right) \qquad \textbf{(11.4-3)}$$

where P_s and P_L are the signal and local-oscillator powers, respectively. The proportionality constant a in (11.4-3) can be determined as in (11.3-6) by requiring that when $E_s = 0$ the direct current be related to the local-oscillator power P_L by $\bar{i}_c = P_L \eta e/h\nu_L$,[7] so taking $\nu \approx \nu_L$

$$i_c(t) = \frac{P_L e \eta}{h\nu}\left(1 + 2\sqrt{\frac{P_s}{P_L}} \cos \omega t\right) \qquad \textbf{(11.4-4)}$$

The total cathode shot noise is thus

$$\overline{(i_{N1}{}^2)} = 2e\left(i_d + \frac{P_L e \eta}{h\nu}\right)\Delta\nu \qquad \textbf{(11.4-5)}$$

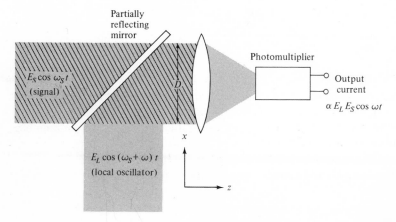

Figure 11-6   Schematic diagram of a heterodyne detector using a photomultiplier.

---

[7] This is just a statement of the fact that each incident photon has a probability η of releasing an electron.

where i_d is the average dark current while $P_L e\eta/h\nu$ is the dc cathode current due to the strong local-oscillator field. The shot-noise current is amplified by G, resulting in an output noise

$$\overline{(i_N{}^2)}_{\text{anode}} = G^2 2e\left(i_d + \frac{P_L e\eta}{h\nu}\right)\Delta\nu \qquad \text{(11.4-6)}$$

The mean-square signal current at the output is, according to (11.4-4),

$$\overline{(i_s{}^2)}_{\text{anode}} = 2G^2\left(\frac{P_s}{P_L}\right)\left(\frac{P_L e\eta}{h\nu}\right)^2 \qquad \text{(11.4-7)}$$

The signal-to-noise power ratio at the output is given by

$$\frac{S}{N} = \frac{2G^2(P_s P_L)(e\eta/h\nu)^2}{\{G^2 2e(i_d + (P_L e\eta/h\nu)] + (4kT_e/R)\}\Delta\nu} \qquad \text{(11.4-8)}$$

where, as in (11.3-9), the last term in the denominator represents the Johnson (thermal) noise generated in the output load, plus the effective input noise of the amplifier following the photomultiplier. The big advantage of the heterodyne detection scheme is now apparent. By increasing P_L the S/N ratio increases until the denominator is dominated by the term $G^2 2e P_L e\eta/h\nu$. This corresponds to the point at which the *shot noise produced by the local oscillator current dwarfs all the other noise contributions.* When this state of affairs prevails, we have, according to (11.4-8),

$$\frac{S}{N} \simeq \frac{P_s}{h\nu\Delta\nu/\eta} \qquad \text{(11.4-9)}$$

which corresponds to the quantum-limited detection limit. The minimum detectable signal—that is, the signal input power leading to an output signal-to-noise ratio of 1—is thus

$$(P_s)_{\min} = \frac{h\nu\Delta\nu}{\eta} \qquad \text{(11.4-10)}$$

This power corresponds for $\eta = 1$ to a flux at a rate of one photon per $(\Delta\nu)^{-1}$ seconds—that is, one photon per resolution time of the system.[8]

Numerical example. It is interesting to compare the minimum detectable power for the heterodyne system as given by (11.4-10) with that calculated in the example of Section 11-3 for the video system. Using the same data,

$$\nu = 6 \times 10^{14} \text{ Hz } (\lambda = 0.5 \, \mu\text{m})$$

$$\eta = 10 \text{ percent}$$

$$\Delta\nu = 1 \text{ Hz}$$

---

[8] A detection system that is limited in bandwidth to $\Delta\nu$ cannot resolve events in time that are separated by less than $\sim(\Delta\nu)^{-1}$ second. Thus $(\Delta\nu)^{-1}$ is the resolution time of the system.

we obtain

$$(P_s)_{\min} \simeq 4 \times 10^{-18} \, \text{watt}$$

to be compared with $P_{\min} \simeq 3 \times 10^{-16}$ watt in the video case.

Limiting sensitivity as a result of the particle nature of light. The quantum limit to optical detection sensitivity is given by (11.4-10) as

$$(P_s)_{\min} = \frac{h\nu\Delta\nu}{\eta} \qquad \text{(11.4-11)}$$

This limit was shown to be due to the shot noise of the photoemitted current. We may alternatively, attribute this noise to the granularity—that is, the particle nature—of light, according to which the minimum energy increment of an electromagnetic wave at frequency ν is $h\nu$. The power P of an optical wave can be written as

$$P = \overline{N}h\nu \qquad \text{(11.4-12)}$$

where $\overline{N}$ is the average number of photons arriving at the photocathode per second. Next assume a hypothetical noiseless pohotomultiplier in which *exactly* one electron is produced for each η^{-1} incident photon. The measurement of P is performed by counting the number of electrons produced during an observation period T and then averaging the result over a large number of similar observations.

The average number of electrons emitted per observation period T is

$$\overline{N_e} = \overline{N}T\eta \qquad \text{(11.4-13)}$$

which, assuming perfect randomness in the arrival, is equal to the mean-square fluctuation[9]

$$\overline{(\Delta N_e)^2} \equiv \overline{(N_e - \overline{N}_e)^2} = \overline{N}T\eta$$

Taking the minimum detectable number of quanta as that for which the rms fluctuation equals the average value, we get

$$(\overline{N}_{\min}T\eta)^{1/2} = \overline{N}_{\min}T\eta$$

---

[9] This follows from the assumption that the photon arrival is perfectly random, so the probability of having N photons arriving in a given time interval is given by the Poisson law

$$p(N) = (\overline{N})^N e^{-\overline{N}}/N!$$

The mean-square fluctuation is given by

$$\overline{(\Delta N)^2} = \sum_{N=0}^{\infty} p(N)(N - \overline{N})^2 = \overline{N}$$

where

$$\overline{N} = \sum_{0}^{\infty} Np(N)$$

is the average N.

or

$$(\bar{N})_{\min} = \frac{1}{T\eta} \qquad \text{(11.4-14)}$$

If we convert the last result to power by multiplying it by $h\nu$ and recall that $T^{-1} \simeq \Delta\nu$, where $\Delta\nu$ is the bandwidth of the system, we get

$$(P_s)_{\min} = \frac{h\nu\Delta\nu}{\eta} \qquad \text{(11.4-15)}$$

in agreement with (11.4-10).

The question as to whether the real limit to sensitivity is imposed by the cathode shot noise or the fluctuations in the incident photon flux is thus academic. An examination of the photocurrent cannot distinguish between these cases.

11.5 Photoconductive Detectors

The operation of photoconductive detectors is illustrated in Figure 11-7. A semiconductor crystal is connected in series with a resistance R and a supply voltage V. The optical field to be detected is incident on and absorbed in the crystal, thereby exciting electrons into the conduction band (or, in p-type semiconductors, holes into the valence band). Such excitation results in a lowering of the resistance R_d of the semiconductor crystal and hence in an increase in the voltage drop across R which, for $\Delta R_d/R_d \ll 1$, is proportional to the incident optical intensity.

To be specific, we show the energy levels involved in one of the more popular semiconductive detectors—mercury-doped germanium [7]. Mercury atoms enter germanium as acceptors with an ionization energy of 0.09 eV. It follows that it takes a photon energy of at least 0.09 eV (that is, a photon with a wavelength shorter than 14 μm) to lift an electron from the top of the valence band and have it trapped by the Hg (acceptor) atom. Usually the germanium crystal contains a smaller density N_D of donor atoms, which at low temperatures find it energetically profitable to lose their valence electrons to one of the far more numerous Hg acceptor atoms, thereby becoming positively ionized and ionizing (negatively) an equal number of acceptors.

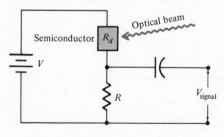

Figure 11-7 Typical biasing circuit of a photoconductive detector.

Since the acceptor density $N_A \gg N_D$, most of the acceptor atoms remain neutrally charged.

An incident photon is absorbed and lifts an electron from the valence band onto an acceptor atom, as shown in process A in Figure 11-8. The electronic deficiency (that is, the hole) thus created is acted upon by the electric field and its drift along the field direction gives rise to the signal current. The contribution of a given hole to the current ends when an electron drops from an ionized acceptor level back into the valence band, thus eliminating the hole as in B. This process is referred to as electron–hole recombination or trapping of a hole by an ionized acceptor atom.

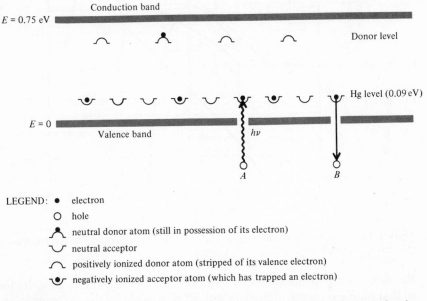

Figure 11-8 Donor and acceptor impurity levels involved in photoconductive semiconductors.

By choosing impurities with lower ionization energies, even lower-energy photons can be detected and indeed photoconductive detectors operate commonly at wavelengths up to $\lambda = 50\,\mu m$. Cu, as an example, enters into Ge as an acceptor with an ionization energy of 0.04 eV, which would correspond to long-wavelength detection cutoff of $\lambda \simeq 32\,\mu m$. The response of a number of commercial photoconductive detectors is shown in Figure 11-9.

It is clear from this discussion that the main advantage of photoconductors compared to photomultipliers is their ability to detect long-wavelength radiation, since the creation of mobile carriers does not involve overcoming the large surface potential barrier. On the debit side we find

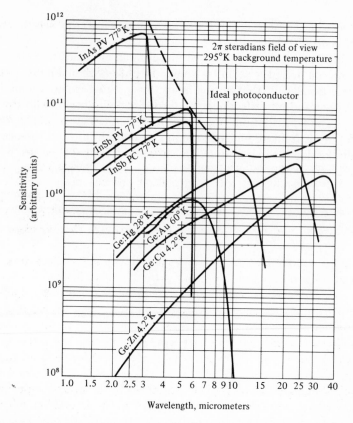

Figure 11-9 Relative sensitivity of a number of commercial photoconductors. (Courtesy Santa Barbara Research Corp.)

the lack of current multiplication and the need to cool the semiconductor so that photoexcitation of carriers will not be masked by thermal excitation.

Consider an optical beam, of power P and frequency ν, which is incident on a photoconductive detector. Taking the probability for excitation of a carrier by an incident photon—the so-called quantum efficiency—as η, the carrier generation rate is $G = P\eta/h\nu$. If the carriers last on the average τ_0 seconds before recombining, the average number of carriers N_c is found by equating the generation rate to the recombination rate (N_c/τ_0), so

$$N_c = G\tau_0 = \frac{P\eta\tau_0}{h\nu} \tag{11.5-1}$$

Each one of these carriers drifts under the electric field influence[10] at a velocity $\bar{v}$ giving rise, according to (10.4-1), to a current in the external circuit of $i_e = e\bar{v}/d$, where d is the length (between electrodes) of the semi-

---

[10] The drift velocity is equal to μE, where μ is the mobility and E is the electric field.

conductor crystal. The total current is thus the product of i_e and the number of carriers present, or, using (11.5-1),

$$\bar{i} = N_c i_e = \frac{P \eta \tau_0 e \bar{v}}{h \nu d} = \frac{e \eta}{h \nu} \left(\frac{\tau_0}{\tau_d} \right) P \tag{11.5-2}$$

where $\tau_d = d/\bar{v}$ is the drift time for a carrier across the length d. The factor (τ_0/τ_d) is thus the fraction of the crystal length drifted by the average excited carrier before recombining.

Equation (11.5-2) describes the response of a photoconductive detector to a constant optical flux. Our main interest, however, is in the heterodyne mode of photoconductive detection, which, as has been shown in Section 11.4, allows detection sensitivities approaching the quantum limit. In order to determine the limiting sensitivity of photoconductive detectors we need first to understand the noise contribution in these devices.

Generation recombination noise in photoconductive detectors. The principal noise mechanism in cooled photoconductive detectors reflects the randomness inherent in current flow. Even if the incident optical flux were constant in time, the generation of individual carriers by the flux would constitute a random process. This is exactly the type of randomness involved in photoemission, and we may expect, likewise, that the resulting noise will be shot noise. This is almost true except for the fact that in a photoconductive detector a photoexcited carrier lasts τ seconds[11] (its recombination lifetime) before being captured by an ionized impurity. The contribution of the carrier to the charge flow in the external circuit is thus $e(\tau/\tau_d)$, as is evident from inspection of (11.5-2). Since the lifetime τ is not a constant, but must be described statistically, another element of randomness is introduced into the current flow.

Consider a carrier excited by a photon absorption and lasting τ seconds. Its contribution to the external current is, according to (10.4-1)

$$i_e(t) = \begin{cases} \dfrac{e\bar{v}}{d} & 0 \leqslant t \leqslant \tau \\ 0 & \text{otherwise} \end{cases} \tag{11.5-3}$$

which has a Fourier transform

$$I_e(\omega, \tau) = \frac{e\bar{v}}{d} \int_0^\tau e^{-i\omega\tau} \, dt = \frac{e\bar{v}}{d} [1 - e^{-i\omega\tau}] \tag{11.5-4}$$

so that

$$|I_e(\omega, \tau)|^2 = \frac{e^2 \bar{v}^2}{\omega^2 d^2} [2 - e^{-i\omega\tau} - e^{i\omega\tau}] \tag{11.5-5}$$

---

[11] The parameter τ_0 appearing in (11.5-2) is the value of τ averaged over a large number of carriers.

According to (10.3-10) we need to average $|I_e(\omega, \tau)|^2$ over τ. This is done in a manner similar to the procedure used in Section 10.5. Taking the probability function[12] $g(\tau) = \tau_0^{-1} \exp(-\tau/\tau_0)$, we average (11.5-5) over all the possible values of τ according to

$$\overline{|I_e(\omega)|^2} = \int_0^\infty |I_e(\omega, \tau)|^2 g(\tau) d\tau$$

$$= \frac{2e^2 \bar{v}^2 \tau_0^2}{d^2(1 + \omega^2 \tau_0^2)} \tag{11.5-6}$$

The spectral density function of the current fluctuations is obtained using Carson's theorem (10.3-10) as

$$S(\nu) = 2\bar{N} \frac{2e^2(\tau_0^2/\tau_d^2)}{(1 + \omega^2 \tau_0^2)} \tag{11.5-7}$$

where we used $\tau_d = d/\bar{v}$ and where $\bar{N}$, the average number of carriers generated per second, can be expressed in terms of the average current $\bar{I}$ by use of the relation [13]

$$\bar{I} = \bar{N} e \frac{\tau_0}{\tau_d} \tag{11.5-8}$$

leading to

$$S(\nu) = \frac{4e\bar{i}(\tau_0/\tau_d)}{1 + 4\pi^2 \nu^2 \tau_0^2}$$

Therefore, the mean-square current representing the noise power in a frequency interval ν to $\nu + \Delta\nu$ is

$$\overline{i_N^2} \equiv S(\nu)\Delta\nu = \frac{4e\bar{I}(\tau_0/\tau_d)\Delta\nu}{1 + 4\pi^2 \nu^2 \tau_0^2} \tag{11.5-9}$$

which is the basic result for generation–recombination noise.

Numerical example. To better appreciate the kind of numbers involved in the expression for $\overline{i_N^2}$ we may consider a typical mercury-doped germanium detector operating at 20°K with the foolowing characteristics:

$d = 10^{-1}$ cm

$\tau_0 = 10^{-9}$ second

V (across the length d) = 10 volts $\Rightarrow E = 10^2$ V/cm

$\mu = 3 \times 10^4$ cm^2/V-s

---

[12] $g(\tau) d\tau$ is the probability that a carrier lasts between τ and $\tau + d\tau$ seconds before recombining.

[13] This relation follows from the fact that the average charge per carrier flowing through the external circuit is $e(\tau_0/\tau_d)$, which, when multiplied by the generation rate $\bar{N}$, gives the current.

The drift velocity is $\bar{v} = \mu E = 3 \times 10^6$ cm/s and $\tau_d = d/\bar{v} \simeq 3.3 \times 10^{-8}$ second, and therefore $\tau_0/\tau_d = 3 \times 10^{-2}$. Thus, on the average, a carrier traverses only 3 percent of the length ($d = 1$ mm) of the sample before recombining. Comparing (11.5-9) to the shot-noise result (10.4-9), we find that for a given average current I the generation recombination noise is reduced from the shot-noise value by a factor

$$\frac{\overline{(i_N^2)}_{\substack{\text{generation-}\\ \text{recombination}}}}{\overline{(i_N^2)}_{\text{shot noise}}} \underset{\omega\tau_0 \ll 1}{=} 2\left(\frac{\tau_0}{\tau_d}\right) \tag{11.5-10}$$

which, in the foregoing example, has a value of about $1/15$. Unfortunately, as will be shown subsequently, the reduced noise is accompanied by a reduction by a factor of (τ_0/τ_d) in the magnitude of the signal power, which wipes out the advantage of the low noise.

Heterodyne detection in photoconductors.   The situation here is similar to that described by Figure 11-6 in connection with heterodyne detection using photomultipliers. The signal field

$$e_s(t) = E_s \cos \omega_s t$$

is combined with a strong local-oscillator field

$$e_L(t) = E_L \cos (\omega + \omega_s)t \qquad E_L \gg E_s$$

so the total field incident on the photoconductor is

$$e(t) = \text{Re}\, [E_s e^{i\omega_s t} + E_L e^{i(\omega_s + \omega)t}] \equiv \text{Re}\, [V(t)] \tag{11.5-11}$$

The rate at which carriers are generated is taken, following (11.1-2), as $aV(t)V^*(t)$ where a is a constant to be determined. The equation describing the number of excited carriers N_c is thus

$$\frac{dN_c}{dt} = aVV^* - \frac{N_c}{\tau_0} \tag{11.5-12}$$

where τ_0 is the average carrier lifetime, so N_c/τ_0 corresponds to the carrier's decay rate. We assume a solution for $N_c(t)$ that consists of the sum of dc and a sinusoidal component in the form of

$$N_c(t) = N_0 + (N_1 e^{i\omega t} + \text{c.c.}) \tag{11.5-13}$$

where c.c. stands for "complex conjugate."

Substitution in (11.5-12) gives

$$N_c(t) = a\tau_0(E_s^2 + E_L^2) + a\tau_0\left(\frac{E_s E_L e^{i\omega t}}{1 + i\omega\tau_0} + \text{c.c.}\right) \tag{11.5-14}$$

where we took E_s and E_L as real. The current through the sample is given by the number of carriers per unit length N_c/d times $e\bar{v}$, where $\bar{v}$ is the drift velocity

$$i(t) = \frac{N_c(t)e\bar{v}}{d} \qquad \textbf{(11.5-15)}$$

which, using (11.5-14), gives

$$i(t) = \frac{e\bar{v}a\tau_0}{d}\left[E_s{}^2 + E_L{}^2 + \frac{2E_sE_L\cos(\omega t - \phi)}{\sqrt{1 + \omega^2\tau_0{}^2}}\right] \qquad \textbf{(11.5-16)}$$

where $\phi = \tan^{-1}(\omega\tau_0)$.

The current is thus seen to contain a signal component that oscillates at ω and is proportional to E_s. The constant a in (11.5-16) can be determined by requiring that, when $P_s = 0$, the expression for the direct current predicted by (11.5-16) agree with (11.5-2). This condition is satisfied if we rewrite (11.5-16) as

$$i(t) = \frac{e\eta}{h\nu}\left(\frac{\tau_0}{\tau_d}\right)\left[P_s + P_L + \frac{2\sqrt{P_sP_L}}{\sqrt{1 + \omega^2\tau_0{}^2}}\cos(\omega t - \phi)\right] \qquad \textbf{(11.5-17)}$$

where P_s and P_L refer, respectively, to the incident-signal and local-oscillator powers and η, the quantum efficiency, is the number of carriers excited per incident photon. The signal current is thus

$$i_s(t) = \frac{2e\eta}{h\nu}\left(\frac{\tau_0}{\tau_d}\right)\frac{\sqrt{P_sP_L}}{\sqrt{1 + \omega^2\tau_0{}^2}}\cos(\omega t - \phi) \qquad \textbf{(11.5-18)}$$

while the dc (average) current is

$$\bar{I} = \frac{e\eta}{h\nu}\left(\frac{\tau_0}{\tau_d}\right)(P_s + P_L) \qquad \textbf{(11.5-19)}$$

Since the average current $\bar{I}$ appearing in the expression (11.5-9) for the generation recombination noise is given in this case by

$$\bar{I} = \left(\frac{e\eta}{h\nu}\right)\left(\frac{\tau_0}{\tau_d}\right)P_L \qquad P_L \gg P_s$$

we can, by increasing P_L, increase the noise power $\overline{i_N{}^2}$ and at the same time, according to (11.5-18), the signal $\overline{i_s{}^2}$ until the generation recombination noise (11.5-9) is by far the largest contribution to the total output noise. When this condition is satisfied, the signal-to-noise ratio can be written, using (11.5-9), (11.5-18) and (11.5-19) and taking $P_L \gg P_s$, as

$$\frac{S}{N} = \frac{\overline{i_s{}^2}}{\overline{i_N{}^2}} = \left[2\left(\frac{e\eta\tau_0}{h\nu\tau_d}\right)^2\frac{P_sP_L}{1 + \omega^2\tau_0{}^2}\right]\bigg/\left[\frac{4e^2\eta(\tau_0/\tau_d)^2P_L\Delta\nu}{(1 + \omega^2\tau_0{}^2)h\nu}\right] = \frac{P_s\eta}{2h\nu\Delta\nu}$$

$$\textbf{(11.5-20)}$$

The minimum detectable signal—that which leads to a signal to noise ratio of unity—is found by setting the left side of (11.5-20) equal to unity and solving for P_s. It is

$$(P_s)_{\min} = \frac{2h\nu\Delta\nu}{\eta} \tag{11.5-21}$$

which, for the same η, is twice that of the photomultiplier heterodyne detection as given by (11.4-10). In practice, however, η in photoconductive detectors can approach unity, whereas in the best photomultipliers $\eta \simeq 30$ percent.

Numerical example—minimum detectable power of a heterodyne receiver using a photoconductor at 10.6 μm.   Assume the following:

$\lambda = 10.6\ \mu$m

$\Delta\nu = 1$ Hz

$\eta \simeq 1$

Substitution in (11.5-21) gives a minimum detectable power of

$$(P_s)_{\min} \simeq 10^{-19}\ \text{watt}$$

Experiments (see References [8] and [9]) have demonstrated that the theoretical signal-to-noise ratio as given by (11.5-20) can be realized quite closely in practice; see Figure 11-10.

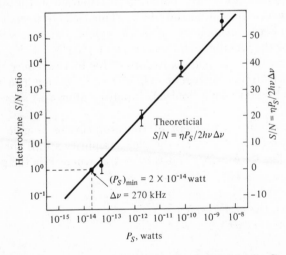

Figure 11-10   Signal-to-noise ratio of heterodyne signal in Ge:Cu detector at a heterodyne frequency of 70 MHz. Data points represent observed values. (After Reference [8].)

11.6 The *p-n* Junction

Before embarking on a description of the *p-n* diode detector, we need to understand the operation of the semiconductor *p-n* junction. Consider the junction illustrated in Figure 11-11. It consists of an abrupt transition from a donor-doped (that is, *n*-type) region of a semiconductor, where the free-charge carriers are predominantly electrons, to an acceptor-doped (*p*-type) region, where the carriers are holes. The doping profile—that is, the density of excess donor (in the *n* region) atoms or acceptor atoms (in the *p* region)—is shown in Figure 11.11(a). This abrupt transition results usually from diffusing suitable impurity atoms into a substrate of a semiconductor with the opposite type of conductivity. In our slightly idealized abrupt junction we assume that the *n* region ($x > 0$) has a constant (net) donor density N_D and the *p* region ($x < 0$) has a constant acceptor density N_A.

The energy-band diagram at zero applied bias is shown in Figure 11.11(b). The top (or bottom) curve can be taken to represent the potential energy of an electron as a function of position x, so the minimum energy needed to take an electron from the *n* to the *p* side of the junction is eV_d. Taking the separations of the Fermi level from the respective band edges as ϕ_n and ϕ_p as shown, we have

$$eV_d = E_g - (\phi_n + \phi_p)$$

V_d is referred to as the "built-in" junction potential.

Figure 11-11(c) shows the potential distribution in the junction with an applied reverse bias of magnitude V_a. This leads to a separation of eV_a between the Fermi levels in the *p* and *n* regions and causes the potential barrier across the junction to increase from eV_d to $e(V_d + V_a)$. The change of potential between the *p* and *n* regions is due to a sweeping of the mobile charge carriers from the region $-l_p < x < l_n$, giving rise to a charge double layer of stationary (ionized) impurity atoms, as shown in Figure 11-11(d).

In the analytical treatment of the problem we assume that in the depletion layer ($-l_p < x < l_n$) the excess impurity atoms are fully ionized and thus, using $\nabla \cdot \mathbf{E} = \rho/\epsilon$ and $\mathbf{E} = -\nabla V$, where V is the potential, we have

$$\frac{d^2V}{dx^2} = \frac{eN_A}{\epsilon} \qquad \text{for } -l_p < x < 0 \tag{11.6-1}$$

and

$$\frac{d^2V}{dx^2} = -\frac{eN_D}{\epsilon} \qquad 0 < x < l_p \tag{11.6-2}$$

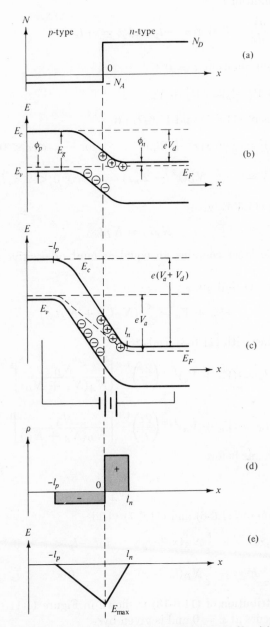

Figure 11-11 The abrupt *p-n* junction. (**a**) Impurity profile. (**b**) Energy-band diagram with zero applied bias. (**c**) Energy-band diagram with reverse applied bias. (**d**) Net charge density in the depletion layer. (**e**) The electric field. The circles in (**b**) and (**c**) represent ionized impurity atoms in the depletion layer.

where the charge of the electron is $-e$ and the dielectric constant is ϵ. The boundary conditions are

$$E = -\frac{dV}{dx} = 0 \text{ at } x = -l_p \text{ and } x = +l_n \tag{11.6-3}$$

$$\frac{dV}{dx} \text{ is continuous at } x = 0 \tag{11.6-4}$$

$$V(l_n) - V(-l_p) = V_d + V_a \tag{11.6-5}$$

The solutions of (11.6-1) and 11.6-2) are

$$V = \frac{e}{2\epsilon} N_A(x^2 + 2l_p x) \qquad \text{for } -l_p < x < 0 \tag{11.6-6}$$

$$V = -\frac{e}{2\epsilon} N_D(x^2 - 2l_n x) \qquad 0 < x < l_n \tag{11.6-7}$$

which, using (11.6-4), gives

$$N_A l_p = N_D l_n \tag{11.6-8}$$

so the double layer contains an equal amount of positive and negative charge.

Condition (11.6-5) gives

$$V_d + V_a = \frac{e}{2\epsilon}(N_D l_n{}^2 + N_A l_p{}^2) \tag{11.6-9}$$

which, together with (11.6-8) leads to

$$l_p = (V_d + V_a)^{1/2} \left(\frac{2\epsilon}{e}\right)^{1/2} \left[\frac{N_D}{N_A(N_A + N_D)}\right]^{1/2} \tag{11.6-10}$$

and

$$l_n = (V_d + V_a)^{1/2} \left(\frac{2\epsilon}{e}\right)^{1/2} \left[\frac{N_A}{N_D(N_A + N_D)}\right]^{1/2} \tag{11.6-11}$$

and, therefore, as before,

$$\frac{l_p}{l_n} = \frac{N_D}{N_A} \tag{11.6-12}$$

Differentiation of (11.6-6) and (11.6-7) yields

$$E = -\frac{e}{\epsilon} N_A(x + l_p) \qquad \text{for } -l_p < x < 0$$

$$E = -\frac{e}{\epsilon} N_D(l_n - x) \qquad 0 < x < l_n \tag{11.6-13}$$

The field distribution of (11.6-13) is shown in Figure 11-11(e). The maximum field occurs at $x = 0$ and is given by

$$E_{\max} = -2(V_d + V_a)^{1/2} \left(\frac{e}{2\epsilon}\right)^{1/2} \left(\frac{N_D N_A}{N_A + N_D}\right)^{1/2} = -\frac{2(V_d + V_a)}{l_p + l_n} \tag{11.6-14}$$

The presence of a charge $Q = -eN_A l_p$ per unit junction area on the p side and an equal and negative charge on the n side leads to a junction capacitance. The reason is that l_p and l_n depend, according to (11.6-10) and (11.6-11), on the applied voltage V_a, so a change in voltage leads to a change in the charge $eN_A l_p = eN_D l_n$ and hence to a differential capacitance per unit area,[14] given by

$$\frac{C_d}{\text{area}} \equiv \frac{dQ}{dV_a} = eN_A \frac{dl_p}{dV_a}$$

$$= \left(\frac{\epsilon e}{2}\right)^{1/2} \left(\frac{N_A N_D}{N_A + N_D}\right)^{1/2} \left(\frac{1}{V_a + V_d}\right)^{1/2} \qquad \textbf{(11.6-15)}$$

which, using (11.6-10) and (11.6-11), can be shown to be equal to

$$\frac{C_d}{\text{area}} = \frac{\epsilon}{l_p + l_n} \qquad \textbf{(11.6-16)}$$

as appropriate to a parallel-plate capacitance of separation $l = l_p + l_n$. The equivalent circuit of a p-n junction is shown in Figure 11-12. The capacitance C_d was discussed above. The diode shunt resistance R_d in back-biased junctions is usually very large ($> 10^6$ ohms) compared to the load impedance R_L and can be neglected. The resistance R_s represents ohmic losses in the bulk p and n regions adjacent to the junction.

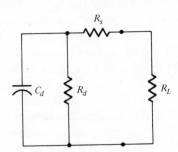

Figure 11-12 Equivalent circuit of a p-n junction. In typical back-biased diodes, $R_d \gg R_s$ and R_L, and $R_L \gg R_s$, so the resistance across the junction can be taken as equal to the load resistance R_L.

11.7 Semiconductor Photodiodes

Semiconductor p-n junctions are used widely for optical detection: see References [10]–[12]. In this role they are referred to as junction photodiodes. The main physical mechanisms involved in junction photodetection are illustrated in Figure 11-13. At A, an incoming photon is absorbed in the p side creating a hole and a free electron. If this takes place within a diffusion length (the distance in which an excess minority concentration

---

[14] The capacitance is defined by $C = Q/V_a$, whereas the differential capacitance $C_d = dQ/dV_a$ is the capacitance "seen" by a small ac voltage when the applied bias is V_a.

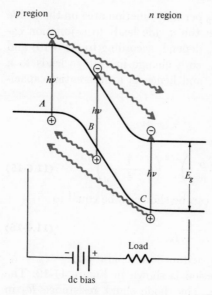

p region   *n* region

Figure 11-13 The three types of electron–hole pair creation by absorbed photons that contribute to current flow in a *p-n* photodiode.

is reduced to e^{-1} of its peak value, or in physical terms, the average distance a minority carrier traverses before recombining with a carrier of the opposite type) of the depletion layer, the electron will, with high probability, reach the layer boundary and will drift under the field influence across it. An electron traversing the junction contributes a charge e to the current flow in the external circuit, as described in Section 10.4. If the photon is absorbed near the n side of the depletion layer, as shown at C the resulting hole will diffuse to the junction and then drift across it again, giving rise to a flow of charge e in the external load. The photon may also be absorbed in the depletion layer as at B, in which case both the hole and electron which are created drift (in opposite directions) under the field until they reach the p and n sides, respectively. Since in this case each carrier traverses a distance that is less than the full junction width, the contribution of this process to charge flow in the external circuit is, according to (10.4-1) and (10.4-7), e. In practice this last process is the most desirable, since each absorption gives rise to a charge e, and delayed current response caused by finite diffusion time is avoided. As a result, photodiodes often use a p-i-n structure in which an intrinsic high resistivity (i) layer is sandwiched between the p and n regions. The potential drop occurs mostly across this layer, which can be made long enough to insure that most of the incident photons are absorbed within it. Typical construction of a p-i-n photodiode is shown in Figure 11-14.

It is clear from Figure 11-13 that a photodiode is capable of detecting only radiation with photon energy $h\nu > E_g$, where E_g is the energy gap of the semiconductor. If, on the other hand, $h\nu \gg E_g$, the absorption, which in a semiconductor increases strongly with frequency, will take place

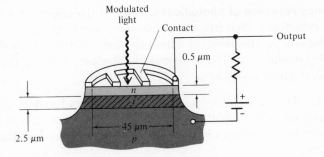

Figure 11-14   A *p-i-n* photodiode. (After Reference [13].)

entirely near the input face (in the *n* region of Figure 11-14) and the minority carriers generated by absorbed photons will recombine with majority carriers before diffusing to the depletion layer. This event does not contribute to the current flow and, as far as the signal is concerned, is wasted. This is why the photoresponse of diodes drops off when $h\nu > E_g$. Typical frequency response curves of photodiodes are shown in Figure 11-15. The number of carriers flowing in the external circuit per incident photon, the so-called quantum efficiency, is seen to approach 50 percent in Ge.

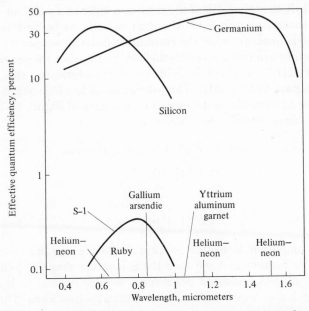

Figure 11-15   Quantum efficiencies for silicon and germanium photodiodes compared with the efficiency of the S-1 photodiode used in a photomultiplier tube. Emission wavelengths for various lasers are also indicated. (After Reference [13].)

Frequency response of photodiodes.   One of the major considerations in optical detectors is their frequency response—that is, the ability to respond to variations in the incident intensity such as those caused by high-frequency modulation. The three main mechanisms limiting the frequency response in photodiodes are:

1.   The finite diffusion time of carriers produced in the p and n regions. This factor was described in the last section and its effect can be minimized by a proper choice of the length of the depletion layer.

2.   The shunting effect of the signal current by the junction capacitance C_d shown in Figure 11-12. This places an upper limit of

$$\omega_m \simeq \frac{1}{R_e C_d} \qquad \text{(11.7-1)}$$

on the intensity modulation frequency where R_e is the equivalent resistance in parallel with the capacitance C_d.

3.   The finite transit time of the carriers drifting across the depletion layer.

To analyze this situation, we assume the slightly idealized case in which the carriers are generated in a *single* plane, say point A in Figure 11-13 and then drift the full width of the depletion layer at a constant velocity v. For high enough electric fields the drift velocity of carriers in semiconductors tends to saturate, so the constant velocity assumption is not very far from reality even for a nonuniform field distribution, such as that shown in Figure 11-11(e), provided the field exceeds its saturation value over most of the depletion layer length. The saturation of the hole velocity in germanium, as an example, is illustrated by the data of Figure 11-16.

The incident optical field is taken as

$$e(t) = E_s(1 + m \cos \omega_m t) \cos \omega t \qquad \text{(11.7-2)}$$

$$\equiv \text{Re} \, [V(t)]$$

where

$$V(t) \equiv E_s(1 + m \cos \omega_m t) e^{i\omega t} \qquad \text{(11.7-3)}$$

Thus, the amplitude is modulated at a frequency $\omega_m/2\pi$. Following the discussion of Section 11-1 we take the generation rate $G(t)$; that is, the number of carriers generated per second, as proportional to the average of $e^2(t)$ over a time long compared to the optical period $2\pi/\omega$. This average is equal to $\frac{1}{2} V(t) V^*(t)$, so the generation rate is taken as

$$G(t) = aE_s{}^2 \left[\left(1 + \frac{m^2}{2} \right) + 2m \cos(\omega_m t) + \frac{m^2}{2} \cos(2\omega_m t) \right] \qquad \text{(11.7-4)}$$

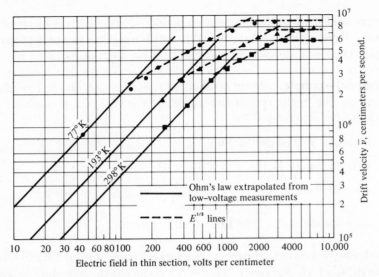

Ohm's law extrapolated from low-voltage measurements

—————

$E^{1/2}$ lines

Electric field in thin section, volts per centimeter

Drift velocity v, centimeters per second.

Figure 11-16 Experimental data showing the saturation of the drift velocity of holes in germanium at high electric fields. (After Reference [14].)

where a is a proportionality constant to be determined. Dropping the term involving $\cos(2\omega_m t)$ and using complex notation, we rewrite $G(t)$ as

$$G(t) = aE_s^2\left[1 + \frac{m^2}{2} + 2me^{i\omega_m t}\right] \tag{11.7-5}$$

A single carrier drifting at a velocity $\bar{v}$ contributes, according to (10.4-1), an instantaneous current

$$i = \frac{e\bar{v}}{d} \tag{11.7-6}$$

to the external circuit, where d is the width of the depletion layer. The current due to carriers generated between t and $t' + dt'$ is thus $(e\bar{v}/d)G(t')\,dt'$ but, since each carrier spends a time $\tau_d = d/\bar{v}$ in transit, the instantaneous current at time t is the sum of contributions of carriers generated between t and $t - \tau_d$

$$i(t) = \frac{e\bar{v}}{d}\int_{t-\tau_d}^{t} G(t')dt' = \frac{e\bar{v}aE_s^2}{d}\int_{t-\tau_d}^{t}\left(1 + \frac{m^2}{2} + 2me^{i\omega_m t'}\right)dt'$$

and, after integration,

$$i(t) = \left(1 + \frac{m^2}{2}\right)eaE_s^2 + 2meaE_s^2\left(\frac{1 - e^{-i\omega_m\tau_d}}{i\omega_m\tau_d}\right)e^{i\omega_m t} \tag{11.7-7}$$

The factor $(1 - e^{-i\omega_m\tau_d})/i\omega_m\tau_d$ represents the phase lag as well as the reduction in signal current due to the finite drift time τ_d. If the drift time is short compared to the modulation period, so $\omega_m \tau_d \ll 1$, it has its maximum value of unity, and the signal is maximum. This factor is plotted in Figure 11-17 as a function of the transit phase angle $\omega_m \tau_d$.

Numerical example.   As an estimate of the limitation on the modulation frequency due to the transit time, consider the case of a photodiode with the following characteristics:

material: p-type germanium

$\bar{v}$ (from Figure 11.16) $= 6 \times 10^6$ cm/s

$d = 10^{-4}$ cm

transit time: $\tau_d = \dfrac{d}{\bar{v}} \simeq 1.67 \times 10^{-11}$ second

We choose, somewhat arbitrarily, the highest useful modulation frequency as that for which $\omega_m \tau_d = 1$. This is the point where, according to Figure 11-17, the detector photocurrent is down to 65 percent of its maximum value. Using the foregoing calculated value of τ_d, we obtain

$$(f_m)_{\max} \simeq 10^{10} \text{ Hz}$$

for the highest modulation frequency as allowed by transit time.

Returning to (11.7-7) we can determine the value of the constant a by requiring that (11.7-7) agree with the experimental observation according to which in the absence of modulation, $m = 0$, each incident photon will create η carriers. Thus the dc (average) current is

$$\bar{I} = \frac{Pe\eta}{h\nu} \qquad \text{(11.7-8)}$$

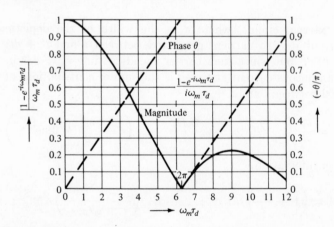

Figure 11-17   Phase and magnitude of the transit-time reduction factor $(1 - e^{-i\omega_m \tau_d})/i\omega_m \tau_d$.

where P is the optical (signal) power when $m = 0$. Using (11.7-8), we can rewrite (11.7-7) as

$$i(t) = \frac{Pe\eta}{h\nu}\left(1 + \frac{m^2}{2}\right) + \frac{Pe\eta}{h\nu}2m\left(\frac{i - e^{-i\omega_m\tau_d}}{i\omega_m\tau_d}\right)e^{i\omega_m t} \qquad \textbf{(11.7-9)}$$

Detection sensitivity of photodiodes. We assume that the modulation frequency of the light to be detected is low enough that the transit time factor is unity and that the condition

$$\omega_m \ll \frac{1}{R_e C_d} \qquad \textbf{(11.7-10)}$$

is fulfilled and, therefore, according to (11.7-1), the shunting of signal current by the diode capacitance C_d can be neglected. The diode current is given by (11.7-9) as

$$i(t) = \frac{Pe\eta}{h\nu}\left(1 + \frac{m^2}{2}\right) + \frac{Pe\eta}{h\nu}2me^{i\omega_m t} \qquad \textbf{(11.7-11)}$$

The noise equivalent circuit of a diode connected to a load resistance R_L is shown in Figure 11-18. The signal power is proportional to the mean-square value of the sinusoidal current component, which, for $m = 1$, is

$$\overline{i_s^2} = 2\left(\frac{Pe\eta}{h\nu}\right)^2 \qquad \textbf{(11.7-12)}$$

Two noise sources are shown. The first is the shot noise associated with the random generation of carriers. Using (10.4-9), this is represented by a noise generator $\overline{i_{N1}^2} = 2e\overline{I}\Delta\nu$, where $\overline{I}$ is the average current as given by the first term on the right side of (11.7-11). Taking $m = 1$, we obtain

$$\overline{i_{N1}^2} = \frac{3e^2(P + P_B)\eta\Delta\nu}{h\nu} + 2ei_d\Delta\nu \qquad \textbf{(11.7-13)}$$

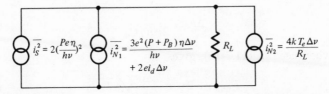

Figure 11-18 Equivalent circuit of a photodiode operating in the direct (video) mode. The modulation index m is taken as unity, and it is assumed that the modulation frequency is low enough that the junction capacitance and transit-time effects can be neglected. The resistance R_L is assumed to be much smaller than the shunt resistance R_d of the diode, so the latter is neglected. Also neglected is the series diode resistance, which is assumed small compared with R_L.

where P_B is the background optical power entering the detector (in addition to the signal power) and i_d is the "dark" direct current that exists even when $P_s = P_b = 0$. The second noise contribution is the thermal (Johnson noise) generated by the output load, which, using (10.5-9), is given by

$$\overline{i_{N2}^2} = \frac{4kT_e\Delta\nu}{R_L} \tag{11.7-14}$$

where T_e is chosen to include the equivalent input noise power of the amplifier following the diode. The signal-to-noise power ratio at the diode output is thus

$$\frac{S}{N} = \frac{\overline{i_s^2}}{\overline{i_{N1}^2} + \overline{i_{N2}^2}} = \frac{2(Pe\eta/h\nu)^2}{[3e^2(P + P_B)\eta\Delta\nu/h\nu] + 2ei_d\Delta\nu + (4kT_e\Delta\nu/R_L)} \tag{11.7-15}$$

In most practical systems the need to satisfy Equation (11.7-10) forces one to use small values of load resistance R_L. Under these conditions and for values of P that are near the detectability limit ($S/N = 1$), the noise term (11.7-14) is much larger than the shot noise (11.7-13) and the detector is consequently not operating near its quantum limit. Under these conditions we have

$$\frac{S}{N} \simeq \frac{2(Pe\eta/h\nu)^2}{4kT_e\Delta\nu/R_L} \tag{11.7-16}$$

The "minimum detectable optical power" is by definition that yielding $S/N = 1$ and is, from (11.7-16),

$$(P)_{\min} = \frac{h\nu}{e\eta}\sqrt{\frac{2kT_e\Delta\nu}{R_L}} \tag{11.7-17}$$

which is to be compared to the theoretical limit of $h\nu\,\Delta\nu/n$, which, according to (11.3-11), obtains when the signal shot-noise term predominates. In practice, the value of R_L is related to the desired modulation bandwidth $\Delta\nu$ and the junction capacitance C_d by

$$\Delta\nu \simeq \frac{1}{2\pi R_L C_d} \tag{11.7-18}$$

which, when used in (11.7-16), gives

$$P_{\min} \simeq 2\sqrt{\pi}\,\frac{h\nu\Delta\nu}{e\eta}\sqrt{kT_e C_d} \tag{11.7-19}$$

This shows that sensitive detection requires the use of small-area junctions so that C_d will be minimum.

Numerical example. Assume a typical Ge photodiode operating at $\lambda = 1.4\,\mu\text{m}$ with $C_d = 1\,\text{pF}$, $\Delta\nu = 1\,\text{GHz}$, and $\eta = 50$ percent. Let the amplifier following the diode have an effective noise temperature

$T_e = 1200°K.$[15] Substitution in (11.7-19) gives

$$P_{min} \simeq 3 \times 10^{-7} \text{ watt}$$

for the minimum detectable signal power.

11.8   The Avalanche Photodiode

By increasing the reverse bias across a p-n junction, the field in the depletion layer can increase to a point at which carriers (electrons or holes)
that are accelerated across the depletion layer can gain enough kinetic
energy to "kick" new electrons from the valence to the conduction band,
while still traversing the layer. This process, illustrated in Figure 11-19,
is referred to as avalanche multiplication. An absorbed photon (A) creates
an electron–hole pair. The electron is accelerated until at point C it has
gained sufficient energy to excite an electron from the valence to the conduction band, thus creating a new electron–hole pair. The newly generated
carriers drift in turn in opposite directions. The hole (F) can also cause
carrier multiplication as in G. The result is a dramatic increase (avalanche)
in junction current that sets in when the electric field becomes high enough.
This effect, discovered first in gaseous plasmas and more recently in p-n
junctions (References [15] and [16]) gives rise to a multiplication of the
current over its value in an ordinary (nonavalanching) photodiode. An
experimental plot of the current gain M[16] as a function of the junction
field is shown in Figure 11-20.

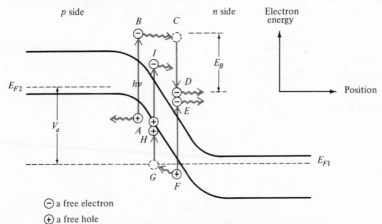

Figure 11-19   Energy-position diagram showing the carrier multiplication
following a photon absorption in a reverse-biased avalanche photodiode.

---

[15] The effective (input) noise temperature T_e is related to the amplifier noise figure F
by $F = 1 + T_e/290$, so $T_e = 1200°K$ corresponds to $F \simeq 5$ (or ~7 dB)

[16] If the probability that a photo-excited electron-hole pair will create another pair during its drift is denoted by p, the current multiplication is

$$M = (1 + p + p^2 + p^3 + \cdots) = \frac{1}{1 - p}$$

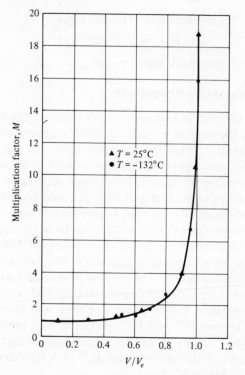

Figure 11-20 Current multiplication factor in an avalanche diode as a function of the electric field. (After Reference [16].)

Avalanche photodiodes are similar in their construction to ordinary photodiodes except that, because of the steep dependence of M on the applied field in the avalanche region, special care must be exercised to obtain very uniform junctions. A sketch of an avalanche photodiode is shown in Figure 11-21.

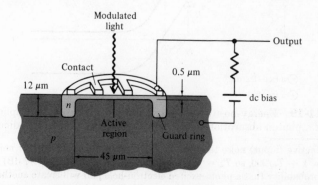

Figure 11-21 Planar avalanche photodiode. (After Reference [13].)

Since an avalanche photodiode is basically similar to a photodiode, its equivalent circuit elements are given by expressions similar to those given above for the photodiode. Its frequency response is similarly limited by diffusion, drift across the depletion layer, and capacitive loading, as discussed in Section 11.7.

A multiplication by a factor M of the photocurrent leads to an increase by M^2 of the signal power S over that which is available from a photodiode so that, using (11.7-12), we get

$$S \propto \overline{i_s^2} = 2M^2 \left(\frac{Pe\eta}{h\nu}\right)^2 \tag{11.8-1}$$

where P is the optical power incident on the diode. This result is reminiscent of the signal power from a photomultiplier as given by the numerator of (11.3-9), where the avalanche gain M plays the role of the secondary electron multiplication gain G. We may expect that, similarly, the shot noise power will also increase by M^2. The shot noise, however, is observed to increase as M^n, where $2 < n < 3$.[17] Experimental observation of a near ideal $M^{2.1}$ behavior is shown in Figure 11-22.

The signal-to-noise power ratio at the output of the diode is thus given,

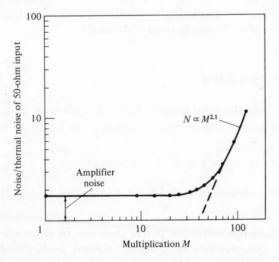

Figure 11-22   Noise power (measured at 30 MHz) as a function of photocurrent multiplication for an avalanche Schottky-barrier photodiode. (After Reference [18].)

---

[17] A theoretical study by McIntyre [17] predicts that if the multiplication is due to either holes or electrons, $n = 2$, whereas if both carriers are equally effective in producing electron–hole pairs, $n = 3$.

following (11.7-15), by

$$\left(\frac{S}{N}\right) = \frac{2M^2(Pe\eta/h\nu)^2}{[3e^2(P + P_B)\eta\Delta\nu/h\nu]M^n + 2ei_d\Delta\nu M^n + (4kT_e\Delta\nu/R_L)} \quad \text{(11.8-2)}$$

The advantage of using an avalanche photodiode over an ordinary photodiode is now apparent. When $M = 1$, the situation is identical to that at the photodiode as described by (11.7-15). Under these conditions the thermal term $4kT_e\Delta\nu/R_L$ is typically much larger than the shot-noise terms. This causes S/N to increase with M. This improvement continues until the shot-noise terms become comparable with $4kT_e\Delta\nu/R_L$. Further increases in M result in a reduction of S/N since $n > 2$, and the denominator of (11.8-2) grows faster than the numerator. If we assume that M is adjusted optimally so that the denominator of (11.8-2) is equal to twice the thermal term $4kT_e\Delta\nu/R_L$, we can solve for the minimum detectable power (that is, the power input for which $S/N = 1$) obtaining

$$P_{\min} = \frac{2h\nu}{M'e\eta} \sqrt{\frac{kT_e\Delta\nu}{R_L}} \quad \text{(11.8-3)}$$

where M' is the optimum value of M as discussed previously. The improvement in sensitivity over the photodiode result (11.7-16) is thus approximately M'. Values of M' between 30 and 100 are commonly employed, so the use of avalanche photodiodes affords considerable improvement in sensitivity over that available from photodiodes.

■ PROBLEMS

11-1 Show that the total output shot noise power in a photomultiplier including that originating in the dynodes is given by

$$\overline{(i_N{}^2)} = G^2 2e\bar{i}_c + i_d\Delta\nu \frac{1 - \delta^{-N}}{1 - \delta^{-1}}$$

where δ is the secondary-emission multiplication factor and N is the number of stages.

11-2 Calculate the minimum power that can be detected by a photoconductor in the presence of a strong optical background power P_B. *Answer:*

$$(P_s)_{\min} = 2\left(\frac{P_B h\nu\Delta\nu}{\eta}\right)^{1/2}$$

11-3 Derive the expression for the minimum detectable power using a photoconductor in the video mode (that is, no local-oscillator power) and assuming that the main noise contribution is the generation–recombination noise. The optical field is given by $e(t) = E(1 + \cos \omega_m t) \cos \omega t$ and the signal is taken as the component of the photocurrent at ω_m.

11-4 Derive the minimum detectable power of a Ge:Hg detector with characteristics similar to those described in Section 11-7 when the average current is due mostly to blackbody radiation incident on the photocathode. Assume $T = 295°$K, an acceptance solid angle $\Omega = \pi$ and a photocathode area of 1 mm². Assume that the quantum yield η for blackbody radiation at $\lambda < 14 \,\mu m$ is unity and that for $\lambda > 14 \,\mu m$, $\eta = 0$. *Hint:* Find the flux of photons with wavelengths $14 \,\mu m > \lambda > 0$ using blackbody radiation formulas or, more easily, tables or a blackbody "slide rule.")

11-5 Find the minimum detectable power in Problem 11-4 when the input field of view is at $T = 4.2°$K.

11-6 Derive (11.6-15) and (11.6-16).

11-7 Show that the transit time reduction factor $(1 - e^{-i\omega_m \tau_d})/i\omega_m \tau_d$ in (11.7-6) can be written as

$$\alpha - i\beta$$

where

$$\alpha = \frac{\sin \omega_m \tau_d}{\omega_m \tau_d} \qquad \beta = \frac{1 - \cos \omega_m \tau_d}{\omega_m \tau_d}$$

Plot α and β as a function of $\omega_m \tau_d$.

11-8 Derive the minimum detectable power for a photodiode operated in the heterodyne mode. *Answer:* $P_{\min} = h\nu\Delta\nu/\eta$

11-9 Discuss the limiting sensitivity of an avalanche photodiode in which the noise increases as M^2. Compare it with that of a photomultiplier. What is the minimum detectable power in the limit of $M \gg 1$, and of zero background radiation and no dark current.

11-10 Derive an expression for the magnitude of the output current in a heterodyne detection scheme as a function of the angle θ between the signal and local-oscillator propagation directions. Taking the aperture diameter (see Figure 11-6) as D, show that if the output is to remain near its maximum ($\theta = 0°$) value, θ should not exceed λ/D. *Hint:* You may replace the lens in Figure 11-6 by the photoemissive surface. Show that instead of (11.4-4) the current from an element $dx\, dy$ of the detector is

$$di(x, t) = \frac{P_L e\eta}{h\nu(\pi D^2/4)} \left[1 + 2 \sqrt{\frac{P_s}{P_L}} \cos (\omega t + kx \sin \theta) \right] dx\, dy$$

The propagation directions lie in the z-x plane. The contribution of $dx\, dy$ to the (complex) signal current is thus

$$dI_s(x, t) = \frac{2\sqrt{P_s P_L}}{h\nu(\pi D^2/4)} e^{ikx \sin \theta} \, dx\, dy$$

■ REFERENCES

[1]   Yariv, A., *Quantum Electronics*. New York: Wiley, 1967, p. 54.

[2]   Engstrom, R.W., " Multiplier phototube characteristics: Application to low light levels," *J. Opt. Soc. Am.*, vol. 37, p. 420, 1947.

[3]   Sommer, A. H., *Photo-Emissive Materials*. New York: Wiley, 1968.

[4]   Forrester, A. T., "Photoelectric mixing as a spectroscopic tool," *J. Opt. Soc. Am.*, vol. 51, p. 253, 1961.

[5]   Siegman, A. E., S. E. Harris, and B. J. McMurtry, "Optical heterodyning and optical demodulation at microwave frequencies," in *Optical Masers*, J. Fox, ed. New York: Wiley, 1963, p. 511.

[6]   Mandel, L., "Heterodyne detection of a weak light beam," *J. Opt. Soc. Am.*, vol. 56, p. 1200, 1966.

[7]   Chapman, R. A., and W. G. Hutchinson, "Excitation spectra and photoionization of neutral mercury centers in germanium," *Phys. Rev.*, vol. 157, p. 615, 1967.

[8]   Teich, M. C., "Infrared heterodyne detection," *Proc. IEEE*, vol. 56, p. 37, 1968.

[9]   Buczek, C., and G. Picus, "Heterodyne performance of mercury doped germanium," *Appl. Phys. Letters*, vol. 11, p. 125, 1967.

[10]   Lucovsky, G., M. E. Lasser, and R. B. Emmons, "Coherent light detection in solid-state photodiodes," *Proc. IEEE*, vol. 51, p. 166, 1963.

[11]   Riesz, R. P., "High speed semiconductor photodiodes," *Rev. Sci. Instr.*, vol. 33, p. 994, 1962.

[12]   Anderson, L. K., and B. J. McMurtry, "High speed photodetectors," *Appl. Opt.*, vol. 5, p. 1573, 1966.

[13]   D'Asaro, L. A., and L. K. Anderson, "At the end of the laser beam, a more sensitive photodiode," *Electronics*, May 30, 1966, p. 94.

[14]   Shockley, W., "Hot electrons in germanium and Ohm's law," *Bell System Tech. J.*, vol. 30, p. 990, 1951.

[15]   McKay, K. G., and K. B. McAfee, "Electron multiplication in silicon and germanium," *Phys. Rev.*, vol. 91, p. 1079, 1953.

[16]   McKay, K. G., "Avalanche breakdown in silicon," *Phys. Rev.*, vol. 94, p. 877, 1954.

[17]   McIntyre, R., "Multiplication noise in uniform avalanche diodes," *IEEE Trans. Electron Devices*, vol. ED-13, p. 164, 1966.

[18]   Lindley, W. T., R. J. Phelan, C. M. Wolfe, and A. J. Foyt, "GaAs Schottky barrier avalanche photodiodes," *Appl. Phys. Letters*, vol. 14, p. 197, 1969.

Interaction of Light and Sound

12.0 Introduction

Diffraction of light by sound[1] waves was predicted by Brillouin in 1922 [1] and demonstrated experimentally some ten years later [2]. Recent developments in high frequency acoustics [3] and in lasers caused a renewed interest in this field. This is due to the fact that the scattering of light from sound affords a convenient means of controlling the frequency, intensity, and direction of an optical beam. This type of control makes possible a large number of applications involving the transmission, display, and processing of intelligence [4].

12.1 Scattering of Light by Sound

A sound wave consists of a sinusoidal perturbation of the density of the material, or strain, which travels at the sound velocity v_s, as shown in Figure 12-1. A change in the density of the medium causes a change in its

---

[1] In this chapter we use the word *sound* to describe acoustic waves with frequencies which in practice may range through the microwave region ($f \simeq 10^{10}$ Hz).

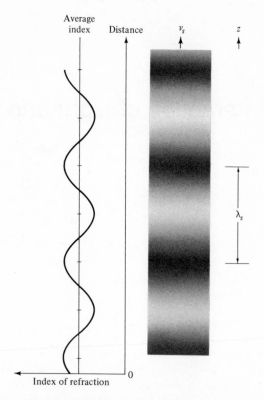

Figure 12-1   Traveling sound wave "frozen" at some instant of time. It consists of alternating regions of compressions (dark) and rarefaction (white), which travel at the sound velocity v_s. Also shown is the instantaneous spatial variation of the index of refraction that accompanies the sound wave.

index of refraction, which, to first order, is proportional to it.[2] We can, consequently, represent the sound wave shown in Figure 12.1 by

$$\Delta n(z, t) = \Delta n \sin (\omega_s t - k_s z) \tag{12.1-1}$$

where $\omega_s / k_s = v_s$.

Next consider an optical beam incident on a sound wave at an angle θ_i as in Figure 12-2. For the purpose of the immediate discussion we can characterize the sound wave as a series of partially reflecting mirrors,[3] separated by the sound wavelength λ_s, which are moving at a velocity v_s. Ignoring, for the moment, the motion of the mirrors, let us consider the diffracted wave and take the diffraction angle as θ_r. A necessary condition

---

[2] This is easily understood in the case where each atom (or molecule) contributes a constant amount to the index n, so the latter is proportional to the material density.

[3] This is due to the fact that the index of refraction is higher in the compressed portions of the sound wave and lower in the rarefied regions. Since a change in index causes reflection the mirrors' analogy follows.

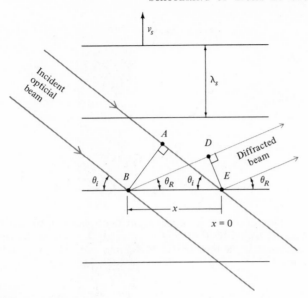

Figure 12-2

for diffraction in a given direction is that *all the points on a given mirror contribute in phase* to the diffraction along this direction. Considering the diffraction from two points, such as C and D in Figure 12-2, it is then necessary that the optical path difference $AC - BD$ be some multiple of the optical wavelength λ for diffraction along θ_r to occur. This condition takes the form

$$x(\cos \theta_i - \cos \theta_r) = m\lambda \qquad \textbf{(12.1-2)}$$

where $m = 0, \pm 1, \pm 2, \cdots$. The only way in which (12.1-2) can be satisfied simultaneously *for all points* x along a *given* reflector is if $m = 0$, from which it follows that

$$\theta_i = \theta_r \qquad \textbf{(12.1-3)}$$

In addition to the requirement that the different parts of a given acoustic phase front interfere constructively, which leads to (12.1-3), we require that the diffraction from any two acoustic phase fronts add up in phase along the direction of the reflected beam. The path difference $AO + OB$ shown in Figure 12-3 of a given optical wavefront resulting from reflection from two equivalent acoustic wavefronts (that is, planes separated by λ_s) is equal to the optical wavelength λ. Using (12.1-3) and Figure 12-3 we find that this condition can be written as[4]

$$2\lambda_s \sin \theta = \lambda \qquad \textbf{(12.1-4)}$$

where $\theta_i = \theta_r = \theta$.

---

[4] The reader may justly wonder why path differences of 2λ, 3λ, and so on, do not lead to maximum diffraction as well as a path difference of λ. This point is considered in Problem 12-6.

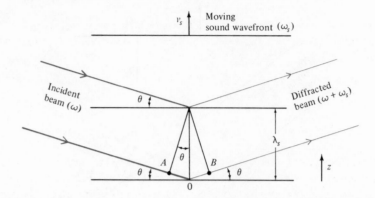

Figure 12-3   The reflections from two equivalent planes in the sound beam (that is, planes separated by the sound wavelength λ_s), which add up in phase along the direction θ if the optical path difference $AO + OB$ is equal to one optical wavelength.

The diffraction of light that satisfies (12.1-4) is known as Bragg diffraction after a similar law applying in X-ray diffraction from crystals. To get an idea of the order of magnitude of the angle θ, consider the case of diffraction of light with $\lambda_0 = 0.5\ \mu\text{m}$ from a 500-MHz sound wave. Taking the sound velocity as $v_s = 3 \times 10^5$ cm we have $\lambda_s = v_s/\nu_s = 6 \times 10^{-4}$ cm and, from (12.1-4),

$$\theta \simeq 4 \times 10^{-2}\ \text{rad} \simeq 3.5°$$

12.2   Particle Picture of Bragg Diffraction of Light by Sound

Many of the features of Bragg diffraction of light by sound can be deduced if we take advantage of the dual particle-wave nature of light and of sound. According to this picture a light beam with a propagation vector $\mathbf{k}$[5] and frequency ω can be considered to consist of a stream of particles (photons) with a momentum $\hbar\mathbf{k}$ and energy $\hbar\omega$. The sound wave, likewise, can be thought of as made up of particles (phonons) with momentum $\hbar\mathbf{k}_s$ and energy $\hbar\omega_s$. The diffraction of light by an *approaching* sound beam illustrated in Figure 12-3 can be described as a series of collisions, each of which involves an annihilation of *one* incident photon at ω_i and *one* phonon and a simultaneous creation of a new (diffracted) photon at a frequency $\omega_d = \omega_s + \omega$, which propagates along the direction of the scattered beam.

---

[5] The beam is of the form $\cos(\omega t - \mathbf{k} \cdot \mathbf{r})$, so it propagates in a direction parallel to $\mathbf{k}$ with a wavelength $2\pi/k$.

The conservation of momentum requires that the momentum $\hbar(\mathbf{k}_s + \mathbf{k}_i)$ of the colliding particles is equal to the momentum $\hbar\mathbf{k}_d$ of the scattered photon, so

$$\mathbf{k}_d = \mathbf{k}_s + \mathbf{k}_i \qquad (12.2\text{-}1)$$

The conservation of energy takes the form

$$\omega_d = \omega_i + \omega_s \qquad (12.2\text{-}2)$$

From Equation (12.2-2) we learn that the diffracted beam is shifted in frequency by an amount equal to the sound frequency. Since the interaction involves the annihilation of a phonon, conservation of energy decrees that the shift in frequency is such that $\omega_d > \omega_i$ and the phonon energy is *added* to that of the annihilated photon to form a new photon. Using this argument it follows that if the direction of the sound beam in Figure 12-3 were reversed so that it was receding from the incident optical wave, the scattering process could be considered as one in which a new photon (diffracted photon) and a *new* phonon are generated while the incident photon is annihilated. In this case, the conservation-of-energy principle yields

$$\omega_d = \omega_i - \omega_s$$

The relation between the sign of the frequency change and the sound propagation direction will become clearer using Doppler-shift arguments, as is done at the end of this section.

The conservation-of-momentum condition (12.2-1) is equivalent to the Bragg condition (12.1-4). To show why this is true, consider Figure 12-4.

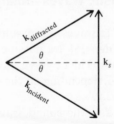

Figure 12-4 The momentum-conservation relation, Equation (12.2-1), used to derive the Bragg condition $2\lambda_s \sin\theta = \lambda$, for an optical beam that is diffracted by an approaching sound wave. θ is the angle between the incident or diffracted beam and the acoustic wavefront.

Since the sound frequencies of interest are below 10^{10} Hz and those of the optical beam are usually above 10^{13} Hz, we have

$$\omega_d = \omega_i + \omega_s \simeq \omega_i, \quad \text{so} \quad k_d \simeq k_i$$

and the magnitude of the two optical wave vectors is taken as k (see also Problem 12-4). The magnitude of the sound wave vector is thus

$$k_s = 2k \sin\theta \qquad (12.2\text{-}3)$$

Using $k_s = 2\pi/\lambda_s$, this equation becomes

$$2\lambda_s \sin \theta = \lambda \qquad (12.2\text{-}4)$$

which is the same as the Bragg-diffraction condition (12.1-4).

Doppler derivation of the frequency shift. The frequency-shift condition (12.2-2) can also be derived by considering the Doppler shift exercised by an optical beam incident on a mirror moving at the sound velocity v_s at an angle satisfying the Bragg condition (12.1-4). The formula for the Doppler frequency shift of a wave reflected from a moving object is

$$\Delta\omega = 2\omega \frac{v}{c}$$

where ω is the optical frequency and v is the component of the object velocity that is parallel to the wave propagation direction. From Figure 12-3 we have $v = v_s \sin \theta$, and thus

$$\Delta\omega = 2\omega \frac{v_s \sin \theta}{c} \qquad (12.2\text{-}5)$$

Using (12.1-4) for $\sin \theta$ we obtain

$$\Delta\omega \equiv \frac{2\pi v_s}{\lambda_s} = \omega_s \qquad (12.2\text{-}6)$$

and, therefore, $\omega_d = \omega + \omega_s$.

If the direction of propagation of the sound beam is reversed so that, in Figure 12-3, the sound recedes from the optical beam, the Doppler shift changes sign and the diffracted beam has a frequency $\omega - \omega_s$.

12.3   Bragg Diffraction of Light by Acoustic Waves—Analysis

In treating the diffraction of light by acoustic waves, we assume a long interaction path so that higher diffraction orders [5] are missing and the only two waves coupled by the sound are the incident wave at ω_i and a diffracted wave at $\omega_d = \omega_i + \omega_s$ or at $\omega_i - \omega_s$, depending on the direction of the Doppler shift as discussed in Section 12.2.

According to the discussion in Section 12.1, the sound wave causes a traveling modulation of the index of refraction given by

$$\Delta n(\mathbf{r}, t) = \Delta n \cos (\omega_s t - \mathbf{k}_s \cdot \mathbf{r}) \qquad (12.3\text{-}1)$$

This modulation interacts with the fields at ω_i and ω_d to give rise to additional electric polarization in the medium which is given by[6]

$$\Delta\mathbf{p}(\mathbf{r}, t) = 2\sqrt{\epsilon\epsilon_0}\, \Delta n(\mathbf{r}, t)\mathbf{e}(\mathbf{r}, t) \qquad (12.3\text{-}2)$$

---

[6] Equation (12.3-2) can be derived using the relations $\mathbf{d} = \epsilon_0 \mathbf{e} + \mathbf{p} = \epsilon\mathbf{e}$, $\mathbf{p} \equiv \epsilon_0\chi\mathbf{e}$, and $n^2 \equiv \epsilon/\epsilon_0$. This leads to $\mathbf{p} = \epsilon_0(n^2 - 1)\mathbf{e}$ so that (12.3-2) follows.

where $e(r, t)$ is the sum of the fields at ω_i and ω_d. The polarization term $\Delta n e$ in Equation (12.3-2) will be shown, in what follows, to cause exchange of power between the fields at ω_i and ω_d.

We start with the wave Equation (8.2-5)

$$\nabla^2 e(r, t) = \mu_0 \epsilon \frac{\partial^2 e}{\partial t^2} + \mu_0 \frac{\partial^2}{\partial t^2} p_{NL}(r, t) \qquad \text{(8.2-5)}$$

where the medium is assumed lossless so that $\sigma = 0$. $p_{NL}(r, t)$ is given in our case by $\Delta p(r, t)$. Equation (8.2-5) must be satisfied separately for the fields at ω_i and ω_d. Writing it for the former case and assuming that both the incident and diffracted fields are linearly polarized result in

$$\nabla^2 e_i = \mu_0 \epsilon \frac{\partial^2 e_i}{\partial t^2} + \mu_0 \frac{\partial^2}{\partial t^2} (\Delta p)_i \qquad \text{(12.3-3)}$$

where e_i is the magnitude of the vector e_i and $(\Delta p)_i$ is the component of $\Delta p(r, t)$ parallel to e_i which oscillates at a frequency ω_i. The polarization components oscillating at other frequencies are nonsynchronous and their contribution to e_i averages out to zero. The total field $e(r, t)$ is taken as the sum of two traveling waves

$$e_i(r, t) = \tfrac{1}{2} E_i(r_i) e^{i(\omega_i t - k_i \cdot r)} + \text{c.c.}$$
$$e_d(r, t) = \tfrac{1}{2} E_d(r_d) e^{i(\omega_d t - k_d \cdot r)} + \text{c.c.} \qquad \text{(12.3-4)}$$

where k_i and k_d are parallel to the direction of propagation of the incident and diffracted waves, respectively. Two differentiations of Equation (12.3-4) lead to

$$\nabla^2 e_i(r, t) = -\tfrac{1}{2} \left[k_i^2 E_i + 2i k_i \frac{dE_i}{dr_i} + \nabla^2 E_i \right] e^{i(\omega_i t - k_i \cdot r)}$$

Assuming "slow" variation of $E_i(r_i)$ so that $\nabla^2 E_i \ll k_i \, dE_i/dr_i$, we combine Equation (12.3-3) with the last equation and recalling that $k_i^2 = \omega_i^2 \mu \epsilon$ obtain

$$k_i \frac{dE_i}{dr_i} = i \mu_0 \left[\frac{\partial^2}{\partial t^2} (\Delta p)_i \right] e^{-i(\omega_i t - k_i \cdot r)} \qquad \text{(12.3-5)}$$

Using the relation $\Delta p = 2\sqrt{\epsilon \epsilon_0} \, \Delta n(r, t) \cdot [e_i(r, t) + e_d(r, t)]$ $(\Delta p)_i$ is given by

$$[\Delta p(r, t)]_i = \tfrac{1}{2} \sqrt{\epsilon \epsilon_0} \Delta n E_d \{ e^{i[(\omega_s + \omega_d)t - (k_s + k_d) \cdot r]} \} + \text{c.c.} \qquad \text{(12.3-6)}$$

Note that in taking the product $\Delta n(r, t) e(r, t)$ we assumed that $\omega_i = \omega_s + \omega_d$ and therefore neglected nonsynchronous terms with frequencies $\omega_d - \omega_s$ and $\omega_i \pm \omega_s$. Substituting Equation (12.3-6) for $(\Delta p)_i$ in Equation (12.3-5) leads to

$$\frac{dE_i}{dr_i} = -i\eta_i E_d e^{i(k_i - k_s - k_d) \cdot r} \qquad \text{(12.3-7)}$$

and similarly

$$\frac{dE_d}{dr_d} = -i\eta_d E_i e^{-i(\mathbf{k}_i - \mathbf{k}_s - \mathbf{k}_d)\cdot\mathbf{r}}$$

with

$$\eta_{i,d} = \tfrac{1}{2}\omega_{i,d}\sqrt{\mu_0\epsilon_0}\Delta n = \frac{\omega_{i,d}\Delta n}{2c_0} \qquad (12.3\text{-}8)$$

An inspection of Equation (12.3-7) reveals that a prerequisite for continuous cumulative interaction between the incident field (E_i) and the diffracted field (E_d) is that

$$\mathbf{k}_i = \mathbf{k}_s + \mathbf{k}_d \qquad (12.3\text{-}9)$$

otherwise, it follows from Equation (12.3-7) that contributions to E_i, as an example, from different path elements do not add in phase and no sustained spatial growth of E_i is possible.

Equation (12.3-9) is, as shown in Section 12.2, the Bragg condition for scattering of light by sound. The difference between Equations (12.3-9) and (12.2-1) is due to the fact that the latter was derived for the case of diffraction from an approaching sound beam so that $\omega_d = \omega_i + \omega_s$ resulting in a "momentum" condition $\mathbf{k}_d = \mathbf{k}_i + \mathbf{k}_s$, while in the treatment leading to Equation (12.3-9) we recall that the sound wave is taken as receding from the incident field so that $\omega_d = \omega_i - \omega_s$.

Assuming that the Bragg condition (12.3-9) is satisfied, Equation (12.3-7) becomes

$$\frac{dE_i}{dr_i} = -i\eta E_d$$

$$\frac{dE_d}{dr_d} = -i\eta E_i \qquad (12.3\text{-}10)$$

where, since $\omega_i \approx \omega_d$, we took $\eta_i = \eta_d \equiv \eta$.

Equations (12.3-10) are our main result. An apparent difficulty in solving Equation (12.3-10) is the fact that they involve two different spatial coordinates r_i and r_d measured along the two respective ray directions. This difficulty can be resolved by transforming to a coordinate ζ measured along the bisector of the angle formed between $\mathbf{k}_i$ and $\mathbf{k}_d$ as shown in Figure 12-5. Defining the values of r_d and r_i, which correspond to a given ζ as the respective projections of ζ along $\mathbf{k}_d$ and $\mathbf{k}_i$, we have

$$r_i = \zeta \cos\theta \qquad r_d = \zeta \cos\theta \qquad (12.3\text{-}11)$$

so that Equations (12.3-10) become

$$\frac{dE_i}{d\zeta} = \frac{dE_i}{dr_i}\cos\theta = -i\eta E_d \cos\theta$$

$$\frac{dE_d}{d\zeta} = -i\eta E_i \cos\theta \qquad (12.3\text{-}12)$$

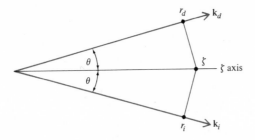

Figure 12-5 The directions and angles appearing in the diffraction equations (12.3–12).

whose solutions are

$$E_i(\zeta) = E_i(0) \cos (\eta\zeta \cos \theta) - iE_d(0) \sin (\eta\zeta \cos \theta)$$

$$E_d(\zeta) = E_d(0) \cos (\eta\zeta \cos \theta) - iE_i(0) \sin (\eta\zeta \cos \theta)$$

Using the correspondence between ζ, r_i, and r_d defined above, we can rewrite the solutions as

$$E_i(r_i) = E_i(0) \cos (\eta r_i) - iE_d(0) \sin (\eta r_i)$$

$$E_d(r_d) = E_d(0) \cos (\eta r_d) - iE_i(0) \sin (\eta r_d) \tag{12.3-13}$$

which is the desired result. It is of sufficient generality to describe the interaction between two input fields at ω_i and ω_d with arbitrary phases ($E_i(0)$ and $E_d(0)$ are complex) and arbitrary amplitudes as long as the Bragg condition (12.3-9) and the frequency condition $\omega_i = \omega_s + \omega_d$ are fulfilled. In the special case of a single frequency input at ω_i, $E_d(0) = 0$, and

$$E_i(r_i) = E_i(0) \cos (\eta r_i)$$

$$E_d(r_d) = -iE_i(0) \sin (\eta r_d) \tag{12.3-14}$$

we note that

$$|E_i(r_i)|^2 + |E_d(r_d = r_i)|^2 = |E_i(0)|^2 \tag{12.3-15}$$

so that the total optical power carried by both waves is conserved.

If the interaction distance between the two beams is such that $\eta r_i = \eta r_d = \pi/2$, the total power of the incident beam is transferred into the diffracted beam. Since this process is used in a large number of technological and scientific applications, it may be worthwhile to gain some appreciation for the diffraction efficiencies possible using known acoustic media and conveniently available acoustic power levels.

The fraction of the power of the incident beam transferred in a distance l into the diffracted beam is given, using Equations (12.3-8) and (12.3-14) by

$$\frac{I_{\text{diffracted}}}{I_{\text{incident}}} = \frac{E_{\text{diffracted}}^2}{E_i^2(0)} = \sin^2 \left(\frac{\omega l}{2c_0} \Delta n\right) \tag{12.3-16}$$

It is advantageous to express the diffraction efficiency (12.3-16) in terms of the acoustic intensity I_{acoustic} (W/m^2) in the diffraction medium. First we relate the index change Δn to the strain s (see Section 12.1) by by [4]–[5]

$$\Delta n \equiv -\frac{n^3 p}{2}\, s \qquad\qquad \textbf{(12.3-17)}$$

where p, the photoelastic constant of the medium,[7] is defined by Equation (12.3-17). The strain s is related to the acoustic intensity I_{acoustic} by[8]

$$s = \sqrt{\frac{2 I_{\text{acoustic}}}{\rho v_s^3}} \qquad\qquad \textbf{(12.3-18)}$$

where v_s is the velocity of sound in the medium and ρ is the mass density (kg/m^3). Combining Equations (12.3-17) and (12.3-18) in (12.3-16) we obtain

$$\frac{I_{\text{diffracted}}}{I_{\text{incident}}} = \sin^2\left[\frac{\pi l}{\sqrt{2}\lambda_0}\sqrt{\frac{n^6 p^2}{\rho v_s^3} I_{\text{acoustic}}}\right] \qquad\qquad \textbf{(12.3-19)}$$

and using the following definition for the diffraction figure of merit

$$M \equiv \frac{n^6 p^2}{\rho v_s^3} \qquad\qquad \textbf{(12.3-20)}$$

(12.3-19) becomes

$$\frac{I_{\text{diffracted}}}{I_{\text{incident}}} = \sin^2\left(\frac{\pi l}{\sqrt{2}\lambda_0}\sqrt{M I_{\text{acoustic}}}\right) \qquad\qquad \textbf{(12.3-21)}$$

---

[7] In the case of interactions using crystals, Equation (12.3-17) becomes a tensor relation and p becomes a fourth rank tensor. In this case we can often simplify the problem in such a way that only one tensor element is important so that Equation (12.3-17) can be used.

[8] The (elastic) potential energy per unit volume due to an instantaneous strain $s(t)$ is

$$\tfrac{1}{2}T s^2(t)$$

where T is the bulk modulus (elastic stiffness constant). The time averaged energy per unit volume due to the propagation of a sound wave with a strain amplitude s is the sum of the (equal) average potential and kinetic energy densities

$$\mathcal{E}/\text{vol} = 2(\tfrac{1}{2})T\overline{s^2}(t) = \tfrac{1}{2}T s^2$$

since $\overline{s^2}(t) = \tfrac{1}{2}s^2$, the bar denoting time-averaging. Using the relation $I_{\text{acoustic}} = v_s \mathcal{E}/\text{vol}$ and $T/\rho = v_s^2$ where ρ is the mass density and v_s the velocity of sound, we get

$$I_{\text{acoustic}} = \tfrac{1}{2}\rho v_s^3 s^2$$

or

$$s = \sqrt{\frac{2 I_{\text{acoustic}}}{\rho v_s^3}}$$

which is the result stated in Equation (12.3-18).

Taking water as an example, an optical wavelength of $\lambda_0 = 0.6328\ \mu\mathrm{m}$, and the constants (taken from Table 12-1)

$$n = 1.33$$

$$p = 0.31$$

$$v_s = 1.5 \times 10^3\ \mathrm{m/s}$$

$$\rho = 1000\ \mathrm{kg/m^3}$$

Equation (12.3-21) gives

$$\left(\frac{I_{\text{diffracted}}}{I_{\text{incident}}}\right)_{\substack{\mathrm{H_2O} \\ \text{at } \lambda_o = 0.6328\,\mu\mathrm{m}}} = \sin^2\left(1.4l\sqrt{I_{\text{acoustic}}}\right) \qquad \textbf{(12.3-22)}$$

For other materials and at other wavelengths we can combine the last two equations to obtain a convenient working formula

$$\frac{I_{\text{diffracted}}}{I_{\text{incident}}} = \sin^2\left(1.4\,\frac{0.6328}{\lambda_0\ \mu\mathrm{m}}\,l\sqrt{M_\omega I_{\text{acoustic}}}\right) \qquad \textbf{(12.3-23)}$$

where $M_\omega = M_{\text{material}}/M_{\mathrm{H_2O}}$ is the diffraction figure of merit of the material relative to water. Values of M and M_ω for some common materials are listed in Tables 12-1 and 12-2.

Table 12-1   A LIST OF SOME MATERIALS COMMONLY USED IN THE DIFFRACTION OF LIGHT BY SOUND AND SOME OF THEIR RELEVANT PROPERTIES. ρ IS THE DENSITY, v_s THE VELOCITY OF SOUND, n THE INDEX OF REFRACTION, p THE PHOTO-ELASTIC CONSTANT AS DEFINED BY EQUATION (12.3-9), AND M_ω IS THE RELATIVE DIF-FRACTION CONSTANT DEFINED ABOVE (AFTER REFERENCE [4]).

MATERIAL	ρ, (mg/m^3)	v_s (km/s)	n	p	M_ω
Water	1.0	1.5	1.33	0.31	1.0
Extra-dense flint glass	6.3	3.1	1.92	0.25	0.12
Fused quartz (SiO$_2$)	2.2	5.97	1.46	0.20	0.006
Polystyrene	1.06	2.35	1.59	0.31	0.8
KRS-5	7.4	2.11	2.60	0.21	1.6
Lithium niobate (LiNbO$_3$)	4.7	7.40	2.25	0.15	0.012
Lithium fluoride (LiF)	2.6	6.00	1.39	0.13	0.001
Rutile (TiO$_2$)	4.26	10.30	2.60	0.05	0.001
Sapphire (Al$_2$O$_3$)	4.0	11.00	1.76	0.17	0.001
Lead molybdate (PbMO$_4$)	6.95	3.75	2.30	0.28	0.22
Alpha iodic acid (HIO$_3$)	4.63	2.44	1.90	0.41	0.5
Tellurium dioxide (TeO$_2$) (Slow shear wave)	5.99	0.617	2.35	0.09	5.0

Table 12-2 A LIST OF MATERIALS COMMONLY USED IN ACOUSTOOPTIC INTERACTIONS AND SOME OF THEIR RELEVANT PROPERTIES. $M = n^6 p^2/\rho v_s^3$ IS THE FIGURE OF MERIT, DEFINED BY EQUATION (12.3-20) AND IS GIVEN IN MKS UNITS (AFTER REFERENCE [6]).

MATERIAL	$\lambda_0(\mu)$	n	$\rho(g/cm^3)$	ACOUSTIC WAVE POLARIZATION AND DIRECTION	$v_s(10^5 \text{ cm/s})$	OPT. WAVE POLARIZATION AND DIRECTION[a]	$M = n^6 p^2/\rho v_s^3$
Fused quartz	0.63	1.46	2.2	long.	5.95	⊥ or ∥	1.51×10^{-15}
Fused quartz	0.63			trans.	3.76	∥ or ⊥	0.467
GaP	0.63	3.31	4.13	long. in [110]	6.32	∥ or ⊥ in [010]	44.6
GaP	0.63			trans. in [100]	4.13	∥ or ⊥ in [010]	24.1
GaAs	1.15	3.37	5.34	long. in [110]	5.15	∥ or ⊥ in [010]	104
GaAs	1.15			trans. in [100]	3.32	∥ or ⊥ in [010]	46.3
TiO₂	0.63	2.58	4.6	long. in [11–20]	7.86	⊥ in [001]	3.93
LiNbO₃	0.63	2.20	4.7	long. in [11–20]	6.57	(b)	6.99
YAG	0.63	1.83	4.2	long. in [100]	8.53	∥	0.012
YAG	0.63			long. in [110]	8.60		0.073
YIG	1.15	2.22	5.17	long. in [100]	7.21	⊥	0.33
LiTaO₃	0.63	2.18	7.45	long. in [001]	6.19	∥	1.37
As₂S₃	0.63	2.61	3.20	long.	2.6	⊥	433
As₂S₃	1.15	2.46		long.		⊥	347
SF-4	0.63	1.616	3.59	long	3.63	⊥	4.51
β-ZnS	0.63	2.35	4.10	long. in [110]	5.51	∥ in [001]	3.41
β-ZnS	0.63			trans. in [110]	2.165	∥ or ⊥ in [001]	0.57
α-Al₂O₃	0.63	1.76	4.0	long. in [001]	11.15	∥ in [11–20]	0.34
CdS	0.63	2.44	4.82	long. in [11–20]	4.17	∥	12.1
ADP	0.63	1.58	1.803	long. in [100]	6.15	∥ in [010]	2.78
ADP	0.63			trans. in [100]	1.83	∥ or ⊥ in [001]	6.43
KDP	0.63	1.51	2.34	long. in [100]	5.50	∥ in [010]	1.91
KDP	0.63			trans. in [100]		∥ or ⊥ in [001]	3.83
H₂O	0.63	1.33	1.0	long.	1.5	∥ or ⊥	160
Te	10.6	4.8	6.24	long. in [11–20]	2.2	∥ in [0001]	4400
PbMO₄[14]	0.63	2.4		long. ∥ c axis	3.75	∥ or ⊥	73

[a] The optical-beam direction actually differs from that indicated by the magnitude of the Bragg angle. The polarization is defined as parallel or perpendicular to the scattering plane formed by the acoustic and optical k vectors.

According to Equation (12.3-19) at small diffraction efficiencies, the diffracted light intensity is proportional to the acoustic intensity. This fact is used in acoustic modulation of optical radiation. The information signal is used to modulate the intensity of the acoustic beam. This modulation is then transferred, according to Equation (12.3-19), as intensity modulation onto the diffracted optical beam.

Numerical example—scattering in fused quartz.   Calculate the fraction of 0.633 μm light which is diffracted under Bragg conditions from a sound wave in $PbMO_4$ with the following characteristics

> acoustic power $= 1$ watt
>
> acoustic beam cross section $= 1$ mm $\times$ 1 mm
>
> $l =$ optical path in acoustic beam $= 1$ mm
>
> M_ω (from Table 12-1) $= 0.22$

Substituting these data into Equation (12.3-23) yields

$$\frac{I_{\text{diffracted}}}{I_{\text{incident}}} \simeq 40\%$$

12.4   Deflection of Light by Sound

One of the most important applications of acoustooptic interactions is in the deflection of optical beams. This can be achieved by changing the sound frequency while operating near the Bragg-diffraction condition. The situation is depicted in Figure 12-6 and can be understood using

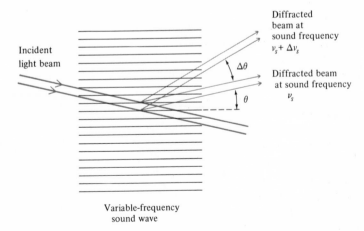

Figure 12-6   A change of frequency of the sound wave from ν_s to $\nu_s + \Delta\nu_s$ causes a change $\Delta\theta$ in the direction of the diffracted beam, according to Equation (12.4-1).

Figure 12-7. Let us assume first that the Bragg condition (12.1-4) is satisfied. The momentum vector diagram originally introduced in Figure 12-4 is closed and the beam is diffracted along the direction θ as given by (12.1-4). Now let the sound frequency change from ν_s to $\nu_s + \Delta\nu_s$. Since $k_s = 2\pi\nu_s/v_s$, this causes a change of $\Delta k_s = 2\pi(\Delta\nu_s)/v_s$ in the magnitude of the sound wave vector as shown. Since the angle of incidence remains θ and the magnitude of the diffracted k vector is unchanged,[9] so its tip is constrained to the circle locus shown in Figure 12-7, we can no longer close the momentum diagram and thus momentum is no longer strictly conserved. The beam will be diffracted along the direction that least violates the momentum conservation.[10] This takes place along the direction OB, causing a deflection of the beam by $\Delta\theta$. Recalling that the angles θ and $\Delta\theta$ are all small and that $k_s = 2\pi\nu_s/v_s$, we obtain

$$\Delta\theta = \frac{\Delta k_s}{k} = \frac{\lambda}{v_s}\Delta\nu_s \qquad (12.4\text{-}1)$$

so that the deflection angle is proportional to the change of the sound frequency.

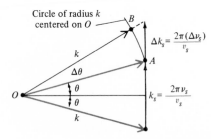

Circle of radius k centered on O

B

$\Delta k_s = \dfrac{2\pi(\Delta\nu_s)}{v_s}$

k

A

$\Delta\theta$

θ

O

θ

$k_s = \dfrac{2\pi\nu_s}{v_s}$

k

Figure 12-7   Momentum diagram, illustrating how the change in sound frequency from ν_s to $\nu_s + \Delta\nu_s$ deflects the diffracted light beam from θ to $\theta + \Delta\theta$.

As in the case of electrooptic deflection, we are not interested so much in the absolute deflection $\Delta\theta$ as we are in the number of resolvable spots—that is, the factor by which $\Delta\theta$ exceeds the beam divergence angle. If we take the diffraction angle as $\sim\lambda/D$, where D is the beam diameter,[11] the

---

[9] The small change in the diffracted wave vector that is attributable to the frequency change is typically about $\Delta k/k \simeq 10^{-7}$ and is neglected. See Problem 12-4.

[10] The violation of momentum conservation is equivalent to destructive interference in the diffracted beam, so the beam intensity will be less than under Bragg conditions, where momentum is conserved. The diffracted beam will thus have its maximum value along the direction in which the destructive interference is smallest. This corresponds to the direction that minimizes the momentum mismatch, as shown in Figure 12-7.

[11] According to (3.2-18), $\theta_{\text{beam}} = \lambda/\pi\omega_0$ is the half-apex diffraction angle, so the full beam diffraction angle can be taken as

$$\theta_{\text{diffraction}} = 2\theta_{\text{beam}} = \frac{4}{\pi}\frac{\lambda}{D}$$

where $D = 2\omega_0$ is the Gaussian spot diameter.

number of resolvable spots is

$$N = \frac{\Delta\theta}{\theta_{\text{diffraction}}} = \left(\frac{\lambda}{v_s}\right)\frac{\Delta\nu_s}{\lambda/D}$$

$$= \Delta\nu_s\left(\frac{D}{v_s}\right) = \Delta\nu_s\tau$$

(12.4-2)

where $\tau = D/v_s$ is the time it takes the sound to cross the optical-beam diameter.

Numerical example—beam deflection. Consider a deflection system using flint glass and a sound beam that can be varied in frequency from 80 MHz to 120 MHz; thus, $\Delta\nu_s = 40$ MHz. Let the optical beam diameter be $D = 1$ cm. From Table 12-1 we obtain $v_s = 3.1 \times 10^5$ cm/s; therefore, $\tau = D/v_s = 3.23 \times 10^{-6}$ second and the number of resolvable spots is $N = \Delta\nu_s\tau \simeq 130$.

■ PROBLEMS

12-1 Derive the expression of the frequency shift, under Bragg conditions, from a receding sound wave.

12-2 Design an acoustic modulation system for transferring the output of a magnetic-cartridge phonograph onto an optical beam with $\lambda_0 = 0.6328\,\mu m$ and $I_{\text{incident}} = 10^{-3}$ watt. Specify the power levels involved and the essential characteristics of all the key components. (*Hint:* Use the audio output of the cartridge to modulate a high-frequency (100 MHz, say) carrier, which is then used to transduce an acoustic beam.)

12-3 What happens in Bragg diffraction of light from a standing sound wave? Describe the frequency shifts and direction of diffraction.

12-4 Show that under Bragg conditions the change in wave vector of the diffracted wave is

$$\frac{k_{\text{diffracted}} - k}{k} = 2\sin\theta\,\frac{v_s}{c}$$

12-5 Consult the literature (see References [4] and [5], for example) and describe the difference between Bragg diffraction and Debye-Sears diffraction. Under what conditions is each observed?

12-6 Bragg's law for diffraction of X-rays in crystals is [7]

$$2d\sin\theta = n\lambda \qquad n = 1, 2, 3, \cdots$$

where d is the distance between equivalent atomic planes, θ is the angle of incidence, and λ is the wavelength of the diffracted radiation. Bragg diffraction of light from sound (see Figure 12-3) takes place when

$$2\lambda_s \sin \theta = \lambda$$

Thus, if we compare it to the X-ray result and take $\lambda_s = d$, only the case of $n = 1$ is allowed. Explain the difference. Why don't we get light diffracted along directions θ corresponding to $n = 2, 3, \cdots$? (*Hint:* The diffraction of X-rays takes place at discrtee atomic planes, which can be idealized as infinitely thin sheets, whereas the sound wave is continuous in z; see Figure 12-3.)

12-7 Design an acoustic deflection system using $LiTaO_3$ to be used in scanning an optical beam in a manner compatible with that of commercial television receivers.

■ REFERENCES

[1] Brillouin, L., "Diffusion de la lumière et des rayons X par un corps transparent homgène," *Ann. Physique*, vol. 17, p. 88, 1922.

[2] Debye, P., and F. W. Sears, "On the scattering of light by supersonic waves," *Proc. Nat. Acad. Sci. U.S.*, vol. 18, p. 409, 1932.

[3] Dransfeld, K., "Kilomegacycle ultrasonics," *Sci. Am.*, vol. 208, p. 60, 1963.

[4] See, for example, Robert Adler, "Interaction between light and sound," *IEEE Spectrum*, vol. 4, May 1967, p. 42.

[5] Born, M., and E. Wolf, *Principles of Optics*. New York: Pergamon, 1965, Chap. 12.

[6] Dixon, R. W., "Photoelastic properties of selected materials and their relevance for applications to acoustic light modulators and scanners," *J. Appl. Phys.*, vol. 38, p. 5149, 1967.

[7] Kittel, C., *Introduction to Solid State Physics*, 3d Ed. New York: Wiley, 1967, p. 38.

[8] Quate, C. F., C. D. W. Wilkinson, and D. K. Winslow, "Interactions of light and microwave sound," *Proc. IEEE*, vol. 53, p. 1604, 1965.

[9] Cohen, M. G., and E. I. Gordon, "Acoustic beam probing using optical frequencies," *Bell System Tech. J.*, vol. 44, p. 693, 1965.

[10] Cummings, H. Z., and N. Knable, "Single sideband modulation of coherent light by Bragg reflection from acoustical waves," *Proc. IEEE*, vol. 51, p. 1246, 1963.

[11]   Yariv, A., *Quantum Electronics*. New York: Wiley, 1967, Eq. (25.4-14).

[12]   Gordon, E. I., "A review of acousto-optical deflection and modulation devices," *Proc. IEEE*, vol. 54, p. 1391, 1966.

[13]   Gordon, E. I., "Measurement of light-sound interaction efficiencies in solids," *IEEE J. Quantum Electron.*, vol. QE-1, p. 283, 1965.

[14]   D. A. Pinnow, L. G. Van Uitert, A. W. Warner, and W. A. Bonner. "$PbMO_4$: A melt grown crystal with a high figure of merit for acoustooptic device applications" *Appl. Phys. Lett.*, vol. 15, 83 1969.

13

Two Laser Applications

13.1 Design Considerations Involving an Optical Communication System

One of the most important areas of application for lasers is that of communication between satellites. One reason is that in this case the problem of atmospheric absorption and distortion of laser beams is of no concern. In addition, the high directionality available with laser beams can be utilized effectively.

To be specific, we will consider a communication link between a system of three synchronous (24-hour orbit) satellites, as shown in Figure 13-1. Each satellite should be able to transmit and receive simultaneously.

Specifically, we agree on the following operating conditions:

    1. The operating wavelength is $\lambda_0 = 0.53\ \mu$m. This wavelength, which can be obtained by doubling the output of a Nd^{3+}:YAG laser (see Section 8-4), is chosen because of the high quantum efficiency of photomultiplier tubes at this wavelength (see Figure 11-4).

    2. The detection will be performed by a photomultiplier tube operating in the video (that is, no local oscillator) mode, as described in Section 11.3.

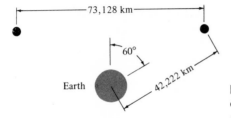

Figure 13-1 The disposition of three earth satellites with synchronous (24-hour) orbits.

● Satellite

3. The modulation signal will be impressed on the optical beam by an electrooptic modulator. The modulation signal will consist of a microwave subcarrier with a center frequency of $\nu_m = 3 \times 10^9$ Hz and sidebands[1] (caused by the information modulation) between $\nu_{\min} = 2.5 \times 10^9$ Hz and $\nu_{\max} = 3.5 \times 10^9$ Hz. The information bandwidth is thus $\Delta\nu = 10^9$ Hz.

4. The electrooptic crystal will be used in the transverse mode (see Section 9.5) and will have an electrooptic coefficient of $r \simeq 4 \times 10^{-11}$ (MKS) and a microwave dielectric constant of $\epsilon = 50\epsilon_0$. The peak modulation index is $\Gamma_m = \pi/3$.

5. The collimating lens and the receiving lens will have radii of 10 cm.

6. The signal-to-noise power ratio at the output of the amplifier following the receiver photomultiplier tube should be 10^3.

Our main concern is that of calculating the total primary (dc) power that the satellite must supply in order to meet the foregoing performance specifications. We will calculate first the optical power level of the transmitted beam and then the modulation power needed to meet these performance criteria.

The synchronous satellites. A synchronous satellite has an orbiting period of 24 hours, so its position relative to the earth is fixed. To find the distance from the earth to the satellite, we equate the centrifugal

---

[1] The information signal $f(t)$, which may consist of, as an example, the video output of a vidicon television-camera tube, is impressed as modulation on the microwave signal. This modulation can take the form of AM, FM, PCM, or other types of modulation. The modulated microwave carrier is then applied to the electrooptic crystal to modulate the optical beam in one of the ways discussed in Chapter 9.

force caused by the satellite's rotation to the gravitational attraction force

$$m \frac{v^2}{R_{E-S}} = mg \frac{(R_{\text{earth}})^2}{(R_{E-S})^2} \qquad \text{(13.1-1)}$$

where v is the satellite's velocity, m its mass, g the gravitational acceleration at the earth's surface, R_{E-S} the distance from the center of the earth
to the satellite, and R_{earth} the earth's radius. The synchronous orbit
constraint (that is, a 24-hour period) is

$$\frac{v}{R_{E-S}} = \frac{2\pi}{24 \times 60 \times 60}$$

We use it in (13.1-1) to solve for R_{E-S}, obtaining $R_{E-S} = 42{,}222$ km.

We employ three satellites so as to obtain coverage of the earth's
surface, as shown in Figure 13-1. The distance between two satellites is
$R = 73{,}128$ km.

Calculation of the transmitted power.   First we will derive an expression
relating the received power to the transmitted power as a function of the
transmitted beam diameter, the receiving aperture diameter, and the
distance R between the transmitter and the receiver.

If the transmitted power P_T is beamed into a solid angle Ω_T and if
the receiving aperture subtends a solid angle Ω_R at the transmitter, the
power received is

$$P_R = P_T \frac{\Omega_R}{\Omega_T} \qquad \text{(13.1-2)}$$

The transmitted beam diffracts with a half-apex angle θ_{beam}, as shown in
Figure 13-2. This angle is related to the minimum beam radius ω_0 (spot
size) by (3.2-18):

$$\theta_{\text{beam}} = \frac{\lambda_0}{\pi \omega_0} \qquad \text{(13.1-3)}$$

The corresponding solid angle is $\Omega_T = \pi(\theta_{\text{beam}})^2$. If we choose ω_0 to be

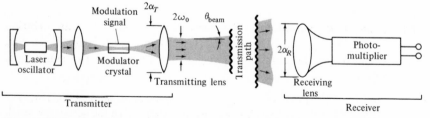

Figure 13-2   An optical communication link consisting of a laser oscillator,
an electrooptic modulator, a collimating (transmitting) lens, a transmission
medium, a receiving lens, and a receiver using a photomultiplier.

equal to the radius a_T of the transmitting lens, we obtain

$$\Omega_T = \frac{\lambda_0{}^2}{\pi a_T{}^2} \tag{13.1-4}$$

The receiving solid angle is

$$\Omega_R = \frac{\pi a_R{}^2}{R^2} \tag{13.1-5}$$

where a_R is the radius of the receiving lens and R is the distance between transmitter and receiver. Using (13.1-4) and (13.1-5) in (13.1-2) leads to

$$P_T = P_R \frac{\lambda_0{}^2 R^2}{\pi^2 a_T{}^2 a_R{}^2} \tag{13.1-6}$$

According to (11.3-11), the signal-to-noise power ratio at the output of a photomultiplier operating in the quantum-limited region (that is, the main noise contribution is the shot noise generated by the signal itself) is

$$\frac{S}{N} = \frac{P_R \eta}{h\nu\Delta\nu}$$

where P_R is the optical power. Using $\lambda_0 = 0.53 \ \mu\text{m}$, $\eta = 0.2$, $\Delta\nu = 10^9 \ \text{Hz}$, and the required S/N value of 10^3, we obtain

$$P_R \simeq 2 \times 10^{-6} \ \text{watt}$$

The required transmitted power is then calculated using (13.1-6), and $R = 7.31 \times 10^4$ meters, yielding

$$P_T \simeq 3 \ \text{watts}$$

Calculation of the modulation power.   In Section 9.6 we derived an expression for the power dissipated by an electrooptic modulator operated in the parallel RLC configuration shown in Figure 9-9. This power is given by

$$P = \frac{\Gamma_m{}^2 \lambda_0{}^2 d^2 \epsilon \Delta\nu}{4\pi l r^2 n^6} \tag{13.1-8}$$

where Γ_m is the peak electrooptic retardation, d the length of the side of the (square) crystal cross section, l the crystal length, r the appropriate electrooptic coefficient, $\Delta\nu$ the modulation bandwidth, and ϵ the dielectric constant of the crystal at the modulation frequency. To insure frequency-independent response of the crystal, the crystal length l is limited by transit-time considerations discussed in Section 9.6 to a length

$$l < \frac{c_0}{4\nu_{\text{max}} n}$$

where n is the index of refraction and ν_{max} is the highest modulation frequency. Using $\nu_{\text{max}} = 3.5 \times 10^9 \ \text{Hz}$ and $n = 2.2$, we obtain $l < 1$ cm.

We will consequently choose a crystal length of $l = 1$ cm. Having fixed l we may be tempted by (13.1-8) to use a crystal with a minimum thickness d. The choice of d is dictated, however, by the fact that we must be able to focus the laser beam into the crystal in such a way that its spread due to diffraction inside the crystal does not exceed the transverse dimension d. The situation is illustrated by Figure 13-3. If the beam is focused so that its waist occurs at the crystal mid-plane ($z = 0$), its radius at the two crystal faces ($z = -l/2$ and $l/2$) is given by (3.2-11) as

$$\omega\left(\frac{L}{2}\right) = \omega_0 \left[1 + \left(\frac{l\lambda}{2\pi}\right)^2 \omega_0^{-4}\right]^{1/2} \tag{13.1-9}$$

Our problem is one of determining the value of ω_0 for which $\omega(z = l/2)$ is a minimum. The dimension d will then be chosen to be slightly larger than the minimum value of $2\omega(z = l/2)$. Setting the derivative of (13.1-9) (with respect to ω_0) equal to zero yields

$$(\omega_0)_{\min} = \sqrt{\frac{l\lambda}{2\pi}}$$

and

$$\omega(z = l/2)_{\min} = \sqrt{\frac{l\lambda}{\pi}}$$

so that choosing d_{optimum} as equal to $2\omega(z = l/2)_{\min}$

$$\left(\frac{d_{\text{optimum}}^2}{l}\right) = \frac{4\lambda}{\pi} \tag{13.1-10}$$

Substituting the last result for d^2/l in (13.1-8) yields an expression for the minimum modulation power

$$(P)_{\min} = \frac{\Gamma_m^2 \lambda_0^3 \epsilon \Delta\nu}{\pi^2 r^2 n_o^7} \tag{13.1-11}$$

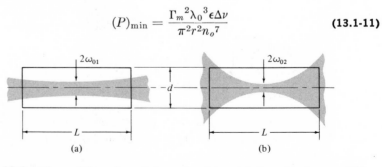

Figure 13-3 The problem of confining a fundamental Gaussian beam within a crystal of length l and height (and width) d. A decrease of the minimum beam radius from ω_{01} to ω_{02} causes the beam to expand faster and "escape" from the crystal.

Using $\Gamma_m = \pi/3$, $n = 2.2$, $r = 4 \times 10^{-11}$ (MKS), $\lambda_0 = 0.53\,\mu m$, $\epsilon = 50\epsilon_0$, and $\Delta\nu = 10^9$ yields

$$(P)_{\text{optimum}} = 10^{-2} \text{ watts}$$

for the microwave modulation power under optimum focusing conditions.

We have thus determined that the laser power output should be approximately 3 watts and the modulation power around 10^{-2} watt. If we assume that the efficiency of conversion of primary (dc) power to laser power is about 1 percent, each satellite will be required to supply approximately 300 watts of primary power.

13.2 Holography

One of the most important applications made practical by the availability of coherent laser radiation is holography, the science of producing images by wavefront reconstruction; see References [1]–[3]. Holography makes possible true reconstruction of three-dimensional images, magnified or reduced in size, in full color. It also makes possible the storage and retrieval of a large amount of optical information in a small volume.

Figure 13-4 illustrates the experimental setup used in making a simple hologram. A plane-parallel light beam illuminates the object whose hologram is desired. Part of the same beam is reflected from a mirror (at

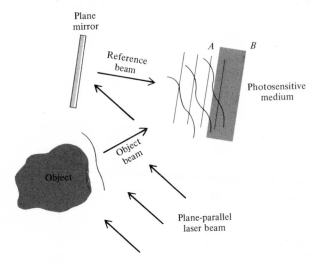

Figure 13-4   A hologram of an object can be made by exposing a photosensitive medium at the same time to coherent light, which is reflected diffusely from the object, and a plane-parallel reference beam, which is part of the same beam that is used to illuminate the object.

this point we refer to it as the reference beam) and is made to interfere within the *volume* of the photosensitive medium with the beam reflected diffusely from the object (object beam). The photosensitive medium is then developed and forms the hologram.

The image reconstruction process is illustrated in Figure 13-5. It is performed by illuminating the hologram with the same wavelength laser beam and in the same relative orientation that existed between the reference beam and the photosensitive medium when the hologram was made. An observer facing the far side (B) of the hologram will now see a three-dimensional image occupying the same spatial position as the original object. The image is, ideally, indistinguishable from the direct image of the laser-illuminated object.

The holographic process viewed as Bragg diffraction. To illustrate the basic process involved in holographic wavefront reconstruction, consider the simple case in which the two beams reaching the photosensitive medium in Figure 13-4 are plane waves. The situation is depicted in Figure 13-6. We choose the z axis as the direction of the bisector of the angle formed between the two propagation directions $\mathbf{k}_1$ and $\mathbf{k}_2$ of the reference and object plane waves inside the photosensitive layer. The x axis is contained in the plane of the paper. The electric fields of the two beams are taken as

$$e_{\text{object}}(\mathbf{r}, t) = E_1 e^{i(\mathbf{k}_1 \cdot \mathbf{r} - \omega t)}$$

$$e_{\text{reference}}(\mathbf{r}, t) = E_2 e^{i(\mathbf{k}_2 \cdot \mathbf{r} - \omega t)} \tag{13.2-1}$$

From Figure 13-6 and the fact that $|\mathbf{k}_1| = |\mathbf{k}_2| = k$, we have

$$\mathbf{k}_1 = \mathbf{a}_x k \sin \theta + \mathbf{a}_z k \cos \theta$$

$$\mathbf{k}_2 = -\mathbf{a}_x k \sin \theta + \mathbf{a}_z k \cos \theta \tag{13.2-2}$$

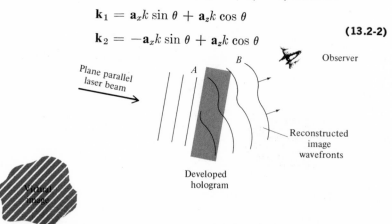

Figure 13-5   Wavefront reconstruction of the original image is usually achieved by illuminating the hologram with a laser beam of the same wavelength and relative orientation as the reference beam making it. An observer on the far side (B) sees a virtual image occupying the same space as the original subject.

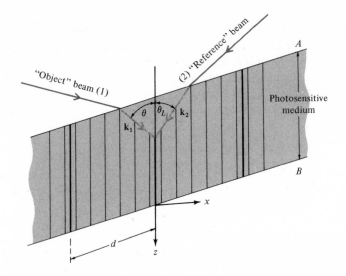

Figure 13-6 A sinusoidal "diffraction grating," produced by the interference of two plane waves inside a photographic emulsion. The density of black lines represents the exposure and hence the silver-atom density. The z direction is chosen as that of the bisector of the angle formed between the directions of propagation *inside* the photographic emulsion. It is not necessarily perpendicular to the surface of the hologram.

where $k = 2\pi/\lambda$, and $\mathbf{a}_x$ and $\mathbf{a}_z$ are unit vectors parallel to x and z, respectively.

The total complex field amplitude is the sum of the complex amplitudes of the two beams which, using (13.2-1) and (13.2-2) can be written as

$$E(x, z) = E_1 e^{ik(x \sin \theta + z \cos \theta)} + E_2 e^{ik(-x \sin \theta + z \cos \theta)} \qquad \textbf{(13.2-3)}$$

If the photosensitive medium were a photographic emulsion, the exposure to the two beams and subsequent development would result in silver atoms developed out at each point in the emulsion in direct proportion to the time average of the square of the optical field. The density of silver in the developed hologram is thus proportional to $E(x, z)E^*(x, z)$, which, using (13.2-3), becomes

$$E(x, z)E^*(x, z) = E_1{}^2 + E_2{}^2 + 2E_1E_2 \sin (2kx \sin \theta) \qquad \textbf{(13.2-4)}$$

The hologram is thus seen to consist of a sinusoidal modulation of the silver density. The planes $x =$ constant (that is, planes containing the bisector and normal to the plane of Figure 13-6) correspond to equidensity planes. The distance between two adjacent peaks of this spatial modulation pattern is, according to (13.2-4),

$$d = \frac{\pi}{k \sin \theta} = \frac{\lambda}{2 \sin \theta} \qquad \textbf{(13.2-5)}$$

In the process of wavefront reconstruction the hologram is illuminated with a coherent laser beam. Since the hologram consists of a three-dimensional sinusoidal diffraction grating, the situation is directly analogous to the diffraction of light from sound waves, which was analyzed in Section 12.1. Applying the results of Bragg diffraction and denoting the wavelength of the light used in reconstruction (that is, in viewing the hologram) as λ_R, a diffracted beam exists *only* when the Bragg condition (12.1-4)

$$2d \sin \theta_B = \lambda_R \qquad \text{(13.2-6)}$$

is fulfilled, where θ_B is the angle of incidence and of diffraction as shown in Figure 13-7. Substituting for d its value according to (13.2-5), we obtain

$$\sin \theta_B = \frac{\lambda_R}{\lambda} \sin \theta \qquad \text{(13.2-7)}$$

In the special case when $\lambda_R = \lambda$—that is to say, when the hologram is viewed with the same laser wavelength as that used in producing it—we have

$$\theta_B = \theta$$

so that wavefront reconstruction (that is, diffraction) results only when the beam used to view the hologram is incident on the diffracting planes at the same angle as the beam used to make the hologram. The diffracted beam emerges along the same direction $(\mathbf{k}_1)$ as the original "object" beam, thus constituting a reconstruction of the latter.

We can view the complex beam reflected from the object toward the photographic emulsion when the hologram is made, as consisting of a "bundle" of plane waves each having a slightly different direction. Each one of these waves interferes with the reference beam, creating, after development, its own diffraction grating, which is displaced slightly in angle from that of the other gratings. During reconstruction the illuminating laser beam is chosen so as to nearly satisfy the Bragg condition

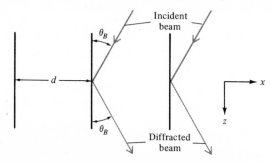

Figure 13-7 Bragg diffraction from a sinusoidal volume grating. The grating periodic distance d is the distance in which the grating structure repeats itself. In the case of a hologram we may consider the vertical lines in the figure as an edge-on view of planes of maximum silver density.

(13.2-6) for these gratings. Each grating gives rise to a diffracted beam along the same direction as that of the object plane wave that produced it, so the total field on the far side of the hologram (B) is identical to that of the object field.

Basic holography formalism. The point of view introduced above, according to which a hologram may be viewed as a volume diffraction grating is extremely useful in demonstrating the basic physical principles. A slightly different approach is to take the total field incident on the photosensitive medium as

$$A(\mathbf{r}) = A_1(\mathbf{r}) + A_2(\mathbf{r}) \qquad \text{(13.2-8)}$$

where $A_1(\mathbf{r})$ may represent the complex amplitude of the diffusely reflected wave from the object while $A_2(\mathbf{r})$ is the complex amplitude of the reference beam. $A_2(\mathbf{r})$ is not necessarily limited to plane waves and may correspond to more complex wavefronts.

The intensity of the total radiation field can be taken, as in (13.2-4), to be proportional to

$$AA^* = A_1A_1^* + A_2A_2^* + A_1A_2^* + A_1^*A_2 \qquad \text{(13.2-9)}$$

The first term $A_1A_1^*$ is the intensity I_1 of the light arriving from the object. If the object is a diffuse reflector, its unfocused intensity I_1 can be regarded as essentially uniform over the hologram's volume. $A_2A_2^*$ is the intensity I_2 of the reference beam. The change in the amplitude transmittance of the hologram ΔT can be taken as proportional to the exposure density so that

$$\Delta T \propto I_1 + I_2 + A_1A_2^* + A_1^*A_2$$

The reconstruction is performed by illuminating the hologram with the reference beam A_2 in the *same* relative orientation as that used during the exposure. Limiting ourselves to the portion of the transmitted wave modified by the exposure, we have

$$R = A_2\Delta T \propto (I_1 + I_2)A_2 + A_1^*A_2A_2 + I_2A_1 \qquad \text{(13.2-10)}$$

The first term corresponds to a wavefront proportional to the reference beam. The second term, not being proportional to A_1, may be regarded as undesirable "noise." Since I_2 is a constant, the third term I_2A_1 corresponds to a transmitted wave that is proportional to A_1 and is thus a reconstruction of the object wavefront.

Some additional aspects of holography, which follow straight-forwardly from the formalism introduced above, are treated in the problems.

Holographic storage. The use of holography for the storage of a large number of images and for their retrieval can be best understood using the Bragg diffraction point of view.

We consider, for the sake of simplicity, the problem of recording (storing) holographically and then reconstructing two objects. The storage of a larger number of images is then accomplished by repeating the procedure used in recording the two images.

An exposure of the photosensitive medium is performed using the beam reflected from the first object and the reference beam as illustrated in Figure 13-4. Next, the first object is replaced by the second one, the photosensitive plate is rotated by a small angle $\Delta\theta$, and another exposure is taken. The plate is now developed and forms the hologram.

During exposure each object gave rise to a "diffraction grating" pattern. The two sets of diffraction planes are not parallel to each other, since the plate was rotated between the two exposures. A reconstruction of the first object is obtained when the hologram is illuminated with a laser beam in such a direction as to satisfy the Bragg condition with respect to first diffraction grating. If the same wavelength is used in making the hologram and in the image reconstruction, the image of the first object is reconstructed when the laser beam is incident on the hologram at the same angle as that of the reference beam (during exposure). A rotation $\Delta\theta$ of the hologram will cause the second set of diffraction planes (that due to the second object) to satisfy the Bragg condition with respect to the incident laser beam, thus giving rise to a reconstructed image of the second object.

■ PROBLEMS

13-1 Show that if a hologram is made using a wavelength λ but is reconstructed with a wavelength λ_R the reconstructed image is magnified by a factor of λ_R/λ with respect to the original object. [*Hint:* Consider the process of forming a real image by placing a lens on the output side (B) of the illuminated hologram and then determining the linear scale of the image in view of (13.2-7).]

13-2 By considering a complex waveform as a superposition of plane waves show that a complex wave $A_2^*(r)$ is that obtained from A_2 by making it retrace its path; that is, the wavefronts are identical but their direction of propagation is reversed. A^* is called the conjugate (waveform) of A.

13-3 **a.** Show that if the hologram is illuminated with a plane wave A_2^* instead of A_2 the reconstructed image is A_1^* instead of A_1.
b. Show that the reconstructed image A_1^* is real—that is, that A_1^* actually converges to an image. (*Hint:* Consider what happens to a bundle of rays originally emanating from a point on the object.)

c. Show that the reconstructed image A_1 observed when the hologram is illuminated by A_2 is virtual; that is, rays corresponding to a given image point do not cross unless imaged by a lens.

13-4 Consider the problem of making a hologram in which the reference and object beam are incident on the emulsion from two opposite sides. Draw the equidensity planes for the case where the beams are nearly antiparallel. Show that the viewing (reconstructing) of this beam is performed in the reflection mode; (that is, the viewer faces the side of the emulsion that is illuminated by the beam.

13-5 Show that in an infinitely thin hologram both virtual and real images can be reconstructed simultaneously. [*Hint:* Consider the problem of light scattering from a surface grating (as opposed to a volume grating).]

13-6 Calculate the reconstruction angle sensitivity $d\theta_B/d\lambda_R$ for transmission holograms (as described in the text) and in reflection holograms (as described in Problem 13-4). θ_B is the Bragg angle and λ_R is the wavelength used in reconstruction. Show that $d\theta_B/d\lambda_R$ is much larger in the case of the transmission hologram. Which hologram will yield better results when illuminated by white light?

■ REFERENCES

[1] Gabor, D., "Microscopy by reconstructed wavefronts," *Proc. Roy. Soc. (London)*, ser. A, vol. 197, p. 454, 1949.

[2] Leith, E. N., and J. Upatnieks, "Wavefront reconstruction with diffused illumination and three-dimensional objects," *J. Opt. Soc. Am.*, vol. 54, p. 1295, 1964.

[3] Collier, R. J., "Some current views on wavefront reconstruction," *IEEE Spectrum*, vol. 3., p. 67, July 1966.

[4] Stroke, G. W., *An Introduction to Coherent Optics and Holography*, 2d Ed. New York: Academic Press, 1969.

[5] DeVelis, J. B., and G. O. Reynolds, *Theory and Applications of Holography*. Reading, Mass.: Addison-Wesley, 1967.

[6] Smith, H. M., *Principles of Holography*. New York: Interscience, 1969.

[7] Goodman, J. W., *Introduction to Fourier Optics*. New York: McGraw-Hill, 1968.

The Electrooptic Effect in Cubic $\overline{4}3m$ Crystals

As an example of transverse modulation[1] and of the application of the electrooptic effect we consider the case of crystals of the $\overline{4}3m$ symmetry group. Examples of this group are: InAs, CuCl, GaAs, and CdTe. The last two are used for modulation in the infrared, since they remain transparent beyond $10\,\mu$m. These crystals are cubic and have axes of fourfold symmetry along the cube edges ($\langle 100 \rangle$ directions), and threefold axes of symmetry along the cube diagonals $\langle 111 \rangle$.

To be specific, we apply the field in the $\langle 111 \rangle$ direction—that is, along a threefold-symmetry axis. Taking the field magnitude as E, we have

$$\mathbf{E} = \frac{E}{\sqrt{3}}\,(\mathbf{e}_1 + \mathbf{e}_2 + \mathbf{e}_3) \qquad \text{(A-1)}$$

where $\mathbf{e}_1$, $\mathbf{e}_2$, and $\mathbf{e}_3$ are unit vectors directed along the cube edges x, y, and z, respectively. The three nonvanishing electrooptic tensor elements are, according to Table 9-1 [see $\overline{4}3m$ tensor], r_{41}, $r_{52} = r_{41}$, and $r_{63} = r_{41}$. Thus, using Equations (9.1-2) through (9.1-4), with

$$\left(\frac{1}{n^2}\right)_1 = \left(\frac{1}{n^2}\right)_2 = \left(\frac{1}{n^2}\right)_3 \equiv \frac{1}{n_o^2}$$

---

[1] "Transverse modulation" is the term applied to the case when the field is applied normal to the direction of propagation.

334

we obtain

$$\frac{x^2 + y^2 + z^2}{n_o{}^2} + \frac{2r_{41}E}{\sqrt{3}} (xy + yz + xz) = 1 \qquad \text{(A-2)}$$

as the equation of the index ellipsoid. One can proceed formally at this point to derive the new directions x', y', and z' of the principal axes of the ellipsoid. A little thought, however, will show that the $\langle 111 \rangle$ direction along which the field is applied will continue to remain a threefold-symmetry axis, whereas the remaining two orthogonal axes can be chosen *anywhere* in the plane normal to $\langle 111 \rangle$. Thus (A-2) is an equation of an ellipsoid of revolution about $\langle 111 \rangle$. To prove this we choose $\langle 111 \rangle$ as the z' axis, so

$$z' = \frac{1}{\sqrt{3}} x + \frac{1}{\sqrt{3}} y + \frac{1}{\sqrt{3}} z \qquad \text{(A-3)}$$

and take

$$x' = \frac{1}{\sqrt{2}} y - \frac{1}{\sqrt{2}} z$$

$$y' = -\frac{2}{\sqrt{6}} x + \frac{1}{\sqrt{6}} y + \frac{1}{\sqrt{6}} z \qquad \text{(A-4)}$$

Therefore,

$$x = -\frac{2}{\sqrt{6}} y' + \frac{1}{\sqrt{3}} z'$$

$$y = \frac{1}{\sqrt{2}} x' + \frac{1}{\sqrt{6}} y' + \frac{1}{\sqrt{3}} z' \qquad \text{(A-5)}$$

$$z = -\frac{1}{\sqrt{2}} x' + \frac{1}{\sqrt{6}} y' + \frac{1}{\sqrt{3}} z'$$

Substituting (A-5) in (A-2), we obtain the equation of the index ellipsoid in the x', y', z' coordinate system as

$$(x'^2 + y'^2) \left(\frac{1}{n_o{}^2} - \frac{r_{41}E}{\sqrt{3}} \right) + \left(\frac{1}{n_o{}^2} + \frac{2r_{41}}{\sqrt{3}} E \right) z'^2 = 1 \qquad \text{(A-6)}$$

so the principal indices of refraction become

$$n_{y'} = n_{x'} = n_o + \frac{n_o{}^3 r_{41}E}{2\sqrt{3}}$$

$$n_{z'} = n_o - \frac{n_o{}^3 r_{41}E}{\sqrt{3}} \qquad \text{(A-7)}$$

It is clear from (A-6) that other choices of x' and y', as long as they are normal to z' and to each other, will work as well since x' and y' enter (A-6) as the combination $x'^2 + y'^2$, which is invariant to rotations about the z' axes. The principal axes of the index ellipsoid (A-6) are shown in Figure A-1.

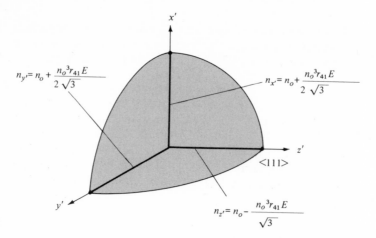

Figure A-1 The intersection of the index ellipsoid of $\bar{4}3m$ crystals (with E parallel to $\langle 111 \rangle$) with the planes $x' = 0$, $y' = 0$, $z' = 0$. The principal indices of refraction for this case are $n_{x'}$, $n_{y'}$, and $n_{z'}$.

An amplitude modulator based on the foregoing situation is shown in Figure A-2. The fractional intensity transmission is given by (9.3-4) as

$$\frac{I_o}{I_i} = \sin^2 \frac{\Gamma}{2}$$

where the retardation, using (A-7), is

$$\Gamma = \phi_{z'} - \phi_{y'} = \frac{(\sqrt{3}\pi)n_o^3 r_{41}}{\lambda_0}\left(\frac{Vl}{d}\right) \tag{A-8}$$

An important difference between this case where the electric field is applied normal to the direction of propagation and the longitudinal case treated in Section 9.2 is that here Γ is proportional to the crystal length l.

A complete discussion of the electrooptic effect in $\bar{4}3m$ crystals is given in C. S. Namba, *J. Opt. Soc. Am.*, vol. 51, p. 76, 1961. A summary of his analysis is included in Table A-1.

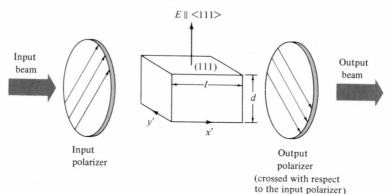

Figure A-2 A transverse electrooptic modulator using a zinc-blende type ($\bar{4}3m$) crystal with E parallel to the cube diagonal $\langle 111 \rangle$ direction.

Table A-1 ELECTROOPTICAL PROPERTIES AND RETARDATION IN $\overline{4}3m$ (ZINC BLENDE STRUCTURE) CRYSTALS FOR THREE DIRECTIONS OF APPLIED FIELD. AFTER C. S. NAMBA, JOUR. OPT. SOC. AM. VOL. 51, 76 (1961).

	$E \perp (001)$ plane $E_x = E_y = 0, E_z = E$	$E \perp (110)$ plane $E_x = E_y = \dfrac{E}{\sqrt{2}}, E_z = 0$	$E \perp (111)$ plane $E_x = E_y = E_z = \dfrac{E}{\sqrt{3}}$
Index ellipsoid	$\dfrac{x^2+y^2+z^2}{n_o^2} + 2\,r_{41} E\,xy = 1$	$\dfrac{x^2+y^2+z^2}{n_o^2} + \sqrt{2}\,r_{41}\,E(yz+zx)=1$	$\dfrac{x^2+y^2+z^2}{n_o^2} + \dfrac{2}{\sqrt{3}}\,r_{41}\,E(yz+zx+xy)=1$
n_x'	$n_o + \dfrac{1}{2} n_o{}^3 r_{41} E$	$n_o + \dfrac{1}{2} n_o{}^3 r_{41} E$	$n_o + \dfrac{1}{2\sqrt{3}} n_o{}^3 r_{41} E$
n_y'	$n_o - \dfrac{1}{2} n_o{}^3 r_{41} E$	$n_o - \dfrac{1}{2} n_o{}^3 r_{41} E$	$n_o + \dfrac{1}{2\sqrt{3}} n_o{}^3 r_{41} E$
n_z'	n_o	n_o	$n_o - \dfrac{1}{\sqrt{3}} n_o{}^3 r_{41} E$
$x'y'z'$ coordinates			
Directions of optical path and axes of crossed polarizer			
Retardation phase difference $r(V = Ed)$	$\Gamma_z = \dfrac{2\pi}{\lambda} n_o{}^3 r_{41} V$ $\Gamma_{xy} = \dfrac{\pi}{\lambda}\dfrac{l}{d} n_o{}^3 r_{41} V$	$\Gamma_{max} = \dfrac{2\pi}{\lambda}\dfrac{l}{d} n_o{}^3 r_{41} V$	$\Gamma = \dfrac{\sqrt{3}\pi}{\lambda}\dfrac{l}{d} n_o{}^3 r_{41} V$

Index